D1555839

A CROSS OF STARS

A CROSS
OF STARS

Patricia Shaw

HEADLINE

British Library Cataloguing in Publication Data

Shaw, Patricia, 1928-
A Cross of stars
I. Title
823 [F]

ISBN 0-7472-2006-9

Typeset by
CBS, Felixstowe, Suffolk

Printed and bound in Great Britain by
Mackays of Chatham plc, Chatham, Kent

HEADLINE BOOK PUBLISHING
A division of Hodder Headline PLC
338 Euston Road
London NW1 3BH

For Lynne and Mary, with thanks.

Chapter One

'They came from beyond that ridge up there,' he said, pointing with his cane. 'A big mob of blacks, about fifty of them, all painted up to glory and brandishing long, nasty-looking spears. Gave us a jolt, I can tell you.

'We were down here, Kelly and me, fencing off a paddock for our horses. Of course there was nothing here in those days, this was our first sheep run, and we were living in a log hut down by the river where the jetty is now. We only had five hundred sheep and an old shepherd called Claude . . .'

'But how did you come to be in such a dangerous situation in the first place?' the woman asked him.

'Land, my dear. Land. It was here for the taking. We drove the sheep from Brisbane and kept going west for a couple of hundred miles until we were well past the boundaries already mapped. From then on, once we found this river and decided where to settle, we marked off a few square miles to start with and drew our own maps. But it didn't seem dangerous at first. The blacks were more curious than difficult, they came by our camp just to stand and stare, as if we'd fallen off the moon, and we'd give them some tucker and they'd wander off. Then they became a bit of a nuisance, too friendly, thinking they had the run of the place. On the one hand they'd bring us wild honey and nuts and fish, but at the same time they'd walk off with our belongings, things we certainly could not spare.'

'Thieves,' the Reverend Billings sneered. 'Famous for it.'

Austin Broderick reacted sharply: 'I wouldn't say that! It's in their culture to share the necessities of life.' Then he smiled. 'Except when it comes to their tribal land. No sense of humour about that at all. Obviously we broke every rule in their book, but there was nothing much we could do about it. We took one look at this endless pasture land going to waste, and set about founding a sheep station. In our ignorance we thought they'd just move over, but it wasn't to be. When they decided we'd outstayed our welcome they started by killing our sheep, not for food, just wanton slaughter, and our threats of punishments were met with blank stares. Even showing them what guns could do had no effect; we still kept finding dead sheep.'

He peered into the distance. 'They had a big camp a couple of

1

miles from our hut, at the bend of the river, and suddenly, one day, the men were all gone.'

'They'd gone walkabout?' the Reverend asked.

'Well . . . that's what Claude said. He was an old bushie, he knew a fair bit about their ways, but in retrospect it was more ominous. A few days later they were back, lined up on that ridge in full war-paint with high, feathered head-dresses which made them all look, from our angle, about ten foot tall, and not a sound out of them.

'Though that day was forty years ago, I remember it like it was yesterday. It was a day like this, hot, blazing hot, not a breath of wind, and we were hard at work. Nothing unusual, the tingling bush all about, the smell of sweat and dust, the constant piping of birds, the zing of cicadas, and then silence. Dead silence, a hush, a sort of waiting in the air.

'At first I thought a bird of prey was hovering, an eagle or a hawk perhaps, but Kelly touched my arm and jerked his head towards the ridge.' Austin rubbed his neck. 'I can still feel how the hairs stood up on the back of my neck. We knew we couldn't run for it, we'd never make it to the hut or the horses, so we quietly downed tools and began to walk slowly towards the hut, expecting a rain of spears, but nothing happened, and when we looked back they were gone. Then we ran!'

'All bluff, was it?' The Reverend gave a thin smile. 'Just blowing off steam?'

Austin Broderick wondered why he was bothering with these people, these blasted missionaries. He'd only agreed to take them for a walk at the insistence of his wife. They'd arrived at Springfield uninvited, but at these big stations hospitality was never stinted. No one, whatever his social standing, was turned away, so Billings and his wife were entitled to the courtesy of his household.

'Sort of,' he replied, losing interest in the telling, though the dramatic tableau he'd witnessed was far from bluff. It had been a warning for them to leave. They'd been given the grace of time.

'Ah, yes,' Billings explained to his wife, 'a cowardly race, if they can be called a race at all. No match for white men.'

'No match for guns,' his host snapped. 'They gave us time to leave but we didn't take it. Instead we holed up in the hut with Claude and loaded our guns. They attacked that night. Spears against guns. Before they retreated we had shot six of their men, some of whom we'd befriended, which was unfortunate. The fight began a hit-and-run war that lasted for years, until they were forced to buckle under. But not before they exacted a terrible payback. We brought in more men, more sheep, and kept going while they hung on, harassing us where they could. That was the situation for a couple of years.

'Then, one awful day, I found my mate Kelly – his real name was Kelvin Halligan – out in the bush, pinned to a tree by five spears with honey smeared all over him to attract bull ants. God rest his soul. After that, troopers came and it was all over.'

'How frightful!' said Mrs Billings. 'Savages! Just like the Maoris back home.'

'And yet you still have blacks on your property?' Billings said.

Austin looked at him, surprised. 'The war's over.'

'But they're still savages, and they live like animals. I've seen their camp.'

'They're the remnants of the tribe. The least we can do is let them live in peace now, in their old ways.'

'Your friend Kelly mightn't see it that way.'

'Kelly was of another time,' Austin said impatiently. 'But he was a true Christian, I doubt *he* would begrudge them now. Come along and I'll show you the tennis court.' He stamped away, leading them over the footbridge that spanned a shallow creek, to an expanse of lawn bordering the fine Springfield homestead.

Reminded of Kelly now, he wondered what his late partner would think of the property in its present state. Originally they'd claimed ten square miles of prime land along the river, then they began exploring further afield, doubling their claim by blazing trees and bringing in a private surveyor to map the area, making sure there could be no argument with the neighbours who were sure to follow. At the time of Kelly's death they were preparing to take up more land on the other side of the river, keeping their surveyor busy.

'Bloody shame,' he muttered to himself. Springfield sheep station had been Kelly's dream, not his. Even the name had been Kelly's suggestion. Now Springfield was famous, head station of a property covering more than 300,000 acres, which was divided into three sections for ease of management.

The enterprise had been a success beyond the wildest dreams of either man, taken up with minimal expense, by leasehold, from a government eager to see the land opened up, and carrying an average of 60,000 sheep in each section. But it was the homestead that would have Kelly gazing in awe now. The two men had graduated from the log hut to a long timber shack that they shared with their stockmen, and outbuildings began to spring up around that central point to cater for what was fast becoming a self-contained enclave of sheds, stables, a blacksmith forge . . .

It was, Austin recalled, at about that stage that Kelly had been killed. Springfield was still primitive, they were just feeling their way, more concerned with their precious sheep than with homesteading. But when their first wool cheque came in, it was such a shock, both Austin and Kelly, celebrating, were drunk for two days. The price of wool had skyrocketed since they'd last heard, and they were in the money! They knew full well that they'd double or maybe treble their income the following year, with natural increase, as they continued

3

to stock the fine pastures. They were right, of course, but Kelly didn't live to see the next wool cheque.

Later Austin built himself a cottage more fitting to his status as boss, but fifteen years on, when he'd finally come to realize, not without a sense of awe, that he was a millionaire, he announced his intention to construct a suitable homestead.

He was married by this time, with three young sons, and Charlotte, his wife, was nervous when she saw the plans he had drawn up. Plans for a beautiful sandstone house, high on a hill, with reception rooms, family rooms, guest quarters and his very own day wing, facing not the river, but back across the valley that he loved so much.

'Can we afford this?' she asked him unhappily.

'This and more,' he'd laughed.

'But it's so big, Austin . . .'

'What does that matter? People in Brisbane live in houses this size.'

'Mansions, you mean. We don't need a mansion right out here. It's forty miles to our nearest neighbours. What will they think?'

He grinned. 'Jock Walker will probably follow suit, if I know him.'

Eventually Charlotte had come to like the house, turning into a martinet in her quest to keep everything in impeccable order. Austin was now glad he'd built his own wing – his refuge, his own office and recreation room, where he could throw off his boots and chuck things down wherever he pleased. Kelly would have loved this house though – proof that he'd known what he was about right from the start.

The tennis court was enclosed by a high brush fence.

'Sounds as if there's a game on,' Austin said to his guests as he made for the gate. 'It's Victor and Louisa playing singles. Do you want to stay and watch?'

Their horrified frowns reminded him that the missionaries disapproved of the game, so he turned back with a smile. 'My daughter-in-law's quite good. She can really race round the court, except when she skids too fast on the grass and upends herself. You're sure you don't want to watch?'

'No, no. No!' They reacted in unison, veering away.

'Oh well,' he shrugged, 'it's time for tea anyway. We'll go back to the house.'

Having delivered the Billings to the garden room where the table was already set for afternoon tea, he edged away, making for his den, but his wife intercepted him.

'What are you up to? You're skulking.'

'No, I'm not. I've got things to do. Would you ask Minnie to bring tea and cake to my office?'

'Where are the Billings?'

'I've done my duty for today. They're lining up for tea. They won't miss me as long as there's food on the table. They eat like horses.'

'Ah, don't be unkind.'

'Who's unkind? You're the one who said they were boring.' He glanced out of a tall window at the end of the long passage. 'Here come the tennis champions, they'll help out. Where's young Teddy?'

Charlotte smiled. Their grandson was the apple of Austin's eye. He doted on Teddy more than he ever had done on his own sons, spoiling the child and monopolizing his company to the irritation of his mother, who complained that he undermined parental discipline. But then Louisa could always find something to complain about.

'Teddy's with Nioka, so leave him be. He's playing with her little boy, Jagga, and Bobbo.'

'Who's Bobbo?'

'Oh, Austin, you know perfectly well. He's Minnie's boy.'

He grunted. 'Teddy'll grow up knowing more Abo than English.'

'Don't start that again. Nioka's a good nursemaid and there aren't any other kids his age to play with. If his mother doesn't mind, why should you?'

'His mother? She only wants him around to dress him up like a girl. She won't even let him have a pony!'

'She thinks six is too young, so leave it be. Now, go on down to your office. The mailman came, a week early instead of a week late, for a change. Victor had words with him – he thinks we should have a weekly delivery, not fortnightly. He put your mail on your desk.'

He was gone, hurrying away, still that powerfully built man Charlotte had fallen in love with so long ago. In its kindness, the light from the window silhouetted his form, darkening the shaggy white hair, disallowing the slight stoop and failing to measure the determined step that now replaced his cool, manly stride. She still loved him, but it had been hard to bear, all those aching years, because, as his wife, she'd had to take second place to all the importances of his life. And there was no end to them. An ambitious man, he was never short of plans and projects, all of which revolved around the betterment of Springfield. His house had to be the best; his sheep, quality merinos; his wool first grade, and so it went on until his sons were old enough to contribute to the Broderick fortunes, at their father's bidding.

Charlotte walked through to the kitchen, gave Minnie, the Aborigine maid, Austin's request, and wandered out to the porch, depressed. Austin was good to her, kind, and she supposed he loved her, but there'd never been any real romance in their life together, more of a convenience. She sighed, telling herself she was silly to be fretting over such schoolgirl stuff, but he did take her for granted, always had.

Your own fault, she said to herself. You knew in your heart that he married you out of loyalty to Kelly, but you didn't care then. You were so smitten by him, so overwhelmed, you rushed in . . .

Her own father had been so much in love with her mother that he had made their lives a joy, romancing his wife to the very end. Charlotte supposed she had expected the same sort of attention from Austin, but it was not to be. When her mother, Mrs Halligan, died, her husband wasn't long following her, so people said that he'd died of a broken heart. Charlotte wouldn't have that; deliberately she fought against such an explanation, insisting that he had died, as stated on the death certificate, of heart failure, because the alternative was too sad, and too close to home. She doubted that Austin would pine away to a shadow if his wife shuffled off this mortal coil. Despite her mood, a small smile crept over her face.

'He'd be too busy,' she murmured, 'arranging the world's finest funeral; as befitting the lady of Springfield.'

If I'm still here, she added silently, because there were times when she contemplated leaving the property and moving to Brisbane, to find a life of her own while there was still time. Another pipe dream, to relinquish her role of housekeeper and hostess in this complicated establishment in favour of a small house and the pleasantries of a city.

She had lived in Brisbane before, and she had liked the town, but she and her brother, Kelly, had been much poorer then. When their father died, Kelly had insisted she leave Sydney and come to Queensland with him.

'A land of opportunity,' he'd said.

It hadn't seemed so at first. They rented a house in South Brisbane and were struggling to survive, with Kelly taking odd jobs, refusing to touch the few hundred pounds left to them by Paddy Halligan.

'It's our nest egg,' he argued. 'Our ticket to the good life when I find the right investment.'

Night after night he studied maps of the settled areas beyond Brisbane, coming up with a scheme that sounded like sheer madness to his sister, until he brought home another dreamer called Austin Broderick. He was so handsome, tall and blond, with blue eyes that lit up with excitement as he listened to Kelly's proposal to take up land out west, that Charlotte surprised her brother by suddenly agreeing with him.

Then they were gone. She went to the stables to see them off with their packhorses, too embarrassed to mention, in front of Austin, that Kelly had left her very little money. Certainly not enough to live on. Right to the last minute she had hoped he would slip her a few more pounds, but he kissed her on the cheek, patted her head, leapt on to his horse and rode off with his new partner.

On the way home, Charlotte called in at a boot factory and managed to secure a poorly paid, miserable job as a machinist, but even that was only part-time work. Kelly had promised to write but Charlotte hadn't set much store by that because he'd never been much of a letter-writer, even to his parents, and if they really did travel beyond civilization then what hope of mail from there?

When he did come home, six months later, Kelly raced in like the conquering hero! They'd done it! They'd taken up their own land as far as the eye could see, wonderful pastoral land, and they were on their way to making their fortunes.

'We'll be rich, Lottie! Rich! I'm sorry you had to get a job but it won't be for much longer, and you'll never have to work again. You can come to live at Springfield.'

'Why can't I come now?' she'd asked, even then with her heart lost to Austin, afraid he'd meet someone else.

'Not possible. We're living rough, in a hut. We've only come to town to buy more sheep.'

'Where will you get the money?'

'We've still got some cash between us, and we're taking out a loan from the bank. Austin arranged that.'

Selfishly, all he could spare for his sister was ten shillings, so she was cross with him when he left the second time, not realizing that that was the last time she'd ever see her brother.

Two letters reached her, full of promise. Soon he'd be in a position to send for her. Soon. Charlotte found another job, less arduous, as a machinist in a shirt factory, but when that closed down at the end of the year, she was forced to write to Kelly for money, reminding him firmly, that she'd seen precious little of their nest egg. But eventually it was Austin who came, looking grave, clutching his hat, stammering the dreadful news, tears clouding his eyes as he tried to console her.

Charlotte was devastated, more so recalling that her last letter to Kelly had been critical. She blamed herself for not having more faith in him, because, as Austin now reported, the sheep station was a reality, a steadily growing concern.

He took over, organizing a memorial service for Kelly, rounding up her few friends and a surprising number of mourners not known to Charlotte, to fill the small suburban church. She had expected a pitiful little service but it was all so beautiful, she wept even more. There were lovely flowers, and wreaths on the altar steps, and a tenor with the most glorious voice sang the hymns that reminded her not so much of Kelly but of their dad. The priest spoke sincerely of the young man, cut down in the prime of his life, whom he had not had the pleasure of meeting, and so forth, but it was Austin who made the most impact.

Stole the show, she recollected now, in more cynical mode. Not that she'd realized it at the time; she was too overwhelmed by his fine oration. Standing beside the pulpit, he told of the bravery and fortitude of his friend and partner, of Kelly's magnificent pioneering spirit, a credit to his family and a shining example to the young men of this country. There were sobs to be heard from the pews behind her, because Austin truly meant every word he said. Until then, Charlotte, in her own misery, hadn't understood that Austin was suffering too. Kelly had been his best friend, the only person he knew who was

7

willing to take up the challenge of venturing into the unknown outback with him, facing not only the backbreaking work but the obvious dangers.

Humiliation was to follow days later, when Austin told her, in his matter-of-fact way, that he had read her letter to Kelly, asking for money.

'I can't just leave you here,' he said, brushing aside her feeble claims that she'd manage. 'Kelly would never forgive me. You do have a stake in Springfield, after all. You'll have to come back with me.'

'Wouldn't it be dangerous?' she fluttered, half hoping she hadn't provided him with an excuse to withdraw the offer. But given the manner of Kelly's death – speared by a black was all that she'd been told at that stage – it seemed an obvious response.

'No. I'll look after you. It's safe enough within the precincts of the head station. But there are no other white women out there. Will that bother you?'

'I suppose not, but where shall I live?'

'I'll build a cottage. I can't go on living in the staff quarters anyway. You can live there with me.'

Charlotte blushed. 'I don't know about that, Austin.'

He stood and walked to the door of her tiny sitting room, staring out with undisguised contempt at the dismal street and its row of workmen's cottages. 'Well, you can't stay in this place. It won't do at all. Kelly never meant for you to be stuck here, he was looking forward to showing you Springfield.'

They seemed to be at an impasse, but Austin, as usual, had the solution. 'Look, Charlotte. We get along well, you and I. And as I said, you do have a stake in Springfield. If you feel it would not be in order for you to live with me, I quite understand, one should respect the conventions. So why don't we get married?'

What had he said? Married? Perhaps she had misheard him, or worse, allowed her daydreamings of this man to conjure up that explosive word. Embarrassment sent her rushing out to the kitchen where she opened and shut cupboards in a panic, for how could she respond when the question might not have been asked? When it was quite possibly only a pathetic slip of her imaginings.

But he followed her. 'What do you say then?'

'To what?' she whispered, unable to face him.

'To our marrying? That is, if you find me suitable. I know I'm only a bushie, but the Brodericks are good stock . . .' He laughed. 'Barring a few rascals earlier on. But I won't let you down, Charlotte, you have my promise on that.'

Goose bumps added to her discomfort, tingling with excitement while an inner voice warned her this was not real. He was just feeling sorry for her. By tomorrow he'd forget all about it. This was only another of his impulsive gestures.

8

To save face, Charlotte decided to turn him down, but at the last second, the words would not come.

Instead she said, 'Isn't this rather sudden?'

'Not at all.' His confidence overwhelmed her. 'I've been thinking about this for days. You're a fine woman, Charlotte, I'd be honoured if you could see your way clear to becoming Mrs Broderick.'

Even though her heart was pounding with joy, Charlotte managed a little resistance. 'I'll have to think about it.' By which she meant he should have time to reconsider. Days later, when she did accept his proposal, Austin hugged her, gave her a kiss on the cheek, and said, 'Good girl. You'll like Springfield, I know you will.'

Well, she thought now, as she prepared to join the others for afternoon tea, he was right on that. Springfield was a wildly exciting place in those days, and she had adored her husband. What more could a girl want?

'You and your romantic notions,' she murmured. 'You should have grown out of them by this.' But there was that other matter. Her stake in Springfield. Another thing taken for granted. Kelly's name was no longer on the original leases. They had been renewed, with the rest of the huge runs, by Austin, and Charlotte never had the temerity to comment. It had seemed so ungrateful . . . But these days, with three ambitious sons, she wondered.

Victor stood when his mother came in, and drew out her chair for her, while the Reverend looked up from plastering butter on hot scones to acknowledge her. Victor disliked the missionaries, especially the prune-faced wife, with her overly genteel mannerisms and whining voice. Her husband was a lean, mean character who managed to introduce God into even the most trivial conversation, as if it were necessary to establish his credentials, and as a result he was regarded by all in this household as a sanctimonious bore.

'I hope the heat isn't bothering you,' Charlotte said to Mrs Billings, making conversation.

The Reverend answered for her. 'God's will, Mrs Broderick. We regard these minor irritations as heaven-sent, to remind us that we are but servants of the Lord. It's too easy in surrounds such as these, the lap of luxury, to forget that all blessings are gifts from the Lord, and temporary.'

'You could hardly call Springfield temporary,' Victor said, ignoring his mother's frown.

'All life is temporary, sir. I was disappointed to discover that there is no chapel here, and wondered if Mr Broderick could be persuaded to build one. I should be happy to return to bless the premises.'

'My husband did consider building a church,' Charlotte told him, 'but there have been differing opinions among visiting ministers as to what denomination it should be. I am Catholic and the rest of

9

the family are Church of England . . .'

'And there are a whole range of religious attitudes among the men on our staff,' Victor added with a grin. 'Try to get agreement from thirty or more men. Too hard.'

'That could be easily solved. Our faith, the Church of the Holy Word, upholds the truth as stated in the Bible. No other religion relies strictly on the Word. I was thinking that a Chapel of the Holy Word would be an excellent beginning for your people here. Later my bishop could come out and consecrate it as a regular church.'

'Oh Lord, there's another one,' Louisa said. 'The last minister, Wesleyan, I think he was, suggested a chapel here for his flock.'

'So you see our predicament,' Victor said.

'I'm afraid I don't,' sniffed the Reverend.

'Did you have an interesting walk this afternoon?' Charlotte asked them.

'Most interesting,' Mrs Billings said. 'We went through the gardens and out to the orchard and on over the creek. Mr Broderick showed us the ridge from where they were attacked by savages.'

'Not that again,' Victor said. '"They came from beyond that ridge . . ." That's his favourite story.'

'But surely it's true.'

'Oh yes, it's true. He could write a book.'

'Then I think Mr Broderick was incredibly brave to live in such dangerous country. Thank God the savages were overcome. At least I hope they have been.'

'That's something I wanted to speak to you about, Mrs Broderick,' the Reverend said. 'We have seen natives strutting about undressed, a shocking state of affairs, and we would hope . . .'

Charlotte put down her teacup, startled. 'Not within the homestead area?'

'No, at a disgusting camp by the river.'

'That's miles away!' Louisa said. 'Did you walk all the way down there?'

'We considered it our duty to investigate these people, so we followed two of the housegirls.'

'Oh, that's all right.' Charlotte was relieved. 'We see to it that any of the blacks who come into the living or work areas are clothed. There are trousers and shirts available for the blacks who work as stockmen, and shifts for the housegirls, so the tribal people can collect something from them if need be, but mostly they don't bother. We don't worry about the children of course, they run about in the buff . . .'

'But this is wrong!' Mrs Billings said. 'It cannot be. The Bible says . . .'

'The Bible doesn't deal with our Aborigines,' Victor laughed. 'They're not even mentioned.'

10

'It does not behove you to be facetious,' the Reverend retorted. 'My wife was shocked. Most of those natives had barely a stitch on. You can't condone this. They're living like animals.'

'They're living as they have lived for thousands of years, Mr Billings,' Charlotte said quietly. 'Before the Bible was ever heard of. God must have approved because He gave them a wonderful country all to themselves. Although I must admit He's let them down of late, relatively speaking.'

Victor smiled. He knew the Reverend and his missus still didn't agree, but Charlotte had shut them up, for the time being at least. To escape them, he decided against another slice of fruit cake and departed, leaving the guests to the women.

'Interfering fools,' he muttered as he strode across the courtyard, making for the shearing sheds. He himself had taken the pair on a tour of the sheds which were now being opened up again, ready for the arrival of the shearers. Together with the merino stud, the sheds were Victor's pride and joy. Designed by his father, in much the same style as a friend's huge wool shed on the Darling Downs, they were each 300 feet long and had cover for about 2,000 sheep. The interiors were an eye-opener to visitors. Each shed had a tramway for fleece and bales down the centre, and there were fifty-two stands where the shearers worked.

'Last year,' he'd told Billings proudly, 'we had fifty-four shearers to shear two hundred thousand sheep. Took them fifteen weeks, a job well done.'

Billings was unimpressed. 'And you don't have a conscience about all this?'

'A conscience? Why should I?'

'You must own a lot of land to run so many sheep. Do you think that is fair? The Lord might deem it greedy for you squatters to covet so much when other men are now searching for arable land.'

'The Lord has nothing to do with it. My father got these runs by hard work, he's entitled to every acre.'

The Reverend scratched his chin and gave Victor a patronizing smile. 'Obviously you've not taken into account the lessons of America. The ranchers of those great plains were soon overrun by hordes of advancing homesteaders. It is said the same thing will happen here.'

'That's where you're wrong. The big stations won't be so easily destroyed here.'

'Inevitable, I would think,' Billings murmured, and Victor let him have the last word, rather than enlighten him as to the steps already taken to prevent such a catastrophe. The Australian squatters, or ranchers as they were known in America, were a powerful force in the land, an exclusive society bound together by common interests. They had made it their business to use their influence in judicial and political circles through appointments and family connections, and were well

11

prepared to face any battle to retain their vast properties.

'It won't happen to us,' Victor repeated to himself as he looked in satisfaction at the trim sheds, all ready for action. The shearers would be arriving next week.

He leaned against a timber railing and lit a smoke, thinking again of Billings. The cheek of the man, to be enjoying their hospitality, sitting back there with the ladies in pleasant surroundings and all the while begrudging his hosts their success. Maybe he was a spy?

'No, he's too stupid.'

Nevertheless, a nagging worry lodged. Obviously Billings was just mouthing stuff he'd heard in Brisbane, or country towns. It was common knowledge that selectors were fanning out across the countryside, demanding that they be permitted to select and buy portions of land leased by squatters, and some government members, driven by socialistic elements, were in agreement. Selection Acts had already been introduced into Parliament but so far, without success.

Austin planned well ahead. He had three sons and they all had to be strategically placed. Victor was settled as his right-hand man at Springfield. The next son, Harry, had set out on a road well paved for him by the Broderick connections, with a safe seat in State Parliament, on the Government benches, and a suitable wife, daughter of Chief Justice Walker.

Then there was Rupert. He was only twenty, and had been away to boarding school for years. Now home again, he'd been bucking at his father's instructions to study law. They'd had fierce arguments over that, until Austin had a better idea. Given these ominous Selection Acts, he had decided they could do with another voice in Parliament. Without bothering to consult Rupe, his father had gone ahead, made a deal with a retiring politician for Rupe to inherit his seat, squared it with the Premier, and announced Rupe's future at dinner one evening.

Rupe had been furious. 'I'm not going into bloody Parliament. There's plenty of work for me here. I'll take over the stud from Victor. And if I can't work here I'll leave and get a run of my own.'

Victor hadn't intervened in the ongoing rows. It wasn't his concern, he just wanted to get on with his own affairs. Coping with Louisa was enough of a problem lately. She was becoming bored living at Springfield . . . He stubbed out his cigarette and flicked the butt into the air. 'That's just too bad,' he muttered. 'This is our home, and here we stay.'

Sometimes Austin thought he might have made a mistake insisting that all the rooms downstairs be panelled in cedar. The result had been rather darker than he'd anticipated, but as Victor pointed out, the rooms were a good size and had high ceilings, so they could carry the timber panels. However, the panelled walls in his own wing never failed to please him: they were eminently suitable for a gentleman's rooms. Here he had his own office and a long room furnished in the manner of a club, with comfortable leather chairs, a billiard table and card table, and above the mantelpieces photographs of his prize merinos, as well as the numerous plaques and awards they had won.

He walked through to the veranda, pleased with himself for dodging the God-botherers, and stood there flexing his arms, doing deep-breathing exercises, because he'd been a little short of breath lately. From the hills beyond the valley, light clouds were drifting forward, but he knew from experience that they were only teasers, they'd not bring a drop of rain to the parched land. He smelled the air . . . no sign of bushfires as yet.

'Maybe we'll be spared this year,' he said. 'We had enough of them last year.'

Minnie brought his tea in on a tray, accompanied by her usual wide smile. She was a cheerful girl of about twenty, who'd been working at Springfield as a maid for many years.

'Missus say you like some cake too, boss,' she commented as she set down the tray.

'Yes. Thank you, Minnie. How are those blackfellers going down at the camp? Getting plenty fish?'

'Moontime,' she nodded. 'Good fishin' now.'

'I thought so,' he grinned. 'You tellum those boys send up a nice fat fish for the boss, eh?'

She giggled. 'I tellum.' She made for the door, then stopped, nervously. 'Boss . . . them prayin' people, they make famblies down there cranky. Sticken noses in, not wanted.'

Austin poured his tea. 'Tell them not to take any notice. The Reverend and his missus will be gone soon.'

'Ah.'

When she left he laughed. 'Them prayin' people! That's a good one.'

He picked up a newspaper from a newly delivered pile on a side table, and read it carefully while he ate his cake, frowning when he found an article referring to that damned Selection Act, now back before Parliament after a number of amendments had been accepted. The writer was obviously in favour of sabotaging the successful rural industry, by allowing any fool or farmhand to chop into station property owned by their betters, despite an editorial which spoke of the big sheep stations as being the backbone of the country. The latter went on to decry this shameful movement, that could only bring ruin to the sheep industry, and warned of the danger to the state's economy.

'So he should,' Austin snapped. 'So why is he letting that other fool write his socialist rubbish? I want that fellow sacked. I'll write a personal letter to that editor, Bernie Willoughby, and tell him to smarten up. It's no good him writing one thing and his staff writing something else.'

13

He turned angrily to the letters page, only to find three contributors supporting the Selection Acts, urging selectors to start choosing their land claims right away, before greedy squatters started snatching the best land.

Bewildered, Austin tried to digest this. What did they mean? Why would squatters like himself be snatching up their own land? They already owned it on legal, well-documented leases.

He hurried into his office to dig out the thin pages of the Selection Act VII, that Harry had sent him. The wording was confusing, full of the usual poppycock of 'heretofores' and 'thereins', designed to confuse any sane man, and knowing, as he thought, the contents, Austin had not bothered to read it carefully. He had been under the impression that these selectors were going about claiming land on properties such as Springfield, and demanding to buy their claims from the squatters.

But now he realized, as he studied the irritating verbiage, that that wasn't the idea at all. These Acts meant that squatters had to transfer *all* their land from leasehold to freehold, by purchasing it from the Government, otherwise leased land would revert to Government ownership, and so could be sold to selectors.

'Madness!' he said, tapping the desk. 'How could I buy all this land, acre by acre? And at a pound an acre, that's the going price, they say. I'd be up for more than a quarter of a million pounds with nothing to show for it but my own land. It'd break me! Bloody fools, the lot of them, if they think we'd fall for that!'

He stormed out on to the veranda and shouted at a passing stationhand to get Victor for him.

'Now!' he added. 'Right now! Tell him to get up here!'

Victor had come back as far as the stables by the time he received his father's order.

'Is he dying?' he asked the messenger, Joe Mahoney, who winked. 'Not that I noticed.'

'Then he can wait. Let's have a look at the mare.' To please his wife, Victor had agreed to a game of tennis, but he begrudged the time. It threw his whole day out. Then, when he did arrive at the court, late, Louisa had complained that he hadn't changed into tennis whites, her latest fad, and that had caused a row. Bloody tennis whites, he snorted to himself. What next?

The chestnut mare was in foal. She was resting in her stall when they arrived and she looked up at them with sad, moist eyes.

'You'll be all right, girlie,' he said, moving in to examine her. 'She's close to her time, Joe. You'd better stay with her.'

'Right, Vic. I'll give you a call if there's any movement.'

'Good.'

Although not qualified, Victor did have veterinary experience. When

14

he was eighteen his father had sent him to Brisbane for a year, apprenticed to a vet, and he'd enjoyed that work, but Austin never believed in wasting time. Considering that veterinary work wouldn't take up all of his time, he'd also enrolled his son in an accountancy course. Victor had been annoyed by this double duty, especially when he found accountancy difficult, but Austin was boss and there was no point in arguing. He was told to bring home a certificate in accountancy at the end of the year or stay there until he could produce one. It had been a busy year but he'd managed to pass the course and came home to a proud parent. Nowadays, he was grateful for Austin's insistence: the knowledge he'd gained was invaluable for his work at Springfield, and he'd furthered his education by studying books on animal husbandry that were sent to him by his friend, the Brisbane veterinarian.

One more call, to check the shearers' quarters, where two black housemaids were opening up the sheds and airing bunks ready for occupancy.

'Some of dese here mattresses no good no more,' one of the girls complained to him, holding up a battered slab with horsehair hanging from the sides.

'Get new ones from the store,' he said. 'These sheds got to be shiny clean or the shearers get cranky. And when they come, you girls keep away from them. You hear me?'

'Yes, boss,' they whispered, as if the strange men might hear them. Shearing time was exciting, with so many strangers converging on the station, but it also meant trouble if there *was* any fraternizing between the black women and the shearers.

Returning to the homestead, Victor strode down a long track shaded by a row of pepper trees, their streaming foliage rustling in a slight breeze that brought promise of a cooler night, easier on the mare.

We're in for a long hot summer, he told himself, judging by this early heat.

The track diverged at this point, with the homestead to the left, and the main gate straight ahead, a clear run across a half-mile stretch of open country. The homestead and surrounding outbuildings were contained in fenced areas for convenience, but apart from a few paddocks, no other sections of the huge property were fenced, and that was a worry for Victor. There were two outstations, where overseers lived, to manage their sections of Springfield, keeping in regular communication with Victor, but the days were coming when the boundaries should be more clearly defined. He shuddered at the thought of fencing, though. The cost would be prohibitive. As it was, their neighbour, Jock Walker, was always complaining that Austin's boundary lines 'up and walked'.

Victor grinned. He was probably right. Austin wasn't averse to fudging a few extra miles of pastoral land if he could get away with it.

15

The land greed was still strong in him.

He cut across a lawn, stepped over a garden bed and vaulted the rail on to his father's veranda. This section was known as Dad's wing, but the brothers referred to it as his den. A great hangout for Austin and his cronies, but a danger zone for the sons, who knew that a summons to the lion's den meant trouble.

'What's up?' he asked cheerily.

'You took your time getting here!' Austin shouted. 'Have you read the papers?'

'How could I? They've just arrived.'

'Well, it would pay you to get your nose in them and not leave it to me. You're supposed to be my manager and you don't seem to have any idea of what's going on.' He slammed a newspaper on the card table, jamming a calloused finger on the offending page. 'Read that! By Christ, I'll have something to say to Bernie, letting this sort of garbage loose in his paper. Do you see what they're trying to pull now? They want us to buy our own leases.'

Victor scanned the article. 'That's what I've been trying to tell you.'

'You've never told me any such thing! You just said those dimwit selectors are lining up to try to buy some of my land!'

'That's right. From the government, unless we freehold. But there's no need to panic, so calm down. The Selection Acts will go on forever, they'll never get passed.'

Austin's face blazed red and his white hair was almost standing on end. 'Don't you bloody tell me not to panic, you bloody upstart! Christ knows what would become of Springfield, left to you lot. I want something done about this now!'

Victor sighed. 'Something is being done. Selectors can't lodge claims until the Acts are passed, and Harry has the matter in hand. They'll keep throwing up amendments until doomsday. He wrote and told you that last week.'

'Harry! He's a bloody lightweight and you know it, swanning round Brisbane like God's gift to the social world, with that brat of a wife of his. I must have been out of my mind to think he'd come in useful. I *should* make Rupe go. He's what's needed down there in the Parliament, bloody-minded, stubborn bastards who kick where they see a head.'

Victor took a cigarette from a pile in a box that were rolled for the boss by Minnie, and lit it, puffing casually while his father raved on. It was always the same. Rupe and Austin clashed like a couple of yellow dogs. But come comparison with his brothers, Rupe was thrown at them like a junior Austin Broderick, a saint, which he was not. Harry, it was true, wasn't making much of a mark in the political world, but Victor resented his father's attitude. He was an excellent manager of this property and he knew his worth. But try to tell that

16

to the old man. All he got was abuse. It was hard to run a station of this size with all its problems – not only of distance but of the necessity to keep a tight rein on the inhabitants, from family and tribal blacks to a predominantly male staff, to high-falutin' visitors encouraged by Austin – and all the time having to suffer the ignominy of having his father circumvent his instructions. Circumvent? he mulled angrily. That's Harry's word. That's what Harry would say, dammit! Austin doesn't just circumvent, he changes. Makes a fool of me in front of the men. Moves the bloody goalposts all the time, like he does with Jock Walker. And everyone else for that matter.

It had been Charlotte's idea that Austin retire and hand over to Victor, and with the gentle, flattering way she had with the old man, he'd come to see it as his own design. Boasting to his mates that he was retiring. Throwing a huge three-day party to announce the retirement of Austin Gaunt Broderick and the handing on to the next generation – duly reported in every Queensland newspaper, as well as the *Sydney Morning Herald*. A giddy time, Victor recalled, that lasted until the final guest left. He was as much in charge of Springfield as Minnie was of the kitchen, where she'd worked for years under the rule of Hannah, the homestead cook.

'Are you listening to me?' Austin snarled. 'Has it occurred to you in any time and bloody space that if one of those Selection Acts gets through . . .'

'They can't,' Victor persisted.

'Numbers, you bloody dolt! Politicians can be bought. A couple could be away sick. Someone could miss the call. And what can happen? Idiots like Harry can be left sitting like knots on a log. Beaten! It only takes one bloody vote!'

Victor shook his head. 'Not possible. You forget, half the opposition is on our payroll. Not to mention the relations sitting pretty as justices of the peace, magistrates, in high office in banks, the police, and even the damn post office. For God's sake, Dad, stop making a mountain out of a molehill. We're their bread and butter.'

Austin moved over to the drinks tray and poured himself a whisky from a trio of decanters, adding ice. 'You want a drink?'

'Yes.' Victor poured his own.

'Two things here you've overlooked,' Austin said quietly. 'And by Jesus, if you've never listened to me before, you'd better listen to me now, mate. Because there are two things you have to look at. One is . . . never underestimate power. Any man in opposition would shoot his grandma to get into government. To get into power. Opposition is ratshit. To hell with the bloody relations. So you can count them out.'

He swallowed a gulp of whisky with obvious enjoyment.

'Right. Now say, just say, that by bribery and corruption or by all manner of heartfelt conviction, added to absences from the House, and persuasion by socialist elements, one of those Selection Acts got

17

through. Became law. What then, Mr Broderick, manager of Springfield? What's your defence?'

He hurled his glass, still half full, into the empty fireplace. 'I'll tell you what happens then, you bloody idiot, with your dimwit brother wringing his soft white hands, we lose! What do they want? They want *us*, you stupid clown. They don't want the bloody land. What bloody use is some penny-hanky block to a sheep man? Expenses are too high, markets too far, you need a range, dozens of big runs like we've got . . .'

'That's right,' Victor agreed, ignoring the smashed glass. Austin often smashed things to make a point. His sons were no longer impressed. 'We should have someone writing an article in Bernie's paper about the risks to their investments from such a futile move . . .'

'You still don't get it, do you?' Austin said softly. 'It hasn't entered your woolly head that they're after us, the squatters. The oligarchy, as they call us. It's to do with breaking the power of the squatter. We explored and opened up their bloody land, and we squatted on it until the government surveyors ventured out this far. We did the fighting, we took the risks, and we earned every penny we own, plus every acre we leased from a government that didn't know such land existed. But we worked, and we paid, not only in rent to a ratshit government, cowering back there in Brisbane, but in lives, Kelly being one of them . . .'

Oh Jesus, Victor thought, not Kelly again. He settled back into a luxurious armchair. Kelly might have been their mother's brother, but the Broderick boys had come to hate him. Another saint listed in Austin's repertoire.

'The second thing is,' Austin said, 'if you happen to be interested, like I won't keep you from your tennis . . .'

'I played today because Louisa needed company,' Victor began, hating himself for needing to explain.

'Good for you,' his father remarked sarcastically. 'In the meantime, Springfield is teetering on the edge of disaster. Let's suppose, then, that one of those sneaky little Acts gets through. Despite my brilliant son Harry, despite all the bastards that we've set up in high places. Did no one ever tell you that a man who can be bought is a man who can be bought again? Doesn't that ring any bells in your dead head?'

Victor stood. 'I've had enough of this. When you've got all this shit out of your stomach I'll try to explain it to you.'

His father smirked. 'No need, my boy. No need at all. Just come here and look at the map. This map. Now!'

He had several maps laid out on the billiard table, detailed maps which, set in place, gave an overview of all the land owned by A.G. Broderick, the boundaries jutting unevenly where he had claimed the best possible grazing land.

'How can we buy back all that?' he asked.

18

'We can't. Anyway, it's already ours. We won't have to.'

'But if push comes to shove and selectors turn up here waving papers to prove this land has been thrown open to freehold? We won't be able to stop them marking off their claims, unless we buy it ourselves, and that's financially impossible.'

Victor shook his head, not bothering to comment. It was all hypothetical. Or was it? Austin was making him nervous.

'You go and find Rupe. Get him in here. We'll have a council of war. We have to mark off our very best land, watered land, along the riverbanks and creeks . . .'

'What for? We couldn't fence all that.'

'Fencing will come later. This is a fall-back plan. We'll map blocks of the maximum size, to the bloody inch, that selectors including ourselves will be permitted to buy under the law. Then if the worst happens, we'll be ready and we'll pounce. We'll at least be able to buy the cream.'

Victor stared at the maps. 'That'll take a lot of work. We'd need a good surveyor to help us.'

'Then get one.'

Charlotte came in. 'Austin, the Reverend wants a word with you.'

'Not now. We're busy. What's he want?'

'I don't know.'

'Well find out. And you deal with it.'

She shrugged and left.

Louisa was left in the garden room with the guests. She had nothing better to do, so she stayed on.

'Why did you want to see Austin?' she asked Billings. 'My husband is the manager now. Austin has retired.'

'I'm quite aware of that, dear lady,' he said. 'But my bishop asked me to see Mr Austin Broderick on church business.'

'No use talking to Austin about building a church. You'd have more luck with Victor.'

'It's not about a church,' Mrs Billings said. 'It's regarding the Aborigines. We feel it is our duty to try to help them.'

'Oh, that's nice,' Louisa said vaguely.

Just then Charlotte returned. 'The men are busy at the minute, Reverend,' she said. 'Maybe I could help you?'

'They want to do something to help the blacks,' Louisa told her.

Charlotte could see that the Reverend wasn't too keen on discussing the matter with her, so she resumed her seat at the table, which had now been cleared by the maids, and looked at him encouragingly. 'What did you have in mind?'

Cornered, he reached into his waistcoat and produced a letter. 'Perhaps you could take this in to Mr Austin,' he said loftily. 'It's from my bishop. He feels it is our Christian duty to reach out to the poor deprived children of those black people who are living in such squalor.'

'Very commendable,' Charlotte murmured. 'May I read it?'

The Reverend hesitated, but he could hardly insult his hostess.

'Of course,' he allowed.

Charlotte read the letter carefully and then looked up with a smile. 'What a wonderful programme. And this has been going on for quite some time?'

'Oh yes,' Mrs Billings said enthusiastically. 'Native children have to be rescued from their pagan environment and brought into the civilized world.'

'They'll be brought up as Christians,' her husband added, 'cared for and taught to assimilate into the white world. It's a charity that's very close to our hearts.'

'Yes, the Bishop explains here. You've already placed more than twenty children? Where do they go?'

'We have a mission school at Reedy Creek, about five miles from Brisbane, run by our lay brothers. Segregated, of course. The children are taught English, and as they grow older we place them with families where they can earn their keep.'

'Are they happy?'

'Indeed they are. They have plenty of company.'

'I've heard of this before,' Louisa said. 'It's a marvellous idea. The Church of England took in a score of children from my uncle's station in northern New South Wales. It's happening everywhere. And about time, otherwise what's to become of them? They can't remain tribal any more.'

'Exactly,' Billings said. 'We've already seen the drunkenness and contemptible behaviour of the blacks who have drifted into the slums of cities. We have to save them from destitution and despair. As many as we can . . .'

'And you want to take some of our tribal children?'

'Unfortunately, at this stage, we can only take three from here, because I don't have room on the wagon. Also, it is only a small school, but later we'll be able to receive more.'

'How old should they be?'

'We've room for boys at this stage. Six-year-olds . . .'

'Six?' Charlotte said, startled. 'Isn't that a bit young?'

'It's the best age. They pick up English quicker than older boys and they're more amenable to a new life. And it is a life we're giving them, a chance to survive in a changing world.'

Charlotte nodded. 'I suppose it would be. I'm sure Austin will approve. Our own boys had to go away to boarding school too. Of course, they were older. We had tutors for them in earlier years. Which reminds me, Louisa, have you decided on a tutor for Teddy? It's time he settled down to lessons . . .'

'I think a governess would be better for him to start with. Victor has been making enquiries through family and friends in Brisbane.'

'Then we'd better put a room aside for a young lady and open up a classroom again. It will be fun to furnish a classroom after all these years. There's so much more equipment available for children now . . .'

The Reverend Billings begged to interrupt for a minute. 'I really should have Mr Broderick's approval as soon as possible. We have picked out three healthy youngsters who should qualify – without mentioning their good fortune to them as yet, of course. So we should be on our way.'

'By all means,' Charlotte said. 'I'll speak to him.'

He'll approve quickly enough, she thought, when he wakes up to the fact that the missionaries want to leave.

'Where was Victor's schoolroom?' Louisa asked her, the plan to educate black children forgotten.

'Only in a shed. This house wasn't built then. Teddy will have a nice room, over this side of the house,' Charlotte laughed, 'so that Austin won't be wandering in to give instructions.'

When they adjourned from the garden room, Tom Billings went to their room to take a nap, but his wife, Amy, preferred to go for a walk on her own. She wished Tom hadn't been so hasty in saying that they would be leaving with the black children as soon as they got Broderick's approval. She had never been inside a house as luxurious as this in all her life – for that matter neither had Tom – and she was in no hurry to leave. Why should they rush? The journey out here in the wagon had taken weeks, a long, tedious, uncomfortable journey in this horrible Australian heat.

Tom and Amy were New Zealanders, from the South Island, where it was always lush and green. They had never had to cope with this dry heat, or the huge distances between villages. They'd undertaken this mission at the request of the Bishop, who'd assured them it would be a most pleasant journey, being springtime.

'Well, if this is spring,' Amy muttered to herself as she pulled her black felt hat down on her head, 'I hate to think what their summer will be like.'

She walked through to the wide entrance hall with its polished floors and expensive rugs and out through the open front door to stand on the porch overlooking the circular driveway that enclosed a superb garden, ablaze with roses.

Cost a pretty penny to keep even that garden going, she said to herself, noting the annuals that bordered the roses. Not that it matters to them, I suppose. They seem to have gardeners everywhere.

Amy recalled their first sight of this house. Prior to arriving here they'd found accommodation more suited to their humble purse, as they travelled through country towns, staying in boarding houses.

Then, as they'd forged into the sparsely populated areas of sheep stations they'd been put up, free, at homesteads, but nothing had prepared them for the homestead at Springfield. The others had only been overgrown cottages, with rooms tacked on for guests, where some of the women had remarked on their good fortune to be going on to Springfield.

'Are you going further out, to Narrabundi? Jimmy Hubbert's station?'

'No. We turn back at Springfield.'

'A pity. That's very nice too. But Springfield's the show place.'

Following hopeless directions, they'd turned down dirt tracks to find themselves at dead ends in this awful bush, or faced with river crossings, impassable in a wagon. They were lost and in the worst of humours, with not a house in sight anywhere, when two riders had found them and delivered them, hours later, to the entrance to the Broderick domain, a long drive lined with pines, welcome shade for the weary travellers.

In gratitude they gave the two men books of daily tracts from the library of the Church of the Holy Word, and set off along the drive.

Tom and Amy had always been Christians, but they'd felt that their local Church of England vicar was too soft on sinners – Tom's words – and had demanded that he take a stronger stand against evil in the community. While the vicar claimed that he quite understood their complaints, he did nothing to combat the evils of drink, gambling and social intemperance that prevailed in Queenstown. Then they met Pastor Williams, a truly Christian man, who agreed with them on every point and had no trouble converting them to the Church of the Holy Word.

When he called for missionaries among his small congregation, Tom and Amy stepped forward with pride. Tom gave up his job as a clerk in the education department, and on one glorious night they gave themselves over to the Holy Word. It was a tearful and uplifting experience, handing over all their worldly goods – the small house in Gresham Street that he'd inherited from his father, their savings, for Amy had also worked, as a laundress – for the glory of the Lord. It was the happiest day of their lives.

For two years they travelled throughout New Zealand, campaigning for Christ, knocking on doors to sell small tracts and Holy Bibles and, where possible, encourage people to join them in prayer. Sadly, few were inclined to give even a minute of their time to the Lord, but a donation was acceptable. They also raised money by holding street meetings, much as the Salvation Army followers did, but without the necessity of resorting to noisy drums and tin whistles. 'They make a fool of the Lord,' Tom always said, 'turning a service into a side show.'

At the close of their probation as lay preachers, Tom was ordained a reverend, a true vicar of Christ, at a special service held at headquarters. They called Pastor Williams' home on the outskirts of Christchurch 'headquarters' because it was from there that all goodness emanated. A humble man, he had declined the offer from Bishop Frawley in Brisbane to be elevated to higher office, preferring to remain pastor and church leader in New Zealand. (Tom had no such inhibitions; he hoped his good works would lead him on to a bishopric one day.) However, the Pastor had been persuaded to accept a suitable brick residence with a drawing room that had been blessed and turned into a chapel for services and meetings. His followers, or rather believers, were housed in timber huts at the rear of the block. They were overcrowded at times, but no one minded, because there were always a lot of comings and goings. Tom and Amy enjoyed their homecomings, meeting up with the others, comparing notes and preparing themselves to set off again with renewed enthusiasm.

Some people complained that Pastor Williams lived high on their earnings but Tom would have none of it. He called their grievances despicable, especially when he discovered that quite a few received commission on the sale of 'holy' objects such as paintings of the Lord and an array of imitation-gold crosses. He considered such things blasphemous and soon spoke to Pastor Williams about them . . .

Come to think of it, Amy mused as she strolled around the Brodericks' rose garden, I never did hear the outcome of that. Too much excitement at the time. That was when Pastor Williams gave us the news that we were being sent to join the Brisbane mission. In Australia!

She remembered that a spiteful woman, jealous of their good fortune, had told her that Bishop Frawley wasn't a real bishop at all. That he'd just started up the church and called himself a bishop! 'He's no better than Pastor Williams,' she'd said.

It was Tom who quashed that talk. 'The real truth is emerging with our church. We have to start somewhere. Keep in mind that St Peter was only a fisherman. Bishop Frawley is just the first of our bishops. One day we'll have many, many more.'

They still lived poor, she had to admit, but it was a sacrifice they were willing to make. On the other hand, they no longer had to suffer boring jobs, or worry about making ends meet; their time was their own and the Lord, through their church, provided for them. Amy smiled. 'Our shepherd,' she said aloud.

'And look where we are now!' she added, turning back to stare at the beautiful sandstone house wrapped about by wide, cool verandas in the colonial style. Further back, as if to allow the house to make its own statement, two matching wings extended to the right and the left from the main building. One of these contained the elegant guest quarters where she and Tom were staying. That wing even had a sitting room of its own, and a large bathroom! Since they were the only guests at present, they had the wing all to themselves. Such luxury!

When they'd emerged from the shadows of the pines at the end of the drive, Amy had gasped to find such a house out here in the wilderness. 'Oh my!' she'd said. 'Oh my! Have you ever seen such a lovely house?'

But Tom had been angry. 'It's an abomination! An insult to the Lord to wallow in such ostentation. Extravagance is the worst of sins, depriving the Lord of his dues. It is a disgusting waste of monies that should go to the saving of souls. Blessed are the poor. Remember that, Amy. These people will find it hard to locate the gates to heaven; they'll be blinded by their own grandiloquence.'

Nevertheless he forged on, driving the wagon right up to the elegant front steps that were guarded on either side by stone lions, while Amy, in trepidation, thought that perhaps they should go round the back. But Tom was made of sterner stuff. This house could not intimidate him.

She hoped he would have a good rest now, because he was in a rather bad mood. She had told him that he should speak to Mr Broderick about their mission while they were out walking, but he'd hushed her.

'I will speak to him in his office. That's where men discuss matters of importance, not prancing about on a guided tour.'

But Mrs Broderick had pre-empted him, thrown his plans out of kilter. The black children were important. They'd been given instructions to bring back three, and by the sound of things that would eventuate, but Tom had wanted to speak privately with Broderick about a chapel, as a lead-in to the all-important question. Broderick was a very wealthy man, and Bishop Frawley had said they could expect a substantial donation from him. As he'd said, 'Men like him won't blink at handing over a few hundred pounds, so don't think small. This isn't New Zealand.'

Now he'd have to try again to get into that office, in private. He couldn't broach the subject through the wife or even the son, it just wouldn't do. And the Bishop was relying on them.

She walked away from the house, towards all the big outbuildings where the real business of the property was conducted, and saw a group of riders galloping back to base across a clearing. Enjoying her walk, she kept going, close enough to watch them dismount and expertly slip the saddles and bridles from the horses before releasing them into a paddock. They were all young, energetic men, at a guess none much more than her own age, which was twenty-eight, and they all looked so manly in their check shirts and dungarees and short riding boots.

Amy blushed, embarrassed at her sinful thoughts. What would Tom say if he knew she'd been standing here admiring stockmen?

24

'Forgive me, Lord,' she whispered, turning away, but a voice behind her startled her.

'Talking to yourself, it's a bad sign!'

It was Rupe Broderick, the youngest son, and he was laughing at her. Amy was so confused she didn't know what to say to him. She tried to hurry away but he caught up with her.

'How are you today, Mrs Billings?'

She could smell the sweat and dust on him, and feel his strength as he fell into step beside her. He was only in his early twenties, but he was already a big man, muscles bulging under rolled-up sleeves, and long legs striding out.

She glanced at his tanned face, just long enough to see those mischievous blue eyes, and muttered, 'Very well, thank you.'

'How are you enjoying your stay?'

Amy wished he would go away. Surely he wasn't thinking of walking all the way back with her? She had no idea how to cope with a self-confident young gentleman like this, even if he was dressed in rough stockman's clothes.

'Very well, thank you,' she said primly.

'Have you seen the stud yet?'

'The what?'

'The stud. Where Springfield's finest merinos live.'

'No.'

'You should. The ram's there at the minute. Austin's pride and joy. Old Silver Floreat Della, purest of the pure, the daddy of them all, and still raring to go.'

Shocked, Amy turned down a path, away from him, and he stood, smiling.

'You'd better come back. That's a dead end. It just leads to the gardeners' sheds.'

'It doesn't matter,' she mumbled. 'It's just somewhere to walk.'

'Oh well, please yourself. See you later.'

At last she was rid of him. Was he deliberately teasing her, talking about the sheep? Trying to take a rise out of her by mentioning such a delicate subject? He had really upset her now. He wasn't a bit like his brother Victor, who was also a tall fellow, but craggy-faced and stern, very much the manager. Victor takes after his father, she mused, pacing away, head down, hat pulled forward like a monk's cowl to shield her face from any further intrusion. In the distance she could hear the rhythmic clang of a blacksmith's hammer. It reminded her of church bells, metal upon metal, and suddenly Amy was homesick. She missed Pastor Williams and their tight little group of dedicated Christians. She found that country folk over here were different, more cynical, less inclined to accept the Holy Word without argument, which was disquieting. Even the women would challenge her on points of doctrine and Amy would find herself floundering, unable to provide adequate responses.

'Then study the Bible more,' Tom had counselled her. 'The answers are all there.'

'Sometimes I think they're laughing at us,' she worried.

'No, they're not,' he said. Tom was always a pillar of strength. 'They're just covering up their own ignorance. They're all descendants of convicts, the criminal classes. What can you expect?'

In a little fit of rebellion, Amy looked back at the big house and considered the Broderick family. If they are descended from convicts, they're not doing too badly, she noted to herself.

Rupe strolled into the kitchen and caught Hannah, the cook, unawares, grabbing her round her plump waist and lifting her up. 'How's my favourite cook lady today?'

'Put me down, Rupe,' she laughed, extricating herself. 'You are a one! I suppose you're hungry?'

'If you've got some of those cold pigs' trotters left, I am. Where are they hidden?'

'Leave them. You'll spoil your dinner. I'll make you a sandwich.'

'Good idea, I'll have both.'

'Oh, very well.' Hannah smiled indulgently. She had been cook at Springfield for more years than she could count. She'd watched the three boys grow up and was very fond of them, but Rupe was her favourite. He'd always been a wilful kid, born to create mayhem, and whenever he was in trouble, it was Hannah he'd turn to. She delighted in the angelic smile that belied his boldness, and so she'd become his backstop. She defended his naughty ways, even hid him when Mr Austin was on the warpath; and in return Rupe amused her, keeping her in fits with his tales of the goings-on round the station.

He nosed about the pantry, returning with a plate of jellied trotters, and stood, sucking at the bones, while she made the sandwiches.

'I just met the black widow out by the horse paddock,' he commented.

'Who?'

'You know. Mrs Preacher. How much longer are they staying?'

'I haven't been told.'

'What are they up to? Why are they hanging about here anyway?'

'There's some talk they want to build a church.'

'Fat chance. No, I've got the feeling there's more to them than meets the eye.'

'Like what?'

'I don't know. Pair of phoneys, if you ask me. Has the mare foaled yet?'

'Not yet. Victor's inside with your dad. They were looking for you a while ago.'

Rupe was leaning against a bench, devouring his makeshift meal, when Minnie came in to help Cook begin preparing the dinner. He watched as she shuffled across the stone floor, barefoot, eyes downcast.

'Now, Minnie my girl,' he said, 'what's with the long face? Haven't you got a smile for me? You know you're my best girl.'

'Don't tease her,' Hannah said. She turned to glance at the Aborigine maid, who normally took no notice of Rupe's banter, and saw she was not her usual cheerful self.

'What's wrong, Minnie?'

'Nuttin',' Minnie said sullenly, and made her way over to the basket of potatoes in the corner of the kitchen.

Rupe shrugged, polished off the last sandwich and left them to it. Having disposed of his dusty work clothes, he took a shower and retreated to his room to throw himself on the bed for a nap.

That was where Victor found him. 'Get up. The old man wants us, he's on a real rampage.'

'What have I done this time?'

'Nothing. He's declaring war.'

'On who?' Rupe jerked up on the bed, running his hands sleepily through his still-damp hair.

'On a world full of conspirators against squatters.'

'Oh Jesus! What next?'

'Don't ask. Just get a move on.'

Chapter Two

Minnie was confused and upset, and she was grateful that neither Rupe nor Hannah pressed her for an explanation, because she hadn't got the worry straight in her mind yet. Even after years working for the white people, she could still have occasional lapses in understanding their language.

Hannah and Victor, not Rupe, were her favourites at the big house. The cook treated her well, often giving her leftovers to take down to the camp where most of her family lived. Victor was always kind, even though he had grown into being a bossman like his daddy.

When she became pregnant with Bobbo – real name Bobburah – there'd been such a fuss, because she'd refused to name the father. He was a stockman who had threatened to beat her if she told, so she kept quiet, and then she'd been shocked to hear that Mr Victor was being blamed, just because he was her friend. They'd grown up together. She could hardly tell any of the white people that neither Victor nor Harry ever came near the black women. Rupe did, though. He was a villain, always chasing black girls, hanging about the camp of nights. They were all glad when there was talk of him going to live in the city, but he never did go. Once he came home from school, he stayed.

She'd thought Victor would have been angry with her over her stubborn silence, but he'd only laughed. 'What have you got there, Min? Black or white?'

'Black piccaninny comen,' she'd blushed, lying to be on the safe side, and it was a relief when the baby was born beautifully black, accepted by her own family without the confusion a half-caste child usually caused. By that time the stockman had left, so the problem just faded away. Minnie's real name was Moomabarrigah. She was Cullya, of the emu people, her mother's clan of the great Kamilaroi tribe that once owned all this land, from far south through to the blue ranges where the sun set. Now, though, the Kamilaroi people were scattered. Minnie's father had been killed by whitefellers, in a raid on a hunting party. They'd said he was a renegade, leader of a bad mob, but his people said that was not true. Sometimes Minnie wished it was. Unlike her sister Nioka, she was a shy girl, but she liked to think of her father as a great warrior, a fighting man, and she hoped he had been a renegade, giving all those whitefellers their own back.

After his death, life had become even more difficult for the Cullya people. Many went north into the hot lands to seek refuge with distant tribes, some just drifted into the white men's towns, but Minnie's immediate family and friends tried to make do in the country they knew. Sadly, that was hardly possible any more, because the whites kept moving them on to make way for their families and all their livestock.

In the end it was Minnie's mother who'd made the decision, after much argument, to 'go in'. Her name could not be mentioned now, because she had died last summer, but in her day she had been a strong, brawny woman, with a loud voice, and the white men soon came to know who was boss in this mob.

She had gone, on her own, to front up to Mr Broderick and demand that they be allowed a permanent camp at the bend of the river, well away from his house camps. In return she would see to it that there would be no more fighting, no more killing sheep and no more stealing from stores.

So they struck a deal. He even agreed to give the mob of about fifty Cullya people two eating sheep per month and occasional presents of tea and flour and tobacco, if they were good.

It didn't always work, though. Every so often the girls would hear their mother engaged in shouting matches with Mr Broderick, as she defended her people, right or wrong, waving her heavy waddy at him, demanding he keep his men away from the black women. He would yell back at her, threatening to throw the whole mob off his property, and that would send her into a rage. She was a fierce woman, standing nearly as tall as he was, and she'd never back down, because, as she'd said, he was a good man, as white men went.

Eventually they'd sit down, have a smoke and a talk, and even end up laughing, to the amazement of the rest of the mob, who'd congregate among the trees, afraid of being expelled from their last campsite.

Only Minnie and Nioka knew the real despair in their mother's heart. When they went walkabout, fulfilling the old laws by visiting the ancient sites, she saw how impossible it was all becoming. Sacred places were being desecrated, land cleared where once they knew they could find nuts and honey in their travels, and the big mobs of emus driven off. That hurt her more than anything else. Emus were their totem, untouchable, never to be harmed, and as the numbers dwindled so did her strength. She cared less and less about their plight, and spent her last days fishing and daydreaming.

But Mr Broderick had come to respect her, and he'd been there, standing vigil outside her humpy as her family mourned, and her life ebbed away.

Minnie had been impressed by this kind act, but not so Nioka. She was more like her mother, fiery, bossy, a fighter. She wanted to drive him away.

'He was not invited,' she cried. 'How dare he intrude! His people killed her heart.'

'Respect, Nioka! He is showing respect.'

'We don't need his respect. You're only saying that because you work for him. You don't want to lose your stupid job.'

'That's not true.'

Minnie left the kitchen and went out to the produce shed, where she chose a big pumpkin, put it on a bench and skilfully whacked it into four pieces with a small machete. She sighed, delaying her return. She wondered if she would have had a different attitude that day if she hadn't been protecting her job.

Mrs Broderick had brought her up to work for her when Minnie was twelve. It had been difficult at first, making sense of a house and a language, but she'd tried very hard and she didn't make too many mistakes now. Other girls had come and gone over the years but Minnie had lasted the longest. She was settled now, and she liked being part of both worlds. Two black girls had jobs as housemaids but Minnie liked the kitchen work best. She was good at helping the cook, who appreciated her.

On the other hand, Nioka had flatly refused to work for the whites. She didn't mind looking after little Teddy because she liked him and he was a playmate for her boy and Minnie's son, but no one could persuade her to go into service, as it was called. She'd play with the three little boys near the house, or take them down to the camp for a swim, and the Broderick people accepted her rule. They knew that Teddy was much loved by the blacks, and no harm would come to him with so many people watching over him, delighted with the white-haired boy.

Dismally, Minnie stomped back to the kitchen carrying the pumpkin pieces and handfuls of beans in a wide enamel dish.

What would Nioka say if she knew?

Hannah took no notice of her as she proceeded with her chores, peeling the pumpkin and stringing the beans with a small knife, or with her teeth when Hannah's back was turned.

What exactly had she heard when she was clearing up after their tea meal? Minnie wasn't too sure. She'd been in and out with trays and had only picked up scraps of the conversation. And that praying man and his missus talked in singsong voices, not straight out like the rest of them, so maybe she'd misunderstood. That happened often enough. But they were saying something about taking the children away. The black children. Not Teddy. But they wouldn't do that, would they?

She knew the Broderick boys went away to school when they were big enough. Teddy would have to go when he was twelve, she supposed. But she'd distinctly heard that man say six-year-olds, because Mrs Broderick had repeated it.

Six? Minnie shuddered. Her boy was six. Jagga was seven. And there were others about the same age at the camp. Minnie was so fearful she wanted to scream.

'You're day-dreaming again, missy,' Hannah said. 'Get on with it. I want some apples peeled too, and then you can get me some milk and cheese from the dairy.'

High on a cliff overlooking the ocean sat a very old man. He wore his hair in a high cone, plastered in place with beeswax and shells, and around his neck hung a cord threaded through a mean-looking crocodile tooth. His dark, skinny frame was clothed only in a loincloth but the body was so laced with cicatrices they almost gave the impression of a garment. A glance at the poor old fellow presented a picture of the cruel ravages of age, but he looked weak and feeble only until his eyes snapped open. Moobuluk did not need to shade them from the strong sunlight; they glistened, brown and bright, as alert as those of a man a quarter of his age.

Beside him sprawled a three-legged dingo. The animal had faced the choice of dying in a white man's trap or chewing off his own leg. He'd decided on life, then, finding that he was no longer boss of the pack, had attached himself to this human, who also seemed to have been left behind to die.

But the dingo was wrong. Moobuluk was no derelict. Far from it. Not only was he a distinguished elder of the emu people, he had been endowed with great responsibilities. The Dreaming had taken him deeper and deeper into the profound secrets and mysteries of his race, and now he was the most famous magic man on this side of the continent, because he had outlived all his mentors. Moobuluk had travelled far beyond his Kamilaroi lands for many, many years. He'd met and conferred with the chiefs of countless tribes, including the wise Jangga people, the strange Manganggai and the fierce Warungas, because he spoke many languages and was known as a listening man. More than this, though, he was always made welcome because his powers were greatly feared, never underestimated.

On this day he gazed sadly at the brilliant blue of the ocean, which hid, he knew, a reef of such colours as would put a rainbow to shame. This was his favourite sitting place in the whole world. His own secrets had taken an age to divine from a lifetime of listening and learning, but his lifespan was trivial compared with the eons it had taken those tiny polyps to build their massive underwater treasure. It was a humbling experience to contemplate time in that context. And amusing. And pleasurable. All about him was such a richness of colour, from that sea-blue, as brilliant as the blue stones he'd found out in the dry country, to the softer blue expanse of sky, to the rich green of the steamy forests of these mountains, lit by an amazing variety of flashy, cheeky birds.

He would be sorry to leave here, but it had come to him on the wind that he was needed elsewhere.

But where to turn these days? There was so much anguish caused by the white invaders, so much despair, that he could hardly contain his own sense of hopelessness. He couldn't hold back the tide; destiny had overtaken the old order and replaced it with ... what? Moobuluk could not reach into his great store of knowledge for the answers, because the whole structure was based on the experience of thousands of lifetimes, passed on to men like him. The white men were not part of the Dreaming, nor were their animals, or even the strange plants they'd introduced, so he had no base to work from ...

He scratched his belly and looked down at the dog. 'The Jangga people are calling me but I can't go that way because those Cullya people are headed for trouble.' That irritated him a little. Obviously the Jangga had much more serious problems than the little mob down south. Taking the lead from his great-granddaughter, they had 'gone in' and settled on a sheep station, so they couldn't be in too much trouble.

But the concern nagged. Something bad was in the wind by that great river. And they were family. Immediate family. It was his duty to respond.

Moobuluk wasn't looking forward to returning to his home territory. Even though peace dwelled there now, it distressed him to visit memories of his childhood by the big-man river, and know that that joyful way of life was lost to his descendants. He found no consolation in realizing that the mob now living under Broderick's laws accepted their lot and even claimed to be content, because he grieved to see the old ways passing.

Oh yes. He knew Broderick. And he'd known the one called Kelly, too. The first white men to enter Cullya country without permission. Not that any of the whitefellers ever asked permission, but in taking those first steps they'd broken tribal law. Normally peaceful people, the Cullya men had been curious at first; then, when it dawned on them that the whites were digging in, they'd tried frightening them off, to no avail. Then they'd harassed them, killing sheep, starting bush fires, stealing their food which, Moobuluk recalled with a grin, was good eating.

In the end they'd attacked in force. The first time they'd met the power of guns. It was all over in minutes, with six men dead and several wounded. Shocked beyond belief, they'd dashed back into the cover of the scrub, where they were forced to face the inevitable. That was the first and last open battle with Broderick.

There were consultations with the elders, arguments and discussions went on for weeks, and then into months, while more and more whites arrived with their huge mobs of animals alien to this Cullya land. Finally it was decided that the guns were too strong; there should be no more attacks, but payback had to be enforced.

All this time Moobuluk, already considered an elder at that stage, had been tracking the two white bosses as they went about their work, and studying them.

He spoke at the meeting when it was agreed that a fitting payback would be to pick off those two men.

'No, just one of them,' he'd said. 'A ritual killing, so that the other boss will know we could just as easily have killed him too. The big feller with the white hair is quieter, a thinking man, leave him in charge. If we kill them both, then who might come after him? Another boss even more savage than this one?'

And so it was.

After payback, when they'd speared one of the bosses, the two men who had been appointed to carry out the killing left the district. There was big trouble as a result, with horsemen raiding the camps, some intent on killing every black in sight, even the women and children, but Broderick had stopped them. He was told by the elders that the culprits had gone, so in retaliation he ordered twenty young men to leave his land, forever.

That had caused huge grief among the people, as Broderick had known it would, but he was adamant. His payback decimated the clan, but at least lives were spared.

Moobuluk had been there when the woman of his kin died, the mother of the two girls. She had called to him as she was slipping away to her Dreaming, and so he'd appeared beside her to show her the way. The old men inside the death humpy had known who he was, and they were proud that the woman could summon up so powerful a man, though they continued their chanting without a sideways glance.

He'd recognized Broderick standing among the trees behind the weeping women, paying his respects, and nodded to himself, relieved that he'd chosen the right man so long ago, but he made no move towards him. Moobuluk rarely associated with white men. It would not do, nor was it necessary. He could, however, understand their language, and that was enough.

Instead he drifted away to stand gazing at his beloved river, and when his great-granddaughter passed over, the dingo howled mournfully. As silently as he'd come, Moobuluk walked away into the night.

He could see a great ship with sails like wings out there on the blue sea, and he marvelled at its grace, but reluctantly he turned away. Duty called.

By the time Rupe made his appearance with his brother, Austin Broderick was ready for them. He sat them down at the table piled with section maps and began: 'Now, this is where we start.'

'Start what?' Rupe said.

'Start protecting Springfield.'

'From what?'

'Jesus Christ! Do I have to go through this all over again? Didn't you explain the situation to him, Victor?'

'I told him you were scared selectors were going to grab great hunks of Springfield.'

'Scared. Who said I'm bloody scared? It's the selectors who'll need to be scared.'

Victor shook his head. 'You never listen to me. I keep telling you the Selection Acts, or the Lands Acts as they call them now, will never get passed. Not a chance in hell.'

'But what if they do?' Rupe said, and his father slammed a fist on the table.

'Exactly. What if they do? There'll be a rush for land that will equal gold rushes. At least land is a sure thing. And this is what we're here to discuss. Have you got any suggestions?'

'Yeah.' Rupe grinned. 'We'll run them off. A few shots up their backsides will soon discourage settlers.'

'And if there is such a law, you'll be breaking it,' Victor said angrily.

'So what?' his father snorted. 'It's my land. My only alternative to keep Springfield intact would be to buy all the leases, which I can't afford.'

Rupe stood back and stretched. 'Of course you can. Freehold the lot, and if you need more ready cash, borrow the money. You're in good with the banks.'

'That's just the sort of stupid thing you would say,' Victor snapped at Rupe. 'You just heard Dad say he can't afford it. We'd be in debt for generations.'

Austin ignored them. 'We have two plans of attack. First we employ more boundary riders to keep out intruders, and secondly we start marking off the best land.' He explained the necessity to identify and map the areas most suited for pasture: 'That way we'll cut off possible selectors from access and essential water, and leave rocky, hilly, scrubby stuff to the scabs who want to get in here.'

'You're talking as if it has already happened,' Victor remonstrated. 'It's not a foregone conclusion, only wishful thinking on the part of selectors who think they're on to a good thing.'

'Which they could be,' Rupe said. 'We'll just have to start deciding on our best grazing areas.'

'That'll be no bloody problem,' Austin said. 'The maps are here. We know this country, they don't. We'll start now. Victor, get some pencils. And rubbers.'

'Now?' Rupe said. 'Why now? We've got plenty of time.'

'Who says so? I don't.'

'But it will take all night.'

'I don't care if it takes a week. We'll work on the maps between us, then you two can get out there and peg boundaries, so we can get surveyors on the job.'

They were all studying the maps, making tentative lines, when Charlotte came in to remind them it was dinner time.

'Our guests are waiting,' she added.

Austin was so involved in his plans, he hardly raised his head. 'You go ahead. We're busy.'

'But your dinner will be spoiled.'

He twisted in his chair. 'Didn't you hear me? We'll eat later.'

Charlotte looked to her sons, but since they didn't respond, she retreated.

Angrily she informed Hannah, who also was not impressed, and took the guests through to the dining room, where they were joined by Louisa.

'Where are the men?' her daughter-in-law demanded.

'They'll eat later.'

'Why not now?'

'They're busy.'

Louisa turned back to the door. 'I'll see about that!'

'I wouldn't,' Charlotte said, and Louisa, taking the warning, sat in her place with an irritated sigh.

'Then I shall say grace,' Billings announced.

Amy sat meekly beside her husband while they were served dinner, a delicious meal of thick soup, succulent lamb chops with bowls of beautiful vegetables, and her favourite dessert, steamed apricot pudding with custard and whipped cream. But she couldn't enjoy it: her back ached, and Tom glared at her whenever she attempted to speak, even to answer questions. She knew her real punishment would come later.

He had been in a very bad mood, frustrated in his attempts to speak to Mr Broderick at the time he had chosen, and his host's absence from the dinner table didn't help. But Amy knew that she had upset him too, and she was very sorry about that, she should have known better.

When she came in from her walk he'd been waiting for her.

'Where have you been? My socks need darning and all you can think about is skipping about this godless place as if you owned it.'

'I only went for a walk. I'll darn your socks now.'

He threw them at her. 'Do you expect me to be like these overindulged sinners? I only have two pairs of socks, I will only ever own two pairs of socks, praise the Lord, one pair in the weekly wash and one pair ready to wear. But what do I find? Holes!'

'I'm sorry. I'll darn them.'

'There isn't time if we are to obey the rules of this house.' He grabbed them back. 'I shall wear them, holes and all, and if they notice, it will be a good lesson in humility for you. Not for me. Who did you walk with?'

The question was so sudden, Amy was nonplussed. 'On my own, of course.'

He punched her in the back and she fell against the wall. 'Liar! I was in the bathroom down the passage. I looked out of the window and saw you walking with a man.'

'Oh no, Tom, I wasn't . . .'

'Lies again!' He grabbed her by the hair and pulled her to her feet, shaking her until she bit her tongue.

'Oh Tom, don't,' she pleaded. 'He walked with me. I didn't invite him. It was only Rupe Broderick.'

'Is that what you call him? Rupe? Since when have you become so familiar?'

'We were told to call the sons . . . Rupe and Victor.'

'I was told. Not you. Have you no shame? You're a married woman. On your knees.'

As his belt lashed her back, Amy clenched her teeth on a towel, so that she would not cry out. She would hate for anyone to hear what was happening, because they wouldn't understand. Tom loved her, it was just that she had trouble keeping up to his standards of Christian living, and she often defaulted. As he had explained to her so many times, in better moods, he had enough trouble fighting the devil himself, without having to fight her battles as well. Amy knew she would have to try harder, that was all, because Tom was a good husband, and he did care for her. He was constantly afeared that he might have to go on to heaven without her unless she learned to please the Lord. A truly caring man. Not too many husbands had the foresight to think ahead as Tom did; they were all too selfish.

The other two women at table with her would hardly have seen Tom Billings as a caring husband. In fact, had they known that he beat his wife, and under their very roof, they'd have been calling for the horsewhip. On the other hand, both women did consider their own husbands selfish. Charlotte because he deprived her of that romantic love she had always yearned for, and Louisa because Victor allowed his father to make the running on everything. Her wishes took second place. He loved her, he loved her dearly, she knew that, and he was so proud of her, always introducing her as 'my beautiful wife', and making a fuss of her whenever he could. But it just wasn't good enough having to compete with that tyrant of a father, who, Louisa was well aware, had disapproved of the marriage.

Grimly she picked up her spoon and attacked the soup, leaving Charlotte to nod wisely at the Reverend, who had once again launched into a monologue about the Second Coming, interspersed with soupy slurpings. He had the worst table manners, and that added to Louisa's irritation. If only the men were here, the women wouldn't have to put up with his sermonizing. What did Rupe call it?

A captive audience.

He thought the missionaries were funny. He would!

Glancing up, Louisa caught sight of her reflection in a gilt-edged mirror on the wall, and was consoled. Victor need never be ashamed of her, even if she was only a storekeeper's daughter, and not born into the Queensland élite like he was. In fact, it was often said that she and Victor could be taken for sister and brother. They were both tall, fair and blue-eyed, but as Louisa liked to insist, there the similarity ended. After all, one didn't need to be likened to a man. Her hair was long and silky, almost to her waist, and Victor adored it, made her promise that scissors would never touch the lovely strands. Her features were fine, her skin was clear and free of freckles, and her mouth was small. 'Like a rosebud,' Victor had said.

She frowned. Her father had warned her, when she married Victor: 'Don't let them put you down, love. You remember, we're as good as any of them. My dad was a free settler. Broderick's grandpa came here in chains. You keep your chin up.'

At the time, Louisa had been so excited at the prospect of marrying Victor, who had been courting her for a year, that she'd considered his advice too silly for words. Victor was mad about her. What else mattered? Plenty, she now thought, sullenly. But there wasn't much she could do about it.

Minnie came in and took the plates one by one, moving slowly as if her feet were lead weights, until Charlotte noticed and frowned at her.

She brought in the chops and vegetables but overturned a jug, slopping gravy on to the crisp damask cloth.

'Oh Lord, now look what you've done,' Charlotte cried. 'What's the matter with you?'

'I'll get a cloth,' Louisa said, jumping up.

'No. Stay where you are,' Charlotte instructed. 'I'll attend to it.'

She took a napkin to sop up the mess. 'Hand me another one, Minnie.' But their waitress burst into tears and dashed out of the room.

Having been told to sit, to stay put, Louisa ignored all the confusion. Just another example of her status in this family.

'I'm nothing here,' she'd told Victor. 'Your father treats me as if I haven't got a brain in my head, on top of making it obvious that his son married beneath him. And Charlotte won't even let me pick up a broom.'

'She doesn't want you to have to worry about anything. She runs the house, you've got Teddy to look after.'

'She runs *her* house, you mean!'

38

She and Charlotte were friendly, but they were not friends. Not like the girlfriends that Louisa had now lost touch with. They'd never even had an argument. Sometimes Louisa wished they could, so she could find out who Charlotte really was, this plain woman with her stringy red hair, who presided over the Springfield mansion with a fussiness that bordered on obsession, all to please her husband. They had nothing in common, except Teddy of course. Charlotte even regarded fashion as giddy, while Louisa adored lovely clothes. She allowed herself a grim smile.

The dress she was now wearing, just to dine in her own home, since the Brodericks dressed for dinner, had cost twenty pounds. An absolute fortune. Her father wouldn't have earned that in the old shop in a week, and yet here she was, swanning through a boring meal in a beautifully cool Swiss organza embroidered with yellow butterflies.

'They should be bees,' she'd commented to Victor when the dress had arrived last week. Bought mail-order from a catalogue.

'Why bees?'

'It doesn't matter,' Louisa had said. Hadn't Napoleon decreed that golden bees be embroidered on to all his raiment? Why not the bloody Brodericks and golden butterflies? It was the same set-up. These squatters and their ilk thought they owned the world. Which they probably did, she admitted. Their world.

So why was she so unhappy? Louisa wished her mother was still alive. She'd tried to talk to her father when he'd last visited Springfield, but he'd been swallowed up by his enthusiasm for her grand lifestyle. By Teddy, his sweet little grandson. By Austin's assistance in extending his store into a warehouse for country people to buy supplies at less than retail prices, as long as they ordered in bulk, which was a necessity for squatters like the Brodericks anyway. Her father, who was now on his way to becoming quite well off, had also become a fan of the great Austin Broderick, no longer a battler, suspicious of the upper classes.

And there was no point in trying to talk to Charlotte, who always had her ears pinned to the doors as if her bloody husband was out there, eavesdropping.

There was more to Charlotte, there had to be, if only one could break through, Louisa mused, turning her nose up at steamed pudding, which she hated. And there's more to me. I'm not going to allow this lot to keep me here, trying to think how to fill in the days. I want my own home. But Austin would never allow Victor to build another house on Springfield, even though there was space to burn. He had built this huge house for his family.

The Reverend was expounding. Still. On the Second Coming.

'When should we expect this?' Louisa asked, in bitchy mood.

'Very soon.'

'But how soon? Like next week or next century? In which case we won't be here.'

'Ha! That is the trap so many fall into. Why should the Lord tell you, a mite in the universe, when He will strike? The truth is in the Bible and only true believers in the Holy Word will be ready to receive His grace.'

'What true believers?'

'The folk we are blessing, baptizing, through our mission, dear lady.'

'And where has your mission taken you, Reverend?'

'From across the Tasman to your fair land.'

Louisa saw Charlotte's eyebrows raised in disapproval. She did not like her guests, but neither did she appreciate carping.

Well, to hell with that, Louisa decided, bravado increased by the absence of frowns from her husband, who chided her occasionally for talking too much.

He had been right, initially. No one knew better than Louisa herself that when she'd first arrived she *had* talked too much. Chattered. Rattled on. Especially at the dinner table, fortified by wine. But that had been sheer nervousness and the awful realization had only made her worse. Gradually, with effort, she had managed to quieten down, but not to the extent of being silenced. Louisa had her own opinions, and considered she was entitled to express them whenever it suited her, despite old Austin's glowers and the twitching of Victor's nose.

'What happens to the people who are not privy to your blessings, Reverend?' she asked suddenly. 'I mean, all the rest of the world? Are the gates of heaven closed to them?'

He sopped up gravy with a crust of bread and smiled at her.

'Ha! Good question. That is why we are working so hard. We want to bring all souls to the Lord.'

'What about me then? As an Anglican, am I doomed?'

Charlotte intervened. 'Really, Louisa, this is hardly the place for such hair-splitting. Remember . . . in my Father's house are many mansions.'

Louisa saw the Reverend's smile turn to a scowl, and she wondered if Charlotte realized she had shot his creed down in flames. You never knew with Charlotte.

'Well, tell me this,' she asked him, grasping the opportunity to tease him further. 'When the black children return, will they be of your religion, Reverend? Or will they be aware, as Charlotte says, of the many mansions?' She refrained from adding: 'and not come back as bigoted as you are.'

Mrs Billings jerked up from her lethargy and seemed about to say something, but her husband overrode her. 'It is our duty to rescue the black children from their pagan existence and lead them into the light of Christianity, since no one else on these stations seemed inclined to do so. Surely you do not begrudge them this God-given opportunity, Mrs Broderick?'

'Of course not,' Charlotte said quickly. 'You yourself agreed, Louisa, that this is an excellent programme. I thought we'd take our coffee out on the veranda this evening, it's so much cooler.' She turned to the guests. 'You'll join us, of course?'

Billings picked up the battered prayer book that he always carried and glanced uncertainly at the darkened veranda.

'I think not. We shall retire now.'

As he intoned grace, Louisa almost burst out laughing. Prior to this, when the men withdrew to Austin's den for port and cigars, the Reverend, being a teetotaller and a non-smoker, had preferred not to join them. Instead he'd produced that prayer book and read to the women in the parlour until sheer boredom had caused them to make excuses and bolt. But there were no lamps on the veranda; they brought hordes of insects. A reading was out of the question. She wondered if Charlotte realized this.

Amy was mystified. When they returned to their room, having missed out on the excellent coffee and tiny biscuits Mrs Broderick served after dinner, thanks to Tom's decision not to partake, he was in a worse mood.

'Godless lot!' he snarled. 'That woman did it on purpose.'

'Did what?'

'Deliberately invited us outdoors where it would not be possible for me to read the chapters I had chosen for this evening.'

'Why not?'

'Because there is no light out there, you stupid woman. But they will suffer, the Lord is vengeful. You mark my words. Now kneel and begin your penance. I haven't forgotten your evil doings of this afternoon.'

Obediently Amy kneeled, facing the wall, at the same time grasping her ankles behind her in an agonizing stance, her neck straining and her back arched.

'Now say after me: "I rebuke you, Satan. I cast out the devil . . ."'

These sessions only ended when Amy collapsed on the floor, begging the Lord for forgiveness, grateful to be able to stretch out, face down, restored to His fold. Though painful, she found the penance heightened her awareness of the Lord, and when she was permitted to rise, she too could cry out 'Hallelujah! Hallelujah!' in harmony again with her husband.

But the question still remained.

As she climbed into bed she reminded him: 'That Mrs Broderick, Louisa. Did you hear what she said about the black children?'

He nodded. 'Ah yes. I heard.'

'She seems to think they're coming back.'

41

'Which just goes to prove the ignorance of the woman. She claims to be an Anglican but knows nothing of theology. And on top of that she has totally misunderstood our mission. These black children have to be removed from the filth of paganism and animalistic ways. If they were brought back they'd only sink into depravity again.'

'That's what I thought. She seems to think they're off to a boarding school like white children. Perhaps you should explain to her . . .'

'Definitely not! We do not have to explain the word of the Lord to a hoyden like her. Did you see that dress she had on? Cut so low in the front it was an obscenity before my very eyes. Her husband should tear it from her. Now remove the sheet.'

Dutifully, Amy settled her long nightdress about her until only her toes peeped out and tossed back the sheet, watching as he climbed over to straddle her in his heavy nightshirt.

'I'm ready now,' he announced. 'Cover your face.'

She pulled out her pillow and settled it over her face so that he could commune with dignity.

'What's so important that they're missing dinner?' Hannah asked, and Charlotte shrugged.

'I've not been informed. But there's a way to find out. Make me up a tray of cold cuts and anything else you can put your hand to, and I'll take it in myself. They can't expect you to sit about all night.'

'The vegetables are soggy now anyway,' Hannah sniffed. 'I'll make a bubble and squeak out of them tomorrow. Minnie, you cut a pile of bread and butter it.'

Minnie emerged from the scullery, her dark eyes red from crying. 'What you say?'

'The bread! Cut the bread! Get butter from the pantry! God help us, girl, what's got into you?'

Charlotte stared at her. 'Are you all right, Minnie? That was just an accident in the dining room. There's no need for you to get so upset.' She reached out to the girl but Minnie cringed away as if she was afraid she'd be slapped.

'For heaven's sake,' Charlotte said. 'You're shaking like a leaf. Are you sick, Minnie?'

'No, missus,' the girl wept.

'I don't think she's well,' Charlotte said to Hannah. 'Let her go off and we'll see how she is in the morning.'

Relieved of her duties, Minnie sped out of the back door and ran down the path behind the guest quarters. As she passed the room where the evil pair slept she heard the woman scream: 'Hallelujah! Hallelujah!' A terrifying scream that rent the soft night air. Minnie stumbled in fear, not understanding the words. She picked herself up and ran, on and on, past the sleeping hut she shared with the other black housegirls and out across the paddocks. Still in a panic, she

42

hitched up her cotton shift and hurdled fences on the run as effortlessly as a trained athlete. When she came to the river she slowed, feeling safer now, in her own environment.

Then she began to trudge along the familiar trail towards the camp, unconcerned by the dark of the moonless night.

Her people wouldn't ask any questions. She was permitted one night a week to return to the camp and they would think this was her night off. They didn't count the days like the whites.

But still she had to be careful. Not say a word yet in case they laughed at her for being such a ninny. Frightened by shades of white talk and screaming women.

She had heard more, though. They were still talking about taking away black children. Once again she'd only picked up scraps of the conversation because she'd been so nervous and spilled things, but Louisa had said something about when the black children came back. Minnie was sure in her own mind that they did intend to send some of the black boys off to school, just as they had done with Victor and Harry and Rupe. And then, like Mr Broderick's sons, they would be brought home again.

But why? Black children didn't belong in those places. What was the point? Nioka laughed at her, but Minnie saw a future for her Bobbo right here on the station. He already knew some English, and when he was older she would ask Victor to teach him to ride the horses. He could be a stockman, have a job here.

Nioka, she admitted, was a lot wiser. She noticed things. She noticed that all the white staff were paid but the blacks were not. And that was true. Not even the boys who worked as stockmen. But their mumma had been angry with Nioka over that, she'd said it was good to get jobs like Minnie had done, it gave them a place to learn, even if they didn't get paid money.

What exactly she achieved by learning to work in the house, Minnie was never sure, because at times, when she was real tired from the long, regimented days, she envied her sister's untroubled life in the camp, coming up to the house to play with Teddy only when she felt like it. Or rather, when Bobbo and Jagga insisted on visiting their playmate. Because, Minnie thought sadly, she rarely saw her own son. Nioka took care of him now, while his mother was miles away, working for the whites.

Surefooted, Minnie stepped out on to a flat rock she knew so well, sat down and paddled her feet in the rushing waters, relaxing in the sudden chill.

That wasn't right, she knew. Many a time Nioka had spat at her, in arguments over Bobbo, that if she wanted him brought up her way, she should be down at the camp with him like a good mother, not prancing away to wait on whites. And what for? For nothing but free feeds and the occasional pat on the head.

'They don't care about you!' Nioka had shouted. 'If you die they'll just pull up someone younger than you and teach her to obey. Slap her until she gets it right.'

And that was true too. Minnie had come in for a lot of slaps from Hannah and Mrs Broderick to help her learn, when she was younger. But then they never hit her as hard as Mumma would, when she was cranky with her girls. Getting a clout from Mumma, with or without her famous waddy, was like being kicked by a horse.

It was all very confusing. Who was right? Nioka or Mumma? Nioka, strangely, was more old-fashioned than Mumma had been. Nioka wanted to keep to the old ways. Even her husband had disagreed with her. He had run off not long after Jagga was born, to see the white man's towns, and word had it that he had caught some sickness and couldn't return even if he wanted to.

Minnie sighed. She supposed she had better get going. It was only a couple of miles on to the camp and most of the people would be sleeping by this. She felt a rustle in the bushes nearby and stiffened warily, her sharp eyes accustomed to the darkness now.

A three-legged dingo padded out of the scrub below her and dropped down the sandy bank to drink. Then it turned and looked up at her, its eyes soft and calm. It shook the water from its jaws and quietly padded away.

Minnie was up and running again.

She plunged through the camp to find Nioka and wake her.

'Nioka, wake up! Wake up! Moobuluk is here! He's back.'

'Shut up!' Nioka was sleeping in her bark humpy by the river bank. She heaved herself up on her elbow. 'Shut up, you'll wake the kids.'

'Moobuluk is here, I tell you. I saw his dog. The three-legged red dingo. The big dog. The same one he had with him when our mother died.'

'What are you talking about? We didn't even see him then.'

'But he was here. Everyone knew that. And you saw his dog, we both did. I'd know that dog anywhere. I saw it tonight back there by the flat rock.'

'You're drunk! Go away.'

Minnie blushed. They wouldn't let her live down the night she'd sampled the residue of bottles and glasses from a Broderick party and become so drunk they'd found her the next day, wandering, incoherent, in the bush.

'I'm not,' she cried, but Nioka was already asleep again, so Minnie crawled in beside the two boys and dozed off, hugging them tight.

Moobuluk, though, was a long way away yet. Worries about those two girls teemed through his brain so that in desperation he cast a spell, only a simple spell, to let them know that their ancient kinsman was with them in spirit, if not in body. Because the old body was frail.

44

According to the white man's measurement of distance, his eyrie, his hidden cave, where he presided over the sacred paintings that told the stories of the Dreamtime – those paintings that had not yet been defiled by the invaders – was hundreds of miles north of the Broderick station, and his original home. In the old days, being fleet of foot, he could cover great distances in a day, even continuing on through the night, but not any more. He knew where he had to go, though, and with the hot, rainy season near, the great rivers would be bloated, surging south to flood the always unsuspecting dry lands, so with good fortune assisting, he could meet river tribes and be carried a long, long way in their dugouts.

Moobuluk nodded to his dog as they plodded down the mountains. 'Why walk when we can ride, old fellow? Even the whites will give an ugly old fool like me a ride on their boats.'

Weeks later he threaded his way through a rain forest, feeling the tingle of expectation all about him as it waited for the monsoon. The undergrowth was dry and brittle, vines hung languidly from thirsty trees, small animals scurried busily under huge leaves, away from the prying eyes of slow-moving snakes, and the old man smiled, talking to them as he travelled on to the river. The level was low. Crocodiles dozed on the muddy banks, and there was an air of decay in the swampy surrounds, but this did not bother Moobuluk. All was as it should be. Stepping deftly over exposed mangrove roots, he followed the river down to where it streamed over a huge fall, splashing into the crystal waters below. In time, he knew, when the rains came, the river would turn into a torrent and thunder over the high rocks, waking up the world.

And so he ambled on with the dog padding beside him. All in good time, as nature decreed, he would visit his kin. He hoped they didn't expect too much of him. Some thought he could hold back time, reverse changes brought about by the whites, but it was not in his power to do so. Logic told him that if there was trouble down there in the open country where the little clan still lived, it would have something to do with the whites again, and he sighed. Maybe it was time to move them deeper inland.

For days, the three Broderick men traversed the huge property, dividing it into separate, numbered runs, but not without heated arguments, because they all had their own ideas on which were the best pasturelands, and Austin's insistence on claiming all the waterholes and courses was turning Victor's attempts to map them in his notebook into a maze of zigzag lines.

But they toiled on, with Austin giving instructions, Rupe blazing trees and chalking landmarks for the surveyors, and Victor trying to make sense of it.

At night they worked in Austin's den, drawing new maps, altering them, redefining the boundaries in what Victor saw as a total waste of time. But Rupe was enjoying himself, not caring that Austin cheated, making runs almost twice the size of the maximum set out in these so-far untested Lands Acts.

'Apart from your obvious cheating,' Victor said, 'you still can't buy up all these runs. Those laws put a limit on the amount of land one man can own.'

'That's no problem,' Rupe grinned. 'We put them in family names as well.'

'Still not enough.'

But his father wasn't to be deterred by such a minor setback. 'Then we use dummy names. Our stockmen, ringers, they won't care, and who's to know? You worry too much, Victor.'

'The boot's on the other foot. You're the one worrying about something that's never going to happen. It'd be chaotic.'

'Politicians create chaos,' Austin said. 'They neither sow nor reap. Tomorrow we start on the other side of the river.'

Over all these days, the Reverend fumed. He felt he was being slighted. He believed Broderick was deliberately dodging him, for what could be more important than his mission? These excuses about being busy all the time didn't wash with Tom Billings. Nor would he stoop to broaching the subject again with the women. But something had to be done, it was not good for Amy to be lazing about this indolent household, it would put notions in her head.

Finally he accosted Broderick when he was walking up to the house from the stables.

'Sir. A word with you, if you please.'

Broderick stopped, took his hat off and wiped his sweating face with a handkerchief. 'Can it wait? I'm a bit tired right now.'

It was true, he did look tired, but as Tom saw it, if a man his age chose to ride about his domain in this heat like some sort of royal duke, then he didn't deserve pity.

'I'm afraid not. Mrs Billings and I seek your permission to be on our way . . .'

Did he note a spark of sudden interest in the man's face? Tom was not sure, but he plunged on, choosing not to be outwardly offended. 'I wanted to discuss with you our plan to take three black boys with us and give them an education.'

'Yes.' Broderick nodded. 'My wife mentioned that. It sounds like a good idea. You will take care of them?'

'Indeed we will, sir. I have a letter from my bishop, outlining the programme. You will see that we are out to rescue as many young souls as we can afford and introduce them to the civilized world. We house and clothe and feed them at the mission school, and they are cared for by our lay people, who are dedicated to the Christian way of life. Of course, all this takes money, and the Bishop was hoping . . .'

46

'You want a donation? How much? Or do you want me to pay for their school fees? I think that would be a better way of doing things. How much per child?'

He began to stride towards the house, and Tom kept pace with him. 'We do not charge for the children, that is our charity work. The same programmes are being carried out by other churches and charitable organizations on a much bigger scale . . .'

'So I'm told.'

'But they too have to rely on donations to keep functioning. A donation direct to Bishop Frawley . . .'

'Never heard of him.'

'He is the head of the Church of the Holy Word and highly respected not only in Queensland but in New Zealand.'

'All right. Drop his letter into my office and the names of the three boys you wish to educate. It sounds like an excellent opportunity. When did you say you were leaving?'

'We could go tomorrow . . .'

'Then come round to my office at six o'clock and we'll fix it up. You'll have to excuse me, I want to have a shower and cool off.'

As the grandfather clock in the hall struck six, the Reverend approached Broderick's door. He knocked several times before he received a response, and when he was finally admitted, he found Broderick, a glass of whisky in his hand, poring over a table covered in maps. It was a very large room, Tom noted, taking in the furnishings, stinking of money, alcohol and tobacco. Typical of the loose-living Brodericks.

'Take a seat,' Broderick said over his shoulder, and Tom stared about him, wondering where he should sit. There were maps scattered everywhere, on tables, chairs and even, he was disgusted to see further down the room, on a billiard table, yet another evil occasion for sin.

'Just push some of those papers out of the way,' Broderick added. 'Would you like a drink? No. I forgot. You don't partake.' Unperturbed, he poured himself another. 'Now, let's see what your bishop has to say.'

He carted the letter and his drink into his office, and sat down to read it, but no sooner had he begun than Victor came through the door.

'Good day, Reverend.' Having acknowledged the visitor, Victor walked past to drop some letters on Broderick's desk. 'A stockman brought some mail in. These are for you. There's one from Harry . . .'

'Well, open it! Christ almighty! What's he got to say? What's happening down there?'

Victor opened the letter and perused it quickly.

'Anything about the legislation?'

'No, he talks about his house . . . they're considering extensions.

47

And a ball at Parliament House . . . and Connie's dad is retiring . . .'

Austin snatched the letter, glanced through it and tossed it aside. 'Typical. Bloody typical! He's not there to be a social butterfly. I ought to pull the fool out. Bring him back. Give him a job as a bloody stockman for a couple of years. Knock some sense into him.'

Billings listened to this tirade with misgivings. He could hardly expect generosity from Broderick when he was in such a mood.

'Don't get yourself into a state,' Victor said. 'Remember, the doctor said you should take it easy, and you've been out on the range all day . . .'

'And don't you be bloody telling me what to do. You answer this letter and tell Harry we don't want to hear any more about his social cavortings; we need day-to-day reports on that legislation, who is for it and who is against. The numbers!'

'If there was any problem he'd know and he'd say so. I reckon it's dead. They can't keep on resurrecting the same old Acts, there's too much more important business in the Parliament.'

'Like what?' Broderick shouted, grabbing the letter again, scrunching it and shoving it at Victor. 'Does he tell us what else is happening in the House? Or does he just go in there to sleep?'

'I'll tell him,' Victor sighed. 'And don't forget, there's no missing dinner tonight. It's our wedding anniversary and Charlotte has planned a special dinner party with champagne.'

Billings shuddered. Obviously he and Amy would have to endure a drunken evening with these people. Maybe he could ask that they be served in their room.

The son disappeared, and Broderick turned his attention back to Billings. 'Now. Where were we? Oh yes, the Bishop.' He read the letter carefully.

'That seems to be in order.'

Billings jumped up and handed him a letter of his own, explaining that they would be taking the boys, whose names were listed below, in their wagon on the morrow, and would deliver them personally to the Bishop.

At the same time, he talked at length about the merits of the boys' home . . . clean surrounds, instruction in English and their prayers, and the learning of a trade.

'A trade, eh? That's good.' Broderick took out a chequebook. 'I've been thinking about this. To tell you the truth, Reverend, I've never heard of your church nor your bishop. I don't want to be offensive, but you're taking three children from here and I have to know that they'll be well cared for. So this is what we're gonna do. I want your bishop to open a trust account in the names of these boys. Who are they again? Let's see . . . Bobbo, Jagga and another little feller, Doombie. The money is to be used for their welfare.'

'It's not really necessary,' Billings said. 'They will be cared for.'

'But you yourself said their upkeep and the upkeep of the home and the lay workers costs money.'

'It does. That's why it is better to pool all donations so that the Bishop may distribute where needed, Mr Broderick.'

'That's as may be. But I want it known that these kids are not exactly charity cases. They're from Springfield. Your bishop may draw on the fund to support the children, and next time I come to Brisbane I shall call on them myself to see how they're doing. Here's my cheque for three hundred pounds. That's one hundred per child, which may be spent on their quarters, clothing and their essentials. Is that satisfactory?'

'Oh, very generous, sir. God bless you. Very generous.'

'Good. Then you take a seat here and write out my conditions, which will accompany this cheque. And you will sign the page on behalf of Bishop Frawley. Put down that I also require an accounting of all expenditure, with receipts. Everything being in order, then, and only then, will I be pleased to make a substantial donation towards the upkeep of the boys' home. Do I make myself clear?'

Three hundred pounds! This was the largest donation Tom had ever achieved. The Bishop would be thrilled with him. And more to come!

'Very clear, sir. Very clear. I shall write down every word, exactly as you require. If I may say so myself, I have a good hand. I shall make the document entirely presentable.'

Pen and ink and fine notepaper were provided, and Tom set to work toiling over rather too wordy an essay, but in a careful hand that would impress the reader, especially this hardboiled gent with his bullying ways. The Bishop would know how to deal with him.

Out of the corner of his eye, Tom saw Broderick pour himself yet another whisky from a crystal decanter and thought he really ought to speak to him about the evils of drink, but one thing at a time.

As he waited, Broderick picked up two more letters that had been left on the top of the desk by his son. The first one didn't seem to interest him; he placed it aside, and using an ivory letter-opener slit the next envelope. As he did so, he remarked to Billings: 'The mothers of these kids are happy about sending their kids off to school, are they?'

Tom's hand jerked on the page, causing him to spoil a letter. The mothers? What did they have to do with it? Or the fathers for that matter? The whole idea was to remove children from the influence of savages. What was this fool of a man, who was probably drunk, thinking of now? The kids would be taken to Brisbane and put into a home until they were old enough to be farmed out to white families. Their origins had to be erased, forgotten.

Using the excuse of his effort to write more carefully, head down, the Reverend was mumbling a reply when Broderick startled him.

49

'Jesus! Oh, by Christ!' he said. 'Look at this!'

'At what, sir?' Tom, having ruined another letter, was worried that he might have to start again, for there was no rubbing out of ink, but Broderick, red in the face, was waving a letter at him as if he should read it.

'This! I knew it would happen!' Broderick seemed so angry he was gasping for breath. 'They're going to do it, the bastards! They're going to do it!'

Bewildered, Tom dropped his pen and took the letter, unsure if he should be looking at it at all, because it was from a bank, and the words PRIVATE AND CONFIDENTIAL were evident across the top of the page.

'Tell me what it says,' Broderick whispered. 'Tell me.'

Reading, as instructed, Tom intoned: '"Dear Austin, I'm sorry to have to inform you that the passing of the latest Lands Act is imminently possible. We should have immediate discussions on the state of your shares and other assets to meet the cost of freeholding. Because of the urgency of the situation this is a short letter, for which I apologize, but I have to warn other pastoralists to be prepared also. I shall write more fully to you as soon as possible."'

He looked up. 'It's signed "Ben Matthews" . . . Are you all right, Mr Broderick?'

'Water,' Broderick gasped, clutching the desk for support. 'Get me some water, quick!' But even as he spoke, he crashed to the floor, clutching at his chest.

Tom leapt up, trying to break his fall, but too late. He rushed over to a silver tray and brought back a jug of water, which he held to Broderick's lips, spilling it down his shirt.

Broderick grimaced in pain. It was obvious he was having some sort of an attack. Tom wanted to run for help, but Broderick clutched his arm, confiding in him: 'I really never thought it would happen,' he rasped. 'I was just trying to keep them on their toes.'

'Who?' Tom asked, reacting politely.

But another spasm of pain caused Broderick to crumple on the floor. 'Oh Jesus!' he cried. 'Here it is again.'

Tom decided he'd better go for help, but before he did so, he grabbed the precious cheque for three hundred pounds from the desk, as well as the document he'd been composing.

With them carefully tucked in his pocket, he ran down the passage, past the grandfather clock, calling for Mrs Broderick, calling for help, knowing that the vengeful Lord, who could not abide sinners, had struck.

Distress held the whole household in its grip. Broderick, confined to the daybed in his den, was in a bad way. His wife and Victor were still in there with him. Rupe had gone to fetch a doctor from the distant village of Cobbside, despite the lateness of the hour. Mrs Louisa Broderick had hurried her young son upstairs, trying to keep him quiet, since the child was complaining bitterly that they'd promised to let him stay up for the party.

Apparently forgotten, Tom and Amy sat in the drawing room, waiting for their instructions. Through the open double doors that led to the dining room, they could see the long table set for a festive occasion with a glitter of glasses and silver and a splendid array of flowers.

'Should we pray for him?' Amy whispered.

'He is in God's hands. There is no need for us to interfere.'

'I just thought . . .'

'Well, don't think. No one's thinking of us. Dinner should have been served hours ago. The staff are very slack, they've no excuse for ignoring guests.'

Though he wouldn't admit it, Tom found mealtimes the best part of the day at Springfield, and he had come to look forward to the excellent fare with greedy anticipation. Knowing that dinner was there, ready and waiting to be brought to the table, caused his stomach to rumble relentlessly. He was so hungry; it seemed ages since he'd last eaten.

At last Louisa Broderick swept into the dining room from the kitchen, accompanied by the black maids, and Tom clutched his prayer book miserably. They were clearing the table!

As he watched, the candelabra, glasses and other gewgaws were removed, leaving plain, everyday settings.

Louisa came into the drawing room. 'I'm so sorry to keep you waiting, but we're all very upset. It was such a shock, I couldn't think of having a party, but if you'd care to come through . . .'

They were on their feet instantly.

'How is Mr Broderick?' Amy enquired solicitously.

'Oh, dreadful. He's been in such pain. He's still conscious but he doesn't seem to be able to talk, although he will keep trying. It's too sad . . .'

'A stroke, it sounds like,' the Reverend said.

'Yes. Look, do go on. Don't wait for any of us. We're taking pot luck tonight.'

'I quite understand. Under the circumstances I feel it would be better if we went on our way in the morning. Would you advise Mrs Broderick that we'll pack up tonight?'

'Yes, of course.' She seemed so agitated that Tom wouldn't have been surprised if she totally forgot his message, but he wasn't concerned. These people lived such charmed lives that some travail would do them good. He marched ahead of Amy and took his usual place at the table, tucking a napkin into his collar. Then he tapped a spoon on a sugar bowl to alert the kitchen to their needs.

Chapter Three

Dawn mists floated wistfully over the river, and water birds on long, spindly legs picked their way through the shallows, mindful of the woman who stood on the sloping bank, gazing, just gazing at the steady flow as if the slow rhythm might calm her fears.

Charlotte had stayed by his side all night, sharing his pain, praying, consoling him, telling him not to worry, that the worst was over and he'd be all right. But would he? His speech was seriously affected and he seemed unable to use his right arm. Worse, he was aware that this had happened to him, and typical of Austin, his reaction was anger, frustrated anger. She prayed the doctor would be here soon. To calm him. Reassure him. Rupe would have ridden hard for Cobbside but would Dr Tennant be home? A country doctor could be anywhere in the district.

'Please God, let Rupe find him, and quickly. I don't know what more we can do here. And what if he has another stroke? Oh God, don't let him die.'

Tears of anguish rolled down her face, and rather than go back and have him see that she'd been crying, Charlotte crouched down and doused her face with the cold river water. It cleared her head too, and she felt refreshed. The chill had replaced the need for sleep.

She turned back to the house reluctantly, because she couldn't bear to see him struck down like this, not Austin, who was so vital, so full of life. But Louisa had been up all night too, and it was time she took a rest.

As Charlotte crossed the courtyard, the Reverend dashed out to meet her. 'Ah, good morning, dear lady. How is the patient?'

'Much the same, thank you, Mr Billings. We're waiting on the doctor. I believe you are leaving us this morning. You don't have to rush away, you know.'

'We must, I'm afraid. I had a talk with Mr Broderick last night, about the black children. He was very enthusiastic about our programme, and very generous, might I say. He dictated a letter to my bishop regarding the care of the three boys, and gave me a generous donation.'

'I'm glad he agreed,' Charlotte said, anxious to be on her way. 'You will keep us informed of their progress?'

'Of course. I hope you don't think that our little talk had anything

53

to do with his bad turn. I didn't upset him, he was in good spirits during our discussion . . .'

'Yes, I'm sure . . .'

'It was the letter that upset him.'

'What letter?'

'The letter from a bank manager, a warning of some sort about legislation. Even as he was failing – in the first throes, one could say – the dear man confided in me. He said: "I really never thought it would happen. I was just trying to keep them on their toes."'

'Where's the letter?'

'By the poor man's desk, I would say. Or maybe on the floor. I'm very sorry, I didn't have time to retrieve it . . .'

'That's all right. What time are you leaving?'

'If we could have an early breakfast?'

'Yes. Just ask the cook, Mr Billings. I must go, I'll come and see you off when you're ready.'

Victor was in the room with Louisa when Charlotte returned, so, whispering, she called him aside.

'Do you know anything about a letter from the bank?'

'No.'

'Then come over here and we'll look for it. I think it might have given him a shock.'

Victor found the page lying innocently on the floor by Austin's desk. He read it quickly, then nodded. 'It's on, Mum. We have to freehold.'

'But Harry said . . .'

'Dad was right,' he grated. 'Harry's a bag of wind. I hope Rupe remembers to send him a telegram from the Cobbside post office to tell him about Dad. I'll wring Harry's neck when he gets home.'

Charlotte hushed him. 'No you won't. We don't want any more trouble. Your father's not up to it. And please don't mention any of this in front of him. He's too sick to even think about it.'

'Like hell he is,' Victor muttered to himself as she hurried back to the patient. To tidy the room, Charlotte had collected all the maps and bundled them into a cupboard, mixing the old with the new. They'd have to be rescued, Victor groaned, and removed to his own office for sorting. He and Rupe had a mountain of work ahead of them. The old man had pointed the way out of this mess, and Victor was determined to carry on. He walked on to the veranda and looked out over the valley.

'Don't worry, old man,' he murmured. 'They won't beat us. Springfield will survive, I promise you.'

Amy was sorry to be leaving Springfield, dreading the return journey and by no means looking forward to their shabby existence in Brisbane. Everything they owned in the world was packed in the lumbering wagon with space to spare. While they were in the city they were allotted accommodation in a rickety boarding house owned by an old lady who was also a member of their church. Rumour had it that she had left it to the Bishop in her will, though Amy didn't think it was much of an asset. The place was alive with fleas and all manner of horrible creeping insects. For the first time since they'd set out on their road to redemption, Amy had complained to Tom that she couldn't live in such squalor, and her fall from grace had shocked him.

He had retaliated on behalf of the Lord by insisting she kneel and take vows of poverty and humility, and as usual, Amy had felt better after that; she hadn't minded the sordid surroundings so much, accepting them as all part of her duty. And admiring Tom for his stoicism. He never complained.

But staying here, in this lovely house, had unsettled her, she had to admit. Humility had certainly not been to the fore when Mrs Broderick had asked her where they lived. Thank God that Tom hadn't been listening to hear her lie, to hear her say they lived in the suburb of Hamilton, not in a dingy city lane.

'How nice,' Mrs Broderick had replied. 'It's very lovely at Hamilton, looking over the river. I've often thought I'd like a place there myself.'

Amy sighed as she watched Tom hitch the horses to the wagon. It was only a small lie. Then she jumped as a man came up behind her and touched her arm.

'Excuse me, missus. I'm the storeman. Mrs Broderick said these are for you. Will I put them on the wagon?'

He dumped two boxes beside her.

'What's in them?'

'Kids' clothes. Blankets. Donations to your charity.'

'Oh, thank you. Yes. Put them on the back if you will.' She called to her husband. 'Look, Mrs Broderick has donated clothes for us.'

'We don't need clothes,' he snapped, misunderstanding. 'Leave them, though, I'll look at them later. Now get on board, Amy, I haven't got all day.'

She climbed up front, tightened the ribbon on her bonnet, opened her umbrella for shade, and put on a brave smile for his benefit. The wagon trundled slowly round to the front entrance of the house, where Tom called a halt, tied the reins and jumped down.

'You stay there. I'll find Mrs Broderick to bid her goodbye.'

The lady of the house came out to farewell them, but none of the others appeared, which Amy took to be a snub. Charlotte shook hands with Tom and was walking over to Amy in the wagon when she saw two horsemen racing up the hill.

'Oh, thank God!' she cried. 'It's Rupe, and the doctor is with him!' She hesitated, seeming to have more to say, but changed her mind. 'You have a safe journey, Mrs Billings. I have to rush now. Goodbye.'

With that she hurried away to greet the riders.

'No need for us to hang around now,' Tom said, boarding the wagon again. 'Let's go!'

He slapped the reins and the wagon moved forward round the circular drive. Just before they reached the row of shady trees, he turned the wagon on to a track that crossed the open paddock to a side gate. Amy jumped down to open and then close the gate, so that they could follow this track through bushland and on to the blacks' camp. It was time to collect the children.

The camp was quiet. To the people, by this hour, four since dawn, the day was well established. The old men were gathered under their favourite tree, women tramped about attending to their business, while others squatted in groups, preparing food or making nets for bags and fishing, nimble fingers flicking in and out. By a low bank away to the right of the track that narrowed to a footpath as it meandered through to the camp, several children played, laughing and screeching as they swung out over the river on a rope, and leapt, splashing wildly, into the water. Most of the younger set, including Nioka, had left earlier, to search for tucker in the diminishing bushland.

They all knew that the boss had taken sick, and being gentle people, they were concerned for him, so this was not a day to let their children go up to the house to play with Teddy. Nioka figured that if Teddy got lonely, as he often did, then Minnie would bring him down here, where they could make as much noise as they liked.

In the meantime she enjoyed these days with her friends, just wandering on for miles and miles, digging at roots with her stick, searching, exploring. There was always something new to see in the bush.

The people remaining in the camp saw the man and his wife come down the track. They knew who they were, the praying man and his missus, so they lowered their eyes and deliberately ignored them. Often white people strolled into their camp like this, mooching about, sticky-nosing, but they never stayed long.

Tom stood, taking in the scene, sniffing in disgust at the stink of dust and sweaty bodies. Two mangy dogs slunk over to investigate the newcomers, and he kicked them away, motioning Amy to follow him upriver to where the children were playing.

He was disconcerted to see two women splashing about with a dozen children in a most unseemly way, and he stopped dead, averting his eyes.

'Those women are naked,' he snapped. 'I can't look upon them. You go ahead and find the boy called Bobbo and bring him up. We need him to start with, because he speaks what passes for English among these wretches.'

Hanging on to tree branches, Amy picked her way along the slippery bank until she was close enough to call to the boy, but it was difficult to find him among all the brown bodies.

A woman stood in the shallows exposing large breasts and a swollen stomach, and Amy gasped. Not only was she naked, but she was pregnant! Never had Amy seen such a disgusting sight. She felt herself blushing, and almost turned to run, but the woman spoke, in a surprisingly soft voice.

'What you want, missus?'

'Bobbo,' Amy replied, trying not to look at her.

But the children were paying attention now, and with a wave of her arm, the woman indicated to Bobbo that he was wanted, and in seconds the child came scampering up to her.

'Oh, heavens,' Amy said, staring at the skinny little body. 'Where are your clothes? Or a towel? Mr Billings wishes to talk to you.'

Confidently Bobbo shrugged, 'No duds here, missus,' so Amy sighed and led him back to her husband.

'Dear God!' he cried. 'Naked in front of a woman! They have no shame. Come here, boy.'

He took his scarf and wrapped it about the grinning child's hips. 'Now, Bobbo, I have something important to tell you. I'm taking you for a ride in my wagon. Would you like that?'

Bobbo nodded enthusiastically.

'Good. Now we can only take three lucky boys, so I want you to go back and get your friends Jagga and Doombie. Can you do that?'

The boy nodded again.

'Then go now, and be quick about it.'

Within minutes the three eager little boys were dancing about them, and Tom led them back to the wagon.

'Look in that box,' he told Amy. 'We can't take them like this. Find something that might cover them.'

Amy climbed on to the tray of the wagon to investigate Mrs Broderick's donations, while Tom endeavoured to explain to the boys that he was taking them for a good long ride in the wagon, and then on to school. Telling them of all the wonders they would see on the way, not that the children were listening: they scrambled on to the wagon like three monkeys and had to be hauled down again.

'There are children's clothes here,' Amy called. 'And they're new!' She tossed three cotton shirts to Tom. 'These will do until I sort something else out.'

With difficulty they managed to get the shirts on the excited children, who leapt on to the wagon again, not about to be left out of this adventure.

Tom breathed hard from the exertion. 'At last. Now we can go.'

But the pregnant woman emerged from the scrub. 'Where you take them?' she asked, curious.

Amy rushed over to stand in front of her. 'You aren't dressed! You

57

can't speak to the Reverend in this state!'

Angrily the woman snatched Amy's shawl and wrapped it round her waist, still leaving her dark breasts bare. 'Now dressed. Where you take them kids?'

Tom walked over to her. 'They are very lucky. God is kind to these boys. They are going to school.'

'What school?'

As Tom explained his mission, the woman kept shaking her head, so Amy intervened.

'She doesn't understand, Tom. I think she wants to know what a school is.' She turned back to the woman. 'School. You know school? Lessons?'

Numbly, the bare-breasted native shook her head again, clearly worried.

'Mr Broderick wants me to take them to school. You understand that? Mr Broderick.'

'Boss say they go?'

'Yes. Boss say.'

'I go get their mummas.'

'No need. You must not interfere.' Tom's voice was forceful now. 'Boss say. I have to do what the boss says. Right?'

She nodded, uncertainly. 'Where this place you go?'

'Oh, for God's sake! Just down the road. I can't stand here all day arguing with her, Amy. Do something.'

Amy took her scarf gently. 'There's nothing to worry about,' she smiled, turning the woman away from his gaze. 'The children will have a lovely time. They get to ride on the wagon. Eat good tucker. It's all right.'

But the woman sensed it was not all right. 'No. Boys stay.'

Amy pointed to the boys. 'Look. They want to go. Happy, see. You go back to the camp.'

Finally the wagon pulled away, with the boys grinning happily, waving to the woman, who stood watching them leave. She began to follow them through the bush, but as it appeared they were making for the big house, she gave up. Looking back, Amy was relieved to see her turn away.

Soon, though, they were moving quickly along the avenue of trees and out on to the road, where the fresh horses responded to the slap of the reins and set off at a fast pace.

At last they were on their way.

They made good time, stopping, hours later, for what Bobbo called a 'picanik' in the shade of a grove of trees. Tom had bought provisions at the station store but the cook had also supplied them with a basket of fresh sandwiches and cake to get them started, and that proved popular with the three boys, who ate heartily.

That night, after a meal of tinned beans and biscuits, they camped out, and the boys, wrapped in their blankets, slept on the wagon, huddled together like puppies, blissfully unaware that they were being taken to another world.

In the morning, though, the trouble started. Jagga cried. He wanted to go home. Despite encouragement from the other two, who were more adventurous, he didn't want to go on. He began to scream, punching at Amy to keep away from him.

Eventually, tired of the tantrum, the Reverend slapped him, causing him to scream louder, frightening his friends. Then, suddenly, he jumped down from the wagon and ran, with Tom hurtling after him. He was no match for Tom's long legs though, and soon they were back, the child struggling under Tom's arm.

So they continued on their way, with Bobbo and Doombie trying to console the child, who was now lashed to the seat, his hands tied behind him. It was no longer a happy adventure for the three sombre piccaninnies.

The doctor spent a long time with his patient, while Charlotte waited outside on the veranda, trying to hear what was being said.

When at last he did join her, Dr Tennant was cheerful.

'The damage could be worse. He's a tough old dog. His speech is badly impaired, and he's lost the use of his right arm and right leg, but that could be temporary. It could *all* be temporary, so rest is the order of the day. We can't leave him on the settee, but it will be easier to keep him downstairs. Could you set up a bed in here for him?'

'Yes, of course.'

'And he has to be kept very quiet, Charlotte. No visitors – not for a week, anyway. He's already fighting his infirmities, distinctly displeased. I think if he could talk he'd be abusing me for not curing him forthwith, so I've sedated him and will leave you a mixture to dose him with once a day, for three days. We don't want another stroke. Otherwise that's all you can do for now, beyond keeping him comfortable.'

'Do you really think he'll get better?' she asked.

'He's not going to die, and later, he shouldn't be treated as an invalid, not that Austin would allow that anyway. We'll just have to wait and see how he progresses.'

As they walked quietly into the room, Charlotte was relieved to see that her husband was sleeping peacefully, but she was so worried about him, she urged the doctor to stay over.

'It's a long ride out here. You need a rest too. Do stay. I'll show you to your room and have Cook send up a tray.'

'That's very kind of you.' Dr Tennant stretched. 'I could do with a hot bath – the old bones, you know. Does Austin still ride?'

'Yes.'

'That's out for a while too, even when he is on his feet. But one

59

thing at a time. You're looking well, Charlotte, that's good to see.'

'Yes. I keep well, thank God.'

As he stretched out in the bath, Dr Tennant admired the large white-tiled bathroom. It was always a pleasure to come to this house, and he was glad he didn't have to face the ride home just yet. He'd leave tomorrow and make a few district calls while he was out this way.

Pity Austin was down. He would have appreciated a good game of cards with the Broderick men. And billiards. Unfortunately the billiard table was in the sick room.

He sighed. Austin and Charlotte were a strange pair, so unalike: Broderick large, handsome, domineering, but an excellent companion, while his wife was gawky, quite unattractive. One wouldn't be so unkind as to say she was ugly, more unprepossessing, with her bony features and carroty hair and that gap-toothed smile. She was a quiet woman, Mrs Broderick, overshadowed by the strong personality of her husband, but as was said by all, she was a very good housekeeper. Springfield was a credit to her.

There was talk, he knew, of Broderick and another woman, which didn't surprise him, because in the old days, even though he was married, away from his station Austin had been quite a lad. Rumour had it now that there was a woman in Brisbane. Only rumour. No one seemed to be able to put a name to her.

Dr Tennant shrugged and hauled himself out of the bath. Conjecture maybe. Just conjecture. Part of the myth of the indefatigable Austin Broderick, who wasn't at his best right now.

A tray was waiting in his bedroom, and Tennant investigated hungrily. Corned-beef sandwiches, warm buttered cheese scones and a pot of tea. Excellent.

'My word, they live well, these squatters,' he murmured. 'I should have leased land out here while I had the chance.'

He munched on a sandwich sweetened with pickles. Then again, if this freeholding scheme goes though, I could afford to buy a run now. All I'd have to do is stock it and put on a manager. Worth considering. They say a lot of this good pastureland will be up for grabs.

Late in the afternoon Austin woke to find himself occupying a bed somewhere, certainly not his bed, and this was not his bedroom. For a minute there, he thought they'd carted him off to hospital, but as his eyes roved the darkened room he made out the glint of a brass lamp beside tall bookshelves, and was comforted. They'd left him downstairs in his den. Good. A better idea than being shoved upstairs, where he'd be out of sight and out of mind.

He tried to call out, to summon someone, anyone. Now that he was awake he wanted the curtains drawn back and a cup of tea to remove the foul taste in his mouth. But his lips writhed and his tongue wouldn't respond, and the guttural sounds that came out scared him. Frantically he fished about in his mind for Tennant's words. What had he said? The stroke. Temporary setbacks. Speech. The arm. And Jesus! The bloody leg too! It had better be bloody temporary, he wasn't going to lie here like a log for the rest of his days.

It took a huge effort, but he managed to push himself up into a sitting position, surprised to find himself sweating, but he forged on, struggling with his legs until he was at last seated on the side of the bed, feet resting on the floor.

That will do for a start, he told himself, but as he moved again into a more comfortable position he knocked over a bedside table, and its contents, medicine bottles, glasses and jug, crashed to the floor.

The door flew open and Minnie came dashing in. Obviously they'd had her standing guard outside.

'Wassamatter, boss?' she cried. 'You alri?'

Too late he tried to warn her there was broken glass on the floor, a danger to the barefoot maid, but a loud screech told him she'd already found it.

Austin could do little but sit numbly as she hopped over to the window to open the curtains, so that she could remove glass from her foot, leaving a trail of blood across the polished floor.

'Ow!' she cried, and 'Ow!' again, as the offending splinters came out. She hopped back to him.

'I get a broom.'

Austin shook his head ruefully. That was Minnie. If she could put her foot in it, she would.

But Minnie's accident brought Charlotte running, and fussing, ordering him to lie down again, calling for the doctor, in a worse state of confusion than the black girl. He wished she would calm down, bring him some tea, take off the damned pyjama jacket someone had put on him – she knew he hated pyjama tops – go away, leave him alone.

Then Tennant was back, irritatingly cheerful, followed by the troops, Victor and Louisa and Rupe, all peering at him and asking him how he was, as if they couldn't bloody see! Young Teddy came flying in then, to leap on to the bed, and his grandpa tried to smile. Teddy could stay.

But Louisa grabbed him. 'Get off there, Teddy! Grandpa's not well.'

'I want to show him the yo-yo!' The little hands threw the red-painted yo-yo but failed to grasp the string, and the toy whizzed past Austin's head.

'There! Look what you've done now!' Louisa complained.

'Take him out, Louisa,' Charlotte instructed. 'Austin needs rest.' She handed her daughter-in-law a litter bin containing the glass she'd swept up. 'And take this too.'

Eventually there was quiet again, and just Charlotte. She reset his bedside table. 'I'm putting a little bell here for you,' she told him. 'So you can ring if you need anything. But I won't be far away. Victor's bringing in that commode chair we had for Justin . . .'

Austin turned away in disgust. Commode chair? What more could they do to humiliate him?

He thought of Justin, his late brother. Justin had died here seven years ago, of cancer. A hard lingering death. Poor Justin. He had always been a shy, conservative sort of fellow. Older than Austin by three years, with prematurely greying hair, he had not been interested in his brother's dreams of owning a large sheep station, preferring to stick at his dreary job as an apprentice to a jeweller. A city bloke really, not interested in the bush.

But eventually he bought his own store in an arcade in Queen Street, Brisbane, and had no need to envy his brother's good fortune, because Justin did well. Then he married Fern, lovely, gorgeous Fern.

Austin had taken his family to Brisbane to attend the wedding and he'd been stunned to meet this beauty. It was almost incomprehensible to him that slow, staid Justin could capture the heart of such an attractive woman, but there it was. The bride wore cream lace that set off her peaches-and-cream skin, the softly curling brown hair and smiling blue eyes. Fern laughed a lot, and those eyes danced in merriment. Austin had fallen in love with her on that very day.

But Fern and Justin had been very happy. Austin had to admit that. Even though he was a sick man, Justin had been determined to see Austin's house finally completed, and had made the journey out here with Fern, only to collapse a few days later.

That had been a harrowing time for everyone. Justin had been in so much pain there was little Dr Tennant could do. It broke Austin's heart to see his brother suffering so much, and in the end his death was a blessed relief.

Austin had escorted his sister-in-law back to Brisbane himself, offering to assist her in any way he could, but Fern was very independent. Instead of selling the store, she took over the management herself, carrying on the good name of Broderick in the jewellery business. Austin had half hoped she'd fail so that he could step in and rescue her from financial ruin, but playing the white knight was denied him.

Whenever he was in Brisbane after that, with or without Charlotte, he always managed to find an excuse to be with Fern on her own. Talking business, of course, enquiring about every aspect of her buying and selling, and then sitting back, delighted to be entertained by this lovely, amusing woman.

Finally Austin Broderick could stand it no longer. One night, when he was dining with her, he broke out: 'Fern. I have to tell you this. I'm in love with you.'

She smiled. 'Oh yes. I know.'

He was flabbergasted. 'Well. For crying out loud! Why didn't you say something?'

'Me?' she laughed. 'What could I say before this? People fall in love. They just do. I love you too, but you're a married man, so finish your dinner, I've got your favourite dessert, strawberries and cream.'

Austin stared. 'Is that all there is to it?'

'Yes, dear. So let's say no more about it.'

He was never happy with their platonic love affair and compensated by buying her extravagant gifts which delighted her. But there the situation remained. Now, consoling himself in his present misery, Austin day-dreamed about Fern and hoped she would feel duty-bound to visit her ailing brother-in-law. She hadn't been out to Springfield since Justin's death; now would be a good time. She could sit with him, comfort him, amuse him with those funny stories about her strange clientele.

Austin was an optimistic man, he could always see a light in the darkness. And thinking of Fern kept his mind off the letter from his banker. He hadn't forgotten that.

Nor had Victor and Rupe. The all-important maps were now rolled and banded, and out of sight in Victor's office.

'When Tennant goes, we'll set them all out in the library,' Victor said. 'That table is bigger anyway, more suited to this job. And we can keep the door locked in case visitors wander in. We've got a lot of decisions to make before we call in a surveyor.'

'Harry will be coming home. I sent him a telegram. He can help.'

Victor stopped, his hand to his head. 'Oh Jesus! I wish you hadn't.'

'What are you talking about? You told me to, and so did Charlotte.'

'But we didn't know about the news from the bank then. He only said imminent . . . there could still be a chance the bill will get knocked back again. Our side will need all the numbers they can get. If Harry misses the vote . . .'

Rupe grimaced. 'And they lose by one . . .'

'Our lives won't be worth living. Austin will kill us all.'

'I'm on my way!' Rupe said, heading for the door.

'Where to?'

'To send a stockman post-haste for Cobbside to telegraph Harry. Tell him Austin said to stay put. That he's over the attack. And listen, we'll go in to dinner when I get back. I don't want Tennant to know anything else is wrong.'

'I hope you warned Charlotte.'

'Yes. She was very good. When the doctor asked what might have caused the attack, she said she didn't know. Not that she has grasped the problem yet . . .'

But Rupe had gone.

Victor lit a cheroot and decided that Austin's illness would give them an excuse not to encourage visitors to Springfield for the time being. He was well aware that investors not only from the Cobbside township, but from the bigger centres like Toowoomba and Brisbane, would already be lining up at the starting gate for a chance to select freehold land that squatters couldn't hold on to. Men like Tennant, who was in the parlour right now, with the women. And storekeepers who had a gripe against squatters for bypassing their expensive little stores and buying wholesale from city warehouses. And managers of big stations who would not miss an opportunity to go it alone on smaller runs that they could afford.

'And all the bloody rest!' he growled. 'All wanting a slice of the cake. We'll need more boundary riders.'

The talk at dinner centred on Austin, with everyone being as cheerful as possible since Charlotte was so upset. They'd had to insist she come and have a meal.

'Harry and Connie will be here in a few days,' she said. 'Austin will be pleased to see them. It will be a terrible shock for poor Harry.'

'He'll survive,' Rupe said, nodding to Victor. Message sent.

The soup was served and there seemed to be some delay with the main course. Charlotte was about to go out to the kitchen to investigate when the screaming started.

'Oh my God,' she cried. 'Something's happened to Austin!' She was out of her chair, running from the room, before any of them could react.

'I'd better go too,' Tennant said, dropping his napkin and jumping to his feet, but Hannah, the cook, burst into the dining room. 'Where's Mrs Broderick?'

'Gone to see what's happened to Dad,' replied Victor, also on his feet.

'It's not the boss,' Hannah puffed, 'it's the blacks. Minnie's throwing hysterics, and there's a mob of them outside the back door.'

When Nioka returned to camp that evening and heard the garbled story about the boss's friends who'd taken her son, her nephew and Doombie off for a ride in the wagon, she was annoyed but not anxious. They were probably up at the house. Minnie would feed them. The Brodericks never minded little kids wandering about, and they knew their way home.

But Doombie's mother and father, who'd also been on the gathering expedition, and had returned with a bag of their son's favourite berries, were not so complacent. They quizzed Djallini, the pregnant woman, and heard the word 'school'.

That was enough to concern Gabbidgee. He was not a young man, and he had suffered a broken leg some years ago that had left him with a limp and the necessity to remain here by the river where life was easier, rather than leave with the fitter men. This was his second wife, and Doombie was the son of that union. His other children were full grown now, some gone, some still here, but Doombie was his treasure. Another reason why he'd stayed. He'd wanted Doombie to be safe under the protection of the white boss.

Gabbidgee knew what a school was but he couldn't think what it had to do with them. The white boys had schooling rooms and teachers and went away to school. Not black kids. Never.

At dusk he took his concerns to Nioka. She wanted to go up to the house right away, but Gabbidgee's wife argued against that.

'You keep away! Minnie said we should keep away with the boss so sick. The doctor is coming.'

Eyes rounded in wonder. They all knew Dr Tennant. He had often visited the camp to check on them and give them medicines, but someone would have to be very sick for him to make a special call.

'He's already here,' someone said. 'He came riding in this morning, with Rupe. Maybe the boss is dying.'

Even Nioka was intimidated now.

'All right,' Gabbidgee said. 'You lot stay here. I'll go and look around. No one will know. I'll find the wagon.'

He ran through the scrub, picked up the wagon tracks and began to follow them, running easily despite his ungainly gait. He fully expected them to head for the big house, but at the turn-off they veered away. The failing light was no hindrance, because his feet read the furrows in the thick dust, but to make certain he squatted, examining the track. Gabbidgee hoped he would find two sets of tracks, to tell him that the wagon had only gone as far as the main gate and back. Someone had said that the praying man had only wanted to take them for a ride, therefore it would make sense to expect return tracks. But there were none.

Anxiously he sped down the drive between the trees, feeling for only the wagon wheels now, for other horses had passed this way since. They were lighter; the vehicle had been moving faster than before. At this point, one road, used mainly as a stock route, turned left, another, centre-tufted with grass, coursed across the valley. His feet searched the fine red dust for the flatter grooves of wagon wheels, and then he stood, staring across the long, empty road.

Where could they have gone? There were no schools around here, and the nearest neighbours were in the opposite direction. They'd been gone all day. Surely they should have been back by now. He scratched his head and hitched at the cord belt strung from his thin hips that kept his laplap in place. Maybe they'd had an accident. Wheels fell off those lumbering wagons. Hadn't he been called on often enough to help stranded whites? But why, then, weren't the whites out looking for them? Why weren't their horsemen out searching like he was? This was a great mystery.

He turned back to the camp with his news.

'That does it,' Nioka said. 'I'm going up to ask Minnie where they are. I don't care if the doctor is there.'

'Me too,' Doombie's mother said.

'Wait for me,' Gabbidgee cried, remembering the rules. He rushed back to a cache of discarded tea chests that contained an ill-assorted collection of articles gathered by the people for no particular reason: rusted pots and pans, a broken teapot, worn boots, bits and pieces of leather, pram wheels, empty tins . . . But Gabbidgee knew exactly what he was looking for. He delved into the jumble and pulled out ragged trousers. To venture within the confines of the big house it was necessary to be dressed.

By the time he caught up with the women, other people, curiosity aroused, had volunteered as well, so they set off in a band, trudging determinedly towards the lights of the homestead.

First in the kitchen, Victor grabbed Minnie and shook her. 'Shut up! Stop this noise. Don't you know the boss is sick?'

It was a blessing that Austin's wing was on the other side of the house. 'What the hell's the matter with you?' he cried. 'Quieten down, you stupid girl.'

'Where my boy?' Minnie cried through her tears. 'What you done with Bobbo?'

Nioka was standing in the doorway, arms folded, jaw jutting, in a pose that reminded Victor of her mother. 'Where our kids?' she snarled. 'Where you got them?'

'You settle down too,' he snapped at her. 'And what's that mob doing outside? Tell them to get out of here.'

Then Charlotte came hurrying back. 'Austin's asleep. What's going on?'

'I think some children are lost,' Victor told her. He turned back to Minnie. 'Now stop your grizzling. We'll find them.' Black kids didn't get lost. He wondered what mischief they were up to.

'Where's Teddy?' he asked Louisa. 'Is he with them?'

'No, he's in bed. I think I know why they're upset. Three of the little kids went off to school today. With the Billings.'

Minnie started to moan again, wringing her apron, but Nioka was stunned. 'What you say? What?'

'Oh, goodness me!' Charlotte stepped in to calm everyone. 'You people go back to the dining room. I'll explain to the girls. Obviously they didn't understand.'

'What?' Nioka snapped. 'What you mob bloody do to our kids?'

'That's enough, Nioka,' Victor said angrily. 'Another word out of you and I'll ban you from the homestead.'

'You gimme Jagga and bloody ban shit!'

Victor motioned to Louisa to go, and Tennant, diplomatically, left too. Then he turned back to Nioka, waving a warning finger at her. 'Behave yourself!'

Charlotte intervened. 'It's all right, Victor. I've been so upset I forgot that the Reverend and Mrs Billings were leaving today. They've taken Bobbo and Jagga and Doombie with them to attend school.'

'What? On whose authority?'

'On Austin's,' she said sternly. 'He had a long discussion with Mr Billings and approved. He even gave him a sizeable donation for the children's upkeep.'

Wailing, Minnie threw herself into Hannah's arms, while Nioka remained in the doorway, gaping.

'You gib dem our kids?'

'Didn't anyone explain to them?' Victor asked angrily.

'Of course. Mr Billings would have explained. It's just that they still don't understand. There's no need for all this, the children will be well cared for. They're very fortunate.'

Victor saw Gabbidgee loom up on the back veranda behind Nioka, and he shivered as if someone had walked over his grave.

'It'll take some explaining,' he snapped. 'There had to be a better way to do this. Why did you leave it to Billings to explain? He's a cold bastard.'

'Don't you start too,' Charlotte said. 'I'm just not up to this right now. You know perfectly well that this programme to educate young blacks has been underway for some time. Austin knew it was in their best interests or he would never have allowed it. Now, take them all outside and explain it properly to them. Make them see it's a good thing.'

'Thanks.'

Rupe had been standing watching all this. 'Seems to me that Billings didn't tell them a damn thing. The parents should have been asked, at the very least.'

But Victor realized that even if Nioka and Minnie, and Gabbidgee out there, had been asked, their reaction would have been the same. Or probably worse. If they'd refused on the spot, there could have been a riot. Maybe Billings knew this. Maybe it was best that he'd just quietly moved off with them.

He walked outside and sent all the blacks, except the parents of the three boys, back to camp, then he squatted under a tree to talk to them.

For an hour he went back and forth over the story, with Minnie sobbing, Nioka furious and poor Gabbidgee and his wife thoroughly intimidated by this momentous happening. He reminded them that he and his brothers had gone away to school, and Charlotte had cried too, when they left. He told them how lucky the boys were, that they wouldn't be lonely, being together. He asked if the boys had cried, not wanting to leave, and was relieved to hear this was not so. He had

Hannah bring them out some hot sweet tea and cake, which only Nioka resolutely refused, so he felt he was gaining ground. He told them the boys had gone to the big city where they would see all the great wonders, and would come home full of stories, enough stories to keep the camp enthralled for months.

'When they come back?' Minnie sobbed.

Not wishing to lie to them, because he had no idea, Victor could only tell them: 'When the time is right.'

Eventually Gabbidgee asked: 'Boss man, your daddy, he say this a good thing? He say boys go school learning lak his boys?'

'Yes.'

The black man nodded miserably, jerked his head at his wife and together they left without another word.

That left only the two sisters. Minnie seemed to have accepted the inevitable, but she was shattered. Nioka was still stonily angry, but she'd just have to get over it, Victor reasoned. Hundreds of black parents were going through the same sadness these days. Change had come upon them. That was all. He understood their hurt, but there was nothing more he could do.

The camp was sullen and silent. Years of intimidation had taken their toll. In a fit of bravado Gabbidgee threatened to go after the wagon to track it down and bring home the boys. The elders warned him of the white men's guns. The fearful times were still with them, and they wept as Gabbidgee sharpened his spear and allowed the women to prepare him for battle by assisting him in the ceremonial painting of his body.

His other children begged him not to go, reminding him of his duties to them and to his grandchildren; there were too few men in the camp as it was. That caused a fight between his wife and his eldest daughter, a ritual fight that required the women to bash each other in turn with heavy waddies, until one succumbed. Battered and bleeding, Doombie's mother could not match the strength of the heavier older woman, and the decision was made for him. Gabbidgee had to remain with his other family; his youngest son was not their concern.

Nioka jeered at him. She claimed that had she his experience as a tracker she would have gone herself. She was not afraid of the white men or their guns. Devastated, mourning for his beloved Doombie, Gabbidgee slashed his body with his bush knife and crept into the bush to suffer for his failure to protect the boy.

It was just as well he hadn't followed the wagon, because Billings and his party had met up with drovers who were moving a huge mob of sheep along stock routes to Toowoomba. They travelled with a dray which was, for these itinerants, a moveable base, and they had no objection to the Billings' wagon accompanying the dray.

Billings was relieved. It saved him having to worry about directions

68

in this wide-open country, and being able to camp with drovers added efficiency to the journey. By no means a bushman, he appreciated their expertise in preparing meals and their knowledge of the district waterholes. They spared him the necessity for detours to find shelter at station homesteads, and explanations about the presence of three black boys.

The drovers had been curious about the children at first, but when they understood their destination, they were pleased.

'From Springfield, eh?' the boss drover commented. 'I'll say this for Broderick, he might have had his wars with the blacks years ago, but he's good to them now. Not like a lot of squatters. It's a fine thing that he cares enough to see kids like this get an edjucation. Never had one meself.'

The boss's wife travelled with them, and she was glad of Amy's company. 'Don't you be worrying, nothing to be afraid of out here in the bush. We'll deliver you and the kids safely to town, and then you only have a straight run on to Brisbane.'

She liked the little black kids, and even jollied young Jagga along so that he no longer had to be tied to the wagon. She allowed them to take it in turns to ride on her dray, and as a special treat, when everything was going smoothly, her husband lifted one of the boys up to his horse, to sit in front of him and travel on horseback. That privilege became such a joy to the little fellows that it even took second place to the treacle toffee the drover's wife made for them.

Although the men were cynical about the Reverend's attempts to convert them, the boss's wife never minded Amy's constant talk of the Lord. It was the female company she appreciated, so she didn't care what Amy talked about. If her new friend was all fired up with religion, that was her business and good luck to her.

Had an irate father come upon this party of six men and two women, it was doubtful that he would have faced guns, just white people who would have chased him away with their horses and stock whips, amused by a blackfellow who belonged in the past.

Minnie would not go back to work. She could not. She was inconsolable, wearing herself down with weeping. In spurts of determination she waylaid them all – Victor, Rupe, the missus, even Louisa – but they all gave her the same answer: not to worry, Bobbo would be all right.

But Hannah was her greatest disappointment. Minnie hung around the kitchen, whispering to Hannah to get her boy back, and though the cook had been more sympathetic than the rest, understanding the terrible sorrow that Minnie was experiencing, she could not help. She tried to encourage Minnie to come back to work, but her efforts met with stubborn resistance.

Then there was Nioka. She railed at Minnie.

'Serve you right. You always said they were your friends. Now look what they've done to you. Taken your boy. Did they tell you when they bring our boys back? No! I think never. We'll never see them again. That's what you get for sucking up to them. It's all your fault.'

Minnie stood staring at the river. If that was true, that she'd never see dear laughing Bobbo again, she had nothing to live for. She might as well throw herself in the river and be drowned for all her life was worth now. This grieving was worse than death.

And then she saw the three-legged dingo loping towards her across the boulders massed at the bend of the river, and she spoke to it.

'What you doing here, poor feller? You lost?'

'No, he's not lost,' a voice said from the trees behind her, and old Moobuluk came creaking out on his bony legs.

Minnie recognized him. There was no one in the world as old as Moobuluk, she was sure. But she was too depressed to care that the magic man had appeared among them again. He'd come too late.

'Why do you cry, little girl?' he asked, and even that pleasantry upset her. She wasn't a little girl, she was a grown woman, and fed up with everyone and everything. She felt that she had failed her son, but her people had failed her too, and this old bloke . . . what was the good of him now? He should have been here, where he belonged, when he was needed.

When she refused to acknowledge him, he circled the boulders, and with the aid of his stick negotiated the slippery banks until he was standing in the shallows, cooling his feet.

'Ah,' he sighed, 'that's better. My feet were on fire. I think the pads of these feet are wearing out.' He looked up at her and cackled. 'Do you suppose the boss up there would give me a pair of boots like he wears?'

Minnie shrugged. The dog, settled on a smooth rock, jaws agape, tongue lolling, seemed to smile fondly at the question.

'I used to think,' he continued, addressing the dog, 'that the white fellers were a weak mob having to wear boots over the earth, but now I'm not so sure. Which goes to prove that a man can't always be right.'

His croaky old voice making trivial conversation goaded her into responding. 'Where were you?' she demanded. But even those few words caused a flood of tears, so she moved to leave, to run away from him.

'Don't go, Moomabarrigah.' Has voice sounded clearer, sweet and gentle. 'When you weep I weep, but I don't know why I weep. You must tell me why, so that I know how deep should be my sorrow.'

He climbed up towards her, reaching for assistance so she had no choice but to give him her strong hand, and soon he was sitting patiently beside her, contemplating the waters.

70

'My boy Bobburah,' Minnie whispered when her sobbing subsided. 'They've taken him.'

'Who?'

'The praying people!' Angry now, she turned on him. 'You should have been here. You could have turned them into crows. Into two old black crows!'

Moobuluk resisted a smile at this simple solution, because this was obviously a very serious matter.

'Tell me all about it.'

The crying started again, but through the tears of fear and anger and desolation the story unfolded. Moobuluk was so distressed, tears coursed unashamedly down his leathery cheeks. She was right. He should have been here. He had taken far too lightly the voices in the wind that had called him home. But who could have foreseen such a terrible thing happening to these quiet people?

'Why was such punishment inflicted on you? What went wrong?'

'That's what I'm trying to tell you,' Minnie insisted. 'They say this is a good thing. They sent our little boys to school. Like their boys go.'

'Ah, but such babies!' Moobuluk grieved.

Minnie's anger returned. 'They don't send their own kids off that young. They say our babies had to go young to learn the English so that they can do school learning proper. I hate all those whitefellers. You go and cast a spell on them, great daddy. Tell them we want our boys back.'

He had her go over this strange story again and again so that he could grasp the enormity of the crime. Already he had realized that Moomabarrigah was the best one to explain this to him because of her contact with the whites. And he was worried about Nioka, the fiery one. Her sister said that she was still in a very savage mood. She could cause trouble that would be difficult to overcome.

As he saw it there were two problems here. First the spiriting away of three little boys, and secondly, how many more would they want? Were all the children in danger from these obsessive whites? He moaned. Haven't they done enough to us?

Moobuluk walked back to the camp with Minnie, calmly accepting the excited welcomes from all sides as if he didn't have a worry in the world, but after a quiet talk with Doombie's parents, he sought out Nioka.

For a long time he sat with her, giving counsel, insisting she wrap her wrath in her hands and put it behind her until he had time to think about this. She was a difficult girl to deal with, given to shouting, even at him, but gradually he had her quietened, for the time being anyway.

That night he sat with the clan elders by the light of their campfire, listening to their sadness.

71

'Can you help us?' he was asked eventually, but he could only give them the same answer.

'I have to think on this.'

Their father was slow to recover. Even though it was more than a fortnight since the stroke, he was still weak. His first effort at sitting himself up on the side of the bed had not only shocked the doctor, it had frightened the patient and used up the last of his strength. He now saw merit in going about this recovery business more slowly, but that didn't prevent him from becoming daily more restless and frustrated.

In the family it was generally thought, but never actually said, that if he behaved himself a little better, ceased his tantrums when he couldn't make himself understood or when his limbs failed him, he wouldn't be so weak. Charlotte was endlessly patient with him, picking up the pillows and blankets he'd testily thrown to the floor; not minding his rage when she attempted to feed him, since he was clumsy with his left hand; bringing him pencil and paper so that he could write notes, and retrieving them without complaint when he flung them away. He couldn't write legibly with his left hand as yet, and the sight of his own scrawl contributed to his frustration.

Charlotte hovered about all the time, irritating the others by vetting even the most trivial conversations with warning frowns and interruptions. They knew they were not to mention the Lands Acts, or those maps, or the ominous letter from his banker. Nor the fact that early shearers were arriving to claim the best sleeping quarters. Nor why Minnie had disappeared. Nor anything, it seemed, to do with the property. He was to stay so cocooned, according to Victor, that they couldn't think of anything to say to him without incurring Charlotte's disfavour.

'The new colt's a sturdy little fellow,' Victor told him. 'Up and about now, kicking up his heels.'

From behind Austin, Charlotte shook her head, and Victor knew she had taken exception to the words 'up and about', in case it reminded her husband of his infirm state. Exasperated, he ignored her.

'A little beauty he is. Louisa got to name him because . . .' He was about to say 'because she missed out on our wedding anniversary party', but realized he was on thin ice here with both of his parents. Austin had chosen that night to have his stroke, and Charlotte would throttle him if he gave that reason, but on the other hand, Austin's steely eyes were hard focused on him, listening carefully. Naming of thoroughbreds was important to him; many a row had erupted over this, not only with horses but with their aristocratic merino sheep.

'Because it was her turn,' he stammered. 'The mare was out of Joybelle so Louisa decided to call him Teddy's Joy.'

He saw Austin's eyes and the left side of his face grimace into a smile, and laughed in relief. Austin was pleased! Teddy had saved the day.

But outside, he grabbed Rupe. 'Did you see his face?'

'Yeah, it's fallen apart.' Rupe hated the sick room; he only called in when duty-bound.

'But his whole face had gone slack. Didn't you see just then, when he smiled, one half of his face worked? The other side is still dragging down, but one side worked!'

'You're imagining things!'

'No I'm not. Do you think I ought to tell him? It will give him some encouragement.'

'Ask Mum. She's in charge. I think she likes having him at her mercy at last.'

It seemed to Victor that his brother wasn't too upset at having Austin incapacitated either. He had a new air of authority about him that made Victor nervous. Until now, with Austin and Victor running the station, Rupe had been apathetic, even lazy, working when it suited him, but now he was all for action, full of ideas to do not only with the proposed new boundaries, but with anything else that came into his head, from the merino stud to the workloads of their outriders. Victor wondered, for the first time, if his brother would start challenging his authority.

'By the way, remember that old Cullya blackfeller that Dad knew, the medicine man? He's back. What was his name?'

'Moobuluk,' Victor said.

'Yeah. That's him. I've seen him three nights in a row, right on sunset.'

'How do you know it's him?'

'Because Austin said he turned up when Minnie's old mum died. He's related to them. And he had a three-legged dingo with him. Well, the old bloke's come home and he stands out every night on that rocky cliff that overlooks the tennis court. We're working out that way and I see him every time I come in, just standing there at the cliff edge with his mangy old dingo like he's cast in bronze. With a stringy beard. What do you suppose he wants?'

'Nothing. He's just come home for a bit. But I wouldn't mention it to Austin.'

Rupe grinned. 'Yes, Charlotte!'

But Victor was worried. Superstition stalked him. As a lad he'd always been fascinated by the mysteries of the Aborigine culture and the stories of the Dreamtime. He and Harry could speak the local dialect almost as well as Austin, because Aborigine children were their only playmates, but for that reason they had been easily spooked by tales of awesome magic men. Some of those dark fears still lingered.

Austin had always been ambivalent about the blacks, depending on his mood. One day they'd be a downright aggravation, but another time Victor would hear him entertaining guests with wondrous stories of their knowledge of the land and their second sight. He always claimed some of them did have magical powers. Often enough Victor had heard the story of a black medicine man, a widgery man, who was seen in two places at the same time. And his father himself claimed that he had seen one of these magic men change himself into a huge dingo with flaming jaws.

Whether that had been a hallucination, or the booze talking, Victor didn't know, but although he had never been fortunate enough to witness such events, he'd heard tell from the blacks of great powers, and he could not totally separate the possible from the impossible.

He worried now about that old magic man whom he had never met. Many were the tales of Moobuluk. His first thoughts were ominous. Had the ancient come to witness death again? Like he had for Minnie's mother, turning up out of the blue as if he had known it was imminent? Fear clutched. Was it Austin? Had those mysterious powers forewarned Moobuluk of the boss's demise?

Victor had to slap his hands together to shake himself out of these morbid thoughts, knowing it was just this sort of mood that spooked the blacks into imagining all sorts of queer events. And here he was doing the same thing, when it was obvious that Austin would recover.

'Bloody old Moobuluk!' he muttered. 'You're not going to spook me.'

Nevertheless, late in the afternoon, on his way home from organizing mobs of sheep to be brought closer to the home paddocks to wait their turn for shearing, Victor detoured towards that high ridge. Sure enough, there was the old wretch with the dingo still in tow. He was standing arrogantly at the point that overlooked the homestead hill, in the age-old pose, one foot resting on a knee, holding a tall stick resolutely in front of him.

No wonder Rupe thought he looked like a bronze statue, Victor grinned. Another trick of the trade. Because Moobuluk was facing the setting sun, his body, bathed in coppery light, made a striking figure from a distance.

Victor wheeled his horse and galloped to the base of the ridge, urging the animal up a steep zigzagging track, but when it clambered on to the flat of the plateau, they were met only by the snarling dingo. There was no sign of its master.

When Victor lashed at it with his stock whip, the dog backed off, growling.

'What do you want, old man?' he shouted in their lingo. 'Boss man sick. You talk to me.'

Gusts of dust-laden wind blew across the ridge, and the dog began to lope away, so, pulling down his hat to protect his eyes, Victor followed, keeping his horse on a tight rein, stepping cautiously. As the dust storm increased and visibility decreased, he peered about him, keen to meet this old bloke face to face, if only to tell Austin he'd finally come across the legendary magic man. He could still see the dingo just ahead, and thought the animal might lead him to Moobuluk, but suddenly the horse squealed and skidded sideways and Victor found himself staring down a deep crevice.

'Jesus!' he shouted, jerking the horse well away from the edge, his heart thumping.

He dismounted quickly, still pulling back, patting the horse. 'Good fellow. By God, we nearly went over there. I should have been watching. Good fellow, you're not that stupid, are you?'

He left the horse and walked back to the edge. 'I don't remember this gap in the rock,' he worried aloud. 'But then I haven't been up here for a long time.' He examined the sides, half hidden by dry shrubs, and shuddered. The dingo had led them this way, an easy leap across for a dog, but a dangerous trap for an unsuspecting horse and rider.

As he rode back down the ridge, Victor was uneasy, disconcerted by his own lack of care. But once out on the track leading round the home hill, he shrugged off thoughts of Moobuluk and let the horse have its head to release the tension.

Rupe was waiting for him at the stables. 'Where have you been? The two new boundary riders have arrived. They want to know what the pay is.'

'I'll tell them at the end of the week when I see how they go. Send them out tomorrow with one of our lads to learn the lay of the land. They have to know our boundaries exactly from one end to the other and across the river. That'll take them at least a week.'

'I told them they could pick up rifles and ammo from the store.'

'You told them wrong. There's no need for them to be armed beyond the usual yet; that will only draw attention to them. As far as everyone here is concerned, they're simply new stockmen on the lookout for stray sheep. Leave it at that. Keep in mind that that bill hasn't been passed yet. It could be a false alarm.'

Moobuluk watched the son they called Victor leave the ridge. He had yellow hair like his father, and he was just as curious, unlike the third son, who had glanced up at him and passed on by. The second son, Harry, did not live here any more, he was informed, so that accounted for all of Broderick's boys.

He had heard Victor's question but had no answer. Not yet. What *did* he want? He didn't know.

Moobuluk had been hovering, unseen, near the cooking camps of the men who worked here, listening to their talk, but the missing black children were never mentioned. And the black girls who worked in the house had said the same thing. No one spoke of them except the child Teddy, who missed his friends, and he was simply told they were gone. True enough, gone and completely forgotten by the whites. It was as if their little lives had touched none of them; they were less important than any one of the countless sheep they nurtured and guarded so solicitously.

He had seen Victor's horse almost come to grief at the fissure in the rock that had been formed eons ago by the snake spirit to hide her young. The wily old dingo had deliberately led them that way for his own reasons: probably payback for the sting of the whip.

So. He wiped eyes, grimy from the dust. What now?

Besides the black housegirls, Moobuluk had another spy. This was Spinner, who was more white than black. On the outside. Result of a union between Gabbidgee's sister and a shearer with hair as yellow as the Brodericks'. Spinner had always been taken with white men's ways, and he loved horses. No one had any idea where his name came from, but it wasn't important. The boy had hung about the stables from his earliest days, a willing helper just as long as he could stay with the horses.

His mother gave up on him, knowing he was safe and happy, when he refused to return to the camp, preferring to sleep in the stables. Then, as he grew up, a fixture, the whites took him for granted. Spinner became a skilful rider, and, joining the other men, had been working on the station for several years.

Since Spinner now lived like a white man Moobuluk conferred with him in the quiet of the bush.

'Where are our children?'

'They've been taken down to the big city.'

'To teach them to live with white men?'

'Yes.'

'Why couldn't they teach them here? Like they did with you.'

'Because they're going to teach them to be Christians.'

'What is that?'

'I'm not sure. But they kneel down to pray. I've seen whites doing that.'

'What is this pray?'

'Talking to the spirits.'

'Ah.' Then later: 'What do they know about the spirits?'

Spinner laughed. 'Buggered if I know.'

'When will they be back?'

Spinner shook his head. 'Beats me.'

'I told you to ask.'

'No one knows. Maybe never. I was talking to this new bloke, a shearer, and he said that's the whole idea. They have to forget about being black in them towns.'

'How can they do that? It is an impossibility.'

Spinner spread his hands helplessly. 'I don't know. I'm as sorry about this as anyone else, but there's nothing I can do.'

'You could go and get them. You've been to their towns.'

'Not that far. Anyway, they'd stop me. Maybe they'll bring them back next year. Give them a year of learnin' and bring 'em back.'

He didn't sound too convinced, but Moobuluk made him promise that if the boys did come back he was to let him know. Immediately.

'Are you staying this time, old man?'

'I don't think so,' Moobuluk said heavily. 'But I will make arrangements for message sticks. You can still do that much?'

'Sure I can.'

'Then you keep your ears open. If you let me down I will not forgive you.'

Spinner nodded, cracking his knuckles nervously. He wasn't that much of a white man that he could afford to break his word to this one. If Moobuluk pointed the bone at him, he wouldn't last a day.

'So . . .' Moobuluk explained to the elders, 'as I see it, this is the only course to take, unless you want to lose more of your children. I will withdraw for the time being, lest my presence cause agitation. If you agree to my suggestion, then put it to the people; it is a hard decision to make, so they must be given the opportunity to discuss it in full.'

The old men listened gravely. For many days after that, they were seen to be deep in thought by their campfire, then they emerged to proclaim that at the next moon a corroboree would take place. This was the usual time for the annual celebration of the trees that produced such bounty, the hard round nuts, sweetest of all nature's gifts after the wild honey, but it was the right of the elders to set the actual date.

They had agreed that this would be the best occasion to introduce a matter of great import to the whole clan.

Chapter Four

Shearing was in full swing and Springfield station was bustling with energy. Thousands of sheep were brought in from the wide pasturelands to be shouldered into pens and thence into the waiting hands of sweating men in the wool sheds. They emerged shorn, skinny-looking now, and bony white, to skip, run and jostle in grateful release to the next pens and on again, follow-my-leader, out of the gates to freedom, with dogs yapping, guiding them towards their home pastures.

Inside the sheds the work went on tirelessly, with everyone watching the blackboards, counting the sheep shorn by the gun shearers, the fastest men on the floor. Honour was at stake here. Older, experienced men were challenged every year by newcomers and young guns, while the rest placed their bets on the daily figures and the overall average. And all looked forward to the entrance of the very last sheep with shouts of laughter and anticipation, because Springfield was known to put on a boomer of a wind-up party.

An extra shearers' cook was engaged for the busy weeks to assist the staff cook, and they operated in a long grub shed attached to the cookhouse. Even so, the women in the homestead did their bit, Hannah baked extra scones and dampers and fruit cakes, assisted by Louisa; housegirls were sent in all directions to lend a hand, in the laundries, the orchard, the dairy and the slaughterhouse, helping the butcher to keep up the supply of meat needed to feed all those hungry men. Though concerned for her husband, Charlotte managed to keep everything running smoothly with her usual efficiency, but by this, Austin was able to leave his bed. He was still hampered by what he called his 'dead' leg, relying heavily on exercise and massage to regain movement in the limb, and Charlotte encouraged him. Despite their complaints, she set up rosters for Victor and Rupe to assist her in keeping up the exercise, and when they became too busy, she brought in a muscular black woman who warmed to the task of slapping the boss's leg into shape, and so was doing a better job than any of them.

Embarrassed by all this attention, and by his own weakness, Austin decided that only 'Black Lily' should stay at the job. He didn't mind her jovial, no-nonsense company, and besides, he was certain that only Black Lily really believed, as he did, that all this effort would make any difference.

She lifted him bodily to his feet, took his arm over her shoulder and lumped him about the room, acting as his crutch. She took him hopping out on to the veranda, where he preferred to take his meals, and even hauled him to the shower and the lavatory, shocking Charlotte, who protested to him. She was not as strong as Black Lily so she couldn't help him, but she felt it was unseemly to have a woman, even a black woman, attending to such personal matters.

'You should wait until I call one of the men, Austin.'

But he disagreed, speaking with difficulty through his stiff jaw and half-clenched teeth: 'No. Work. Leave 'em. She all right.'

He became so dependent on the forty-year-old Aborigine woman, who was at his beck and call from early morning until he retired, that Charlotte felt herself being pushed into the background again. His main interest, naturally, was the progress of the shearing, so his sons had to report to him every night, but not once, to any of them, did he mention the letter from the banker, nor did he enquire about the parliamentary debates regarding yet another Lands Act. He seemed to have forgotten that problem.

Charlotte had a wheelchair sent out, which he would not be seen in, and crutches which he could not use. She was mortified when Black Lily had to explain to her that the boss was working on his arm.

'He got to get that right first, missus, else them sticks no good. That arm same bad leg. Can't hold no stick on that side. Boss fall down bang crash.'

The woman massaged his fingers and his arm endlessly with a foul-smelling potion, and on his instructions, which she seemed to understand better than any of them, tied weighted dilly bags to his arm to rebuild his muscles, and all the time, Charlotte could only stand back and watch. Austin's determination to regain use of those limbs had become an obsession with him, almost to the point of exhaustion, but he would not cut down on the routine that he and Lily had established.

Harry wrote, concerned for his father, explaining that he would have come out to Springfield when he received the first telegram from Rupe but then another arrived insisting he remain in Brisbane. Should he come home or not?

That infuriated Austin, who made it plain to Victor that his brother should stay where he was needed. Then another letter arrived announcing that Harry and Connie would be home as soon as the House rose from this sitting. No mention of the Lands Acts.

Not really understanding what the fuss was all about, Charlotte was upset when Austin crumpled the note angrily and threw it on the floor. But fortunately he did not refer to it again.

The mailbags brought stacks of letters from Austin's friends and colleagues, all wishing him well. There was even a letter from the Premier of the State of Queensland, which impressed Charlotte but not Austin. 'Bloody fool!' he gritted. 'Losin' his grip!'

And then there was a letter from Fern Broderick, who wondered if perhaps a visit from her might help to cheer up the patient.

Fortunately the envelope was addressed to Charlotte, who saw no necessity to show it to her husband; it was just one letter among hundreds. She didn't dislike Fern, but she was inclined to be jealous of her. The woman was so elegant, so self-assured, that she made Charlotte feel inadequate. Austin was always talking about how clever Fern was, running that business so well after her husband died.

And why shouldn't she? Charlotte thought crankily. I'd have done the same in her place. After all, her husband had taught her the trade. What else could she do? Sell out and try to support herself on the capital and the small amount of ready money Justin had left her? Apparently, according to Austin, he'd invested a great deal of money in that lovely house on Wickham Terrace before he'd become aware of the sickness that had finally overtaken him.

'It's too big for her on her own,' Charlotte had said. 'She ought to sell it and get a smaller place.'

And she'd been stunned by Austin's retort: 'You've got a big house, why shouldn't she?'

That's as maybe, Charlotte said to herself now, as she sat at Victor's desk answering all the letters on her husband's behalf. But Fern owns her house *and* the jewellery business.

When the first panic over Austin's stroke had subsided, Charlotte had found Austin's keys and opened the safe in his inner office. This room in his private wing, off his main club-like area, was more akin to a pantry, with banks of shelves from floor to ceiling. They contained the history of Springfield; the careful station records of stock, land and water supply, weather reports, the bloodlines of horses and, in leather-bound volumes, the more important lineage of the stud merino sheep, the darlings of the station. The records also noted the rise and fall of wool prices, and a wealth of information gleaned by Austin on the husbandry of sheep and the treatment of wool, going right back to Macarthur's days. Investigating Austin's office while he was away in Brisbane one time, Charlotte had been astonished and impressed at the meticulous study her husband had made of sheep breeding. No wonder he'd made such a success of the big property when so many others had failed.

But this time, with Austin drugged and snoring out there, she'd investigated the safe. He had a lot of cash in there. Thousands of pounds, probably to defeat the intrusions of irritating taxation clerks who made shambling visits from time to time. And there was a wad of notes attached to a gold tie-pin, fastened with a band and with a note in crayon.

'For Teddy, from his Grandpa.'

Charlotte smiled at that. It was sweet. Typical of Austin. But the

81

money didn't interest her. Victor's safe, which she'd also checked, contained a lot of cash too, necessary for wages and the purchase of stores.

Then she found Austin's will. Simply written and duly notarized.

Springfield station was left to his sons, in three equal shares.

She noted that she was entitled to life residency in the homestead. 'How kind,' she muttered bitterly. 'I'm allowed to stay in my own home.'

Reading this confirmed the suspicions that had been bothering her for some time, since she'd begun to realize that Austin only ever referred to the station as his legacy for his sons. No mention of his wife's rights to Springfield should his death precede hers. Charlotte made up her mind that she would eventually have to talk to him about this. But not now. She couldn't possibly mention the subject until he was completely well again.

There were several other bequests. Hundreds of pounds to family retainers like Hannah, two overseers, Carter, the old storeman, and an elderly blacksmith, who had since died, and five thousand pounds to his widowed sister-in-law, Fern Broderick, in memory of his beloved brother, Justin.

No, Charlotte didn't dislike Fern – she was quite a nice person – but she had damn good reason to.

What had happened to Kelly's share in the station? Kelly had worked hard for this dream, and had died a horrible death. For that reason, Charlotte had never been able to take to the blacks. They'd murdered her brother. Under her husband's instructions she'd accepted them, trained girls, put up with their irritating presence, but she'd never had the courage to tell him she didn't care whether they lived or died. Any of them. She so desperately wanted Austin to love her that she'd completely sublimated, discarded, her own opinions rather than offend him, or cause him to think less of her. Charlotte knew that she wasn't much to look at – the mirror told her that – but she had won, married, the most handsome man in all the world, and that had to count for something. Didn't it? She'd seen how flirty women looked at him, but he was hers. She wasn't backward in reminding them.

But his will . . . She owned nothing. It was taken for granted that her sons would care for her. But which one? And which wife would she have to contend with? Neither of her two daughters-in-law had a real stake in Springfield, not like she did. If her husband died, would she end up in the back room like a maiden aunt?

'Like hell I will,' she said aloud, as she took the scissors and very neatly cut up that letter from Fern Broderick.

Fern was very concerned about Austin, so she decided to call on her nephew, Harry, at Parliament House to see if he had any news. Only yesterday she'd heard Harry was still in town, which was surprising, since she'd taken it for granted that he and Connie would have left for Springfield weeks ago. But then she guessed that if Austin had any say in it, his son would remain solidly in his place while the House was in session. Fern saw that as a promising sign.

She walked through the main gates and across the wide courtyard, passing small groups of men huddled in earnest conversation, and smiled benignly as some gentlemen took the time to raise their hats to this elegant lady.

Although she'd visited this gracious building many a time, it never failed to impress her. Palms and jacarandas in the forecourt added lustre to the tall freestone walls, lacing them with delicate shadows, and modifying the ornate façade of gothic windows and low balustrades. Instead of entering the main lobby, Fern followed the arched colonnades to the private entrance used by Members.

The clerk on duty recognized her. 'Lovely day, Mrs Broderick. How nice to see you again.'

'Thank you, Linus. And are you keeping well?'

'Indeed I am. What can I do for you? Looking for young Mr Broderick?'

'Yes. I was hoping to catch him before the afternoon session.'

'Time yet. He could be in his room. But if not, come back and I'll send a page for him. You know where to go? Do you want me to escort you?'

Several men had arrived, requiring his attention, so Fern shook her head. 'Thank you, Linus, but I think I can find my way.'

She walked down the passage and turned left, admiring the cedar woodwork rubbed to a satin finish, and the gleam of brass lamps and doorknobs.

'It's all so beautifully as it should be,' she remarked to herself as she studied the gilt figures on the row of doors.

Harry's room, on the ground floor, was number 35. He was lowly yet, but as his career progressed, Fern, loyal to the Brodericks, had no doubt that he would rise to higher office. 'And offices,' she grinned, knowing that the ministerial suites were upstairs.

Tentatively she raised a gloved hand to knock on Harry's slightly open door, but hearing voices, drew back, rather than intrude. Polished benches were placed outside the Members' rooms to accommodate people waiting their turn to see the great men, so she took her cue and sat quietly by the door, nodding politely to the occasional passer-by.

She recognized Harry's voice – it had that same deep resonance as his father's – but she could not hear, nor did she wish to, the details of the conversation taking place between him and another gentleman. As their voices were raised and became more heated, however, Fern could hear them clearly. They were arguing about a vote.

Nothing unusual in this place, she mused.

'I can't give this legislation the nod,' Harry was saying. 'It's impossible. I've been against it from the very beginning. You've got a cheek to be asking me, James.'

'Get it through your head, I'm not asking you, Harry. I'm advising you. These amendments are the best you're going to get. Trouble with you, Harry, you haven't been round the traps long enough to see the wood for the trees. Times are changing; you have to go with changes or you'll get left sitting on your thumbs.'

'But they say freeholding will be the ruination of the squatters.'

'Jesus! They say . . . They said we'd never get telegraphic communication from London! They said Brisbane was a swamp, fit only for convicts. They said we'd never be able to separate from New South Wales and be self-governing here in Queensland, didn't they?'

'Yes, they did, but freeholding is a different matter.'

Fern heard a match strike and caught a whiff of cigar smoke. Then the other man, James, spoke again. His voice sounded familiar, and she wondered if it was James Mackenzie, a union man and an influential spokesman for the opposition parties.

'No, it's not. We're offering squatters like your father security of tenure, but they can't see that. They're against change, spooked by anything new. Don't you remember the shouts of bankruptcy when this very building was planned? Look at it now . . . magnificent! And the state isn't bankrupt.' He sighed. 'No, you wouldn't remember, you're too young. And that's your trouble, you're lining yourself up with the old guard.'

'That's rubbish!' Harry snapped. 'I'm voting with the Government, with my own party.'

'Then you'd better look again, old son. The squatters haven't got the stranglehold they used to have . . . Look round the front benches; you've got doctors, lawyers, big merchants who are beginning to lean on the Treasurer. Leasehold of all that land brings in a pittance; they're saying what I'm trying to tell you, before you end up out of step. The state needs money to survive. They want to sell that leasehold land outright, get some cash in the coffers, and at the same time, I repeat, give the squatters a fair go, a chance to buy their land.'

'How can they bloody buy their land?' Harry said angrily. 'Look at Springfield. We have hundreds of square miles on one side of the river alone. How could we afford to buy all that?'

James laughed. 'Typical! From the farmer to the squatter, always crying poor mouth. Austin could afford to buy half of Queensland.'

'That's ridiculous. I can't speak for the rest, but my family couldn't afford to go freehold. It's too much to ask of us.'

Fern was listening intently now, and she nodded. Good for you, Harry.

'Why? Has Austin fallen on bad times?' the other man said silkily, and Fern heard menace in the voice.

'Of course not. Why would you say that?'

'Because I was wondering why he won't help you out. It's common knowledge, Harry, that you're up to your neck in debt, on top of what you owe me.'

'That's nothing to do with my father.'

'Well, it's a lot to do with me, mate. You trade on Austin's name at the tables, but when it comes to settling, suddenly he's not there any more. You can't have it both ways.'

'I'll find it,' Harry grated. 'I just need time.'

A chair scraped across the boards as one of them stood, so Fern sat quickly upright to give the impression that she was not eavesdropping.

'Where will you find it? The only income you have comes from Daddy. Unless you sell that palatial house of yours and live like the backbencher you are. Or does that belong to Austin too?'

'None of your business!'

James relented. 'Listen, Harry, don't let it get to you. I'm a reasonable man. I like a flutter too, as you well know, but I have friends who'll back me up. You shouldn't have to flail about like a goose waiting for the axe. As I told you in the first place, this bill will go through. If it doesn't, you can expect tougher amendments. As it stands, the bill states that a three-hundred-and-twenty-acre selection will cost two hundred and fifty pounds, but there are voices claiming it should be more. Austin won't thank you if you procrastinate until the going price skyrockets, with the Treasury men rubbing their hands.'

Harry muttered something that Fern couldn't hear.

'All we want to do,' James said evenly, and Fern had to strain to listen, 'is to get this bill out of the way. There are more important decisions waiting in the wings. If you give an indication that you're ready to vote for security of tenure for squatters, then I'm sure I could find friends who will give you a leg up.'

'In what way?' Harry asked nervously, and Fern found herself chewing the fingertip of a glove.

Don't ask him to spell it out, she urged silently. Don't even listen!

'Your slate could be wiped clean,' James said firmly. 'Clean, Harry. And from my sums, that'd buy a lot of drinks *and* take you off the debtors' list at your club. But it's up to you, mate. You can go down with the old guard or make your mark in the House as a responsible, forward-thinking parliamentarian . . .'

'I'd cop a lot of criticism.'

James laughed, as if relieved. 'Don't we all? But you'd be in good company . . .'

Fern Broderick fled. She couldn't face Harry. She'd deliberately eavesdropped on a private conversation, and true to the warnings about such an ill-mannered pastime, she'd gained more than she'd bargained for.

She was so upset she didn't notice she'd taken a wrong turning, maybe several, in the labyrinth of corridors, until a clerk passed her, ringing a warning bell to advise Members that the afternoon session was about to commence. Desperately she opened a door and found herself outside, on the river side of the building. Rather than re-enter and try again, Fern made for the path that led right down to the banks at the bend of the river. She'd had quite enough of Parliament House.

From here she knew her way back into town, along the track that led under the bridge. Back to her jeweller's shop. But she was in no mood to face anyone.

'Harry,' his father had told her, 'is a bloody dunce.'

'That's unfair, Austin,' she'd said. Hadn't she? 'You don't give him a chance. Every one of us is a new chum until we start to get a grasp on what we're trying to do. Even you. You made some terrible mistakes when you started the station, so don't pretend to be so clever. I remember Justin telling me some of those stories . . .'

'Like what?'

'Like when you insisted on shearing too early and the poor shorn sheep died in an overnight cold snap.'

'I can't be blamed for the weather.'

'I'm just saying give Harry a chance. Parliament must be hugely intimidating for young men unless they're pumped-up blowhards, and they don't last.'

'I know that, but I have to listen to him. And you'd think he'd just joined the best club in town, the way he goes on about the bloody social life.'

'Well, he has,' she'd laughed. 'He has. Give him time to settle down.'

That had been three years ago. Harry and Connie were now well known in the Brisbane social set, entertaining lavishly in the riverside house Austin had bought them for a wedding present. Fern had often been invited to soirées and musical evenings there, but not to the more formal functions that required a partner.

Only now did she realize that Harry was better known for his parties than for his impact in the House. Come to think of it, though he featured often in the social pages, she doubted if any of his speeches had been of enough moment to be reported in the papers. If he had even made any, outside of his maiden speech. All the family had been there, his aunt included, when Harrison J. Broderick, MLA, had made that maiden speech.

About the iniquities of the Lands Acts!

'Oh my God!' she said, standing staring across the softly flowing river. 'Is he changing his mind?'

Austin had talked about the proposed Lands Acts at various times but was confident that they'd never be passed.

'But what if they are?' Fern had asked.

'I'll be in a bit of a fix, but don't you worry your pretty head about it.'

'Pretty head!' she snorted now, stepping out briskly. His wife was so self-effacing, so obedient to his whims and opinions, that he seemed to think all women had heads of cotton wool. Fern remembered him begging her to sell the shop, terrified that she'd go broke overnight. Even now he liked to think he was guiding her finances, not noticing that though sometimes she took his advice, on most matters she relied on her own judgement.

Ever since Austin had mentioned the Lands Acts, she'd been following their progress through the papers as best she could, trying to keep up with the constant debates and amendments, and it seemed to her that the fellow talking to Harry was right. The tide was turning, slowly, inexorably, towards freeholding, but Harry had missed the point, as the sly James Mackenzie – she was positive now it was him; who else could it be? – had meant him to. Certainly a great deal of money was involved, but there were to be restrictions on the area of land – or runs, as they were called – that one man could own. Therefore, Fern reasoned, Austin would have to relinquish a great slice of Springfield. It would break his heart.

Loyally, she was firmly on the side of the squatters, and believed that the men who wanted to fracture the great estates were bent not so much on giving small selectors their chance as on breaking the power of the squatters. They had no appreciation of the huge contribution the sheepmen had made to this country by hard work and careful breeding of their stock. It was said often enough that Australia had ridden to success on a sheep's back, but that didn't seem to matter any more. Not to them. But Harry? What was he thinking of, to even consider turning his back on his father?

She walked up busy Queen Street, grateful for the shade provided by the awnings over the footpath. She was so cross, she'd been walking too fast, and now she felt all hot and bothered. What could she do about all this? Nothing really. Even if she did admit she'd overheard the conversation, she could hardly accuse Harry of accepting a bribe when it hadn't happened. And if he did accept it, those sorts of men had ways of covering up such corrupt practices by making the rewards appear normal transactions. Difficult to prove wrong-doing. And would she want to accuse Austin's son of such a thing? Of course not.

The Brodericks' high-stump house in Paddington was large and airy, with a square floor plan, a parimeter veranda and a high, steep, iron-sheeted roof. The exterior timbers were white-painted, as were the cast-iron balustrades and the latticework panels, with a light touch of green for the gutterings. The intricate cast-iron decorations lent opulence to this otherwise plain house and were carried through as railings for the wide timber front steps that led from ground level up to the front door. The Brodericks' home was a typical Queenslander, as the style was known.

Early Brisbane houses were built at ground level, but when houses raised on stilts began to appear on the river flats, builders took note. They realized that not only did these houses with headroom underneath provide protection against seasonal flooding, but they were cooler; they caught the breezes, an important factor in the oppressive Queensland heat. They became fashionable, even in hilly areas such as Paddington, because they sat higher than the shrubbery that nursed low-flying mosquitoes, and, what was more, they were able to provide spectacular views. Metal caps were placed on the high stumps, effectively deterring termites, and the raised floors kept out snakes, the bane of the housewife in tropical lands.

Wooden latticework either side of the front steps hid the vacant area underneath the houses which provided extra space for storing implements and odds and ends, and for erecting clothes lines, which were made good use of during the rainy season. Using stilts also made it cheaper to build houses on sloping sites.

Connie Broderick loved her house. The site itself was high, looking down over the city and its winding river, but the added height of the stilts made it feel very special – quite superior, in fact. She and Harry had gone to a great deal of expense to make their house more attractive than other houses of the type. They installed large canvas blinds on the veranda that could be lowered for shade and for protection against monsoonal rains, and that meant they need not worry about the summer furniture that they'd lavished on the outdoor living areas.

Their front door, of latticed timber, led only to the veranda, so the first view the visitor had of Connie's domain was this cool sprawl of double cane chairs and lounges with floral cushions, occasional tables and potted palms.

The door to the main house, which was rarely closed, was only a few steps across the veranda, and it afforded a first impression of care and high polish. The floors gleamed, soft Persian rugs were scattered throughout, grand mahogany furniture inhabited every room, softened by rich lace ceiling-to-floor curtaining that need not stoop to being functional, for the wide verandas took care of shade and privacy. Across from the formal parlour, a grand piano in full flight occupied the music room, and the dining room boasted a table that could seat twelve.

That bothered Connie. She had furnished this house, down to the last detail, from pictures in a London magazine, but the dining room was a disappointment. Harry was an important man, and as his wife, she had her position in society to uphold, but that room was just too small for really smart dinner parties. One day she would have a bigger house and a more adaptable dining table. It was difficult being confined to only ten guests at a time when they had so many important friends.

When Harry came home he was alone. That was disappointing. It was Thursday afternoon, and he usually brought a couple of his friends home with him on the last day of sittings, to talk and laugh about their week in the House over a few drinks. They were such gay company, especially Sam Ritter, who was not only divinely handsome, but was also an outrageous flirt. Connie adored him; he always made her feel so special. Last week he had complimented her on her beautiful dress, the softly flowing pink organza with deep flounces, so she was wearing it again today, just to please him. She primped her dark curls in a gilt mirror before coming out to greet her husband, just in case the others were following on later.

He took off his jacket, threw it on a table and plumped down on one of the chairs on the veranda to take off his shoes.

'Oh, Harry,' she cried. 'Not here. Go inside if you wish to undress. You're not in the bush now.'

'I'll undress where I like,' he retorted, throwing down his shoes, taking off his tie and removing the studs from his stiff collar.

Hurriedly she picked up the discarded clothes. 'You can't sit here in your shirtsleeves. I'll get your smoking jacket.'

'It's too bloody hot. Forget the jacket, bring me out a whisky and cold water.'

'You could say please. Is anyone else coming?'

'No. I have to go back. Committee meetings.'

'But you can't. We're dining at the Pattersons'.'

'It's been cancelled. She's sick or something.'

'Oh, well thank you very much. I'm the last to know. I've given Cook the night off.'

He sighed. 'The whisky, Connie? Do you think you can do that without her help?'

She brought out the drinks tray that was already prepared and placed it carefully on a table. 'Help yourself. And I'll have a glass of the white wine, if it isn't too much trouble.'

By the time he handed her a glass of wine she had arranged herself in her favourite chair and sat facing him, sulking.

He gulped down his drink, poured another one, and eventually decided to talk. 'I've got to make a decision.'

'What about?'

'The Lands Acts. There's another vote coming up again soon.'

'That old thing. Haven't they got anything else to talk about?'

'I'm being lobbied to vote for it this time. It's not such a bad idea really, but Austin will throw a fit.'

'Why do you always have to do what he says? You're the one in Parliament, not him.'

'Because it will affect Springfield. And it's hard to explain it to him; he doesn't understand what's going on. Besides, he's sick, this wouldn't be the time to try to explain.'

'Would he be very angry if you just went ahead and voted the way you want without telling him?'

Harry stared at his drink. 'Livid is the word. He's likely to cut me off without a penny.'

'Good God! It can't be that important.'

'It is.'

'Then forget it. Haven't you been voting against those bills before this?'

'Yes. But now there are extenuating circumstances. I really should vote with the ayes this time.'

Connie was shocked. 'You're crazy, Harry. You'll have to vote no again.'

'Didn't I just hear you saying I shouldn't always do what he says? You've made a quick switch.'

'Well, I don't claim to know what these bills are all about, but I know your father's temper. And so do you. You can't risk Springfield. He wouldn't go that far, would he?'

Connie was frightened. She knew in her heart what the answer would be, and Harry's nod confirmed it.

'Then you stay with the noes, Harry. I don't care whether it's a good idea or a bad idea; Springfield is your heritage.'

She frowned when he poured yet another drink but did not dare criticize.

Harry lounged back, his long legs stretched out, lost in his thoughts. Finally he turned to her.

'We're broke, Connie. Flat broke.'

'What are you saying? We can't be. You've got plenty of money.'

'Did have,' he shrugged. 'Not any more. I owe everyone. Even your father.'

'What have you done with it? Both Austin and Daddy made substantial settlements on us when we were married, and then there was that legacy I got from my auntie . . .'

'Don't ask me what I've done with it,' he snapped. 'Austin bought us this house but you haven't stopped spending since you got in the door. Nothing was too expensive for you: imported furniture, the best silver and china, and even the bloody piano that neither of us can play, not to mention your clothes . . . You've got more dresses than my mother ever had in her whole life.'

Coldly, she shouldered that tirade aside. 'Our money was invested to bring us a reasonable income. If I've been overspending you could have said so. Why did you borrow money from Daddy? Don't tell me. You've been gambling again. You had that row with Austin a year ago about your gambling, I heard it. You promised to stop.'

'What difference does it make?' Harry said. 'We're broke.'

'It makes a lot of damn difference. It *is* your gambling. I won't let you turn me into a pauper! You're a fool, Harry Broderick.'

'I see.' He smiled meanly. 'And what do you propose I do about it?'

'Borrow from Austin. You could borrow from Austin.'

'More debts. And he won't lend me any more. I already owe him too. It's funny really. If I vote no, I get his approval and no cash. If I vote yes, there are friends who'll wipe out my debts and, if I lean hard enough, get me on boards that pay for my services. Friends on the other side of the House, of course,' he added.

'Madness! I'd back Austin against them.'

'That door's closed. You could go to your father for me. Tell him we've had a lot of extra expense lately . . .'

'I will not. I absolutely refuse to be humiliated like that.'

Connie shut herself in the silence that followed, wondering if her husband shared the thought that had just come into her head: if Austin had succumbed to that stroke, their troubles would be over. Harry would own a share in one of the biggest sheep stations in the state . . .

'Do you want anything to eat before you go back?' she asked at length.

'Just a sandwich. I'm not very hungry.'

She saw him fed and out of the house before she cut some bread for herself, slicing impatiently, cross that the knife wouldn't cut straight. She piled it with butter and jam, searched the pantry for some cake, added that to her tray with a glass of lemonade, and took it through to the parlour where she could at least be comfortable if she had to stay home on her own. Again.

'It's just not good enough,' she mumbled as she picked up some journals to try to take her mind off their troubles while she ate.

But the pages couldn't hold her interest, and she threw them on the floor. 'How dare he blame me! I've got something to show for my spending. What's he got but gambling debts and a drawer full of unpaid bills?'

Connie remembered now that only recently her mother had murmured something to her about Harry and the races.

'It might be better if you didn't encourage him to attend the race meetings so often, dear. Surely there are other things you can find to do of a Saturday afternoon?'

'I enjoy the races, Mother. All our friends go. We have a lovely time.'

Was that a warning? What did she know that she couldn't come straight out and tell her daughter?

'Damnit!' Connie snapped. 'I should have insisted he tell me just how much he owes.'

But then, she worried, what good would that do? Only upset her more. Broke? What did that really mean? Didn't they have any money at all? Fear flooded again. She'd known of a couple who'd dropped out of society altogether, sold their house and disappeared to some country town because they'd lost all their money, and she was terrified that it would happen to her.

'Oh no it won't!' she declared. 'I'm not going to my parents to beg for money for him. I'd be better off leaving him and going home to them if things got that bad.' The solution sounded reasonable to her. Girls went home to their mothers, leaving their husbands for reasons that were never discussed in polite circles. It was just accepted that the husband was some sort of a cad. The more Connie thought about this option, the more she liked it, but the timing was important. If Harry was facing ruin his wife had no intention of sitting about until bailiffs turned her out of her own home. That would be the ultimate humiliation. She'd have to have her bags packed and be well away before the axe fell.

Harry really was stupid to have got them into this mess. The obvious answer – the only answer really – was for him to throw himself on his father's mercy, so what was he thinking of to be even listening to those lobbyists? But that was typical of Harry: short-term solutions that always backfired, like betting more to recoup losses. And losing more.

Well, if he wouldn't write to Austin, she would. No need to antagonize her father-in-law further by mentioning that blasted vote.

But then again, why not? She'd been so busy concentrating on these options that she hadn't grasped the true implications behind this offer of assistance from friends. She considered it would serve Austin right if his meanness caused Harry to further his career by opposing his father's opinion. In refusing to help Harry out of his financial difficulties, he was leaving his son no other choice.

A letter from Victor had explained that Austin was recovering. He was left with some paralysis from the stroke, but his mental capabilities were not impaired, so he would have no trouble understanding Harry's situation.

She heard a knock at the front door and froze, her imagination running riot. Did bailiffs come at night? Was it a creditor calling to demand payment? It occurred to Connie to hide, to refuse to answer the door, but then a familiar voice called: 'Yoo-hoo! Anyone home?'

It was Sam Ritter.

Frantically she pulled on the shoes she'd kicked off, tried to collect the journals, looked at the miserable remains of her bread-and-jam dinner and thought how awful that must appear. She straightened her dress, rushed to a mirror to tidy her hair and hurried out, closing the parlour door behind her.

'Why, Sam! How nice to see you. Do come in,' she said, escorting him into the music room.

He strolled in, standing easily by the piano to look at her. 'My word, you are a picture, Connie. You're getting prettier by the day. Where's our Harry?'

'He had to go back to the House. More meetings.'

She saw him blink. 'Meetings? Ah, yes, of course. The bane of our lives.' And she knew Harry had lied. Where was he then?

Sam made no move to leave so Connie, glad of his company, asked him if he'd care for a sherry.

'Good idea. I'm on my way to supper at Newstead House, a deadly affair to honour some old gent in the Royal Historical Society, so I'm not in any rush.'

While he waited for her to pour the drinks, he ran his fingers expertly over the keyboard. 'I adore this piano, you know. I've only got an old upright.'

Connie laughed. Everyone knew that Sam Ritter was wildly wealthy in his own right, having inherited a great deal of money from his late father and made good use of it by becoming an importer of luxury goods. He had huge warehouses near North Quay, and a lovely home at New Farm, overlooking the river.

'Play something for me,' she said. 'I need cheering up.'

He was just about to seat himself on the piano stool when he caught her words, and was genuinely concerned. 'Why? What's the matter?'

'Oh, nothing much. Just worries.'

'There's no such thing as just worries, dear heart. They're real or imagined. Now, which is it?'

'They're real all right,' she said miserably.

He picked up his sherry. 'Well then, the first thing we do is drink to our good health. Come on now . . . chin, chin . . . drink up, in one go!'

Sam demolished his sherry and laughed as she took a few extra sips to finish hers. 'Right. Now, come and sit over here with me and tell me all about it.'

But as soon as they were seated on a sofa, Connie burst into tears. She couldn't possibly admit they were broke. For all she knew, Harry might owe Sam money too. Besides, it sounded so pathetic. Then she recalled her original plan.

His arm went round her, consoling her as she sobbed into her handkerchief. 'Come on, dear heart, tell old Sam all about it.'

She shook her head, 'I can't,' and the tears became more real in a rush of self-pity.

Sam held her closer, kissing her on the cheek. 'Don't cry. It can't be that bad. What's upset you?'

'It's Harry,' she whispered. 'He's perfectly horrible to me. He makes my life a misery. I dread him coming home these days.' And she truly did, she told herself, because he was the bearer of horrible news.

'Good Lord,' he said softly. 'I had no idea. Why? I mean, how? Does he ill-treat you?'

'Don't ask me to talk about it,' she sobbed. 'It's too awful, Sam. I'm just so glad you're here, I don't know what to do.'

'Oh, my poor love,' he murmured. Suddenly she was in his arms and he was kissing her, and his lips were soft, wonderfully soft. Sam was an elegant man, not tall and rangy like Harry, and that added to his appeal. He was always cheerful, and had such a jolly face, with twinkling blue eyes, but now those eyes were serious, hurting with concern for her, and she was comforted. More than that, she loved his kissing and caressing, so desperately needed right now, and she responded, thrilled at her own daring as he crushed her to him.

'Oh, Connie,' he murmured, 'I love you, my darling. I've always loved you. You must know that.'

She was excited, impressed beyond words that she'd made such a conquest, that Sam had really cared about her all this time and she hadn't known, and when their lovemaking became more intimate it was Connie who made the decision. If they were to really make love then she didn't want to have to cope with this hard sofa. She wanted to show him that she really was worth loving.

In the comfort of the soft double bed, Connie met his passion with an excitement she'd never known before, astonished that he was such a marvellous lover, listening to him tell her how much he loved her, over and over again, revelling in his total lack of inhibition and her own waywardness . . .

And then Harry walked in.

There had been a meeting, but not at Parliament House. It was held at James Mackenzie's cottage in South Brisbane, where the four men drank beer and went over and over the pros and cons of the legislation that was due to come before the House the following week.

Harry listened, argued, worried. He knew there were opportunities here for him to break free of Austin's financial stranglehold, but would it be worth the revenge his father might visit on him?

'And keep in mind,' James said, 'that any day now, other legislation will be passed to pay Members for their expenses. If you stick with us, Harry, we're taking it a step further. Labor Party policy is that all Members of Parliament should be paid, and paid handsomely, for the vital burdens they have to shoulder as representatives of the people. Rich men on the Government benches don't need to worry, or care, that most of us have to sacrifice a great deal to attend to our duties and our electorates, leaving precious little time to earn incomes.'

'Yes,' Harry nodded. 'Quite.'

'We know that money really isn't a consideration for you, Harry,' another man said. 'But you young blokes have to realize that you were elected to represent all the people, not just – with respect, Harry – the whims of rich men.'

'That's really what you're up against, Harry,' James added. 'Do you rely on your integrity and vote for the people, or do you uphold the outmoded interests of the élite? You're in a difficult situation, family interests as against the interests of Queensland. It could even be said that you have a conflict of interest that should, in a fair society, make your vote illegal.'

'I'm an elected Member the same as you,' Harry said angrily. 'My vote could never be illegal.' He stood up. 'I have to go. I'll think about this over the weekend.'

When he left, the Labor men nodded. 'He's nearly over the line, James. You keep at him.'

One man was cautious. 'I don't get this. He might be deep in debt, but what's the problem? His father will haul him out.'

James grinned. 'Then again he might not. I heard a whisper that old Broderick has lowered the boom. Shut down the coffers. Since then he's had a stroke. They say he's in a bad way, but not on his death bed. It'll take time for him to be in good enough shape to hear Harry's woes. That's why it's imperative we keep the pressure on the lad. What about Ned Lyons? Harry owes him a bundle. Can you get him to help?'

'Sure. He'll send one of his chaps round to give him a nudge.'

'Make it tomorrow, and more than a nudge.'

'You don't want him roughed up?'

James laughed. 'No. Worse. Make it clear that if he hasn't paid up by Saturday, he won't be able to put so much as a shilling on a horse. That'll send him into a panic . . . make him look a right fool in the Turf Club.'

'Do we need him that bad?'

'Yes. The numbers are close; we could make it this time. My son and a lot of his mates are already out there waiting for the starting gun. It'll be better than a gold rush when all that land is opened up to selectors.'

'And not before time. Them squatters have had it too good for too long. Let's go over the numbers again, we've only got four days.'

Harry forgotten, they searched their lists, looking for more possible defectors from the Government stand, planning to make sure that none of their supporters was absent, choosing their best speakers to lead the debate, worrying over the important bill late into the night.

Fern Broderick closed her shop and walked slowly up the hill to her home on Wickham Terrace. She was so tired, she found herself counting the steps, and breathed a sigh of relief when she reached her front door. All the way home she'd been tempted to hail a passing cab and have the driver take her out to Harry's place, feeling she ought to have a good talk to that young man, but her weary bones were just not up to it.

'Maybe it's time I retired,' she said to her maid, Bonnie, as she slumped into the nearest armchair in her sitting room. 'I'm really feeling the strain.'

'You shouldn't have walked home. It's a steep hill, that. On your feet all day, you should have taken a cab.'

Fern smiled, unpinning her hat. Bonnie had been into the jeweller's often enough, but she still saw her mistress as a shopgirl, never seeming to notice that Mrs Broderick occupied an office with glass panels at the rear of the shop. A very comfortable office, where she conferred with gem merchants and her special customers. Two experienced salesmen, who had been with the Brodericks for years, were her frontline troops.

Gratefully, she took off her shoes and sat drinking the tea that Bonnie brought her, trying to make a decision. When she'd finished the tea she made for the bathroom. She had in mind calling on Harry after dinner, uninvited, but first a long, warm bath, to reinvigorate body and spirits.

Bonnie was surprised when she came down to the dining room in a grey suit. 'You going out again, Mrs Broderick?'

'I might. I'm thinking about it.'

Fern ate in the dining room even when she didn't have company, but she never felt alone. To her, it was the best part of the day: a good meal, a glass of wine, no more rush . . . She looked out at the greenery that surrounded her house, listening to the birds settling and the evening song of the currawongs.

Now, as dusk drew shadows, she reconsidered her plan. Connie would be home. She could hardly expect the wife to vacate, or to be able to broach the subject in her presence. The last thing she wanted to do was to cause any trouble in the household. Then again, Harry might be offended by her interference. Especially when it was based on a spot of eavesdropping.

In other words, Connie admitted, she was backing off, talking herself out of confronting her nephew. After all, he wasn't a child. Did he need his aunt turning up on his doorstep? To do what?

She shuddered. To tell him she knew he had problems and ask if she could help. How? He'd be within his rights to show her the door.

'No, I'm not going out after all,' she told Bonnie, who was relieved. 'But I'll have my coffee at my desk.'

Austin had been horrified that a lady had a rolltop desk in her sitting room, but Fern liked it there. She'd moved it from the back room where Justin had liked to work, right up here where she didn't feel so isolated.

Now she sat, pen in hand, staring at an empty page. If calling on Harry wasn't the best move, then she ought to appeal to his mother.

She could hardly write to Austin; it would be cruel to upset a sick man.

Fern recalled that she had written to him, wishing him well, and there'd been no reply, but that didn't bother her. She guessed that Charlotte had enough to do without answering all the letters that would have come from his friends.

Dear Charlotte, she wrote.

I hope you are well and Austin is feeling better. Connie told me he's on the mend. This is a hard letter for me to write because I don't wish to be interfering, but I have become aware that Harry has financial problems . . .

'No,' she said. 'That's awful. Telltale. Horrible.'

She screwed up the page and dropped it into the waste basket.

'This isn't stuff one should write about,' she admitted.

'Bonnie,' she called. 'How would you like to come with me to visit the Springfield sheep station?'

'Me? When?'

'In a day or so, when I get things sorted out at the store. Early next week.'

'Lovely. And the best news to hear you're going to take a holiday at last. How do we get there?'

'It's a long journey. Train and coaches.'

'Doesn't sound much of a holiday, bumping about in them coaches. Are you sure this is what you want to do?'

Bonnie was right. A long, uncomfortable journey like that was hardly what a doctor would prescribe for a weary middle-aged woman, even if she could enjoy the comfort of Austin's home when they finally made it. And then there was the return journey, which always seemed longer.

'No,' she said, surprising Bonnie. 'But I feel I ought to.'

'Ah. You're worried about Mr Austin?'

Fern nodded. That and his damned son. What would she say when she got there? Tell them their son was heading for trouble? Maybe it would be better if she just had a quiet word with Victor. He had more sense than the other two.

Or maybe you should just stay home and mind your own business, she told herself. Are you sure you're going out there to try to help? Or is this really an excuse to see Austin?

Harry was standing in the doorway of his bedroom with his tweed jacket hitched on his shoulder and his tie in his hand. He'd dumped his shoes on the veranda. He felt stupid being there in his socks, staring at the bed, his bed. At the two people in his bed, two bodies, sheets rumpled, pillows on the floor, no light except from the lamps in the passage behind him.

He was the intruder. Embarrassed, his first reaction was to back away, apologize, leave, close the door behind him. He was already upset and depressed, but this had him disoriented. He stared about him. This was his room, wasn't it?

There was frantic movement on the bed. Disentanglement. A clutching of sheets. He shook his head, blinking, as the awfulness of this scene began to register, and his voice came out as a croak. 'What's going on here?'

'Harry!' the woman screamed. The woman. Connie. His wife.

The man was scrambling out of the bed, lunging about. Nude. Bloody nude! In his house! Grabbing for clothes. But still Harry couldn't move. He needed someone to explain, to tell him what to do, because while his mind was beginning to focus, his limbs were weak and loose, like jelly.

Then the man spoke from over there in the corner by the dressing table, hopping about, struggling in the dim reaches of the large room. Harry didn't catch what he said, but a light snapped on in his head and he saw only too clearly what was going on. And he realized that the man hopping about over there, with his white bum turned towards him, was Sam Ritter.

Harry exploded. 'You bastards!' he shouted, and rushed away to do what any red-blooded man would do in these circumstances. He skidded round the polished passages to the hall cupboard where he kept his guns, bypassed the slim rifles and grabbed a double-barrelled shotgun and cartridges, stumbling, slipping on his way back as he loaded the gun.

They were both half dressed by this. Sam had his pants on and his shoes, and was fumbling with shirt buttons. She was already in that flowy dress of hers but her hair was all mussed up. Looked like a rat's nest, he noted, and that reminded him.

'You pair of rats,' he shouted. 'Get out of my house!'

She cringed back there by her mahogany dressing table with the huge mirror that had cost him a fortune, while Sam kept the bed between them.

'Listen, old chap. I can explain. Put the gun down. There's no need for that.'

She echoed him, her voice high-pitched, unreal. 'Please, Harry. Put the gun down. Don't be stupid.'

'How dare you call me stupid, you stupid woman?' he shouted, waving the gun from him to her. 'Didn't you hear what I said? Get out of my house.'

Sam's voice was calm. 'All right. I'm going. I'm going. You take the gun and move out of the way, and I'll leave.'

Harry hadn't thought what to do next. He was confused. Outraged. But then he heard a shower of rain begin to patter on the iron roof, and he was pleased. Brisbane badly needed rain. He listened as the rain became heavier, wind accompanying it, rattling the loose guttering that he should have had fixed months ago.

'If you take that gun and go into the parlour,' Sam said, 'I'll go, Harry. We can talk about this tomorrow.'

'What?' Harry was jerked back into this nightmare. His wife! His best friend! He felt like weeping but instead plumped for vengeance. It made him feel stronger, and the gun helped. Come to think of it, he realized with wonder, never in his life had he been in such a position of strength. All his life he'd had to jump to other people's commands; now it was his turn.

'You're not going anywhere,' he told Sam. 'Neither is she. I'm going to shoot you both. And I'll get off, too.'

To prove his point he pulled the trigger, aiming at the bed that he'd never sleep in again, smashing to smithereens the mahogany bedhead and causing a cloud of feathers to billow out in all directions. The noise was deafening. They were both hiding somewhere on the floor. He reloaded.

She was screaming. Sam stood up when the feathers subsided.

'Be sensible, Harry. You can't shoot us. And don't kid yourself. You won't bloody get off. They'll hang you.' He was up and walking, step by step, around the shattered bed. 'Give me the gun.'

'I told you to get out of my house!'

'So you did and I'm going. But not with a bullet in me. So you back off! Get out of the way!'

Harry was shocked at this turnabout. Sam Ritter, with all his parlour manners and bonhomie, was always the life of the party, but now he sounded like Austin. Where had that come from? Harry felt bereaved. Not only had his friend dishonoured him, but now he was the voice of authority. The hated authority he'd had to bow to at home, at school, and in the Parliament, where all the Premier's men, his father's mates, told him daily what to do, where to sit, how to vote. Until lately, when he was figuring on breaking away. If he could.

He stared at Sam, who was now standing firmly facing two steely barrels. It was sad. Nothing would ever be the same again with him and Sam. His dear friend. He didn't really want to shoot him. He'd rather shoot *her*. The whore.

'Get out then,' he said, relenting. Then, his mind churning, Harry thought that if he did shoot Connie, instead of both of them, he would hang. But honour was at stake here.

'Get out,' he said again. 'And take her with you.'

She clambered out from under the bed and ran to Sam, who stood in front of her.

'Now! Get out now!' Harry screamed at them, prodding them down the passage. Connie was dressed but barefoot, and Harry felt a marvellous surge of power. 'I won't shoot if you get out. You have my word. But don't look back, either of you.'

'Let me get my shoes. My coat,' she called. She was crying, for God's sake! He was the one who should be crying. As if he didn't

99

have enough on his mind without all this. It was teeming outside now, and Harry liked that.

He let loose another blast, wrecking the hall stand and showering plaster over them as they scampered towards the front door and out on to the veranda.

'Keep going,' he thundered, enjoying the spectacle of his wife, the whore, near to fainting, being lugged along by her lover, across the veranda and out into the rain, stumbling down the steps and running out along the path to the gate, while he stood there, his trusty shotgun resting on his hip, the protector, the defender of his hearth and home.

'Good riddance!' he shouted after them, and slammed the door.

Connie clung to Sam. 'Oh God, I feel sick. What are we going to do?'

'Ah, Jesus! I don't know.'

'We can't just stand here. I'm getting drenched.' It dawned on Connie then that they weren't alone. All along the street neighbours, having heard the gunshots, were out in their front gardens, staring at this dishevelled pair, curiosity craning.

'I have to go,' he said. 'I'll come and see him tomorrow, sort this out. I'll fix it, Harry's weak, he'll settle down.'

'But what about me?'

'Just go back and tell him you're sorry.'

'Sorry? Are you mad? He's got a gun.'

'Harry won't shoot you.'

'Oh, really? Maybe he won't shoot me. Maybe he'll just beat the life out of me. I'm not going back in there. I'm coming with you.'

She ran down the street after him. 'Sam, stop! I can't keep up.'

Angrily, he turned on her. 'I told you to go back.'

So there they were, standing at the corner of the street in the teeming rain, arguing.

'I'm coming with you. Over to your place.'

'My place!' he yelped. 'You can't. Look at you! You're not dressed.'

'What does it matter?' she wept. 'I thought you loved me.'

'Well, I do.' Conciliatory. 'But my mother's there. She's visiting from Melbourne. God, Connie! You don't know her. She'd take one look at you and order you out.'

'We could explain we got caught in the rain.'

'So what? She'd put you in a cab and send you home. So go home, for God's sake. Just tell him you're sorry. Anything.'

But Connie dug in. 'I'm not sorry. I don't give a damn about your mother. I haven't got anywhere else to go. I'm coming with you. Tomorrow we'll send a servant over to my house, to collect all my things. We'll be all right, Sam. It might cause some talk for a while but if we love each other it won't matter. We belong together, you and I. We proved that tonight. You love me and until we were together there, tonight, and it was so glorious, I didn't realize how much we meant to each other.'

He grabbed her, shaking her, looking at the sad flimsy dress clinging to her. 'Stop it, Connie. Stop! You're upset, and understandably so, but you're raving. You're a married woman; I can't take you home. For God's sake, have a bit of sense. Now, where the hell am I going to find a cab out here in this weather?'

'You can't mean that,' she screamed. 'You said you loved me!'

'And you said Harry was out!'

At yet another corner they stood and argued again, with Sam trying to shake her off and Connie, crying hysterically, hanging on to him.

Eventually, when they'd tramped almost into town in the driving rain, he managed to hail a cab, but by this time he wanted no more nonsense from her. 'You're not coming home with me. Get that through your head. Where do you want me to drop you?'

'Nowhere! In the street! What do I care?'

'Be sensible, Connie. Where do you want to go? Can I drop you at your parents' house? You can make up some story.'

'No!' She was shrieking again. 'Looking like this? My father would go straight round to Harry, and he'd tell him what happened. I'd rather face your mother after this than him.'

'Then this cab will drop me off and take you back to your place.'

Connie's tears had dried up. 'Harry was right,' she spat. 'You are a bastard, Sam Ritter! A rotten, filthy bastard! Take me to Wickham Terrace.'

'Who lives there?'

'Fern Broderick.'

'Harry's aunt?'

'What do you care?'

Only Austin – and Bonnie, of course – knew that in the privacy of her own parlour, Fern enjoyed a fine cheroot. In fact, Austin had bought this box for her. Justin would never have approved, but then he never did have Austin's sense of humour.

So now she sat at the desk, smoking quietly, mulling over this problem, beginning to back away from her rather rash idea of visiting Springfield, since Charlotte had neither responded to her last letter nor issued an invitation. Over the desk was a portrait of the brothers, both looking very serious and devoid of personality in a formal pose, Justin seated and Austin standing by him, hand on his brother's shoulder.

It was still a source of wonder to Fern that both brothers had loved her, and she missed them both so much.

She glanced fondly at Austin in his high-buttoned suit and stiff collar. 'What can I do? I know you'd tell me to throw protocol to the winds and just come on out to Springfield. You'll be hurt if I don't make the effort. But what then? Often enough you've discussed Harry with me . . . How could I not tell you what he's up to now? I know you, Austin Broderick, you might be under doctor's orders to stay quiet, rested, but you won't appreciate me confiding in Victor instead of you.'

Fern knew that if she did that, Austin wouldn't be cross with her – he was never cross with her – but he would surely take it out on Victor for not informing him. Austin had to know everything that was going on in the family or there'd be hell to pay.

'Oh, I don't know,' she sighed. 'Maybe I ought to go to see Harry after all. Let him tell me, if he will, what that conversation was all about. I might be overreacting.'

She was just stubbing out the cheroot when she heard someone thumping on her front door. In a guilty reaction, she waved her hands about, creating a flimsy breeze to try to rid the room of tobacco smoke, and shut the rolltop desk quickly. Only then did she wonder who on earth would be calling at this hour, and on such a wet and windy night.

Anxiety accompanied her to the front door, the sort of fear engendered by telegrams, the usual bearers of bad news. Her first thought was for Austin. Had he had another stroke? Had he died? Please God, no.

She opened the door in a flutter of agitation, fully expecting a bulky policeman in heavy black oilskin to be standing on her porch with a long face and an apologetic manner, but that was not so. It was a slight woman, barefoot, drenched to the skin.

For the second time that night, someone stared at Connie, not believing the scene. Not recognizing the fastidious, fashion-conscious young socialite in her new role, barely comprehending her presence.

'Yes?' Fern asked, relieved, but now bewildered.

'Let me in, for God's sake,' the drenched woman snapped, and Fern gaped, wishing she'd roused Bonnie to open the door as the stranger pushed past her, black hair streaming wet, her soaked dress almost diaphanous now in the light of the hallway.

Fern stared. 'Good Lord! It's you! Connie!'

With that Connie burst into tears and threw herself into Fern's arms with a torrent of words that didn't make any sense. No sense at all.

'All right. Calm down, Connie. You're all right now. What on earth happened to you? You poor girl. Wait until I call Bonnie. We have to get you out of those wet clothes before you catch a chill. Oh my Lord! What a night to be out!'

Connie felt better. More in control. She'd had a hot bath, stepped into one of Fern's rather fetching satiny nightdresses and a Japanese kimono, had her hair towelled dry by Bonnie, Fern's nice maid, and drunk two cups of hot sweet cocoa, all of which gave her time to think about what she should say. She didn't know Harry's widowed aunt very well. At social and family functions they'd conversed rather than talked. Nevertheless, Fern herself was highly respected, even though she did have a shop; she was always escorted by couples, never gentlemen, and the right people at that. In short, Connie was rather in awe of this woman, and it was only desperation that drove her to this particular door.

Finally, sitting on the edge of a single bed in a very pleasant room, Connie stared down at her hands as her hostess came in.

'How are you now, my dear?'

'I'm so sorry to have barged in on you,' she whispered, 'but I didn't know where else to go. I'm feeling much better, though, thank you.'

'What happened, for heaven's sake?'

'He went berserk!'

'Who did?'

'Harry. It was awful. I was terrified.' She considered not mentioning the gun because it might point to the truth, but decided that there'd be talk, the neighbours would see to that, so best not to leave it out.

She whimpered, 'He had a gun, a shotgun, he was shooting up the house.'

'Oh my God! Harry?'

'Yes, Harry,' Connie said fiercely. 'Wait till Austin hears about this.'

'But I don't understand. What brought on such a rampage?'

Connie sighed. 'He just seemed to go mad. He came home from a meeting and started going on about how broke we are.'

'Broke?' Fern echoed, nervously registering surprise.

'Yes, broke. You can imagine how shocked I was. To tell you the truth, I didn't believe him at first, because he'd been drinking, but he kept talking and raving on about all his debts, and I realized he'd been gambling again.' She hesitated. 'I'm sorry, I don't want to burden you with all this, it's so sordid.'

'It's all right. Just tell me quietly what happened.'

'Well . . . I don't know if you are aware that Harry gambles, but he does. And now we don't have anything left, all our investments gone . . . everything. He owes money all over the place.'

She began to weep again, and Fern handed her a handkerchief. 'Bear up, my dear. I might as well hear it all.'

'He was raving, shouting that we'd come to the end of the road, we'd lose the house, go bankrupt. He was quite out of his mind. I suppose the worry of it had driven him mad. I tried to calm him down but then he turned on me.'

'Why?'

'Because he started to blame me. It's so unfair,' she wept. 'He said I was a spendthrift, that I had caused all this, and I tried to explain that I had no idea we were in any financial trouble at all, honestly I didn't.'

She saw Fern nod her head, understanding.

'But that only made him angrier. He raced off and got his shotgun, that's when he started shooting. You should see the hall stand: it was imported, so expensive, and he blew it to bits.'

'The hall stand! Good Lord!'

'Yes. Imagine how terrified I was. I tried to make him put the gun down but he threatened to kill me. He was in such a state, so I ran, just as I am now, out of the house, as fast as I could to get away from him.'

'Why didn't you run to a neighbour?'

'Oh, Fern. I was so humiliated. They were there, standing out in front of their houses, watching as if we were a circus. I couldn't bear to face any of them so I just ran and ran down the street. I didn't care about the rain, somehow it seemed to hide me from all that shame.'

'Surely you didn't run all the way up here?'

'No. I was so puffed out and scared that when I saw a cab I hailed it and jumped in.' Suddenly Connie saw a flaw in her story, but overcame it quickly. 'The driver was so nice. When we got here I had to tell him I didn't have any money on me. He told me not to worry about it, he was on his way home anyway.'

'That *was* nice of him.'

'When I first got in the cab I intended to go to my parents' house so they could pay the driver, but I decided against it. Can you just see my father's reaction to have me turning up in such a state? He's a quick-tempered man. He'd have gone over there after Harry, and God knows what would have happened.'

'Yes. More mayhem. It was very wise of you to avoid further trouble. Now, I think the best thing for you to do is get a good night's sleep. You've had quite enough for one evening.'

'What about Harry?'

'These things blow over. With you out of the house he'll have no one to argue with so he'll probably calm down and realize how stupid he's been. We'll go and see him tomorrow.'

'No! Definitely not. I'm not going back there.'

'All right. Don't upset yourself. I'll put out the lamp and you go to sleep.'

Fern closed the door, feeling very sorry for Connie. With her prior knowledge, she could well understand how Harry had reached breaking point. Being in debt was one thing, but to grind to a halt and find yourself broke would be dreadful for a man in his position. She hadn't realized, despite the conversation she'd overheard, that the situation was so bad, but now it made more sense. Harry had been considering the propositions made to him by opposition Members because he needed money fast. And a lot of money, by the sound of it. Even if the man could pay his debts, he'd still need funds to live on.

She went into her bedroom, lit the lamp and closed the curtains. If Harry was declared bankrupt that would be the close of his parliamentary career. She wondered if those cunning men had thought of that angle, and realized that of course they would have. If he refused to vote for the Lands Act there were other ways to kill a cat. Pounce on him and have him ousted from the House, thereby losing a vote against the bill, and achieving the same result. Did Harry understand that? Probably. No wonder he'd erupted as he had. But there was no excuse for turning on his wife.

Fern hoped he would be all right. There was nothing she could do beyond going out into the night herself to try to find a cab to take her over there, but they'd be scarce at this hour. Besides, the rumpus would have alerted the law, she guessed. Police would have investigated, or one of the men in the neighbourhood.

But in the middle of the night she awoke with a start, terrified that Harry in his depressed state might do himself harm. After that she hardly slept a wink.

The sun rose giddily through scuds of gilded clouds in the wake of the storm, and the wind still blustered about, almost spent. Harry sat on the back steps of his house, holding his head. With good reason. After they'd left, were ejected, he put the gun away and blundered through the wreckage in the hall to find the whisky decanter and sit alone with his rage.

For hours he thought about them – what he should have said, what he should have done – and when the bottle was empty he opened another, cursing them for their rottenness, their disgusting, foul behaviour, vowing never to forgive them. At times he wept, overwhelmed by his misfortunes, and then he slept, waking sprawled in an armchair as the dawn seeped in to find him. His stomach woke too, rebelling, and in the nick of time he rushed through the house to vomit on the back lawn.

After that he used his remaining strength to drag himself back up as far as the top step. He could go no further. He collapsed to nurse his thumping head and was still sitting there when Cook and the morning maid came through the back gate.

'Are you all right, sir?'

He didn't look up to see which one spoke, just waved them past him with an impatient grunt. Then he heard their cries of dismay, of astonishment, and had to focus very, very hard to recall the night's events, because by this, it was all a blur.

They stampeded back out to him. 'Mr Broderick! What happened? Things are smashed in there! The house looks as if a cyclone hit it! Where's Mrs Broderick? Are you all right?'

Harry stood, with quite some effort, and glared at them. 'We had a party. Clean it up.'

'But how can we? There's furniture smashed. The bed . . .'

'So what?' He shouldered past them. 'Bring me some tea. And a sandwich. In the dining room.'

He changed his clothes, washed, but made no attempt to shave, ignoring the maid, who was furtively collecting smashed timbers in the hall, as he strode through to the dining room. Food. He needed food to recover, then he'd be able to think.

After breakfast he repaired to the parlour, where he sank gratefully into the couch. He was soon asleep.

The maid woke her master to find him in a murderous mood. 'Get away! What do you want?'

'There's a gentleman to see you, sir.'

'I didn't tell you to invite anyone in.'

She flinched. 'You didn't tell me not to, sir. And he's only in the hall.'

When Harry saw who it was, he felt ill again. The bruiser was one of Ned Lyons' men, a nasty piece of work, and he delivered his message without delay.

'Mr Broderick, sir. I come from Mr Lyons. He said to tell you you won't get no bets on at the course tomorrow if you don't clear your debts today. He says you can pay me now if you like and I'll take the money to him right away, then there's no more problem, like.'

Harry shook his head. 'I'm not well. I can't think now.'

'I can see that, sir,' the man said stodgily. 'You don't look too good at all. But what will I tell Mr Lyons?'

'No need to tell him anything. Come back this afternoon.'

'What time, sir?'

'How do I bloody know? Come back this afternoon, I said.'

'Three o'clock then.' The fellow dumped his cap on his head, nodded to Harry and left.

'Ah, Jesus!' Harry said, making for the parlour again, but the maid intercepted him. 'I don't know what to do about the bedroom, sir. I don't know where to start.'

'Then don't start,' he shouted. 'Get out! Go home! Do what you bloody like!'

She threw down her broom. 'Righto. I'll do just that. I'll come back tomorrow when the missus is here! You've got Cook out there not knowing what to do.'

'Can't she just get on with her work?' he snapped.

'Not until the missus tells her the menu. She's not a mind-reader.'

With that the girl stamped away, and Harry returned to the couch to try to rest, but now all his woes were crowding in on him.

Eventually he realized that the house was unusually quiet, and when he went to investigate, he found that both the cook and the maid had

106

bailed out, leaving the mess to him.

Later there was another knock at the front door. He stole round to the side veranda to see who it was this time, and was stunned to see his aunt, Fern Broderick, standing there.

'What the hell does she want?' he muttered, keeping well out of sight. He let her knock and knock again, then he heard her call to him, but he was in no mood to be bothered by her, so he remained quiet until she gave up and left.

The aftermath of all that alcohol, and his miserable recollections, had him so distracted he couldn't think what to make of this day; what to do with it, or himself. He considered locking himself in a spare bedroom to take refuge in sleep, but there were no locks on the doors and a barricade would be unseemly.

'Unseemly!' he groaned. 'Right now this has to be the most unseemly house in town.'

Mortification came at him with a rush, and he recoiled, moving to the rear of the house for fear of another knock at the door. He wouldn't be surprised if neighbours had reported the disturbance to the watch-house and the police turned up, and God knew who else might decide to visit. Harry wasn't ready to face anyone. He shuddered. What if Connie came back with her lover to collect her clothes? What would he do about them?

Suddenly he made a decision. For the second time that morning he had to wade through the chaos in his bedroom to find the clothes he needed – cotton shirt, dungarees, hunting jacket and riding boots – then he dressed in the passage, grabbed his bush hat and ran across the back yard to escape into the lane. It was a short walk to the stables where he kept his horse, and soon he was back at his house with the animal, sneaking in like a thief to raid the pantry. He packed a knapsack, rolled a few necessities into a swag, grabbed a rifle and ammunition and left.

Riding away, Harry felt light-headed, free. Comfortable on horseback, he headed for the river and began following its course along suburban roads, then along bush tracks.

He rode all day, keeping the wide, picturesque river in view, sometimes across farmland, sometimes through more difficult scrub, until, with a sigh of relief, he came to his destination.

Perched on a high bank overlooking a bend in the river was a one-roomed timber hut, almost hidden by acacia trees. It was a lonely, deserted place but Harry loved the view from that point – that was why he'd built the hut there, with the assistance of a hired labourer. Although it had no amenities, no fireplace, not even glass in the one slim window, he called it his hunting lodge. Not that he did much hunting. Occasionally he'd shoot a scrub turkey, for a change of diet, but he preferred to fish. The only person he'd ever brought up here with him was Sam Ritter, but Sam never came a second time. He didn't appreciate the solitude, or the beauty of the surrounds, and he was a rotten fisherman.

'Rotten right through,' Harry added, reminded of that fellow, and slid the bolt to open his hut.

Everything was just as he'd left it. When the hut was completed he'd brought a few requirements upriver by boat, because there was no actual track leading here, and he'd never felt the need to improve on the basics. He stepped across the earthen floor, past the table and benches to a canvas roll in a corner, pleased to see that his fishing rods and tackle were intact.

Harry Broderick, MLA, stretched, smiled, and went outside to see to his horse.

That night he sat by his campfire under the stars with a bottle of rum and a good Cuban cigar, trying hard, though without much luck, to concentrate on the warm rush of the river and the settling sounds of the bush. The very thought of returning to Brisbane and facing all of his woes kept him deep in melancholy.

The next day the cook and the morning maid came and went. With no instructions, and worse, no money, Saturday being payday, they cleaned up the hall but not the bedroom, tidied the rest of the house and the kitchen and left a note on the kitchen table stating that they would return on the Monday, and requesting their pay. By this time they were well aware that there'd been a hell of a bust-up in the Broderick household and were vastly amused, except for the matter of their pay.

It wasn't until Sunday that Fern could persuade Connie to at least visit her house, and hopefully Harry, to try to sort out their problems.

'I'll come with you,' she offered, insisted, and Connie couldn't talk her out of it. She was terrified that Fern would hear the truth from Harry, which she had already decided to deny, but she did need her clothes. She couldn't stay hidden in Fern's house forever. She'd been shocked when Fern told her that she had gone over to Paddington on her own, but that Harry was out. What if he'd been there and told his aunt what had really happened?

She was so distraught she didn't think to ask why the maid hadn't answered the door. That thought caused her even more humiliation. Had the maid seen the mess? Oh God! It would be all over town. She blamed Harry entirely, closing her mind to the episode with Sam Ritter. If there was to be any gossip, Harry was the cause . . . Harry with his debts and his demented behaviour.

Bravely, for Fern's benefit, she strode up the path to confront him, dragging crankily at a skirt that was too long for her, and looking neither to the right or the left for fear nosy neighbours would be lurking about.

The house was quiet. Neat as a pin. Connie never required staff on

108

Sundays. It was their day off, so she considered it was hers too, her day for visiting, dining out, socializing.

'That's where the hallstand was,' she told Fern as she passed by the space. 'I don't think he's home.'

In a way she was sorry that the wreckage had been removed, for she would have liked Fern to see the evidence of his monstrous behaviour. Expecting the bedroom too to have been restored to order, she was unprepared for the sight that met her eyes in the doorway. In her rush to get out of there she'd had no clear picture of the chaos. Now that she saw her bedroom in the cold light of day, it shocked her, and she screamed.

'Good Lord!' was all Fern could offer, peering over her shoulder.

'I told you, didn't I?' Connie shrieked. 'Look at it! Look at this! And he doesn't even have the decency to do something about it! He's a pig! An absolute pig!'

She heard a man's voice in the hall and clung to Fern. 'I can't see him. I don't want to see him. Tell him to go away.'

'Anyone home?' the voice called again and Connie almost fainted.

'Oh, hell!' she wailed. 'It's my father.'

Judge Walker was appalled. 'A fine thing to hear about on a Sunday morning! Where is your husband?'

'I don't know and I don't care,' Connie sulked.

'If I catch him, I'll horsewhip the rascal! I'm very grateful to you, Mrs Broderick, for taking care of Connie, but she should not have involved you in this sordid business.' He turned on Connie. 'Why didn't you come home?'

'She was upset, confused,' Fern said. 'It's a very difficult situation.'

'Oh no it's not. Not any more. You pack your things, girl, you're coming home with me. I don't know what your mother is going to say. She is not accustomed to such disgraceful behaviour. What sort of a household have you been running here, girl? And where's the hall stand gone? I had nowhere to hang my hat!'

'He shot that too,' Connie whispered.

'He shot the hall stand! Have you gone mad, the pair of you? Mrs Broderick, I believe that's your cab outside. I wonder if you would kindly excuse us now. I shall wait for my daughter to collect her effects. And her wits, one hopes. But there is no need to delay you any longer. I am indebted to you for your kindness.'

As Fern was leaving, he added, 'If you see your nephew, would you be kind enough to request him to present himself in my rooms tomorrow morning at nine sharp. I require an explanation of this, and a few other matters.'

'If I see him,' Fern agreed, but she thought it most unlikely.

While her father waited, Connie took a quick tour of the house to make certain Harry wasn't there. She saw the note in the kitchen and tore it up, not even bothering to read it properly. She had just noticed that the cook and the maid were asking for their pay, and that was enough for her. She couldn't have her father angered more than he already was by the servants' trivial problems.

She had planned to leave Harry and go home to her parents, but not like this. The Judge had no pity for her at all; he was so stiff-necked he saw only the damage to his own reputation caused by gossip about gunshots in his daughter's house, and he was now fuming as he watched curious neighbours gathering again, to stare at his well-known carriage.

'Get a move on, you wretched girl,' he shouted. 'You're making a spectacle of me too.'

As the cab spun across the quiet Sabbath streets Fern was inclined to ask the driver to take her down to the Botanic Gardens, since she was already out and about, but regretfully she decided against it. Often of a Sunday she would stroll down to the kiosk in the gardens for morning tea with friends. They called it their 'elevenses', although there was no set time and no prior arrangements, and it provided an opportunity for her to catch up with people after her busy week.

Maybe not today, though, she mused. Gunshots in sedate Paddington were not everyday events, and news travelled fast, especially where public figures were involved. She did not feel like answering questions about her nephew, that Member of Parliament.

And as for Springfield, that idea was fading fast too. Not even Fern Broderick would be brave enough to break the news to Austin or his family that Harry was not only deep in debt but was now being accused of going berserk in his home with a gun. And to top that off, it seemed his wife had left him.

'Oh dear,' she murmured, 'best I keep out of it.' And a letter was out of the question, she decided. 'Let's hope it all blows over.'

On the Monday morning, Judge Walker waited, but there was no sign of his son-in-law.

'Not even man enough to come in and offer some sort of explanation,' he muttered angrily. 'But never mind. I know where to find him tomorrow. He can't dodge me there.'

It was with a great deal of difficulty that the Judge managed to rearrange his schedule to give him time to walk over to Parliament House, but he was a determined man, and by three o'clock he was climbing the steps to the public gallery so that he could spot his prey and wait on him.

He found that one of those damned Lands Acts was being debated again, and since this issue was of singular importance to his family, with their grazing interests, he became so involved in what the speakers were saying that he almost forgot to look for Harry Broderick. When

110

he did, peering over the balcony at the half-circle of eminent gentlemen below him, he was unable to identify Broderick, although there were many familiar faces.

The debate was becoming more heated, noisier. Insults were shouted, the speakers heckled, interrupted, while the Speaker of the House banged his gavel time and again, calling for order. Two men in the gallery shouted their comments and were promptly warned by a clerk to desist or be asked to remove themselves.

As the clerk was about to step back, the Judge asked him where Mr Broderick was seated.

Happy to oblige, the clerk leaned forward to point him out. 'He sits there, sir. But he's not in his place at present. He must have stepped out.'

'Thank you,' said the Judge, and glowered down at the noisy floor. There were only a few empty seats. 'Trust Broderick to be missing when the Lands Act is being debated,' he muttered. 'Austin will like to hear about this.'

The Speaker was addressing the House. 'The time for this debate has elapsed and there will be no more extensions.'

There was a sudden flurry, more calls to order, and the Premier was on his feet, angrily demanding a further extension, while the opposition Members shouted at him to sit down. The Speaker droned on, replying stolidly to points of order, and eventually the call came: 'The House will divide . . .' and the floor exploded into uproar as the Members began moving about. Some were standing arguing in the aisles, other men were downright abusive as colleagues forced a way past them, and all the while, the Judge, standing now, searched for Harry Broderick to the left of the Speaker, where he would have to take his place.

The count went on but the Judge was certain Broderick was not present. He could hardly miss the tall blond fellow among the array of mostly grey heads.

He put on his glasses and was still searching when the Speaker announced: 'The ayes have it.' For a minute, the Judge didn't digest the result because the expected cries of anger followed, but then it hit him. The ayes! The Lands Act had been passed! The affirmative vote had confused him, but there it was. The attack on the squatters had begun.

Too late, he tried to identify who had voted for this outrageous bill, but the Members were dissolving from the crowds back to their seats, or making for the exits.

He was convinced by this that his son-in-law, a traitor, must have voted for the bill, otherwise he'd have seen him in his rightful place. He joined the rush of onlookers who were exiting the gallery now that the debate was over, and downstairs in the hallway began the search for Broderick, finally enquiring of a friend.

'Broderick!' The parliamentarian was livid. 'I don't know where the hell he is. He wasn't in the House today, of all days. I'll strangle him when I get hold of him. One vote! We lost by one bloody vote! The bastard.'

Judge Walker made his way to Harry's office in a state of bewilderment, hardly acknowledging the greetings of friends and acquaintances in the long polished corridors. His world seemed to have been turned upside down, not only by the delinquency of his son-in-law – a dreadful embarrassment – but by the passing of that legislation. His family had huge leaseholds on the Western Downs, his father's station was adjacent to Austin Broderick's holdings, and he still retained substantial shares in another property. A true gentleman of the squatter hierarchy, the Judge knew that freeholding those lands would create immense financial difficulties for squatters, but he was more concerned by the inevitable outcome of such upheavals. A way of life would be disrupted, and that, to him, was a great loss.

Some men were milling about a staircase, congratulating each other, and he had no need to ask why.

'Shame on you!' he snorted, and stormed past.

He expected to find Harry Broderick in his office, and was anticipating an explanation for his absence from the floor. Would he be asleep? Or drunk? Ill, maybe? Surely he had to be in the House somewhere.

Instead, a gentleman whose name he could not recall was standing grimly in the empty office.

'Good afternoon, Judge,' he said. 'Perhaps you could enlighten me as to the whereabouts of Mr Broderick.'

Walker realized that the fellow was the Government whip, and he could understand his chagrin, but he resented the man's tone.

'It appears he is not present. No one absents themselves from the House without good reason . . .'

'Or without advising me,' the Whip interrupted bluntly.

The Judge continued: 'Therefore I can only surmise that Mr Broderick has encountered an accident or a similar unfortunate event. Good day to you, sir.'

On his way home the Judge called by the house in Paddington again, but it was deserted. By the time he arrived at his own residence, he was in the foulest of moods, ordering his daughter to his presence forthwith.

'Where is he?' he demanded. 'The fellow has neglected his duties this day and I won't have it. Do you understand? I won't have it!'

'I don't know where he is,' she cringed. 'He could be at his club. Anywhere.'

'Then you will sit down, this minute, and write down the addresses of his club, his cronies, and any other of his haunts. I shall send my manservant to call at any or all of those places and dig him out. Dig him out! Do you hear me?'

Connie wrote a list, deliberately excluding Sam Ritter, and handed over the page for his perusal.

'Huh! Typical of your associates, the town loungers and layabouts. You two will be changing your ways, my girl, if I have any say in it. I won't have this disgusting behaviour in my family. And you will return to your home in the morning. I shall not make excuses for your presence here, on top of everything else. Now go to your room.'

Connie ran weeping to her mother. 'I can't go back. What if he starts shooting again?'

'The Judge knows best. He'll give Harry a good talking-to. You can't stay here, it will just create more gossip.'

Chapter Five

The wool shed dance was a joy for all. Some young people, and others not so young, had ridden more than fifty miles to join in the annual Springfield celebrations. Because of the presence of so many shearers, who could now relax after weeks of hard work, there was a shortage of women. But where there's a will there's a way, and many a young lady saw this as an advantage. Every year, with the Springfield 'bash' in mind, girls from as far away as Brisbane made a pilgrimage to the homes of friends and relations within striking distance of the Brodericks. Others found it a convenient time to visit folk already working on the station, as well as managers and overseers on the Springfield outstations. The latter led lonely lives in their far-flung cottages, in charge of smaller sheep stations and reporting to Springfield, the head station, so they welcomed visitors. And then, the young ladies who were headed for Springfield never lacked for girlfriends to accompany them, on this occasion which ranked in the social scene as being more important than Christmas. Romance was in the air.

Victor's proposal that visitors not be encouraged because of the efforts to begin guarding the boundaries was forgotten as friends arrived at the homestead, taking the hospitality for granted, and Austin had no intention of relinquishing his role as boss. He made it very plain that despite his disabilities he was not an invalid, although he would not attempt to sit at table with his guests. He still had difficulty feeding himself so he preferred to dine in private.

He sat in state in the parlour, welcoming guests, rarely able to say much but enjoying all the talk just the same, and old friends were delighted to join him. Despite doctor's orders and Charlotte's misgivings, a few whiskies made him even more amenable.

To tell the truth, he admitted to himself, the end-of-season celebrations, which he'd dreaded, were not turning out to be so bad after all. In his darkest hours he'd feared being seen in public, a poor wreck of his former self, unable to make himself understood without the constant effort of forcing words to form. Unable to do so many things . . .

But he had adjusted. He was carried from room to room. His old mates, now ensconced at Springfield with wives and daughters who rushed about with bundles of fluffy dresses to be ironed, did not patronize him. Instead they joked. They took him in their stride. They were better, in fact, he thought, than his own family, because they didn't fuss. These men had seen worse. They knew he wasn't about to die, he still had a life ahead, and they talked to him about normal things, not how he was feeling.

Only once, so far, had he nearly made a fool of himself, Austin recalled as his wife helped him to dress before the night's celebrations were to commence. Earlier, Victor had taken him over in the dray so that he could watch the setting-up of the big barbecue area, where everyone would join in, from the lowliest workers to his most distinguished guests. Austin was very particular about the Springfield barbecue. The beef on spits had to be cooked to perfection, carving tables put close by, other serving tables set in line for ease of access, beer kegs set under the wattle trees. So many details . . .

Victor went off to find a good solid chair, because he'd forgotten to bring one from the house, so that Austin could oversee arrangements. He left his father perched on the open tray of the dray.

Austin didn't mind waiting. He didn't get out of the house much these days, and with dusk setting in, it was pleasant to just be there.

A shearer came past, a stranger. He saw the man stuck there, legs dangling, one arm limp at his side, and walked over to touch Austin on the shoulder, give him a gentle nod and a smile and a 'How you goin', mate?' before moving on.

The kindness, the refusal to intrude or patronize, the encouragement in that small gesture, which Austin understood well in the world of laconic bushmen, touched him so much that tears rolled down his face. He had only just managed to scrape them away when Victor returned to assist him down.

Sentimental old fool, he chided himself now, remembering, but he knew that the tears weren't for himself but for the men that he loved, hard-working, hard-drinking, honest-minded men, the salt of the earth. And he determined that this night would be called the best ever at Springfield.

The barbecue was a riotous success and later the dance got underway with fiddlers, and an accordion player calling the tune. The shed had been cleared out and the oiled floor was perfect for dancing. Austin was seated in a grand old armchair on a raised dais, and he'd had no objection to that at all. If he couldn't join in he should at least be able to see what was going on.

It was a great night. A great turnout. Everyone was having a ball. Austin downed his whisky and watched, pleased, as the floor was cleared for the lads. With a male-to-female ratio of five to one at these dances, he had introduced an opportunity for young men to take to the floor without partners. The fiddlers set up a merry reel and the lads bounced out, eager to participate in the one dance set aside for their pleasure.

116

This had become a highlight of the Springfield wool shed dance, and Austin was delighted. The young men, fit as all getout, gave a great display. Some, with thumbs stuck in their braces, tapped out intricate steps; others gave Celtic reels; braver souls jigged and leapt and cavorted to thunderous applause from the audience, but as the boss watched and cheered, he felt something was missing.

What had he overlooked? What had *they* overlooked?

He presented a bottle of Scotch whisky and a bonus cheque to the top shearer, and another bottle of whisky to the old bloke who'd come second in shearing the most sheep. He gave a garland of flowers and a huge box of chocolates to the belle of the ball, a lovely girl from Toowoomba, and when the dancing commenced again he peered about him, determined to track down the reason for his concern.

And then it hit him.

He turned to Charlotte, who was seated beside him, but old Jock Walker intervened, pulling up a chair to join them. Jock was the grandfather of Connie, Harry's wife, an eccentric old villain, do you for tuppence, but Austin liked him. He would be eighty if he was a day, but he still insisted on wearing his faded old kilt and a pair of greying buckled slippers.

He refilled his whisky glass from a drinks table set up on the dais for the benefit of Austin and special guests, and at a nudge from his host, refilled Austin's too.

'Great party, Charlotte,' he grinned. 'You've done yeself proud, me love.'

'Thank you, Jock, I'm glad you're enjoying yourself.'

'Ah, milady, I always do that. But it breaks an old Scotsman's heart that I'm getting too old for all these pretty gels.'

Austin gave a snort of laughter. 'You never saw Scotland in your life,' he gritted.

It was probable that Austin's speech was too mashed to have come out clearly, but it didn't bother Jock. This was normal banter with them.

'I'll have you know I left the auld country when I was twenty and not a day before!' he objected. 'On a great grand sailing ship.'

'In chains, more like it.'

Unconcerned, Jock leaned over to Charlotte. 'Would ye care to dance the light fantastic with me?'

'Oh, thank you, but I don't think . . .'

This amused her husband. Wilfully, he pushed her: 'Go on.' Charlotte was a poor dancer and Jock was manic on a dance floor; they should make an interesting couple.

'Delighted!' Jock said, taking her hand while Austin looked about him for Victor or Rupe. He couldn't spot them in the crowd. He looked again at the doorways of the wool shed, now garlanded with gum tips and streamers. Usually they were crowded with blacks who came up from the camps to watch the show, but unless his eyes were deceiving him, they were not out there tonight.

This bothered him. Come to think of it, they hadn't been at the barbecue either, but in all the excitement, and his own concerns at having to be assisted from place to place, their absence hadn't registered. The Springfield blacks, except for the few who had progressed to work on the station, were still tribal. They couldn't be invited to join the guests, but they were always there in the background, and when the outdoor dinner was over and everyone had had their fill, all the leftovers, even the charred carcasses, were taken to the far table where the blacks could help themselves. There was always plenty of tucker left over, because Austin insisted that the cooks, both staff and household, cater for them as well. And the Aborigines loved it. They were always just as excited about this big occasion as everyone else; a feast was a feast in anyone's language.

The blacks weren't there tonight though. Austin was sure of it. What was wrong? Had someone died? That would explain their absence, for they were great mourners.

Finally he managed to sight Victor, and beckoned him up.

'Where are the blacks?' he mouthed.

Victor shook his head and shrugged, and it was obvious to his father that he, too, had noticed but didn't want Austin to be bothered.

'Well, where are they?'

'I don't know.'

'I can see that! So what's going on?' Anger, he knew, made his attempts at speech far more difficult, but he had no remedy for that. 'Bloody well find out!' he shouted.

'I'll check them tomorrow.'

'Now!' Austin demanded, then, with a stroke of luck, saw young Spinner, the half-caste stockman, on the floor. At any other time he would have smiled to see Spinner in his Sunday best, boots polished to a shine, working manfully at a barn dance. Someone had been teaching the kid, who was now counting, lips moving, one, two, three, and watching his feet instead of the ladies, but Spinner was needed.

Austin sent Victor to fetch him, and saw that the lad wasn't too upset at being rescued from the intricate business of dancing. He spoke carefully to the stockman, enunciating each word. 'Where are all the mob? What is wrong?'

Spinner was distressed to see his beloved boss struggling to talk, and his dark-brown eyes rolled sadly. Further, he was pretty cranky that the whole mob had gone, just gone, without telling him a bloody thing. He was hurt, but in a way pleased, because by not informing him they'd placed him firmly in the white man's camp. Where he belonged.

Just the same, he couldn't admit to the boss that he had no idea where they were. He'd gone down to the camp late in the afternoon,

118

to show off the new shirt and dungarees that he'd be wearing to the dance, the white man's dance, and was stunned to find the camp deserted. The fires were dead, humpies vacant, not even a cook-pot left among the debris of habitation, and there was an eerie silence, as if they'd all been suddenly spirited away. The camp gave him the shivers, and more so when he saw that the one clan treasure was missing. The tall carved totem pole that spoke of their particular place in the Dreamtime. He'd never, never known of that being moved. It was said that the totem had guarded the emu-people-who-dwelled-by-the-river since the beginning of time. And now it was gone.

Fearfully, he had run from there.

'The boss asked you a question,' Victor urged.

'Ah, yeah,' he smiled. 'They all gone walkabout, boss.'

'All of them?' Victor said. 'That's not usual. Why did they all go?'

'Ah!' Spinner said, searching for a plausible reason to protect his good name. 'All had to go, boss. Totem time. That big feller totem, he had to go to the sacred places again to get straight with the spirits, see.' He could tell that they knew about the totem pole, so it was just as well he'd mentioned it. He began to improvise. 'Long time Dreamtime rule, see. Old blokes got to speak up, young blokes get special ceremonies. Big corroboree time way out in the bush.' He grinned. 'I bet them mob real crook on missin' the feast, but they gotta do this walkabout or the evil spirits grab them.'

'Where did they go?' Victor asked. 'Where's this big corroboree?'

Spinner feigned disinterest. 'Bush place. Long ways, I think. They come back. Be back for next year feast, I bet!' he grinned.

'Thank you,' Victor said politely, and the lad was allowed to escape them.

'Well, I'll be damned!' Austin muttered. 'I never heard of that before.'

'They've often gone walkabout.'

'But they usually leave someone to guard their camp from evil spirits taking over, and they never move that totem pole.' Austin realized that he'd been muttering to himself and what he'd said was probably unintelligible, so to cover his embarrassment he waved Victor away and pretended to be more interested in watching his wife try to cope with old Jock's fancy jigs.

When she returned, he said to her, 'I didn't see Black Lily today. Where is she?'

'I don't know. She didn't come up.'

Economical with words, he added, 'Housegirls too?'

She sighed. 'I didn't want to worry you. The blacks have moved camp and the silly girls must have gone along too. Today of all days. They'll be in trouble tomorrow. We can do without Black Lily, with so many people in the house, but it has been very difficult without the maids. I ought to sack all three of them. Louisa has been so good, working really hard helping Cook. The ladies have been giving a hand too, doing their own rooms, but it has all been very inconvenient.'

He sighed. Moved camp? Where to? Austin was more inclined to believe Spinner. The mob had gone walkabout. He'd send Rupe to check tomorrow. But it was a pity that they'd chosen to leave today, or last night, or whenever. It seemed to take the shine off proceedings. He liked to see them laughing, enjoying themselves, squizzing at the antics of whitefellers in party mood.

Jock came back, attracted by the Scotch whisky, poured himself another drink and leant over Austin. 'Let me give ye a tip, man. I've seen plenty of strokes in my day, and the best way to get yourself talking clear again is to practise in front of a mirror.' Then he chortled. 'But don't be lettin' them see ye, or they'll be thinking you're vain.'

He straightened up and surveyed the room as the fiddlers picked up their instruments again. 'Do you think I ought to give the belle of the ball a dance now?'

'Yes.' Austin snorted with laughter, motioning him to hurry, then sat back, thinking that maybe it was time he went back to the house. The dance would go on until dawn, and the seat was getting hard.

By late afternoon the next day the shearers had straggled off to the next job, some riding, others sprawled on the flat tray of an old brewery wagon, and the house guests were packing up.

Rupe rode in with some stockmen to report to Victor.

'No sign of the blacks anywhere. We couldn't find another camp. They've just disappeared into the scrub, the whole bang lot of them. Do you reckon we ought to get Spinner to track them?'

'Spinner couldn't track a mob of bullocks on a wet day. Anyway, if they've gone walkabout they won't come back until they're good and ready. Send a couple of blokes down to clean up the campsite and burn all the junk while we've got the chance.'

Some of the people were upset at the day chosen by Moobuluk for them to begin their trek. They didn't want to miss all the fun, or the feast, but he was adamant. He had a point to make, disdaining the white man's bounty.

They crossed the river and struck west, filing over the plains and into the hills, gathering food as they journeyed on, and gradually they began to enjoy this walkabout, released from the confines of the old camp. Many days later they emerged from the shelter of the hills to string out over flat country again, only this time they headed north, padding along in quiet determination. The men roved abroad, hunting; women with babies slung across their backs in dilly bags strode ahead; others foraged; children plunged sturdily on, sometimes accepting a ride on broad shoulders; and the elders brought up the rear.

Only Minnie was still not convinced this was a good idea. She understood that the other children should be removed for their protection, but she had wanted to stay at Springfield to be there when they brought little Bobbo back. Eventually Nioka managed to convince her that Moobuluk had seen to it; he would know when the boys came home and then they would go and get them. None of the persuasions, though, could disperse her misery. She missed Bobbo too much.

'Don't you think I miss Jagga too? I feel sick thinking about him. But we'd miss them just as much back there. We're not leaving them; we'll get them back when the time comes. You have to cheer up or you'll make yourself sick, and Bobbo wouldn't want to come home and find you all thin and weak.'

They travelled unchallenged across lands stocked with cattle and sheep, and burgeoning farmlands, but nevertheless, when they came to Baruggam territory, they made camp and, observing tradition, waited for permission to enter. Some of the young ones thought that was futile these days, because the whites never asked, but their elders insisted on the traditional mark of respect.

'While we still can,' they added glumly.

Their eventual destination was, in Moobuluk's estimation, about a hundred and fifty miles north of their own base, not too close and not all that far away. More importantly, they were met by members of the Waka Waka clan and allowed to sit down with them in forest country by a wide lake.

Moobuluk introduced his elders, and after deep discussion it was agreed that the two clans, having no serious totem or ethical difficulties, could share the benefits of this remote valley hidden between the peaks of the great eastern mountains. The Waka Waka people, too, were scattered, and this mob accepted the newcomers with kindness, arranging for a corroboree to be held to welcome their new friends.

The old man stayed long enough to see them settled and then he left. He had business with the Badjala people who lived in beauteous rainforest country on the coast, and who had the added good fortune of being the keepers of a large island as well. They were rather aggressive people, closer in spirit to the warlike tribes of the far north, but they still had the usual clannish difficulties that had to be sorted out. They'd taken him over in their fast canoes to visit the island, and being mostly a land-fellow, Moobuluk was delighted. There in the deep, clear water, he'd seen the coral fields for the first time, and discovered the gorgeous fish that inhabited the most serene of worlds.

He was looking forward to another visit.

Springfield should have settled back into its normal routine now that the shearers and the guests had departed, but there seemed to be tension in the air, and Austin was edgy. He tried to analyse his feelings but only ended up worrying even more, because on the surface everything seemed just fine. There had been no problems with the shearers, the weather had been kind to the newly shorn sheep – that was always a worry – and the wool clip looked like being a record.

He missed Black Lily, but knew he shouldn't be relying on her; he had to work this out for himself. Surreptitiously he practised working his jaw and his lips with the aid of his shaving mirror. With no housegirls, Charlotte and Louisa were kept busy, but that didn't bother him either. A bit of housework wouldn't kill them.

The absence of the blacks still rankled, even though he kept telling himself that walkabout was nothing unusual. He wondered if the sudden departure had anything to do with old Moobuluk, who'd been hanging about for weeks before they left.

And then there was the ever-present spectre of those blasted Lands Acts with their interminable amendments. He hadn't forgotten the letter from his banker but none of his guests had been concerned. He'd heard Jock discussing the legislation with his neighbour Jimmy Hubert, dismissing it as unworkable, not worth worrying about, so he'd kept quiet about the warning he'd received, thinking the banker might have overreacted.

All in all, Austin decided, everything was under control. He should be concentrating on reviving his muscles instead of mooning about over nothing.

The bad news came without warning.

Since he wasn't using enough energy during the day, and he didn't have Lily to tire him with her pounding and pummelling, Austin was having trouble sleeping. He so looked forward to the dawn and the sound of movement that he began to organize his own routine. He decided, despite Charlotte's protests, that Victor should get him up at five and help him to shower and dress before he went about his own duties. He would have his breakfast around six in the morning, the same time as his sons, after which Rupe could give him a hand with his exercises.

The plan worked more or less, though Rupe was no Black Lily. He seemed to believe that the exercises were a waste of time and his father would do better to rest.

'You're too bloody lazy, that's your trouble,' Austin griped. 'Help me stand, I've got to put some weight on that leg . . .'

He knew Victor took his efforts more seriously, but he didn't see why Rupe shouldn't help.

The only problem with his system was that the days seemed long and empty after all the excitement of the previous weeks, and to cure his insomnia he flatly refused to rest during the day. To fill in time he turned to the pile of newspapers that Charlotte had placed neatly on a low bench. Austin never read much at all, and he rarely opened the copies of the *Brisbane Courier Mail* that arrived with the post in weekly bundles, because he considered the paper a rag, full of tripe and city doings. The ladies liked it, though, for the social news and advertisements for the latest shipments of dress materials and fancy wear, and Victor watched stock prices.

With a sigh he picked up the first one, a fortnight old, and found himself engrossed in all the ongoing sagas of the goldfields. One article gave a lengthy account of the Cape diggings, pointing out that prospectors should be aware that the diggings were much further than 200 miles from Bowen; on foot, rather than as the crow flew, they were more like 320 miles from the coast.

'From Bowen!' he murmured. 'That little coastal town has to be at least a thousand miles north of here. It'd be wild country and bloody hot. They can keep it!'

In another paper he was astonished to read that of the ships departing England an average of 600 per year were shipwrecked, and an average of 1500 souls lost, not to mention millions of pounds.

When Charlotte came in with his morning tea, he pointed out the article and said: 'That can't be right.'

'If it says so in the paper . . .'

'Just proves what I always say. You can't believe a bloody word they write.'

He ploughed on, reading without interest of the Governor's latest speech, and then he came across a letter from a C.G. Graham, who claimed that proposals in the Lands Acts to charge one pound per acre were far too expensive. That pleased him, until he read the rest of the letter.

Only greedy squatters can afford to pay that, C.G. Graham went on.

'Who says so?' Austin demanded aloud.

The letter continued: *You may say that if the land is cheaper, to help the working man to purchase, it would only be swallowed up by the squatters, but that is not necessarily so if the size of the runs is limited. If you look at the present picture, the squatters under leasehold are only paying threepence and a halfpenny per acre. Is that fair?*

'Of course it's fair,' Austin reasoned crossly. 'We don't have security of tenure. Who is this fool? They shouldn't publish these ratbag opinions.'

But C.G. Graham had thought of that. *You also may say that the squatters have no certain tenure, which only underlines the rottenness of the system, because the squatter has practical possession of the land and makes few permanent improvements beyond his own homestead luxury. He won't redirect streams to stabilize soil for fear that by doing so he may create good fertile land which the government might regard as better for agriculture. He just uses square mile after square mile for his sheep or cattle to chew over, wasting good downlands that should be available to a working farmer.*

'Bosh!' grunted Austin although he knew it was true to a certain extent, if you overlooked the fact that it was the export of wool, not local consumption of carrots and cabbages, that paid the country's bills.

123

What annoyed him most about these papers was the wordiness. Anyone who had anything to say, including the editor, filled up long, skinny, tightly printed columns with thousands of words on the one subject. He could never understand why they couldn't get their opinions off their chests instead of waffling on and on, wasting the reader's time. Worse than Parliament.

He read that the French and the Prussians under Bismark were lining up for a fight, without bothering to even glance at the lengthy explanation, and forged on, turning page after dreary page.

In the afternoon, his interest in these pages began to sag, until he came to an editorial which claimed that committees, working all day and through the night on various clauses to do with the Lands Act, had to cope with the imbecility and ill-temper of the Minister for Lands.

That made him sit up. Victor had said that this paper favoured selectors not squatters, and here it was out in the open, because the Minister for Lands, J.J. Prosser, was a fair man and had given these innovators more than their share of his time.

Austin looked at his covered billiard table and wondered if he could fill in time by learning how to play with a gammy arm, supporting himself on a chair. Then he had a better idea. He wasn't going to be stuck in this room day and night. If they put him on a horse, he could ride. No reason why not.

That night he put the suggestion to Victor, who, surprisingly, agreed. 'But not yet. Give yourself a chance.'

'For what? To sit here and have cobwebs grow on me?'

The next day, in sour mood, he worked through more of the papers, appalled to read about a petition to Parliament by 'farmers, storekeepers, and other inhabitants of the district of Toowoomba' begging for the rights of small freeholders.

The long petition stated that the alienation of large areas of land for grazing was inexpedient and antagonistic to the interests of small freeholders.

'Like yourselves, you covetous scoundrels!' he snorted, and hurled the pages away. 'Enough of newspapers! Bloody worthless waste of time.'

He manoeuvred himself out of the heavy armchair, so that he could stand, leaning against it, to test his weak leg, pleased to find that it would take a certain amount of weight.

That gave him heart. By the process of dragging and shuffling, inch by inch, Austin was moving about the room when Rupe came in with a bottle of olive oil to carry out his duties as masseur.

'Pick up the papers before your mother comes in,' Austin said. 'And straighten them up. They're only fit for lighting fires, but she likes to read about the smart set. In my day, getting your name in the paper was nothing to crow about . . .'

While he talked, Rupe collected the scattered papers, not bothering with any particular order, and placed them under the latest editions that were still intact, obviously as yet unread by his father.

One small heading caught his eye. 'What's alienation of lands?' he asked.

'A new-fangled excuse for grabbing our land.'

'It says here "Alienation of Lands Act Passed".'

'Where? What does it say? Show me.' Austin lowered himself into a chair by a table as Rupe planted the page in front of him.

'There. See?'

His father was stunned that such a grave pronouncement should occupy a few bare lines. Sentence had been passed on the great stations of south Queensland without so much as comment. The paragraph was followed by a treatise on the Oaths Bill, which was a stumbling block for non-Christian Members.

He found himself, stupidly, dwelling on this, mystified. 'Who but Christians go into Parliament?'

'I don't know. What was that bill about?'

'It means we have to freehold,' Austin replied. This time, he was determined there'd be no physical reaction. He had to stay calm. 'We'll talk about it later. Get your oil and give this gammy leg a good hard massage.'

Rupe looked up, amazed, realizing that his father was managing to get through sentences – not without effort, and a slurring of the words, but getting there.

'I'm astonished at how well he took it,' Victor told Louisa that night. 'I walk in the door and he casually tells me to take a look at the paper. Rupe had ringed the article with one of Teddy's crayons. Well, you could have knocked me down with a feather. I couldn't believe it! All over, and so damned sudden!'

'What happens now?'

'I'll have to go to Brisbane . . .'

'Marvellous! Can I come too?'

'I don't see why not. I'll have to see lawyers and the bank so we can start lodging claims.'

'When can we leave? It'll be so exciting for Teddy.'

'Leave? Not yet. It will take a while for the bill to get the Governor's assent, and then our lawyers will have to go through every single clause with a fine-tooth comb so that we know exactly where we stand. Then there's Christmas. We'll go early in January.'

'Maybe the Governor will refuse his assent.'

'Not likely. He's only a rubber stamp. In the meantime I'll employ more men to make sure that all of our boundaries are clearly marked.' Angrily he took off his shirt and threw it on the bed. 'Especially the best blocks. I'll even throw up a few fences.'

Louisa stared at him. 'You can't fence blocks that size!'

'A couple of strips of fence in the vicinity of waterholes won't keep the selectors out, but they'll deliver a message. Damnit! I just realized that every single section will have to be described for the surveyors too. I'm beginning to see how much extra work all this is going to take.'

'What did your father say about Harry?'

'About the vote? Not much he can say. Harry's only one voice. But he's more than displeased that we haven't heard from him. He could at least have sent us a telegram instead of leaving us to read it in the paper. We could have missed it, end up being the last to know. If we're not already. I wouldn't like to be in Harry's boots when the old man catches up with him.'

The youngest Broderick son took a different attitude. To Rupe, this was war. After dinner that night he went down to the men's quarters and called a meeting in the mess hut to break the news to them.

'If Springfield is broken up into sections, half of you will end up working on smaller runs owned by bunglers like shopkeepers and farmers,' he said tersely. 'You won't have the amenities or the backup of Springfield. You'll be living in huts like the old-time shepherds, miles from a friendly face.'

He was pleased to hear the growls that the news produced, and warmed to his subject, describing as looters men who would now be rubbing their hands at the prospect of grabbing sections of Springfield.

'They'll be running mad about the district now,' he said, 'thinking they're gonna be squatters, owning half-arsed runs, with no bloody idea of what they're doing.'

The head station overseer, Jack Ballard, was there to back Rupe up. 'I reckon they think running a sheep station is a piece of cake. They're in for a bloody shock.'

'Too right,' Rupe laughed. 'But they can make their mistakes somewhere else. I say we keep 'em off Springfield, until we can get it all secure.'

'How long will that take?'

'A year or so, maybe,' Ballard said. He winked at Rupe. 'I wondered why you and Victor were out there marking off blocks. Did you know this was in the wind?'

'We thought it might be . . .'

'No flies on the boss,' Jack laughed, 'even if he is sick.'

Rupe was slightly taken aback. Standing up there in front of all these men, he was feeling like the boss, and he didn't appreciate being reminded that he was in Austin's shadow. He pressed on.

'Anyway, what we have to do is to keep selectors from nosing about Springfield land. So the question is, are you with me?'

'Yes!' they cheered.

126

A voice at the rear was heard. 'How do we do that?'

'Easy,' other men laughed, but Rupe spelled it out.

'Very easily. You bail them up at gunpoint and escort them off the property!'

'What if they won't go?' the same voice queried, and a tall stockman had the answer.

'Start with shooting one of their horses,' he said laconically. 'That should work.'

Rupe grinned. 'Why not? They're trespassing. I think this calls for drinks on the house.' He turned to the storekeeper: 'We can spare a few bottles of rum, can't we?'

Sunlight filtered through the trellis on to the veranda, dappling it with light and shade, and perfume from the big frangipani tree wafted in on a gentle breeze. A lovely day, a perfect day, but not for Connie, who sat hunched in a cane chair, chewing her knuckles. She felt caged. The weave of the wooded trellis seemed like prison bars, because she could not go out there into the cruel eye of the public while Harry's disgrace lingered. To his colleagues and many of their friends, he was a pariah, a traitor to his class, and by association, so was she, judging by the curt notes hand-delivered to their door.

Inside, the servants were only filling in their hours. They didn't have much to do with only the mistress in the house, and a total absence of visitors. Their very presence intimidated Connie. She was sure they were laughing at her.

Cook had called in her husband with his dray to remove the wreckage of the imported mahogany bed so that the maid could do the room, and Connie could still hear his hoots of laughter. It had been so humiliating, and only a small part of the worst week of her life. Her father had given her some money to tide her over until Harry came back, and most of it had gone on pressing household bills; she only had enough left to pay the women today.

Then what, she asked herself anxiously.

I'll pay them off, she decided. Get rid of them. I can't stand their insolent stares any more. When he comes home I'll get new servants.

Connie had learned, from the nosy maid, of course, that Harry had taken his horse from the stables and she guessed that he'd gone home to Springfield since no one had seen him in Brisbane. The rat. The coward. The fool. She shuddered as she roved over every nasty name she could call her husband, but even they were overshadowed by the Judge's furious outburst when he had learned that Harry had disappeared.

Connie sobbed. Her father cared more about Harry missing a session of Parliament than he did about him deserting his wife. And the Judge was even more enraged to see that voting list published in the paper with no mention of Harry at all. Several Members were noted as being absent from the crucial vote through illness, but no such excuse was provided for Harry.

'Bloody fool,' the Judge had roared, tearing out the page. 'I'm sending this to Austin Broderick. With a letter insisting that if his son can't attend to his parliamentary duties, then he should at least see to his domestic responsibilities!'

Connie was glad about that. Austin would be just as angry. He would send Harry home pretty damn quick, and hopefully with some money. That reminded her. When the servants left, she had no choice, she'd have to walk over to her parents' house and make them give her some more money.

After all, none of this was her fault. As far as they knew, anyway.

Sick at heart. That was how Harry felt. Sick at heart. On the first night he'd had to rely on the rum for sleep, but after that, less and less as the peaceful surrounds calmed him and fat fish sprang easily to his bait. For a few days he managed to keep the aggravations at bay by refusing to accommodate them. This was his haven, his blessed sanctuary, and they had no place in his routine. He swam in the clear, tingling waters of the river, lay naked on the sandy shore soaking up the sun, took long walks in the bush and returned to the cheerful company of his camp fire, but after a while he realized that bravado had set in. He was having to force himself to turn away from reality.

Bit by bit, his worries returned, ruthlessly refusing to leave him alone no matter how he battled, until all of his waking hours were taken up with wild plans. He would have his revenge on Sam Ritter. And his whoring wife. He would borrow some more money from the bank. Better still, he would tell Austin he needed part of his inheritance now. Why wait until his father died? He would look at that bill and vote the way he wanted. He was sick of people telling him what to do. And he would invest in gold mines. They were the thing these days . . . He became so enamoured of all these grandiose solutions that, aided by a few rums, he was in a highly excitable state by the time he retired.

Morning brought remorse and a nasty feeling of disquiet that badgered him until a dip in the river cleared his head.

Harry Broderick, MLA, stood waist-deep in the velvety current and panicked.

'Jesus! What day is it?' He began counting, trying to pin down the nights, until he finally worked it out. Thursday!

'Oh, Jesus! It's Thursday and the House has been sitting for three days. Oh, God! What have I done now?'

Despairing, he stumbled up the bank to drag round his few chores in a daze, then he slumped into a chair, nursing a mug of black tea.

'That's torn it. I'm in real trouble. I'll probably get expelled from the party.' He wondered if the Lands Act had been debated again, or even been put to the vote.

'If it has, I'll be as unpopular as the rats from all sides.'

It seemed as if the whole world was sitting in judgement on him, and he bowed his head miserably.

'So now what?'

As if in response, a kookaburra's loud hooting laugh broke the quiet of the morning, and Harry studied the high trees, trying, without success, to spot the bird.

'Ah, what the hell!' he said. 'Looks as if I can't get anything right.'

Then he added, 'That's the truest thing you've said in a long time.'

In the depths of depression, with no one to disagree, Harry began to take note of his own shortcomings and found it a sorry tale. He had never taken Parliament seriously, too interested in living the high life. 'Too many pals and too many parties,' Austin had warned him some time back, but he'd ignored the advice. His debts were his own doing, the turf and the tables. Connie and Ritter were another story, but in his outrage at their behaviour, he'd completely forgotten that Harry Broderick wasn't exactly a saint himself. What about those stag nights with his mates at Madame Rosa's? And what about pretty little Pearl at the plush Albert Hotel? And her girlfriend, the other barmaid? They had always been obliging.

'And you scream at your wife!' he muttered, trying to overcome an imbalance here, because Connie *was* his wife, and he was still shocked at finding her in bed with Ritter.

'So what do you do?' he asked himself. 'Make a real bloody fool of yourself, shooting up the house. You've hit rock bottom, old son, no doubt about it.'

Slowly, deliberately, he cooked the last of the bacon with a tin of beans, and stared at the rifle leaning against the wall. That would be a quick, clean end to it all.

The thought of ending it all was, surprisingly, a welcome release to Harry Broderick. He enjoyed what was to be his last day without a care in the world. A marvellous day. Fondly, he took his beloved horse swimming in the river, explaining that he would soon release him in the bush, and someone would find him. Jovially he tried his hand at making damper with flour and water and a touch of salt, and when he lifted it from the camp oven, he congratulated himself: well done. He ate it all, hot, covered in treacle, and sat back, content.

Who'd care if he died? No one. He was just an embarrassment to the family.

That night, in a strange euphoria, he polished off the last of the rum. He'd decided he'd barricade the hut later and use the rifle in there, where his body would be safe from bush scavengers. But first the night. It was a lovely clear night and Harry searched the skies for the Southern Cross, which had intrigued him from childhood. He found the 'saucepan' and the big pointer star and let his gaze travel over to the Cross.

There it was, huge, towering above him. All his life Harry had wanted to watch the Cross turn over; it was talked about in the bush all the time, but somehow he'd never got around to it, never been out that long, never cared enough. But suddenly it was important. The only thing in his life he'd really wanted to do. He put his feet up and sat back, watching, waiting. It would take hours, he knew, for the Cross to move across the sky and turn over; all night, maybe. But he had the time.

Irritation replaced his determined content as clouds began to scud over the dark skies, reaching out for the Cross as if to thwart him even in this, such a small request. Then, suddenly, there was a scuffle in the bush and his horse screamed.

Harry grabbed his rifle and ran, crashing through the scrub to a small clearing. The horse was still screaming, rearing and plunging, backing into the bush as it tried to fight off dingoes, hobbles preventing it from escaping. Harry fired a shot in the air but the dogs, snapping and snarling, moved swiftly about. They seemed to know that safety meant keeping close to the horse, using it as cover, so Harry, too, had to move closer for fear of hitting the horse. He fired again and a dingo yelped in pain. Wounded, it dodged away, still yelping, and Harry saw two others slinking away.

Thinking that was the last of them, he went over to the frightened horse and patted its sweating flank, but the animal's head jerked up, and just in time Harry turned to see a dingo running at him from the undergrowth, teeth bared. He swung the rifle butt, smashing the dog over the skull, and it went down without a sound.

Quickly, he uncoupled the hobbles and pulled the horse out of the scrub, leading it back to the hut.

By lamplight he sponged gashes on the horse's belly and another on its hind leg, which was bleeding heavily. Then he put a halter on it and tethered it to a rail.

Harry grinned. 'Not that you need the halter, old chap. You'd rather stay right here with me, wouldn't you?'

He reloaded the rifle in case the dingoes decided on a return attack, unlikely though it was, and sat outside watching the dawn light the eastern sky, telling himself it was important to guard the horse.

Harry knew that wasn't quite true: he needed the company, and the presence of the animal comforted him.

He began to find the situation ludicrous. 'I can hardly shoot myself with you standing watching,' he said. 'And I'd have a fat chance of shooing you away even if I do take the halter off. You're not silly enough to go too far from my protection, stinking of blood. The dingoes will be on your track in a matter of minutes.'

Eventually he made a decision. 'It's Friday. I think I'd better take you home. Looks like I'll just have to face the music.'

Though his absence had obviously created even more problems

130

for him, Harry was calmer now. Allowing for the horse's injuries, he rode slowly, giving it a rest now and then, as he mulled over a course of action. Or, as he saw it, a course of non-action. He didn't care any more. No point in trying to please everyone. In attempting to keep up with the social life and the Parliament. Austin always said he was stupid. He made no bones about that. And he was probably right. Victor and Rupe were the smart ones.

He stopped at a country pub, bought a pint, ate a couple of pickled onions from a jar, pleased to be anonymous. No one in the bar would have taken this unshaven, unkempt bushie for a member of their State Parliament. Idly he turned the pages of newspapers on the bar but stopped when he saw the results of the vote on the Alienation of Lands Act, mildly surprised that it had been passed, shuddering at the absence of his name from the lists.

'Austin will just love that,' he shrugged. 'Now he really has got something to yell about. That will make him happy.'

Moving so slowly along the river road, Harry had time to notice how the town was spreading out, new streets, new houses quite a long way from the centre of Brisbane.

A rather large house took his eye, an ugly timber building on bare stumps, with no effort made to hide the gaping space underneath. No trellis, not even bushes. It was the signs outside that interested him.

By the gate was a large black board with gilt printing that announced: CHURCH OF THE HOLY WORD, and the times of services held by a Bishop Frawley.

'Never heard of that lot,' he commented, thinking that it was an odd-looking church.

On the other side of the gate was a large FOR SALE sign.

Shaking his head, Harry rode on by. As he headed for town, he mused that there were a lot of new-fangled religions turning up in Brisbane lately.

'Absent? What do you mean, absent?' Austin roared, forgetting his resolve to live calmly and therefore longer.

Rupe noticed that his diction was definitely improving. 'Just what I said. He wasn't in the House when the vote was taken. It was in a newspaper.'

'Where was he?'

'No one knows.'

Austin's eyes narrowed. 'Was that in the paper too?'

'No.'

'Then how come you're telling me? Where did you get it from?' He stumbled on the last few words and slammed the table with his fist, as much in frustration as anger.

Rupe shrugged. 'There was a letter from Judge Walker, he's pretty

131

hot under the collar about it. And a few other things.'

'What letter?'

'They didn't think you ought to see it. Victor and Mum. They didn't want you to get upset.'

'Get it!' Austin hissed.

Rupe dodged around to Victor's office, found the letter from Harry's father-in-law and read it again with a grin. The old bloke was ropable, words scorching the pages as he listed all Harry's sins. Not only had Harry missed that crucial vote, the bastard, he had debts all over town, was flat broke, and, to top it all off, had terrorized his wife with a gun. Charlotte and Victor were all for keeping the letter quiet, but Rupe disagreed. Why shouldn't Austin know that Harry had ratted on them, before Harry got here with his excuses. Walker had written that he was on his way home.

'There'll be no welcome for you here if I have any say in it,' he muttered, and took the letter back to Austin. He was well aware that news like this could cause his father to have another stroke, but he excused his actions by telling himself that Austin would find out sooner or later. Sooner probably, when Harry came bleating for money to buy himself out of the mess.

Rupe didn't believe the bit about Harry terrorizing Connie with a gun – he thought it was just her father raving on – but it added grist to the mill.

He handed the letter over. 'Now take it quietly,' he warned Austin, knowing that that advice was a waste of time.

As Austin read, the colour rose in his face. He shuffled the pages, rereading, shaking his head as if he couldn't believe this, and then hurled them away.

'He's coming home!' he snarled.

'Looks like it.'

'I don't want him here!' he shouted.

Charlotte came rushing in. 'What's going on?' She picked up the pages, recognized them and turned on Rupe.

'How could you? I specifically said . . .'

'My letter!' Austin yelled at her. 'How dare you hold my mail?'

'It was for your own good. Please, Austin, settle down. You know what the Judge is like. He's always criticizing Harry. When Harry comes home I'm sure he can explain it all perfectly well.'

'The House is still sitting,' Rupe said meanly. 'He should be there, not running home to mother.'

'He is our son, and he's entitled to give us his side of the story before anyone starts condemning him. He's probably not well.'

'He's no son of mine!' Austin snapped. 'I won't have him here.'

'Oh, you don't mean that,' she said. 'I'll get you a cup of tea.'

That night Austin insisted his sons take him over the plans for the dissection of Springfield under the new laws, and show him, again, the list of family and dummy names that would be used to lay claim to the best pastoral blocks. He studied the plans carefully, making sure that the list coincided exactly with the numbered blocks, then he sat back.

'Cross out Harry's name. He's not getting one bloody acre.'

Rupe was delighted. He kept his head down, pretending to study a section map, but Victor protested.

'You can't do that. And what's the point? Springfield will still be yours. We're not breaking up the property, this is all just on paper.'

Until he dies, Rupe thought. Then we'll see who owns what.

'Take his name off!' Austin gritted.

'We can't. Everyone in the family, and that includes Louisa and Connie . . .'

'Take her off too!'

Victor was exasperated. 'Will you listen to me? We've marked off the maximum land each one of us will be permitted to own, even if we can afford to freehold all of it. That in itself will take some figuring. The outer blocks are already in dummy names – Jack Ballard and a couple of our men. We can trust them. You can't replace Harry. We'd have to give good land over to another dummy name, and I can't think for the life of me who else we can trust.'

He turned to Rupe. 'You know that. Look, here, out on the boundaries, there's land we decided to let go because we don't know anyone else we can trust to be a dummy owner and be loyal enough to accept that in reality it belongs to Dad.'

'It does belong to Dad,' Rupe said. 'You seem to be forgetting that. Harry let us down with a bang. We're the ones who are going to have to work our way out of this mess, not him.'

'That's not the point!' Victor said angrily. 'He's still family and he stays.'

But Austin threw what amounted to a tantrum. Handicapped by his disabilities, unable to stand or even to grab the pencil from Victor, he raged at them.

'It *is* my land! It is mine! I'm not bloody dead yet! Take his name off! And hers! Or yours will bloody go too.'

Victor took the list and slammed it on his desk. 'Very well. Who will we put in Connie's place?' He sat poised, challenging his father to come up with a name.

'Teddy!'

Rupe was startled. That would give Victor a triple holding. The bulk of the property. 'He's too young!'

'His father can be trustee!'

Victor went ahead and replaced Connie's name with that of his son. 'Now who? There's Harry's share.'

Rupe watched, knowing his father was stumped. There was no one else. He wished he had a wife. Maybe it wasn't too late, though.

These were only preparatory plans. He'd have to look about.

'Righto,' Victor said at last. 'You've punished Harry by taking his wife's share off, now let it be.'

'No.' Austin was tired, but he struggled on. If Harry had as many debts as Walker claimed, there'd be no helping him. Every spare quid would be needed now to hang on to Springfield. The fool could end up a bankrupt so there wouldn't be any point in claiming he owned blocks here. Creditors would grab them. And he could never forgive Harry for missing that vote and embarrassing his father to this extent. Where the hell was the bugger when he was needed? In a gambling hall, probably. Miserably, Austin wondered what he had done to deserve a son like this. Hadn't he done the best he could for him? And his silly wife. They'd already cost him a fortune, keeping up appearances in Brisbane. And twice he'd settled, or thought he had, Harry's debts. Obviously he'd owed a lot more than he'd admitted. According to Walker, the couple were now flat broke. Austin was bewildered. How could they be flat broke? What the hell had they been up to? He was even further embarrassed to have Walker demand from him the money that he had loaned his son-in-law. Well, he could go jump! That letter was damned insulting, as if he was to blame for the situation. Time Walker looked at that social-climbing daughter of his, Harry's wife.

But that didn't alter the fact that Victor was now waiting on him, waiting for him to capitulate. No one could fill in for Harry.

'Never,' he stormed. 'Never! I'll put Spinner's name down before I let that bloody useless Harry ever own one acre of Springfield. He's done his bloody dash now. He's no son of mine.'

And then the answer came to him. An inspired choice! Someone he could always trust.

'Fern Broderick,' he said triumphantly. 'Put her down for his block. She's family. And now that's settled, get me a brandy, Rupe. Doctor's orders.'

Charlotte finally managed, through friends in Toowoomba, to employ two more servants, white girls, and they weren't too bad, although less pliable than the black girls. Of course, they required better accommodation, which meant giving them Cook's room and shifting her to a guest room, which pleased her no end.

Old Jock had offered Charlotte three black gins from the mob that lived on his station, but strangely they had all refused point blank to come to Springfield. They would be neither persuaded nor ordered to go over to Springfield, weeping hysterically when he insisted, so in the end he'd given up, not displeased that his blacks preferred to remain on his land. Flattered, in fact.

'They'd probably be lonely here, with the others all gone walkabout,' Victor explained. 'They don't like to be totally cut off from the tribe.'

134

So now Charlotte had the two white girls, Maisie and her sister Alice, working fairly well in their black dresses and white aprons. She rather liked the idea; it raised the standard of her household to have real servants. Austin wasn't impressed, though, when he heard that they had to be paid each week.

'Do you think I'm made of money?' he'd growled. 'We're supposed to be tightening our belts.'

Charlotte ignored him. She was in the best of moods these days. Everyone was upset about these confusing Lands Acts, and she'd often sat in when Austin and the boys were drawing up the complicated maps and plans to protect their huge holdings. And that was where she'd learned that her name was now on a block adjacent to Austin's first choice, which naturally took in the homestead area, and his beloved valley. Her block was prime land, big enough to carry thousands of sheep. In her own name!

This was all she had wanted from the day that Austin had promised her a share, Kelly's share, and now it had happened, if only by accident. Although, she reminded herself, she was really entitled to a larger block. However, she had to admit that, thanks to the machinations of the government, not even Austin could legally lay claim to more. He had simply turned his land into a chequerboard of blocks to confuse the Lands Department, and dumped names on it like pawns.

Nevertheless her name was there. Charlotte Broderick. She was no longer just the wife. Charlotte thought no further than that. She didn't understand that the names listed were only part of a paper chase, that Springfield in its entirety still belonged to Austin. She'd heard mention of them forming a company, not realizing that they were investigating a plan for a pastoral company that could hold and control all of these blocks as separate sheep stations, with Austin at its head.

Then came the terrible news about Harry, and Charlotte was devastated. Although she'd always been careful to hide it, Harry was far and away her favourite son. Victor was nice, but stolid. A good man, hard-working, but he lacked Harry's flair. She sighed. Rupe had the flair all right, and he was the most handsome of her boys, with a dazzling smile and intense blue eyes that too often spelled trouble. Rupe was . . . well, Rupe.

But Harry. Poor Harry. His mother had already replied to Judge Walker, taking him to task for his libellous remarks and demanding that in the name of good family relations he should desist from such outrageous scribblings until Harry was given a chance to speak for himself.

She blamed Connie. She knew that Austin was right . . . Connie was a social-climbing little minx, not a patch on Louisa, although Connie came from the ranking Walker clan, élite even among squatters because they traced back to the Macarthurs of Parramatta. Harry could not have become so poor without the wild spending of his wife.

135

Why was he not in the Parliament? Connie would know. There was more to this than met the eye. And as for threatening his wife with a gun? Charlotte was the only one to really ponder that question. Unlike Rupe, she knew there had to be some truth in it. A judge would not dream of making such a wild statement in writing. Why would any man in his right mind threaten his wife with a gun?

'An old story,' she mused thinly. 'His wife and who else?'

Harry was coming home, the letter said. No mention of Connie coming with him. Odd. One would think she too would wish to visit Austin since he'd been so ill. To Charlotte these tales did not ring true. She would get the truth out of Harry when he did come home. And whether Austin liked it or not, this was his home.

The three of them had worked in Victor's office last night until all hours. Charlotte took Maisie in there to clean up the mess that only her husband and two sons could make. Glasses all about, dirty ashtrays, some empty bottles, papers strewn, but as Maisie tidied, Charlotte sorted the pages on the desk, looking for the one that made her so happy; looking for her own name on the all-important list.

When she found the list she was distressed to see the mark of a purple indelible pencil through Harry's name. And through Connie's, typical of Austin's ridiculously angry reactions. But when she saw who had been nominated to replace her son as one of the owners of Springfield, she was shocked.

Fern Broderick! How dare he! Fern Broderick! What right did she have to one inch of this station?

Charlotte had always been suspicious that there was something going on between Fern and her husband, and now she was sure of it. If you took this plan at face value, she, Charlotte, was said to own no more and no less of this property than Fern Broderick. Who had no right to any of it.

'Do you want me to mop the floor, madam?' Maisie asked.

'What? Yes,' Charlotte responded vaguely.

She stared down at Victor's list, misinterpreting her sons' part in this, thinking this was what the three of them had decided upon. She was hurt, dreadfully hurt. And angry.

'We'll see about this,' she murmured as she shut the desk.

The tribulations of the previous day and the late-night session with his sons had cost Austin dearly. In his wearied state he was hardly able to speak at all, and when Teddy wandered in he was even further depressed. He liked to have the boy with him, but he wasn't much company today.

'Aren't you getting up?' Teddy asked.

Austin shook his head, and the child sighed. 'Tomorrow then. Will you take me for a swim? Nioka's gone and everyone else is busy. You're not busy.'

He investigated Austin's breakfast tray. 'You didn't eat this bacon. Can I have it?'

At his grandfather's nod, the boy took the bacon, chewing on it as he toured the room in idle contemplation.

'It'll be Christmas soon,' he announced suddenly. 'How soon?'

'A few weeks yet,' Austin murmured.

'Yes, a few weeks. And Harry will be home. He promised to bring me a train. Not a real train, a toy train, but a big one. A great big one. You ever been on a train, Grandpa?'

'Yes.'

Still chatting, Teddy roamed out on to the veranda, obviously bored, and Austin realized how much the child must be missing his black playmates. He wished he could make it up to the kid, but in his present state there was little he could do. He was just as bored as Teddy. Except when it came to thoughts of Harry. He wouldn't be coming home this Christmas, or any other Christmas.

'I'll buy you a train,' he managed to say to Teddy.

'Will you? That's good. I'll have two. We can race them!'

Austin gave up and allowed himself to doze.

Connie's visit to her parents was decidedly unpleasant, but she did manage to prise ten pounds out of them. A miserly ten pounds! She felt she'd earned that, and more, having to listen to their endless gripes, and had escaped their clutches as soon as she'd snapped the money firmly in her purse.

When she returned to the empty house, she hung her coat and hat in the horribly bare bedroom. Tired after that long walk in the heat, she decided to make herself a cup of tea, but just as she walked into the kitchen, a tall, unkempt man loomed up at the back door.

Connie froze. For a minute there she thought it was a tramp breaking in to rob her, but the shadowy figure against the sharp sunlight was too confident, and she realized it was Harry.

Struck speechless at first, Connie didn't take long to burst into a tirade of abuse.

'Where have you been? You rotter! Have you any idea how much trouble you've caused? Your name is mud in the town. My father is absolutely livid with you. And, my God! Look at you. You look like a deadbeat! And how dare you go off without a word, leaving me without a penny? I've had to put the servants off. That'll be all over town as well. The broke Brodericks!'

As he moved into the kitchen, she had a flash of memory and backed off. 'You keep away from me. Do you hear? My father has taken all the guns out of the house so you can't bully me any more, and if you raise a hand to me, I'll scream . . .'

'The stove's cold,' he said, leaning over to take some deal and paper from the woodbox to rekindle the fire. That was too much for Connie. She rushed at him, thumping him on the back, shouting at him about the week she'd endured, with so many people, including creditors, looking for him, the mailbox filling up with bills, the humiliations . . .

Harry stood up and took her arm in a firm grasp, leading her to a kitchen chair. 'Sit down and shut up.'

She remained there, weeping, while he put the kettle on, searched the pantry for some bread and cheese and a jar of pickles and calmly began making himself a meal. 'Do you want some of this?'

'No!'

He shrugged, bit into the rough sandwich and waited calmly for the kettle to boil.

'You want a cup?'

She did, but she couldn't bring herself to accept, so she had to endure watching him pour himself a good strong cup of tea before he joined her at the table.

'I need some money,' she snapped.

'All in good time.'

'Where have you been? I thought you'd gone to Springfield.'

He ignored that, annoying her even more. 'What have you got to say for yourself?' she snapped.

'I should ask the same of you. I thought your lover would be taking care of you. He's not short of money.'

On the defensive, Connie fought back. 'Your place was in the Parliament. You should have been there this week. You let them down, they'll probably throw you out.'

'They won't have to. I'm resigning.'

'You're what? No one resigns from Parliament.'

'Yes they do. Now tell me about Sam Ritter.'

'What about Sam Ritter? I haven't seen him.' She didn't add that in desperation she'd called on Sam, only to be told by a servant that he and his mother were not receiving. Another rat, she decided. Both he and Harry were rats.

'How long has the big love affair been going on?'

Connie jumped up from the table. 'It wasn't going on at all. I don't want to talk about it. Leave me alone.'

He nodded. 'I'm not surprised you don't want to talk about it. Neither do I. There are more important matters to discuss.'

He talked for a long time, refusing to even consider any of her arguments. His mind was made up.

'So that's it,' he said finally. 'I'm resigning from Parliament, selling the house and all this fancy furniture – that should cover some of the debts – and I'll get a job, a paying job.'

'Where will we live?'

'My contacts are good. In the bush, that is. I won't have any trouble getting a job as a manager on a sheep station . . .'

'I'm not going to live like that. Just the wife of a manager on some damned outback station.'

'Then don't. You're free to please yourself. You can come with me or go where you like. I'm fed up with town life. I want to live in the bush where I belong.'

'Where will I go?'

'Up to you,' he shrugged. 'Now I have to shave and clean up, and get going. I have to see a lot of people, starting with the Premier.'

'Your father will have something to say about this!'

Harry smiled. 'I daresay he will.'

Anger hid Austin's distress. Charlotte was convinced that Harry had suffered a nervous breakdown but the calm tone of his letter belied that. And what would have caused a so-called breakdown? His own profligacy, that was what! And the shaming of the Broderick name. The man was a quitter, running out on his responsibilities to his party, his constituency and, worst of all, his family.

'He is still concerned for you, though,' Charlotte said. 'He hopes you won't be upset by his decision, and he's coming to see us as soon as the house is sold.'

'No he's not.' Austin was adamant. He ordered Victor to reply, telling Harry to stay away. He was not welcome.

'But he always comes home at Christmas. He's entitled to a hearing.'

'He's had a hearing! In that damned letter.'

In the end it was Rupe who replied, as instructed. Austin knew that Charlotte would have written to him too, but she could say what she liked. Harry was still banned from Springfield.

The letter was no surprise to Harry. The old man was acting true to form. But at least he was recovering fairly well from his stroke, according to Charlotte, who begged Harry not to take Austin's attitude too seriously. He'll get over it, she'd written. Harry doubted it.

His mother had apologized that she was not able to help him financially, as she had no money of her own, and that upset Harry more than any of it. Was it only money that had kept them all under Austin's thumb? Austin had always been generous when it came to handouts. He kept a cashbox in his office and if any of them, wife or sons, needed money for shopping or outings, they only had to ask to be given more than they required. But they had to ask. And Austin had set him up well in Brisbane when he married and entered Parliament.

Victor had not fared so well. Because he and his wife lived at Springfield, Austin had not deemed it necessary to give them the same allowance. Harry knew that rankled with Louisa, but Victor had never commented. Maybe he realized that Harry needed funds to live in town.

Anyway, he sighed, his funds were all gone now and the well had dried up, so he had to look ahead.

139

A terse Premier had accepted his resignation from Parliament and, dismissing Harry, turned his attention to a by-election for his seat.

He called on his aunt, Fern Broderick, to thank her for looking after Connie for those few days, apologizing for his behaviour but not mentioning Sam Ritter. There was enough turmoil, he had decided, without introducing that incident.

This was the first time he'd ever sat down and really talked to Fern, and he found her surprisingly unperturbed about the whole mess. Even about the gun. She brought that up herself.

'I hope there'll be no more late-night gunshots.'

He reddened. 'I'm so sorry, that was just plain stupid.'

'Are you sure that's all it was?' she asked him pointedly.

'Yes.'

'Oh well. Good. Now, what are your plans?'

'Josh Pearson has bought Tirrabee station, near Warwick, and he's looking for a manager. I'll see him this afternoon.'

'What about his son? I thought he bought Tirrabee for him?'

'He was killed in a fall from his horse, poor Andy. Broke his neck.'

'Oh dear. I am sorry.'

Before he left, Fern pressed a wallet of money on him. Harry was embarrassed.

'I can't take this, Fern. I've vowed never to borrow money again.'

'It's not a loan. It will tide you over until you get on your feet again. What does Connie think about going to Tirrabee?'

'She's not keen on the idea, but it's a beautiful station and the homestead's all right. No palace, but we can smarten it up. If I get that job we'll be very lucky. It's the best I can offer.'

Fern watched him leave, pleased that he'd faced his problems squarely and was setting out in a new direction, even though his father disapproved. It was typical of Austin to ban his son from Springfield, and ridiculous. She had no qualms about helping Harry with a few hundred pounds; his father had spent enough on her. Now she could put some of Austin's generosity where it was best needed.

She decided to write to Charlotte and Austin to tell them that she had seen Harry, and not to be worrying about him, he was fine. Then, at last, she added her own news. She hoped Austin was feeling better, because she would be coming to visit Springfield shortly. Probably in a few weeks' time.

The response from Charlotte was swift and very curt.

Fern was quite shocked.

Thank you for your letter. Austin is as well as can be expected. We were pleased to hear news of Harry, but he did write to us himself. As for your visiting Springfield, it is not a good time. We are all very busy these days.

I remain . . . Charlotte Broderick.

Chapter Six

Hannibal Frawley, self-appointed bishop of the Church of the Holy Word, had hay fever. He stood by the FOR SALE sign, sneezing and snuffling into his handkerchief, then he pocketed it again and went back to his task of removing the sign from the gatepost. One last blow with the hammer and he managed to dislodge it, grabbing it quickly and trudging back up to the house. He ducked under the heavily flowering wattles and threw it among the debris that had accumulated beneath his house.

With a sigh of relief he dusted his soft pink hands and marched up the wooden steps to stand, satisfied, surveying the overgrown garden.

Were it not for this torment of hay fever, Hannibal would have been a very happy man. This was his last night at the church that also served as his residence, because the property was sold, and he'd done very well out of it. Sold it to a parishioner, in fact, a virtuous gentleman with a large family who had been thrilled to acquire a home already blessed by the Lord. He had promised, one hand on the Good Book, to treat the house with respect, as demanded by the Bishop, a condition of sale, understanding that such a property could not be sold to just anyone.

'It's a sad day when a church has to be closed down,' the parishioner had said, but was cheered by the Bishop's answer.

'Definitely not,' Frawley told him. 'It is a great day. It's time I built a real church. It will be magnificent, next door to our mission home on the slopes of Mount Nebo. We have so many children there, and our dear lay people. They need their bishop to be on hand all the time.'

'Ah, God bless you, Bishop,' the gentleman said as the money changed hands.

'And bless you too,' Hannibal grinned now, remembering, as he stepped into the house and made for the brandy decanter. The fool had paid well for the privilege of sharing his house with the Lord, far more than the Bishop had expected to receive, giving him a handsome profit on his investment.

As for the mission house, that was closed too. The children had been dispersed to an orphanage or to the care of the lay preachers who had been cut loose to fend for themselves. As Hannibal had pointed out to them, ever so kindly, this was only a temporary setback, because the lease had run out on the mission premises, and could not be renewed. They were so gullible. They had actually believed that he was negotiating to purchase much more pleasant premises on the beach at Redcliffe, and were looking forward to a grand reunion there in four weeks' time.

Brisbane had been kind to him; his followers had worked it well. Dedicated fundraisers, they'd amassed a small fortune on his behalf and he was extremely grateful to them, presenting each one with a beautiful scroll, their names inscribed in gold ink, as newly ordained pastors of the Church of the Holy Word. Their tears of joy had almost touched his heart.

But now it was time to move on. Hannibal poured himself another brandy, savouring it and his new plans. The Holy Word was a good idea, but the real killing was in faith healing. And in a big city. Sydney was the place . . .

He was startled to hear the creak of his old wrought-iron gate, and the sight of horses hauling a dusty wagon into his drive brought on another fit of sneezing.

Who the hell was this?

By the time he met Tom Billings and his wife and the three black brats they had in tow, Hannibal had recovered his equilibrium but was not in control of his snuffling.

'My dears,' he said, sniffing and sneezing, but arms outstretched in welcome, 'how wonderful to see you. I bless the Lord who has brought you safely home!'

He had totally forgotten this pair of New Zealanders whom he'd sent into the bush in the hope they'd find good pickings among the squatters.

'Are you all right, Bishop?' Mrs Billings asked him anxiously. 'You don't look well.'

'Dear lady, thank you. I'm suffering from the most awful flu. Please forgive my disarray, but I have been bedridden for days. I am embarrassed to receive you in my shirtsleeves. Do come in, though. I shall change.'

But Billings came to his rescue. 'Goodness me, no. We are intruding, Bishop. A man in shirtsleeves is no less a man in God's eyes. We are in no position to complain, having travelled far these last few weeks.' He smiled his thin smile. 'I fear we are hardly dressed for the occasion, but on our way to our lodgings I wanted to let you know that we have carried out our mission . . .'

'With great success,' his wife interrupted.

Billings frowned at her. 'With the grace of God.'

Hannibal had no choice but to take them into his parlour, apologizing that his housekeeper was off, doubling up on the coughing and spluttering and holding his head as if in a fever, for surely the

142

appearance of these zealots, along with three skinny, miserable-looking piccaninnies, was enough to give any man in his position an attack of fever. Especially now.

'You poor man,' Mrs Billings said. 'Can I get you anything?'

'No. I just fear that I might give you this influenza, it's a plague in Brisbane at present. Just bear with me.'

He listened, his hands pressed into a steeple, to Billings' account of their travels and travails, and the only thing that stopped him interrupting and sending them on their way – for what right did they have to barge in on their bishop? – was that triumphant glint in Tom's eyes. There was more to this than the collecting of three wretched black children to be Christianized.

The boys huddled, petrified, in an armchair, like puppies, and Hannibal tried not to stare. Jesus! How old were they? No more than seven, he was sure. He could remember giving a sermon to his lay preachers that he'd copied from something he'd read about getting black kids young so that they'd pick up English more easily, but none of them had actually turned up with piccaninnies. The children at the mission had all been at an age where they could be put to work, labouring or housework, none of them any younger than eleven or maybe twelve.

But this damned Tom Billings! Hannibal remembered now that Billings took every word he uttered as gospel. Come to think of it, he wouldn't be a bad offsider to take with him. Idiotic. Unquestioning. Fanatical.

What were his own meetings, his God-searchings, all about? They were to dig out, unearth, identify and call in the unquestioning, the believers, the fanatics. The heartlands of his ministry. To work for him. To bring in cash and go back for more! Billings was ideal.

Hannibal permitted Mrs Billings to scrounge about in his kitchen, make tea and deliver it to the adults, with biscuits and water for the kids, while he listened, waiting for the good news that her husband was already flagging. And then it came. The cheque from a squatter, from Austin Broderick, no less.

Billings handed it over with a flourish, plus a bag of coins that amounted to all that remained of their other collections, less expenses. As he did so, he lost all chance he'd had of going on to glory and good fortune with his bishop, for he also had instructions from Austin Broderick specifying the care of the black children, and Hannibal wanted no part of it.

In magnanimous mood, he returned the bag of coins to Billings, telling him it was God's reward for an honest man, and endeavoured to send them all on their way, but Tom couldn't do that.

'We can't take black children to our lodgings. It just wouldn't be permitted, Bishop. You've no idea the trouble we've had bringing them here, after we left the drovers. No lodgings, even in the country, would have them – we had to lock them in sheds – so there's no way town boarding houses would take them.'

'Even so, even so,' Hannibal murmured, in his best pastoral voice, but Mrs Billings had a solution.

'I know it's an imposition,' she said, 'especially when you're not feeling well, Bishop, but we'll have to leave them here with you. We have no choice now that we're back in town. We'll take them out to the mission tomorrow.'

'Yes, I think that's best,' Billings concluded. 'Then I can write to Mr Broderick and inform him that the children are placed as we agreed. He had a stroke while we were there, you know. Too much good living, I'd say. The man drinks. They all do.'

Hannibal was relieved that he'd had the presence of mind to hide the brandy decanter.

In the end, desperate to be rid of his lay preachers once and for all, he agreed to keep the kids, even to place them at the mission himself. With his blessings, he gave Mr and Mrs Billings a week's leave to rest up after their long pastoral journeys.

He led the prayers, as on their knees they thanked the Lord for their daily bread and the continuance of the Church of the Holy Word, and he nodded sombrely as Billings intoned: 'This is only the beginning. The Word will be heard all over Queensland. We will have a chapel in every town and every village, and a pastor to minister to the lambs of God. Amen, I say, and amen again.'

'Amen,' Hannibal echoed as he ushered them out of the door and turned back to the babes in the armchair, who were picking at biscuit crumbs. He didn't need this complication. He'd had everything worked out perfectly. The nice fat cheque from the squatter was a welcome bonus, and it would be cashed first thing in the morning, but the kids were a damned nuisance. He wondered if he could just let them go. Turn them loose.

'Well, it was only a thought,' he chided himself.

They cringed further into the folds of the chair as he approached, obviously scared stiff of him.

'I'm not going to eat you,' he growled. 'Any of you speak English?'

'Me spik real good,' one of them said.

'What about your mates?'

'No like English. They cry.'

He looked at their big dewy eyes and nodded. 'Well, they can stop now. Nothing to cry about. Do you want some tucker?'

That had the desired effect; they were suddenly alert, so he carted them out to the kitchen to see what was left in the line of food. The Bishop was not standing on ceremony this night. He found some cold lamb and potatoes, tomatoes, beetroot, a tin of beans and stale bread that he plastered with dripping, and dumped it all on the table, helping himself first then leaving them to devour the rest.

Their spokesman, the boy called Bobbo, seemed to know his way about a kitchen. He found cups and got them drinks of water, waited until they'd demolished every scrap of food and then wiped his mates' faces and hands with a damp cloth.

'That Mr Billings, he comen back?'

'No. He's gone.'

Bobbo smiled. 'Good. He a bad man. He belt us. We go home now?'

Hannibal smoothed his fine grey locks, a gesture he was apt to use whenever he was searching for an appropriate lie. 'Not just yet. You have to get some sleep.'

He left the mess in the kitchen – it wasn't his problem any more, the house was sold – and took them into a back room. 'There's a bunk and blankets. You sleep there.'

By this time all three of them were almost asleep, tottering in without a word.

He went back to his brandy bottle, still trying to figure out what to do with them. He couldn't just leave them here; that would cause the new owners to come looking for him. Nor could he dump them at that Catholic orphanage where the nuns had already taken some of the mission children, after giving one of his lay preachers a tongue-lashing for their treatment of the kids. Maybe he could separate them, and put each one of them in a church, but he guessed that would cause a riot. The way they clung to each other, they'd scream their heads off if he left one behind.

Finally he had the answer . . . the Home for the Destitute. Or, as it was more commonly known, the workhouse. It would take some fancy footwork – they didn't take little kids – but they'd be stuck with them, the same as he was.

Before he went to bed he peered in at the boys, hoping they'd have climbed out of the open window and bolted, but they were still asleep, bundled up in the blankets, but not on the bunk, on the floor.

At first light, he found them aimlessly wandering about the house, so he gave them a cup of milk to share and set to, packing his belongings into his gig. As part of his plan, he put into a bag some apples and a box of toffees that had been given to him by a kindly parishioner, and placed it under the seat of the gig. Then, with the horse in harness, he called to the boys to jump on board, and they were soon away, clip-clopping down the back lane.

The gate in the stone wall of the workhouse was open, so he pushed them inside and told them to sit down there and wait.

'Don't go away,' he told Bobbo. 'You've been very good, so here's a present for you.'

Their eyes popped when they saw the toffees, and as he hurried away they were happily sharing the spoils.

'You'll be all right now,' he muttered as he hopped on to the gig. 'They'll have to place you!'

His duty done, the Bishop never gave them another thought. Dressed in his best ecclesiastical clothes – black jacket, cravat and breeches, boots highly polished and with his cocked hat firmly in place – he strode into the bank, cashed the cheque, drew out all of his considerable funds and closed the account.

Next stop, the shipping office.

The Reverend Billings did not fare so well. He was disappointed to find that none of his colleagues were in residence, but more important, that the boarding house was under new management and the rates had doubled.

'We can't stay here,' he told his wife. 'It's too expensive. But there's no point in moving until we see Bishop Frawley and get our next assignment.'

A week later, he was pleasantly surprised to find several workmen busy at the Bishop's residence. Gardeners were toiling in the grounds, painters giving the house a much-needed coat of paint, and inside, he could hear carpenters hammering away. All very inspiring to know that the Church of the HolyWord was becoming a force to be reckoned with. By the looks of things, this house would be much improved, a boost for impressionable parishioners.

A gentleman approached him. 'Can I help you, sir?'

'I wanted a word with Bishop Frawley.'

'I'm sorry, the Bishop has left. He doesn't live here any more.'

'What? Where is he?'

'He's building a new church and residence next door to the mission, on Mount Nebo, I believe. Beautiful surrounds there, it will be a joy for us all.'

'Ah, yes. Of course,' Billings said, backing away. 'I forgot. Good day to you, sir.'

'And he forgot to tell me,' he muttered angrily, heading back to his horse. 'Still, he wasn't well, and we did land on him without notice. It was very kind of him to receive us at all.'

An hour later the Reverend was riding up and down Mount Nebo Road. He couldn't find the mission house, or any buildings that looked remotely like it, and eventually he was forced to enquire of some road workers, who told him the mission house had been pulled down. Razed to the ground.

'It was over there on that empty block,' one of them said, leaning on his pick.

'Oh, I see,' Billings replied knowingly. 'That's where they're building the new church.'

The labourer scratched his head. 'Not that I heard of, mister. That land belongs to the Forestry Department. Those old cottages were

146

only leased to them churchies. They're going to build worksheds there when we finish fixing up this road.'

'That can't be right,' Billings spluttered. 'That's church premises.'

The man shrugged, 'Have it your own way,' and went back to work.

Tom Billings was a worried man. 'I can't find any of our people,' he told Amy later that day. 'I've no idea where the Bishop is.'

'We'll just have to stay here until he contacts us, then.'

'It's far too expensive.'

'But if we move, he may not be able to find us. We've been away for a good while. Things change.'

He stared sourly out of the window. 'I knew we shouldn't have stayed so long at that den of iniquity. Now you see what lolling about in luxury with those awful Brodericks has done to us. We're being punished. You thought it was a beautiful place. Now I hope you're satisfied. For all I know Bishop Frawley may have decided we're not worthy to carry on in his flock.'

'Or the rest of them are just being mean, freezing us out.'

Weeks later the Reverend and Mrs Billings had just enough money left to purchase steerage passage back to New Zealand, sharing disgusting quarters with abominable people during a stormy crossing of the tempestuous Tasman Sea. Amy was violently ill all the way, Tom slipped down a gangway and broke his leg, and when they finally arrived in Wellington, trying desperately to organize the rest of their journey home, they heard that Pastor Williams had died, and his church with him.

Finding abandoned kids in the cobbled yard was nothing new to Buster Giles; he got them all sizes and colours, from wee babes to knobbly-kneed ragamuffins, white, black and yellow. People seemed to think the workhouse was a safe haven, if they cared at all. But it was far from that.

'Far from that,' he echoed his own thoughts. 'More like a madhouse, if you ask me.'

Buster, an ex-pugilist, retired from various occupations because of the drink, had been glad to get this live-in job as assistant to the supervisor, because he'd been down on his luck. His sister was matron of the women's section and she'd found the job for him, making him promise to give up the grog because, the way she put it, this was a very responsible position. But it didn't take him long to realize that apart from Molly Giles, no one was responsible for anything much round here, except for getting their pay and keeping the inmates from killing one another. His supervisor, a former bank manager with a history, spent his days in his office poring over detailed journals, ledgers and files, rarely deigning to step outside, let alone invite contact with the inmates.

So Buster was his runner. He handed out rosters to the staff, conveyed instructions to the hopeless workers in the so-called shoe factory, informed inmates that they had to leave, dodged the stinking kitchens and stopped fights. In all, he decided miserably, it was a horrible place, but like the rest of them, he had nowhere else to go. And at least he got his five bob every week.

The wonder of it, though, was that the workhouse seemed to be able to drive anyone to drink. There was no shortage of grog; even his supervisor sucked on bottles of rum for his nerves, and the rest bartered, fought, stole, lay on their backs, begged, for anything that even smelled like booze, while the few non-drinkers cowered away from the chaos.

Buster, still good with his fists, became their protector, at the same time discovering that he'd lost the urge for the grog himself. A revelation that was. Sickened by his surrounds, Buster Giles was now a teetotaller, and he felt good about it. That was why he was beginning to believe that he could make a go of this job.

But for now, these piccaninnies.

'Where'd you kids come from?' he asked.

'Bush, boss. We come outa bush,' one of them said.

'Where? What bush?'

Small hands pointed in all directions.

'Who brought you here?'

'White boss. He takin' us home.'

'Where's home? Where your mummies?'

At that the other two started to cry.

'Back at the camp,' the spokesman said, and as he questioned them Buster guessed that they really were bush blacks. Two of them could only jabber in their own language.

'This is bloody lovely,' he muttered, and took them down to his sister in the women's quarters.

'You can't leave them here!' she said.

'I know that. I'll just have to do the rounds again.'

Then it was the same old story, appealing to churches and orphanages, to private schools, to anyone who would listen, but these boys were harder to place than babies, who were sweet, and bigger kids, who could work. So for weeks, Bobbo, Jagga and Doombie, families unknown, remained in the workhouse, cared for spasmodically by poor women who could offer the tiny outcasts little but time.

Summer brought torments of suffocating heat, mosquitoes and flies and hordes of huge cockroaches to the overcrowded dormitories and sheds of the workhouse, and with them debilitating sicknesses and fevers, that seemed, to Matron Giles, to be in plague proportions. The women could no longer care for the three black children, and she certainly didn't have the time, so they were left to their own devices, roaming about the maze of buildings, scavenging for food where they could.

At last her brother was able to place young Bobbo in a Methodist orphanage, but only because he could speak English. They flatly refused to take the other two.

Separating the boys would be difficult, they knew, so Bobbo was spirited away during the night. In the morning his two pals howled for hours when they discovered he really was gone, adding to the moans and groans of sick women, but there was nothing much Matron could do to comfort them.

Jagga adjusted to their new circumstances within a few days, trailing about the corridors clutching an old red cushion that someone had given him, but it was all too much for Doombie, who wouldn't budge from a heap of discarded blankets that had become their home in a far corner of a dormitory.

Matron herself was becoming desperate. She suffered from recurrent fevers and she knew she couldn't cope with this mayhem much longer. The only bright spot in her day was the visits of the charity ladies, who brought baskets of food and medicines for the inmates. They were a group of well-off women who really were trying to help, appalled by conditions in the workhouse, and Matron had come to rely on their generosity.

She was aware that some of the women came, as she put it, 'for show'. Simpering, silly women, impressed by their own good deeds, who rarely ventured beyond the stone receiving rooms into the tumbledown wooden structures beyond. But the others were of stronger stuff. They visited the sick, kneeling by the bunks to spoon soup into them; they went to work with brooms and mops cleaning sheds, even the long communal lavatories. They demanded that doctors visit patients; they had no inhibitions about charging into the men's quarters and demanding the staff clean up; and they invaded the kitchens. But best of all, they gave the lazy supervisor hell, harassing him with justified complaints about the refuge.

Matron Giles loved them. The salt of the earth, these formidable ladies. They didn't threaten, they *did*. They wrote a report about conditions in the workhouse and presented it to the Premier, demanding that the supervisor be sacked and be replaced by a competent administrator. It would happen, Matron knew, but too late for her. She wasn't well enough to stay much longer.

One morning when she met the ladies in the lobby as usual, Jagga had taken it into his head to trail about with her. He hung on her skirts peering at the newcomers as they lugged in their baskets, and some memory must have come out of his past. Most of the women wore black and businesslike aprons, but one of them, obviously on her first visit, was decked out in a pretty blue dress which set off her fair hair and complexion. Jagga burst free of the matron and ran forward, throwing his arms about her billowing skirts.

'Miz Louisa!' he cried joyfully.

149

The lady smiled, delighted to be singled out.

'Who are you, dear?' she asked kindly.

'Teddy!' he cried. 'Teddy!'

Matron laughed, reaching out to retrieve him. 'No you're not, you're Jagga.' She looked up. 'Never heard him speak English before. Now come on, Jagga, let the ladies past.'

'What's he doing here?' one of the older women asked.

'Oh, he's just adorable,' Jagga's new friend said. 'Such big eyes and lovely curly hair.'

'He's one of the trio I told you about,' Matron replied to the questioner. 'They were dumped on us. We couldn't abandon them, but we've only been able to place one of them so far.'

'Is he an orphan?' the pretty woman asked.

'Seems so. No one's come to claim him.'

'But he's so sweet. Such a dear little thing.'

Buster was stunned when his sister came to him later in the morning with her news. 'I've found someone to take Jagga. One of the charity ladies. She wants to take him home and keep him. She's married, hasn't any other children. I'm too busy. Will you find him and clean him up, give him a good scrub? Be quick about it before she changes her mind.'

'Good God! Just like that?'

'Yes. Fortunately Jagga has taken a liking to her.'

When Buster presented the buffed and polished child in ill-fitting shirt and long trousers, the lady was ecstatic.

'What a little darling! You're coming home with me, Jagga, with your new mummy.'

'Louisa,' he intoned, correcting her, and she giggled.

'No, Mummy. And I shall call you Jack. We'll have a lovely time.' She looked back at Buster. 'Isn't it gorgeous? I shall have my very own blackamoor.'

Buster thought that must be a breed he was not familiar with. 'No, he's an Aborigine.' He looked down at Jagga and placed a heavy paw on his head. 'Now you be good for the lady.'

This time there were no tears. The bonds of brotherhood between the three children had been severed by the disappearance of Bobbo.

'You haven't been looking too good lately,' Buster said to his sister. 'You ought to rest up a bit.'

'I'll do better than that. I've decided to retire.'

'Retire?' That required some thought. The concept was bewildering. In Buster's experience there were sackings or quittings that occurred with varying degrees of unpleasantness. Working-class people couldn't retire.

'Can you get another job?'

Matron shook her head wearily. 'I don't want another job. I've had enough, I'm too old now. Time I retired.'

'What will you do for money?'

'I've saved enough to get by. And I've still got my little house at Camp Hill. I can always fall back on midwifery if I need any extra. It'll be lovely. You can come and stay any time you want.'

'Well, I'll be blowed. When is this goin' to happen?'

'At the end of the week. I've told the super I'm leaving. He got nasty about it, said I couldn't leave. He wouldn't give me a reference.' She grinned. 'All he knows! I don't need references any more.'

'Well, I'll be blowed!' Buster repeated. 'If I save up, can I retire too?'

She took his arm and walked to a side door, gazing out at the glare of the day. 'You're doing a good job here, Buster, so you might as well stay on as long as you can. But you will always be welcome to come and live with me, as long as you stay off the grog.'

They were interrupted by a woman pushing through with a laundry basket. 'Hey, Matron! They've been lookin' for you down in the dormitory. That black kid's sick, they say.'

Doombie was ill, burning up with a fever. Matron bathed him in warm water laced with vinegar, cleared a small bunk for him, and gave him a few drops of tonic and some of the medication she kept for cases of influenza, but she was worried. He seemed so little and frail she doubted the medicine would help.

That night he developed a rasping cough, so she rubbed his little chest with eucalyptus and wrapped him in soft cloths to keep the soothing ointments near his throat and chest. Then she lifted him up and nursed him to her. Though he was barely conscious, she could feel the fear in him . . . a lost and lonely child caught in a terrifying environment. Matron knew that the fretting would aggravate his illness, depriving him of the will to live, so for days she hardly left his side, talking to him, singing little songs, rocking him to sleep.

The women in the dormitory fell silent, willing Doombie to live. Even in these rough and heartless surrounds, they could muster pity that transformed itself into a measure of defiance against a hard world. They prayed, they kept vigil, they relieved Matron when necessary, they even found a half-caste woman who squatted beside Doombie murmuring to him in her almost-forgotten language. As she told them, he talked a different lingo, but her words were distinctly Aborigine so they urged her to stay with him.

On the fourth day they found the fever had stolen away during the night, and Doombie was suddenly awake, staring at them.

When he was feeling a little better, Matron asked the Aborigine woman to talk to him, to try to find out more about him, but she shook her head. 'I come from up north, missus. Can't unnerstan him much, but he say he come from the bush. Big river bush. That all he know.'

151

'That was all Bobbo knew too,' Matron sighed. 'My brother has already asked among the Aborigine people here in Brisbane if any of them are missing three kids, and they spread the word, but no one has claimed them. They obviously have come from a tribal mob, but where in the bush? It's hopeless.'

Buster was all smiles the day his sister retired. He was proud of her. He even borrowed a horse and cart to take her and her belongings out to the tiny two-roomed timber cottage in Camp Hill, and Doombie sat up front between them. He was still thin and weak, but now he had a home. After nursing him back to health, Matron Giles couldn't bring herself to walk away and leave him in that place.

'He'd end up out in the streets on his own,' she explained to Buster, who smiled benignly, knowing his sister had become fond of the kid. She'd be lonely without him now, and Doombie would be well looked after.

It was all a very happy ending. He was looking forward to his own retirement, and in the meantime he could visit them when he got a day off. They were a family of three, after all their years of going it alone.

The workhouse had outer walls, stone walls, but Bobbo had never noticed because inside, there were no restrictions on their movements. He truly believed, as he told his mates, that this was only a stopover camp on the way home. The kind man had rescued them from the clutches of the evil ones who had stolen them, and he would come back for them. This view was reinforced by Buster, who became their next keeper. He never bashed them, or tied them up or gagged Doombie when he screamed in his dreams. And he let them explore all the ins and outs of this huge camp on their own until it became a game to them, hunting and hiding and chasing about the busy grey complex, with all its strange and peculiar stinks.

Nevertheless Bobbo kept an eye on the gates, which were always open, with people coming and going, knowing they could run away if they wanted to, because there was no one to stop them.

But now he was in a new place. Spirited away in the night when he was half asleep, by a new family of devils, taking him from his only friends.

This place had walls too, high timber walls, and heavy gates that were always locked, and that frightened him. It began to dawn on him that they'd all lied, all the whitefellers. They weren't going to take him home after all. Jagga and Doombie might be able to go home, but he'd missed out.

Every day brought new shocks. He was camped in a long hut with a mob of boys, mostly white, who were ruled over by white bosses wielding straps.

Right from the start Bobbo hated the bosses. He didn't know how to make his bed or use eating tools or even get his clothes straight, and that was only the beginning. There were so many regulations, so much bashing and shouting, that he became totally confused and lost his grasp of English. How was he supposed to know that this was the worst crime of all? Every time he spoke in his own language he was punished, locked in cupboards, deprived of meals or strapped, until forcibly, and with the help of other kids, words gradually came back to him.

There were prayers and lessons and jobs to be learned, and a million other things, and for the first few weeks, to avoid punishments, he tried very hard, but it didn't seem to matter to the bosses; Bobbo was known as the dunce. Despairing, he began to fight back. When they tried to drag him about, he kicked and spat and bit, inviting more beatings. He soon picked up what the white kids called swear words, and shouted abuse at his captors, screaming his little lungs out when they locked him in dark rooms to teach him to behave.

The troublesome piccaninny lost the title of dunce. That didn't seem to fit the belligerent, defiant Bobbo, who wore his cuts and bruises with a scowl. But this was an orphanage, the end of the line. The staff knew that in time this skinny black kid would have to settle down – the years would take care of that – but in the meantime it was their duty to reform him, to turn him into a God-fearing Christian, and they went about it the only way they knew. With the strap.

Jagga, on the other hand, was living in luxury at the house of the pretty lady and her husband. He slept in an iron cot on their back veranda, and every morning he was bathed and powdered and dressed in funny crampy clothes. Very nice to look at, he thought, but too uncomfortable to wear, especially the strange hat. So bit by bit, each day, he discarded them, leaving them in the garden or anywhere about the house, much to the lady's annoyance.

She fed him well, patiently teaching him how to eat with tools, how to sit on chairs, all sorts of things that were like a game to Jagga to start with.

The trouble first began with shoes and stockings. The clothes were bad enough, but Jagga got fed up with having to wear things on his feet. The stockings were hot and the tight shoes hurt. Dressing him became a battle of tears and threats.

'Let him go!' the husband said, sick of the fuss. 'Forget the shoes.'

'No, he has to learn,' the lady insisted.

Jagga didn't mind the man. He seemed to think the clothes were a joke, and would occasionally wink at him. Sometimes he would sit down with the child and teach him English words. But then he was away a lot, and it became clear to Jagga that the lady was the boss in this house. She too gave him lessons, helping him to scrawl things on a slate, and that was familiar to him. He remembered Teddy had had one too.

The best part of this life, though, was the animals; the two dogs and the cat who became his friends. The dogs slept in his cot with him, refusing to allow the cat the privilege, so it curled up, sulking, on a nearby chair. They had two bright parrots in a cage too, but they complained so much to Jagga about being locked up that he let them go, delighted to see them winging their way to freedom.

This upset the lady so much she was really angry with Jagga and sent him to bed without his tea, which didn't bother him at all. These people had so many mealtimes it was hard to keep up. He put on weight, grew stronger, but when he heard the word 'home', he recognized it from Bobbo's questioning and he began to question too. Asking her when he could go home. Receiving the same answer.

'This is your home, Jack.'

He pined for his own family. He fretted for Bobbo and Doombie. He tired of being hauled out on show for visitors in his startling clothes, and instead of smiling and bowing low, as he'd been taught, he began to sulk. He wet his pants and was smacked. He ran and hid when he heard the doorbell and had to be dragged out from under the bed.

For her part, his pretty lady, Mrs Adam Smith, wife of the Inspector of Customs, was becoming very tired of this naughty boy, who wouldn't learn the tiniest duty of a servant, such as carrying trays to her guests. She resented her husband's attitude.

'I told you so. He's a kid, not a toy,' he said.

But she would lose face with her friends if she got rid of him, so she simply had to grin and bear it, pleased at least by their approval of her charitable deed.

Gradually she lost interest in dressing him up and he became a nuisance, so she put him in the charge of her housekeeper, who was kind to him.

'I don't know why you feel sorry for him,' Mrs Adam Smith said angrily. 'How many other orphans get such good treatment?'

'You're right, madam, of course. But I don't think he is an orphan. He keeps saying he wants to go home to his mummy. I think her name is Nioka.'

'Yes, and she's probably dead. And we don't know where home is. Do we?' Mrs Adam Smith wished she did know. She would gladly deliver the child to his home. Her friends would approve of that.

Though humid clouds gathered in the distance, tables were set up under the shaggy pepper trees within view of the river, in the hopes of a breeze. For Christmas Day was always hot, the land baking, thirsting for rain, and already the sun was climbing heavily over the massive sandstone ridge.

Glancing up, Victor shuddered. There were times when that ancient

154

ridge seemed arrogant, even insolent, as if disdaining the fragility of the mortal span at its base, and today, more than ever, it depressed him. On the surface, everything seemed normal. Excitement had been building on the station as the big day drew near, and at last there was evidence that their traditional Christmas dinner would go with a swing. Everyone working on the station sat down with the Brodericks right on noon because Austin regarded this as a family occasion, and to him, they were all family.

But despite arguments with Charlotte, two regulars were missing. He would not lift his ban on Harry and Connie.

Charlotte's Christmas dinners were famous. Linen cloths covered long tables, her red and silver decorations were brought out of their boxes to lend colour, and gaudy streamers were strung from tree to tree. She even wrote souvenir menus to place on the table beside little individual baskets of sweets and nuts, although the fare never changed. Cream of chicken soup, fillet of fish with lemon sauce, roast chicken with baked vegetables and greens, wine trifle, plum pudding with brandy sauce.

Victor picked up a menu, smiling at her stylish writing. She had stuck to her tried and true menu, working hard, but he knew she was very upset with Austin. Furious, in fact, and that was rare. She'd even gone behind his back, writing to Harry, who was now managing Tirrabee station, telling him to come anyway, but Harry had declined. He had wished them all, including Austin, a merry Christmas but said he did not wish to cause any more bother. For that, Victor was grateful. There would have been trouble, for Rupe had sided with his father, taking a hard line against Harry.

'I don't know why you're so incensed,' Victor had said. 'What's done is done.'

'He sold us out,' Rupe said angrily. 'You're weak. We don't want him here.'

'I'm not weak. I just can't see the point in carrying on about it.'

Harry hadn't forgotten Teddy, though. He and Connie had sent a big wooden train for the boy. It was painted red and Teddy loved it, pulling it everywhere he went. Victor appreciated the thought.

But Austin, with his stubborn attitude, had not lost out in the upset department either, Victor mused. His father was missing the blacks.

'Where are they?' he'd asked Victor, on several occasions.

'I don't know. No idea.'

'But they like Christmas,' Austin had said testily. 'They don't know anything about our calendar but they know the seasons and they never have to be told when Christmas Day is near. I've never known them to miss our Christmas. They sit in the shade by the river, and have their own feast and singsong. We always have extra tucker for them. So where are they?'

'Probably too far away to get back in time,' Victor offered, to shut him up.

This morning, though, when he had discovered that not one of the blacks had returned, Austin was in a very bad mood. He seemed to regard their absence from his Christmas Day, his family party, as a personal insult.

Victor shook his head. He'd be glad when it was all over. There was nothing he could do about Harry and Connie, or the blacks. He went over to help some stockmen set a barrel of beer on a stand ready to serve their eager mates.

Far to the north, Minnie hadn't forgotten Christmas, the birthday of a white spirit who now lived in the sky. It was a time of fuss and fun, with everyone in good moods, proving that the Jesus was a good and kindly spirit. Remembering him now, she wasn't above appealing to the Jesus to bring back her son, her hands flat together the way the whites prayed, fingers upright, making a shape like an anthill.

But he was no more help than all the other spirits she'd invoked, and her depression worsened. None of the others seemed to care. They were content with this new mob, and with the valley which was still forested and a better natural food source than Springfield, which had been overrun by sheep. There was some doubt about ever returning to their old camp and when Minnie heard that talk she fell on the ground in an uncontrollable fit.

Days later, when she emerged from heavy sleep, induced by a foul-smelling white liquid the women had made her drink, Nioka was cross with her.

'You have to stop this playing-up. It is making everyone upset. You never do any work or look for food. You don't even fish, you just lie about feeling sorry for yourself. Look how fat you're getting! The people don't like it. You are an embarrassment to us. They don't see why they have to feed you.'

Minnie was furious. 'They don't have to feed me. I don't care. And I know all about you! You've got a new man. You're the one said no more men to mess up your life, and I see you mooning about with Rangutta all the time.'

'That is no secret. I have decided he will be my husband.'

'So you can have more babies and forget about poor Jagga!'

'That's not true. I will never forget Jagga. He'll come home one day.'

'How?' Minnie screamed. 'How will they find us? They are only little boys.'

Nioka sighed. 'Rangutta has been speaking to the elders of his people. They know more about this than we do. They say it often happens that the whites take black children for their own.' She took a deep breath. 'To keep.'

156

'What? I don't believe you. They took them to the white people school and they will come home for their holidays just like the Broderick boys.'

'No,' Nioka said sadly. 'We were wrong to think that. They don't bring back the black kids. You have to face that, Minnie. You must. Today you can rest but tomorrow you must get up and do some work like the rest of us.' She poked her sister gently, trying to cheer her. 'Work off some of that fat.'

'First you say I must find food, now I'm too fat. You don't know what you're talking about. None of you.' She struggled to her feet. 'I'm going to find Moobuluk.'

'Don't be silly. We don't know where he is.'

'Then I'll fast until he comes.'

'That won't help Bobbo.'

Minnie lashed out at her sister with her fist. 'Get away from me, you liar. You say Bobbo isn't coming back. You lie to get me to work. Well, I won't.' She began to weep, great heaving sobs. 'There's nothing for me any more. I've lost my darling boy. I've even missed Christmas.'

'Christmas!' Nioka was incredulous. 'What's that got to do with it?'

'Go away. I hate you. I hate this place too.'

Minnie did fast. She flatly refused to find her own food, so for a while they let her be, until Nioka became worried. She brought her sister cooked meat, flat bread patties with honey, nuts and her favourite berries, but Minnie flung them all away.

Gabbidgee came to plead with her, talking about his son Doombie, begging her to eat and sustain herself, and when that failed, he called in their own elders, who sat with Minnie, trying to persuade her to eat. But she had only one question for them.

'Is it true that the white people keep our babies? You dare not lie to me or the spirits will strike you down.'

'It is true,' they said sadly, finally. 'It is true.'

Sometimes Minnie disappeared into the bush for days, wandering aimlessly, until someone brought her back to sit by the lake in determined silence.

Nioka was sorry now that she had accused Minnie of being fat, because the flab was fast falling away. Her sister was so haggard and unkempt, she was becoming the butt of cruel jokes in the camp, and children called her the mad woman.

'Why is she doing this?' Nioka asked the wise men. 'It won't bring Bobbo back. It is so stupid.'

'She is punishing herself. She feels she failed the boy by not protecting him.'

'But we didn't know. We thought the boys were safe, they were with the families. And they thought the praying man was just letting them ride on their wagon.' She wept. 'How could we have known such a monstrous thing would happen?'

157

'You could not have known. There is no blame.'

'How long can she go on like this?'

'Long time, to starve the body, but weakness invites other sicknesses to attack. We will talk to her again.'

But they found Minnie had slashed her breasts in mourning and would not permit their intrusion on her crying time.

'Maybe this is a good thing,' they reported to Nioka. 'If she observes the traditions then she should be able to put down her crying when the time is past.'

That made Nioka feel better. The summer rains came and the valley steamed in the heat, and the brittle forest became lush and green, reflecting the brilliant colour in the lake. With love in her heart for her new man, Nioka was overwhelmed by the beauty of the valley, and her worries about Minnie receded.

For Rupe, this Christmas was simply a time to be endured. Christmas Day was just another day during which he had to sit through a long, boring midday meal and an exchange of bland presents, from socks for the stockmen and new stock whips for the overseers, right through to a classy tweed jacket for Austin, who complained it was too expensive. The women exchanged fancy goods, Teddy got more toys, Rupe and Victor were duly presented with a variety of shirts, and the afternoon dragged on.

But at last it was all over and the household returned to normal. An exciting new year began, and this was what Rupe had been waiting for with carefully concealed impatience. Victor was preparing to leave for Brisbane with Louisa and Teddy, so that he could commence discussions with their lawyers about the real ramifications of the new regulations under the Alienation of Lands Acts, and Rupe thought they would never go. As if his brother didn't exist, Victor stretched out the days, making certain everything was in order at Springfield before he left, issuing instructions to the overseers, checking his journals and stud books to see that they were up to date, checking everything down to the last blade of grass, it seemed to Rupe. But at last their luggage was packed into the spring cart and they were off!

As a courtesy, Rupe rode beside them all the way across the valley, teasing Louisa, who couldn't hide her excitement, and on into the foothills that constituted the outer boundary of Springfield. There he stopped, asking solicitously: 'Will you be all right from here?'

'Of course we will,' Victor laughed. 'And don't you go forgetting the horses. Some of the stock horses could do with a spell. Check the whole mob, I think we could do with some fresh animals. If so, see what Jock has over there.'

'You've already told me that. On your way now. And have a good time!'

Rupe watched until they were out of sight and then he wheeled his horse to head back, galloping wildly down the long sandy road. Victor was out of the way, Austin was confined to the house and now he, Rupe Broderick, was in charge. He was the boss!

In the morning he was up earlier than usual to muster the men for his own purposes. Routines were abruptly changed. Only those with urgent jobs to do were released from his plans.

'As you all know,' he told them, 'the Government has passed an Act to break up good working stations like Springfield, so it's time we did some acting ourselves. The new boundary riders are learning the lay of the land, but I want to make sure that the rest of you know exactly where Springfield begins and ends.'

Rupe knew that eventually, when all the sections of Springfield were clearly defined, some of the rougher country would be excised and there would be new boundaries to learn about, but for now, the property was intact.

He divided the men into four groups, two of them to report to the overseers of the outstations.

'Tell them they are to familiarize you with their boundaries, and from now on, no strangers are permitted to cross our land.'

One of the men was confused. 'But roads go through there, Rupe. We can't stop everyone.'

'You can and you will! The same goes for the road on through this valley. They're closed to strangers. We built those roads for our own use, and we've always allowed travellers to use them. But not any more. If the Government's so damn smart, they can build their own roads, and not through Springfield.'

'It will inconvenience a lot of people.'

'So what?' Jack Ballard said. 'This is private property. Austin has let traffic through as a favour, but no one's doing *him* any favours now. Besides, we can't spend our time working out who is a genuine traveller and who is prospecting for land, nosing about for good pastures.'

'Exactly,' Rupe nodded. 'The roads are closed, and I want you all armed, to make sure they get the message.'

'How long do we have to be out there?'

'Only for a day or so, to get to know your territories, assuming that there's nothing to stop intruders coming cross-country. After that we'll just roster enough riders to keep a constant watch on the property.'

'Why don't we block those back roads and be done with it?' Rupe was asked.

'Why not?' he grinned. 'It won't stop riders, but it'll sure stop the rest. And word will get out that Springfield doesn't provide roads or trails any more.'

He sent the third group across the river and kept the others with

159

him. 'We'll patrol the main route east. We can't block our own access into the valley, and you all know this area fairly well, so we'll just have a look around today so that you know what you're doing.'

Rupe felt very proud, riding out with a troop of armed stockmen, letting them know he meant business.

There was never a lot of traffic on the outback roads, so all was quiet for a few days. Then the trouble started. Horsemen were turned back at gunpoint; wagons were bailed up on the outskirts of the property, demanding access to proceed west; other travellers who needed to be able to cross the river at the causeway that Austin had built were turned away. Only the presence of armed men prevented fights, even though not a few of the men they were confronting were also armed, for peaceful reasons.

As the reports came in, Rupe was jubilant. 'That'll teach them,' he told Jack Ballard. 'I sent a drayload skidding back up the road myself.'

'But that was a family,' Jack worried. 'I heard they only wanted to go through to visit relations on past our river runs.'

'That's what they said. You can't trust anyone these days.' He was adamant, there would be no relaxing of his orders.

Their supply wagon came in, the driver bewildered. 'What the hell is going on?' he asked Rupe. 'They say at Cobbside that all these roads are closed, and I can tell you, they're getting very nasty about it.'

'Let them. Springfield is not a public thoroughfare. Never was.'

'But you're jamming up half the district, Rupe. Tell Austin to ease up.'

'I'll decide if there's any easing-up to be done! You let them know in Cobbside, and right on to Toowoomba, that selectors won't get a chance to eye off any of Springfield.'

'But they're not all selectors.'

Rupe stared at him. 'What did you say?'

'You heard me.'

'You said they're not all selectors. Not all. So some of them are?'

'Maybe. I dunno. Maybe they just want to compare pasturelands. To learn what to look for. Springfield has a good reputation.'

'I'll say it has, and we don't like strangers. Compare pasturelands? Do you think we're that stupid? Tell them to learn in the botanic gardens.'

Austin had to hear, of course, but not from his own men. Jock Walker rode in with some of his men and his own complaints.

He came straight to the point, unconcerned that Austin looked bleak and lonely on his side veranda. 'What the hell do you think you're doing?'

'About what?'

'Ha! You can talk now, man, can you? Just as well. About stopping access through Springfield.'

160

Austin had no idea what he was talking about, but pride wouldn't allow him to admit it. Anyway, Jock wasn't short of a word, and he soon made things clear.

'You can't keep this up, man. They're detouring through my land like bloody Brown's cows, and I don't know who's what. Bloody bad-tempered coots straying all over my place, cursing you and your roadblocks.'

'Selectors, are they?' Austin asked carefully.

'Some of them could be. How do I know? And there's folk blaming me for this flaming jam-up. No one wants to have to reroute more than fifty miles to bypass Springfield. It won't do. You put a bloody stop to it, I say.'

'Doesn't the Alienation of Lands Act bother you?'

'Of course it does, but there's no need to antagonize people.'

'Then you do it your way and I'll do it mine.'

They talked for a long time about the Act, and Austin discovered that Jock, with his large holdings, was already up to some of the same tricks, sectioning off his best land, preparing to dummy blocks, even damming and rerouting streams back into his best land. They had a good time plotting, the pair of them, over several whiskies, then Jock remembered Harry.

'He's not in the best of shapes with my son, the Judge,' Jock grinned.

Austin wasn't amused. 'Nor with me.'

When Jock had left, Austin waited angrily for Rupe.

'What's this about roadblocks?'

Rupe didn't get much chance to explain, with his father shouting at him. 'This is my property, not yours, you ingrate. Where do you get off pulling these stunts without my permission? Did you think I wouldn't find out? That I'm a bloody imbecile not fit to know what's going on in my house? You don't give any more orders round here. You send Jack Ballard to me every night, when he gets in. I don't care what time it is. Do you hear me? I'm the boss here and don't you forget it.'

But when Rupe had left, Austin grinned. Bloody little upstart, but he's on the right track. Victor's too soft. He'd never have pulled a stunt like this. I don't care what Jock does, that's his worry. But if Rupe has closed up Springfield then I'm all for it. Shut the bastards out . . .

Charlotte brought in his dinner, surprised to find him in such a genial mood, believing that Jock's visit had done him the world of good. He was still sleeping downstairs in his own wing, and even though his health had improved considerably and he could move about with the aid of a crutch, there was no mention of him returning to their own room. Their bed. She hoped she wasn't imagining this, but she had an awful feeling that he preferred to be right where he was.

★ ★ ★

161

For a week it rained, warm, welcome rain, and the greening of the wide pasturelands began again. The sluggish river, nudged by heavier flows from the catchment areas in the hills, bustled into life and soon swept by its banks with a purpose, as if it knew these torrents had to be delivered smoothly to the far reaches of its course before even heavier rains came, causing an overload – in human terms, floods.

Not that Austin would have minded minor floods, as long as the sheep were safe; like grass fires, floods were nature's bounty, rejuvenation. He sat on his veranda, smiling in childish delight. He loved rain, loved the dull thudding on the roof, loved to watch it closing in on the valley accompanied by distant rolls of thunder, satisfied that, for another year at least, it looked as if they had beaten the perennial enemy, drought.

In this sodden weather, only the rostered boundary riders were out on the job, patrolling their sections, assisted by the river which, at some crossings, had become a barrier in itself. Only hardened bushmen, who could swim their horses across, would bother with the river roads; vehicles would have to stick to the muddy tracks well away from the water. Knowing this, Rupe repositioned his men to watch the open roads, while he himself kept watch on a well-worn trail that led down to the river.

Since there had been confrontations with travellers, word was out that Springfield roads were closed, and few now ventured their way, so the men were bored, riding aimlessly, it seemed, from one vantage point to another, and out along the lonely roads. Not Rupe, though. Clad in a cowhide hat and a black oilskin cloak, he was unmindful of the rain as he actively sought out intruders. Far from being bored, he enjoyed this role, buoyed up by the knowledge that, despite his outburst, Austin approved of his decision to close off Springfield.

Finding no starters, he even rode towards Cobbside for a while, hoping to turn back wayfarers before they even approached Springfield, but he met only the mailman, who complained that his cart had been bogged twice on the muddy roads.

'Seen anyone else?' Rupe asked. 'Any strangers about?'

'Quite a few, as a matter of fact. Riders. Scouting about all over the district.' He grinned. 'And I don't think they're out to visit their grannies, Rupe. There's a lot of talk about selection rights now, and I reckon those blokes mean business.'

'So do I. They needn't bother looking in this direction.'

'Then you keep your eyes peeled. They're getting plenty of support in Cobbside and other little towns.'

'Why? What's it got to do with them?'

'Plenty. The more settlers and their families they get out here, the better the shopkeepers like it. Good for the town. Can't say as how it will suit me, though, having to detour all over the place. Next thing they'll be breaking up my run and tendering it to new chums and you know who'll come off second best? Me. I can see it coming. Progress, they say, but I say leave things be. Everything's working real good out here now. I don't see why we need change.'

Rupe sent him on his way, still grumbling. The news about more riders on the roads interested him. He turned to ride cross-country towards the straggling river roads, lost in thought.

If I knew the main accesses across Springfield station were closed, what route would I take? he asked himself.

The river. I wouldn't expect anyone to be on watch there in this weather. It's flowing well, past the old ford, but not in flood yet. Easy enough for horsemen to cross.

He put his horse to a canter through the sparse scrub, allowing it to take small creeks in its stride, at the same time thinking angrily of the townspeople of Cobbside.

'Bloody ingrates,' he growled. 'If it wasn't for big stations like Springfield, the town wouldn't exist. Now they're turning on us.'

He emerged from the scrub on to a stock route as low clouds dissolved into drizzling rain, occupying himself with the host of irritations that, lately, had beset him. There was no great hurry; his theory, of riders coming this way, was only a possibility. He doubted any of them would have the brains to figure it out.

When he came to the old ford, where a small peninsula of land jutted into the river, he dismounted and took shelter with the horse under a slab of ti-tree branches. This construction leaked; it had six bough poles to support the roof, and no sides, and was intended to give respite from the sun, not rain. But for now it would do. He undid his saddlepack, took out his lunch and began munching on thick sandwiches of corned mutton and mustard, idly surveying the river. Remembering Austin's plans to appear to break up Springfield by placing sections in family and dummy names, he was irritated by the unpleasant fact that he was nominal owner of only one section, while Victor had three, taking into account his wife and young Teddy. That still rankled. What if Austin died? He might have left the station to his two sons now, with Harry out of the way, but would Victor have a controlling interest? Rupe worried that he should have gone to Brisbane himself. Victor could be up there feathering his own nest. He'd have to watch this situation.

Rupe hadn't forgotten, either, that it would be in his interest to marry as soon as possible. He could then claim, on behalf of his wife, the section set aside for Fern Broderick. That would be a start, and a child would even up the tally. One of these days, he resolved, when Victor came back, he would have to take some time off and go a-courting. Several girls he knew came to mind, preferably from station families who would be able to provide considerable dowries. That was important. So was his sex life, which had been nonexistent, except for a couple of forays into Cobbside, since the blacks left. He missed them. Rupe grinned. Black velvet, nothing like it for a lonely man.

He lit a smoke and stood by the warmth of his horse, dreaming in the quiet of the bush of the pleasures of married life. All at once he thought he heard something. He walked out on to the road that came to a stop at the river and then, throwing down the cigarette, rushed back and swung on to his horse. The sound was unmistakable: the thud of hooves on the heavy track.

Rupe pulled his rifle from its holster, loaded it and rode out on to the rim of the sandy bank, squarely facing the road, waiting for riders to come over the hill. He was pleased with himself. They'd get sent back with a flea in their ears just like the rest. Friendly folk wouldn't be coming this way. This lot were in for a real surprise if they thought they could snoop around the Broderick property as they pleased.

Then he saw them. Two riders came into view, their horses plodding steadily down the slope. The rain had eased to a fine mist but they still had their hats pulled down over bearded faces, and the collars of their rough jackets up around their ears. Even from that distance, though, Rupe could see rifles slung by their saddles, so he lifted his gun, resting it in front of him as a warning. Then another rider appeared, moving a little faster to keep up. This one wasn't a bushman like the other two, and the figure seemed younger, clean-shaven. His hat was new and natty, and the coat was tailored.

'Who might you be?' The first of the trio, noting Rupe's stance, didn't bother with a greeting. This was a challenge, and Rupe was suddenly uneasy, but he managed to keep his voice firm.

'Rupe Broderick. You're on our property. Springfield station.'

'So what?'

'So you'll have to turn back.'

'Grow up, sonny. We've come this way many a time.'

'I don't know you.'

'Then we're quits. We don't know you either.'

Rupe, backing down just a little, nodded towards the river. 'You can't cross here. It's too deep now.'

'Let us worry about that, mate.' The other bearded man had nothing to say; he just sat his horse, grinning at Rupe. Annoying him.

'What's your business here?' he asked angrily.

'Whatever it is, it's none of yours.' The man turned back and yelled to the third rider. 'Come on, Charlie. This is where you get your boots wet.'

The one called Charlie joined them. He seemed very nervous. A townie, Rupe thought, noticing the expensive high boots which were probably the butt of jokes with this pair of bushies. Too fancy for this country in this weather.

'Excuse me,' he said, moving past the other two, 'I am Charles Todman. We don't want any trouble. What right have you got to be barring our way?'

164

'He's the boss's son,' the other man laughed.

'Exactly. And you are trespassing.'

'It is not trespassing to be using common routes.'

'Then why aren't you using the more common routes?' Rupe crowed. 'Any fool would know the river is up. Why are you sneaking about out this way?'

He saw Charlie's eyes flicker for a second before he responded: 'Because we need to go in this direction. The other roads are miles out of our way.'

'Is that so? Why do you need to go in this direction? Who are you anyway, Mr Charles Todman?' Rupe looked again at the odd trio, and suddenly knew for a certainty that he'd caught a real fish, not just snags this time. 'It's my bet you're a surveyor, and this pair are just your offsiders.'

'Half right, mate,' the big bearded man grinned. 'This here's our boss,' he indicated the other rider, who seemed content just to observe proceedings, 'and he's come a long way from the north to take a look at the countryside. You wouldn't want to disappoint him, would you?'

'This is private property. Look somewhere else.' Rupe raised his rifle, pointing at the spokesman, because Todman wasn't armed. 'I'm ordering you to turn back. You're trespassing.'

He shifted his gaze to the boss, to appeal to him, and then he quaked. Rupe found himself looking into hard, mean eyes. This man would have been about forty. His skin was heavily tanned and the clipped fair beard jutted like an extension of his jaw. Resisting a need to swallow, Rupe stood his ground. 'I don't want any trouble. I'm just asking you to turn back.'

'If you don't want any trouble,' the boss drawled, 'then you'll put down that popgun.'

Rupe reacted quickly. He fired a shot into the ground and the horses reared, swerving away.

'You're crazy!' Todman screamed. 'Get out of the way, you damned fool.'

The boss was still calm. 'You lookin' for a gunfight, son? You're outnumbered, you know.'

Bravado pushed Rupe on. 'I'll shoot the first one that tries to cross.'

'Jesus!' the stranger sighed, turning his horse away, and Rupe felt a surge of excitement. He'd won. They knew as well as he did that the crossing wasn't worth killing for.

Then he heard the shot.

It came from the nearby bush. In that split second he cringed, expecting to be hit. His horse stiffened, shuddered and began to crumple beneath him.

Rupe, confused, leapt clear, losing his grip on his rifle. As he turned back, in horror, to see his horse roll over with a scream, he saw, from the corner of his eye, another rider emerging from the bush.

One of them scooped up his rifle, but Rupe didn't care. He ran at the rider, shouting at him, 'You bastard! You shot my horse. You bastard!'

But the man shoved him aside with his boot. 'Count yourself lucky it wasn't you.'

They were heading for the river, and there was nothing he could do to stop them.

The big man was yelling at Todman: 'Get off the horse, dopey! You can't ride him across, the saddle will slip. Hang on to him. He can swim better than you!'

As they plunged into the stream, Rupe screamed abuse at them, threatening Todman, the only name he knew, with the law.

'You'll pay for killing my horse, you bastards! You'll pay!'

Not one of them looked back. They were busy manoeuvring themselves across the currents. Rupe hoped they would drown. Todman was struggling, shouting to the others for help, but they kept going, their horses swimming strongly.

Gleefully, Rupe watched as Todman lost his grip on the bridle and slipped back behind his horse. He willed the animal to swim faster, away from the man, leaving him to fend for himself, but he was denied that vengeance. Somehow Todman managed to strike out, grabbing the horse's tail and clinging on.

From the far side, one of the men turned his horse and re-entered the river to help the surveyor make it to safety.

Rupe looked back at his dead animal, already a target for a mass of flies, and dropped, stunned, to the river bank.

They'd shot his horse. He couldn't believe anyone would do such a thing. He recoiled from remembering the grim jokes of weeks back, when one of his own men had suggested doing the same thing to intruders' mounts. Such an act hadn't seemed real then, just all talk. Bravado again. He was so shocked he felt like weeping, anger and frustration building.

The men had disappeared, free to roam the huge property at will. He couldn't see what direction they had taken, and anyway, what difference would it make? By the time he alerted his own men the intruders would be well on their way. Rupe had no doubt that the surveyor would have a district map of Springfield and, riding inland from the river, wouldn't waste any time in spotting billabongs and waterholes, essential for any claims.

'It won't do you any good!' he shouted into the distance. 'We'll have them all tied up!'

But would they? He'd been so set on his brilliant plan to keep out strangers, needing to lead the men himself, that he hadn't continued with the work that he and Victor had undertaken, blazing trees and identifying landmarks to apportion all those sections of the property. And Victor would be back any day.

166

He'd better get back to the homestead. And fast.

Then it hit him! He'd have to walk. He was a long way from home. He wouldn't make it before nightfall.

Sadly he stared at the horse. It had been a good stock horse, that fellow. Cursing, he dragged leafy branches from the scrub to make some attempt to cover the poor thing, found his rifle in the bush where one of the men had thrown it, after unloading it, and strode into the bush, away from the winding river. It meandered on to eventually pass the homestead, but it was quicker to head across country.

Those men had made a damn fool of him, but back home there would be such outrage at the killing of his horse, they'd forget that Rupe himself had failed to keep strangers out. Anyway, he could change the story a bit, tell them he'd been bushwhacked. That the horse had been shot from under him while he was riding along by the river.

Only now did he recognize the futility of trying to bail up three men, let alone four. What would he have done if they'd decided to ignore him? Shot one of their horses? Shot one of them?

He doubted it, and the thought made him cringe.

It was just unfortunate that they were such rotten bastards, he told himself, because otherwise he'd have been forced to let them pass.

Maybe he could still find them tomorrow, with blacktrackers.

What blacktrackers? Rupe tramped on furiously. The blacks had gone. He'd have to bring one in, and that would take more time.

What a bloody mess he'd made of things! Austin would be furious over the horse, and he'd be blamed.

'Yes,' he said, shoving heavy bush aside, 'I'll get the blame, you can bet on that. Austin's big on blame. I'll never hear the end of this.'

'Bushwhacked? *You* were? While you were supposed to be on guard? While you were asleep, more like it! And they shot your horse? Tell me another.'

Austin's speech was only slightly slurred these days, but there was nothing wrong with the volume. As the expected tirade continued, Rupe responded angrily, when he could get a word in. He wished that the stroke his father had suffered had been more severe, leaving him with no power of speech, because then there'd be some peace in the house.

To make matters worse, Victor had arrived home late that afternoon. Now he was getting an earful of this and was already interfering.

'If they bushwhacked you, how did you know that bloke was a surveyor?'

'I guessed he was. He was dressed better than the other three,' Rupe gulped. He'd almost blurted out the surveyor's name.

'They shoot your horse and you calmly let them cross the river?' Austin snarled.

'Would you rather I let them shoot me?'

'They shot your bloody horse, you fool. That's still a crime in this country. You could have fired on them from cover.'

Victor intervened again. 'Am I missing something here? What were you doing out there in the first place? And why would they bushwhack you and calmly ride away? Why *were* you there?'

Rupe began to explain the necessity to patrol the boundaries, and Victor gaped. 'Are you out of your mind?'

'Didn't you see anyone on the road coming in?' Austin asked Victor.

'Yes, a couple of stockmen gave us a wave. Don't tell me they were guarding that road too?'

'Well then, they were doing their job,' Austin said, pleased. 'At least someone was,' he added, glaring at Rupe.

'They were not doing their jobs hanging about out there. They are stockmen, they've got work to do.' Victor was incensed.

'This is a turnabout,' Rupe accused him. 'You were all for protecting Springfield from intruders, so what are you complaining about?'

'Not like this,' Victor snapped. 'You'd need an army. A couple of extra boundary riders wouldn't be out of place, given other jobs at the same time, but I only meant for all the rest of the men to be on the alert, to watch out.'

'No you didn't, you were as keen as we were.'

'I didn't have time to think it through,' he admitted. 'But you've shown by your bloody stupidity that it won't work. Has there been trouble anywhere else?'

'Only a few arguments on the roads. They're closed. Dad wanted them closed too, so don't go picking on me.' Rupe was beginning to squeeze himself out of trouble. 'Anyway, how did you get on with the legal johnnies?'

'They agree. Now that the law is passed we have to resort to splitting ownership here. Have you finished those maps? They're going to lodge our claims for us so that they're all legal, and work out just how much we can afford to freehold for a start.'

'I haven't had time,' Rupe muttered.

'That figures! You're bloody hopeless, Rupe.' Victor turned to Austin. 'Aside from all that, the news isn't good. When I can get Rupe to do something constructive for a change, we'll finish the maps. The lawyers will lodge all the claims together and then they'll start stalling. The Lands Office won't accept every one of them without bickering about size and position, so our lawyers will spin it out by doing plenty of arguing themselves, but the bottom line is we'll have to start paying.'

'But we're dummying lots, *we* won't have to pay for them!' Austin was appalled.

Rupe realized that his father still couldn't see the gravity of the situation. He still thought he could run roughshod over any rules that applied to his property.

'They will all have to be paid for,' Victor said quietly. 'Sooner or later; much later, I hope. The Lands Office will be swamped so it could take years, but even the dummy claims . . . someone has to pay for freeholding them. There's no way out of it. I suggest we pay for the homestead land first, to give the impression we're eager to settle.'

Austin slumped back in his armchair. 'Sack those bloody lawyers. They don't know what they're talking about.' But they could see his heart wasn't in it. He looked pale and tired.

Victor shook his head. 'No point.'

'They know, don't they?' Austin asked wearily. 'This surveyor fellow that Rupe says he saw, and all the rest of the vultures, they know we can't afford to freehold all of Springfield.'

'Not hard to figure it out,' Victor agreed.

'Then we're ruined.'

'No. We'll hang on.'

Austin glared at Rupe. 'You should have shot the bastards!'

After all that, worn out from his long trudge back to the homestead, Rupe had to face his mother, who rounded on him for upsetting Austin.

'You don't seem to care about your father at all. He's not well, can't you remember that? He looks terrible. You didn't have to tell him about the horse, did you? Couldn't you have let that pass? Deal with it yourself, don't come back to him with tales.'

'I will deal with it,' he retorted. 'And he only looks pale because you've got him penned in that damn room. You should let him get out more. He could sit a horse if you'd stop treating him like a cripple.'

'How dare you speak to me like that?'

'Somebody has to. Now leave me alone!'

From Rupe's point of view there was only one bright light on the horizon. Victor and Louisa had brought a young woman back with them, Teddy's governess.

'She'll be down shortly, so you be nice to her,' Louisa told Rupe the next morning. 'God knows what she must think of us, what with you men shouting and arguing last night, and Charlotte charging about in a foul mood.'

'I'll be nice to her. But who is she?'

'Cleo Murray. Her father owns big sugar farms up north . . .'

'They're called plantations.'

'Whatever. She has excellent references, especially from her school . . .'

'Halleville College for Young Ladies?'

'You know her?'

'Met her a couple of times at house parties in Brisbane.'

169

'Good. Listen, Rupe, before Victor comes in. How *did* your horse get shot?'

'Cripes! Don't you start.' He drank his tea, grabbed a slice of toast and headed for Victor's office to make a start on the maps.

Cleo Murray. He didn't actually know her, but she'd been a boarder at Halleville at the same time as he was boarding at Grammar, and he'd come across her occasionally at socials. She was a shy girl, rather plain if he recalled, more spoken of than spoken to, because it was said her old man had pots of money. He'd heard later that he had taken her on the Grand Tour of Europe, and it was said, rather spitefully, that he'd hoped to marry her off to an acceptable title.

Rupe grinned. Obviously that hadn't worked.

He found the mapwork dreary, now that they were concentrating on the outer sections of the property, sections that they'd probably lose anyway, so he simply agreed with everything that Victor suggested to get it over and done with. Later, when he saw Miss Murray walking by the side of the house, he made some excuse and hurried out to catch up with her.

'Good morning, Miss Murray. I'm Rupe. Remember me?'

She turned to him with a smile. 'Why, Rupe. Of course I do. How nice to see you again.'

As he made small talk with her, welcoming her to Springfield, he studied the governess. She was still quite plain, with straight dark hair tied back with a black bow, a sallow complexion and pale eyes, but she was no longer shy. The eyes were cool and direct, and the over-wide mouth was now her best feature, because those lips were full, and very inviting. He smiled, recognizing real possibilities here. Cleo was a good catch, and he already had a head start. It was obvious that she was happy to see him, delighted with Teddy, and thrilled to be at Springfield.

'I hope I can do Teddy justice,' she was saying. 'He's such a dear little boy and really keen to start his lessons.'

'You'll be fine. From what I recall you were always quite the scholar.'

'How nice of you to say that.'

He walked her round to the new schoolroom, where Louisa, with Teddy's excited assistance, was unpacking boxes of children's books and other such paraphernalia in front of a new blackboard. Rupe would have stayed to join in the fun had he not remembered that Victor was waiting for him.

Why bother searching further afield for a wife? he asked himself. Here was one for the taking. And Cleo liked him, that had already been established. But he'd have to go very quietly, not appear interested, not for a while, anyway . . .

Austin had not forgotten about the horse. He was still angry, and insisted that Rupe lodge a complaint with the police sergeant in Cobbside.

'I'll write a report this afternoon and send it in,' Rupe told him.

'No you won't. You'll go into Cobbside tomorrow and see what else you can find out about those bastards. I want them charged.'

Pity Cleo had only been at Springfield for a couple of days, Rupe mused as rode towards Cobbside. This would have been a nice day out for her. They couldn't expect the governess to be chained to the place. He wondered if the lessons only took place on weekdays, and what Cleo would be expected to do at weekends. Sundays were dead days on the station; maybe he could take her riding. After a reasonable interval, of course. Wait for her to find out how boring the place was.

'Especially after Europe,' he laughed.

Most stations had governesses for the young children. In some cases tutors were employed, but Louisa had insisted on a female teacher for Teddy. Probably because she needed company herself, he mused. She and Charlotte weren't exactly bosom pals. He hoped Cleo played tennis; that would please Teddy's mother. A handy partner at last.

Then again, Rupe worried, a lot of the young women who went out to the stations as governesses didn't last the distance. They found their new homes too lonely, too quiet, too far from the city lights, in fact too boring, and they soon quit. He hoped Cleo would stay on.

'As a matter of fact,' he announced, talking to his horse, 'we'll have to see that she doesn't get lonely, won't we? I'll have to find her a pretty little horse for her own use, and if she doesn't ride, I'll teach her.'

This time, Rupe was riding his own horse, a fast thoroughbred that would cover the distance to Cobbside easily, instead of the stock horses he used at home. Nevertheless, the death of that good animal still hurt. He'd be watching for those men from now on. For ever, he thought furiously.

He turned on to the deserted sandy road, riding into the sun, pleased to see the bush was beginning to glow again, gum tips looking sprightly, delicate red and orange blossoms peeping out from the fragile greenery, all with the compliments of the recent rain. Overhead a party of brolgas sailed past, their long necks and legs extended, trumpeting their presence, and he saluted them, knowing they were returning to their mating grounds by the river at Springfield. They came every year, these tall, stately birds, to perform their courting dances with bows and leaps and high steps, and no one at Springfield would ever dream of disturbing them. It was considered a great honour to be able to sneak over and watch them.

Sourly, Rupe remembered that he'd had a pet brolga when he was a boy. The lovely grey bird was only a youngster when Austin found him, injured and malnourished, and nursed him back to health, but by then the bird had decided that this was home and made no attempt

171

to leave, although his shallow wings had recovered. Rupe claimed the bird, called him Brolly, delighted to find that Brolly followed him about, tamer even than his pet magpies. He'd only had the bird for a year before disaster struck. A boy called Luke had been visiting Springfield, and when Brolly had come flapping towards him, Luke, a city kid, had thrown a stone at him, breaking his spindly leg. The bird had to be put down.

Rupe had been so angry, he took to that kid and really whipped him, but then Austin had given his son a belting too. It was no consolation for young Rupe Broderick to hear his father's explanation: 'If you want to fight, son, you fight with your fists. You don't use a riding whip. That lad didn't stand a chance.'

Bad luck, Rupe thought. He was still glad he'd drawn blood.

He had no conscience at all in telling his tale to Sergeant Perkins in Cobbside, in whipping up outrage at the killing of his horse, and the crime was duly entered on the books to be investigated.

'They say Springfield is out of bounds these days, Rupe.'

'Any wonder, with bastards like this roving about?'

'What do you think they were up to?'

'You tell me. Snooping to select on our land, or sheep stealers? We've got a lot of valuable merinos in our stud. The horse was bad enough, but if any of our stud sheep go missing there'll be hell to pay.'

'Lot of strangers about these days,' the sergeant said moodily. 'I don't know what the world's coming to. How's your dad?'

'Fighting fit again now, and very savage about the horse. You know Austin, he won't let a crime like that pass.'

'No. I'm real sorry about this, Rupe. Say hello to your dad for me. I'll come out and have a pint with him, next time I'm out your way.'

That done, Rupe headed for the pub, mildly irritated by the cheerful ambience of the village. Cobbside now had a new bank, a draper's shop, a bicycle shop, of all things, and further down, an office of some sort. As he strode along under the new awnings, checking these signs of progress, he spotted the white print on the office window: E.G. TODMAN & SON. SURVEYORS.

He forgot that his story had changed a little. He forgot that he hadn't mentioned in his report to the police 'guessing' that there was a surveyor with the bushwhackers, to make his story more feasible. It sounded better to say he'd been ambushed by strangers who'd high-tailed it across the river on to his land. The interrogation he'd suffered at the hands of Austin and Victor, who were still suspicious, had taught him that. The police sergeant had swallowed it whole.

And now he was standing in front of Todman's office!

Without giving the matter another thought, Rupe barged in, to be met by a middle-aged gent wearing a striped shirt and bow tie and a clipped moustache.

'What can I do for you, sir?' the gent asked.

Rupe looked at his cheap clothes, his almost bare office, and took him for a spiv of the first order.

'Where's Todman son? Charlie Todman?'

'You mean Charles?' The voice was as oily as its owner. 'He's not here at the minute. Can I help you? Maybe you're interested in taking up some land round here? I'm a land agent too, you see, it's there on the door.'

Everyone in the district knew who the Brodericks were. Ever since he'd left his horse at the police station, to walk into the town, people had bade him 'G'day, Rupe.' But not this fellow, and Rupe was further incensed.

'You've got a bloke from up north wanting to buy land here.' It wasn't a question, it was a statement.

He saw the watery eyes waver and heard the lie. 'I dunno about that, mate. Who would that be? What did you say your name was?'

'Where's Charlie?' Enraged now, Rupe considered smashing the place up, but he saw a neat jacket hung over a chair and another on a hook on the wall, and knew the owner of one of those townie coats couldn't be far away.

Leaving the office abruptly, he loitered about the bicycle shop, feigning interest in the machines by the door, until he saw Charlie Todman coming up the street.

When he stepped out, confronting the surveyor, Todman was surprised, but he recovered quickly. Too quickly, Rupe thought.

'Excuse me, sir. Would you move aside, please?'

'Don't you remember me, Charlie?' Rupe asked, pleased that he was a lot taller than this bastard.

'No, I'm afraid I don't.'

'You should. Your mates shot my horse.'

'I don't know what you're talking about. Step aside, please.'

'Where are your mates? The boss from up north and his trigger-happy offsiders? The ones you took on to my land. On to Springfield?'

Rupe had intended to collar this character, drag him up to the police station, charge him over the horse and make him give up the names of his mates, but when Todman shrugged and grinned at him with: 'You're mistaken, sir. I've never set foot on Springfield, wherever that is,' Rupe lost his temper. The horse, the humiliation, the long trek home and his subsequent attempts at explanations caused him to explode. He grabbed the nearest weapon, a lump of lead piping, and slammed into Todman with it, enjoying his revenge, until people in the street dragged the surveyor away from him.

'I don't care, he was worth it,' he told the sergeant as he was led into the lock-up.'

'But you said you didn't know any of them.'

'I recognized him, that's all. He was one of them.'

173

'But he never carries a gun. He couldn't have shot your horse.'

'One of his mates did.'

'What mates? He says he was never anywhere near Springfield. You must have got him mixed up with someone else.'

'No I didn't.'

The sergeant scratched his head. 'Well, I dunno. You broke his arm in two places. They're charging you with assault and battery. You'll have to stay here until I get in touch with Victor.'

'That's great! Bloody marvellous! They kill my horse and I'm the one gets locked up.'

'Yeah, well, you Brodericks had better learn you're not the law round here any more.'

'And you'd better start doing your job. Those bushwhackers must have been in this town. If you kept out of the pub you might have noticed them. Time we got some real police here, not a boozer like you.'

'Do you know your trouble, Rupe?' the sergeant drawled. 'You're too big for your bloody boots. One of these days you'll find they don't fit. I'll stable your horse; you stay there and cool off.'

Chapter Seven

They found Minnie face down in the mud by the lake, clutching a dilly bag of her few possessions with a garland of rusting white frangipani round her neck. The white flowers denoted her passage from life in gentle transition, but her discoloured, bloated body spoke otherwise, and Nioka was distraught. She blamed herself for failing to take more care of her dear sister, for being too immersed in her new love, for her selfishness; and no one could console her. She was shocked beyond belief that her mother and her sister did not exist any more. They did not exist. She wept for them, knowing it was useless, but she still wept, tearing at her breasts just as Minnie had done despairing for her lost son.

Nioka's days were full of pain. She spurned her lover, rounding on him with a fury that astonished him. She waded, swam, far into the lake, crying out to the spirits who had watched her sister destroy herself, cursing them for not delivering her back to shore sooner. For deep underneath there was another pain, a cruel, menacing pain that told her this was the children's revenge. Those three babies would never forgive their mothers for forsaking them. That was where the fault lay. She went in search of Doombie's mother and berated her, screaming abuse at her until Gabbidgee had to intervene, begging her not to make their suffering any worse, for every day in his life, poor Gabbidgee grieved for his son.

There was talk at the lake that Nioka was going the same way as her sister, another mad woman, and the elders were called in to cast spells that would relieve her crying, but nothing worked, and one day they realized that Nioka had gone from them, just like Minnie. Maybe drowned in the big lake or, more likely, dead out there in the deep forests.

Keening, they searched the shores and the forests, calling on the birds of the air and the nocturnal creatures of the bush to give a sign, but they would not. The disappearance of Nioka became a mystery to the tribal people and heartbreak for her lover, who, in desperation, requested the elders to send for the awesome magic man, Moobuluk, who was known to be her kin.

In his sleep, Bobburah, known as Bobbo, witnessed his mother's passing. He saw it as beautiful, as she had intended; he saw her sleeping

175

in the gentle waves, smiling at him, fragrant flowers floating by her long dark hair, and he heard her call his name, so sweetly . . . 'Bobburah. Oh, my Bobburah,' and in the beauty of it he forgave her for letting the whites take him. He saw her lovely brown eyes and through them he saw, too, her kitchen, the familiar kitchen, and the veranda outside where he'd often played with Teddy. And the big men with their horses, and the silly woolly sheep. He smiled. Those silly woolly sheep with their soft, burrowing heads and their sweet lambs, nuzzling into buckets of milk. Spilling. Guzzling. No one to boss or bully them. Dear, happy times. Where was that?

His mother closed her eyes, she was very sleepy, but when he asked that question she opened them again, surprised that he should ask.

'Springfield,' she said. Clearly. 'Springfield.'

And then she drifted away, contented, into the Dreaming.

Bobbo awoke with a jolt, with the word 'Springfield' on his lips. Shivering with cold, he joined the ragged groups of boys delegated to mop and clean their sheds before assembly outside in the hard bitumen yard for roll call and morning hymns. He trudged into breakfast, slopping down the thin porridge, and waited in line for his basket. This was hard work for a seven-year-old, but there was no point in giving coloured boys like Bobbo lessons, so he worked in the vegetable garden. The orphanage had acquired an extra block of land and it had to be made ready for planting.

On this day Bobbo didn't mind being led out with other boys to the field, where they toiled, clearing the soil of rocks and stones, because this field wasn't fenced. It was outside the walls of the orphanage. When he had enough stones to fill his shallow basket, he lugged it up to the steadily growing heap where other boys were dumping their collections, and then dragged it round to the other side. He got rid of his stones and the basket, and, hidden by the rocky mound, if only for a short while, walked away.

Bobbo didn't run, he walked quietly towards a lane that bordered the rear of the paddock, but once free, he broke into a sprint, diving into the first yard he came to, rushing across it to scale a low fence. From then on he felt he was flying. He zigzagged through private properties, ducking under wire fences, hurtling over timber ones, on and on, crossing a road and running down it as fast as his dark little legs would carry him. Then he flashed into another lane, cobbled this time, racing, racing away from the bosses. He ran for hours until he found shelter in an overgrown orchard, helping himself to a couple of grub-ridden apples. To Bobbo they were delicious, the best food in the whole world, so he sucked and sucked on the cores, while he waited.

He watched the sun move across the trees, watched as it moved to the west, away from this big town, because he believed the sun would take him home, take him back to the country. Then, with a determined sigh, he was on his feet, hurrying away, trudging towards the afternoon sun.

That night he slept in some scrub by a road. In the morning he found himself crossing farmland, so he walked boldly up to the house and banged on the back door.

A woman opened it and stared at him. 'Who are you?'

'You got somethin' for me to eat, please, missus?' he asked.

Taken aback, she gaped at the ragged little figure. 'Where are your people?'

He pointed. 'They gone on down the road. You got jus' a little bit for me?'

The woman laughed. 'Oh, all right, but don't you be hanging about here, and don't touch anything. Wait a minute.' She came back with a honey sandwich, neatly cut in half.

'Here you are.'

His brown eyes lit up in delight. 'Tank you, missus. Tank you.'

'Goodoh, now scat! Off you go!'

He wolfed down the sandwich as he ran, convinced he was on his way home and aware now of how to find food, remembering that kitchen door at Springfield where his mother had worked before she went to the Dreaming.

Doombie was still with Matron, feeling better these days, and content to be her little boy, to belong to this kindly woman. They both looked forward to the weekends when Buster came for Sunday dinner with news of the goings-on at the workhouse.

'There's no money to fix it up,' he told his sister, 'so it looks as if it'll be closed down. They reckon the whole building is gonna be pulled down.'

'Best thing that could happen to it,' she sniffed.

'Yeah, but what about me? I'll lose me job.'

'Never mind, you can come here. There are new houses going up round here all the time. Getting quite suburban, it is. And I've been asking about. No shortage of odd jobs for a man like you.' She smiled. 'And no shortage of young families here either. I'm becoming accepted as a responsible midwife.'

'So you should,' Buster said proudly. 'Not too many real good nurses out this way, I bet.'

Mrs Adam Smith was upset at having the black boy in her house now that she was pregnant. That had come as a shock; the doctors had told her she couldn't get pregnant, and here she was three months along. But at least it had forced Adam to make a decision. 'We can't bring our child up with a black kid. What if it's a girl?' he worried.

'Boy or girl, it wouldn't make any difference, Adam. It is just not appropriate. He'll have to go.'

'Yes. I'll see what I can do.'

His enquiries led him to discover that there was a new reserve for blacks out past Ipswich, on the road to Toowoomba. Quite a large reserve, to hold black families who were being rounded up from various districts.

'An ideal place for them,' he told his wife, 'and I'm assured that any of the black women there would be happy to take Jack. He'll be better off with his own people anyway.'

But Cook was sorry for him. She packed all his clothes in a smart new suitcase, after dressing him in his best little sailor suit with its white straw hat, insisting that he wore his good shoes and socks. She gave him a basket with Devon sausage, fruit cake, biscuits and bananas, and pressed two pennies into his hand with a kiss.

Jagga was thrilled. He thought he was being taken back to Bobbo and Doombie, having forgotten that Bobbo had left before he did. He took the suitcase for granted but was delighted to be the owner of the picnic food, so he hung on to that as the pretty lady patted him farewell and helped him into the gig beside Mr Smith.

It was a long journey over the river and out into the country, so he was soon curled up in a rug under the seat, dozing happily. They stopped at a big town and the little man was fussed over in a café when he sat up sturdily to have a meal with Mr Smith, displaying the nice manners the lady had taught him. He could see that Mr Smith was pleased with him: he smiled and joked all the time, and even bought him a strawberry ice.

They set off again on this great day, out on a long, flat, sandy road, and Jagga sniffed the air. Somehow this road smelled familiar.

'We goin' home?' he asked suddenly.

'Yes. I'm taking you where there are plenty of boys and girls just like you. You'll have lots of playmates.'

'Real home?'

'That's right.'

But they stopped at a very strange place. A big gate and a lot of huts and plenty of people walking about, but not his people. Jagga was frightened.

'This not my place.'

'Yes it is, these are your people.'

Jagga clutched at him. 'No fear. I don't know dem.' Having no concept of skin colour, Jagga saw only strangers, and he had to be dragged down from the gig.

'He doesn't look like an orphan.' The administrator peered at the black boy dressed up like a doll.

'We've been looking after him,' Smith explained. 'But I'm advised he will be better off here.'

'Yeah, I guess so. What's his name?'

'Jack. He's a good little boy. An extremely well-behaved child.'

178

'If you say so, mate. Leave him with me.'

Mr Adam Smith, his duty done, was only too pleased to release his charge into the care of another public servant. He was looking forward to breaking the journey home with an overnight stay at an Ipswich hotel. It was Saturday, and he'd heard that the Ipswich Playhouse had an excellent vaudeville show running. Mrs Smith abhorred vaudeville, but Adam loved it. This was a chance not to be missed.

He patted the cringing child on the head, told him to be good, and vanished.

'Now what am I gonna do with you?' the administrator asked Jagga, much as Buster had asked the three waifs.

He stuck his head out of the window and spotted a large Aborigine woman sitting cross-legged in the dust beside a hut.

'Hey, Maggie. Get over here! Come and see what I've got.'

She climbed to her feet with an agility that defied her size and strode over. 'What you want, Mr Jim?'

He left the kid inside and brought out his basket. 'Take a look in there. Real good tucker.'

She opened the basket and grinned. 'This tucker for me?'

'Yes. But the owner goes with it.'

'Who the owner?'

As soon as she saw the child quivering behind a desk, her heart went out to him. 'Ah, dear little feller! And all pretty too. Where his mumma?'

'He's an orphan and his name's Jack.'

Without a moment's hesitation she scooped him up and held him close. 'Poor little chap. Got no mumma. Doan you worry. Maggie, she take care of you. One more kid doan matter.' She plumped him on to her wide hip. 'That your tuckerbox there, Jack? We take it wid us.'

'You can take his suitcase too,' Mr Jim told her. 'For an orphan he's well set up.'

Having disposed of the kid, Mr Jim went back to his easy chair on the narrow front veranda to read his paper. He didn't bother to enter Jack in the records. As Maggie had said, another kid didn't matter. Here, there was a mix of tribes and clans from all over the place, and trying to sort out family names was beyond him. They were hard enough to spell, let alone keep in any order.

It was Doombie's father, Gabbidgee, who insisted that Nioka was not dead.

'She's not like her sister,' he said. 'She's a strong woman. A warrior woman. She has just run off.'

He wanted to continue the search for her but his wife became angry. 'Why are you making such a fuss over that woman? Have you

179

got eyes for her? Don't lie to me. Now you want to go off searching for her. She has always been trouble. You bring her to this humpy and I'll kill you.'

So Gabbidgee waited until Moobuluk came, respectfully remaining in the background as the traditional welcomes for this awesome magic man were observed, listening to the elders as they gently broke the news that two women of his kin had died.

He even joined in the renewed mourning led by Moobuluk, for indeed Minnie was dead. But only Minnie.

Eventually he managed to seat himself behind Moobuluk at his campfire and whispered to him, 'The woman Nioka is not dead.'

For an instant Moobuluk was shocked. It was taboo to mention the dead woman's name.

He turned and glared at Gabbidgee. 'What is this you say?'

'Forgive me, old man. Forgive me,' Gabbidgee stammered. 'But she is not dead.'

'How can this be? I have spoken with her elders. They should know. Death has been here, the spirits are satisfied. Why do you take on so? This is a cruel thing to say to me.'

'I am not satisfied.' Gabbidgee was astonished at his rudeness but he pushed bravely on. 'You are wrong, old man, you spoke only to the spirits of one sister.'

Moobuluk's eyes misted. He was hurt by this tragedy, feeling he had failed his kin. He'd been sure they'd be safe here but other elements had intervened.

'I'm sorry,' Gabbidgee mumbled. 'I should not have said that to you.'

'It is possible for me to be wrong, my brother. But no one would lie to me. Why do you say otherwise?'

He listened without interruption to Gabbidgee's story of the dead woman's despair and her sister's reaction.

'At first she did despair too, but I saw her despair turn to rage. Over the lost sister, over the lost children. Nioka is not dead.'

'Then where is she? Her lover grieves. Would she leave him of her own accord? I believe she loved him dearly.'

'That is truly said. But Nioka raged. I think she has gone back for the children.'

'But they are not there at the old camp, nor anywhere near the Broderick house. If they were, Spinner would have sent me the message and I'd have come quickly to this lake. Both of the sisters knew that. They knew I would not let the matter rest.'

'Maybe she thought Spinner would forget.'

'He would not dare.'

Gabbidgee shuddered. That was true. Spinner would not dare. If the children were back they'd all know by this. For Spinner to forget his duty to a man like this would be absolute madness. To have

180

Moobuluk, of all people, take umbrage and point the bone would mean certain death.

'No,' he admitted. 'The children are not there. But I still think Nioka has gone home, and I will not be released from that belief until she or her remains are found.'

The old man looked down at his three-legged dog and nudged it with his foot. 'It seems we must go back and see for ourselves, otherwise Gabbidgee shall have no rest.'

'Do you want me to come with you?'

'No. I don't think your wife would approve. But if you are right, I will have cause to thank you for returning one of our girls to me.'

Sometime during the night, Moobuluk drifted away.

'Rupe is where?' Louisa was appalled. Jail! No one she knew had ever been to jail, had ever been near a jail.

Her husband pulled a pair of polished riding boots from a cupboard and reached for a clean shirt. 'I told you, he's in jail. He got into fight, by the sound of things.'

'How do you know?'

'A stockman on his way to Jock's place stopped by to tell me. I have to go to town and bail him out.'

'I can't believe this. Are you people determined to embarrass me? What on earth will Cleo think of us? Nothing but rows and arguments since she got here, and now Rupe's in jail like a common criminal and it doesn't seem to bother you at all.'

Victor hauled on his shirt. 'Of course it bothers me. It bloody infuriates me. I don't know what the idiot has got himself into this time, and I've got better things to do than having to trail into town and get him out.'

'You ought to leave him there!'

'Don't be ridiculous. That will only start more talk. Anyway, Austin wants him home, now!'

'Austin! I'm sick of hearing that man's name. And if I hear his raised voice again I'm going in there myself to tell him to shut up.'

Victor grinned. 'You do that! I don't care. We should have stayed in town longer. We'll know better next time.' He kissed her on the cheek. 'Cheer up. It can't get any worse.'

'I wouldn't bet on it. What happens when your sainted brother gets home? There'll be more eruptions.'

'That might be a good time for you to take on Austin,' he laughed. 'Or get Cleo out of earshot.'

'You think I'm joking, don't you? Well, I'm not!'

By the time he rode into Cobbside, Victor was hot and thirsty and far from amused. He was hungry too, having left home before lunch, so he decided to let Rupe stew in jail for a bit longer. The pub looked more inviting than the local lock-up.

181

As soon as he walked into the bar he was greeted by some station hands from Jock's property.

'Come to bail out Rupe?' they laughed. 'Bring him back here for a drink and we'll celebrate.'

'Celebrate what?'

'Rupe making his mark! He's a hero.'

Victor shook his head. 'You've lost me. I haven't found out what happened yet.' He called the bartender to bring him a pint, and decided it might be better to hear the story from these men than from Rupe, whose versions of things were never all that reliable. Like the story of the ambush, which Victor hadn't believed for one minute.

'What went on here anyway? Was there a brawl?'

'No.' The spokesman was Bert Fleming, who'd been in the district for years. 'I saw it meself. Rupe had some sort of an argument with one of the new surveyors, Charlie Todman . . .'

'He says his name is Charles,' one of the other men chortled.

'Next thing, Rupe grabs a piece of pipe and goes for young Charlie. Boy, did he give him a hiding! Bashed hell out of him. Broke his arm in two places.'

'Oh, Jesus!' Victor muttered. 'What the hell did he do that for?'

Bert sucked on his pipe. 'We pulled Rupe off Charlie in case he might have killed him, then Todman Senior comes galloping out of his office, shouting for the police. And at the same time Rupe's yelling that they shot his horse from under him.'

Victor's head jerked up from his drink. 'His horse?'

'Yeah. Did Charlie shoot his horse?'

'Someone did. Strangers. Trespassers. But Rupe didn't know who they were.'

'Well, he does now. And those surveyors and their mates might get an idea of what they're up against out here! Old Jock's real worried; he heard that since leasehold land was thrown open for claiming, there are queues lining up at the courthouse in Toowoomba to put their names down for any blocks that aren't freehold.'

'I know that, but what's it got to do with Rupe?'

'Every bloody thing. Hanging on their coat tails are these mongrel surveyors, in for the quick quid. They've got offices springing up everywhere like the one down the road. Todman and Son. Didn't you see it?'

'No.'

'You rode right past it, mate. But Todman's story is that his son never set foot on Springfield. Rupe says he did. Either way, they've got the message. We let old man Todman know that if he brings selectors anywhere near Jock's place they'll get more than a thumping.'

The barman interrupted. 'Just the same, Victor, your brother's up on a charge of assault and battery, and to top it off he gave Sergeant Perkins plenty of lip. That didn't help.'

'Good on him,' Bert said, swallowing his beer, but Victor wasn't impressed. He'd hoped a chat with Perkins might have put an end to the incident, but obviously Rupe and his big mouth had put the sergeant offside.

For all the cheerfulness of these blokes, Rupe's attack with a weapon on an unarmed man was a serious matter, worse than just the street brawl that Victor had first guessed at. Rupe was no stranger to brawls, usually over women.

He had a few more pints with the men, and persuaded the barman to rustle him up a cold meal from the kitchen, since lunch was finished, while he tried to figure out his next move. If the Todmans persisted and this went to court, Rupe would lose. Too many witnesses. And no available witnesses to the shooting of the horse, a far worse crime. But anyway, it had no bearing, as far as a court was concerned, on Rupe's case. The fool.

Sometimes Victor thought Rupe lived in the past. He was too vulnerable to all those hell-raising tales that Austin fed him, of the days when Austin was the law. When the squatters ruled their lands like grass dukes, and no one dared come up against them. But those days were long gone, and if Rupe saw himself as a latter-day Austin Broderick it was time he woke up to reality.

Maybe not today, though, Victor thought grimly. This charge was no joking matter, neither was a conviction. Instead of heading for the police station, he turned left and walked back up the road to find this surveyor's office.

As he walked in the door he was annoyed with himself because he knew he was about to behave just as Austin would advise in these circumstances. But he couldn't think what else to do.

He introduced himself to Todman Senior, with the expected reaction.

'Broderick, did you say? Related to that wretch who assaulted my son? He's still in hospital. What sort of people are you? Get out of my office!'

'His brother,' Victor said calmly. 'And consider yourself lucky that it was only Rupe who got into a fight with your kid.'

'There was no fight,' the grey-haired man spluttered. 'Get out of here or I'll call the police.'

'By all means call the police. When I'm finished. Someone shot one of my horses . . .'

'Charles didn't. He doesn't carry a gun.'

'So I hear. But you sent him on to Springfield with the men who did . . .'

'I won't listen to this!'

'Yes you will. Sit down.' Victor waited until the surveyor backed into a chair. 'Now, on our land, boundary riders don't ride alone. Especially not family. Rupe was not alone when that horse was shot,

183

so we have a witness.' He was playing this by ear, because he knew that, in between Rupe's version and the surveyor's, there had to be some truth. There was no doubt in his mind that Rupe had recognized the townie who had been with the bushwhackers. And that they had entered Springfield. Trespassing.

'Have you got any idea how the land lies out here?' he asked menacingly. 'Stealing a horse is worse than stealing a man's wife. Shooting a horse, killing a fine animal, is even worse. You'll get no sympathy from anyone here, because the truth is out. I've been in this town for two hours and I've already heard that Charlie ought to be lynched. He mightn't have shot the horse, but he condoned it and he lied about it.'

He paused, 'Put it this way, Mr Todman. If I were you I'd get Charlie out of town as soon as he is released from hospital. Or he could suffer a great deal more damage.'

'Are you threatening me?'

'Yes. Prove it. I've just come here for a chat. You retract those charges against my brother – a broken arm is little enough to pay for a good stock horse – or your troubles are only just beginning. This is not a threat, Mr Todman, it is a promise.'

Todman stuttered and stammered before he could get the words out. 'The least you can do is pay for my son's medical expenses.'

'And the best you can do, sir, is thank your lucky stars they're both not in jail, because Rupe would only cop a fine, which is chicken feed to us, but Charlie would do time.'

Todman fiddled nervously with his tie and jerked his waistcoat into place. 'I'm sure we could come to some amicable arrangement, Mr Broderick,' he said, a wheedling tone in his voice.

'Of course we can. You withdraw the charges against my brother and I'll guarantee that Charlie leaves this town without further accidents.'

'This is grossly unfair, sir.'

'No. Your kid is getting off lightly. And keep this in mind. If anyone connected with you lays claim to one inch of Springfield, then we'll have you. In a nutshell, Mr Todman, you and your son appear to keep particularly bad company. Now, if you don't clear this up within the hour, I'll prefer charges against Charlie. For a start.'

Rupe, ignoring the scowling Sergeant Perkins, was jubilant when he swaggered out of the police station with Victor.

'I knew that charge wouldn't stick. Where have you been anyway? I thought you'd have been here hours ago. I could have been out on bail long before this. That Charlie Todman, the bloke I hit, he was the surveyor I was telling you about. I spotted him as soon as I came into town. Let's go to the pub. We don't have to go home tonight. I've been stuck all this time in Perkins' filthy lock-up.'

'Get on your horse, we're going home.'

Despite Rupe's angry complaints, they rode out together, heading home. For a while Victor listened to his brother's boasts about how he'd given that Charlie Todman the beating of his life, until, sickened, remembering the bullying that he'd just handed out to a weaker man, he turned on Rupe.

'Shut up, will you! That bloke didn't shoot your horse and you know it. You weren't ambushed. I reckon that you took on more than you could handle, big-noting yourself. And you got the horse killed . . .'

'Whose side are you on?'

'Not yours. You bashed that bloke before he had a chance to defend himself, you bloody gutless wonder.'

'Then how come they withdrew the charges?' Rupe smirked, but Victor nudged his horse into a gallop to put some distance between them. He'd had enough of Rupe. He began to think that Harry was now better off than any of the brothers. He'd chucked the life he didn't want or need, and was, by all accounts, doing a good job at Tirrabee station. Better still, he was his own boss, spared the interference and disruptions that his brother had to put up with.

Victor wondered how Connie was enjoying Tirrabee, though.

Connie was surprised to find life at Tirrabee station quite pleasant. She was well aware that not too many husbands would have forgiven her that awful business with Sam Ritter, no matter how badly they had behaved as a result, and she was grateful to Harry that he'd never mentioned it again.

He'd sat her down the day the house was sold and suggested they ought to call a truce. After all, they were down to basics now; they only had each other.

She shuddered, remembering that her alternatives had been bleak at the time, with no prospect of returning to her parents' home even if she'd wished to do so, and absolutely nowhere else to turn.

But Harry had been very sweet, he really had been. He understood her predicament, apologizing to her for making such a mess of things.

'I don't want you to feel I'm forcing you to come with me, Con . . .'

'I've no choice,' she'd wept.

'Try not to look at it like that. I want you with me. I love you. Don't you care about me at all, even a little?' He put his arms around her. 'Stick with me, love. You won't regret it, I promise you. We'll start again, just you and me.'

Then it dawned on her that she really would hate to lose Harry. She was comfortable with him, and she'd been cured of flirting forever. What would she do without him?

'Just a little bit?' he murmured, kissing her.

'A little bit, yes, I suppose so,' she allowed, and he laughed.

'Try harder.'

She was being courted all over again by the Harry she'd known when they first met, handsome, cheerful Harry Broderick, and it was all too much for her romantic soul. Even though she had reservations about living in the bush, Connie quickly realized that they were both now free of the two men who had dominated their lives.

'We've been disowned,' she giggled suddenly. 'Austin has dumped you and my father has shown me the door. We're a couple of outcasts.'

'So we are,' he grinned. 'What a horrible shame. We ought to celebrate. There are still a couple of good wines in the cellar.'

That night they made love in one of the single beds in their guest room, neither of them caring to recall the madness that had brought them so close together.

And Tirrabee wasn't so bad after all. It was a peaceful station with undulating green pasturelands only a few hours from Toowoomba, a very pretty country town that was well on its way to becoming a city.

And the homestead was such a relief . . . a timber house nestled into the side of a hill, white-painted, with a red roof. Surrounded by a fenced garden, it had a welcoming feel about it as the new manager and his wife drove up in their jinker. The furnishings were plain but comfortable, and it was immaculate, thanks to the wife of one of the stockmen who was there to greet them.

'I didn't know exactly when you'd be here,' she said, 'so I've been coming in every day to keep it neat for you.'

'That's very kind of you,' Connie said, knowing they were over the worst. She had expected an untenanted house to be overrun with all sorts of creepy-crawlies.

The woman, Clara Nugent, took them into the big kitchen. 'The stove has a mind of its own, Mrs Broderick, but I'm sure you'll get it under control!'

When Clara left Connie turned on Harry. 'You didn't tell me I'd have to do my own cooking!'

'No cooks or housekeepers on a spread this size. We're too small for such luxuries.' He patted the cold stove. 'I want you to meet my wife, the cook.'

'Very funny. I wonder if there are any cookbooks in these cupboards?'

'Consider it a challenge, my love.'

Connie smiled. 'Some challenge. You're the taster, remember. You're in for some strange meals, Mr Broderick. The first thing you'd better do is show me how to light the damn thing.'

Fortunately, Clara did the cooking for the men in their quarters and was always around to rescue Connie from her initial disasters, until the boss's wife, a determined woman, began to understand the rudiments of country cooking and took control of that contrary stove.

Connie liked Clara, and she also began to enjoy cooking, explaining to Harry that at least she knew what things *should* taste like, from the heady days at Brisbane's best restaurants. She didn't mind the bit of housework she had to do in their one-bedroomed house; in fact, it was another bonus being free of the snippy maids at their big house in the city.

All in all, Harry and Connie were very happy. The men liked Harry, who had taken to the job as if he was born to it – which of course he was – and they were very respectful towards his attractive wife, who seemed to have a good sense of humour about being a new chum in the bush.

On Connie's birthday, Harry arranged a surprise party for her in the wool shed, and presented her with a pony and trap of her very own so that she could take herself on excursions about the station, or even to visit neighbours when she felt experienced enough to go off on her own.

That night Connie told Harry that she thought she was pregnant, and he was delighted. 'I must write and tell Mother.'

'No. Wait until I'm further along. Plenty of time.'

'All right. If that's what you want.'

Connie lay in his arms, contented, wondering why she had fought against such a pleasant, easy-going existence, wondering why she deserved such happiness.

Though Rupe was home again, Louisa was not comforted. Those damn Brodericks seemed to have changed sides again, and Victor was on the outer. Austin thought Rupe's escapade amusing; Charlotte did not, but she did not appreciate Victor sending Rupe out to work as a stockman while he stayed in the office. They seemed to be constantly bickering about something.

'It's Rupe,' Louisa explained to Cleo. 'He gets into all sorts of strife and Victor has to get him out of it. So don't take any notice of them. Actually, this used to be such a peaceful house, until all the trouble about freeholding started.'

'Oh, yes. It's the talk of Brisbane. Such a shame. My father says the Government won't want to try it in the north. The cattle men won't stand for it.'

'But I thought your father grows sugar?'

Cleo nodded. 'He does. He's not worried. He had to buy his properties – too much investment in agriculture with sugar cane to take a risk on leasing land. But a lot of his friends are cattle men. Those big stations are leasehold.'

'They wouldn't have to worry anyway. They're too far from civilization to care. Our problem is that settlers are spreading out from Brisbane, Ipswich and Toowoomba, and the big stations are in their way.'

'That's bad luck.'

'Yes, so you can see why the men are upset. And Charlotte too. Her brother and Austin opened up this land. I just wanted you to understand, Cleo, why things are a bit peculiar here. They really don't seem to know what to do for the best. But be warned. Give Rupe a wide berth – he's trouble – and Austin can change like the wind. One day people are in his good books and the next they're on the outer. It's Victor's turn this week.'

'Oh well, I suppose Mr Broderick is worried,' Cleo said gently. Louisa seemed to her to be making a mountain out of a molehill, just to make the governess feel at home. Cleo had three brothers herself, and they were always arguing, far more violently than these men. But then, plantation work was heavy in that hot clime, and tempers were apt to boil more easily. She found life in this lovely house far calmer than her own rowdy household and wished Louisa would stop apologizing. Cleo found her attitude rather demeaning to the highly respected Broderick family.

And as for Rupe, she had her own opinion. Cook had told her all about the drama in Cobbside. How Rupe had beaten the man who shot his horse, and been arrested for doing what any man in his place would have done. Why Louisa was embarrassed, Cleo would never know. So what if Rupe had been tossed in jail overnight? It was worth it. Some women simply didn't understand the difference between polite behaviour and standing up for one's rights. Cleo was a rebel; she believed that women like Charlotte and Louisa were far too immersed in grand living and dressing for dinner to be regarded as country women any more. She had written to her father telling him how fortunate it was that she'd brought with her some of the dresses she'd purchased in London, because these people set great store by the formalities of dress, and he'd been amazed.

She knew, too, that her Brisbane schoolfriends gossiped about her being taken overseas to find a husband, and were meanly pleased that this had not happened, but the truth was quite different. Cleo's mother had died some years ago, and her father had taken her simply as his companion.

'You might as well come with me,' he'd said. 'See the world before you settle down.'

By which he meant 'before I bring you home to marry Tom next door'. His best friend's son. Amalgamating two large plantations.

On her return, Cleo had flatly refused to marry Tom Curtis. She didn't even like him.

Her brothers hadn't helped. 'You're no oil painting, Cleo. Who else will marry you?'

That was all Cleo had needed to quit the plantation and come down to stay with an aunt in Brisbane until such time as she'd landed this job as a governess. She hadn't bothered to tell Louisa that every letter she received from her father contained money, his way of apologizing. And to make doubly certain that his only daughter was no longer angry with him, he'd placed a substantial amount of cash in a Brisbane bank account in her name.

'Poor Daddy,' she sighed. 'I can't see myself going back up there to live. The tropical north might be very exotic but I really can't stand that heat, and months of monsoonal rain are no fun for ladies.'

The governess had drawn up a daily schedule for Teddy: the three Rs in the morning, and art and craft for a couple of hours in the afternoon, depending on his attention span. And depending on what interested him. Cleo took her job very seriously. She felt it was important to have the family understand that her timetable had to be adhered to. She wanted to succeed with Teddy, to prove that she really was an excellent teacher, even though she'd had no training.

If Teddy's parents were happy with her, then Rupe would appreciate her as well. Cleo knew that a lot of governesses, young and old, went out to the stations in search of husbands, good pickings on the male-dominated properties, and she didn't want anyone to put her in that category. Or rather she hadn't, until she'd come across Rupe Broderick again. He'd grown into a handsome man, tall and fair like his brother, but much better-looking than Victor, finer-featured. Being of independent mind, Cleo hated to admit that she was already in love with the youngest of the Broderick sons, and she was still cross with herself for going all gaga over him the first time they'd met out here.

That won't happen again, she told herself. That's exactly the way to scare him off, and make a fool of myself. After that mistake, Cleo had been secretly thrilled every time she came in contact with Rupe, but was deliberately distant with him now. Even to the point of avoiding any opportunity to be alone with him. She already knew that men like Rupe, who were inclined to arrogance, expected women to fall at their feet. Well, Cleo Murray would not. Better to keep him guessing for a while.

'If I can,' she murmured as she opened up the schoolroom and walked to the window looking out over the river.

This really was a beautiful house, and the view from here was a delight. How fortunate that her aunt had known Fern Broderick, who had made the connection. Apparently there'd been another governess in the running, someone known to Judge Walker, but there seemed to be some family fuss going on there, so the Brodericks had looked elsewhere.

Cleo grinned. This family appeared to have their fair share of fusses, despite Louisa's avowals to the contrary.

Teddy came rushing in, still enthusiastic about his lessons, and pushed into his brand-new desk. 'What we doin' today, Miz Murray?'

His governess shook her head. 'You say "Good morning, Miss Murray." Not "Miz Murray".'

She looked up to see Louisa smiling her approval. 'I'm afraid he picked up his odd speech from the black kids.'

'What black kids?' Cleo asked. She hadn't seen any.

'Oh, they've gone now, thank God.'

Cleo was right about Rupe. He couldn't understand why she was so standoffish. She'd seemed to be genuinely pleased to see him when she'd first arrived, and now she treated him like a stranger. He realized that she had to observe protocol in the household – after all, she was in their employ – but there was no need to be so stuffy about it. She was very pleasant at mealtimes, quite good company, they all agreed, and she never failed to address him, so she wasn't ignoring him, but she kept her distance. She always seemed to be busy, and of an evening, after dinner, when the others made for their bedrooms, she disappeared too.

For a while Rupe found her attitude annoying. Then he decided she was scared of him – the little governess and the big bad wolf of a Rupe – so he started teasing her, deliberately sitting next to her in the parlour, bumping into her in the passageways, waylaying her on the staircase to ask some silly question, but none of that fazed her. She was polite, cheerful, and never seemed to notice.

But Louisa did. 'Have you got a crush on Cleo, Rupe? You could do worse, you know.'

'Don't be stupid,' he growled.

Louisa's intervention, unknown to Cleo, was a setback for her because it meant that the tables were turned. Rupe began to avoid her. His pride hurt, he was even curt to her at times, but Cleo was up to it. She had her fall-back position of just getting on with the job of teaching, becoming an excellent tennis opponent for Louisa and enjoying the late summer at Springfield. The next move had to be Rupe's. Win or lose. She was, after all, the only single girl on the property and that gave her a sporting chance, as her brothers would say.

Cleo began to take more care with her appearance, encouraged by Louisa, who taught her how to dress her hair in styles, rather than dragging it back with a ribbon. Who pointed out that the dumpy gathered skirts did little for Cleo's figure, and that it wasn't really necessary for her to dress like a schoolteacher. Despite her much-lauded European tour, Cleo had never owned any dress sense, and gradually, under Louisa's supervision, the unbecoming clothes were discarded and a more attractive young lady began to emerge.

Because Louisa had her own plan. One that she didn't even mention to Victor. She was sick of having Rupe under their feet all the time, causing trouble, needling Austin to blame Victor for anything that went wrong, turning to Charlotte whenever he couldn't get his own way. He should be married and out of the house.

190

That wasn't as difficult as it sounded, she told herself. There were always the outstations. He could replace one of the managers out there. Austin couldn't object if it was decided that a manager's cottage should be replaced with a decent house to accommodate Rupe and his wife. And Victor certainly would not. But the first thing to do was to get Cleo and Rupe together. So far, Cleo didn't seem interested. Louisa wished she hadn't been so quick to criticize Rupe in front of her. The girl had really taken her at her word, giving him a wide berth. And why wouldn't she? Cleo's family were well-off. She'd travelled the world. Why would she want to settle down in the bush? She was only here because she really liked teaching. That part was obvious. Teddy adored Miss Murray.

Well, I can but try, Louisa told herself. Anything to get rid of Victor's young brother.

She had always preferred Harry to Rupe. It was a pity their situations weren't reversed.

But all of her plans were forgotten when their lives were overturned by the worst thing that of them could ever have imagined.

Chapter Eight

The claims were lodged to break Springfield into separate properties, most of which were substantial holdings in their own right, being of the maximum size permitted by the Government. Each one to be freeholded by a Broderick was an excellent sheep run, and claims by the dummy names were considered by Austin to be secondary in value.

That also annoyed him. Freeholding laws did not differentiate between good pastureland and less arable country; the blocks had to be paid for by the acre. He would have to pay the same amount for what he saw as second choice as he would for the best.

It was small comfort to him that he was leaving unclaimed large areas useless to graziers, whether they be Brodericks or other claimants. Most of these were on the outskirts of their land: rocky or hill country, or dry blocks too far from water or wells. To Austin they were still breaking up the huge sweep of land that belonged to him, that was Springfield, and it could never be the same again.

Victor dreaded the day when he'd have to ask his father for bank drafts to start paying for these claims, and when, eventually, the lawyers advised that the first claim had been processed he had no choice but to broach the subject.

'They want the money already?' Austin snapped. 'That can't be right.'

'This is for your claim. The most important section surrounding the homestead. I wanted to get that set in stone first. There'll probably be arguments about the rest because we've lodged some peculiar-looking maps, but the valley is the heart of the station.'

'And what do I get for my money? My own land! I call that right generous of the bloody vultures in that Government. I won't pay it! They can go to hell.'

'It has to be paid, Dad. You won't miss this money. For the next claims we can start selling some of our shares . . .'

'I won't miss it! Typical of you! Don't you know how hard I had to work to get that money in the bank? To keep you lot in the lap of luxury? Don't you tell me I won't miss it as if we're talking about a few cakes of soap that someone's stealing from me.'

It took days for his anger to subside, and all the while Charlotte remonstrated with Victor. 'Couldn't you have broken it to him more

193

gently? Did you have to dump it on him like that? You've given him a terrible shock. You know he's not well.'

'Mother, he has known it's coming for a long time now. There's no getting out of it, and no way I could have made it any easier for him.'

As usual Rupe took the opposite view. 'You could have suggested paying a small amount first, a deposit, and the rest later.'

'We're not dealing with an ordinary buyer; this is the Government. Either we want to freehold or we don't, so get off my back. Anyway, he can afford it. He can afford to buy back quite a few of our blocks before he starts to feel the pinch, and then I'll have to talk to the bank about a loan. We'll have the collateral of the purchased land. He has to start paying now, there's no way out of it.'

He talked to Austin about security of tenure. 'At least we'll own the land outright; we won't ever have to go through this again. And Springfield will go on earning well. We won't have to reduce sheep numbers and the wool cheques will keep on coming in.'

'Don't patronize me! Don't you think I know that?'

In the end, after weeks of stubborn refusal, Austin signed, but the decision left him tired and depressed.

'He'll get over it,' Victor said.

'Until next time,' Rupe added.

'We'll see. We just have to get on with running the place. You and I will have to work a lot harder now.'

'I don't see how I can. You can get out of your office for a change.'

'I intend to, and I'll be cutting back on expenses wherever possible. Sooner or later money will get tight, so we might as well start economizing. I'll be looking at every single aspect of the property now, to see what can be done.'

Rupe shrugged. He knew that their plan was to buy the blocks emanating from the focal point, the valley, and that Victor's claims would come next. It still rankled with him that Victor would own three blocks and his name would only be on one, even though it was only on paper. And what economizing? He had no idea how Victor would go about this, but he didn't like the sound of it.

'We could cut back on staff,' Victor told his wife as they took an evening stroll in the garden, the air heavy with the almost liquid fragrance of jasmine and frangipani. 'Starting with the gardeners.'

'Charlotte won't like that.'

'She doesn't seem to like anything these days. She's permanently cranky. I don't know what's got into her.'

'She worries. And she's upset that Austin won't forgive Harry.'

Victor shrugged. 'Austin has never grown up, that's his trouble.'

'Who has?' Louisa murmured, wishing her husband would take a firmer hand with his father, instead of caving in to all his demands and then coming to her to gripe about it.

He didn't seem to hear. He opened the gate into the orchard but

194

stopped her as she walked through and drew her to him. 'You look beautiful tonight. And I love you so much. Don't let any of this freeholding business worry you. As a mat f fact, I feel better about it now. At least we know what we're do . The uncertainty about what was going to happen has been har g over our heads for far too long.'

Louisa kissed him. 'I'm sorry. I haven't been much help, have I?'

They moved on, taking the path that skirted the trees, enjoying the quiet and the stillness of the night until distant thunder rumbled in the hills, giving promise of rain and welcome relief from the heat.

The overnight storm sweetened the air, damping down, for another day, the familiar haze of dust. Wakened by kookaburras, the harbingers of dawn, flocks of restive sheep began moving about to meet the warmth of the sun; thousands of parrots swept into action, screeching across the sky in their gaudy mischievous revels, and the land-bound natives, kangaroos and wallabies and their kin, peered warily at the morning with soft and gentle eyes. Horses blew and stamped and nudged at the damp grass, and from the staff quarters, yawning men emerged to nod thoughtfully at the morning, satisfied that the storm had been a help not a hindrance.

Charlotte, too, always awoke with the birds. She climbed out of the large four-poster bed and padded along to the bathroom, from habit banging on Rupe's door as she passed. He was hard to wake in the mornings. Or reluctant, more like it, she smiled.

Back in her room, she dressed quickly, then brushed her hair and yanked it into a bun, securing it with pins. She paused to study her face in the mirror, and then, almost furtively, she took a pot of face cream from a drawer and rubbed it into her skin, producing a sheen – though temporary, she knew – on her dry cheeks.

Charlotte had finally come to thinking that she ought to do something about her appearance, to please her husband. To hopefully make him pay more attention to her. The image of Fern Broderick loomed large these days, because on several occasions recently he'd asked why Fern hadn't come to see him. Each time Charlotte had shrugged off the question.

Now she studied her fading red hair, lightly sprinkled with grey, and wondered how it could be cut so that she wouldn't have to wear it pulled into a bun all the time. How it could be made to look more attractive, and thereby soften her stern features. Louisa would know, she was always changing her hairstyles, but Charlotte could never bring herself to ask. She was too shy. Too prideful. Although she hadn't commented, she had watched with interest the way Louisa had improved Cleo's appearance from a dumpy, dull-looking girl with hair that always looked as if it needed a wash, into quite a smart young lady. Louisa was good at stuff like that; she didn't have much else to do.

195

With a sigh, Charlotte turned away from the mirror, tied a fresh apron over her serviceable brown dress and went downstairs to the kitchen. She always liked to take Austin's morning tea in to him herself. It was her place to do so, her right.

A little while later, with the glittering sunlight edging over the hills, the whole of the household was shattered by her screams.

Doors were wrenched open, voices called. Disturbed, Teddy woke crying, afraid of the day. Outside, men halted in their tracks, looking about them, shocked by the suddenness of it. Some began to run towards the house.

Victor found her sitting on the daybed, rocking back and forth in anguish.

'He's dead!' she wept. 'He's dead.'

Victor had to prise her away. 'Hold on, Mother. Let me see. Just a minute now. Let me see.'

But Austin Broderick *was* dead. Died peacefully, they would be able to say. In his sleep.

Dead.

As the others crowded in, Victor, stunned, stood back, hardly able to take this in. Louisa came to him, put her arms around him. 'Darling, I'm so sorry. So very sorry.'

He looked at her, totally at a loss, as if defeated by such an inexplicable event, his voice a nervous whisper. 'He's dead. What do we do now?'

Louisa heard the voice of the son of the man, and she was silent, understanding Victor's confusion as Austin's dominance ebbed away, wondering what sort of a person would emerge now, in his own right. She looked at Rupe, who was comforting Charlotte, and thought she saw an expression of satisfaction in those cool blue eyes, but then she might have imagined that. Rupe was as shocked as everyone else.

Cleo was sorry too, but she'd not had much contact with the great man, except when she'd trailed along with Teddy on visits to his grandfather, or on family occasions when he'd deigned to emerge from his private wing, so she couldn't feel a great deal of concern. It was interesting, however, to watch the reactions of these people. They didn't seem to realize it, but they were all strong personalities, even the wives, and she was intrigued.

As a mark of respect, she suspended the lessons and spent more time in the kitchen, helping Cook prepare for the expected influx of visitors and listening to the gossip.

'Harry will be home soon,' she was told. 'He and that silly wife of his. He'll be broken-hearted, poor lad. Never had a chance to make it up with the old man. I always thought they would, you know. Mr Broderick was a bombastic man, but he cooled off in time.'

'I thought you said he cut Harry out of his will.' Cleo didn't mention

196

that she'd heard even juicier gossip about the Harry Brodericks in Brisbane. Of Harry in a jealous rage threatening to shoot his wife and her lover. It had been the talk of the neighbourhood where her aunt lived; several people claimed to have seen him ordering them out of the house. And yet the pair of them were still together. Cook had said he'd be bringing his wife.

'That's right,' Cook was saying. 'He did that all right, cut Harry out, but that's only the slash of a pen. Given time, poor feller, Mr Broderick would have set it to rights. He had to make his point, you see. Bark worse than his bite. He'll be turning in his grave now, realizing what he's done. Went too far this time. But they're all three his sons, so the other two will do the fair thing. The missus will see to that.'

Cleo was on the front veranda trying to keep Teddy quiet by reading to him when a gig pulled in and a big man with the familiar thatch of blond hair strode around to assist a woman down from the vehicle.

She didn't have to guess who this was, and Teddy confirmed her recognition by racing away from her to welcome him.

'Uncle Harry! Grandpa's gone to heaven!'

Cleo saw the real hurt in Harry's eyes as he picked up the child, and she warmed to him, understanding the cruelty of his situation. His wife, too, must have felt his pain as he stood numbly outside his father's house.

'Come on, darling, we'll go in.'

Teddy delayed them, insisting they meet Miss Murray who would read them stories, but then Charlotte appeared in a gush of tears to cling to Harry, speechless, and the miserable little group made their way into the parlour, so Cleo thought it best to take Teddy for a walk down to the stables.

Rupe stood angrily at the parlour door. 'What are you doing here? Didn't you do enough damage while he was alive? There's nothing here for you.'

Harry lifted his head from his hands as if to answer, but just shook his head instead.

It was Connie who reacted. 'Don't you dare speak to him like that! Go away and leave him alone.'

Harry took her hand. 'It's all right, Connie. He's just upset.'

'Where's Mother?' Rupe asked. 'Does she know you're here?'

Louisa came back into the room. 'I've just taken her upstairs to lie down. She shouldn't have been up. And yes, Rupe, she knows Harry's here.'

She watched Rupe storm away and looked to Connie. 'What was that about?'

Harry stood up. 'Nothing, Lou. We've come a long way, Connie must be tired. We'll go upstairs. Our old room?'

'Yes, of course.' Louisa glanced at Connie. 'You're looking well

197

even after a long journey like that.' It had occurred to her that Harry looked more weary than his wife, but now Connie smiled wanly. 'Connie, my dear. Don't tell me . . .'

Connie blushed. 'Yes. A baby.'

'Oh. How lovely!'

Then they were all quiet, aware that this was a grandchild whom Austin would never meet.

'Where is he?' Harry asked.

'In his den. Hannah and the doctor's wife laid him out.'

Harry nodded. 'I'll be down later.'

Victor was sitting on Austin's veranda, nursing a whisky, when Harry entered the study, but he didn't hurry out there.

Harry was appalled to see his father's favourite room turned into a mausoleum, the big mirror draped in black, portraits turned to the wall, his precious trophies hidden away, and in the middle of the room, Austin in a dark suit lying in state, surrounded by white flowers. Chrysanthemums, he noted, realizing for no particular reason that it was May. They always came out in great clumps in the Springfield gardens in May.

For a minute he closed his eyes at the scene, knowing this was only Charlotte's overreaction, her perception of duty, her usual misunderstanding of Austin's tastes. Dad would have hated being left in this floral display like a bridegroom . . . Then he stood, looking down at the still, handsome face, and whispered: 'I'm sorry, Dad. I'm so sorry.'

He blinked away the tears, searched in a cupboard for a glass and went out to join Victor, not caring about the reception that could await him, it was just somewhere to be.

'How are you?' he asked Victor.

His brother pushed the whisky bottle towards him. 'I don't know. It doesn't seem real. Him in there. He was all right the night before. We had a game of cards. He beat me. And Rupe. He was even talking about inviting old Jock and a couple of his mates over . . . Maybe we stayed too long. Wore him out. I thought he was over the worst.'

Harry let him talk out his remorse of what might have been, of what he might have, should have, done, trying to ease him away from this futile guilt.

'Mother says we kept him up too late,' Victor said despairingly.

'Sounds as if he went out smiling. He liked to win.'

'Yeah.'

'Charlotte's overreacting, distraught. Don't take any notice. She's just looking for blame. The same way he always did. She can't blame God, because he's in there dead.'

Victor poured himself another whisky and Harry passed him the silver water jug, but he waved it away, preferring his drink neat this

198

time. 'Springfield will never be the same again,' he mourned.

'Self-pity doesn't help.'

Victor jerked up angrily. 'All very well for you to say. You weren't here to see him fall apart, to see him dragging himself up, day by day, to the man he was, fighting all his disabilities without a word of complaint . . .'

'That'll be the day.' Harry watched as his brother dissolved into tears. 'Have another drink. We might as well have our wake tonight and get it over with.'

Louisa put Victor to bed. Then she gave Charlotte another dose of the sedative the doctor had prescribed, to try to make an end to her mother-in-law's hysterical weeping.

She saw Harry walking out towards the men's quarters, and took a supper tray up to Connie.

'Is it true that Austin cut Harry out of his will?' Connie asked.

'How did you know that?' said Louisa, embarrassed.

'We heard. Rupe's a big talker. Station gossip. Is it true?'

'Yes.'

'Oh well. Good luck to you all.'

'It's nothing to do with me, Connie.'

'I know that. I just wanted you to confirm it. Harry doesn't care.'

'Really?' That surprised Louisa.

'No. He has changed. He just wants to get on with his own life without complications. He had a breakdown, you know.'

'I'm sorry. I didn't know.'

'Well, you wouldn't, because nobody cared to enquire or come to visit us. Not even Charlotte. Her husband was too important.'

'We didn't know, Connie. We just thought he'd quit Parliament because he missed that vote, but . . .'

'Never mind about that now,' Connie said firmly. 'It's behind us. We're happy at Tirrabee, it's the prettiest station . . .'

'So I've heard.'

'And Harry wants, needs, the quiet life.'

'That's good then.'

'Is it?' Connie put the tray aside, tightened the belt on her pink silk dressing gown and walked to the French windows.

'I said Harry doesn't care. But I do. My child will be entitled to his or her inheritance. The grandchild of Austin Broderick. You think about that, Louisa, and you tell Victor that my child has the same rights as Teddy. So if he and Rupe think they are going to cut us out, they've got another think coming.'

She smiled sagely. 'Nothing personal, Louisa. I've always liked you. And thank you for the tray. I must drink my cocoa before it gets cold.'

Victor was sprawled on their bed, too drunk for any hope of conversation, so Louisa went downstairs and slept in a guest room.

199

Connie, though, was busily writing to her father. To tell him again that they were very happy at Tirrabee and that her husband had asked her to apologize to him unequivocally – which he had not – for any inconvenience and upsets he had caused. Because Harry was now a reformed person, a loving husband who took his duties seriously. Then came her good news, that she was bearing his first grandchild.

Darkly then, frowning over her pen, Connie related the bad news – which he probably already knew, Austin being a rather famous person – the reason for their presence at Springfield. After which came her plea to the Judge for advice. How could it be possible that because of a temporary breakdown in his mental capacities Harry Broderick had been struck out of his father's will? That Harry and her child should be denied their true inheritance of one third of Springfield?

Again she begged his advice as a loving daughter, knowing that her avaricious father, son of old Jock on the station next door to Springfield, would fight tooth and nail to unite Harry's share of Springfield with the Walker estates.

She sealed the letter with a quiet smile and drank the cold cocoa thinking how she would love to see Rupe's face when he came up against the powerful legal might of Judge Walker. That would teach him to tell Harry he wasn't welcome in his own family home.

Rupe and Cleo dined alone. He was jumpy and insecure, apologizing for the rest of the family who had deserted them, seemingly unable to concentrate on any conversation until he suggested they have a bottle of wine.

'I need a drink,' he stated. 'Do you have any objections?'

'No. Why should I?'

'My brothers are out there getting stuck into a bottle of whisky. I wasn't invited. But my opinions don't count. Anyway, you don't drink whisky, do you?'

'No.'

'Then wine it shall be. The best. My father was never one for the miseries. We should drink to him. Not to his good health, though, I suppose.'

She sat back quietly. 'Rupe, you don't have to make excuses. Get the wine. I'll keep you company.'

'Why? Because I'm the odd one out?'

'No. Because you're upset and we're the only two here.'

She sipped the dry white wine, wishing she'd stayed in her room with a book and a snack from the kitchen, because she was finding it difficult to cope with him, and the maid was agonizingly slow in serving. It seemed to Cleo that Rupe's grief included anger with the world that his father had died, and her heart went out to him, but he kept slumping into silences, and she didn't feel she should make any attempt to cheer him up.

200

Eventually he pushed his chair back. 'Do you want to go for a walk?'

Cleo was taken aback. She would have preferred to escape from him, but she couldn't think of an excuse.

'If you feel like it.'

'We might as well,' he shrugged.

They walked to the front of the house and followed the gravel paths that circled the garden beds. She was relieved that now Rupe made an effort to talk, asking her about her home in the north, the plantations, the seasons, the crops, anything, she felt, rather than mention the subject of Austin Broderick, and he seemed very interested, as any country man would be, in her answers. So much so that they strolled round a second time, and when they arrived back at the front steps he touched her arm.

'Thanks, Cleo. Sorry if I was a bit cranky before. It's just that . . . Oh, well, never mind. You'd better go in.'

At the open door she turned back to see him trudging away, his hands thrust in his pockets, and she realized how lonely he was. His father had been his only real friend.

But Rupe was by no means lonely. He was pleased with himself. He'd finally broken the ice; she wouldn't avoid him now. The more he saw of Cleo, the more he liked her. Enough to marry her anyway, keeping in mind that her family was wealthy and she could be expected to come with a substantial dowry, plus her eventual inheritance.

'Damn the Government!' he muttered. He had a half-share in Springfield now, and it was just his bad luck that it had come to him when those blasted politicians were busy draining all the funds from the coffers. Having to pay to pretend to be breaking up the Broderick holdings was an appalling waste of money. It was only when Victor had started talking about economizing that the finality of these huge payouts for security of tenure had sunk in. Now he was shocked. It wasn't Austin's money that was being handed over to the Government; it was his own!

He leaned against the far fence and stared back at the house, the sandstone almost white in the moonlight. He'd always imagined that when Austin died, they'd be able to leave Victor here to run the place, which was what he'd always wanted anyway. Harry would stay in Brisbane and Rupe, the youngest son, would be free to get out in the world and enjoy himself, relying, like so many other squatters, on his share of the wool cheque to pay his bills.

And with Harry cut out of the will, he and Victor would have had all that lovely money to themselves.

'Bloody bad luck!' he snorted. It had now become imperative to marry a wealthy girl. And none of her money would be going to Springfield. That would be their own. His own.

Rupe began to wonder about the necessity to buy all of Springfield.

Austin had wanted to keep it intact, but he had gone, and with him the silly pride of trying to hang on to land that would keep them short of money for years.

That's what we'll do, he decided. To hell with the dummy runs, we'll just freehold enough to have a decent, manageable property, and let the rest go. Victor won't have any choice. I'll just refuse to buy. We'll keep the best and get rid of the outstations so that we don't have to pay the managers. Springfield will just be smaller, that's all.

Feeling better, Rupe strode back to the house and slipped through to his own room. He didn't want to meet up with Harry again; there was nothing to talk about. And tomorrow there'd be people arriving from all directions for the funeral the day after. Already the women were busy making arrangements for the biggest crowd Springfield had ever seen. The place would be bursting at the seams.

He nodded. 'When it's all over, *I'll* be telling Victor what we have to do.'

Charlotte awoke in the grip of the most dreadful depression she had ever experienced. Her head ached and her body felt heavy, a ton weight, as if she'd never be able to lift herself from this bed again. She heard a dry, rasping sob before a wave of nausea swept over her and she was forced to quell the rising bile.

The room was silent, not a rustle of breeze from the open windows, and the whole household was quiet. Very quiet. Ominous. No voices, no clang of activity, nothing.

Today they would bury her husband.

She wanted to weep, but there were no tears left. Only this awful heartbreak. Because Austin had gone without a word. Without ever fulfilling her dreams by turning to her, telling her how much he really did love her. She re-entered that fantasy of leaving him, moving to Brisbane so that he could come after her, beg her to return to him, his wife, his love, showing the world how much she meant to him, and stayed there awhile to comfort herself.

Yesterday she'd heard the horses, the spin of wheels on the gravel drive, and the constant murmur of voices on the front porch directly below her bedroom, as they came to pay their respects, so many of them, and there'd be more arriving today. She knew she should have been down there to greet them but she couldn't face anyone. It was too hard. Better to stay here until they all left. No one cared about his wife. The visitors would be his mates, his admirers, his friends in the upper echelons of society, all duty-bound to make the trek to his last resting place, up there beside Kelly, where he'd always wanted to be buried.

Names came to mind, names of important people who would be coming to her home, some of them probably installed in the guest rooms already, or crowded into other rooms, somehow. And that gave

202

her cause to worry. How was Louisa coping? Did she know the right thing to do? Had she taken care to see that the house was tidy? Everything in its place. Charlotte doubted it. Her daughter-in-law was not the tidiest of people herself. And what would people think? Coming to Springfield and finding it in disarray? Worry turned to fright, as a score of details that she was sure Louisa would overlook nagged and nagged, until she knew she would have to get up. Go down there. Take charge.

But it was easier said than done. She had to make a huge effort to drag herself from the bed, and standing made her dizzy. She looked to the gilt bell on the wall and moved to press it, to call a maid, but couldn't bring herself to do so. The depression was isolating her, encouraging her to remain in this room, their room, with Austin and their memories, and she almost succumbed, but her pride in her household kept her moving. Slowly, in a daze, she went to her wardrobe to lay out her best black dress, a grand silk dress, and all the other pieces she would need, as the tears began to flow again.

They were clearing up from breakfast in the busy kitchen when Charlotte appeared at the door, looking tired and wan, but composed.

'Louisa. It's ten o'clock and the parlour hasn't been touched yet.'

'I know, Charlotte. We're in a bit of a rush this morning. Are you all right? Can I get you some tea?'

'Not just now. I want the front of the house done first, please.'

Louisa reported to Victor that his mother had come down and seemed very much in control. 'Thank God.'

'Good. I was wondering if she'd be up to attending the funeral. I'll go and see if there's anything I can do to help her.'

Cleo was amazed at the big crowd that attended Mr Broderick's funeral and touched to see that so many ordinary stockmen from other stations had joined the throng to say farewell to a pioneering spirit. Charlotte, her face hidden by a dark veil, stood stolidly by the grave all through the service, flanked by her three sons, their blond hair adding lightness to the sombre scene.

Full voices joined in hymns that rose and fell with the wind over the valley, and Louisa sang 'Now Thank We All Our God', as the others listened, because she had such a sweet voice.

And then it was all over.

The guests repaired in a quiet, respectful manner to the household for afternoon tea, and later, Charlotte took her place on the porch to thank and farewell people as they left. But that night, when the remaining ladies gathered in the parlour, Cleo fled to her room, and was surprised to hear singing coming from outside.

She went to the window and listened, realizing that the men were holding a wake of their own down by the river. She could see the flicker of campfires and catch the aroma of eucalypt-filled smoke,

203

and she found it all very comforting. The songs were not hymns, they were ballads, as familiar as old friends, reminders that Austin Broderick would not be forgotten either.

'You don't have to leave yet,' Charlotte said to Harry the next morning. 'Can't you stay awhile?'

'Not really. Too much work piling up back home. You'll have to come and visit us, a holiday will do you good.'

'Oh, there's too much to do here . . .'

He put an arm about her shoulders. 'Come on now. Austin wouldn't want you to be miserable. You've got through all this like a real trouper, but now you have to take it easy. What if I come back for you in a fortnight? Will you come and stay with Connie and me then?'

She shook her head. 'Don't rush me, Harry, I can't think about leaving Springfield just now. It's hard enough to get through the day.'

'I know,' he said gently. 'You come in your own good time.'

Charlotte turned to him, urgency in her voice. 'Please, Harry, don't go yet. Stay just one more day. I need you here. William Pottinger won't be leaving with the others this afternoon, he's waiting for the last of them to go so that he can read the will. He wants to make it official.'

'All the more reason for me to leave. Rupe has made it plain that I'm not included.'

'Oh, what does Rupe know?'

'But it's true, isn't it? Look . . . I don't want to upset you, Mother, or anyone else. It was Austin's decision, I'll abide by it.'

'I still want you to stay. I need you with me. The others don't care about me.'

'Yes, they do. Where's this coming from?'

'Tell me you'll stay,' she insisted. 'Just this once do something for me.'

He was surprised when Connie agreed, not only to stay but to attend the reading in the parlour. 'I thought you'd find it embarrassing to have your husband sitting in there like a spare wheel.'

'Oh, no. I want to hear it for myself. With my own ears.'

He shrugged.

Louisa nudged Victor when Harry and Connie walked in to hear the verdict, and he looked over at them nervously. Rupe ignored them, and Charlotte nodded to Pottinger. 'You may begin.'

Pottinger looked more like a farmer than a lawyer, with his lean, tanned face and large hands, but as they all knew, he was a keen gardener. He shuffled pages about on the polished desk that Charlotte had provided for him, tossed back his coat-tails and sat down, obviously unnerved by Harry's presence.

He coughed. Read the date of the will and coughed again, as if to give them time for that to sink in, since it evidenced the fact that this

204

was a new will, written after Harry's spectacular fall from grace. Then he intoned the words: "'This is the last will and testament of I, Austin Gaunt Broderick, being of sound mind . . .'" and turned to Charlotte to see how she was holding up, but her face was turned to the windows as if something more interesting had caught her eye outside.

He proceeded with the bequests, which were accepted in silence, making a small remark about this being a simple, uncomplicated will, not like many others he'd had to deal with, then hurried on to announce that Austin had left all of his estate, goods and chattels to his sons Victor and Rupert, with the proviso that Springfield be regarded as the home of Charlotte Broderick for the term of her life.

No one spoke, so he began gathering up his papers, obviously feeling that his usual expressions of goodwill to the two fortunate sons would be inappropriate in this company.

Finally Rupe stood. 'Thank you, William. Is that all?'

'We have to go into the details of your exact inheritance, Rupe, the financial assets and so forth, but we can do that later. Since you're both living here, it's only a matter of course.'

Pottinger saw Charlotte lean forward, begin to speak, stop, take a deep breath and try again, and he felt sorry for the widow. Whatever it was she wanted to say was taking a great effort.

'Yes, my dear?' he asked solicitously.

She gulped. 'Where is my share?'

Pottinger stared. 'I beg your pardon?'

'My share.'

'Oh, you're taken care of, Charlotte. This is your home. That's very clear.'

'Is it?' she asked angrily. 'Then let me tell you, the lot of you, that my brother opened this station with Austin. They were partners, together they owned all of the land in this valley before Kelly died, before Austin struck out in other directions.'

'I don't think that's relevant now, Mother,' Rupe said, but Harry growled: 'Mother is speaking, Rupe. Please don't interrupt her.'

She looked at them, anguish in her voice. 'Don't you understand? Austin always said I was entitled to my fair share, as my brother's next of kin. His heir,' she added bitterly. 'You know that word. But he never did give me my fair share. He kept it all for himself. And now he has cut me out again.'

Victor was stunned. 'Mother. Please! You mustn't feel like that. This is your home.'

'And if I want a pound I have to beg from you, the same as I had to do with your father.'

'Oh, come on now. You're just upset. Austin never begrudged you a penny or a pound, Mother, and neither will we. If you wish we'll make you an allowance . . .'

'You're missing the point,' Connie intervened, enjoying this. 'Your

205

mother is saying that she is entitled to property and income, not handouts from her sons. Isn't she, Harry?'

He was flabbergasted. 'Well, I don't know. I've never thought about it.'

'We'll look into this another time,' Victor said unhappily, embarrassed by this ignominy in front of the Toowoomba lawyer, one of Austin's best friends.

But Charlotte had spoken up at last, and she knew that if she gave in now it would be difficult to gather the courage again.

'I want it discussed now. I want you to look into this, William, because I require my share of Springfield. I demand it.'

Nonplussed, he shook his head. 'Charlotte, I'm acting for your late husband and his heirs. I can't act for you too. If you do wish to proceed with this, er, attitude, then you shall have to engage another lawyer.'

'You don't understand, do you? Any of you? I've seen the maps of the claims that you men were lodging, to give the impression that you are complying with Government laws.' She turned to the lawyer. 'Do you know that Austin allotted me the same amount of land as Fern Broderick?'

Recalling that, she became so angry they were all astonished, but she pushed on. 'You look at those maps, William. I am entitled to only as much as a dummy name. And I regard that as an insult.'

Pottinger sat down warily. 'Now, Charlotte, Mrs Broderick, you are confusing inheritance of Springfield as a whole with the requirements of the Alienation of Lands Act. Whatever the gentlemen here have chosen to do – through city lawyers, I am advised – to gain the best possible advantage over the known expense of freehold is up to them. But I should caution you, most sincerely, that mention of dummy claims should not be made outside of this house. That work is beyond my expertise and indeed, though I can commiserate with graziers faced with such problems, I do not want to be part of any illegal plans. I have forgotten that you made any mention of dummy claims.'

'In other words, you don't care that I feel I have been cheated of my rightful share of Springfield?'

'Not at all, Charlotte. If you feel that way, then you have every right to challenge the will.'

'What?' Rupe was on his feet.

'Sit down!' Harry glowered, and he did so, with a thump.

Pottinger continued: 'As I said, you have every right to engage another lawyer.'

'Who?' she asked.

'That's up to you, my dear.'

Connie smiled. 'Why, Judge Walker, of course. I'm sure my father would be honoured to assist.'

'Oh my God, no!' Harry was appalled, but he saw his mother

nodding gratefully at his wife, the first time they'd really had anything in common. He sat back to allow the confusion and arguments in the family parlour to bypass him, saddened to think that all this time Charlotte must have been fretting over her rights to a parcel of Springfield. He wished she'd talked it over with Austin, but then that wouldn't have been easy for her. Austin never talked things over with people; he talked them down.

The lawyer prepared to leave, bidding farewell to each family member with studied politeness, almost backing out of the room to make his escape with as much haste as possible. Charlotte accompanied him.

'I hope you will give this matter more thought,' he said to her as she helped him into his white dustcoat. 'Challenging Austin's will could cause quite a scandal.'

She gazed out over the gardens to the long bank of trees on the far side of the valley, now gilded by the glow of the afternoon sun. 'I think it is a scandal that I was overlooked,' she sighed. 'But I mustn't keep you. Goodbye, William, and thank you for that lovely wreath you brought. It was very much appreciated.'

Victor turned to Harry. 'You're at the bottom of this! Is that why you stayed? You put Connie and Charlotte up to this!'

'Not me. I'm just a bystander!' he grinned.

'Then how come Connie is demanding a share for you as well?'

'First I've heard of it.'

Rupe stormed over. 'You're a bloody liar. You're just trying to cause as much trouble as you can . . .'

He didn't get a chance to finish the sentence. Harry grabbed him by the shirt front and slammed him against the timbered wall. 'And I've had as much cheek from you as I'm going to take. You shut your mouth or I'll shut it for you.'

Connie was enjoying this, pleased that Rupe had rattled Harry enough to make him react, and maybe put up a fight for his share of Springfield, but Louisa was upset.

'For God's sake, you three! Your father is hardly rested in his grave and you're at each other's throats! You will stop this right away.'

The men moved apart, but no one seemed inclined to vacate the room. There was too much at stake here. Finally Harry offered a solution.

'There should be no need for Mother to have to demand a change to the distribution of Austin's assets. We all owe her an apology. None of us, including Austin, gave a thought to what she wanted. If you two offer to split three ways with her, and make it legal, then there'll be no problem.'

'What about when Springfield is broken into sections?' Victor asked. 'It will be too complicated.'

'Come off it, Victor,' Harry said. 'You know perfectly well that no matter what happens with all those so-called new runs, the management, the stock control, the cash, will all come through a central point, your office right here. All I'm saying is that you two give her one third.'

'We can't afford it.'

'Yes you can. She's not asking for cash. Just equal ownership. That's not too hard to understand.'

Rupe hung back by the French windows. 'If I'm permitted to speak, someone should tell Harry that we are simply abiding by Austin's will. And I intend to follow it to the letter.'

'Not even to include your mother?' Harry asked tersely.

'Austin didn't forget her. She has the house to live in as long as she wishes. He knew we would look after her. Maybe he thought that if he left her a share, she would complicate things by remarrying. Austin knew what he was doing and he was right.'

Victor was uncertain. 'If we do give Mother a share, are we leaving ourselves wide open for you to claim a share too, Harry?'

'Of course not.'

'Excuse me.' Now Connie took her turn. 'You be careful what you say, Harry Broderick. You're not just passing up your rights to a penny-ante farm. This is Springfield, not little Tirrabee station, where you are only a manager. Victor knows full well that there's someone else involved here . . .'

'Like who?' Rupe snapped, but Connie ignored him.

'. . . Louisa would have reminded him. So don't let him get away with pretending he doesn't know, trading off a share to Charlotte to get you to drop your claim.'

While she was talking, Harry had walked across the room to pour himself a whisky from the silver drinks tray on the sideboard. 'Am I the only one who has missed this part of the plot?' he asked languidly.

Charlotte was standing at the door. 'No, dear. You aren't. I apologize. I didn't think of it either. Connie's quite correct. If you won't fight for your child's inheritance, Austin's second grandchild, then Connie and I will.'

She walked shakily across the room and Victor jumped up to support her as she made her way to the chair she had recently occupied. 'Would you like a brandy, Mother?'

'Yes, please. With water.'

Harry poured the drink and handed it to Victor, who rushed it across to his mother. 'You're not up to this now. Why don't you go up and rest, Mother, and we'll talk about it when you're feeling better?'

She gulped the brandy. 'We'll talk about it now. I want this decided. Victor, you and Rupe obviously have the same attitude as Austin did. I can't blame you, it's the way he brought you up. I never spoke about this to your father because he had a patronizing attitude to women, but I can't and I won't tolerate it from my sons.' She paused. 'Harry is beginning to understand, but what about you two? I want your answer.'

'It's a very difficult time to be talking about splitting the property three ways, Mother,' Victor said.

'Four ways,' she corrected him.

'Splitting it at all,' he continued, 'with the necessity to freehold hanging over our heads. Can't you wait until we get all that over and done with?'

Oh yes, she thought. Until Fern Broderick's name is listed in the Lands Office as owning property the same size as mine.

'What about you, Rupe?'

'I think it would be wrong, a sad thing, for anyone to try to overturn our father's last will and testament. He was of sound mind and he understood the huge problems that Victor and I have to face to protect his land, and your home, Mother.'

Charlotte sat nursing her brandy glass, taking a sip now and then as they waited for her reaction.

'So,' she said at last, 'that's it, then. I have become a boarder in my own home.'

Louisa was upset. 'Oh, no, Charlotte! Please don't even think like that.'

Charlotte folded her hands. 'Harry and Connie will be going home in the morning. I shall be leaving with them. There's nothing to hold me here now. I'll visit Tirrabee, then I'll be going on to Brisbane.'

'Where will you stay there?' Harry asked. 'There's no need for you to leave Tirrabee.'

'I'm not exactly a beggar. You heard Victor say he will provide me with an allowance. I am fully aware that both Victor's and Austin's safes contain a great deal of spare cash, for a rainy day, as Austin used to call it. What I do and where I stay will be my own business.'

That night, in the privacy of her room, Charlotte was so lonely, she wept herself to sleep. She couldn't imagine her life without Austin, and the family arguments that she had incited were only temporary distractions. She didn't care that they were all upset. None of them could ever understand the enormity of her loss. What did they know about love? Austin might have been selfish and patronizing, but to his mind that was expected of a man like him. A boss man. He knew how much she loved him. Well, he knew, he just wasn't able to reciprocate. Romance, sentimentality, were not part of his make-up. As they'd aged, she'd hoped he'd mellow – some men did – but it was not to be. Time had robbed her of that last joy.

Her dreams were consoling; sweet, lovely dreams with her handsome man beside her again, holding her to him, safe in his arms, whispering how much he loved her, making up for lost time, and she awoke mildly irritated by what she regarded as the trivia of real life.

In the morning she felt stronger. Austin now had his place in her heart, never to be ousted, and so that was settled, but now she had to look to her own life and defend her interests with the same tenacity that her husband had shown. If nothing else, Charlotte had learned from him how to get her own way. You did not falter. You never backed off. And you never, never, relinquished your right to rule. That attitude had built Austin's dukedom on these great pasturelands despite confrontations with Aborigines, other graziers, stockmen and shearers in their turn. He'd maintained his stance and he'd won.

Sadly, she thought that he might have allowed himself to slip away because he'd known the next fight would be too tough, and the loss too hard to bear.

Despite all their plans, Charlotte was aware that her sons would have an uphill battle to hold on to all of Springfield, but she wasn't inclined to feel sorry for them now. Not when Rupe and Victor were trying to slink out of allowing her a share.

She dressed and packed a trunk, taking her time because she knew no one would disturb her for a while yet, giving a great deal of thought to her plan of action.

In Brisbane, she would see Judge Walker and have him guide her claim to upset Austin's will. And she wouldn't falter, because she had another card up her sleeve. It wouldn't be all that long before they freeholded the section of Springfield allotted to Austin's wife. Prime land. Plumb in the centre of the property.

Never falter. That land was registered in her name, and if she didn't get her way, she would sell it. Chopping a great hole in their best holdings. Splitting Springfield irrevocably, while she still held access to the house any time she wished.

And she wanted Fern Broderick's name removed and replaced by Harry's. A lot of plans would have to change now.

She put on her hat and secured it with a silver pin. 'You're just children,' she said to her absent sons. 'I've been taught by an expert. Don't try to cross me. I'll win or I'll break you.'

The diminished household created such a calm and pleasurable existence that Louisa was in seventh heaven. Victor and Rupe were getting along remarkably well, and it was obvious that Rupe was courting Cleo, who had already become one of the family. Every night they dined together, a foursome, a young foursome, free from the restrictions of the older generation, and they had such fun, enjoying each other's company. The men, even Rupe, worked hard, six days of the week and the seventh, constantly checking on the mobs of sheep, examining water holes, throwing up small stretches of wired fencing as visible signs of permanent occupancy, riding restlessly with their stockmen throughout the property like old-time shepherds, determined to provide the best possible conditions for their valuable flocks.

No longer were the women excluded from the men's respite at the end of the long, hot days. No longer was there a last-minute rush to dress for dinner. Life was simpler now, more at ease. Louisa had decided that the dining room should be kept for special occasions, so they took all their meals in the breakfast room, which was much cooler, and Hannah had no objections.

'Less work for the maids,' she said. 'It's a job on its own keeping those big tablecloths starched and pressed all the time.'

Despite the easing of formalities and the more companionable atmosphere, guilt lay heavy with Victor. It was pleasant to come in of an evening and find the girls waiting on the veranda with ready smiles and beer well chilled, but he felt that this cheerfulness had been gained at the expense of his father. Almost as if they were pleased that they were at last rid of Austin. He found that hurtful, and in his quieter times, on lonely rides through the scrub, often conferred with him, apologizing, explaining. But what to say about the awful situation with Charlotte? What would Austin have said about that? A lot, he thought, a bloody lot!

Of course it was all Harry's doing. He'd put Charlotte up to this. Opposing the will would never have entered her head if Harry hadn't been pushing his own barrow, deliberately interfering to cause as much trouble as possible. And he'd encouraged Charlotte to leave with them.

Victor recalled the blazing row he'd had with Harry before they left. He'd begged Charlotte not to be so hasty, not to go, but she was adamant.

'There are four heirs to Springfield, not two. Unless you accept that, Victor, I will go.'

When that final argument reduced Charlotte to tears, Harry intervened. 'For God's sake, Victor, leave her be. I don't want a share, it doesn't matter to me, but surely Mother is entitled. Can't you see that?'

Enraged, Victor had shouted at him: 'All I can see is your determination to wreck this family. You caused enough trouble in Brisbane and you're doing the same thing here. You get out of this house and stay out! You weren't welcome when Austin was alive and you're not welcome now. Don't ever come back here again.'

Later, when he'd calmed down, he'd written to Charlotte, hoping that when she was rested and had had a good holiday she would return to her home, so that they could talk things over.

She didn't reply to that letter, and, no doubt encouraged by Harry, had travelled on to Brisbane to consult with solicitors.

Six weeks later, a package of story books arrived for Teddy, and with them a response from Charlotte. She was well, quite enjoying Brisbane, but looking forward to coming home. In the meantime she

211

was awaiting legal advice on her right to ownership of her home.

Victor sat in his office, the door closed, morosely smoking his pipe. It was late and the house was still, the best time for him to concentrate on station bookwork these days, but too many worries intruded.

He quaked now at the thought of Charlotte coming home. He hadn't been able to bring himself to caution Louisa against making too many changes for fear of upsetting her, with the result that his wife now seemed to believe that she was the lady of the house. Furniture had been switched around, heavy drapes taken down to make the ground-floor rooms brighter and airier. Everything seemed different. Much improved, he had to admit, but would Charlotte approve? He doubted it. In fact he was sure she would not.

Then came the letter from William Pottinger, regretting to advise that Charlotte had rejected his efforts to mediate. She seemed determined to upset Austin's will if necessary.

'Damnation!' Victor had never felt so frustrated. Rupe had come up with the excellent suggestion that they sell off several of the less fertile sections of Springfield, and even part of the outstations, which would relieve them of the necessity to keep managers working there. Victor, though regretting the loss of thousands of acres, was very much in favour. Right now they needed the money more than that land.

He wondered if they should agree to give Charlotte a third share. After all, it would only be nominal, she'd be living here anyway. He could make it a condition that she persuade Harry to give up any claim against the will.

'That's the answer!' he said at last. 'That's it.'

He set to immediately, carefully penning a letter to his mother, wishing her well and agreeing to her claim on the one condition. 'That will sort them out!' he grinned, pleased with himself, despite, once again, that quake of worry. Charlotte would be coming home. Louisa would be displaced, and their easy-going lifestyle would be short-lived.

But Rupe was as stubborn as their mother.

'You don't look to the future, Victor. Say we do cut Mother in. What happens when she dies? She won't leave Harry out. We'll be back where we started.'

'I'll worry about that when the time comes.'

'No we won't. And what gives you the right to send a letter like that? Forget it, Victor. The answer is still no.'

Judge Walker was only too pleased to assist Broderick's widow. They had invited her to stay with them, but since she had indicated by letter that she did not wish to be a burden on anyone, he had found her rooms at the very respectable Park Private Hotel, overlooking the botanic gardens. Quite a few elderly ladies had permanent residence

212

there so he deemed it suitable for a country woman without a female companion.

After spending a Sunday afternoon with her, the Judge decided that Mrs Broderick was rather a foolish woman; she didn't seem to know what she wanted. Understandably grief-stricken at the loss of her husband, apt to become tearful at the mention of his name, she still insisted that she should have been left a share of the property.

Connie had acquainted him with the contents of the will, finding that, after all, she did need her father's advice.

'These young people,' he said to Mrs Walker, 'they think they know everything. And now look what happens. The first time anything goes wrong she comes rushing back to me. Typical of that irresponsible husband of hers not to care about his inheritance when he has a family to support.'

'I'm only glad she had the good sense to write to you before it was too late.'

'Yes. A dose of decent country living must have unscrambled that brain of hers. But I don't know what they expect me to do about Charlotte Broderick. One minute she's bemoaning his death; the next she wants to besmirch his good name by claiming he was unfair to her. Was Austin the only one in that family with any semblance of self-respect?'

'It seems so. Connie hasn't a good word for either of the other two sons. What is Charlotte's position anyway?'

'Exactly as I tried to explain to her. Possession is nine-tenths of the law. He was not unfair to her. She has a beautiful home and sons to run the property for her. She is established there and no one can shift her.'

Mrs Walker shifted uncomfortably in her chair. 'I think she means she is now beholden to her sons.'

'Nothing unusual about that. It's just her bad luck they're peculiar people, which is not to say they are incompetent in running the property. Jock tells me that Victor is a very capable manager, with expert knowledge of sheep breeding. She should be grateful for her late husband's wisdom, not hanging about Brisbane, sulking.'

Privately, Mrs Walker was glad she didn't have sons to oust her from her inheritance if the Judge passed on. He wouldn't dream of leaving all of his considerable property and assets to a daughter, especially Connie.

'Oh dear,' she nodded. 'What will happen, then?'

'With the widow? Nothing. I'll have a barrister explain to her in the clearest of terms that she hasn't got a case. Austin did provide for her in the will, in the normal manner. She has a home and upkeep. Imagine what confusion she could cause out there if she owned a share and remarried. It doesn't bear thinking about.'

'And Harry? Apparently the brothers upset him. Connie says he is

213

willing now to lay claim to a third share.'

'Pity about him! He's upset enough people in his day. Were it not for the child Connie will have, I'd have said serve them right, but I have to defend the rights of my grandchild. Harry will get his share, as stated in the original will, or I'll see to it that this case drags on for years.'

She smiled. 'I think you might be doing this for Connie too.'

'Of course I am. If Harry doesn't make a go of it at Tirrabee, keeping in mind that he is unstable, we'll have them back on our doorstep again. One third of Springfield is not to be sneezed at.'

Chapter Nine

Spinner was thinking of taking a wife, but there were complications. He had chosen Dixie, a smart young gin who worked as a laundress over at old Jock's place, and she was thrilled at the prospect. There weren't too many men of her tribe who had steady, respectable jobs as stockmen. The problem arose when they had to decide where to live.

He couldn't bring Dixie back to Springfield. There were no quarters for black women, and the Springfield mob had long deserted their riverside camp, so she couldn't join them.

'You'll have to come and live here,' Dixie told him.

That would be a wrench for Spinner. This station was his home; he loved Springfield, knew every inch of it. But by this time he also loved Dixie, he was mad for her, so he allowed her to make enquiries.

The next time he rode over to visit, Dixie ran out to greet him with exciting news. 'You've got the job. The missus says she doesn't want to lose me, so you can work here as a stockman. She'll arrange it with your Mr Victor. And guess what? She said we can have the old shearer's hut out past the stables to live in! The other girls are helping me to clean it up and make it nice! We'll have our own home.'

That was stupendous news. Spinner was delighted. And flattered to think that the missus – Mrs Crossley, old Jock's widowed daughter – would help them. He would be able to raise a family in a proper house. He would be better off than most of the white stockmen who lived in dormitory-style men's quarters, finding women where they could because married quarters for whites were kept to the minimum. To Spinner, the shearer's hut was a step up in the world, a godsend; he'd be living the way he'd always wanted, just like a white family. He wouldn't have to resort to camping with his own mob down by the river once he took a wife.

He was glad they'd gone.

Everything was arranged. Everyone at Springfield knew that Spinner was leaving to get married, and while they teased him unmercifully, he knew they were happy for him.

But then he changed his mind. He refused to leave Springfield.

Dixie was upset and bewildered. Mrs Crossley was sorry for her. She sent a note to Victor asking him what was wrong, but Victor replied that he had no idea. He couldn't get any sense out of Spinner, except that he did still love Dixie, and yes, he still wanted to marry her, but he didn't want to leave this property.

Amused, Victor put it down to old clannish ties, maybe a sort of homesickness, and told them not to worry. Spinner would get over it and make the break one of these days. A little patience was required for the time being.

But Spinner had remembered the kids, Bobbo, Jagga and Doombie, and his promise to Moobuluk. His promise to watch out for them, to listen about and report any word of them. He knew that he could ride over occasionally to see if there was any news of them, but that was only the letter of the law. It was not what was expected of him. He was the last clan member left on Springfield and he had to stay here. He dare not leave.

But when *could* he leave?

In passing, he managed to strike up a seemingly innocuous conversation with Jack Ballard about young Teddy, who happened to be in the storeroom with Victor.

'He's gettin' a big boy, that Teddy. When's he goin' off to school?'

Jack laughed. 'Not for a long time. He's got a teacher here. You know, the governess. The girl Rupe's sweet on.'

'Yeah,' Spinner nodded. 'When do you reckon Bobbo and them other kids finish school?'

'God knows.' Not interested, Jack strode away to talk to Victor, and Spinner still had nothing to report to Moobuluk beyond what had already been discussed. That the boys might never come back.

When the boss died, Spinner was even more worried. He sensed that with the passing of that man, his clan had lost a valuable tie with the whites. He was sure the boss would have known where the kids were; he wouldn't just have let them be taken and dropped in a well somewhere, he'd have known. Now he too was gone.

During all the fuss of the funeral, Spinner disappeared, unnoticed. He rode north for a full day until he came to the camp of the warrigal people, dingo totem, at the two-river junction, and there he left a message to be passed on to Moobuluk that Boss Broderick had died. He didn't suppose that the ancient would care, but it would remind him that Spinner was still loyal and would perhaps provoke a response. For Spinner dearly wished to be released from that promise.

Moobuluk received the message when he climbed into the great range of hills that formed the spine of the east coast and gave direction to the people. He visited old friends among the hill tribes and sent out scouts to enquire if anyone had sighted the woman, Nioka, but no one had any word of her. That wasn't surprising, given the distances she had to cover. If indeed she was journeying south. He set some days aside to meditate, endeavouring to align his mind with hers, to probe her secrets, and was very much disturbed to find only rage. No

216

hint at all of where she might be, but she was alive. Very much so.

He turned his thoughts to the death of Boss Broderick, and that did affect him. It gave him indigestion, reminding him that his days too were numbered, a sad fact when there was so much to do.

Since he could now assure himself that Nioka was still in the land of the living, that she hadn't spent her own life as her sister had done, he felt there was no hurry to locate her. Better to let her walk off that rage her own way. Sooner or later he would find her. In the meantime the hill people had many problems that required his wisdom. Decisions had to be made as to which of their elders should be appointed as keepers of the song; which fathers had achieved enough seniority to carry out the most important initiation ceremonies; on totem and marriage disagreements, all the usual matters, as well as the current concerns about the relentless advance of the whites.

He heard with horror that people from all clans and tribes were bundled together into huge whitefeller camps called reserves, and forbidden to leave. There was one, he heard, at Yarrabah, and another outside a white town called Ipswich, a place he knew well. It was on the plains that led up to the great plateau of grasslands, his own home territory.

He heard of all the poor people who were being brought to these places, even shipped south from their own lands, to be herded and confined just like sheep, with no care or understanding for tribal taboos, wherein various clans may not share the same campfires.

'I will have to go to these places,' he said, 'for my own understanding, for surely the stories are very hard to believe. I must see for myself.'

Yarrabah was far to the north, but the other reserve was closer. He decided to follow the chain of hills south and enter the great plateau from the west through Boss Broderick's sheep country. Spinner was still there. Although, obviously, he had no news of the children, he might have seen Nioka. It was possible she had returned in the hope of finding them.

'Faint hope,' he mourned, 'if they are now rounding up whole families of blackfellows as well as the children.'

Tears ran down his old scarred face. 'What is to become of us?'

Nioka had not taken the same path home. She had headed straight for white settlements, villages and towns, keeping to herself, searching desperately for the children.

The plan had come to her in a dream, a nightmare in which she had found herself fighting with her sister, trying to defend herself from savage blows from Minnie's heavy waddy. And yet they were in that lake, drowning, with a storm raging about them.

'You find my Bobbo!' Minnie was screaming at her.

'I can't. Get away from me. I have to get to the shore.'

She was swimming desperately, furious with Minnie, sobbing in

217

fear, crying: 'I don't know where to look.'

'You do, you lazy bitch. If you'd been minding them while I was working they wouldn't be lost now.'

Demons joined with Minnie, hammering blows on Nioka as she struggled for a shore that was now out of sight.

She awoke in a rage of frustration, damp with sweat, to find all was quiet in the solitary humpy she had built for herself in the forest above the lake, but she knew the demons still hovered. Furious, she was on her feet, charging into the scrub, shouting at them.

'Leave, you foul creatures,' she shouted. 'You let my sister rest or I will call the spirits down on you. My sister was weak, I am not. My mother was not.' She shook her fist at the shuddering trees. 'We are high-born. Kin of great chiefs. I will find her son, and my son, and Gabbidgee's son! I do not need your howling, or hers.'

The words shocked her, but she could not back down now, so she stamped back to the shade of the humpy and sat chewing on a mouthful of nuts.

What right did Minnie have to say she knew where to look? How dare they blame her?

Where would she look anyway?

And then it came to her. Among the whites, of course. Somewhere. They had to be somewhere.

She decided to cut down from the hills, making for the lights of the white men's houses, and start from there. Following roads that always led to other camps and towns, she would scour every inch of them. That would shut her sister up.

As she set off she was angry with Minnie, with the demons, and most of all with that white praying man and all his kin, and it was this rage that kept her going.

At the first village, aware of white men's ways, she stole a blouse and skirt from a line, swam in a creek to wash off the travel dirt and bunched her hair back with a ribbon torn from the bottom of the blouse. Barefoot, but dressed, she plodded along the street, giving the impression she knew where she was going but watching, peering all about her listening for children's voices.

Soon Nioka learned to recognize schools, but they seemed to be only for white children; she noted praying men in their black clothes with the turned-about collars and followed them to their prayer houses. One of them, a white-haired old man, even invited her in to see his church, but she was afraid to enter, afraid he would ensnare her. He surprised her, though, by asking if she was hungry, and that she couldn't deny, so he asked her to wait. Warily, she hung back under a tree, ready to bolt, but he returned with a billy of warm soup, which she drank greedily.

'Where are you from?' he asked her kindly.

'No place.'

'You don't live here?'

'No.'

'Just going walkabout?'

'Yes.'

'On your own? That's not usual. You seem a good type of girl. There are dangers for young girls like you, wandering about on your own. Serious moral dangers. You should come and talk to my wife. She might be able to find you a job . . .'

Nioka couldn't understand all he was saying, except for the part about the job, and she had no time for that, but she felt that he meant well, so she let him talk on, gathering courage to ask him her question.

'Where the black kids' school, mister?'

'The black kids' school?' he echoed. 'Oh, well now. There isn't one here. They don't have to go to school. It's not necessary for them. No. Not necessary. Why? Do you have children with you?'

Nioka left. She'd heard all she wanted to know. No school here for her boys. She had no more time for this old fellow.

Outside of the small towns she often found black communities, sad, miserable camps, dens of despair, too late to go back to their hunting grounds and too soon to try to engage the mysteries of the ruling white world. Humbly Nioka accepted their shelter and their poor fare, seeing with her own eyes the effect of grog on their young men, remembering the warnings of her mother, and, she had to admit, of Boss Broderick. Both of them had barred grog from the black camp, and any stockmen or shearers who brought it in were immediately expelled from Springfield.

But among these people she learned about missions where children were taken. And reserves where whole families were swept in like dust. No more than dust. Everywhere she went, her people feared they would be next, and they warned her to beware of police and troopers.

As she trudged on, Nioka wondered if the reserves could be any worse than those barren, dusty camps where all they could do, all day, was hope that someone would bring in some food or grog. But then they would not be free to walk away from reserves if they wished, and that was frightening, almost as bad as being in jail. Their greatest fear. She could imagine the turmoil that would arise at being thrown under the same roof as wrong totems. The sort of thing that would send the spirits into a frenzy, and thoroughly confuse the people.

Alone, nearing the lights of yet another town, Nioka crept into a barn and wept. She had seen too much. This trek had been a terrible mistake. Protected at Springfield, and again, thanks to the wisdom of Moobuluk, in the lake country, she'd had no conception of the world that now engulfed her. Her clothes were worn and dirty, and for the first time in her life, Nioka felt inferior, a horrible new sensation. All the blacks she'd met knew so much about the world, about so many things. She realized that to them she was just a tribal black, lost, lonely and not too bright.

Her mother came to her that night, not to console her but to demand: 'What did you expect? Would you listen to me? No. You wanted the world to stay still for you. Now you sit about sorry for yourself. You didn't want any place in the white world and that's what you've got. To them you don't exist.'

But Boss Broderick was there too. He never agreed with Nioka's mother. 'Come home,' he said. 'You belong at Springfield.'

He seemed sad. 'Why did you leave? Why did you all go? You were not there, any of you, to sing me on my way, and I missed you. I never wished you any harm.'

Moobuluk was right. Nioka had walked off her rage. The strange worlds she had encountered had burned the fire from her, confusing her into submission, because she had no answers to all the questions that battered her, almost as if she was like Moobuluk himself.

What is to become of us? she kept asking herself, not knowing why the question should haunt her. She was only a no-account black gin. She resumed her travels through the outskirts of a town until she was confronted by a river.

Now that she was vulnerable, the demons pounced. 'Come and see. This is a big river. Wide and exciting. Give yourself to the river spirits, they will take you into their hearts . . .'

They were right. This *was* a great river, fast-flowing, making for the wonders of the oceans beyond, oceans that Nioka had heard about and never seen. It would be easy just to dissolve into the warm, creamy waters.

She sat on the end of a jetty and contemplated slipping into the Dreaming for the sake of peace, so easily, so simply, freed from all these terrible confusions.

'What are you doing here, girlie?' a fisherman asked her as he settled down to throw a line into the river.

Nioka turned her gaze on him.

What was she doing there? What had happened to her? Had she forgotten why she had left the lake? She thought she heard the boys weeping. No one else was looking for them. Minnie was dead. Gabbidgee had given up. Would she forsake them too?

'What is this place?' she asked him wearily.

He grinned. 'Why, it's Brisbane, missy. This is the good old Brisbane River, and a mighty good river at that.'

Nioka looked down along the river and was terrified at what she saw. This wasn't a village or some small town. There were buildings crowding the banks and a big, big bridge towering from one side to the other.

'Are you all right?' he asked.

She shook her head. 'No, boss. Reckon I be lost.'

220

'Where do you want to go?'

'Springfield.'

He chewed on his pipe. 'Can't say as I know that town.'

'Not town. Plenty sheep place.'

'Ah, well. It wouldn't be nowheres near here.'

Nioka could hardly believe that she had sunk so low as to ask a whitefeller to show her the way to her own country, but it had to be done.

Tears dribbled down her grimy cheeks. 'I want go home.'

'Now, now, there's no need for that. Here, you eat this bun, and when I've caught our dinner, I'll have a talk with my missus. She might know. Not much she don't know; but never you tell her I said that.'

Freda Omeara stood in the narrow lane outside the row of shanties and flapped her large apron impatiently.

'Get inside, you kids!' she shouted, and her ragged brood quickly disengaged from the push and shove of their street game to gather behind her skirts, curiosity delaying them, for their father was coming down the lane, past the empty beer casks lined up at the back gate of the pub. They knew the apron flapping was for him; she always flapped like that when she was angry. It was near to dark and he'd be late for his nightwatchman job.

They nudged and grinned, waiting for the explosion, for wasn't he always late, their pa.

'You'd be late for your own funeral!' she always said.

They weren't disappointed. 'You've been in the pub, you wretch!' she shrilled as he neared. 'Would you be losin' this job as well? And us behind in the rent. Have you no thought for these little ones?'

Pa never took her seriously; he never seemed to take anything too seriously at all. Mischievously he lunged at her with his fishing rod, causing her to swerve aside and the youthful assemblage to paddle sideways with her.

'Not the pub, me darling, but the fishing, can you not see? And look here in the basket, everythin' but the loaves.'

But she was staring past him at the tall, bedraggled black gin, who she'd thought was just a passer-by, but who was now standing, stopped, if you don't mind, in the middle of the Omeara family.

'Who's that you've got with you?' she demanded.

'Ah, now. This here's Nioka. And a great fisherlady she is. Caught yabbies for me. Look at 'em! Nice fat yabbies. Along with the fish and all, it's a great feast we'll be havin'.' He turned. 'Say hello now to Mrs Omeara, me girl, and we'll go on in.'

As Nioka nodded shyly, the kids looked to their mother.

'What do you mean, bringing home a black gin? Have you gone off your head?' she hissed.

Then a rare thing happened. The smile disappeared from his broad face and the twinkling blue eyes went flat.

'Only fair, Mrs Omeara. She got us the yabbies.'

'Then give them to her and send her on her way!'

He hesitated, looked from one woman to the other, and then the kids breathed a sigh of relief as the stormclouds vanished. He took his wife's arm, the way he did when he wanted to cool her down, and beamed on her.

'We can't do that, there's somethin' else. She's lost, you see, and I've been tellin' her that my darlin' wife is an educated woman who can read and write with the best of them. Who could sort this out with the greatest of ease, had she a mind to.'

They could feel their mater relenting. She was proud of her education, but in their poverty had little enough chance to use it, beyond battering the letters and sums into her kids with slates and spit and chalk.

'What can I tell her?' she allowed.

'First we'd better get in, or I'll be late for work,' he murmured with a sly grin.

They all trooped into the two-roomed shanty with its shingle roof, taking the black girl with them.

'First things first,' Mrs Omeara snapped, not ready to give in too easily. This was her domain and they knew their place. He was sent out the back to clean the fish and peel the shells from the yabbies, the older girl was directed to stoke the stove and heat the gruel and her sister to bring out the weevily flour and the fat tin and start cooking the fish as the boys brought them in.

The dark-skinned girl hung by the door, as if about to take flight.

'Nioka, is it?' Mrs Omeara asked firmly.

She nodded.

'Speak English?'

'Some,' she whispered.

'Well, that's something. But I have to tell you, I have rules here. And I can't have you in my house smelling like a garbage bin. I don't care what he says. You come with me.'

She led Nioka out the back, past the bench where he was cleaning the last of the fish with the help of the two lads, and on to the laundry, closing the rickety door.

'Do you know what that is?' she asked, pointing at the large tin bath.

'Yes, missus.'

'Good. Because you're going to have a good wash down from top to toe.' She went to the door, calling to one of her daughters. 'Sheila, bring the bucket and the sandsoap. Now!'

Her attitude was beginning to annoy Nioka, whose temper was never too far from the surface. She was lost and depressed and very hungry, but she had her pride too. She watched coldly as they lugged in buckets of water, enough for a few inches in the bath, and then the missus sent Sheila to give her father his dinner.

'You get in now and get yourself clean,' Nioka was told. 'Hair as well. Understand?'

Nioka drew herself up and looked down at the dumpy woman. 'I need a towel.'

The woman stood back, astonished. 'What? Yes, I suppose you do. I'll get you one.'

The only towels Nioka had ever seen were the lovely soft ones in the laundry at Springfield, and she deliberately looked askance at the pathetic piece of cloth the woman brought her, taking it with no show of gratitude.

Inside, Mrs Omeara slammed plates on the table for the kids.

'She's a hoity-toity miss, that one. Putting on airs, if you don't mind.'

Her husband looked up from his meal. 'Bravado is all. You see if you can give her a hand.'

'What do you think I'm doing? Now, do you see, I can't put her back in those filthy clothes. It's burning they need. What'll I give her to wear?'

'You're a kind woman behind all your ferocities. You'll find something.'

'Ah, God help us!'

She was shocked to find the girl had no bloomers, just a skirt and blouse, and the godliness in Mrs Omeara found her searching through the tin trunk for some pink bloomers, a black jersey and a faded brown skirt that she'd intended to cut up for patches. She placed the garments hurriedly on the little stool in the laundry, carefully averting her eyes from the girl in the bath. It was the first time she'd glimpsed the polished black body of a naked Aborigine woman. As she walked away, she blushed, for hadn't that glance shown her a smooth elegance of line and limb that could almost be called beautiful.

When they were all fed in their turn, including the donor of the dozen fat yabbies, and he'd gone off to work, Mrs Omeara planted the lantern on the small scrubbed table.

'Now, what's this all about?'

Nioka took a deep breath, which came out as more of a sob, worse luck. She had hoped to be able to ask about the boys, but the gentleman had gone and left her with this bullying woman and her staring kids, and they intimidated her.

'The gentleman, he say you know where is Springfield.'

'Huh! Gentleman, is it? He's come up fast in the world. Is that where you live? Springfield?'

Nioka nodded her head. Live? Yes, that would do.

'And you want to go home?'

'Yes, missus.'

'Well, let me see. He said it was a sheep station. Is that right?'

'Yes, missus.'

'How come you're in Brisbane?'

'Got lost.' That seemed the best explanation, but the woman didn't think so.

'I didn't know you people could get lost. Thought you could follow your noses. But it looks like you lost yourself well and good. Nary a sheep station in these parts. So where is it?'

Nioka thought that a stupid question. If she'd known where it was, she wouldn't have to ask. She just looked blankly at the woman.

'What direction from here? North? South?'

'Don't know.'

'Dear God! A pin in a haystack. Sheila! Bring me my map!'

The girl ran into the other room and came rushing back with a large folded page. 'Is this it?'

'Yes. Lay it out here now, while I look. Here, now,' she said, addressing them all, opportunity for a lesson emerging, 'is my map of Queensland, that I bought with my own money, because I'm a person who likes to know where I am. Can you read, girl?'

'No, missus.'

'Well, I wouldn't expect you to, I suppose. But you kids pay attention. If she could read she wouldn't be having this trouble. She could just take a map and find her way home. That's what becomes of people who can't read. Do you hear me?'

'Yes, Mater,' they chorused earnestly.

Her eyes waded over the map with care. 'It's a great grand state this is, bigger than forty Irelands, where your pa and me came from. Maybe fifty even. But she couldn't have come from up top there or she'd have no soles left on her feet. We'll look round the bottom part. Right here's Brisbane, that's where we are, see. On the river.'

She sat back so the kids could crowd the table and peer at her finger, and Nioka, fascinated, leaned forward too.

Then they were ordered to move back as Mrs Omeara searched for the name, her finger sliding backwards and forwards, stopping, studying, pressing on, and Nioka realized with a wry smile that this boss lady was enjoying the chase. And also that she was now seeing another side to the woman, a cheerfulness that replaced her botherations.

She reminded Nioka of Hannah, the cook at Springfield, who was often bossy and testy, but much nicer of a night when all the work was done. Kind then, kind to Minnie and the kids, and generous with handouts of leftovers.

She looked about the tiny kitchen, dominated by the stove, with its stone floor and rickety scraps of furniture, and wondered what this white woman would think of the huge kitchen at Springfield, bigger than this whole house. It was a wonderment to her how some white folk could be so poor.

Mrs Omeara was still searching, shaking her head.

'Can't you find it, Mater?' one of the boys asked anxiously.

'It's not necessarily here at all. Not all them big farms are mentioned on the maps. Only towns. Now listen here, girl. There must be a town nearby. You tell me the name of the town.'

Nioka blinked. 'Town?'

'Yes. There has to be a town where they buy their provisions. You must know that.'

The name flashed in front of Nioka's eyes like a falling star. 'Town,' she squealed. 'Yes. Town! I know, missus. It's Cobbside.' She intoned it carefully. 'Cobb Side.'

The finger chased back and forth again, up and down.

'Fetch me the ruler, Johnny,' Mrs Omeara called, and the boy ran to the dresser drawer to bring it to her so that she could move it down the page ever so slowly, agonizingly slowly, while they all waited, breathless with suspense.

'Can't say as I've heard of it,' she muttered. 'And me who has studied this map a million times but never remember seeing Cobbside. Are you sure you've got it right, Nioka?'

That was the first time she'd used her name, and Nioka felt proud. Accepted.

'Yes, missus.'

'A little place, is it? Maybe too small, too insignificant to earn a place on a great world map. We'll have to try again. Would you be knowing another town out there?'

The children sighed as Nioka shook her head, but this woman was faced with a challenge to her knowledge, to her expertise, and she wasn't one to give in, especially with them all there to witness a failure and report to himself. Who had such faith in her.

'Tell you what we'll do. I'll call you names of towns and you tell me if they ring a bell.'

Nioka wasn't sure what ringing bells had to do with it, but she got the drift, and waited as the missus pored over the map and began calling names.

In her travels Nioka had discovered that she knew a lot more English than she'd thought she did. Half the time, back at Springfield, she'd deliberately tried to shut her ears, and the rest of the time she'd pretended she didn't understand, to annoy Minnie.

Now, though, she was flummoxed by the names that the missus threw at her. Random words.

'Maryborough. Sandgate. Redcliffe . . .'

They didn't mean a thing to her, but when Gympie was mentioned she felt she ought to contribute something.

'Stinging tree,' she translated, wanting to be helpful.

'What? Is that the place?' the missus asked expectantly.

'No.'

'That's what it means?'

'Yes.'

'Well I never! What about this? Gayndah.'

'Thunder,' Nioka grinned, and so began a game.

Yarraman was horse. Kingaroy, red ants. Nambour, ti-tree. Bundaberg, home of Bunda people.

Mrs Omeara clapped her hands in delight. Here was a new lesson, something not to be learned in books. Later she would write them down. She began pulling out other native-sounding names for the fun of it, temporarily forgetting the chase.

'Maroochy?'

'Black swan.'

'Indooroopilly?'

'Many leeches in creek.'

'Mareeba?'

'Don't know. Another language.'

'Toowoomba?'

'Big swamp. Water underground.' She almost missed it. The name almost flitted by her, so intent were they on this game. 'That's the town. Toowoomba. Big town. Boss Broderick, he go there a lot. Plenty people there, I reckon.'

'Glory be to God! We've got you placed! Look here, right here. How far is your station from Toowoomba?'

Nioka had no concept of the measuring of distance except by days, and what was more, she'd never been to Toowoomba, she'd only heard about it. She racked her brains and took a guess, rather than appear too stupid.

'Three days,' she announced blithely.

'Three days' walk, that's a long way. But it's even further from here. Never been there meself, for it's more than a couple of hundred miles away.' Mrs Omeara grinned, proud of her success. 'There'd be sheep stations out there, all right, but bless my soul, you're way off the track, my girl. We'll have to ask himself what to do about this.'

Nioka had been lost, but more in her head than her surroundings, despairing as she became aware how feeble were her attempts to find the boys in the great maze of streets and houses. Fear kept her from mentioning them to any white people. She was afraid that they would regard her search as wrong-doing, and become suspicious of her. Even hide the boys deeper in their big towns.

Now, though, she was caught up in the excitement of this family as they rushed to tell the man, when he came home in the morning, that they had found where Nioka lived.

He beamed on the children. 'Did I not always say your mother is a remarkable woman?'

They talked to Nioka about Springfield, asking questions, for none of them had ever seen a sheep station and were keen to learn, and she answered them as best she could. Yes, big house, much land. Many, many sheep.

Kangaroos?

Nioka grinned. 'Plenty kangaroos. And wallabies, the little ones.' She was more knowledgeable discussing the wildlife, and they were enthralled.

'Ah, what a great life it must be,' the missus sighed. 'We have to see about getting you home.'

Home? Nioka wondered. It was hardly home any more, but their enthusiasm was infectious, and now she was eager to go back. Maybe this was a sign. The boys could be home by this and they would be waiting, bewildered to find all the people had gone.

As the days passed, while the man made his enquiries, Nioka became convinced that the spirits had heard her cries, and were now preparing to return her to Springfield. She was in their hands.

In the meantime, however, finding that the missus took in washing, she shed her opposition to white women's work and gave a willing hand, proving a strong, competent worker. She grinned as she hauled heavy, steaming sheets from the copper and dumped them in the basket, knowing that her sister, who would be watching from her spirit home, would be astonished. But these people were kind to her, they let her sleep by the stove, wrapped in a blanket, and they shared their food with her, so helping in the laundry was the least she could do.

When the great day came, the family gathered at the end of the lane to see her off. Clutching her dilly bag with some food for the journey, and a brown paper parcel containing her washed and patched blouse and skirt, Nioka was hoisted aboard a brewery wagon to sit atop the heavy kegs. She waved as the gallant draught horses heaved and snorted, pulling away.

'You come back and see us!' Mrs Omeara called, and Nioka nodded, sadness wilting her confidence because she was alone again, except for the lorry driver, who seemed not to be interested in her at all.

They crossed the river and set out into the country as the sun melted the morning mists. Nioka studied the route, noting landmarks. Taking her lead from Mrs Omeara, she felt she should learn more, and the first thing to do was to know exactly where she was going. It was necessary these days, she told herself resolutely, to understand where all these roads led.

They stopped in the town of Ipswich late that afternoon, and the driver allowed her to sleep in the stables with his horses. In the morning they were off again. The horses clattered over a bridge and sped merrily back into the countryside, but when they came to steep roads, climbing high into the hills, they worked hard, dragging the heavy load, and Nioka, frightened, hung on for dear life.

Eventually they made it, puffing and snorting, on to a long, flat road, and the driver called to her: 'This is Toowoomba, missy. This is as far as I go.'

He directed her to the road that would lead her to Cobbside. 'You might as well start walking. When you get out on the road, someone will give you a lift.'

Once out there, tramping the sandy road, it took a while for Nioka to pluck up the courage to do as he suggested and hail passing wagons. Most ignored her, but in the end a man and woman let her sit on the back of their dray, and she was on her way again, marvelling at the simplicity of white travel. For the first time in her life, Nioka wished she had a horse. She'd seen enough of them on the station but had taken no notice. Now, as she watched riders galloping past, she appreciated the sleek animals. This long journey from the lake country was proving a real eye-opener to her. A good lesson, as Mrs Omeara would say.

At a crossroads the dray halted and the woman swung around to her. 'You'll need to be getting off here, we're turning in to Cobbside.'

Nioka jumped down. The air was already familiar; this was her own country all right. 'Thanks, missus.'

'You one of the Springfield blacks?'

She nodded, her feet tingling for her own bush lining the road.

'Is Mrs Broderick back yet?'

'Where's she been?' the driver of the dray asked his wife.

'I told you. After Austin died she left with Harry. They reckon she was heartbroken and needed to get away for a while, but I heard different. I heard there was ructions in that camp. Over the will.' She looked to the black girl for an answer.

Nioka had no idea, but she was desperate to go on up the road, so she made a guess. 'No. Not back yet.' That seemed to satisfy them.

Before the dray was even out of sight, Nioka was off and running, diving into the bush past a big old wattle tree that glowed with yellow blossoms. She skittered through the scrub, so excited to be on home ground again that she must have travelled for miles before she slowed, breathing in the welcoming sweet smells, climbing down into a gully, recognizing every tree, every old crumbling log that littered well-known tracks.

There was no hurry now, she was home. This was her bush and she knew exactly where to find food without ever having to rely on anyone else again. Her mind turned back to the conversation with that couple.

Did they say that Boss Broderick was dead? And that Mrs Charlotte had left the property? That was a monumental piece of information.

It didn't affect her, or her intentions, but she wondered about his death. To Nioka, Boss Broderick was Springfield. She couldn't imagine that place without him. What would all the white people do now? Mrs Charlotte's presence, or absence, was not important, except possibly to watch out for the three little boys when they came home. There was always Mrs Louisa. She would look after the boys.

Who would bring them home? she asked herself. The praying man? Nioka hoped that was so, and savoured the punishment that he could expect for taking them away in the first place. She would bash him. She could make a spear and kill him. Or belt him with a tomahawk. They were pleasurable thoughts.

But what if the boys were already there? The spirits were bringing them together, of that she was sure. Nioka began to hurry again. It was a long way to the river, to the old camp, and from there to the homestead. With joy in her heart, fuelled by wishful thinking, by the certainty that she would find the boys waiting at Springfield, she kept going, even when the sun went down. Darkness was no hazard as she plunged on through the familiar scrub, as sure-footed as the many nocturnal creatures that scuttled out of her path. With the stars for company, she crossed open country where sheep nestled and dingoes prowled, and keeping to the straight line climbed rocky outcrops from where she could see the shimmer of the river in the distance.

Gaudy red bottlebrush adorned the side garden, and flashy lorikeets, even more colourful, shrieked and shoved through the greenery and wobbled along the branches like toy soldiers, quaffing the nectar. White cockatoos perched and fluttered angrily in the nearby treetops, their screeches louder and more raucous than the smaller birds, hoping to drive them away, but there was safety in numbers and the lorikeets could afford to ignore them.

Louisa loved the birds, but the racket was giving her a headache. She closed the French windows firmly to shut out the noise and went back to sorting out her clothes because summer was fast approaching and the light dresses would need airing.

The room was quieter now but the headache persisted. It wasn't only the birds that worried her, it was the war of words that had erupted between Victor and Rupe, causing constant upsets in the household.

'I knew everything seemed to be too good to be true,' she muttered crossly. 'Rupe would have to spoil everything, as usual, he's so damned selfish.'

But it wasn't only Rupe, it was Charlotte. They were both pigheaded, both wanting their own way, with poor Victor failing to achieve a compromise.

Lawyers on both sides had advised the silly woman that she could not win her claim against Austin's will, but she still wanted her day in court, thereby preventing her sons from selling some of the outer blocks to release much-needed cash. Victor had decided to give in to her, but Rupe would not.

'You capitulate too easily,' he argued. 'She can't win. Let her go to court.'

'That will cost us more money.'

'And her too. Where will she get the cash to fight us? She hasn't got a bean.'

That bothered Victor even more. 'It doesn't say much for us to be admitting that our mother hasn't got a bean, after all the years she has spent working at Springfield, long before this house was built. She pulled her weight.'

'And she has the run of the place for life.'

'But no money.'

'If she behaves herself she will have money. An allowance.'

'I still say we cut her in, on condition she makes Harry withdraw his claim, because that's in the wind too.'

'No. Definitely not. Springfield is ours. We'll just have to sit them out.'

'Don't be so bloody stupid. We haven't got the time to sit them out.'

Louisa agreed with her husband. It upset her to see him so worried. She had tried to talk to Rupe and was shocked by his attitude.

'You keep out of this. You don't want Mother back here at all. You've been having a great time playing the lady of the manor. If she gets a share she'll be here for life and you'll be the also-ran again. As long as she doesn't get her share, she'll stay away on principle. You ought to take a good look at where your bread's buttered, Louisa. If you haven't already done so.'

The awful part was that Louisa knew he was right, and she was embarrassed that he could spell it out so starkly.

She sighed. Left the clothes scattered on the bed and went down to find a cup of tea.

When the mail came in, a few days later, Louisa took the letters into Victor's office and began to open them. This was a new role that she enjoyed, being able to assist with the office work, cutting down on his workload. His father would have regarded her secretarial work as an intrusion. To him, the men ran Springfield station, and all the bookwork involved had to be overseen by the boss, even though Victor wore the title of manager. As far as the station books were concerned, Victor had really only been his secretary. Now Victor had an assistant of his own, who was finding all the books and journals extremely interesting.

She set aside newspapers and country magazines, filed bills carefully, read a cheerful letter from her father, and perused circulars containing the latest information on wool and stock sales. Then she looked up

230

and smiled. At last she'd found an occupation she enjoyed.

'What a relief,' she breathed. 'I've got myself a job.'

Two months since Austin had died, and Charlotte still missed him so much. The ache in her heart seemed permanent. It wasn't that she needed his company in Brisbane – she was far too busy for that; the hurt went much deeper, leaving a void, a cruel emptiness. She still found it hard to believe that he was dead.

She knew that Judge Walker, and other friends, thought it peculiar that she wished to countermand Austin's precise last instructions and yet still professed to be grieving for him. In fact, it was fairly obvious that they regarded her as rather a hypocrite, but she couldn't be worried about them. How could she explain that this had been on her mind for years but she'd never been able to pluck up the courage to confront him over his will?

Now, of course, Charlotte wished she hadn't been such a mouse. But it had never occurred to her that her sons would refuse to remedy the situation. Often enough they'd complained to her about Austin's old-fashioned ideas and attitudes, and this was a perfect example. What a fool she'd been to believe she could rely on them.

Her rooms at the Park Private Hotel were very comfortable and had a lovely view over the botanic gardens, where she often strolled of an evening before dinner, but she missed Springfield. This place seemed unreal, a sort of limbo, neither here nor there. Neither pleasant nor unpleasant. She had made the acquaintance of several ladies who lived here and were exceedingly kind to the newly-widowed Mrs Broderick. Some of them were also widows, and they rallied to give her support in various ways, but Charlotte avoided them as much as possible. Their lives seemed to consist of daily rounds of meals and teas and card games and shopping expeditions, which didn't interest Charlotte at all. She missed the bustle of Springfield, the responsibility of the household, the endless activity outside . . . Charlotte had never confined herself to the house.

She realized that in this sterile atmosphere, she missed the maleness of a sheep station. Men at work. Horsemen coming and going. The mustering of sheep. A blacksmith hard at work but always ready for a chat. Horse breakers whistling and snapping whips behind the high fences. The serious discussions down at the stud, with spoiled pedigreed sheep showing off their fine coats. The laughter of stockmen. The excitement of shearing time in the big wool sheds. All of those things were her life, not mincing about here like a hothouse flower.

She had consulted the barrister recommended by Judge Walker, anxious to be done with this argument so that she could go home. But when he had given her his opinion, after several meetings Charlotte was aware that he was avoiding her.

Yesterday, though, she'd sat him out. Busy he might be, but so was she, having had to study, with great care, the opinion he'd foisted on her. An opinion that gave her little hope of upsetting Austin's will.

When she finally seated herself in his office, he was impatient.

'Do you really feel you want to take this matter to court, Mrs Broderick?'

'I insist. It is my opinion that my sons will see how foolish they are being. They won't go to court. Victor would regard airing family disagreements in public as scandalous. He won't fight me, sir. Once he knows I am quite determined, he'll settle.'

'In other words, you're bluffing?'

Charlotte tucked a wisp of hair under her hat. 'I suppose you could say that,' she admitted.

'Well, I'm afraid it isn't working.'

'What do you mean?'

'I have here correspondence from their solicitor in Toowoomba. He states that if you insist on placing this matter before the courts, then his clients will, naturally, oppose.'

Charlotte was stunned. 'They'll fight me in court?' she whispered.

'I'm afraid so.'

She sat in silence for a while, clutching her handbag, and then gave her response. 'Very well. So be it. As I have told you, I believe I am entitled to a share in that property, not only from my husband, but from my brother, the original partner. We will take them to court.'

'Mrs Broderick, might I remind you that I am not at all sure that you will win this case, and such litigation is expensive. Perhaps you should give the matter more thought.'

'There's nothing more to think about. I don't have any choice now. I'm very sorry about this, it is a great pity. I honestly didn't believe it would come to this.'

For a while there he seemed to be engrossed in the papers on his desk, head down, his fine white beard brushing what appeared to be important documents, and then he lifted his head, bushy eyebrows beetling over his spectacles.

'There is a note here from their solicitor that you should be made aware of before we go any further. Mrs Broderick, do you have a private income?'

'No. That's obvious, isn't it? If I had a legal right to a share in that property I would have my own income.'

'And who is paying for your accommodation at the Park Private Hotel?'

She felt a flush seep over her face. 'Victor. He is giving me an allowance.'

'I see. But apparently your other son, Rupert, disagrees. He claims that unless you drop this matter, the allowance will cease. Also, I am instructed to inform you that the two owners of Springfield, as things stand now, have no intention of providing you with the finance necessary to fight them in court.' He grunted, choosing not to look at her. 'I'm sorry, but that's rather to be expected. Logically speaking, one might say.'

Charlotte sat bolt upright in her chair, refusing to wilt before this blow. She wondered if she could ask him to let her owe his costs, until the case was heard, and remembered that somewhere along the line he had mentioned that if she lost, the costs could be awarded against her.

He reached for his pipe and put it down again. 'My expenses to date can wait,' he said kindly, 'but perhaps you should give further thought to the matter now, and let me know . . .'

Charlotte knew she was beaten, but was horrified at the thought of this fellow treating her as a charity case.

'What are your expenses to date?' she snapped, scrambling through her handbag for her purse. 'I'll pay you here and now!'

He stood. 'That's not necessary, Mrs Broderick. I know you're good for it. There's no hurry. I think the best thing to do is to patch up these disagreements with the lads, and everything will work out, you'll see.'

'Patronizing wretch,' she muttered to herself as she stalked from his offices into Queen Street, to be met by gusts of rain-filled wind. She was so angry she marched off ignoring the rain, not caring that she had no umbrella and that her hat was flopping round her face and her dress was becoming soaked.

Fern Broderick saw her sister-in-law charge past the shop, a grim expression on her face, no doubt caused, she thought, by being caught in the storm. It was raining hard, sending pedestrians scattering for shelter. She grabbed an umbrella from a stand by the door and rushed outside to offer it to Charlotte, but she had turned a corner and was gone.

Seeing Charlotte reminded Fern that she really ought to call on her. She had heard she was staying at the Park Private Hotel, and also rumours that the Brodericks were at odds over Austin's will. She was very curious to know what that was all about. More importantly, under normal circumstances she should have called on Charlotte before this, but she knew that for some reason she was in Charlotte's bad books. She'd been snubbed prior to Austin's death, and her very sincere letter of condolence had been answered by Louisa. Not a word from Charlotte again; she hadn't even let her sister-in-law know she was in town.

'I don't know what's got into her,' Fern mused, when she returned to her office. 'I'm her only relative in Brisbane, and she'll be broken-hearted at losing Austin. I'd better make the effort to see her, or next thing she'll be saying I ignored her.'

As Mrs Broderick swept into the foyer of her hotel, shaking her dripping hat, the desk clerk rushed over to assist her.

'Oh my goodness, madam, you're soaked. Shall I send a maid up with you?'

'No. A bit of rain never hurt anyone.' She stormed past him, heading for the stairs, but he called after her.

'There's a letter for you, Mrs Broderick.'

Charlotte stopped. 'A letter? What now?' she asked crossly, but she waited until he brought it to her, then went on up to her rooms.

The letter was from Harry, but she left it on the table while she changed out of her wet clothes, shivering a little at this unseasonal weather. It was after five o'clock, one hour to the dinner bell, but already the room was dark, as the storm thundered on, so Charlotte lit the lamps, wishing she could just put on her dressing gown and stay in her sitting room. The last thing she wanted was to have to face all those people downstairs. They fussed so much every time she put in an appearance, she was finding them absolute pests. Especially the widowed variety, with all their sugar-sweet advice. She was never even permitted to eat alone, which she much preferred.

Eat alone? That struck a chord. She recalled one of the women saying that when she wasn't feeling well, she had her meals in her room. Realizing that such a service was readily available, Charlotte decided to try for it.

She rang the bell, and a maid was at her door within minutes.

'I'm not feeling the best,' she said. 'Could I have dinner sent up?'

'Certainly, madam. What would you like? Tonight we have pea soup or oxtail soup . . .'

'Whatever! Just a meal, thank you.'

But old habits died hard. Charlotte could not allow anyone, not even a maid, to see her improperly dressed for dining. She plastered her hair back into a knot, took out a severe black dress that buttoned up to a high collar and placed herself by the table in her sitting room.

Time now to see what Harry had to say. More bad news, no doubt. But Harry just wanted to tell her that he had withdrawn his claim on Springfield. He was sorry that his decision had upset Connie, and her father, but they'd get over it.

A passing whim on my part to agree to it in the first place, Mother, made from all the wrong reasons. More from my anger with my brothers than from proper consideration. My father was of sound mind, he had every reason to be upset with me, and I want to respect his wishes. This is my way of saying that I always had great respect for my father and leave it at that.

On the other hand, I do believe that had Austin understood your feelings, he would have made better provision for you. Had he given it any thought at all, he would have made better provision for you. I am willing to bear witness to this effect.

By withdrawing my claim to Springfield, I hope that my brothers will be more amenable to your request, which I believe is morally sound.

The day had been too much for Charlotte. She put down Harry's letter and wept.

No matter what Harry said, or did, she had lost. She couldn't afford to take Victor and Rupe to court, something she had dreaded anyway, and even if she did, according to that barrister it seemed certain she would lose. And have to pay costs. Now what could she do?

Nothing.

Nothing except creep back to Springfield, beaten. Having not only antagonized her sons, but made the most horrible fool of herself. What would life be like back at Springfield now? Charlotte knew it wasn't in her nature to accept defeat gracefully. She could go back, and make their lives hell if she wanted. But what sort of a life would that be? And, she warned herself, that attitude could be a two-way street.

It was all so unfair. If Austin hadn't died, everything would have gone along so peacefully.

Then Charlotte gave way to real grief, weeping uncontrollably, wishing she had died first . . .

A knock at the door gave her a fright. The maid! She mustn't see her like this.

'Just a minute,' she called, embarrassed to hear a sob in her voice as she mopped at her eyes with a fresh handkerchief. Then, making a determined effort to compose herself, she opened the door a few inches, turning away to allow the maid to bring in her tray.

But it wasn't the maid. It was Fern Broderick.

'What are you doing here?' Charlotte demanded.

By the time she arrived at the door, Fern had convinced herself that she was at fault, inexcusably at fault, for not having called on Charlotte as soon as she'd heard her sister-in-law was in town. Now Charlotte would have every reason to feel hurt and neglected in her time of sorrow. She had dismissed Charlotte's previous snubs as simply unfortunate, fits of moodiness, perhaps . . .

So she was completely taken aback to be met by such belligerence.

She blinked. 'Well . . . I wanted to see how you are. How you're getting on.'

'Now you've seen. And I'm quite all right.'

Charlotte could hardly slam the door in her face; instead, she stood, scowling, waiting for the visitor to leave. But Fern, having come this far, decided to stand her ground. If she walked away now, the rift would have to be permanent, because she would not countenance this rudeness a second time. And that would be a great pity.

'I hoped we could talk. I am so sorry about Austin's death.'

'Oh yes. You would be, wouldn't you?'

'For heaven's sake, Charlotte. What's got into you? It is perfectly

235

normal for your sister-in-law to call on you, and I'd prefer not to be left standing here in the passage.'

Unwilling, but given no choice, Charlotte allowed her into the neat sitting room, and as she turned, Fern saw that Charlotte had been weeping, and was instantly apologetic.

'I'm sorry, Charlotte. This is a bad time. I didn't realize you were upset.'

'I am not upset,' Charlotte cried angrily, but she was unable to stop another flood of tears.

Just then the maid arrived at the door with a tray, and Charlotte rushed to the other side of the room, pretending to be staring out of the window, rather than have the maid see her distress. Fern took charge, placing the tray on the table and thanking the girl.

She peeked under the steel covers. 'Your dinner, Charlotte. It looks very nice. Come and have your soup while it's still hot.'

'I'm not hungry.'

'You're paying for the meal. You might as well eat it.'

Quietly, treating Charlotte like an invalid, she coaxed her into taking some of the soup, but couldn't convince her to have any of the roast lamb.

'I can't face it,' Charlotte said wearily. 'You eat it.'

With a grin Fern picked up a roast potato and bit into it, grateful that this interruption seemed to have broken the ice between them. 'The potatoes are delicious, nice and hot. You have the other one.'

Charlotte shrugged, and the two women began to pick at the meal with their fingers, like a couple of schoolgirls.

'There's a pot of tea here. Shall I pour for you?'

'If you like.'

Charlotte caught sight of herself in the gilt-edged mirror and shook her head miserably. Her face was blotchy, her eyes bleary, and her nose red from snivelling. Normally she would have hated for this attractive woman to see her like this, but now she didn't care. Nothing mattered any more. She even admitted to herself that she was glad Fern had stayed. She did need company after all, and this woman was at least an improvement on those widows downstairs. Then she remembered that Fern, too, was a widow.

'Oh, God!' she said.

'What?'

'Nothing.' She slumped into an armchair by the window, watching as Fern poured the tea and brought her cup over to her.

'Austin always thought more of you than he did of me,' she said suddenly. 'Was he in love with you?'

Fern reacted swiftly. This was no time for the truth. 'Good Lord, Charlotte! Where did you get that idea?'

'I would have thought it was obvious.'

'Then you're doing Austin an injustice. He was not in love with me. Nor I with him. So put that out of your mind. He could be a busybody,' she smiled, 'when it came to my business. Always giving advice. I don't think he approved of women in business.'

'I know he didn't,' Charlotte said angrily.

'Why? Didn't you approve either?'

'I didn't care what you did. But you were very fortunate,' she said grimly. 'You didn't have sons to grab your inheritance from under you. To turn you out into the street.'

Fern was startled. 'Oh, my dear, surely not. Austin wouldn't have allowed that.'

'Wouldn't he? He left me penniless.' She looked at Fern with tears in her eyes. 'How can I grieve for a man I loved so much, yet hate him at the same time for his total disregard for my status?'

'I don't understand. What has happened?'

Astonished, Fern tried to make sense of the Springfield débâcle as Charlotte's recital fluctuated between self-pity and righteous rage. She railed against Victor and Rupe, against a government that was trying to ruin squatters, against solicitors and barristers who were nothing but overpaid clerks with no respect for women, even against Judge Walker, who had promised to help but was just an old windbag. She wept when she told Fern how she'd come down in the morning and found Austin dead. How he had died alone, with no one by his side.

Fern let her talk. It seemed to her that with the suddenness of Austin's death and the equally sudden confrontation with her sons, followed by her hasty departure from Springfield and the move on to Brisbane, with all these difficult legal discussions, poor Charlotte had not been afforded a quiet time to grieve. With the loss of her husband her world had fallen apart, and she was in a state of utter confusion.

She slipped outside to find a maid and order coffee for two, and some brandy for medicinal purposes.

'But madam,' the girl said, 'this is a private hotel.'

Fern smiled. 'I quite understand, but I'm sure the housekeeper will oblige Mrs Broderick.'

She felt she needed a brandy as much as did Charlotte. She hadn't bargained on walking into this tale of woe. Nevertheless, some of what Charlotte had been telling her did make sense, and it was appalling that Victor and Rupe should have made their mother so upset. Strangely, there had been no mention of Harry, and Fern wasn't inclined to ask about him for fear of sending Charlotte down another trail of recriminations. She was a very difficult woman to deal with. Always had been. Touchy, easy to offend.

Remembering Charlotte's accusation about her and Austin, Fern shuddered, hoping that that subject was closed.

When she returned, Charlotte was waiting to tell her all about the

237

sectioning of Springfield to defeat the restrictions of the new laws.

'Yes, so you said,' Fern responded. 'How awful. I believe it's the only recourse that station owners have, to hang on to their holdings.' She preferred not to discuss that subject because it could lead to reminders of Harry's delinquency, but Charlotte persisted, and Fern had the impression that her sister-in-law's anger was beginning to turn her way again.

Fortunately the maid arrived with coffee, accompanied by the housekeeper with a small carafe of brandy, two crystal glasses and a deprecating smile. 'Ladies, this is against the rules, but since it is for medicinal purposes, one should try to do one's best. Poor Mrs Broderick, my dear, I do hope you are feeling better. We did miss you at dinner . . .'

Fern edged her out.

'I hate that woman,' Charlotte growled.

'Never mind. We got a brandy out of her. Here's yours.'

Charlotte sipped her brandy, nodding approval. 'As I was saying, Springfield has been split up into sections, with family members each holding the maximum amount of land. Do you understand what I'm saying?'

'Yes.' How many times did she have to be told this bit?

'I, of course, as Austin's wife, have been allocated one block. But Victor, with a wife and child, has three blocks.'

'There's no need to get upset about that. You yourself explained, Charlotte, that it's only on paper. Springfield will remain intact, with the family holding all the land.'

'Really? Then perhaps you can explain to me why your name is on the block adjacent to mine? Why your share is equivalent to mine?' Charlotte's voice moved to a higher pitch. 'Explain that, Mrs Broderick!'

Fern was stunned. And annoyed. 'I can't explain it and I don't choose to. I would have to see the overall picture before I'd go jumping to conclusions like you are doing.'

Damn Austin, she thought. Why did he have to include me? Sentimental reasons? She hoped not. Then she realized that it wasn't real in any case. None of this sectioning was real. It was a fake.

She turned on Charlotte. 'It's time I went home. I've had enough of this! From what I can make out, it was an appalling oversight on Austin's part to leave you beholden to your sons, but to be attacking me because he used my name, just another family name, in an attempt to hang on to his land is not fair. What difference does it make if my block is the same size as yours? It's all part of the whole, specifically designed to stay intact.'

Fern refrained from adding that she found Charlotte's attitude offensive, because she knew her own argument was based on a lie. Austin had loved her.

She reached for her gloves and her handbag, preparing to leave, but Charlotte, in yet another of her mood swings, was staring at her. 'What did you say?'

'I was trying to explain to you that it is immaterial whose names are on those sections . . .'

'No. About Austin. Do you think I'm wrong to be upset about his will?'

'I didn't say that.'

'You think *he* was wrong?'

'Indeed I do. I think it is outrageous. If I'd had a son and my husband had bequeathed all his assets to him, leaving me nothing but a roof, I'd be furious.'

'I didn't think you agreed with me.'

'Because you were too busy trying to pick a fight with me, Charlotte.'

'I'm sorry. It's just that no one sees my side of it except Harry, and he's got no say in it. Austin cut him out of the will and he doesn't care. I have, on what they call good authority, advice that I haven't a hope of overturning the will.'

'What if you drop all these legal people and appeal direct to Victor and Rupe?'

'Harry did that. They insist that Austin's instructions must stand. And to make matters worse, they're threatening to stop my allowance if I don't toe the line.'

'Good God!' Fern said. No wonder her sister-in-law was in such a state. 'Charlotte, if you need any money, let me help.'

'A loan would only postpone the inevitable,' Charlotte said. 'But it's kind of you to offer.'

'Would you like to come and stay at my house?'

'Thank you, no. Let them cut off my allowance to stay here if they dare!'

'That's the spirit. Don't let them get you down. I really must go now. But you try to rest, and tomorrow night you're coming to dinner at my house. We'll have a slap-up meal, just the two of us, without having to worry about people staring at the Broderick widows. Promise me you'll come.'

'I might as well.'

Fern had to be satisfied with that unenthusiastic response, but when she left, Charlotte had a great deal to think about. Fern Broderick had turned out to be her only friend. That was a turn-up for the books. The last person she would have expected to agree with her, given the woman's great friendship with Austin. And Fern, who was a wealthy woman, had offered her financial help. Charlotte hated the idea of a loan, but she needed help, and there was every possibility that Fern would back her.

The next night, over a splendid dinner and some excellent wines, the two women really got to talking.

This time, to clarify the situation, it was Fern who asked the questions, and Charlotte answered timidly. Fern was truly outraged to hear that the barrister had humiliated her sister-in-law by pointing out that she had no money to bring a case against the will.

'Yes you do,' she said gallantly. 'I will pay the bills. Tell him that.'

Charlotte shook her head. 'It'd only be sending good money after bad. It's obvious I'll lose.'

'So what happens now? Can't Harry talk to them again?'

'They're not on speaking terms.'

'Oh dear. Austin would be turning in his grave.'

'Why would he?' Charlotte said angrily. 'He's the cause of this.'

Fern sipped her wine. 'No. Austin never really thought he'd leave. He was the boss. Dead or alive, he expected to remain the boss and everything would go on as usual.'

'Fat lot of good that does me.'

'True. I wish I could think of an answer for you, Charlotte. It infuriates me to feel so helpless, so I can understand your frustration. You don't have to go back to Springfield if you don't want to. You can come here.'

'But that's the trouble. I do want to go back. I'm horribly homesick, Fern. I need my own home.'

Charlotte could not recall when she'd enjoyed an evening as much as this one. She was slightly tiddly when Fern's driver dropped her back at her hotel, and she didn't care one whit. They'd had quite a night, she and her sister-in-law. They'd drunk champagne and wines and port, and commiserated over Charlotte's unfortunate circumstances, and even smoked cigars over more port, abandoning themselves to a measure of hilarity.

'If Louisa could see me now, she'd faint!' Charlotte had laughed.

'What about Louisa?' Fern thought for a minute there that they might have had an ally.

'Louisa? Whither Victor goes, goes his wife. Besides, would you be rushing to have your mother-in-law back in the house? It's my bet she's hoping I'll stay away.'

Fern sighed. 'Why are we women always at odds?'

'Because there has to be only one boss. Victor and Rupe will find that out too. Won't they?'

It was quite a night.

Charlotte Broderick made it to her room in studied dignity, then flopped into the armchair.

Tomorrow was another day, and there was every chance that with luck, and Fern's money, she could turn the tables on them.

For her part, Fern found it difficult to believe that Austin's sons would not accommodate their mother in this matter. Thinking that since

Charlotte wasn't renowned for her tact she could easily have contributed towards the divisions in the family, Fern wrote to Victor and Rupe, in kindly tone, suggesting that they ask their mother to come home to Springfield so that the problem could be discussed without the necessity for legal intervention.

She also hoped that they would show their goodwill by bending to Charlotte's request for part-ownership of the property. *Generosity has its own rewards*, she added, *and everyone will be happy to see family harmony restored.*

Unfortunately, the day Fern's letter arrived, Rupe was on hand to open it, since Victor had taken Teddy and the two girls into Cobbside for the day. His immediate reply was similar to the response Fern had received from Charlotte when Austin was first taken ill. Cold and abrupt.

Thank you for your interest but we are quite capable of handling our own family affairs. Mother knows she is welcome to come home at any time.

That day Cobbside township celebrated the opening of its first town hall, a modest brick building hidden behind a rather grand portico, from where several gentlemen, aspiring mayors, were able to address the small community.

A very important guest, the Hon. Mike Howland, MLA, stood on the top step, scissors in hand, to declare a holiday, to officially open the country fair, already evident in the gaily decorated main street, and to cut the ribbon across the entrance to the proud hall.

All the important people in the district, professional and business men and squatters, and their wives, had been invited to a banquet luncheon in the town hall, and soon the fortunate invitees were crowding, rather ungraciously, through the front door to claim a good seat at the long tables. It was well known that more acceptances had come in than these tables could hold.

The Brodericks, of course, were invited, but Rupe wasn't interested in attending such a bunfight with all those bumpkins and pushy townspeople.

'We have to go,' Louisa argued. 'It won't be just townies, all the station people will be there. It will be lovely to see them all again.'

Later, though, Victor took her aside. 'Don't encourage him. We'll go. It'll be fun. And we don't want him getting into any more arguments.'

As the day progressed, Louisa had time to wonder if Rupe had become aware of public feeling about the Brodericks. He ranged about the district a lot more than Victor did, buying and selling sheep or horses, always on the lookout for good breeders, talking to wool buyers, watching wool prices. Victor never minded. It was always hard to keep Rupe on the job at home, and he needed the information Rupe could glean from other graziers. Besides, he preferred to oversee the

241

day-to-day management of the station himself, keeping an eye on everything.

At this hectic function, Victor noticed nothing untoward. With Teddy on his hip before they went in to the luncheon, Victor laughed and talked with the men he'd known all his life. Louisa and Cleo followed him in, looking about them happily, and Louisa introduced Cleo to some of the station wives.

At first Louisa thought she imagined a chill in the air. The women were perfunctory in the greetings. They were polite to Cleo, but they soon moved away. When she found four seats together, Mrs Toby Black from Strathmore station, who had attended Austin's funeral, actually snapped at her.

'They're taken.'

Like Victor, Cleo saw nothing amiss. When they found seats, she put Teddy in the chair beside her, admonishing him to sit still or he'd lose his place in the crush.

'I think he'd better sit on my knee,' Louisa said nervously. 'I don't think they want a child taking up a chair.'

'Leave him for the minute,' Victor laughed. 'He can get up if need be.'

Birds of a feather, the station folk drew together at their tables, the élite of the district, while the others found their own level.

The four-course banquet was excellent fare, and everyone seemed to be having a marvellous time, especially since the town fathers had not stinted on the liquid refreshments, but it soon became obvious to Louisa that she was being studiously ignored by the women. Whenever she addressed them they appeared not to have heard, carrying on jolly conversations as if she was not present.

She wanted to tell Victor, but it wasn't something she felt she could put into words just yet, and then she wondered if he would believe her. He didn't seem to be having any problems, nor was Cleo, talking animatedly down there to ladies sitting near her. Hideously embarrassed, Louisa kept her head down, wanting to run from the hall but not daring to move, wondering why this was happening to her. Or was it? Confused, she tried to convince herself it was all in her imagination, as the hours dragged on into lengthy speeches.

Finally the guests were leaving, taking their time. Victor, enjoying himself, was in no hurry, but it had all been too much for Louisa. She jumped up, excused herself and made for the door, only to run into a group of women in the lobby who were standing talking to Mrs Crossley, old Jock's widowed daughter.

The women glanced at her, and Louisa knew they'd been talking about her. One of them nudged Mrs Crossley, a formidable woman at the best of times, who took the hint and confronted Louisa.

'You must be pleased with yourself, Mrs Broderick.'

'I beg your pardon?'

'So you might. I see you got rid of Charlotte very smartly.'

'What?'

'You heard. Charlotte Broderick has a lot of friends here. She was a pioneer of this district. She earned a place here today. Not you and her jumped-up sons.'

Louisa pushed past them and fled, hurrying down the street past cake and produce stalls, and clowns with balloons, and a line of sideshows, not knowing where to turn.

Her husband found her sitting on a lonely bench under a row of pine trees.

'Where did you get to? We've been looking everywhere for you.'

He was astonished as she sobbed her humiliation. 'That can't be right. You just took them up the wrong way.'

She was furious. 'Oh, yes, I imagined it all. You men don't give a damn about anything as long as the stock are safe and the weather holds. But I tell you, the women are savage, Victor. Bloody savage. They're all on Charlotte's side.'

'Oh, Christ, let them. It's a five-day wonder. Don't take any notice of them.'

'All very well for you to make light of my troubles. I had a beastly time, and then I got told off! This is all your fault. Am I to be ostracized because you lot can't sort out your arguments?'

'For heaven's sake, don't make such a fuss. Who cares what that old biddy has to say?'

But Louisa did care. Knowing that she could be in for the same treatment at other social functions, she became increasingly irritated with the two men for placing her in this position, adding to the tension in the house. Not that she had a solution to the impasse; she just wanted it ended. She had been planning to give a Sunday luncheon party for Victor on his forthcoming birthday but now thought better of it, for fear she would be inviting wholesale snubs.

It was Cleo who told Rupe about the incident, but he only laughed. 'Mrs Crossley thinks she's the queen of the social set out here, when in fact she's thoroughly disliked. She's sulking because Charlotte was her only real friend.'

'Louisa seems to think you knew people would be upset about your mother being . . . away.'

He was genuinely surprised. 'Me? I'm not psychic. How would I know what lurks the local peasants get up to? Where are you going anyway?'

She smiled. 'I thought I'd sneak down to the orchard while Teddy's upstairs with his mother and see if any of those apples are ripe. I have to keep him away for a while because he's dead keen to pick them no matter how green they are.'

'Good. I'll sneak with you.'

No sooner were they through the gate, enclosed by shady trees and the warm, sweet scent of fruit, than Rupe slipped his arms about Cleo's waist and drew her to him. He had waited all this time to be sure of himself, and of her. In fact, for the last few weeks he'd been very much aware that Cleo was fond of him, and to tease her, excite her, he'd deliberately flirted with her but made no move to touch her.

Now the tables were turned. When he felt her responding, his passion was released and he kissed her breathlessly, becoming more intense, more demanding, until, flushed but by no means upset, Cleo had to pull away from him.

'But I love you,' he whispered impetuously.

'I know. And I love you too, Rupe.'

For a long time they stayed in the orchard, kissing and caressing, with Cleo unable – or maybe unwilling, he couldn't tell – to stop him unbuttoning her blouse and exploring her smooth, lovely breasts.

'Come to my bed tonight,' he pleaded with her, over and over, but she smiled.

'No, I mustn't. I can't.'

'Yes you can.'

She straightened her clothes, tidied her hair, and they walked back, the apples forgotten, both looking circumspect, even parting at the gate to avoid drawing attention to their romance.

They were observed, though, by a person who was drifting by as dusk settled, on her nightly inspection of the homestead. She'd only been back a few days and was gradually overcoming the crashing disappointment at discovering the boys were not back yet. No sign of them anywhere.

However, Nioka found she was a lot stronger in her mind now, and could cope more easily with setbacks, probably because she was home again and away from the tragedy at the lake that had been pulling her down into the same pit of despair. Also, she had the good and bad experiences of that long trek to occupy her thoughts. She had seen so much more of the world.

After the first few nights at the old camp by the river, she'd awoken to the comforting, familiar surrounds and remonstrated with herself for being overly optimistic.

Silly fool, she told herself. Boys who go to school come home at summertime, for their Christmas. All the Springfield blacks had known that Christmas was for feasting and presents, when the family gathered to sing and dance, and so she simply replaced one dream with another. All she had to do was to wait. Dispassionately, from a hiding place in the tall grass, she watched Rupe lovemaking with a strange lady. She had all the time in the world and wouldn't make a move in case they saw her. She was living the way it suited her, like a solitary ghost, keeping out of sight of all these white people whom she despised, emerging from the deep bush at dusk to amuse herself by stealthily touring the homestead.

They had white maids now, she noted, thinking that she ought to tell Minnie, but she quickly changed her mind about that. She didn't want Minnie's spirit disturbing this idyll. Or anyone else, for that matter. She had plenty of company. Nioka knew all the birds and the furry creatures that came gently by her hidden camp, and at night the old owl with his steady gaze watched over her.

Sometimes she saw Teddy running about, and that saddened her. He'd lost his playmates but it didn't seem to bother him. Like all the rest of the whites here, he'd forgotten Bobbo and Jagga and Doombie. Nioka turned to the good spirits for support, hoping that the little boys hadn't forgotten their mothers.

Chapter Ten

'Do you recall offering to lend me some money?' Charlotte asked Fern in her usual gruff manner.

Fern nodded. 'I certainly do. How much do you want?'

'A fair bit, but you'll get it all back.'

They met on a pleasant Saturday afternoon at the kiosk in the botanic gardens. It had become a favourite haunt of Charlotte's, but she still couldn't bring herself to accept Fern's invitation to join her and her friends there of a Sunday morning. She wasn't up to meeting strangers, especially since she'd become aware – thanks to snide remarks she'd encountered from some of the ladies at her hotel – that her claim on the family property had become hot gossip in Brisbane.

Obviously it was not the done thing. Not that Charlotte gave a damn. It was her business.

'They haven't stopped your allowance, have they?' Fern asked, worried.

'Not yet. But this isn't to do with the allowance. I have engaged a new solicitor, a very nice fellow. A Mr Craig Winters. Do you know him?'

'No. Where did you find him?'

'On one of my walks. He has an office up on the Terrace. He's new to Brisbane.'

Fern was concerned. 'Really, Charlotte. You ought to be more careful. I could have recommended another chap to you.'

'I'm quite happy with Mr Winters. He's extremely courteous, and ready to proceed exactly as I instruct, which is a nice change.'

'You're not going to take the boys to court? I don't mind lending you the money, giving you the money, if you feel that's what you have to do, but you have already received the best legal advice on this matter. If your Mr Winters is indicating that he can succeed in breaking the will for you, that is very cruel of him. And quite wrong.'

Charlotte spooned more whipped cream on to her plate. 'I am becoming addicted to this passion-fruit sponge cake, Fern. It is absolutely delicious. Even better than the chocolate cake. They must have an excellent cook.' She finished her cake, dabbed her lips with a napkin and drank some more tea.

'I haven't mentioned that subject to him. No point. I have accepted that I can't win. Victor and Rupe know that by now. They must think me the most awful dunce.'

'I must say I am truly upset by their attitude, but I'm sure they don't think that of you.'

'Botheration. Let them! If you help me they're about to come down to earth with a bump. If I learned precious little from Austin, I did learn you never give in. If you're mean enough, you'll win. And he could be very mean.'

Fern didn't respond. It was true that Austin had been well known as a tough, even bloody-minded businessman, but she could hardly agree with his widow.

'So,' Charlotte said, 'if you agree, it's all arranged.'

'What is?'

'Well, you know that Springfield has been broken up into large blocks, big enough to survive as individual stations . . .'

'Yes.'

'The claims have already been lodged to protect Springfield and Victor has freeholded a couple of them, but he's using delaying tactics to raise the money to buy all the rest.'

'Yes?'

'Well, as I mentioned to you, one section, next to Austin's, is in my name. And I intend to buy it.'

'But you can't!'

'Yes I can. Mr Winters has been down to the Lands Office and has studied the claims that have been lodged. It's there in black and white, Fern!' Charlotte cried excitedly. 'They've done it for me. All I have to do is pay for the freeholding and I own the heart of Springfield. The land beyond the valley, beautiful pastoral land.'

'What does your Mr Winters say about this?'

Charlotte grinned. 'I think he's a tiny bit suspicious. We've had several talks, and it wouldn't surprise me if he has checked on my background, because he did hint a little about family problems. But he's a gentleman, acting for me. And he's ready to freehold that land in my name.'

She ordered another slice of cake. 'Victor and Rupe are out there watching their boundaries for fear selectors will get in and lay claim to their precious land. It hasn't occurred to them that they've left themselves wide open to my claim.' Charlotte sat back. 'Now who's the dunce?'

'You wouldn't? I mean, is it legal?'

'Don't look so innocent, Fern. You know perfectly well it's legal. And binding. And if you won't lend me the money, Mr Winters says he'll have no trouble raising the finance for me. After all, I still retain the title of the lady of Springfield. That house is my home for life, it is included in the section that Austin apportioned for himself. Already

248

freeholded. As Mr Winters says, my good name is collateral in itself.'

The waitress returned. 'I'm sorry, madam. There's no passion-fruit cake left. Would you like something else?'

Too immersed in her story, Charlotte waved the girl away. 'No thank you.'

Then, to Fern: 'Well. What do you think?'

At first Fern was nervous. A throwback, she knew, from the explosive reaction such an outrageous suggestion would have received from Austin, from the boss of Springfield. But he was gone. This was a new era.

'He'd be furious,' she said softly, almost like a conspirator, and Charlotte knew immediately who she meant.

'Serve him right. He dudded me out of my brother's hard-earned share. Will you lend me the money?'

'I don't know. It's a radical idea.'

'Don't go soft on me now. It's not an idea at all. It makes sense. Otherwise I'm lost. Ruined. They'll take over the house, if they haven't already done so. I'll end up in the back room, having to live on their handouts.'

They talked for a long time about the ramifications of this move. Fern had to agree that it was Charlotte's only chance, but what it would do towards restoring good family relations was anyone's guess. She'd had no reply from Victor to her plea for reconciliation with Charlotte. Only that caustic note from Rupe.

'It's obvious that once I own that land I shall be able to repay you,' Charlotte added, 'if that's what you're worrying about. Mr Winters said he would draw up a formal loan agreement for us. With interest if you wish.'

'He thinks of everything,' Fern murmured.

'So?'

'So, yes, Charlotte. To be honest I can't see any other way out of this, but I hope we're doing the right thing.'

Magnanimously, Charlotte paid the bill. 'There's just one other thing, Fern. Could you afford to buy that other block too?'

'What other block?'

'The one Austin sectioned off in your name.'

Fern was startled. Her sister-in-law really meant business. She wasn't about to let her sons ride roughshod over her. Fern applauded the decision.

'I think I could probably afford to buy the other block too,' she said. 'You'll need as much leverage as you can get.'

To Fern's dismay, Charlotte threw her arms about her and hugged her, while people stopped to stare. 'You're a darling, Fern. A dear, good friend. I'll never forget you for this. Will you come and see Mr Winters on Monday morning?'

★ ★ ★

Cleo didn't come to his room that night, or any other night, and that angered Rupe.

'If you loved me you would,' he argued. 'No one would know.'

Not much, Cleo thought. She knew very well from her brothers that men talked about these things – crowed, in fact – much more than women did, and she had to avoid embarrassments. Louisa couldn't help but notice that she and Rupe spent a lot of time together, and she seemed quite happy about it, but Cleo knew her place. She was still only the governess. There was enough tension in the Springfield homestead without adding to it.

Besides, she was hoping that Rupe would propose to her. Some days he was so loving, she felt he was on the point of doing so, but then he would draw back, using his frustration as an excuse for ill-tempered remarks.

'You're just a tease,' he complained angrily, but she was patient with him.

'I don't mean to be. Maybe we ought not to be together so much. Alone like this.'

'You're right,' he said, punishing her. 'Anyway, I'll be away for a few days.'

She wouldn't give him the satisfaction of asking where he was going, but she soon found out, from Louisa.

'There's a three-day race meeting at Jock's station. We usually go, it's an annual event,' Louisa told her. 'But I'm not going. Victor can go if he wants to, but I'm not about to give that old witch Mrs Crossley the chance to insult me again.'

In the end Rupe went, on his own, without even bothering to say goodbye to Cleo.

She was disappointed. Country race meetings were great fun, and if Louisa hadn't been so upset with the Crossley woman, they would all have gone. As for Rupe, she hoped he'd have a rotten time, although that was a faint hope. Single girls from all over the district converged on these gatherings.

As usual, though, Cleo shrugged off her concerns. Rupe was keen on her, but if it was only for sex, not commitment, then time would tell.

The Walker family were engaged in the same complicated freeholding arrangements as were the Brodericks, to preserve the huge holdings pioneered by Jock. They were fortunate to have the ubiquitous Judge Walker, Jock's son, presiding over the gradual transfer of leased blocks into family names. And the names of obliging retainers.

Everyone in the Lands Office, from departmental heads to the most junior clerk, soon came to recognize the imposing figure of the Judge and tried to find urgent work in other directions, because he terrified them.

In the first place, Judge Walker was livid at the colossal amounts of money his family coffers were being forced to hand over to the Government, and the very thought of that was enough to put him in a nasty frame of mind whenever he approached the building. Which was often. He was determined not to let them get away with this without making the staff account for every acre and every penny. He studied each map carefully, often with a magnifying glass, insisting that the official copies were exact in every detail, often calling in surveyors to back up any disputed boundaries. He was a master of harassment, shouting down suggestions that some of these blocks were peculiar in shape, far removed from the accepted practice of Government surveyors, who opened up land for settlement, to draw rectangular-shaped blocks. Like Austin Broderick, the Walkers knew their land and made sure each of their blocks had access to water, but the counter staff could only guess that was the intent.

When it came time to begin making payments on the blocks, he would not condescend to deal with cashiers, insisting on more checks, and receipts from the upper echelon, which gave him the opportunity to abuse them, calling them daylight robbers and traitors to their country.

But still he wasn't finished. While he was freeholding blocks, one by one, stalling for time to raise the necessary cash, he watched, wolf-like, over the rest of his brood of blocks for any sign that a selector was showing interest in them. He also kept an eye on his neighbours' blocks, requiring the clerks to haul out dozens more maps that really had nothing to do with him, but they had learned it was easier to acquiesce.

The Judge's interest in other properties was part duty and part curiosity. He was eager to know how the others were making out, how far they could afford to go before they started feeling the pinch.

He saw that Austin Broderick's chosen patch had been officially freeholded before he died and that Victor had continued to purchase a couple more, in his own and Louisa's names. Another was in Rupe's name, and more recently Charlotte was listed as an owner. Also Fern Broderick. That gave him some grim satisfaction. Obviously Victor had already started swinging in family names, dummy names, to beat the new laws. Fern Broderick had no need of land out there.

Nothing for Harry Broderick, though, and that rankled. The fool had no sense of responsibility. Not only was he not on the list of claims submitted for Springfield, he'd backed off from challenging Austin's will.

'Spineless, that's his trouble,' the Judge muttered as he barged out of the Lands Office and made for his club. That office was bad for his blood pressure; a few good Scotch whiskies were an excellent remedy. From there he could send a report to his father, with friends who were going out to the annual race meeting next week. This year he

251

and his wife would not be attending. Jock knew it was far more important for him to stay here and watch over the dissecting of their station, the way they wanted it to turn out.

The Walker station was titled Lochearn after the home of Jock's forebears in Scotland, but few knew how to pronounce it to his satisfaction, and anyway Jock always referred to the station as 'my place'. For a long time it was the joke of the district to call the station just that. Everyone knew where 'my place' was. Years weathered the name to 'Jock's place', and except for officialdom, that was how it was now known.

Being a lover of thoroughbred horses, Jock had a private race track on the flat beyond the homestead. At first he would challenge his mates to bring over their best mounts and they'd ride their own horses round the makeshift track, but the race soon became an event, and other station people, starved of entertainment, began to arrive, to take part or just to watch.

Nowadays it was a three-day event, with jockeys and bookmakers and all the trimmings of a gala occasion, complete with a final-night ball. The paddock by the excellent track was transformed into a tent city by the time Harry and Connie arrived, to a hearty welcome from old friends.

When they made their way up to the homestead, where accommodation was found for family and close friends, Ada Crossley had already heard they'd arrived and was standing out front waiting for them.

She embraced her niece, Connie, delighted that she'd survived the long journey without mishap, in her condition.

'Come along in, my dear. I've given you the west bedroom, it's quiet so that you can go off and rest when you wish.' Childless, she was thrilled that Jock was at last to be blessed with a great-grandchild, and that she would have a great-niece or nephew to love and spoil.

'How are you, Harry?' she asked firmly as he brought up the rear with their bags.

'Fine thanks, Ada. And you?'

'Never better.'

She ushered Connie into their room but held him back. 'Just a minute. I want a word with you. You're looking remarkably well, young man.'

'Thank you.'

'Not a compliment. They say you had a breakdown. I expected you to be looking a bit pinched.'

He laughed. 'Country air, Ada. You can't beat it.'

'Well, you're not too popular over that vote, you know. But that's history. And the Judge is still angry that you didn't take on Austin's will.' She jerked her head at the bedroom. 'For Connie's sake, you see.'

Harry sighed. 'You can't please everyone, Ada. I learned that the hard way.'

She nodded. 'So you did. But you backed your mother, and in my book that cleans the slate. We won't say any more about it, but you've got guts, Harry. You'll do me. Now get in there and look after your wife.'

For Ada Crossley, that was the best she could do in expressing her feelings. Unlike Charlotte, who'd been brought in as a bride, she'd grown up in the district, competing with her brother for Jock's attention. She loved to recall that by the age of twelve she'd been one hell of a rider, outstripping her older brother at every turn.

'The heart of a lion!' Jock used to say.

Her mother was different. A gentle Scots woman more interested in home and hearth, she greatly feared that Ada would have an accident, racing mad with the horses.

She'd complain to Jock: 'Here's Clarrie, seeing to his lessons, and that girl no more than a tomboy. It's not right for a girl to be out there birthin' sheep and listening to the talk of shearers. She ought to go off to boarding school.'

Ada wouldn't hear of it. Nor would Jock. Their son's education was more important.

Clarrie went and he never came back, except for holidays. He went on to become a famous judge and they were all proud of him. Too late, Ada realized her mother was right. She'd grown up a rough-and-ready bushie, while her brother lived the high life in Brisbane society. He'd even taken his bride on the Grand Tour of Europe, thanks to family money. And she, Ada Crossley, had never been anywhere.

At the age of thirty-one, against her mother's advice, she'd married a shearer. A drunken wretch who'd moved into the house and behaved as if he owned it.

One night he'd gone too far. In a fit of drunken rage he'd taken to Ada with his belt, but being Ada, accustomed to the tough life of these men, she'd fought back, wrenching the belt from him and slashing at him. She was no match for him, though, and he'd punched and kicked her, blackening her face with bruises and breaking several ribs.

When it was over, with Ada lying battered in a corner, he wept, for fear, begging her forgiveness. Then he ran for his life.

His fear was well placed. Jock went after him with a shotgun. The rest of the story was forever unclear.

It was said that he grabbed a horse and made for Springfield, for sanctuary, while all the men from Lochearn were out searching for him. It was also said that he died from a fall from his horse, trying to jump a blind gully on Springfield. But Ada doubted that. His body was brought back to Lochearn for burial, but the casket was closed. She wasn't permitted to see it, not that she wanted to.

Not long after that Austin Broderick and Jock stopped arguing about a lovely piece of pastureland on their boundaries. It was handed over to Austin without a murmur.

What did she think? She believed that Austin and her father had taken care of the man who had almost killed her. And she didn't want to know any more. She was rid of him.

Ada never remarried.

Now she considered Charlotte's situation. Being more forthright than Charlotte, and dealing with her father rather than a man she was absolutely cuckoo about, Ada had demanded to know her place in Jock's will after her mother had passed on, and was relieved to learn that she and her brother would hold equal shares in Lochearn. Plus she would have this homestead as her residence for life.

Ada had always looked up to Charlotte. Charlotte had taught her how to socialize after her mother's death. How to appreciate the work of country women's clubs and associations, and how to support women and their children on isolated properties. Until then she'd never realized how much Charlotte did, in her own quiet way, to help so many people. Typically, and with Charlotte's blessing, she'd taken over the work. Now Ada was the president of various associations; she'd drawn up lists of trusted midwives, banning the incompetent; her home was the centre for the Ladies' Lending Library; and she herself paid for a nurse with actual medical experience to check on the health and diet of small children.

Ada was a powerhouse in the district now, and proud of it, and the huge turn-out at these race meetings gave her yet another opportunity to gather the women for closed sessions in which they discussed their problems and offered solutions.

But she would never remarry. Never.

When she heard that Austin had left Springfield to his two sons – three, if Harry hadn't upset him – leaving Charlotte to have to live like a housekeeper in her own home, she'd been outraged. Before she could go over to visit Charlotte she'd heard that her friend had left the property. The rest she'd gleaned from her brother, Judge Walker, and she regarded the attitude of Victor and Rupe Broderick as despicable.

Normally the Brodericks were billeted in the Lochearn homestead. Near neighbours and best friends, they had priority. When Ada saw that well-known rake, Rupe Broderick, striding towards the house, she hurried down to meet him. It occurred to her to immediately order him off the property, but that would have caused a commotion, possibly annoying her father, so she greeted him coolly.

'Good afternoon, Rupe. Are Victor and Louisa coming?'

'No. They're flat-out busy these days.'

I'll bet they are, she thought, remembering her last encounter with Louisa Broderick.

She sighed. 'Just as well. We're absolutely packed out this year. Far too many starters. If you go on down to the single men's quarters, I'm sure you'll find a bunk.'

Rupe was stunned by the rebuff, but he ran his hand through his unruly blond hair with a grin. 'By all means. Thank you. I was just wondering if William Pottinger has arrived yet?' giving himself an excuse to be heading for the front door of the homestead.

'Not yet.'

'Then I'll catch him later.' He sauntered away with forced joviality, his knapsack slung over his shoulder, to join the lads already settling in.

He claimed a bunk, handed his clothes to one of the Chinese laundry boys to be pressed and went out to the veranda, where several of his friends were sharing a bottle of rum as they ogled the girls strolling about in their finery.

'It's a real fashion show, isn't it?' he said cheerfully, unconcerned now that he'd been denied homestead company. He could have much more fun down here.

'Where's your girl?' he was asked.

'What girl?'

'Come on, Rupe. The governess. I heard you're going steady.'

'Don't talk rot. Let's see what's happening in the marquee.'

Soon he was caught up in the carnival atmosphere, flirting with the girls, studying the parade of horses in search of winners, drinking too much, falling about in a hilarious tug-of-war, sobering up with a barbecue lunch and lining up at the rails when the races started, waving winning tickets.

He was having a great day until he spotted Harry and Connie in the crowd. Rupe was so accustomed to the whole family from Springfield attending these races together that he'd taken it for granted that this time he'd be the only Broderick representative.

He swaggered over to his brother. 'The boss give you time off, did he?'

Harry ignored the snide remark. 'How are you, Rupe?'

'Just fine! I've backed two winners already.'

'Good for you. Have you given more thought to Charlotte's request?'

'Request? Demands, more like it! No need. She's come to see that we're in the right. Just as you did.' He saw Connie walking towards her husband then suddenly turning away, obviously avoiding Rupe's company.

'Connie still sulking, is she?'

'Don't push your luck, Rupe,' Harry growled. 'Is Victor coming over?'

'No. He couldn't be bothered. But why would you care?'

'Because he's got bit more sense than you, and I want to know what he's doing about Charlotte.'

255

'We don't have to do anything about Charlotte. She's welcome to come home when she feels like it.'

Harry had had enough of him. 'That's very generous of you, Rupe. Let's hope she chucks you out when she gets there.'

'Fat chance.'

Rupe strode away, unsettled now. His next horse lost, and the next. He joined two girls from Ballymore station, but their company bored him, so he wandered back to the marquee, standing idly about, glass in hand, aware that everyone would know he was on the outer, while his brother was lodged in the house. He kept telling himself that Harry was only there because Connie was a member of the Walker family, but he knew that wasn't strictly correct. Ada Crossley was a tough old bird. If she hadn't wanted Harry in her house, she'd have let him know.

That night Rupe joined friends round campfires near the tents and covered wagons. They were all enjoying the adventure of camping out, but Rupe couldn't raise any enthusiasm. He was missing Cleo, and was riled that Victor and Louisa had been smart enough to stay home. Later, as the gaiety subsided, to be replaced by the usual singsong, he wandered off to bed, past the homestead that was still ablaze with lights, trying not to face the fact that for the first time in his life, he was as lonely as hell.

The next day his confidence returned. He decided to ignore Harry and the Walker snub. It was either that or take himself off home, and he certainly wouldn't retreat, so he plunged into the partying with a vigour bordering on bravado, even romancingWilliam Pottinger's lanky daughter.

This seemed to please the lawyer, who invited him to share their table at afternoon tea under colourful umbrellas. Pottinger droned on about the wonderful turn-out, and how good it was to see all the young people enjoying themselves. He was too tactful to mention any of the problems at Springfield, but did observe that he was pleased to hear the freeholding was progressing.

Rupe didn't know what he was talking about. Charlotte and Harry's threats to challenge the will hadn't eventuated, butVictor was waiting for the official distribution of assets before he purchased any more land. Pottinger had arranged for them to have a working account, to keep the station viable, but they hadn't freeholded any blocks lately. Until the titles office gave them the all-clear, the other bank accounts and shares were frozen. It was only a matter of days now, but they certainly hadn't been 'progressing', as William called it.

'We have only freeholded the four blocks,' he said. 'We are observing the strictures you yourself put upon us. But I daresay we'll be moving fast once we are free and clear.'

'I thought you two lads must have been using your own money,' William said.

What money? Rupe thought bitterly. Thanks to Austin, neither he nor Victor had much money of their own.

'No. We're prepared to wait until we hear that my father's will has been processed.'

'That's very strange. Are you sure those Brisbane lawyers of yours haven't gone ahead without your permission?'

Rupe laughed. 'Not them, William. They wouldn't move an inch without money up.'

'Well, you'd better talk to Jock. He assures me that you have picked up two more blocks.'

'Where did he get that from?'

'Judge Walker. You know him, he never misses a trick. He says that two more of your blocks have been freeholded. Only last week.'

Pottinger stopped. Clutched his hand to his face. 'Oh my God, Rupe. You don't suppose selectors have got in under your guard?'

Rupe went in search of Jock, who was out in the stables, bewailing the fact that his best horse had gone lame. He was not in any mood to be bothering himself with Springfield business.

'Listen, son,' he said eventually. 'If the Judge says they're bought – two of your blocks, last week – then they're bought! Victor probably forgot to tell you. Will you look at my beauty here? How did this happen? That's what I want to know. She's a champion galloper. No horse in the state could beat her . . .'

He was almost weeping as Rupe strode away towards the single men's quarters to collect his gear. Forgetting that he had offered to escort Marie Pottinger to the ball, and that he had some winnings to collect from a bookmaker, he found his horse, saddled up and rode away from Lochearn as the last race of the second day raised shouts and cheers from the enthusiastic racegoers.

It was late when he arrived back at Springfield to find Victor and the two girls playing cards in Austin's den. They were surprised to see him, but Rupe wasted no time.

He confronted Victor. 'Did you buy two more blocks last week?'

'What the hell is this all about? Of course not.'

Rupe slumped into an armchair. 'Oh, Jesus! Selectors have got in.'

'What? How? Where did you hear this?' Victor was stunned.

'At Jock's place. He heard it from the Judge.'

'It can't be right.'

'They say it is.'

'Oh, Christ! What blocks?'

'Jock didn't know. He thought you'd bought them.'

'How will you find out if it's true?' Louisa asked.

'I'll telegraph Brisbane on Monday. Nothing we can do until then. They've probably got it all wrong.'

'Judge Walker?' Rupe asked incredulously.

257

'No. Jock's probably confused.'

'How was the race meeting?' Louisa asked after they'd exhausted that subject.

'More hangers-on than ever,' Rupe said. 'But I was enjoying myself until this came up. The Walkers seem to have money to burn. More marquees than a circus, and everyone dressed up as if they were at Ascot. It doesn't feel like a country meet any more. Too formal. That has taken a lot of the fun out of it.'

'Were Connie and Harry there?' Louisa asked.

'Yeah. But I didn't see much of them. Can I get something to eat? I'm starving.'

Cleo jumped up. 'Hannah's gone off, but I'll forage for you, Rupe. Come on, we'll find something in the pantry.'

Victor winked at Louisa as the pair departed. 'Do you think that was really why he came home? Sounds a bit far-fetched to me.'

She smiled. 'He could be missing Cleo. They were as thick as thieves before he went away. I was surprised he didn't invite her to go with him. Did he stay in the house?'

'I don't know. He didn't say.'

'Victor, did you talk to Rupe about taking over one of the outstations? Building his own home there?'

Her husband, not anxious to broach this subject with her, began shuffling cards and turning them over one by one, as if waiting for the others to return. 'That's not feasible any more, Louisa.'

'Why not?'

'Because we've decided to sell the outstations to make Springfield more compact. We have to tighten up.'

'Sell the outstations? Your father would have had a fit!'

'He never really had to face freeholding. They'll bring a good price. We've always had more land than we know what to do with. We can't afford the luxury of outstations any more.'

Louisa sat back in her chair and glared at him. 'So what now? You and Rupe own the place. When he marries there'll be two wives here. And I gather we can expect Charlotte home any time it pleases her.'

'I don't know what you're fretting about,' he sighed. 'This house is huge. So what if we have one more woman in the place? If it's Cleo, which I hope it is, she's already here. It's not as if we have Austin ruling the roost any more.'

'No, only Charlotte. And there's a big difference for a woman being a governess and then promoted to a wife. Can't you understand that?' She was upset. 'Why did you let me go on thinking we could move Rupe out?'

Victor moved to put an arm about her. 'It'll work out, love, don't be looking for trouble. For the time being we'll just take one day at a time.'

'You can,' she muttered. 'I think Harry had the right idea all along.

258

He got clean away. I can't think what would be worse, being stuck with my mother-in-law for the rest of my life, or that brother of yours. Cleo thinks she can handle Rupe, but she doesn't know him like I do. I ought to feel sorry for her.'

'That's uncalled for, Louisa. He's a bit headstrong, that's all. Too much like Austin.'

'Like Austin, nothing!' Louisa flared. 'At least, from what I hear, *he* respected the black women. You can't say the same for Rupe. Just as well for Cleo the blacks have gone.'

Victor was furious. 'Where did you hear that sort of talk?'

'It's common knowledge, so don't lie to me. This is Charlotte's home, nothing I can do about that. But I want Rupe out of here, Victor. You're asking too much of me. He goes or I do.'

'You said something like that about having to live with my parents, if I recall,' he retorted. 'Why don't you admit you just don't like living at Springfield?'

Louisa, with a swipe of her arm, swept all the cards on to the floor. 'I married you, not your whole bloody family. I don't give a damn about your precious Springfield, I want my own home. Why can't you understand that?'

She stormed from the room, leaving him to pick up the cards.

The two women had become firm friends, united in the excitement of their conspiracy, as Fern called the transactions they had concluded that day.

'So what happens now?' Fern asked, as she settled Charlotte into an easy chair on her front porch, and, rearranging some cushions, sank into another chair beside her guest. She was fond of sitting out here on the long tiled porch when the sun went down, watching the world go by.

Charlotte sighed. 'I'm not sure. I hope I've done the right thing.'

'Good Lord, it's a bit late for that. Mr Winters said we are now the proud owners of prime grazing land. Does that make us squatters in our own right?'

'Hardly. Grass dukes are born to the cloth. One doesn't just buy into that fraternity. Do you know, there are station people on the Downs who bought out the original owners years ago, and they're still not accepted as members of the squattocracy.'

Fern reminded herself that Charlotte must have been behind the door when sense of humour was being handed out.

'I was only joking,' she said, understanding her sister-in-law's anxiety. After all, it was a big step, and a rather bizarre one at that, but necessary, given Charlotte's situation. And anyway, as Fern had told herself while she watched developments with a keen business eye, it wasn't irreversible. No need to mention that just yet. Better to keep Charlotte firm in her resolve to break the impasse with her sons.

'But of course,' she added, smiling, 'you're already one of the élite . . .'

'Don't remind me. Do you know that one of those awful women at the hotel referred to me as the dowager Mrs Broderick. Isn't that revolting?'

Fern burst out laughing. 'I told you you should have moved in here.'

'Thank you, but I prefer to sit it out in the hotel.'

'Being the martyr?'

'No. It's quite comfortable, but as long as I stay they will have to keep paying. It would suit them fine if I moved in here, save them money. I want them to sweat.'

'They're about to do that anyway. But you still haven't told me what happens now. We own those properties. How do we manage them?'

Charlotte looked up at the fading blue sky, watching an echelon of ibises gliding silently above the treetops, making their way home, their white wings tinged pink by the sunset. 'I have given this a great deal of thought. There are several ways. Victor will have to move their stock off our properties so that we can restock and employ a manager. But we won't have access to the big shearing sheds at Springfield. However, I doubt Ada Crossley would turn us away from the use of her sheds.'

'Who's she?'

'Jock Walker's daughter, on the neighbouring station.'

'The Judge's sister?'

'Yes.'

Fern shuddered. 'Oh, I see.'

She listened as Charlotte explained that they were, in fact, selectors, and outlined in detail how selectors would go about establishing their sheep stations. Tiny, in comparison with Springfield, but excellent runs. Until now, Fern had not really grasped the immense size of Austin's station, in some sections fifty miles from boundary to boundary, and she was impressed by Charlotte's cool appraisal. She seemed to know exactly how many sheep each run, as Charlotte called their holdings, could carry, and about natural expansion of their flocks as against losses, and so many other things, that Fern had to call a halt.

'You sound like Austin!'

'Yes. I had a good teacher. I wasn't always the lady of the house. In the old days we used to be out there in all weathers, fighting to save new-born lambs, protecting newly shorn sheep from the cold and wet. And we used to go together to buy stud rams, bring them home and spoil them like our own babies. I can pick class sheep a mile off. That's what upsets me. Austin turned me into his housekeeper and my sons would have me shoved into the back shed like a broken-down nag.'

260

'Not the place for a dowager, eh?' Fern twinkled.

'Not at all,' Charlotte said seriously. 'Because after all that, Fern, there's a much simpler way of running our properties.' For the first time that evening Charlotte managed a smile. 'We lease them back to Springfield.'

Fern breathed a sigh of relief. 'Oh, for heaven's sake. Why didn't you tell me that in the first place?'

'Because I think it will take a while for Victor to wake up to that possibility and make an offer, if he does at all. That will give me an income and you your rent. In the meantime, we don't have to restock unless it suits us. We have bought the land. That's enough for now.'

'I wonder how they'll react when they find out?'

Charlotte shook her head. 'Not well. I wish I didn't feel so sick about all this. They'll hate me.'

'Just a minute.' Fern went inside and returned with a tray holding a decanter and two small crystal glasses. She handed Charlotte a sherry. 'Not another word until we have had a glass of my best. You're making me nervous too.'

Charlotte drank half of her sherry in a gulp. 'I wrote to them today. Victor and Rupe. I didn't want them to hear it from anyone else. To make fools of them. I explained that they left me no choice.'

'Oh God. I think "not well" is probably the understatement of the year.'

Charlotte's letter arrived the same day as a rider was sent into Cobbside to telegraph the Brisbane lawyers, enquiring about any recent freeholding of Springfield land.

The rider was Spinner, who was pleased to have the day off, since he'd been instructed to hang about the town waiting for a response.

It irked him that although he was treated like any other stockman at Springfield, he could not join other blokes in the pub. He was a blackfeller and the pub was off limits. But he had money, being a proud paid worker now, and so he persuaded a white stockman to buy him some grog, which he took down to the park by the new town hall where a few black folk liked to congregate.

They were keen to know about his marriage but he refused to discuss the subject.

'You gone shy of takin' a wife, Spinner?'

'That girl too much for you, eh? She too smart?'

'Why you wanna stay at Springfield? Big boss gone. Them other bosses, they doan care 'bout you.'

Everybody in the black community knew everybody else's business, and he was considering going back to wait by the store which doubled as a post office when one of the old men spat a chaw of tobacco and had his say.

'Maybe Spinner wait for his own people. They comen back, eh?'

'Who says so?' he growled.

The old bloke nodded, grinned, scratched his thigh. 'Them comen back. People see. People say.'

'What do they see?'

'Emu people see honey gone. Fish traps. Little camps. All in your country. You not a blackfeller no more or you would see. People there orright.'

'Where? Springfield country?'

'What I bin tellin' you? People walkin' through. Goin' other places. They see signs. Blackfeller living there orright. Movin' about. First one side of the big river then other side.' He cackled in delight at Spinner's bewilderment.

'Ah, bullshit! If they was back I'd know!' He left them and walked into the town, where he could buy himself a proper meal, a big meat pie, from the back door of the baker's shop. He sat down right there, on the stone stoop, and devoured the pie, worrying about what he'd heard.

It was true, he wouldn't know if blackfellers, home people or strangers, had moved on to Springfield, but the tribal mob would. They travelled about all the time, unhindered by boundaries, which were only made by white men anyway. They would notice eggs missing from birds' nests, nut trees that had been plundered recently, every little thing, even a blade of grass trodden by bare feet. That was why they were such good trackers. But Spinner had lost the art. Not that he cared. In his job he didn't need to know these things.

He finished his pie and wished he could afford to buy another one, it had been so good, plenty of meat and drippy gravy. He licked his fingers and considered this news. If the people had seen clear signs in the scrub then they'd be right, they were as obvious to blackfellers as words in a newspaper, but what did it have to do with him? Had Boss Broderick been alive, Spinner would have been only too pleased to be able to bring him this information, as proof of his expertise. Old Mr Austin would have liked that. He could have told the boss that he'd spotted all those signs himself. Made a big feller of himself. But Victor and Rupe? They didn't give a hoot about the blacks. For all he knew, they mightn't want the people back.

Best to say nothing. Forget about it. The only one he had to worry about was Moobuluk, and he was damn blast sure that if that old magic man wanted to talk to him, he wouldn't be snooping about. He'd rear up in the bush like a dingo with fire in his fangs if he was angry, and so far there was nothing for him to be angry about. There was no sign of those little boys. Of that, at least, Spinner was certain.

Just before five o'clock he was handed a telegram to take back to Victor Broderick. He couldn't read and it was of no interest to him, but he rode on through the night, despairing of his lost love, calling out to the spirits to prevail on Moobuluk to release him from the

262

impossible duty of watching for children who would never return.

From her latest camp, Nioka saw the horseman taking a short cut through the scrub towards the homestead, but she made no move to approach him. It was only Spinner. She did not need him or his company. She would wait for Christmas to see if her boys came back, and after that another two or twenty Christmases if need be. They would come home. They would.

There was an edge of melancholy in her thoughts now, as the days began to drag and loneliness niggled like an irritating wasp. No matter how often she chased it away by keeping herself busy, it always returned, for the euphoria of her homecoming was wearing off. At first it had been fun to find herself the lone occupier of the old tribal grounds, well nurtured by an oversupply of staple food. It had been bliss to roam the virgin bush, to camp where she pleased, to climb up into the high forests and look out over the expanse of grasslands, reunited with all the natural beauty of the land and its creatures, but even that freedom, that sense of power, had begun to pall.

Truly, she admitted, coming home had restored her confidence. She had never been the same person away from here, among strangers, even though the mob by the lake had been kind to her. She'd found love there too, only to have it diminished by the tragedy of her sister's death and the constant worry about the boys. Nioka had no doubts at all that turning her face back to the old river country had been the right thing to do. She felt her own person belonged here, the strong woman, rid of the devils of misery and uncertainty.

On the other hand, after weeks of proud solitude, she was missing people, and that frailty was mortifying, totally at odds with her grand plan of residence here until the boys returned. She wished the others would come back, but she knew they would not. They were too afraid of losing their children as well.

She supposed she could go and visit the blackfellow mob who lived over at Jock's place. She could even stay with them, they would make her welcome, but Nioka's innate contrariness held her back. There would be too many questions, and the whites would be curious too, wanting to know where she'd come from and where the other clan people were, and she was in no mood to tell them anything. What her people did was their own business, nothing to do with the whites.

Deep in the bush she found a young kangaroo hopping about on its own, separated somehow from its mother, which was probably dead, killed by dingoes, so she picked it up and nursed it for a while, grateful for the company. Soon her nimble fingers were twisting a reed dilly bag into shape until she'd made a pouch big enough to hold the small creature. She slung it over her shoulder, appreciating the warmth of the furry body.

The reply telegram, brought back by Spinner, confirmed the contents of Charlotte's letter, and her daughter-in-law was pleased.

'What a relief,' she told Cleo. 'The men were worried that selectors had infiltrated Springfield, but it was only Charlotte and Fern Broderick pinning down more blocks in the Broderick name, keeping the station intact.'

'That's good. I can't help being aware of the animosity between you people and Mrs Broderick over the will. Do you suppose this is her way of making a peace offering?'

'Could be. And it's about time. There was no need for any argument at all, Austin made his instructions quite clear.'

'Yes.' Cleo agreed with that, but she had her reservations about the fairness of the situation. Given time to consider the widow's point of view, she couldn't help feeling that Austin Broderick had been far too generous with his sons, at the expense of his wife. What had he left her? Just the right to live in the homestead. Nothing else. Cleo couldn't blame the woman for being angry. For trying to retrieve a more solid foothold on the home territory. But it was not her place to comment.

With the heat of the day on the wane, she took Teddy for a walk along the homestead slope, looking out over the wide valley.

'There's Daddy,' Teddy cried, pointing at a group of horsemen riding across the floor of the valley. From this distance they seemed so graceful, keeping to a steady gait, and shading her eyes, Cleo was thrilled to see that the lead horseman was not Victor, but Rupe. She wished she could capture the scene in a photograph, the men so much at ease, the sheen of the horses through the fine clouds of dust, the winter grasses fading to yellow, and beyond, the brooding greenery of bush covering the slopes on the other side of the valley.

'That's Uncle Rupe up front,' she said, a tinge of pride in her voice.

'My daddy's there. He's riding the grey.'

She peered out again. 'So he is. Shall we walk down to meet them?'

'Yes! Yes!' He grabbed her hand. 'Come on, Cleo. Run. Or they'll get there before us.'

Victor was the first to hear. 'What do you mean, it was only Charlotte?' He took off his hat and flipped it on to the sofa.

'And Fern Broderick. It wasn't selectors after all.'

Irritated, he turned on Louisa. 'You're not making any sense. Who bought what?'

'I told you. Jock Walker was right. Two more of our blocks have been freeholded, but only the ones assigned to Charlotte and Fern.'

'Who paid for them?'

'They did, I suppose.'

'Where's Charlotte's letter? And the telegram?'

He read them both and, shades of Austin, stormed to the window and shouted for Rupe, who was just coming up from the stables with Cleo.

'Will you come and see my drawings?' Teddy asked him.

'Not now. You go and tell Rupe I want him. Now!'

Teddy sped away. Louisa was bewildered. 'I thought you'd be pleased.'

'Pleased? Haven't you grasped this at all? They've bought part of Springfield. We don't own it any more!'

'But that's only on paper. You told me that yourself. You said all this dividing-up of Springfield was just to keep to the letter of the law . . .'

He fumed. 'Only if we freehold the blocks ourselves.'

'So what's the difference? They're still Brodericks.'

Victor met Rupe at the door. 'Come in! Come in! Would you kindly tell my wife where we stand if Charlotte has bought the block assigned to her on our freeholding list.'

He laughed. 'She couldn't. She hasn't got any money.'

'Oh yes she has. She's in cahoots with Fern Broderick. They've bought their two blocks. Obviously with Fern's money. She probably put Mother up to it to get back at us.' He handed Rupe the letter from their mother, which was short and to the point. No apologies. More of an advisement.

Rupe stared at it. 'I don't get it. How did they manage that?'

'Very simply. We lodged the claims in their names. They took advantage. They went ahead and freeholded these two blocks and now claim ownership.'

'But we were going to do that anyway.'

Victor exploded. 'Why can't I get through to either of you! We would have bought those blocks with our money, as the owners of Springfield, under our original plan . . .'

'That's right,' Rupe said. 'And now they've saved us the expense.'

'Don't be such a bloody dunce! Can't you see? They haven't saved us anything. They've grabbed one block right in the heart of the station, and another outlying one that we meant to sell. We now have a bloody big gap in the middle of Springfield that no longer belongs to us.'

Rupe slumped into a chair. 'Oh well. Charlotte will just have to sign them back to us. We've got stock on that land.'

The implications had finally dawned on Louisa. 'Oh, Lord. You wouldn't give her a share of the property, so she has bought her way in.'

'Brilliant!' Victor snapped sarcastically.

'Don't talk to me like that! It's all so damned complicated. So she now owns good pastureland. So what? Your mother won't cause any trouble.'

'She has stolen our land!' Rupe said angrily. 'She couldn't break the will so she went behind our backs. And she's in the box seat to cause us as much trouble as possible.'

'Like what?' Louisa asked.

Victor stared at Austin's portrait on the wall as he lit a cheroot. 'In the first place, she or that bloody Fern could sell if it suits them.'

'If we don't toe the line, you mean,' Rupe added. 'We're being punished just because Charlotte couldn't get her own way. They could order our stock off their land. They could restock. Demand fencing. Put in managers, who would need their own residences.'

'Forget the block Fern owns,' Victor said. 'It's Charlotte's I'm worried about. We could in fact have another station inside this one. The thing is, what are we going to do about it? We can't let her get away with it.'

At dinner, the subject was still very much on their minds, and Cleo listened politely. She thought it was rather funny but kept her opinions to herself because they were all so angry, and confused.

In the end it was decided that Victor should write to Charlotte, expressing their outrage that she could be so underhand as to take advantage of their freeholding plans.

Later that night he completed the letter after working on several drafts, to satisfy his co-owner, Rupe.

He advised that since she could afford to purchase such a large block of land, she had no need of an allowance from her sons, which would cease immediately.

He also pointed out that her block would be denied access through Springfield. Although he doubted that would hold up in court, denying her access to their wool sheds *was* their legal right.

Prompted by Rupe, Victor added further draconian measures that would make it extremely difficult for anyone to manage a station inside Springfield boundaries.

And finally, heeding Louisa's suggestion, he wrote that he hoped there could be an end to this unseemly situation. In a rather belated attempt at goodwill, he apologized for any problems that existed between them, feeling sure that they could work things out and return to happier days.

Victor understood much better than Rupe or Louisa the problems that could confront them, and he was jittery. Charlotte was on the warpath and was proving a formidable foe. On the quiet, Rupe had told them about the snub he'd experienced at the hands of Ada Crossley, and that made him even more nervous. Charlotte could call up a great deal more support in the district if she wished, and he hated even to contemplate where that would lead.

Before he sealed the letter, he placed a little note at the bottom of the page without telling the others.

Teddy misses his grandmother.

When Jock rode over to discuss the merits of his new stud ram, Victor was surprised to see Ada Crossley riding with him, and wondered what she was up to.

She was a hefty woman in a bulging riding suit, her big hat held over her tanned face with a muslin scarf, but she slipped down from the tall thoroughbred as lightly as any youngster.

'How're you going, Victor? I thought we'd see you at the race meeting.'

'Too busy these days,' he said firmly.

'What bad luck. It was a great show. Rupe left early. Why was that?'

'I've no idea. Rupe's his own man. He comes and goes as he pleases. I'll let Louisa know you're here.'

Given Louisa's report of Ada's rudeness to her in Cobbside, Victor expected Ada to refuse, but she did not, so he sent a stockman up to tell his wife they had guests.

'What's she up to?' Louisa demanded of the cook. 'She treats me like dirt in town; now she calmly arrives for morning tea. I ought to pretend I'm indisposed.'

Hannah shook her head. 'You can't do that, it's too late. Victor would have said you're not well. And she has to observe the protocols. It's expected that she and Jock would be treated to morning tea. Just as well I've got fresh cake and plenty of cream. I'll whip up some pikelets, Jock likes my pikelets with blackberry jam. Don't worry. I'll give them a real treat.'

As she walked with Victor and her father round the front of the house, Ada kicked at the scattering of dead leaves littering the gravel path. She made no comment, but the state of the front garden irritated her.

'Oh dear! Look at the poor rose bushes. They could do with a drink, Victor. And those bedraggled flowerbeds! They're annuals. They need replacing.'

'He's got better things to do,' Jock snapped.

'Of course he has. I quite understand. These were Charlotte's gardens.'

Victor caught her meaning but trudged on. His business was with Jock, not with her.

Morning tea, laid out in the sunny breakfast room, was a treat. Louisa had set the table herself with the best embroidered tablecloths and napkins, shining silver and Charlotte's favourite china tea set. Lacking fresh flowers, she'd decorated the table with a few sprigs of blossom from the orchard and used the ornate tiered silver cakestand as a centrepiece.

As soon as Ada walked in and spotted it, Louisa knew what she was in for. She could have kicked herself for producing it.

'Ah!' Ada said. 'That cakestand. I've always adored it. Threatened to steal it, in fact. In my cups. It was a gift from the Premier, you know, on Austin and Charlotte's tenth wedding anniversary. What a party that was! Do you remember, Jock?'

'So many parties at Springfield. I can't be expected to remember them all now.' He chortled as he sat down at the table. 'I probably couldn't remember them the next day.'

'What do you call these little pancakes again?' he asked, heaping his plate without further ado.

'Pikelets,' Louisa said.

'Ah, that's right. Hannah knows my weakness. Pass me that jam, there's a good girl. And the cream. You have to eat them hot.'

Louisa breathed a sigh of relief as the tea progressed, grateful that Hannah was such a good cook and that the men were still involved in their usual haggling over the merits of various merino sheep, but inevitably Ada had her say.

'And when can we expect to see Charlotte again?' she asked, reaching for another slice of iced sponge cake.

That triggered something in old Jock's brain as he slurped down his tea, as Louisa was sure the question was intended to do.

'Charlotte?' he asked, looking up. 'What's this I hear about your mum cutting the ground from under your feet? She beat you to the punch, did she, Victor?'

'About what?' Victor asked coolly.

'Ah, don't play the innocent with me, son. Charlotte's bought herself a chunk of Springfield. Didn't you know?'

'Yes. Of course I know. That's not a problem.'

'If you say so,' he grinned. 'Time we were getting along, Ada.'

'Indeed it is,' she responded. 'You've eaten them out of house and home.' She nodded at Victor and Louisa. 'Thank you for a charming morning. I'm so pleased it doesn't bother you that Charlotte has invested in Springfield. Do tell her that your neighbours will be happy to give her every support.'

'They were laughing at us,' Louisa complained to Victor when they'd left.

Victor shook his head. 'No. Jock was. She wasn't. She was throwing down the gauntlet. You have to realize that old Jock isn't the boss any more at their place. She is. After Springfield, they own the biggest station on the whole of the Downs. If they lower the boom on us we could be in one hell of a mess, and she knows it.'

'What can she do, besides being rude to us just because she's Charlotte's friend?'

'Isolate us. Ban shearers. If they work here they don't work at her place, or any other. I've seen that happen before. Austin lowered the boom on a station owner years ago because he was stealing sheep from neighbouring properties. They forced him out.'

'But that's different. He was stealing sheep.'

'Maybe. But squatters are a tight-knit community. Austin was always popular but we took Charlotte for granted. It never occurred to me that they might gang up behind her . . .'

'Whipped up by Ada Crossley?'

'If they think we've done the wrong thing by Charlotte. I think she gave us fair warning today. We're in trouble, Louisa.'

He tried to make Rupe take their situation seriously. 'What we should do, before all of this gets out of hand,' he said to Rupe, after reporting the conversations at lunch, 'is call a truce with Charlotte.'

'How?'

'We agree to her original claim. That's all she wants. To be one-third owner of Springfield. It's my guess she wants it in name only. She'd be content to let us run the place. She just feels left out. All we have to do is give her what she wants, on condition she signs over the land she and Fern bought.'

Rupe poured himself another whisky and studied the glass. 'We give her one third of Springfield in return for one tenth, combining those two blocks. I was never very good at sums but that seems to me a lousy deal. She'll have to do better than that.'

'How?'

'That's her problem.'

Ada Crossley wasted no time. She did not embarrass Charlotte Broderick by letting her know that her friends were in full support of her stand against her greedy sons. That would be unforgivable. She owned the only hotel in Cobbside and she instructed her manager to declare it out of bounds to Springfield stockmen.

That caused fights in the town, but she wasn't concerned. Springfield men were jailed for creating a disturbance. The magistrate was her cousin.

New committees were suddenly formed in various agrarian associations, and the Brodericks were dropped. Tennis competitions, usually held at Springfield, were switched by club members to other venues. The butcher and the fettler, who worked for both Springfield and Lochearn, found they had too much work at Jock's place to be able to come over to Springfield any more. And so it went on.

Victor begged Rupe to back off. He knew that sharing management of the station with his brother would be difficult enough without inviting all these extra problems. And it had also occurred to him that if Charlotte came home, she would accept him as the boss, not Rupe, and maybe act as a buffer between them.

But Rupe remained adamant. He was cockier than ever, glorying in his new role as a fully paid-up member of the landed gentry.

'We don't need the local yokels. I've decided to invite some of my Brisbane friends out for a weekend house party. Longer if they wish. We could organize a hunt, or a bit of fishing, and have a slap-up dinner party on the Saturday night.'

'You'd better check that with Louisa.'

'Why?'

'As a matter of courtesy.'

Rupe frowned. 'Let me explain something to you, Victor, once and for all. This is my home. I don't have to seek Louisa's permission to invite guests. I will have who I like here, when I like. And if Charlotte comes home, the same rule will apply to her. We have a cook and maids. I need only tell them to be prepared.'

'Like hell you will!' Victor grabbed Rupe by the shoulders. 'This is Louisa's home too, and you will treat her with respect! She runs this household . . .'

Angrily Rupe shoved him away. 'Don't try standing over me, mate. I might have a wife of my own here. She won't have to ask permission either!'

'What wife? What's this? Are you going to marry Cleo?'

He shrugged. 'I didn't say Cleo. I didn't say who.' He strode over to the door and looked back. 'So you see, Louisa may not be boss lady for too long either.'

Rupe wandered round to the wing which had once been his father's quarters. They all used the billiard room now, but he had taken over the adjoining office, and sitting in here, idly leafing through old journals and ledgers, gave him a sense of power.

He lit a cigar and put his feet up. That had given Victor a jolt. He had deliberately said 'if Charlotte comes home . . .' to further worry his brother, but he knew that once they stopped her allowance she would have to return home. Then, when he married Cleo – because, to Rupe, that was only a matter of time now – there would be three Mrs Brodericks in the house. He grinned. Louisa would hate that.

Looking out of the window, he saw a flock of cranes gliding towards the river. At this time of the year thousands of birds congregated on the Springfield water courses and billabongs, and they made quite a show, delighting guests.

'We should have visitors here now,' he said, as if to the birds. 'The trouble with my family,' he added, 'is that they don't think ahead. Any fool could see that whether Austin was still with us or not we'd end up with three women running this great hunk of sandstone. They moved Harry on, but what about me? Did they think I'd turn into another old country bachelor?'

Rupe was convinced that Louisa was the key to his plans. Victor might be determined to economize so that he could freehold as much land as possible, but he could be forced to free his brother too. He laughed at his own joke.

All he wanted was a decent allowance, so that he and his wife could travel in appropriate style where and when they pleased. Rupe yearned for the life of a gentleman squatter. He had no intention of spending his days locked in here with his miserable family, doing the same old things day after day, season after season. And three women would achieve that for him. If he rattled Louisa enough, she'd insist that her husband give Rupe and his wife enough money to leave. He was entitled to a half-share of the profits; unlike Charlotte, his allowance was his due. Whether he stayed or left, he was still entitled.

So why not? As for Charlotte, with two women instead of just one under her feet, she'd have no objections to ridding herself of one of them.

No, Victor old son, you can't win this argument. You may have to sell a couple more blocks, but I'll be on my way soon, with my wife and your blessing.

Charlotte's reply served to reinforce Rupe's conviction that his brother could no longer cope with all these problems. Victor was a farmer at heart. It was immaterial that his flocks of sheep ran into the hundreds of thousands; he was used to that. He still had the responsibility of marking the seasons, seeing that his sheep were fed and watered and shorn and protected; of watching over his pastureland as well as domestic cultivations, and the all-important welfare of his stud sheep and a hundred or more horses. Victor needed a quiet life. The peaceful life of a dedicated farmer. If he had his way, Charlotte could come home, be a silent third partner in the firm and mind her own business. Let him get on with the job.

But three women in the house would not permit him that bliss. And now Charlotte *was* coming home!

Not only that. Her response was fair warning that the battle lines were yet to be drawn.

After acknowledging their letter, she returned fire very swiftly: *You forget that you are living in my home. I hope everything is in order, for I shall be returning shortly. Apparently your selfishness knows no bounds. I will not permit you to cancel my allowance. It will continue when I return to Springfield, be sure of that, otherwise as mistress of Springfield homestead I will be making some changes in the manner of your accommodations.*

That brought a yelp from Louisa. 'What does she mean?'

'God only knows,' Rupe said. 'Maybe she's going to bung us out into the staff quarters. You'd better put her curtains back.'

'I will not!'

Victor was too distracted to care about the curtains. 'She can do what she likes with the house. Didn't you read the rest of the letter? She says that if we can't come to an agreement about her share of Springfield when she does return, then she may consider selling her block! Selling it!'

'She's only bluffing,' Rupe yawned.

'Was she only bluffing when she saw her chance to buy that block? It's one thing to have Mother owning it, quite another to have strangers move in on us. They'd be almost at our front door, and they'd own river frontage.'

'She's off her head!'

Victor gnawed at his thumb. 'All the more reason to be very careful

271

of her. We won't cancel her allowance, and when she gets here we'll make her welcome, and hope she settles down. Louisa, it wouldn't hurt to replace some of her stuff.'

'I will not. If you want things put back, do it yourself. I've made the place look much better, less like a museum.'

'I'm just asking for a little co-operation.'

'No you're not. You're just bowing to her threats. She can bully you, but she's not going to bully me. First Austin, and now her. Personally I think your sainted father caused this whole bloody mess because he never thought of anyone but himself and his great big bloody property.'

'Big as an English county,' Rupe grinned, quoting one of Austin's favourite sayings. 'Not that he ever saw one.'

Victor fumed. 'Why don't you shut up! Austin left us a property that we can be proud of, and I'm watching it disintegrate while you two don't seem to care.'

'Nor does your mother,' Louisa snapped. 'It'd be a real slap in the eye for Austin, for leaving her out of the will, if she did sell. Payback time, as the Aborigines say. I think that's what she's been up to all along, otherwise why would she bother to buy the block?'

Rupe left them to their quarrels, but he too was a little unsettled. He had been annoyed to hear that Charlotte had burrowed herself into their land, and that interfering Fern Broderick as well, but on thinking it over, with a cooler head than Victor's, he had decided it wasn't a great problem. They could always lease it back from her for a few pence and leave her dignity intact. But she couldn't be allowed to sell. That was top grazing land, the loss would definitely make a hole in the profits. And profits were all that mattered.

He decided not to worry about it until Charlotte arrived, and if that really was her intention, then it might be a good idea, as a last resort, to get Harry over to have a chat with her. She'd listen to him.

Chapter Eleven

On the Sunday afternoon Rupe sat on a high-railed fence with several stockmen, watching a horsebreaker trying to tame a defiant brumby. The horse was a chestnut, tall for a wild one, and a beauty. Good breeding in there somewhere. But a fair devil, putting up a real fight.

The breaker, Marty Donovan, was a black-bearded Irishman with a silky brogue that Austin had always claimed charmed horses, but he was earning his money the hard way on this day. The angry horse plunged, pitched, lashed out at his tormentor with his back legs in a bucking frenzy when Marty tried to rope him in, but still the breaker was patient. He was sweating as much as the horse, both caked in dust, as he paced about, leaping aside to dodge bared snapping teeth, ducking back to the rails for safety and talking all the time.

'Come on now, there's a good feller. Easy now, me boy. And what a fine feller you are . . .'

Marty was gentle. One of the few breakers Austin had allowed to work at Springfield, his whip was noise, not pain, and when his work was done, his horses stayed 'broke', as the saying went. Not like the rough breakers, who would hand over horses half-broke that would revert to their old tricks as soon as they saw a chance.

By this, Marty was managing to stay on the end of the rope, the horse keeping its distance, wild, wary eyes watching the breaker as it cantered about the perimeter of the ring, occasionally venting its spleen on the rails by charging them, unseating stockmen, who had to scramble out of the way.

This procedure would go on for a while yet, so Rupe decided he ought to go and see what Cleo was doing. He slipped down from the fence and ran up the hill to the house.

She was sitting, reading, in the shade of the side veranda, and his heart lifted at the sight of her in a soft white muslin dress, her long dark hair tied back in a satiny ribbon, curls falling gently on to her shoulders.

He closed his eyes for a second, as if to shut out feelings too strong for him to control. He did love her, in his way, but he didn't want to. Seeing her now, looking so sweet, so damned lovable, he had to turn away to prevent himself from rushing up and taking her in his arms. He wanted Cleo, but it annoyed him to have to admit to the weakness of actually falling in love with her. For that matter, he wondered if he really knew the difference between lust and love. Who did?

He turned away with a sigh, as if the steps he was now taking were pre-ordained.

He showered, shaved and brushed back his thatch of blond hair, which Louisa had said needed cutting but which Cleo preferred to be longer, curling up a bit at the nape of his neck. He put on a fresh shirt, chose a pair of moleskins that were tight on his solid thighs, pulled on short leather riding boots that were more fancy than serviceable and strolled round the veranda, coming across her as if by accident.

'What are you reading?'

'Dickens. *Pickwick Papers*. Have you read it?'

'Not if I could help it. We had that stuff at school. Do you really like Dickens?'

'Yes. Don't you?'

He considered agreeing with her to make her happy, but it was not in his nature. 'No. I couldn't be bothered with all his soppy talk. We all thought it was sissy stuff.'

Cleo laughed. 'I suppose it would be, to a mob of wild lads in a boarding school. Who did you like?'

'I don't know. Can't remember. I did get to read some good books but I don't know who wrote them. But you shouldn't be sitting here on such a nice afternoon. Would you like to come for a walk? I'll take you down to see the birds.'

She was delighted. 'Would you? Hannah said they're out there by the millions, but it's quite a long way.'

'Hannah? She would. Walking from the kitchen to the dairy is a long way for her. It's not that far if we cut across the orchard. Years ago there used to be lots of birds picking about the river right out front of the house, but there's too much activity here now, so they stay in the quieter reaches.'

'Oh, good. Then let's go.'

When she jumped up he noticed her shoes. 'The river's starting to recede so it could be a bit muddy. Birds love swamps. You'd ruin those nice shoes.'

'Hang on a minute. I'll change.'

She rushed inside and was back quickly, unconcerned that black boots looked odd with her frilly dress. Rupe liked that. He was silently mourning his own fancy boots that would soon suffer for his latest bright idea, but that was well worth the opportunity to get Cleo far away from the house on her own. It wasn't all swamp. The grasses were dry and green, and that area was very, very private.

Just then Teddy came round the corner of the veranda.

'Where are you going, Cleo?'

'To see the birds.'

'Can I come?'

'No,' Rupe said. 'You go back to your mother.'

'She's taking a nap. Can't I come?'

'Of course you can,' Cleo said. 'We'll have a lovely time.'

Teddy slowed their walk, so Rupe piggy-backed him most of the way, setting him down when they came within earshot of the persistent shrill of the feathered residents. They followed a track through the bush to a high mound overlooking the river, from where they could view hundreds of birds all busily engaged in the search for food. Ducks in pairs sailed out on the wide river, sandpipers scratched about the shores, cranes picked delicately in the shallows and despite the crowded, noisy scene right along the river it seemed very peaceful.

Except for Teddy's excited questioning.

'What are they doing? What are they eating? Why don't they fly away? Where are their nests?' On and on . . .

Cleo was impressed by Rupe's patient replies. 'They're fishing, or eating insects and plants. Most of them are summer birds, they come from the far, far north and they go back in the winter. They hide their nests in the bush.'

He pointed out a sacred kingfisher, with its rich green cap and wings. It was watching the river, ready to pounce on any fish that dared flip to the surface, and that brought more questions, but eventually Teddy tired of the birds and began prodding about the scrub with a stick, in search of birds' nests.

'If you see any, don't touch them,' Cleo warned. 'Come and show us. We'll just be sitting here.'

Rupe took her arm as she gathered her skirts, prior to dropping down on the grass. 'Just a minute. What about me? Teddy's getting all the attention.'

'Oh, you poor thing,' she laughed, gladly turning to him.

He kissed her, softly, lovingly, and Cleo responded with passion, thrilled by the romance of the setting. The afternoon sun had tinged drifting clouds deep pink, casting a rosy glow over their surrounds, and Cleo glowed too, with love.

'You're looking very beautiful today,' Rupe murmured.

'Thank you.' Her voice was only a whisper. She didn't want to disturb the moment.

Rupe was whispering too, holding her close, caressing her face and her neck with his lips. 'Will you marry me, Cleo?'

'Yes.' She was breathless. 'Yes,' she sighed.

It had happened! He had asked her! This man was to be her husband. In a flurry of excitement they were kissing, tumbling about, slipping down on to the grass, laughing. In love. To be married. He ruffled her hair, tickled her, teased her, caressing her breasts through the soft folds of muslin, kissing her. He slid a hand down under the layers of skirts to meet the warmth of her thighs, but Cleo stayed his hand.

275

'No, don't, Rupe. Teddy might see us.' Suddenly she sat up. 'Teddy! Where is he?'

'He's just there, poking about with his stick.' Rupe had no intention of allowing Teddy to spoil their lovemaking. Not now. Not at this time.

But Cleo was on her feet. 'Where?' She began to run about, searching for him. Calling him.

Reluctantly Rupe stood up, adding his voice. 'Teddy? Where are you? Oh damnit! He's wandered off into the bush.'

'He might have gone down to the river bank.'

'No. We would have seen him.'

Cleo didn't reply. She knew she wouldn't have seen him, and she doubted if Rupe would have done either. She ran down to the banks but there was no sign of the boy. Rupe was still up in the bush, calling to Teddy, and Cleo was frantic. The river was deep and flowing strongly. What if he'd fallen in? Oh, God, no! As she stumbled and slipped all along the banks she was screaming his name.

'Don't panic,' Rupe shouted to her. 'The little bugger has just taken off through the scrub. I'll find him.'

While he searched up there, Cleo, weeping hysterically, scrambled further along the muddy banks, hanging on to branches and tufts of grass, realizing that if Teddy had come down here, he could easily have slipped into the water. Not far down, the river rounded a bend, sweeping away towards the homestead paddocks. Cleo kept going. She could hear Rupe above her, on higher ground, calling Teddy's name as he continued to scour the bush for his nephew.

Finally she climbed up and ran after Rupe, catching her dress on a thorny bush and ripping it free. It was already covered in mud.

'Haven't you sighted him at all?' she begged, hoping he had at least caught a glimpse of the little fellow. 'He's not down there anywhere.'

'No!' Rupe plunged on angrily. 'He must be round here somewhere.'

She clutched at him. 'Rupe, do you think he's fallen in the river? He could have fallen in the river!' Terror pitched her voice to a scream.

'Calm down, for Christ's sake! He knows he's not allowed to go near the river.'

'But we brought him here!'

'The water, I meant. The water! Go through that way to the clearing and I'll come round the other way. He must be lost somewhere here in the scrub. Once he finds his way through to cleared land he'll probably take off home.'

Cleo hesitated, wanting to search those banks again, but Teddy was wearing a red-checked shirt, she couldn't have missed him if he was playing down there, so she too headed into the bush. When she came across the track, she ran. The rough bush bordering the river was less than a half-mile wide. It hadn't taken them long to cover that distance coming in, but now the track seemed miles long, endless.

When she finally burst out of the scrub, panic causing her to gasp for breath, she stood shading her eyes against the sun dipping on the horizon as she searched across the paddock, but still there was no sign of him. Beyond the paddock was the neat line of the orchard. Could he have travelled that far already? 'I hope so,' she sobbed. 'God, I hope so.'

Rupe was running back to her along the edge of the bush. He was very angry now; blustering, but she could hear his fear. 'The little wretch. Where's he got to? We'll go back the other way, towards the birds. You keep going along here so you can spot him if he comes out this side, and I'll work along the river. He'll have to be between us somewhere.'

'What if he has fallen in the river?'

'He'd have yelled. We'd have heard him.'

'Not if he was too far away from us!' she screamed. 'He could have drowned!'

Cleo was weeping uncontrollably. Rupe grabbed her and shook her. 'Stop that! I haven't got time for your tears. Now make yourself useful. Go look for him!'

She kept to the edge of the bush, making short inroads, calling and calling, even resorting to the bush call, 'Coo-ee!' which Teddy knew, hoping for a response because Teddy was quite proud that he could coo-ee as well as anyone. But a quiet was settling on the bush as the birds began to disperse, and there was no response from Teddy.

Rupe began to search again, starting at the high bank above the river where they'd stood to observe the birds, where he'd asked Cleo to marry him, an eternity ago. He cursed himself for letting Teddy wander off. For forgetting him, because guiltily, he knew that was true. He'd forgotten about Teddy.

Carefully he walked into the bush, into the last place he'd seen Teddy prodding at the undergrowth with his stick, a small branch Rupe had broken from a tree and stripped, handing it to his nephew as he set him down from his back, to use as a walking stick or even, like the blacks, just to fossick with. Teddy had been very pleased with his stick.

By this Rupe was frightened. He allowed himself to detour round the spot where he and Cleo had been, gradually easing in an arc towards the river as a naughty child could have done if he'd wanted to keep out of sight of the grown-ups. Or if he just found himself drifting in that direction.

Then he saw it! Teddy's stick. It was jammed in a burrow close to a short, sharp bank above the water.

Rupe didn't touch the stick; he bent down to examine the bank, noticing a tuft of grass torn loose, but he kept his head. It was fresh with soil, but Cleo could have done that in her mad rush along the banks.

No she didn't, he told himself. She'd have to have been in the water to have pulled that out. Almost unwillingly, he turned his attention to the couple of feet of muddy sloping bank between the grass and the surface of the water, and saw the marks on the smooth, glassy surface of mud. Something had slid down here.

He tried to tell himself it was an animal. A platypus, maybe. But a platypus left tracks. Here the mud was churned up, and there were claw marks. No, not claw marks. They could have been caused by a child's hands!

The truth hit him like a hammer but he still wouldn't allow it. He leapt up, shouting across the water for the boy, and then he crashed along the banks, following the current just as Cleo had done, but he was faster, sure-footed. He crashed round the bend of the river and dived in, mad with fear, as if somehow he could locate the child in the swirling waters.

The current shot him wide from the bank, almost to the other side, as it washed heavily at the turn and sped over the rocky, cavernous depths to carve its way ruthlessly to its meeting with a great river sixty miles hence.

Rupe didn't come back to meet her and Cleo was frightened. The sunset was scarlet now, fearsome, flaunting colour before the day died. She waited for ages, calling him, calling Teddy, afraid to re-enter the bush to search for them, afraid of disobeying Rupe, not knowing what to do but wring her hands and pace up and down the rim of that awful bush.

She heard the mournful 'kur-lee, kur-lee' of curlews, and the occasional screech of a flock of birds as they lifted above the trees, and she saw two emus coursing across the paddock. All the birds were heading home. It was late. Very late. They should be home by this. Louisa would be angry. Teddy had his bath at five o'clock.

When Rupe didn't appear, all sorts of explanations rained through her head. He might be hurt. He might have found Teddy but couldn't bring him out. Maybe Teddy had been bitten by a snake. Maybe . . . Cleo didn't know and she didn't wait any longer. She had to run for help.

Hannah was shocked when Cleo burst into the kitchen right on dusk. The girl was in a dreadful mess, covered in mud and absolutely hysterical. Hannah shouted for Victor, but he was over in his office. It was Louisa who came running.

'What's happened? What's wrong?' She took one look at the dishevelled governess and screamed. 'Look at you! You're a mess. Where's Teddy? How dare you take him out without telling me? I was

278

looking for him everywhere until one of the stockmen told me he saw you and Rupe . . .'

She stopped, realizing that Cleo was babbling at her through her tears. 'What's wrong? Where's Teddy?'

But Cleo was incoherent.

Louisa slapped her. Hard. 'You tell me what's happened, Cleo. Right now! Shut up that snivelling.'

'Teddy,' Cleo whimpered. 'We couldn't find him. He got lost. And Rupe too. I couldn't find him either.'

'Where?'

'Down by the river. We were only watching the birds. And Teddy, he wandered away . . .' She collapsed in tears again, but that was enough for Louisa. She rushed out of the back door and clanged and clanged on the big bell that hung there for emergencies, for fire or any other disaster, knowing it would alert any man within earshot.

First came Victor. He picked up on the situation quickly and ran after his wife, who was already racing towards the orchard.

'Stop, Louisa. Wait.' He held her close. 'Now calm down.'

'They've lost Teddy,' she screamed. 'Let me go!'

'No. We'll get horses. It'll be faster. And lanterns. It'll be dark soon.'

He persuaded her to wait in the kitchen for a few minutes while he went out and spoke to the men who were already hurrying up to the back door. Cleo was still there, slumped over the table.

Louisa stood over her. 'If anything has happened to my son, I'll kill you. Do you hear me?' she shouted. 'I'll kill you! What were you doing? Smooching with Rupe? Why did you have to take Teddy with you?'

'Now, now,' Hannah said. 'Everything's going to be all right. Rupe will look after Teddy. I think Cleo must have just got lost and scared. I'll make a cup of tea.'

But Louisa didn't bother with her tea. Victor was out back with her horse. She ran down the steps and hauled herself up into the saddle, glancing fearfully at the darkening sky. They skirted the orchard and raced across the paddocks in the wake of the posse of horsemen who were fast bearing down on the swathe of bush hiding that section of the river.

By the time they'd dismounted and hitched their horses to trees beside all the other mounts, the men were already spreading out to search the bush. Victor and Louisa made for the track that would take them through to the river.

The sudden invasion caused a flurry in the bush as small animals dived for cover and irritated birds fluttered skywards, adding their shrill complaints to the shouts of men tramping through their domain.

Teddy's parents were frantic. They stumbled helplessly along the banks calling to their son, their voices mingling with the plaintive cries heard all about them as they gazed in terror at the darkening waters.

279

It was Victor who found Rupe squatting forlornly by the river, his head in his hands.

He screamed at Rupe, dragging him roughly to his feet. 'Where's Teddy? What happened? You're soaked. Did he fall in the river? Where *is* he, you bastard? Did you let him fall in the river?'

'I don't know,' Rupe wept. 'I can't find him. Didn't he go home?'

'Of course he didn't bloody go home! You're not making sense. Where is he?' Victor was in such a rage he shook Rupe, slapping him, until Jack Ballard came upon them and dragged Victor away.

'Let me talk to him. Louisa's coming, you see to her, Victor.'

Lanterns were lit as the light faded, and the search of that area wound down, so it was widened to follow the river all the way back to the homestead and in the other direction as far as a child might have travelled.

They all knew that there was little chance of the boy being lost in the bush on this side of the river. The belt of greenery was too narrow, giving way to open pastureland. On the other side it was a different story. The bush was rugged over there, and no one had bothered to clear it, since there was already a surfeit of natural grassland on this property. That meant the river was the only real danger, so while they continued to search, the men gravitated to the banks of the river, watching miserably, afraid they might find a small body resting there.

Shaken from his state of shock, Rupe joined the searchers, telling himself that it was possible that Teddy had simply wandered on and on, losing track of time, or even that he'd become tired and fallen asleep somewhere, as did happen with children.

Louisa was exhausted, close to collapse, so at Victor's insistence, Jack Ballard took her back to the house.

'They'll find him,' he told her as he ushered her into the kitchen. 'The lads will find him, Louisa. Come on in and we'll get you a brandy. You're shivering.'

But when she came in, Cleo was there, waiting apprehensively, afraid to voice the question, for the answer was only too evident.

Louisa collapsed into a chair, struggled to hold the brandy and then drank it all in a gulp.

When she regained her breath, she leaned across the table to Cleo, menace in her voice. 'Get out of my house! Get out!'

Sobbing, Cleo twisted from her chair, dragged up her bedraggled skirts, and fled.

'Ah, now,' Hannah said, putting an arm round Louisa, 'she's terrible upset, the poor girl.'

'Upset?' Louisa screamed. 'So she ought to be! Jack, she can stay tonight but I don't want to see her. In the morning you get her out of my house. Someone can take her as far as Cobbside and she can find her own way from there, the bloody bitch.'

Jack nodded. 'All right. I'll arrange it. Don't worry. Would you like

280

to lie down for a bit? Hannah will make you a nice cup of tea.'

'No! I'm staying here. You go back. I want to wait here with Hannah.'

They searched all night in an ever-widening arc, even searching the homestead and all the outbuildings, in the faint hope that the child might, somehow, have returned.

Jack sent one of the men to ride fast for old Jock's place to bring back a blacktracker, even though he was aware that so many men trampling the scrub would have left little to help a tracker.

Jock Walker, shocked by this catastrophe, came with Simon, a tall, grim Aborigine. 'He's the best tracker we've got, he'll find the boy now the sun's coming up,' he told Victor.

Weary men came back for a bite to eat and mugs of hot tea before setting out again with renewed hope, aided by daylight, but Rupe did not go with them. He couldn't face it.

They brought Simon to him so that he could show the tracker where he had last seen the boy.

As Jack had expected, the tracker shook his head when he saw the results of more than twenty men beating through the bush all night, but while Rupe and Victor watched, he began searching about the high bank.

Rupe knew that stick was still stuck in the burrow – he had passed it so often he'd lost count – but he dared not point it out to them, nor could he remove it. He had wanted to grab it and throw it into the river, tear it out of his sight, but fear and guilt had immobilized him.

Squatting down, Simon examined the mound where Rupe had sat with Cleo, mercifully making no comment. Then he moved inch by inch into the bush nearby, examining the ground while they stood well back, waiting.

'The men have been through here, I'm afraid,' Victor said to him.

Simon looked up. 'Men beat high, not looking too low, boss. Someone here bin turnin' over lumps of dirt. Leavin' little lines. Using a diggin' stick, working low on the ground. Who do that?'

All eyes were on Rupe. He cringed. Jock, Victor and Jack Ballard stared at him, not understanding the importance of the question. It was Simon who spoke.

'Who had a diggin' stick?'

'Teddy did,' Rupe whispered. 'In there. He was poking about.'

Simon nodded and went back to work. Slowly, inevitably, it seemed to Rupe, he picked up, not Teddy's trail, but the tracks of that stick, however minute. He went further into the bush on his slow, tortuous search, down the slope and around, sighing when he met difficulties but moving on relentlessly, and then he emerged at the low bank.

He sat back on his haunches and pointed.

'What?' Victor shouted. 'What?' Only about a foot of the stick was visible.

Simon waved his hand at them to stay back as he inched forward to circle close to the stick, not touching it.

Rupe knew that Simon would not take long now to see those marks, if they were still there. The clump of grass certainly was. Dried and fading, it seemed to shout for recognition. He prayed that Simon would draw a different conclusion, that the black man would move on, following a trail that Teddy could have taken down along the bank towards the birds. He prayed. Begged the Lord to help. Hoped against hope that someone would come crashing through the bush to tell them Teddy had been found, to put a stop to this agony.

Sadly Simon shook his head. He stared and stared at the water and when, at last, he looked back to Victor, there were tears in his eyes. 'I'm thinkin' Teddy gone in right here, boss.'

The Brodericks were in shock. Everyone was in shock. Victor had men dragging the river. He would not give up until they found Teddy's body, but it was a difficult job. The river was full of snags, trees and bracken washed down by floods and caught in the rocky depths. With Victor shouting frantic instructions at them, they kept at it, while other men scoured the shores further down, knowing that if the small body hadn't been dragged down, it could easily have been swept away by the current. But so far none of them had had any success.

When Rupe tried to help, Victor snapped. He grabbed a tomahawk and charged at his brother in a blind rage. Only Jack Ballard's swift intervention saved another tragedy. He wrestled the tomahawk from his boss and had the men physically restrain Victor while he rushed Rupe away.

'Come on. Back to the house. You'd better get some rest.'

'Oh, Jesus, I'm so sorry,' Rupe kept sobbing as Jack shoved him on to a horse, leading him across the paddocks. 'What can I do? What can I say?'

Jack had no answer for that. Instead of the house, he took Rupe to the cookhouse and left him shuddering by the stove in the care of the Chinaman who cooked for the staff. There was Louisa to contend with yet. Teddy's mother. Jack hoped Hannah had managed to put the poor woman to bed.

No such luck. She was still in the kitchen, totally exhausted but refusing to budge. She seemed to think that this was where she had to stay to wait for news. Good or bad.

'He hasn't drowned, has he?' she begged Jack pitifully. 'Not Teddy. Please, Jack. Tell me it's not true. Only this morning he was playing with his train and I said his daddy would make him some carriages to hook on to it. Was it this morning? No, it was yesterday!' She began to scream. 'How long has he been missing now? All night out there in the dark!'

Jack spoke firmly to Hannah. 'Take Mrs Broderick to her room, Hannah. Now! She has to lie down.'

'She won't go!' Hannah said desperately.

'Yes she will.' He would not permit any argument. Between them, he and Hannah took Louisa upstairs, but as they passed Cleo's door, Louisa began screaming again. 'Is she still here? I want her out of my house!'

Jack found Cleo sitting nervously in her room, her bags packed. 'Has there been any word of Teddy? No one has told me and I'm going crazy sitting up here.'

Jack patted her on the shoulder. 'Bear up, love. It's not good news. It looks as if he did drown. I'm sorry to have to tell you this but I think it would be best if you did leave. No one's blaming you, the missus don't know what she's saying, but . . .'

'Of course they're blaming me,' Cleo wept. 'I'll never forgive myself. I'll go, Jack, but could I just go to Louisa and tell her how terribly sorry I am.'

'Not a good idea right now,' he said slowly. 'You come on downstairs with me and we'll work out what's best to do.'

He trudged back to the cookhouse to find Rupe. 'I've got a job for you.'

'What?'

'Louisa's terrible upset with Cleo, she being his governess and all. We have to get her out of here. I can't send her to Cobbside and leave her in that one-horse town. I want you to take her on to Toowoomba, book her into a decent hotel and arrange for her to travel on to Brisbane.'

'Why me?' Rupe growled. 'You trying to get rid of me too?'

'Not a bad idea. You took them to the river.'

'It was her job to mind Teddy. Not mine. I thought she knew where he was.'

'You asked me what you can do. Now I'm tellin' you what you can do. Blame won't bring Teddy back, but you saw what a state his parents are in. Give them a break, Rupe, ease out for a while.'

Rupe didn't budge. He sat scowling at the pots heating on the wide stove, and the cook, sensing trouble, slid out of the back door.

'I'm asking you to take Cleo to Toowoomba, Rupe.'

If it had been anyone else, Rupe would gladly have taken the opportunity to flee from this awful situation, but not with Cleo. He never wanted to see her or talk to her again. He had managed to convince himself that this was all her fault, and he couldn't retreat. Besides, what would they talk about on a long ride like that? Go over it all. How they had managed to forget Teddy. How he had drowned. Drowned! The very idea of such an inevitable conversation filled him with horror.

Finally he spoke. 'You don't seem to understand how I feel. Teddy was my nephew. I loved him too.' He could feel a wail building up in his voice but he couldn't control it. 'Why the bloody hell don't you leave me alone!'

'You won't take Cleo?'

'No, I won't. I won't run.' He sighed. 'Jock was here a minute ago. He's saddling up now, taking Simon back with him. I'll go over to his place for a while.' He shrugged helplessly. 'If they don't want me here.'

'I suppose that will have to do, but I thought Cleo was your girl.'

On the way back to the house Jack met Spinner. 'Hey! Come here. Do you know where Tirrabee station is?'

'Yeah. Long ways, boss. Harry running that mob now.'

'That's right. Now I want you to get a good horse and go tell Harry we want him back here.'

Spinner rolled his eyes. 'You want me to tell him 'bout poor Teddy?'

'Yes, bring him back. Plenty quick.'

'Righto, boss. I find him for you.'

Since Rupe wouldn't take Cleo away from Springfield, and she could hardly ride out, even with an escort, Jack arranged for the gig to be brought round to the front door, and instructed a stockman to drive the lady to Cobbside. It was the best he could do.

'Go to the pub,' he instructed her. 'They'll look after you until the coach comes through. Do you need any money?'

'No thanks, Jack. But I would like to see Rupe before I go.'

'He's not here, Cleo. Probably over with Victor,' he lied. 'I'm real sorry about this, but under the circumstances it's wiser to give Louisa a chance to . . . I dunno, think more clearly. She doesn't know what she's saying now.'

'Yes she does. It's all too terrible.'

He took her down to the gig for a sad, lonely farewell. Not even Hannah, or one of the maids, came out to see her off.

'Send us your address,' he told her before she left. 'The police will need a statement from you.'

He watched as the gig spun round the gravel drive and off down the road, past the row of tall pines that Austin had planted so long ago.

'Just as well you went first,' he said, thinking of Austin, 'or this would have broken your heart.'

But there still had to be a reckoning. Louisa had wanted Cleo dismissed, and that was done. Victor was in a dangerous frame of mind, blaming Rupe, so it was best that he was, for the time being, out of range. Soon, however, one or both of them would have to give an explanation of what exactly had happened on Sunday afternoon. What were they doing that they lost sight of Teddy?

The general consensus among the men was that they were canoodling. Forgot about the boy.

'Jesus,' Jack muttered, looking back at the big house. 'When Victor

284

comes down to earth Rupe will need to be further away than the property next door.' He hoped Harry wouldn't waste any time getting back to Springfield.

And then he remembered Charlotte.

Teddy was her grandson. She had to be informed.

The men were straggling back from the river, shaking their heads, sending another shift down. No sign of the boy, and his father behaving like a madman, threatening to shoot anyone who even suggested giving up.

'Oh, Lord, give Harry wings,' Hannah said as she and Jack retreated to the pantry to try to compose a suitable telegram to send to Charlotte.

'How can we break it kindly?' she asked him anxiously.

'I don't know. I'm no good with words.'

'I never had to send a telegram as bad as this in me life,' Hannah cried.

'She has to be told.'

'More than twelve words costs extra.'

'Bugger the cost!'

Finally, after several attempts, Hannah transcribed their message on to a clean sheet of paper.

Regret to inform you that Teddy has met with an accident. Yours very sincerely, Hannah.

She gazed at the page. 'That's the best I can do. They haven't said yet whether he drownded or got lost or what.'

'He drowned all right.'

'So he might have, the poor love, but I'm never sending a telegram with "drowned" in it. It's not right. Too cruel. The poor woman will find out sooner or later.'

Within minutes another rider was hurtling down the road towards Cobbside.

The telegram was delivered to Charlotte at her hotel at nine o'clock the next morning, only a few minutes after the office opened. Since telegrams were famed for being the bearers of bad news, all of Charlotte's new acquaintances were agog as word spread through the hotel. Ladies followed the clerk to her door, worrying about her, and eventually tapping gently to ask if there was anything they could do.

They found her stunned, for once in need of their concern.

'I have to go home,' she cried. 'Something has happened to my grandson. What does this mean? An accident. It's worse than that. It has to be. Otherwise why would she use "regret"? I have to get home.'

She was upset. Sobbing. Trying to pack. But even in this travail Charlotte Broderick had spirit. She was accustomed to giving orders, and now they came thick and fast. One lady who volunteered to help her pack was instantly given the job. Another was sent to inform Mrs

Fern Broderick. Another to book her a first-class ticket on the train to Toowoomba. The very next train.

At twelve noon the ladies handed Charlotte a picnic basket to sustain her on the long train journey out through Ipswich, for which she thanked them kindly. Fern was there too, to see her off.

'Let me know what's happened, Charlotte, as soon as you can. It might not be too bad. Servants panic. You know how it is. I'll send them a wire to let them know you're coming.'

'No need,' Charlotte said stiffly. She was very frightened, wondering why it had been left to Hannah to contact her. And she knew Hannah. That woman wasn't the type to panic. Whatever this accident was, it was bad.

'But they'll send someone to Toowoomba to drive you out to Springfield if they know you're coming,' Fern argued.

'I said no need. I shall stay at a hotel for the night and hire a coach to take me on. I can't be sitting about waiting for a Cobb and Co. timetable. Don't worry about me, Fern. I do know my way home.'

That night Mrs Charlotte Broderick, well known in the district, was afforded the best rooms in the Victoria Hotel, Toowoomba. Her host, delighted to have her stay in his establishment, sent a fine meal up to her room. A meal that Mrs Broderick hardly touched.

Downstairs a young lady, also staying in the hotel, went into the dining room for dinner, but she, too, hardly touched her food. Cleo Murray was too shattered to face a meal.

In the morning she took her suitcase and lugged it down to the railway station where she sat miserably, waiting for the train to Brisbane.

What had happened to Teddy? She still wasn't sure.

What about Rupe? Why hadn't he come to see her? He'd had time to at least call in on her at the house. To see how she was. Did he still want to marry her?

She didn't know.

On the train she wept for Teddy. Prayed.

So did Charlotte. He was constantly on her mind as she sat fuming in the hotel foyer, only to be met with the news that the carriage was not available. Broken axle. To make matters worse, the publican was unable to find her another driver and vehicle because the town was busy celebrating its annual country fair. Charlotte knew she could call on friends to escort her out to Springfield, but that would mean arriving with guests and that might not be appreciated at this time. In no mood to socialize, she remained in the hotel, stubbornly refusing to appeal to Victor. Instead she telegraphed Ada Crossley at Lochearn that she was in Toowoomba, at the Victoria Hotel, on her way to Springfield, but delayed by lack of suitable transport, adding a request for information on Teddy Broderick's accident.

Only a few hours later she had Ada's crisp response: 'Stay where you are. I shall come for you myself.' No mention of Teddy.

Even more agitated, Charlotte had no recourse now but to wait for Ada. She tried to tell herself that if Teddy had been seriously hurt Ada would have said so. She would have enquired. In which case why hadn't she answered the question? Charlotte blamed herself for the too-casual wording of her own message. Telegrams were so difficult. Too sparse half the time to make any sense. She knew she could not expect Ada until the next day, so she spent dreadful hours pacing her room, listening to revellers celebrating after the fair.

Chapter Twelve

There was a nostalgia, a pride, in his return to the river country, but it was no longer a homecoming. This was where his father had grown to a man, and all the fathers before him, honouring the laws that were, in themselves, guardians of the earth and its creatures. Observance of duty meant preservation of the tribes and the land, and brought good men forward to a spiritual awareness, a deeper understanding of the secrets of nature. Remembering the great content that sweetened a man's life at that stage, Moobuluk smiled wanly. Those memories were as precious to him now as every step he took. For his steps were numbered, he knew, fewer each day, and the days left to him were not many.

Everywhere he had been in the past year had constituted a homecoming because he loved the earth so dearly, and was greedy for the feel of it on his hardy, searching feet. The beauty of his surrounds had become more intense from the lake country through to the billowing blue coast, and south over the hills to the grassy plains where once he'd been able to run great distances in a day, carrying messages to other clans.

'I was fast,' Moobuluk told his faithful dog as he stood on the plateau looking down on the Springfield house. 'I could run like the wind. And you could too, I'm sure, before a white man's trap maimed you.'

That, too, made his final journey more distressing. He was grieving in his farewells to family and friends, not for himself but for their poor, bewildered faces. He had heard shocking stories from the very mouths of displaced people. He knew that tribal people to the north had drawn battle lines, refusing to retreat before the invaders, and he could only leave them to their destiny. Bad enough it was that he could not offer solace or even a grain of his famed wisdom to the clamour. There was shame in that. He felt very deeply that he had let them down. Somewhere in the magnificent lore of nature that he knew so well, that he'd been honoured to learn, there should have been a warning.

'Maybe there was,' he admitted humbly. 'And I was too proudful. I could have missed it.'

He wondered what the elders, long gone, would think of the new age that was enveloping their land. The age of desolation. For it wasn't just the scattering of the people. There was too much sadness in the

289

clans for Moobuluk to mention to them that this unprecedented upheaval, unlike any tribal battles through the ages, would also bring the demise of precious species of birds and animals that could not cope with the constant march of so many new breeds.

That night he sat under the stars, denying the waste of hours in sleep, to commune with the spirits of his clan, talking over this pathetic end to a long career in their service. Explaining that he was only here on one last piece of business, in the hope of locating the girl Nioka. He spoke on her behalf, as a good, strong woman, asking for her protection from the demons of depression that had wilfully taken the life of her sister in a wasteful, useless manner.

In the morning, the golden rays of the sun swept over the grey skies and Moobuluk wept with joy. What did he know of the tragedies that had overtaken the peoples of the earth throughout the eons of time? Who was he to think he might have had a hand in destiny? The spirits had scolded him for pride, and for entertaining the ignorant devils of lost hope. They grieved, too, for the miseries of their race, but Moobuluk had learned from them more about the world and the great universe than he'd ever thought possible. Knowledge that he couldn't possibly hold in his head, but then there was no need. He was retiring from the world, not in the company of devils, but into the hearts of men and women who understood. The knowing ones, beside whom he was just a mortal for a few more hours.

Moobuluk wished he had the strength to go back, to go back to sit by all those campfires and tell the people of hope, that from the Dreaming he had seen them and their children, smiling, recovering, the old times remembered, not lost, the new times beckoning. Travail was the earth, like storm and tempest, flood and famine. It passed. He was filled with a new energy. His body was lithe and light, his smooth black skin shone with the ripple of muscles as he explored Springfield station with the dingo that had lost its limp. He wanted to talk to Spinner, to ask him about the children, but there was no sign of him. Nor had the children returned. He visited the old grave of the man called Kelly, which was surrounded by an iron picket fence, and found another grave there, that of Boss Broderick.

But he was puzzled. Only Victor and his missus were living in the house, along with their servants. The boss missus, called Charlotte, was away, and so was Teddy.

'The child has probably been sent away to school,' he told his dog darkly. 'Like they sent our boys.'

As he moved quietly about, he sensed misery, as if devils had invaded the place. The men were not working, just hanging about. Even the horses, who understood white men as easily as dingoes did black men, were listless and nervy. They shied away in fright as he approached.

He went down to the river to sit in silent commune with all the birds that he knew so well, listening to the chattering cockatoos, hundreds of them, perched on high branches like dazzling white blossoms.

Then he saw the brolgas coming. A huge flock of brolgas, more than he'd ever seen in his life before, and his heart gladdened as they soared above him, trumpeting their arrival as if to say to all the other birds gathered beneath them: 'Make way! Make way!'

Their long journey from far-off lands ended, they were in no hurry, gliding down in the thermals, turning about, reaching high into the sky again to slide, in play, down that invisible chute of air.

Moobuluk laughed at their cheek as the regal birds began their final descent. Humbler birds fluttered away, deciding to call it a day; bolder cockatoos lingered, watched them balefully then, squawking crankily, retreated, two by two.

Squads of brolgas came in to land on their stilt legs, and now that they were earthbound again they resorted to hoarse croaks, not nearly as pleasant to the ear as their soaring song. But then, they had to be about the business of renewal. Just like everyone else, as the spirits had reminded Moobuluk.

Harry had ridden through the night with Spinner, changing mounts at various stations on their way. He was broken-hearted at hearing of Teddy's death by drowning, but Jack Ballard, who met him at the stables, warned him that there was more trouble brewing.

'Victor is threatening to kill Rupe.'

'Why?'

'Because Rupe and his lady friend took Teddy down to the river in the first place. Without bothering to tell Louisa.'

'Where's Rupe now?'

'Over at Jock's place.'

As the story unfolded, Harry was close to tears. 'What were they doing so far from the house?'

'The birds. They went off to see the birds.'

'Ah, yes,' Harry sighed. He used to look forward to the return of the birds himself. 'Many brolgas this year?'

'A few wandered in months ago. It must have been too dry wherever they came from. But yesterday a big mob moved in, hundreds of them.'

'That's good to hear. Well, I suppose I'd better go up to the house and see what I can do.'

As he expected, Victor and Louisa were devastated. They had no reaction at all to Harry's presence. It was as if he'd been there all along.

'Have they found him?' Victor asked. 'I'd be still down there but I had to come back to see to Louisa. Try to get her to have a cup of tea or something. Have they searched the far banks too?'

'Yes. I'm sorry, Victor. No news yet.'

Victor looked haggard and drawn, his eyes bleary from tears. 'If it had just been an accident, maybe it wouldn't be so bad, but they were there with him. They took my boy down there . . .'

'It was still an accident,' Harry said gently.

'They've gone, haven't they? Rupe and Cleo?'

'Yes.'

'I don't want Rupe back here ever again. Do you hear me? Never. You tell him that. As for that girl, she'd better not show her face either.'

Louisa was curled up on the couch, wrapped in a rug. She took no part in the conversation, seeming to be too dazed to comprehend what was going on.

Harry sat beside her and nodded at a tray set on a nearby table. 'These sandwiches look good. Do you mind if I have one?'

When she didn't answer, he picked one up and ate it, then he took another, breaking a piece off. 'It's Hannah's famous cheese and gherkin mix, still the best I ever tasted. Here you are. You try, Louisa.'

She shook her head, but he persisted, and gradually fed her small scraps. He was about to remark to her that it was like feeding a little bird, but decided against that. What to say to her? Or his brother? He had no idea how to console them.

Naturally Ada took Rupe in, their previous difficulties forgotten. She couldn't do enough for him in the face of this terrible tragedy, but she had to chase after Jock to ask the obvious question.

'What's he doing here, though?'

When the situation was fully explained to her she was shocked. 'Ah, the poor things, the lot of them. They're blaming Rupe, I suppose?'

Jock nodded. 'You can say that again. Victor's fit to be tied, and Louisa threw the governess out. We figured Rupe would be safer here until Victor cools down. These things happen, they'll have to understand that. Blame does no one no good.'

'What about Charlotte? Have they advised her?'

'I guess so. And Jack sent Spinner to fetch Harry. He might be able to keep things calm.'

The following day Ada was edgy herself, with Rupe wandering listlessly about her house not knowing what to do with himself.

'It'll pass,' she said to him. 'You never know with kids, they can get away from anyone. It's no use blaming yourself.'

His reply stunned her. 'I'm not. Victor's blaming me. I'm as upset as they are. I loved Teddy. I would have done anything for the boy. I didn't want to take him down there. I said no, he couldn't come. It was Cleo who insisted we take him. Don't you see, Ada? It's not my fault at all.'

'Of course not,' she said, disturbed that this young man, while salving his own conscience, was pointing the finger of blame at the girl. She did not appreciate his attitude. Local gossip had it that he'd been romancing the governess for quite a while.

'Whatever becomes of her, she's well rid of him,' Ada muttered to herself. 'And Charlotte's got a time ahead of her, with her sons tossing blame about like a hot potato.'

She went in search of Jock. 'You'd better send for the Reverend Whiley. Get him over to Springfield. That family's in dire need of the word of the Lord.'

'I'll do that, but a rider just brought in a telegram from Charlotte. She's stranded in Toowoomba. And she wants news of Teddy. She must have heard a rumour, poor thing.'

Ada questioned Rupe, who had not known that his mother was in Toowoomba, or even if she'd been advised about Teddy. Nor did he seem relieved that Charlotte was on her way home. Rather the opposite. 'What can she do but cause more confusion?'

'Your mother cares,' Ada snapped. 'Obviously she knows something's wrong or she wouldn't be appealing to me. But don't you put yourself out. I'll see to it.'

Ada had a new light carriage, beautifully appointed and, more importantly, well sprung to cope with rough roads, and now she had a chance to put it to good use. She sent the rider back with her response, which she knew was inadequate, but like Jack and Hannah, she couldn't bring herself to tell Charlotte the cruel truth.

'Better I break it to her myself,' she told Jock.

'Her son's here. Send him.'

'Not on your life. God knows what that whingeing pup would have to say. Leave him here. Don't mention where I've gone. Get the horses hitched up and I want Charlie to drive, he understands the vehicle.'

Rupe stared through the front windows as his hostess hurried out of the house and climbed into the fancy coach he'd noticed when he'd been over here for the race meeting. Few people owned elegant coaches like that, not even the Brodericks, who were content with well-upholstered gigs with weatherproof roofs.

Must have cost a fortune, he said to himself, then he found himself grinning for the first time since this nightmare began, because there was Charlie, a stable hand, sitting up top, reins in hand, dressed in green livery and a matching peaked cap, looking more like a page at court than a plain old bushie.

'Thinks she's a bloody duchess,' he muttered, and wandered into the parlour to try to concentrate on some country magazines. The worries were returning. He wondered, anxiously, if they'd found Teddy's body yet, pushing away those recurring awful glimpses of a child floundering in swirling waters. He could not allow himself to think about that, it was too terrible.

293

It was already time to let the men get back to work. With willing hands from other stations assisting the search, they'd dragged long sections of the river several times, and Harry knew they were only going through the motions now. It was a hopeless job anyway. The banks were littered with the sodden debris they'd hauled up, mud-caked wraiths, ghoulish in their dereliction. As the thick clay on retrieved branches dried, they stiffened into sharp, surreal shapes, adding their eerie silence to the scene.

Victor was so distraught he hardly knew what he was doing, rushing down to the river to harass the men, hurrying back to sit with Louisa, shouting at the maids, ordering them to search the house over and over again until Harry had to intervene, trying to calm him with a few brandies.

When Louisa spoke it was only in whispers, and when anyone addressed her she flinched, withdrawing to her refuge under the rug in the corner of the large leather couch, so Harry was surprised when she suddenly spoke to him.

'You'll find him, won't you, Harry? You will, won't you?'

He had to agree, not knowing whether she meant dead or alive, and distressed beyond words, he wondered why he'd come. There was nothing he could do; never in his life had he felt so helpless. He tried to write a letter to Connie, but even that was beyond him, so he took himself off to the river, through the orchard and down that worn track to where Teddy had last been seen, following his feet rather than his instincts, for somewhere to go.

Earlier he'd visited his father's grave, holding his hat in silent homage, promising he'd call at Springfield more often in the future, rather than allow himself to be summoned by death. Victor had been trying to tell him something about Charlotte interfering, causing the ruination of the whole property, but the tale became so confused in the telling, and besides, was so preposterous, that Harry set no store by it. He just let his brother talk while his mind drifted. Hannah had advised Charlotte that Teddy had met with an accident, and Harry had no doubt that she would be on her way. He expected to hear from her any time now, because she'd be needing transport. He dreaded having to break this terrible news to her. And later, much later, he'd have to talk to her quietly about this misfortune that seemed to be causing Victor added distress. If that were possible.

As he neared the river, a dingo charged from the bushes, barring his way. The animal was crippled but a good size, so those bared fangs were enough to make Harry back away cautiously, surprised that a dingo would bail him up, unless he'd interrupted its feeding. Then a sharp whistle caused the dog to relent and, reluctantly, allow Harry to proceed, sniffing suspiciously at his heels.

Curiosity kept Harry striding along, to see who owned the beast that was pacing him so carefully. He would have liked to kick the mongrel out of the way but thought better of it.

When he saw the old blackfellow seated comfortably, cross-legged, on the bank, he wasn't all that surprised. Few white men had pet dingoes, and certainly none as ancient as this one.

'Hello!' he said amiably, dropping down to the bank. 'What are you doing here, boss?'

'Waiting.'

The dog settled himself beside his master in agreement.

'When are all the mob coming back here?' Harry asked.

The old man's hair was as white as his straggling beard, and the leathery face was grained with age, but it managed a gummy grin. 'You Harry. Boss Broderick's boy.'

'Yes!' Harry stared at him. 'Good God! Moobuluk, you old villain! I thought you'd gone to the stars years ago.'

Moobuluk nodded, pleased. Harry was the only one of the three sons he'd ever got to know, because this son had always been poking about. Even from a little lad he'd traipsed around with the people, picking up their language, learning all the earth things, but he'd never had the awe of the magic man that was inherent in tribal people. He'd even barged up to Moobuluk one day and said: 'My dad reckons you're a medicine man.'

Now his old eyes glittered with amusement as he asked Harry the question he'd always wanted to ask, but which in those days pride would not have allowed him to stoop to enquire: 'What is a medicine man?'

Harry blinked. Then he remembered, and burst out laughing. 'What a memory you've got! The boss used to say that about you. A medicine man is a magic man, clever. Very clever. Fix people. Cure the sick ones.'

'Ah.' That pleased him also, but the cracked old voice was suddenly serious. 'Another question. Where are our babies?'

'What babies?'

The gnarled hands stretched out and Moobuluk counted on his fingers, very slowly. 'Bobbo. Doombie. Jagga. Where are they?'

Harry was bewildered. 'I don't know. Didn't they go on walkabout with everyone else?'

'No.' It was difficult for Moobuluk to have to admit to this white man that he had failed in his duty to his kin, that he was unable to give them a proper account of the event. He hung his head as he did his best to explain it to Harry, who obviously had no idea that a prayer man had taken them away. Miserably, the old man saw the truth in that. No one cared about the little black boys; they hadn't even bothered to tell Harry, who'd grown up with their parents.

By patient prompting, Harry managed to extract the story from him, helping Moobuluk with his English and using his own, almost forgotten, grasp of the clan dialect. He was not unaware of the programme instituted by various state and church groups to remove black children from tribal families and have them assimilated into white society, but until now, to his regret, he'd not been interested. He'd simply taken it for granted as the right thing to do, until Moobuluk now confronted him with the suffering it caused. Until that programme had encroached on his own life.

'I'm so sorry,' he said. 'So very sorry.'

But Moobuluk hadn't finished. 'Sorry. That nothing. Bobbo's mummy she so sorry, she throw herself in the lake and drown.'

'Minnie?' Harry cried, appalled, and then he had to bow his head in shame, for he knew he should not have mentioned her name.

'Sorry,' he whispered again, and his apology was accepted.

Moobuluk continued. 'Gabbidgee, he broken man, all sadness, and Nioka, she run off crazy. What they do with our little boys, Harry? They never come back.'

Harry felt a prickling of fear on the back of his neck. He knew about the Aborigine payback; their stories and Austin's stories had always intrigued him. Teddy had been in the back of his mind all along. After they'd completed the pleasantries of conversation, which had turned out to be far from pleasant, he'd hoped to ask Moobuluk how long he'd been here and what, if anything, he knew about Teddy's death. Maybe he'd seen something.

It had not occurred to him that the old man, or any Aborigine, might injure Teddy in any way, they all loved the white station kids as they did their own, but . . .

Their own? He felt himself sweating, and worse, Moobuluk's cold, steady gaze gave him no solace. Three black children, Teddy's age, had been abducted from Springfield. Now their playmate, a white child, had drowned. Jesus! Payback. Was this payback? His voice was so hoarse he had to almost tear it from his throat when next he spoke, repeating the question the old man had ignored.

'Where are the rest of the mob? Have any of them come back with you?'

Moobuluk looked surprised. 'They can't come back. Me, I tookem them away so the white men can't steal their children too. You unnerstand, Harry? They had to go.'

'Oh, Jesus! Why didn't my father stop this? Or Victor? Or my mother? What were they thinking of?'

'No one care. Only black kids!' the old man spat.

Harry kept the conversation on the boys, promising to search for them, to bring them back, relieved that after Moobuluk's bitter tale he was gaining his trust again, but watching for some hint of payback, of Teddy, of anything. No one needed to tell Harry, in his fearsome suspicions, that he was up against a wily and dangerous foe if Moobuluk had given an order for payback. He would be obeyed.

It was growing late. 'Do you want some tucker?' he asked. 'I can get some for you and bring it back. And a feed for the dog too.'

Moobuluk scrabbled in a dirty dilly bag and brought out some squashed berries, handing some to Harry, who ate them politely, refusing to gag. 'A good feed,' he said genially, seeming to find that amusing. 'A good time for a good feed, eh?'

He pointed downriver. 'Why you blokes all the time fishing down there?'

Now it was time. Harry moved closer to him, ignoring the anxious growl of the dingo. 'They're searching for Teddy. He fell in the river. He drowned. You're a wise man, Moobuluk,' he added intensely. 'Can you tell me about that?'

Moobuluk's eyes squinted and he looked at Harry quizzically. 'Teddy? Your brother's boy? The little one. He drown?'

'Yes. They've been searching for his body for days. My brother and his wife and everyone here . . . we're all heartbroken.' The appeal in his voice was real.

Moobuluk reached out, gesturing for Harry to help him to his feet. Only then did Harry realize how very old this poor fellow was. His skinny legs would hardly carry him. Nevertheless, Moobuluk moved forward with wobbly steps, leaning on his stick. He gazed up and down the river, not seeming to notice the background noise of the settling birds. His thick nostrils extended as he sniffed the air, and his left hand waved forward as if to feel for information. For a long time he stood there, and then turned back to Harry.

'No death here. No death. Who tell you that story?'

'It's true. He's gone. Drowned. He was playing here and he fell in the river.'

'You all wrong. Nothing here speak of death. Nothing.'

'Then where is he? We can't find him.'

It was then that Moobuluk knew where Nioka was. She was here somewhere. He looked across the river at the darkening scrub. Oh, yes, she'd come home. Her presence was as strong now as the perfume from night-blooming flowers. And if the river didn't have the boy, nor the white people, who else? He gazed at the crimsoning sky and saw her dark, powerful eyes. And he also saw a woman who had to be protected. Voices of the spirits hammered at him. Nioka was important to them. She had to carry on the family, gather them to her, show them the way through these strange times. She was his kin, a clever woman, she would know what to do. Nioka must not be harmed.

But if she had taken that child, the white men would have no mercy. If they found out. Moobuluk shuddered. Could he go to his Dreamtime a traitor to his kin?

The answer was equally unnerving. 'What is this?' voices raged at him. 'The white men took your children. Three of them. What does it matter if they have lost one? This is not your business. When you

297

leave, Nioka will take your place. She has to live to deep old age. You must not interfere.'

Harry was pleading with him. He had forgotten the good food, asking about the boy, asking if anyone had seen him. Asking when Moobuluk had returned to Springfield. That question slipped in like a thorn underfoot. The implication hurt, and the old man turned away.

'You go now. We talk tomorrow.'

'What about Teddy?'

'I will think on him. We talk tomorrow.' He settled down on his haunches, closing his eyes, shutting Harry out.

As he walked slowly back to the house, Harry was confused. The old man was in his dotage, he had to be. He looked as if he'd cleared a century of years. But then those old rascals knew things. Exactly what things Harry couldn't define. What if Moobuluk's instincts *had* told him that no death had occurred in the vicinity?

'Impossible!' he muttered to convince himself. He remembered the food he'd offered and then forgotten. He sighed. He really had messed up that talk. Moobuluk was a proud man, and touchy. He shouldn't have voiced his suspicions by asking when Moobuluk had arrived back in his old stamping ground. It was too obvious that he was trying to discover if the old man had had anything to do with Teddy's disappearance. He should have known better. Hadn't Moobuluk just told him no death there? He'd been surprised by the search. Not the reaction of a guilty man at all.

'Damnit!' Harry strode on, deciding not to mention the meeting to anyone at Springfield. There was enough misery in the house without introducing this confusing information. Victor knew who Moobuluk was; he'd go berserk, crashing down there with the tact of a stampede.

No. Tomorrow, at dawn, he'd go back. This time with a peace offering of some food, something soft, since the gummy old mouth wouldn't be able to chew much.

But he did talk to Hannah about the children.

'Is it true Bobbo and Jagga and Doombie were taken off to school?'

'Yes,' she said, taking it for granted that Harry must have learned about them from someone on the station. 'A preacher and his wife took them. They were staying here for a while. We were glad to see the end of them, a miserable Bible-thumping pair they were.'

'What did Minnie have to say about that?'

'Oh. She played up. They all did, the blacks. Came up here to the kitchen door, yelling and screaming. Your mum had to get Victor to shut them up. Have a talk to them. Explain it was for the best. That damn preacher made it worse, he just sneaked off with them, took them from the camp, kidding he was taking them for a jaunt in his wagon, but never turning back. They never even got a chance to say goodbye.'

She moved some pots about the stove. 'Then again, I don't suppose that would have helped. Only caused more screaming and wailing. Come to think of it, not long after that, they all packed up and left. All the blacks. We thought they'd just gone walkabout. Your father was real upset about that, I can tell you.'

'But he let them take the kids.'

She turned about to consider this, hands resting on ample hips. 'As I recall, he was sick at the time, when they left. Yes, it was after his stroke. But he did give his permission. Before that. And your mother agreed. It was talked about for a few days before they actually drove off.'

Harry stood staring out of the window. 'It must have been a wrench for them, never having been away from the station before. And terrible for their parents.'

'Ah,' she said softly. 'You're thinking of poor little Teddy. And Victor and Louisa. But it's a different thing altogether. Little Teddy's gone. The black kids are being given a chance to make something of themselves. You mustn't get morbid about them. You know it was for for the best. Lord heaven, Harry, you kids went off to boarding school yourselves, it didn't do you no harm.'

'But we got holidays. And we knew we'd be coming home. Those kids have gone for good. I used to think the removal of black kids was for the best too, but now I'm not so sure. I never stopped to think about it before. I feel bad about this, Hannah, I really do. Their parents must have been frantic. They'd be heartbroken having their kids abducted by strangers and never knowing what became of them. They wouldn't be able to write letters . . .'

She shook her head. 'Come on now, Harry, don't be letting those things upset you. Remember, you haven't been well yourself.'

'What if that had been Teddy, though? What if some stranger had abducted him and we knew we'd never see him again? How would we feel? How would his parents feel? They'd go crazy with grief, just like they're doing now.'

Hannah placed her hands firmly on the table. 'There's no comparison! You're just down in the dumps! Dinner's ready and I'm serving trays in the parlour because Victor has to stay with Louisa. She won't budge from there. You go in and sit with them. They need someone to talk to.'

Moobuluk came to Spinner in a dream. He was a frightening figure, tall and vigorous, in white and ochre ceremonial paint, but his voice was gentle.

'Have you seen any of our people here?'

'No. But someone was around, people say. They see the signs in the bush.'

'You tell the white men?'

299

'No. Not me. I don't tell them nothin'. They never brought back the kids neither. I have to go from here meself. I got a woman to marry but she won't come live here with the people gone. Can I go?'

'Not yet. I need you here. We have to wait.'

'What for?'

But then he awoke to the snoring and snorts of other sleeping men, trying to recall the conversation, worried that Moobuluk might be here to cause trouble.

From the other side of the river, Nioka had seen them, Rupe and his lady love, standing up on the headland looking down towards the big corroboree of birds. Then Rupe had lifted Teddy up to get a better view, smiling, pointing, and Nioka's heart ached. Would her boy, Jagga, ever see the beautiful birds again? Jealously she watched the little blond-haired boy in his delight. She'd seen him round the station, and how he'd grown. A hand-span taller, she thought, and so Jagga would be that height too. Teddy was a bit on the plump side, and he still had that puppy fat on him. Jagga was reedier, but firm-boned. She hoped those bad men were feeding him properly; boys needed good tucker, plenty fresh meat and fish and growing food. She wished he was here now. There was such an abundance of bush nuts and berries, even a child could feed himself. He could fill his own dilly bag in no time.

Her keen eyes fixed on them, she saw Rupe and the girl draw close together but lost sight of Teddy. They were canoodling now, petting and kissing, and Nioka remembered sadly the lover she'd left behind at the lake, wishing he was here with her, because she needed that loving too. Day after day, her resolve had been weakening. Was her plan to stay here until the boys came home just plain stupid? What if they never came back? She was sorry now that she hadn't asked her white friends in Brisbane to help her find the boys. Maybe they could have helped. But she'd been too set on coming home, as if she could track them from here. Had that been possible, Gabbidgee would have said so.

Nioka nodded, impatient with herself. Pretty stupid to be just hanging about here.

The lovers were now entwined with one another and Nioka was not surprised to see them sink to the ground, hidden from the river by a low bush, to get on with their passion. White folks were no different when it came to loving. And Rupe was cheeky with girls, everyone knew that. She giggled, wondering if the white girl knew that Rupe was after her secret places . . .

She was distracted by the sight of Teddy's red shirt moving mistily down through the bush. She squinted, trying to follow his course, but he kept disappearing until at last he emerged in the clearing by the river, poking about with a stick.

Why weren't they watching him?

That was easy. They were too busy with the loving. She looked to the headland, waiting for them to remember the boy, who was playing too close to the river, and then switched her eyes back to Teddy in time to see him slip, grabbing for a hand grip, grabbing, slipping so fast.

Nioka hit the water on the run, panic driving her on. The silent death, they called it. Drowning of children. They went into the water so fast, so surprised, they never had time to cry out. She sped under water a long time and came up to see the child threshing, sinking, but travelling in the same current bearing her downriver. She struck out strongly, every stroke long and powerful, defying the current with a massive burst of speed, keeping her eye on the blotch of colour as the current bore him towards her in preparation for its swerve round the bend. She saw him disappear, and dived again, smashing at underwater snags that tried to obstruct her, and came up close to him.

Teddy was limp, heavier than she'd imagined. She dragged him to her and looked about, as together they bobbed downriver. Her own shore was closer; it was too dangerous to try to take him back with the river swirling and rippling into whirlpools at the bend, so, keeping his head above water, she used the current and her pounding legs to keep battling for shore, while her left arm struck out again, seeking, relentlessly, the shelter of a jumble of rocks at the bend.

She rushed him ashore, carried him over the slippery rocks to safe ground, laying him out, terrified because he'd turned a sickly green colour. Pounding on his chest. Cleaning out his mouth. Weeping. Blowing life-giving air into his lungs. Unable to see him clearly through her tears. Watching him spew. Turning him over to help him spew more water and bile. Hearing him choke. Pushing more air into him. He was alive, but he had to work to live. She picked him up and ran with him to her fishing camp, where she wrapped him in blankets she'd stolen from the Springfield stables. Knowing he was in shock, she nursed him to her, giving him her warmth, listening for his heartbeat, patting the frail little back, cuddling him, singing to him.

All through the night Nioka held him to her, though her own back, uncovered, felt the chill. His breathing was raspy and irregular, so she kept adding air from her own lungs. She didn't know what else to do.

In the pitch darkness of the night, she nursed him by sound, her body stiff and aching, for she dared not disturb him. She could only yearn for the morning, for the precious rays of heat from that profligate sun that took so very long to come up for them.

It was the kookaburras that woke him, always the first to tell the world so arrogantly, with their racket, that soon would come the dawning, and she clung to him, warming his face with her own.

'I feel sick,' he said suddenly, and he tried to vomit. Dry-retching

301

as she released him. Then she was weeping, relieved, laughing, smothering him with kisses, calling his name, telling him what a good boy he was.

He was exhausted. He needed to rest properly now, Nioka decided, so she took him deeper into the bush and laid him down in her bark humpy, still ensconced in the heavy horse-blankets. Then she waited. Occasionally, when Teddy stirred, she dribbled honey-sweetened water into his mouth as if he were a baby again, pleased to see his tongue move along those dry lips, relishing the honey.

Reward came eventually. He stared at her with sleep-glazed eyes, then, focusing, he struggled up. 'Where's Jagga?'

Nioka was in a thrall of delight. Not only had Teddy recognized her, he remembered her boy, and rather than spoil that pleasure, she swept sadness from her voice to tell him that Jagga had gone away to school. She was amazed that she could say such a thing so glibly, but at all costs this child, recovering from his ordeal, must not be upset.

Later he roused himself again. 'I fell in the river,' he announced, with a mixture of surprise and awe.

'Yes. You play too close, but you orright now.'

'What's that in the bag? It's moving. Is it a snake?'

'No, it's a joey.' She removed the cover and allowed the little animal to peer out.

Teddy was entranced. 'Aaaah! Can I hold him?'

'Yes. He strong now, but only a baby. Like you,' she grinned.

'I'm not a baby!'

But to her he was. Just a little boy. Just like her Jagga. How wonderful it would be to be able to sit and talk to her Jagga just like this. Her heart ached while she treasured this time with Teddy, charmed by him, by the matter-of-fact conversation so natural to a boy this age. Another joy denied to her as a mother. A small thing, she mused, but everything.

'Did you pull me out of the river, Nioka?'

'Yes.'

'I thought so. That was lucky. Can I have something to eat? I'm hungry.'

Nioka wished she could go back to the river and find him some yabbies or eels. Cooked, they made good eating, but she did not dare leave him, for fear he might wander back to the river. She only had some plump green grass seeds, wild berries and round nuts that she'd broken from their casings, so she pushed the rush basket over to him, relieved to find he was content to pick through them, chewing them cheerfully as he nursed the joey.

'When you better, we go find yams and maybe witchety grubs, eh?'

'I'm better. I only sicked up.'

Eventually, at his insistence, they set off, moving slowly into the bush towards a lonely creek that Nioka knew still held just enough clear water for their needs, and would maybe provide them with more substantial food.

Teddy chattered all the while, at ease in her company, finding it a great adventure to be on the search for blackfeller food again, asking all manner of questions about the rest of the people, where they were, when they were coming back. Nioka answered him truthfully, evading only the why of it. She told him about the beautiful lake where the mob were living now with other families who built canoes so they could skim over the lake like the wind.

'Will you take me there, Nioka?'

'No. It's too far.'

'We could ride horses. Get there real fast.'

She laughed. 'We doan have no horses.'

But Nioka had her own questions. Children were truthful. They might get things mixed up, but they could answer, devastatingly, to the point. When she lit the campfire to cook she learned that Teddy was having lessons now, and the girl whom she'd seen with Rupe was his teacher.

'Why couldn't she learn our boys too . . . my Jagga, and Bobbo and Doombie? Why did they have to go away to learn?'

'Because they're black kids. They don't have governesses.'

'What's a governess?'

He sighed, as if she should know these things. 'A teacher. She teaches me for a while then I go to a real school.'

'The same school as the boys? Our boys?'

Teddy considered this. 'No. I don't think so. They don't have black kids at the grammar school.'

'What's a grammar school?'

'Where they teach grammar, I suppose. You know, sums and spelling and things. Can I eat now?'

He relished the fat little grubs with their nutty taste, while she picked the roasted yams from the hot coals, and prised the cooked flesh from the shellfish, handing it to him as it cooled. He didn't like the eel, turning his nose up at it as smelly, so Nioka ate that as she dusted ash from the toasted crusts of her bush bread.

'What did your mother say about our boys? When will they come home?'

'They have to stay away.' He nodded confidently. 'They have to grow up white.'

'Why?'

'For the best. They all say that. It's for the best.'

'Like Spinner?'

'No. He's a blackfellow.' Teddy scratched his tousled head. Apparently it was beyond him too, but it didn't matter. Nioka had heard enough. They were not coming back. Minnie was right. She'd lost her son.

Reminded of his mother, Teddy was concerned. 'Will Mum be angry with me for falling in the river?'

'No. Long as you're safe she won't be angry.'

'Good. You've burnt the bread.'

She broke some off for him. 'Better that way. More taste.'

The delight was still with her. That joy, like a romance, of loving again. She adored the child, adored being with him, feeding him, listening to him, spoiling him, keeping him happy, she was his servant, his slave. His mother. Niggling thoughts skimmed and pricked at her, they tried to tug at her heart, they lingered on the beauty of this child, with his thick white hair, and his fair skin with a bloom of pink on his cheeks, and his eyes of mid-morn sky, and they loitered about through the heat of the day, but she would not permit them to intrude on this idyll. Not for one second. A blink shut them out. That was all it took. One blink.

Nioka knew what they wanted. This child was not hers. A full day had passed, a night and a day, but she wouldn't even contemplate time. Here was now. Here with a son again. Charmed beyond measure.

Teddy was interested. 'How are we going to get back across the river?'

'We have to walk down to the crossing. Long ways. Better you get sleep.'

'My father's got a boat but I don't suppose he'll hear us from here.'

'No. I'll make us a humpy to sleep in. You want help me?'

'Yes. I'm good at that. Bobbo showed me.'

He was hardly good at it, she smiled, but she encouraged him to help her make a shelter from brush, only to find he was more interested in making one for himself, a tiny hideaway which he called a playhouse, that lacked a roof.

'Do you want sleep in that, or mine?' she asked when she'd completed her task and the birds were beginning their retreat over the evening sky.

He twisted his face into a comical question. 'Do you get any snakes in yours?'

'No fear.'

The little man made his own decisions. 'Then I'd better bunk in with you, Nioka.'

But that night, while the child was sleeping, cuddled into her with the joey in his arms, Nioka's demons returned, more hostile than ever.

'The child is yours. You gave him life. You took him from the river death. He is yours. They don't care. They let him drown. He is yours.'

And Minnie's devils joined in, more persistent, more demanding. 'You have him now. A life for a life. The waters took your sister and gave you a son. Go. Take him while you can. Bring him back to the lake. To your people. You cannot deny destiny is kind to you. The

304

water spirits have responded to your pain with true magnificence. See how much you are loved.'

In her dream, Nioka saw the happiness in a mist of forest dawn. She saw herself walking among the people by the lake with her much-loved son. She heard their cries of welcome and astonishment and joy that she had returned with him; and how they loved him too, a great gladness sweeping over the camp at the miraculous return of Jagga. And how proud she was, not only of her boy, but to be able to tell them that she would go again and she would bring back Bobbo and Doombie to reunite them with their families and introduce them to their new friends. It was all so exhilarating that Nioka was puffed up with her own importance until she remembered something, and that woke her with a start.

This was not Jagga. It was Teddy. A white boy.

Distressed, let down by the dream, Nioka examined the story. It was hard to relinquish the sublime satisfaction of that dreamscape, but wakening forced the confrontation. This could not be. No one took any notice of a forlorn black gin trudging the roads, but all eyes would be on an Aborigine woman with a talkative child who had white skin and hair like straw. Black, white or Chinee, they'd all stop and stare. And question. It was not possible. There was not enough bush left to hide them. Troopers would halt her. Recent Aborigine lore was awash with the fear of troopers, sometimes called police. They couldn't differentiate.

The next day was tranquil, lazy, because he was tired after all his adventures, so that night Nioka curled in to Teddy, pulling the blanket over him again. They were sleeping on a mat of reeds that sucked and returned their warmth, the brush overhead dipped protectively as the leaves died, and the moon glimmered silver around them. The little joey, sensing his nocturnal birthright, stirred and peered out at her, so she teased him with the tips of gum leaves, which he munched for a few minutes until he nodded off again. As did Nioka, overcoming the disquiet.

Then the devils came back, vicious and full of their own importance, claiming that her sister was with them.

'That child is yours. You took him from the water. We gave him to you. A life for a life. She is here, your sister, and in great despair. Why do you forsake her? How can she pass on to the other life when you are so weak? She says a life for a life. Even that is not enough. Our clan has lost three children, and your sister. It is payback time.'

'No,' she screamed.

Then she saw Boss Broderick, and Victor and his wife, and all those white people lounging on the lawns by the house while Teddy played with a wooden contraption that had wheels . . .

'Look at them,' the voices harped. 'They took your child, our children, and threw them away somewhere. We will never see them again. Look at those white people. They don't care. Cruelty is their nature. They despise us. Our children will die somewhere and they'll never find their way to the Dreaming. They must be punished. Who knows better than you, Nioka?'

She nodded. She was weak. She knew it. Once she'd been all fired up with hate, with that same need to punish them for their crimes, but somehow it had dissipated, been lost along the way.

The bush all round her crackled with the fires of fervour, and there was excitement in the air as Nioka felt herself being raised up beyond mortal bonds. It was a heady experience; she was being given the power of life and death.

The beings were all about her. 'Is it not payback time?'

She nodded, humbly accepting the all-too-logical outcome of the outrage that had beset them. Payback had to be or the emu people would disintegrate into dust like so many weakened clans before them.

'You took him from the river, now you put him back,' the voices acclaimed. 'Only *we* will know that the law has been fulfilled. This is why we gave him to you. Can't you understand that, or are you too insensitive to our laws? You have been given the privilege of revenging your sister, and she stands here, waiting. Put him back in the river.'

'No!' Nioka shrieked, but she made no sound. The child was still sleeping. The bush was creeping alive with the dawn. Kookaburras cackled. Small birds twittered. Yellow light filtered. A snub-nosed lizard gaped and scuttled. Frogs plopped in the creek, eyed off by a sleek crow.

She was dazed, overwhelmed. She thought she heard Louisa calling to her, but the voice was faint, far off in a world of strange beings, and she couldn't understand what she was saying. Her head was still resounding from the persistent demands of the spirits, and she was desperately afraid of them. They were monsters, they could inflict fearsome punishments on anyone, or anything, that defied them.

Whispering, she woke Teddy. 'Come on. We must go.'

'Where?'

'Down to the river.'

As he stumbled to his feet, crows set up a loud cawing, shattering the morning.

'Damn crows,' he mumbled, gathering himself up obediently. 'Can we bring Joey?'

'No! He big enough to mind himself now. Hurry!'

In the same dawn Harry raided the kitchen even before Hannah appeared, and set off, running, to find Moobuluk again. He knew he was allowing foolish superstitions to raise his hopes, but there was just a chance that old Moobuluk might know something about Teddy, even, he admitted sadly, where the body lay.

He wasn't surprised to find the ancient sitting in exactly the same place, as if he'd been there all night, in no need of shelter. Typical of Moobuluk to pull a stunt like this, he thought. These magic men were past masters at the art of the dramatic to impress lesser mortals.

Harry pretended not to notice, though, refusing to be taken in by any clever tricks. Today he would get his answers.

He handed over the food and Moobuluk dug into the paper bag, nodding his thanks. He had soon made short work of a couple of hard-boiled eggs, bread, and cold meat loaf.

'Good,' he said.

'I want to talk to you about Teddy.'

Moobuluk shrugged. 'Better we talk about our boys. What you do with them, eh?'

'I wasn't here but I asked about them. They've gone away to school.'

'Stolen,' Moobuluk said angrily.

Harry tried to explain. 'It wasn't meant to be that way. My people at the house, they thought they were doing the right thing. I'm sorry. I really am.'

Ignoring Harry's obvious impatience, Moobuluk ordered him to sit. 'Now you tell me all about this school.'

Ashamed, Harry had little to tell. He could not lie to this man, so he had to admit that he did not know where the school was, or who the people were who had taken charge of the three young lives. He fell back on explaining the necessity for schooling, miserably aware of the grief in the old eyes.

'They learn them your language?'

'Yes.'

'What fathers teach them their Dreaming?'

Numbly Harry shook his head, knowing how much cultural awareness meant to Aborigines. Stronger than religious bonds, to them this was life itself, all part of the earth and universe in some unfathomable manner.

'They are lost,' Moobuluk whispered.

Deliberately, Harry pretended to misunderstand. He knew that Moobuluk was not speaking in a physical sense, but he had to offer some hope.

'No. Not lost. They are in Brisbane, I'd say. In the big city. At a school. Like I went away to school.'

As soon as he said that, Harry realized it wouldn't work. So did Moobuluk. He stood up without the slightest effort and his voice had gathered strength.

'When they come home?' he demanded.

Harry sat awhile, staring at the river. 'I don't know,' he admitted, finally.

'You get them!' Moobuluk snapped, his face contorted with rage. 'I say you get them. Bring them back!'

'I don't know where they are.'

307

'Better you find them!' Moobuluk threatened, and despite himself, Harry cringed. Was payback coming? Not in bone-pointing or any of the so-called spells that Aborigines, not whites, were so afraid of. But if the Springfield mob came back, bent on vengeance, stirred up by this powerful old fellow, they could create havoc.

'I don't like being threatened,' he said quietly. 'It is possible that I could find them. I might be able to bring them back. I can't promise.'

Moobuluk took his stick and drew a line in the sand. 'You promise. Make good joss for you.'

'What good joss?' He echoed the word the local Aborigines had picked up from various Chinese cooks.

'First you promise.'

'All right. I'll go looking for them.' Why shouldn't he bring them home? he mused. The poor kids would be completely out of their depth at some half-baked church school, and scared stiff of their strange surroundings. Charlotte or Victor would know what school. The minister and his wife had been staying at the house, after all. But he'd do it for his own reasons, not because an old villain like this was trying to bully him into it. Or bribe him, he recalled.

'What good joss you got for me, old man?'

'You think better on your own boy. Show him proper ways now, and him grow up big fine feller.'

Instantly Harry was alert. 'Who? Teddy?'

Moobuluk shook his head and grimaced as if it was difficult to be dealing with such stupidity. 'No, no! Your boy, the one comen.' He sniffed. 'You forget him a'ready? Like you forget our children. No good, that.'

But Harry was staring at him. Connie was expecting. He hadn't forgotten that for a minute. But girl or boy? That was in the lap of the gods.

'How did you know my wife was expecting a baby?' he asked, realizing the question was futile. He was caught up in one of those wildly improbable situations concerning blacks that had become part of local folklore, but at the same time Harry felt a surge of joy. That was real, very real, and a mischievous side of him was already accepting bets from his mates as to the sex of his unborn child. Bets that he knew without any doubt that he would win. He was to have a son.

The dingo came trotting along the river bank with its ungainly three-legged gait, and Moobuluk turned to watch as it shook water from its fur. Harry surmised it must have been in the river to cool off, or maybe catch a fish. You never knew, with dingoes, what they were up to. It sidled up to the old man, its brown eyes the epitome of devotion, and Harry was touched, knowing Moobuluk had a staunch friend there.

The old man fondled the dog, spoke to it in his own language and resumed his cross-legged position on the bank. He reached over to

Harry and took his hand in a strong grip, forcing him to edge closer.

'We bin waitin' for you, Harry. Waitin' long time. Things to tell.' His eyes misted. 'You allatime good boy, Harry. You bin sick but you orright now, eh?'

'Yes.' Harry held his breath, not daring to interrupt.

Moobuluk nodded. 'Boss Broderick, he good feller too. No more war. Me and him, we both warriors, take no cheek, us. No bloody fear. He up there on the hill now, not goin' no place either, me and him. This our home.' The grip on Harry's hand tightened uncomfortably. 'Boss Broderick he say kids not in any bloody school.' His voice rose. 'You hear this, Harry? Boss, he tell me kids not in any bloody school! You unnerstand?'

Harry felt the pinpricks of hair on the back of his neck. He could have sworn those words, 'not in any bloody school', were Austin's. They sounded like Austin's voice, deep, intense, angry, not the voice of a croaky old centenarian. And no, he didn't understand any of it.

'You go now.' He released Harry's hand. 'You remember ol' Moobuluk and you remember his children, eh? This my sleeping time.'

'I'll remember, but please, I thought you'd be able to tell me about Teddy.' Despairingly Harry looked around him. 'Please. No one else can tell me.'

Moobuluk blinked. 'I tell you. No death here. Only life.' He poked Harry. 'Life of your boy too, eh? Good joss. You do this ol' man one more present.'

'One more favour?'

'Yes. You get Nioka and mind her proper. She a good woman, she tell you 'bout the other boy.'

'Oh, Jesus! Where is she?'

Moobuluk pointed. 'Down there.'

'Where?'

'The dog take you. He know. Better you go help her.' He reached out again and stroked Harry's arm wistfully. 'This a good day for walkabout, eh?'

Harry tried to take his leave of Moobuluk politely, given that he was frantic to get away, but his words were unnecessary, for the old man had closed his eyes and drifted into reverie. The dog, though, was on its feet, looking at Harry expectantly.

'Go!' he shouted, and the dog sprinted up the rise. Running and stumbling, Harry went after him, wondering if this was all a cruel fantasy, wondering if he would even find Nioka, and if he did how he was supposed to help her. What did she know? That kept him going. That kept him pushing along through the jumble of scrub and rocky headlands that bordered the river, afraid of losing sight of the elusive animal, afraid it was just racing nowhere in particular.

Nioka had further to go, a lot further. She and Teddy had wandered far inland, and the river twisted and turned as it forced its way cross-country, swirling round solid rock and slicing through softer sandstone over the ages until it found the flat, where it could eddy along at its own meandering pace. The child was despondent, less enamoured of this adventure if they had to be battling through the scrub in such a rush, leaving behind the joey, and his playhouse, and the unopened nuts that he himself had picked.

He objected to her pulling him along, so she slowed, looking over her shoulder, terrified of the demons. In her heart Nioka was wailing. If she had to put the child in the river, she would go too, she couldn't leave him, they would slip under together the same way her sister had gone. All hope lost.

'Why are you crying?' he asked, suddenly, solicitously. 'I told you we were going too fast. You'll be all worn out.'

Nioka hugged him, speechless, and set him back on his feet, but every time she saw the river, she veered away again, scrambling through the bush, searching for old tracks that seemed to have been obliterated from her mind. He was slowing her down even more, glimpsing the river himself, telling her they were going the wrong way, as if the devils were leading him on, not her; asking her to make him a bush-walking stick so that he could beat off snakes; wanting to examine holes in the ground as if they were only on a bush walk; hearing the distant clatter, wanting to go see the birds; anything to delay her, she felt. Anything to slow their progress.

He didn't know that they'd passed the bird sanctuary; she kept telling him it was up further, and by then he was tired, his little legs almost giving way beneath him, so she put him on her back for a while, as he recalled that Rupe had given him a piggy-back too.

'I expect he'll be looking for me now,' he commented. 'And Cleo too. I'd better get back to my lessons.'

When they finally did burst out on to the bank, Nioka sobbed with relief. She had found the crossing, littered with rocks, that slowed the river into a series of low waterfalls. But the current was still strong, waters running freely as they did until the dry season set in and it was possible to wade over.

She took his hand and began racing towards the river, excited that she'd outrun the devils, exhilarated now that he was nearly home, but Teddy, remembering, pulled back, screaming.

'No! No! I'll drown again. I won't go in there.'

Nioka had a tight hold on him. Battling his struggles, she threw him up over her wide shoulders, yelling at him, trying to calm him as she waded deeper and deeper into the river, bruising her hips against boulders, using them to steady her. By the time the water was up to her chest he was clinging to her, sobbing, giving her advice now. Navigating. Lurching with her against more rocks, helping to push them clear, complaining, trying to wriggle free of her grasp. She wanted to whack him, to make him stop as she stumbled, smashing her toes against sharp rocks, but she gritted her teeth and plunged on, seeing that shore coming closer and closer, away from those devils.

'They can't get him now,' she exulted as the wash swirled about her waist. Moobuluk's dog was before her, panting excitedly in the shallows. Moobuluk had come! He was there. She could see him now, standing behind the dog. He would protect them. He would never let anything happen to Teddy or her. He was more powerful than all of the devils in the world. Nioka was sobbing as she reached out to him.

Harry saw them crossing the river. A black woman, with a child thrown over her shoulder like a sack of potatoes, ploughing through the current with the stride of a titan. He'd stopped for breath. He'd almost given up on this wild chase, running after a dingo like some sort of fool, taken in by a blackfellow's mumbo-jumbo. He'd been so intent on following the dog, he'd only glimpsed them in the river through a break in the bush, but now he raced, tearing ahead, shoving branches out of his way until he found the track that led down to the crossing. He was crying as he ran, sobbing, tears streaming. He skidded down to the water's edge and plunged in, surprised, thrown slightly askew by the force of the current that had seemed to be mild, but he was only waist deep, and Nioka lunged towards him to shove Teddy into his arms.

For the rest of his life Harry would recall that moment. He grabbed for Nioka, pulling her to him, and enveloped them both in a bear hug, unable to release them in case this wasn't real, unable to stop weeping from sheer joy, until Teddy, fed up with the fuss, protested.

'I nearly fell in the river again. I hate that river!'

Nioka looked at Harry gratefully, as if he had rescued her, instead of her wonderful deliverance of Teddy and they stumbled ashore.

He hugged her again. 'Nioka! How can we ever thank you? I have to get you both up to the house,' he said, picking Teddy up, afraid to leave him now. 'Can you walk the distance, Nioka? You look worn out.'

She nodded, watching the dog disappearing into the bush, disappointed that Moobuluk had vanished. Suddenly aware that she would never see him again.

It was Jack Ballard who saw them coming across the far paddock, Harry and a black woman! But then he tipped his hat back and squinted, thinking that maybe the light was playing tricks on his eyes, elongating Harry's already tall figure. Curious, he nudged his horse in that direction, allowing it to trot while he steadied his gaze, until he gave a shout, more a roar, and put his horse to the full gallop, not even realizing that he was still shouting as he raced towards them. It was Nioka, for God's sake, and Harry. And Harry had Teddy, young Teddy, perched on his shoulders!

'God Almighty!' he yelled at them, totally lost for any other words. 'God Almighty!'

Teddy filled the emotional vacuum as Harry handed him up to ride in front of Jack. 'I fell in the river,' he announced proudly, settling himself astride.

'You take him on,' Harry said, but Jack shook his head. 'No, you found him, we'll go up together.'

'I didn't find him. Nioka did.'

Jack grinned at her. 'Looks like you came home just in time, Nioka. Everyone is going to be mighty pleased to see you.' He peered at her. 'You're looking weary on it, girl. What if I hop down and put you up here with Teddy?'

'No. No,' she grinned. 'Teddy more better with you.'

Teddy agreed. 'Yes. Nioka can't ride.'

'Then we'll have to teach her,' Jack said, as he turned the horse towards the house, holding it back to keep pace with the pair trudging beside them. He was bursting with excited questions, overjoyed that the child was safe and obviously none the worse for wear, but Nioka was quiet, leaving it to Harry to explain what had happened.

'He did fall in the river, but thank God, Nioka saw him. She was on the other side, and by the sound of things she didn't waste a second. She went in after him, caught up with him midstream and managed to get him back to her side of the river.'

'I sicked up,' Teddy added. 'I nearly drownded.'

'So you did. Nioka tells me you were very sick. Swallowed too much river, you silly chump. Anyway, Nioka nursed him and then brought him down to the crossing where I met them. She carried him over.'

'But what took so long?' Jack asked. 'It's been days.'

Nioka hadn't explained the time lapse to him, so Harry took it upon himself to explain. 'He was weak, been pretty knocked about.' He moved closer to Jack and winked, lowering his voice. 'Someone was damned scared of the river by then. She had to give him time to recover and then march him a couple of miles down to the crossing. Even then, he wasn't too keen on taking it on again. By the sound of things they had quite a struggle at that point. But what does it matter?'

He put an arm about Nioka. 'We're proud of you, missy. You did all right.'

There was uproar in the house. People came running from all directions, screaming the news.

Louisa flew from the parlour down through Austin's room, out on to the veranda, hurdling the rail to sprint down the path and through the gate, to run and run, tears streaming, arms outstretched, shouting Teddy's name, shouting for Victor.

She swept her son up in her arms, cuddling him to her in a fierce embrace, kissing him, smothering him, asking him if he was all right.

'Oh, my darling,' she wept, 'my darling. Where have you been? Oh, Mummy's been so frightened. We missed you so much.' And all the while, Teddy, unimpressed by this fuss, struggled to be free. But then his father arrived and he too had to hold the child to him to make sure that this was real, that a miracle had happened.

Weeping, he reached out to Harry. 'Thank you, Harry, thank you . . .'

'Don't thank me, thank Nioka. She saved him from the river.'

Both of Teddy's parents practically fell on her, hugging her, thanking her, tears of joy overflowing as stockmen and house staff crowded in, sharing their excitement and gratitude.

Eventually they moved up to the house, where Victor invited everyone in to share a glass in celebration and thanksgiving. Louisa couldn't bear to let go of Teddy for a minute. 'I'll take him and bath him and put him to bed, he'll need a rest after his ordeal. And something to eat. Hannah, you look after Nioka. She'll need some clothes. And put her in the guest room.'

Hannah raised her eyebrows. 'Do you mean Minnie's old room out back?'

'No. I said a guest room. We owe Nioka a debt that can never be repaid. I want her to be comfortable. Would you like that, Nioka? Bed rest in the house?'

Nioka shrugged. She was suddenly too shy to cope with all this attention, so she allowed herself to be led away by the cook.

'How is Minnie?' Hannah asked kindly.

'She die. Too much broken heart over Bobbo.'

'Oh, Lord. I am so sorry, Nioka. The poor girl.'

'You know where our boys are, Hannah?' she asked wistfully.

Hannah shook her head. 'I'm sorry, my dear. I can't say I do exactly. At school. They'll be taken care of, though, don't you be worrying. I'd better get you something to eat. And Teddy too. I'll bet you're hungry.'

The black girl nodded listlessly.

A small wonder crossed her mind at the difference between this large white bathroom with all its polished fittings and the old tin bath lodged in a shed that she'd used in Brisbane, but she was too tired to think on it. She was immensely relieved that she'd beaten the devils, knowing in her mind that they had gone forever. Knowing too that somehow Moobuluk had made her safe, that she was under his powerful protection.

Eventually Hannah came down with fresh clothes for her, surprised to find her still sitting on a little wooden stool.

By then the cook had heard more of the rescue and her gratitude knew no bounds. She ran a bath for Nioka, allowing her to soak while she collected towels. When Nioka was dressed in a Sunday shift and

313

cotton bloomers, she set about pampering the girl, drying her hair and brushing it until it shone, then tying it back with a pretty ribbon.

'You ought to stay with us now,' she said. 'Not go wandering off again. You could have a job here.' Then she grinned, remembering that this was the feisty black girl who would have no part of domestic service. 'Or maybe you still don't like housework. But then, all the mob have gone. You can't live down there at the camp on your own. You're a good-looking girl, Nioka. You should stay here. Find a husband . . .'

While she chatted on, Nioka hardly heard her. She kept thinking of Moobuluk. Her mind was clearing of all the hurt and worry. He knew why she had clung to the white child for so long, and he forgave her. Nioka needed that, because now she realized that she'd conjured up her own devils. They were not Minnie's, they had emerged from her own conscience to punish her for withholding Teddy from his mother's arms. From the minute she'd brought Teddy ashore she'd refused to see Louisa's face, blotting her out as if she did not exist. Needing only the child.

She supposed that the Brodericks would punish her for her selfishness, for being so cruel to his parents, and that had to be accepted. She didn't care what happened to her; there was still one thought uppermost in her mind: those three children. They had to be found.

Harry, too, had to change out of his muddy clothes, so he excused himself from the party when the euphoria had died down and headed for his room, but detoured to check on Nioka.

He was amused to see her perched awkwardly on the edge of the bed, as if she'd been placed in a prison cell, obviously intimidated by the room.

'Well, now!' he laughed. 'Look at you all gussied up. Bit better than being soaked in that river, eh?'

Nioka nodded, eyes downcast, staring at the patterned carpet. 'I'm sorry,' she said.

'What for?'

'You know.' Her bare feet twisted uncomfortably.

Harry did know. He'd known Nioka all his life and he understood how hard it was for the proud girl to apologize to any white man. She was like her mother, more inclined to stand tall and stare down white boys. He remembered she'd cracked Rupe with the back of her hand once, a gross insult, when he'd made a pass at her. He and Victor had laughed their heads off, delighted to see Rupe put in his place by a sassy black. But now she wasn't just a sassy girl; she had matured well, a good-looking woman with firm features and dark, brooding eyes.

'Are we talking about the missing days here?' he asked gently.

She nodded again, squirming.

'I think you only borrowed the boy for short time, eh? Look after him. Care for him. Only borrow.'

When they'd come back into the house Teddy had been all talk about Nioka taking him fishing and letting him build his own humpy, so Harry knew this story had to be sorted out quickly.

'*You* didn't let him fall in the river,' he added, to encourage her.

'Only borrow,' she admitted, looking up at him. 'He very sick boy, Harry. I get him better, make him happy.' She sighed. 'Make me happy too. You tell Louisa I'm sorry.'

'I'll tell her, don't you worry. You saved his life, Nioka, nothing else matters.'

He suddenly remembered the old man. 'Oh, God. I almost forgot. I wanted to tell you I spoke to Moobuluk. He knew Teddy was still alive, he said to find you. I have to go back and see him. I have to thank him too.'

She stared at him. 'You can't do that. Him gone. Not good to mention his name now.'

Harry knew what that meant. It was his turn to stare. He felt the familiar pinpricking on the back of his neck and decided not to pursue that complicated subject, but made a mental note to send Spinner down to the riverside to find Moobuluk. Just in case Nioka was wrong.

'You're still worried about your own boys, aren't you?' he asked, shuddering at the pain that suddenly coursed through her eyes, matching it with the recent fears for Teddy.

'Where are they?' she pleaded.

'I don't know, but I'll try to find out.'

'You'll do that?' She jumped off the bed and grabbed his hand. 'I'll work,' she sobbed. 'I'll be a good worker, you see. Never bold no more. You tell them, Harry. I'll be good. Only bring back our babies.'

He was embarrassed, backing away, distressed that she should be brought down, tamed, in such a cruel manner. Nioka and her mother had always been the talk of the station, and a source of great interest to the Broderick boys, who knew and appreciated that the woman and the growing girl would think nothing of standing up to Austin. So much so, to their astonishment, that he enjoyed them. He always said they'd never tame young Nioka.

Sorrowing, he saw that Austin had been wrong. Nioka could be tamed.

He pulled her to her feet and hugged her. 'Don't give up now, Nioka. You hang on. I'll try to find them. I promise.' He sighed, remembering that he'd already made that promise. 'It might take time, but I'll go to Brisbane and find them.' He gave a grim laugh. 'I used to be quite important there. Maybe I can still use a bit of muscle.'

As he walked down the passage to the main house, he felt a wave of nostalgia for Springfield, for his father, for the blacks who'd once owned this territory. But the halcyon days of his own youth were gone now. The Aborigines who were his friends had all departed, and according to Victor the station was in danger of being decimated, broken up in the name of progress, like so many other great properties in the south of the country, where the population had expanded at such a rate.

The day had seemed like a year to Harry, but it was only lunchtime. Everyone else had gone about their business and Louisa and Victor were in the dining room, still celebrating, they eyes brimming with happiness.

'Teddy's asleep,' Victor called to him. 'Come and join us. We've opened the French champagne. This has to be the best day of our lives! I think I'm a bit drunk already, but who cares!'

'I'm worried about Charlotte. We haven't heard from her.'

'No need,' Victor grinned. 'Jock said Ada went to collect her in the grand carriage.'

'Why Ada?'

Louisa laughed. Nothing could upset her today. 'What does it matter? Have some champagne.'

'I'll have a glass to please you,' Harry said. 'But I have to find Spinner. I want him to do an errand for me.'

'No point in looking for Spinner,' Victor said, pouring champagne into a wide crystal glass with gay abandon. 'He's gone over to Jock's place. Blackfeller business.'

'What sort of business?'

'You remember that old bloke Moobuluk, who used to hang about here? Apparently he's dead, so they're having a wake for him, all the blacks in the district.'

'When did he die?'

'How would I know? Have a drink. You're a hero.'

They talked and talked about Teddy, about his brush with death, about the terror of the days, about his miraculous rescue, and not once did Harry hear any criticism of Nioka. They seemed to take it for granted that Nioka had done the best she could, being a bush black, resting him, feeding him – at that they laughed – with witchety grubs and yams until he was well enough to travel.

Louisa was all gaiety. 'She gave him cooked eel, he told me, but it smelled funny so he didn't eat it. Can you imagine trying to give a kid eel?'

'I've eaten eel,' Victor said. 'Austin used to push it on to us when we were kids. And tripe. God, how I hated tripe.'

They were so merry and it was all marvellous.

'Thank God Nioka is a strong swimmer,' Victor said. 'When we were kids she used to show off. Swimming right across the river and back again, knowing perfectly well we'd never attempt it.'

'Thank God she was there!' Louisa said. 'That's the miracle. Apparently she saw Teddy fall in. That is amazing.'

316

'No it's not,' Harry said. 'She was watching him from the other side. If you recall, she has lost Jagga to your bloody religious maniacs. So what you had was a childless woman, full of love, watching another dear child, enjoying watching him. Then when he fell in, she reacted like any mother would. She went in after him like a flash. The difference is that she's as strong as an ox and she can swim like a fish.'

'While Rupe and Cleo forgot him,' Victor growled.

'Neither of them would have been able to save him at that point. He would have been swept away in the current. He's safe, he didn't drown, let that be the end of it.'

'You want me to forget that Rupe let my son fall in that bloody river?' Victor snapped.

'I would think he has suffered enough, Victor. I can't imagine how terrible he must feel. And the governess too.'

'Then try to imagine what they put us through,' Louisa said angrily. 'I'll never forgive them.'

'Ah, Jesus!' Harry was annoyed. 'What the hell is this family coming to? You're not going to forgive Rupe. Victor and Charlotte are at loggerheads. You say she's threatening to sell the heart of Springfield, but you people won't give her a fair share. Austin would turn in his grave.'

'No he wouldn't,' Louisa said. 'He was the one who threw the spanner in the works. But I refuse to worry about all that today. More champagne, Victor. Make yourself useful. Thanks be to God, our little boy is home and safe. And thanks to Nioka.'

The sadness went too deep for Spinner to be pleased that he was now free to move to the neighbouring station and marry his girl. He felt the loss of the old man far more severely than he could have imagined. It was as if a mountain had been suddenly removed from the landscape. A bewildering experience for a man who considered himself more white than black. And unnerving. He began to worry that he might be taking too much for granted. That maybe he was still expected to stay and watch for the three boys; he hadn't actually been relieved of duty.

Worried, he found the window to Nioka's room and asked her to come out and talk to him, since he would not dream of entering the big house.

He was startled when she came running out to throw her arms about him. They'd never been real friends.

'Spinner! How good it is to see you again. And you're looking so well! You've got taller, haven't you?'

He couldn't know that Nioka was bursting out of her self-inflicted loneliness, desperately needing to communicate with someone, so, quite flattered, he sat down with her under the old flame tree, happy to be appreciated by this woman who was now a hero. The whites

317

were singing her praises to the treetops.

First things first, though. He explained his predicament to her, and she was so grateful that he'd been a silent watcher for the boys all this time that she hugged him again.

'You needn't worry any more. I'll be here. I won't leave. I'll wait here for them. Harry promised to find them for me. They'll let me stay. I'll get a job here.'

'You will?' Spinner was astonished.

She laughed. 'Yes. It doesn't matter any more. Nothing else to do. I've been living in the bush over there on my own . . .'

'We knew,' he said, not admitting that they hadn't known *who* had been camping in the bush. 'But we never told no one. Just as well, eh? Or you wouldn't have been there to save Teddy. By gee, Victor's real savage about Rupe. I reckon he'll strangle that brother of his when he gets his hands on him. But where's Minnie? Why didn't she come back with you?'

Nioka told him about her sister, and he apologized for barging in on her grief like that.

'But you all left without telling me,' he accused. 'Where did you go?'

Nioka explained that they'd left for fear the other children would be stolen, and told him that they'd found a lovely safe place to live now, with people from another clan.

His face clouded. 'Nowhere is safe now. Is this good country? Tell me about it. Do you see many white people? How far from farms and villages?'

When she'd told him all she could, he shook his head. 'It's no good, Nioka. It won't last. More and more white people come, and they need land like that with plenty water for their stock and their crops. You'd better tell our mob to come on back here.'

'They can't! It's too dangerous for our children.'

'It'll be just as dangerous up there among strangers. And it won't be just the kids. You'll all be put in reserves.' He let her sit quietly to think about all this. To try to work out the best thing to do.

In the end she clasped her hands together, thumping them back on her chest as if it were possible to rouse answers from these impatient movements, but nothing seemed to come.

'I'll have to ask Harry,' she said.

'Better make it quick. He doesn't live here any more. Since the boss died, big changes. Black people not the only ones getting overrun. More white people come, they want to live on Springfield, build their own houses here. They say Brodericks got too much land, just like the blackfellers.'

'No!'

'It's true! Same thing happening on old Jock's place. Big trouble, I tell you!'

318

Nioka gaped. How could this be? The world was turning upside down. She couldn't even think on this, because another invasion of the valley and the open grasslands beyond was too much to contemplate.

She sighed. 'You go now, Spinner. Don't forget to bring your girl back to see me.'

Meanwhile, Victor and Louisa had unexpected guests. Sergeant Perkins from Cobbside had heard about the drowning and come to investigate; and the Reverend Whiley had arrived to offer his services and condolences.

Both men were delighted at the good news, and only too pleased to join in the celebrations.

Then a maid brought Teddy down. 'I'm sorry, madam. He says he doesn't want to sleep any more.'

Louisa laughed, sweeping Teddy up on to her knee. 'Never mind. He can stay. He's our guest of honour.'

The news, for Rupe, was overwhelming. It came with such suddenness that his knees almost crumpled beneath him, so Jock poured him a brandy.

'I'll have one with you. A great day this is! What a bloody relief. You must be on top of the world!'

Rupe was, of course, but he still had to face Victor. He couldn't hang about here any longer. Teddy was safe, he couldn't use his grief as an excuse to remain away from Springfield now. He would have to go home.

But not just yet. He lingered over a second brandy, trying to think of an excuse to delay his departure, but none would come.

That afternoon, Ada Crossley had her driver pull in at the general store on the outskirts of Toowoomba so that he could give her carriage a good hose and swab. She was pleased that they had made good time, with an overnight stop and a change of horses at a friend's house, so a short delay was of no consequence now.

When they drew in at the hotel, Charlotte was there waiting for her. 'Thank God!' she cried, getting in the way of the driver, who was trying to hand Ada down as he'd been taught. 'I've been nearly out of my mind. No one here knows anything. I thought you'd never get here.'

'I came as fast as I could!'

'What about Teddy? What in God's name has happened?'

Ada took hold of her. 'Come inside. I hope you booked me a good room. We'll go straight up and have tea and a little talk.' She postponed breaking the news to Charlotte until they were behind closed doors, and as expected, Charlotte almost collapsed in shock.

'Teddy?' she screamed. 'That dear little boy. Dead? Drowned! How could that happen? Oh God, no!'

For hours Ada sat with her, trying to comfort her, praying with her, trying to explain how it had happened, doing her best to console Charlotte in her extreme distress. It wasn't the first time Ada had shared this abject misery with a bereaved friend, but it never seemed to get any easier. Later, despite Charlotte's objections, she sent for a doctor to administer a sedative to the poor woman to help her sleep, promising that they would leave for Springfield first thing in the morning.

As the carriage spun out on to the long country roads, Ada tried to get Charlotte's mind off the tragedy by asking her about Springfield. Had her difficulty with her sons been resolved?

'Who cares about that now?' Charlotte snapped. 'Victor and Louisa must be devastated. And Rupe too. I'll never forgive myself for causing them so much trouble. Where was I when they needed me? Sulking in Brisbane. Had I been there I'd never have allowed that blasted governess to take Teddy anywhere near the river . . .'

'You weren't to know. It's God's will, Charlotte. We all have to bend to His wisdom.'

'His cruelty, do you mean? First my husband. Now my only grandson. And poor Victor. He has lost his father and his son. I have to stand by him now. I've been totally selfish. He can have the property. And my block. I'll give it all back.'

Ada sighed. She wouldn't dream of disagreeing with her friend at this stage, not when she was in such a state, but she thought Charlotte was being rather hasty. The selfishness was coming from the other side of the family.

Eventually Charlotte took her bonnet off and settled back to doze as they climbed through the hills. Ada too was tired, but she had never been able to sleep in a moving vehicle, not even this one. She ranged through her own problems. Jock was ageing fast these days but would not let go of the ropes. He was still the boss in his own eyes, but not according to the three overseers that they employed to manage their outstations. They were constantly at odds, elbowing for precedence, and muttering among themselves that Jock ought to retire the field and nominate one of them as manager.

She'd been surprised, when the last guests left from their race meeting, to have Jock confide in her.

'You know, Ada, Austin Broderick, God rest his soul, got it wrong. Harry was never cut out for politics. He's a born bushie. He should have insisted that Rupe go. He'd know when to put up his hand and when to sit on it. The youngest is a real tricky customer.'

'His mother's finding that out,' Ada retorted. 'And as for Harry, it's all very well to use hindsight. Harry and Connie just got too big for their boots and came down with a thump. Not to mention missing that damn vote. He'll never live that down.'

'Ah, they've forgotten already. Water under the bridge. I never knew Harry that well, he was away so much, but I liked having him here, him and Connie. Family around the place again, and her with a babe coming on. Your brother, the Judge, never deigns to visit much any more. I'm betting his next visit will be for my funeral.'

'What's this talk about? What are you getting at?'

'I'll tell you, my girl. Had I known Harry was going to take on Tirrabee station, I'd have grabbed him myself.'

'What for?'

'To manage this property, of course. He'd make our three jokers sit up and behave, don't you reckon? I can't go on forever, and you're not getting any younger. Which one of them three overseers would you hand the whip to?'

'None of them,' she said bitterly.

'Then you'd better think about it, Ada. Better the devil you know. And better family than the rest. Harry and Connie are just what you need, the next generation and another on the way. That was an excellent dinner. Pour me a port, will you?'

She poured two and sat sipping on her drink, unwilling to reply until she'd thought this through. She had enjoyed the company of her niece and her husband, but there were other considerations.

'I will think about it, Pa, but on one condition. I want your will iron-bound. You leave this property to me, lock, stock and barrel. I'm not going to end up like Charlotte.'

'It's supposed to be shared between you and your brother.'

'He's had enough. You've been paying him like a blasted remittance man all his life. The Judge is well off now, don't worry about him. Fair go, he's never lifted a finger here, and always gets a yearly cheque from the wool profits. A nice fat cheque too. It's your money and I never minded, but leave him half the property and you'll create chaos. He likes cash money. He'll want to sell. You know that.'

Ada watched as Jock fingered his bushy white beard, noting that it needed a trim. This was a subject she'd been wanting to introduce for a long time, but she'd been waiting for the right opportunity. Now it was on the table and Jock was in a very good mood.

'Tell you what,' he said. 'I'll write a new will, and I'll leave you the station, lock, stock and barrel. But it will have to include my instruction that on your death it goes to my granddaughter, Connie Broderick, and her husband.'

His wily old eyes glinted at her, and she knew she was missing something, but she agreed.

'That's fair. The Judge can't complain. His own family end up recipients, since I'm not likely to produce any offspring at my age. Yes. We'll do that. And thank you, Pa. Thank you.'

'That doesn't alter the fact that I want Harry Broderick here as

321

manager. I reckon I could lean on Harry without feeling any hurt. What do you say to that?'

She laughed. 'I say first catch the chicken before you start counting the eggs. Harry has another job and seems very happy at Tirrabee. But we could ask him.'

Sadly she realized now that they would see Harry sooner than they'd expected. At Teddy's funeral.

When Jock finally remembered the name of Charlotte's hotel in Toowoomba, Harry was immensely relieved. He was only staying on now to see his mother. A rider was dispatched to wire her the good news that Teddy had been found, but when he arrived in Cobbside, the messenger found that the post office was closed for a half-day, to facilitate removal to new premises. So by the time the telegram arrived at the Victoria Hotel the next day, the two women had left. They made the same overnight stop, where Ada retrieved her own horses, but they bypassed Cobbside, missing a last opportunity to be made aware that all was well.

As the carriage sped across the valley, Ada's heart sank. She dreaded the encounter with Teddy's parents, wondering what on earth could be said to console them. It would be even worse than trying to deal with Charlotte's pain. She noticed Charlotte shrinking back into the leather upholstery when the driver turned into the long, familiar drive, and took her hand, offering encouragement for the ordeal ahead.

Aware of the solemnity of the occasion, her driver slowed the horses almost to a walk as they rounded the large circular garden, making for the front entrance to the Springfield mansion. Ada noticed that Charlotte's garden, the centrepiece of the landscaping at the front of the house, was even worse for wear now than it had been on her last visit, but her friend had no care for such trivia at this time. Tears had begun to flow again and she was desperately trying to compose herself, scrabbling in her large handbag for a fresh handkerchief.

Charlie opened the carriage door quietly and helped them down to the gravel path as gently as he could, and the two women gathered up their skirts to mount the steps to the open front door.

They had just reached the top step when Teddy came flying out, yelling; 'Grandma! Grandma's here!'

Charlotte stopped, stared in disbelief, then fell back in a dead faint. It was a nasty fall. She toppled all the way down the steps with a horrifying crack of bone on stone before either Ada or Charlie could stop her.

Ada's loud screams brought everyone rushing from the house, where Hannah had been about to serve dinner.

Charlotte was lying at the bottom of the steps in front of Ada

322

Crossley's carriage, black-clothed, limp, unconscious, and Ada was frantically trying to support her.

Victor and Louisa were first to their side, but Ada was furious.

'You rotten lot!' she screamed. 'How could you do this to your mother? Do you realize what you've put her through?'

'What? What?' Louisa was crying as the men lifted Charlotte up to carry her inside. She started to follow, then ran back to assist Ada, who pushed her away.

'We ought to send for a doctor!' Hannah cried, edging along behind Victor and Harry as they bore Charlotte into the parlour to place her on the couch.

'What happened?' Victor wailed, bending over her. 'Mother? Are you all right?'

'Oh, get out of the way!' Ada snapped, still angry. She could smell liquor on them. It seemed to her that she'd brought her friend home to a madhouse. And there was Teddy, looking as fit as a fiddle, watching in awe.

Charlotte's forehead was bleeding from a gash across the hairline, so Ada snatched the cloth that Hannah was proffering and dabbed at the blood, murmuring soothing words. At the same time she waved her free hand at the others to stand back, give the woman air. She loosened Charlotte's collar and moved her to try to make her more comfortable, then she whispered tersely, 'Send for a doctor, she has broken her arm.'

'Is she dead?' Teddy asked. His mother swiftly shushed him, but the voice had stirred Charlotte.

Her eyes opened warily. 'Is that Teddy? Ada, was that Teddy?'

'Yes, dear. He's all right. He's right here. But you have to be still for a little while. You've taken a fall. We'll try to make you more comfortable.'

She ordered the men out of the room while her experienced hands made a more careful examination of the patient. 'No more bones broken, thank God, but Hannah, get me a dressing for that cut on her head. It might need stitching, I fear, but in the meantime some adhesive tape would help. Have you got any?'

'Yes.' Hannah rushed away.

Upset, Louisa leaned down to comfort her mother-in-law, only to have Ada intervene. 'She doesn't need to have alcohol breathed all over her!'

Louisa was shocked, and too intimidated to attempt to explain that she had only had a small pre-dinner gin, Charlotte's favourite tipple. She pulled away with a jerk, hating this woman, and ran out to Victor, who put his arms about her.

'Don't worry, darling, Harry's gone for a doctor. She'll be all right.'

Louisa wondered about that. What would be all right now? Charlotte was home. And with her that awful Crossley woman. All the joy of finding Teddy safe and sound had been whipped away. Her head ached.

Old Jock didn't seem to notice that Rupe was in no hurry to return to Springfield. But Jock was like that, Rupe mused. You could hang about his station forever, for all he cared, as long as you could discuss horseflesh with authority and spend time putting his prize mounts through their paces. Taking advantage of this knowledge, Rupe lingered, playing for time. It wasn't difficult to praise the magnificent horses or their luxurious stables; for that matter, they'd make any man envious. Rupe had often tried to talk Victor into concentrating more on their own thoroughbred horses, but Victor had a one-track mind. Sheep. Their merinos were famous, but for sheer pride and joy, you couldn't beat horses. He even persuaded Jock to let him take the nifty black Arab called Dynamite round the track, and that wonderfully swift ride revived his spirits. He swung down from the saddle, exhilarated, and slapped Jock on the shoulder.

'What a mount! A gift from the gods. Who wouldn't be proud to own a winner like that?'

All of which had given him time to make a decision. The answer was simple. Victor wouldn't easily get over the near tragedy with Teddy, and now it was time to use just that as an excuse to leave.

'It's plain to see,' he rehearsed, 'that you don't want me here. Neither does Louisa. So I'll go. I'm only a spare toe here anyway. You run the property, you've been doing that for years. And you never appreciate any of my ideas. But that's beside the point. I won't stay here and be treated like a pariah because I happened to ask Cleo, not Teddy, to come down to see the birds.'

While the stable hands began settling the horses for the night, Jock, ever watchful, shared a bottle of beer with Rupe, who was busy playing out a scene with his brother.

'You don't want me here, so I'll go. I don't know where' – although he had Europe in mind – 'but you don't have to worry about me. I won't interfere any further in your plans for Springfield. I might be half-shares, but it's yours to run as you like. The way you've always wanted. Now you've got your wish. You're the boss of Springfield. I'll need something to live on, of course, so you split the wool cheque with me every year, on the knocker, and neither of us has got anything to complain about. You have the house, a home, a mansion if you please, and your upkeep, but I don't begrudge you that.'

He knew his request was not unusual. There were plenty of recipients of the fat wool cheques lording it in London, and not just immediate families. Even cousins of wealthy graziers managed to stake their claims via maternal pressure for a small share of the stakes, and were oft heard to be making their way to that great city, the centre of the universe.

That reminded him of Cleo. What on earth had he seen in her?

Proximity, that was all! He shrugged. Her family money would have been handy, but once he was set loose with his own income, there would be other ladies. His only worry was the size of that income, thanks to the necessity to freehold.

So we just sell more land, he decided.

'We'll go up to the house,' Jock said, 'and I'll show you Dynamite's pedigree. He's got ancestors you'd kill for.'

By the morning, Charlotte was resting in her own bed, with her arm in plaster, a bandage nursing the cut on her head which, after all, did not require stitches, and a ferocious headache. All of which added to the fact that the lady of the house had returned and was in an extremely bad mood. Ada was by her side to comfort her.

Victor tried to explain to the two women what had happened. His wife tried too, but she became so angry that she was forced to snap at these unreasonable women.

'Anyone would think, by the way you're behaving, that you'd have preferred to find that Teddy had drowned.'

Charlotte pursed her lips. 'How dare you say that! I get a telegram telling me that Teddy had had an accident. Next thing I hear he had drowned. And all this time neither of you thought to let me know what was happening, one way or another. It was only Ada who cared.'

'Who sent you a telegram?' Victor asked, nonplussed.

Confronted by Victor and Louisa, Hannah was in tears. She did not implicate Jack Ballard, who had helped her to write the telegram to Charlotte; instead she offered to resign. Indeed, as the very trying morning progressed, she decided she would leave anyway. Just pack her bags and go. The doctor was now ensconced in one of the guest rooms, next door to Nioka. Or where Nioka was supposed to be. Unhappy in that room, as Hannah had known she would be, she'd removed herself to the shed where her sister had lived, and was awaiting her fate, refusing to come out. Hannah was fed up with them all.

Because the maids were both at sixes and sevens, answering to several women, not knowing who to obey first, Hannah took tea and scrambled eggs up to Harry, who was, strangely, still in bed. Admittedly, he'd had a long ride last night, chasing up the doctor, who wasn't in Cobbside but visiting another property, and then on his return he'd stayed up until his mother was settled comfortably, but even so, it wasn't like him to stay abed so late.

'Don't tell me you're sick too,' she said, dumping the tray on his bedside table.

'No,' he grinned. 'I figured it would be safer up here. You're a darling, Hannah. I was just thinking starvation might force me up.'

'Well, make the best of it, because I'm leaving. I never heard such goings-on in all my born days. They're at each other's throats, the whole bang lot of them.'

325

'You can't leave. Just keep your head down awhile. They're blowing out the tension. They'll settle down. What about my poor wife back there at Tirrabee? I have to get home, but we must restore some sort of order here first.'

'You could start with getting rid of Mrs Crossley.'

'It would take a braver man than me to uproot Ada. You just hide out in your kitchen for a while and I'm going to enjoy this meal. It's all over, really.'

'It better be.'

She closed his door and marched along the passage to the front stairs, deciding, in a fit of defiance, to go down that way, rather than making for the less imposing back staircase. As she descended, hanging on to the polished cedar banisters, she saw Rupe striding in through the front door, tossing his hat on to the hall stand.

Now Hannah wasn't given to taking the Lord's name in vain in normal times, but this was too much.

'Oh, Jesus Christ!' she said under her breath. 'That's all we bloody need,' and she sped back up the carpeted staircase to make for the plain wooden steps that would return her safely to her own domain.

Chapter Thirteen

In contrast, the small homestead at Tirrabee was a sunny and peaceful place. Smoke twirled idly from the chimney, the red roof had a rosy glow in the afternoon sun, and the greenery of trees surrounding it was speckled with pink and white blossoms. Hens scratched and dipped in the sparse grass outside the home fence, and a piglet trotted about among them trying to discover what it was they were eating. An old sheepdog, proving he was still master, burst from the bushes where he'd been dozing to bail up the two riders dismounting at his gate, with a ferocious volley of snarls and barks that brought Connie out on to her veranda.

She was weeping when she ran down to him, but Harry was all smiles. 'No need for tears, my love. They found Teddy. He's as fit as I am, and giving cheek.'

She stood back. 'What? What? Spinner told us . . .'

'I know, and I can't apologize more for upsetting you like that, but it was all a false alarm. Kiss your husband and tell him you forgive him.'

She kissed him fondly, but was crying again, smiling, trying to contain her emotions because Harry wasn't alone.

'You remember Jack Ballard, don't you, Connie? From Springfield?'

'Oh, yes. Of course. I'm sorry, Jack. I wasn't thinking. Harry, why didn't you telegraph that Teddy was all right? I have never been so upset!'

'Because we're here, aren't we? A telegram would have taken more time. It's a long story, I'll tell you all about it if you ask us in.'

'Oh, dear. I hope you don't mind, Jack. The parlour is in a mess. Clara has been teaching me how to make a patchwork quilt and we've got pieces everywhere.'

'Clara's the wife of one of the stockmen here,' Harry explained. 'She's been a good backstop for Connie. As a matter of fact, her husband is good value too. He used to be a carpenter but they were looking for a live-in job so they came here. We might promote him, give him a bit more responsibility.'

Connie blinked, wondering why Harry was discussing staff in that manner with a visitor. Perhaps he meant to employ Jack as an overseer, but that would be a comedown from Springfield, and besides, this property surely couldn't afford a manager *and* an overseer. But right now there were other things to think about. Like dinner. What would she give them?

'Tell me about you,' Harry said as they went inside, obviously concerned about her pregnancy. 'Have you been keeping well? You look positively blooming.'

'Thank you,' she smiled. 'I feel extra well. No troubles at all.'

As it turned out, she didn't have to worry about dinner. The two men took over the kitchen, insisting she sit down and talk to them while they took great delight in cooking slabs of steak with eggs and fried onions and a large pot of potatoes, and while they worked and joked she heard the story of Teddy and Nioka, and the calamity with poor Charlotte. As well as the sacking of the governess and the serious rift between Rupe and Victor.

'The way things were, I couldn't do any more,' Harry explained as he plonked the necessities of salt and pepper and Worcestershire sauce on the table, along with a loaf of bread and a generous slab of butter. 'They'll just have to sort themselves out. Again,' he laughed.

It was only after dinner, when he was sitting back drinking coffee and slicing at a hunk of cheese that had now become the centrepiece of Connie's table, that Harry began to enlarge on the story, and even Jack was surprised.

'You never mentioned old Moobuluk before.'

'I don't even know who he is,' Connie said.

'He's a magic man, as old as the hills. Or was.'

'A magic man!' Connie laughed. 'I don't believe all that stuff.'

Jack nodded. 'Fair enough. But they carry a lot of clout among the blacks.'

'And they know a lot of things we don't about mother earth,' Harry added.

Connie took his hand. 'If you say so, my darling. Get on with the story. You talked with this old bloke before you found Nioka. What's so strange about that? He knew she was there and obviously he knew she had Teddy with her.'

'I suppose so,' Harry admitted, but it hadn't seemed like that at the time. He was now coming to the most important part of his tale and he had a feeling that Connie wouldn't like it. The black children.

He took a while outlining his conversations with Moobuluk: the old man's concern for the missing boys, his worry that all of their children would be spirited away in the same manner.

Jack lit his pipe. 'Well, I'll be blowed! Is that why the mob upped and disappeared from Springfield? They never said a word. They just took off.'

'They were terrified.'

'How sad,' Connie exclaimed. 'And how awful for the parents. Imagine if they took our little one from us.'

'Our son,' Harry said absently.

328

'Oh, you! How do you know I'm having a boy? It might be a pretty little girl.'

Jack was dismayed. 'And Minnie killed herself?'

'Yes. That's why Nioka is back. She is looking for her son and the other two. She's tougher than the rest of them. She wants those kids! So did Moobuluk.' He took a deep breath. 'In fact, he made me promise I'd find them.'

'Why you?' Connie wanted to know.

'How would I know? Because I was there. At the right time at the right place, maybe.' He was becoming a little irritated at having to explain something he'd much rather not discuss. Finally, he said, 'I think it was a sort of deal. The boys for Teddy.'

'Did he threaten you?' Jack asked.

'No.'

Connie wouldn't have it. 'You said that when you found Nioka she was bringing Teddy back. It wasn't as if you had to help them really, she'd made it across the river. By the sound of things she's a strong woman, she'd have got him safely home.'

'And she'd never have hurt Teddy,' Jack argued. 'I think he pulled a fast one on you, Harry. That old villain knew she was bringing him back, so he was putting pressure on you while he could.'

It hadn't been like that, Harry knew, but it was useless to try to explain, so instead, he moved to firmer ground. 'I did promise Moobuluk, but more to the point, I also promised Nioka. Don't forget, she did save Teddy's life. That stupid pair let him fall in the river, they didn't even know he was down there. He would have drowned, there's no doubt about that. Nioka saved him. We owe her that.'

'You mean Victor does,' Connie said warily, beginning to understand what was happening. She turned on Jack. 'Forgive me, I don't mean to be rude, but why are you here? Are you just visiting?'

'No. Harry said he needed me, he had to go away for a while . . .' Jack's voice trailed off and he looked to Harry for support, because he truly did not know where Harry had to go.

'You're leaving again?' she accused her husband.

'I have to go. I've got to try to find those kids.'

'Not you,' she insisted. 'It's nothing to do with you. Harry, you weren't even there when that minister and his wife took the boys. You're not to blame. Victor is, and Louisa, and yes, your mother as well. Charlotte was there. Let her go. They all allowed those children to be kidnapped.'

'They thought it was for the best,' Jack said guiltily.

'The best?' exclaimed the mother-to-be. 'I never heard of such a thing, grabbing kids from their mothers and dumping them in some horrible orphanage. Aren't there enough orphans around already without scouring the countryside for them? And from what I hear, they don't look after orphans too well either!'

'It's Government policy,' Jack tried to explain to her, and Harry let them argue the subject because, unwittingly, Jack was helping his cause. He had asked Victor to lend him the overseer for a while to help him at Tirrabee station, without bothering to go into an explanation, and Victor had been only too pleased to oblige. He still saw Harry as one of Teddy's rescuers and his gratitude knew no bounds.

Jack hadn't minded either. For him, a change was as good as a holiday. On the long ride back to Tirrabee, Harry had taken the opportunity to defer to this man's experience, which far outweighed his own knowledge of the business, and Jack was willing to take a good look at the station and offer advice. This was a golden opportunity for Harry to have such help, and he was sorry that he'd have to leave, but maybe Jack would stay on for a while when he got back.

Harry already knew that the black boys had been taken to a school run by the Church of the Holy Word – Louisa had at least been able to tell him that. All he had to do was to get back to Brisbane, collect the kids, bring them by train to Toowoomba, hire a vehicle of some sort, since they were too little to ride, and take them to Springfield. He estimated a week to ten days at the most by the time he made it back to Tirrabee. It was a nuisance, traipsing back and forth over these long bush roads, but he had promised. There was no getting out of it.

Even though Harry had been considerate enough to bring Jack Ballard back here to watch over her and the property, Connie was still not convinced that it was his problem.

'They know where those kids are! They let them go. Let Victor get them. You can hardly ask your mother to go since she's got a broken arm – I forgot about that for a minute. It's up to Victor if he really wants to thank Nioka. Or Rupe. What about him? It's just ridiculous, Harry. They caused the problem, let them fix it.'

They argued late into the night. Harry was upset. He understood that this was the very worst time to be leaving Connie, when she was having her first baby, and he wrapped her in his arms, almost ready to capitulate. He felt that at this time it was too much for Moobuluk to be asking of him.

But somewhere deep in his mind, another voice was arguing with him, and not just his conscience for having made the promise. He dreamed that he saw Nioka's mother, that muscular black woman who'd put the fear of God into all the kids, both black and white, and she was laying down the law, thumping the ground with her waddy. He saw her slap Victor aside, and Rupe, and point at him, but she was talking to Austin. Not talking to him after all, shouting at him. Blaming him. Austin didn't seem to be perturbed; he simply turned to Harry and said something which Harry couldn't recall.

When he awoke he realized that even if he could persuade Victor or Rupe to go and find those children, their hearts wouldn't be in it.

330

Would they bring them back? Maybe not.

Before he left Springfield he'd sat with Charlotte, trying to mollify her, because she had still been cross with the family, and with herself for having fallen down in a heap and broken her arm. He'd changed the subject, asking her about the black children, and she'd told him that Austin had actually given his permission for those people to take the boys, and had even given a donation to the church. She'd seen nothing wrong with the arrangement. Like everyone else, she'd thought it had been for the best. In her current confused state she could only recall that the couple were the Reverend Billings and his wife, not the name of the church. Louisa had filled in that gap.

Standing under a cold shower, Harry recalled the dream, and was not surprised, after all, to hear that black woman shouting at his father, and Austin seeming unconcerned.

He could now fill in that elusive response: 'It was for the best.' By this time Harry felt that if he heard that again, he was likely to strike someone. At least Connie didn't see it that way. If only she'd understand why he felt it was his duty to find the boys. Sadly, as he towelled himself dry, Harry knew that until Connie gave her permission, he could not leave her again. She'd been stoic about coming to Tirrabee, and she was making the best of a lifestyle that fell far short of her expectations. His flight to Springfield because of a family tragedy was acceptable, but leaving her again, with strangers, on this isolated property . . . Did he have any right to do that?

The next day, while Harry took Jack Ballard on an inspection of the property, Connie poured her heart out to Clara Nugent over a cup of tea. Over several cups of tea. Clara was fascinated. Interested to the point of interrupting with a volley of questions, which Connie was glad to answer where she could.

'It's really too much,' she said eventually. 'Why should my husband have to take off more time, sorting out these stupid situations his family get themselves into? Just think how awful it must have been riding all that way to Springfield in a state of misery, only to find that his nephew was all right.'

'Ah, but he didn't find that. He entered a household in deep mourning.'

'Well, you know what I mean. Anyway, it's all too ridiculous. His father cut him out of the will. His mother tried to have his inheritance restored but his brothers won't hear of it, the lousy pair. And now he wants to sort out their troubles with the blacks. He even said to me this morning that he doubted his brothers would keep the promise to Nioka. Well, she's there. I say it's up to her to make them.'

Clara looked at this woman, whom she'd come to like. Mrs Broderick was a bit scatty, hopeless, still, in a domestic capacity – she couldn't even make a bed straight – but she was fun to be with. Clara had never met anyone like her in her life. Disarray didn't bother her.

Burned meals were hilarious tragedies to be shared with her husband as they resorted to whatever the pantry held. She laughed a lot, an infectious, giggly, delightful laugh, mainly at her own incompetence. There was such warmth and gaiety about Mrs Broderick that the men, who'd scowled at first at a missus who didn't know one end of a horse from another, now grinned benignly as she approached, almost ready to give her the Raleigh treatment and throw down their coats before those neat little shoes.

'I bet she was a tiger in society,' Clara's husband commented one day.

'Why do you say that?' Clara asked, interested.

'Oh, she's got a real way with her. She'd have all the lads twisted round her little finger in no time.'

'I suppose so,' Clara said wistfully. Not that it really bothered her. She was blonde too, fair, more than fair in the summer, her hair bleached by the sun, long and straight and held back by cord. And tall. The opposite of the lady of the house. And she could ride. She never said much about this to Mrs Broderick, but she'd won prizes in rodeos for trick riding and roping. The ribbons were carefully packed in their own satin-lined box.

Mrs Broderick did indeed have a way with her but she was far more self-contained than most people realized because she had books. Boxes of books. Clara thought the house could be on fire and she wouldn't notice if she was reading. And now she was passing on some of those books to a stockman's wife, as if that was the most normal thing in the world.

Not only had Clara found a friend to whom she could talk about the maddest things in the world, but she'd found reading, and was devouring books as fast as the boss's wife handed them to her.

Clara jerked her mind back to the subject at hand, because Mrs Broderick was demanding her opinion on this impasse.

'I think the boss is a very generous man,' she said.

His wife shrugged. 'He can't afford to be generous these days. Not enough cash around.'

Clara stared out of the open window, hardly noticing the thick dust being stirred up by westerlies. 'There's more to generosity than money. My father used to say that generosity of the heart was the greatest of virtues. He was a school teacher, and a good one they say, although he didn't do much for us kids. It was the drink, you know. They fell on bad times, Mum and Dad . . .'

But Connie wasn't listening to the story. She heard only those few words, from a girl her own age, a woman with goodness in her heart, and she was mortified. Clara had seen something in Harry that she'd overlooked, never noticed, never cared to notice. They'd both made awful mistakes, but now they were closer than they'd ever been. They were so much in love and yet they'd wasted a night last night arguing this thing. What was a week or two in their lives if Harry felt he really had to do this? Didn't she have enough generosity of heart to let him go – no, send him – after those kids? Hadn't she argued bitterly with Jack Ballard about them, for them, in spite of Government policy or whatever they called it? Someone should go and get them.

When Harry came back, thankfully without Jack, she drew him into the bedroom and put her arms about him. 'You're a lovely man, Harry Broderick.'

Later, when, inevitably, the subject came up again she blinked at him. 'Did I say you couldn't go? I meant you shouldn't have to.'

'Yes, I should,' he answered truthfully. 'And I love you, Connie.'

The railway line from Toowoomba to the coal-mining town of Ipswich passed only a few miles from the reserve set aside for indigenous peoples, but Harry had no idea it existed. Not too many whites knew about it, except farmers in the district who complained bitterly about this imposition. They resented having hundreds of blacks dumped in their midst, even though the area was cordoned off, but by the time they found out, it was a *fait accompli*, carried out with the silence of a pen by Brisbane bureaucrats. A German woman from a pioneering family in the ranges behind Nerang wrote a tearful letter to the *Courier Mail* accusing the Government of causing unnecessary hardship, not only to the blacks, forcibly removed from her district, but to the small community, because the Aborigines were their friends. She claimed the pioneering families owed a great debt to the local blacks for their kindness and support over those hard years when they had had to learn to live off the strange land, and she begged that they be allowed to return, but the letter was never published. Maybe, she worried, years later, her English had not been good enough.

There were farmers, too, who looked on the reserve with astonishment. They had no quarrel with Aborigines, they simply asked the obvious question. These plains were excellent farming areas, ideal for crops and dairying, but how could so many people survive in such a small area? They thought in terms of farms. Originally they'd imagined that this would be a farming project, but they soon saw that would be impossible, as more and more black families were carted in there, ostensibly to grow their own food. Instead, the reserve became a jumble of market gardens, huts and store sheds from where food could be obtained through confused systems of coupons, hand-outs and soup kitchens, and smuggled grog became both currency and solace.

Knowing nothing of this, Harry saw only a well-populated area of farmland, and understood why farmers and graziers were reaching out for more land. Both Toowoomba and Ipswich were growing fast. Within a few years they'd be cities in their own right, and the west would have to make room for an influx of settlers. Only in the far north of the country, where distance was the enemy, would the huge stations be able to survive.

At Ipswich he walked over to the Railway Hotel, downed a couple of beers and boarded the train again, making for Brisbane to carry out his mission, deciding that the Anglican archbishop might be able to direct him to the Church of the Holy Word.

Jagga had plenty of kids to play with at his new home, and he was not sorry to be able to discard his funny clothes, especially the shoes, which Maggie sold. She gave him food when she was sober; the rest of the time he ate wherever he flopped, mostly in lean-tos outside the miserable huts. Few people slept in these dilapidated constructions; they were used only as shelter from the rain, because most residents preferred to sleep under the stars.

Soon, though, he became aware of the necessity to keep clear of trouble. There were constant fights between clans, between the people who nurtured their vegetable gardens and those who stole the produce, between drunks, between men and women . . . no end to it. And the kids joined in, throwing stones at perceived enemies and suffering the consequences by being chased and beaten. As a result, Jagga became a wiry little brat, street-smart, knowing the best hiding places to store his provisions, accepted or stolen. Thanks to Mrs Smith and her cook, his command of English had improved considerably, so he hung about the main office listening to the administrator, Mr Jim, talking to his staff, which had now grown to a complement of five clerks. Eventually they found a use for him. He became their runner, their messenger boy, dashing through the confusion to locate individuals whom the clerks wouldn't even recognize. In return he was given the odd orange or boiled lolly, even scraps from their meals, which raised envy among his friends. Kids called him a spy and struck out at him, but he learned to hit back with the one weapon he possessed. He threatened to tell Mr Jim on them, and have them put in the lock-up, an ominous building that had recently been erected to house drunks and troublemakers.

Jagga was a survivor. The Smiths had been good to him, so he lacked the innate fear of the white bosses, and it stood him in good stead. His earlier years at Springfield were lost in the mist, and his mother, Nioka, was only an unidentifiable yearning, but he had one dream. Whenever new people were brought in, Jagga was at the gate, examining the children carefully. He never gave up hope that his real family, Bobbo and Doombie, would come walking back into his life.

Only a few weeks after Matron Giles retired from the workhouse, the charity ladies were up in arms because the new matron was far from suitable. She was a coarse woman with no nursing experience and little idea of what was required of her beyond a daily round of inspections, more to emphasize her status than to attend to the deteriorating conditions, which she didn't appear to notice. Often, when the ladies asked to see her, they found she was off-duty, a regular occurrence, it seemed, no matter the hour. Complaints to the superintendent were only referred back to the new matron, since he claimed that he was not her boss, although it was whispered that she was a personal friend of that gentleman, and he had offered her the position.

Plans to close down the complex had stalled in the cubby holes of cluttered desks after laborious journeys between the Health Department, the Welfare Department and the offices with the responsibility for Government buildings, deep within the Department of Housing.

Exasperated, the ladies stormed the steps of Parliament House with their petitions, demanding action be taken.

Finally, due to some miracle, they agreed, something did happen. The superintendent and his matron were both sacked. A manager was installed, and with him a stern young female supervisor, both of whom, determined to make their mark, called in practical assistance. Fumigators went through the buildings, followed by carpenters and painters, and, thanks to a comfort drive organized by the ladies and several church committees, fresh bedding, linen and blankets were delivered by the wagonload to the front door.

All of this was a relief to the inmates and gave a great deal of satisfaction to the charity workers, but one lowly fellow found no reason to rejoice. The new manager did not need an assistant, nor did he need so many male staff, who, it seemed to him, only took up space. The women could cook, clean and sew, and were paid lower wages. He only retained a couple of groundsmen.

Buster found himself unemployed again and went to his sister, Molly, with the shattering news.

The former matron took it in her stride. 'It's bad luck, but you mustn't let yourself get upset or you'll be reaching for the bottle again. You've got a home here with me and Doombie, and I've told you before, there's no shortage of odd jobs round this suburb.'

'But what will they do without me?' he worried. 'There's the two cripples I used to carry out to sit in the sun, and old Mrs Sparkes who's too fat to do much for herself, and the mad woman, Polly, she was scared of everyone but me, she wouldn't let no one near her. I used to bring her food to her. What will they do? And all the rest of them that need me?'

'Shush, now. Kind people have taken over. They'll look after them, don't you be worrying. You did a sterling job there and I'm proud of you . . .'

'You are?' His face brightened. 'I never thought no one ever noticed.'

'I did, and I was the matron, remember. I knew your worth and that's all that matters. We've done our bit there.'

'I suppose we did.'

But Molly wasn't so much worried about her brother as about Doombie, whom they both loved dearly. At this point she didn't dare tell Buster that she feared for the child. He was a happy little fellow, but sickly.

After a while Buster began to notice. 'Why don't you let him go out and play?'

'He can go into the yard if he wants, but he's just not up to it right now. He's tired.'

'But he's always tired. And he's skinny. A growing boy, you have to feed him up. Give him plenty of tucker.'

She had. Doombie got the best of fare – milk, eggs, thick soup, chops and all the vegetables she could find. It was no trouble feeding him, for the little chap was fond of his food, but she couldn't put the necessary weight on him. She sat him in a chair in the mornings, wrapped in a blanket, and left him outside under the trees for the fresh air, and in the afternoons she let him play with his toys in her tiny sitting room, hoping he would voluntarily venture outside but he always seemed too weary.

At first she thought he was fretting for his parents, whoever they were, and in gentle conversations discovered that his 'dadda' was called something like Gabi Gee, but from his replies to her questions about them, he didn't appear concerned. Only vague. Molly knew the world had swallowed up that part of his life, so she tried to compensate. When she was home, she nursed him to sleep in her arms, telling him all the fairy stories he loved. When she had to go out on her rounds as a midwife, she put him down in her bed with picture books, and on her return she always found him sleeping surrounded by the cheap little books, clutching the teddy bear she'd found in a welfare box. He loved that teddy bear, and to see him in repose like this was a lovely homecoming, because she worried about having to leave him in the house on his own.

Now that Buster was living here, she cheered up. They could share the caring for this delightful child, with his black curly hair, dark skin and dazzling smile. The illness which she was sure he had didn't seem to bother him, apart from his lethargy. He was always full of questions, always the why. Always wanting to know who these people were in the books and why they did such silly things. His little mind worked like a forge picking out illogicalities, she told Buster. How could Red Riding Hood not tell the difference between her grandma and a dog?

'He's smart all right,' Buster agreed. He was immensely flattered that Doombie was happy to have him move in 'for good'. This being only a two-bedroomed house, Buster slept on the back veranda, but Doombie knew he was there, and would often call out to him to make sure. To be reassured. Although neither brother nor sister ever

336

discussed their feelings, both being of shy dispositions, Buster knew that his childless sister loved the boy like her own. For his part, he had come upon a totally new and joyful experience. Doombie loved him, and what was more, he made no bones about it. He chose Buster's company, sitting by his knee, following him about, so much so that Molly teased them.

'Easy to see, men stick together. What chance have I got in this household? I'm just the cook and bottlewasher.'

Humbly, Buster began to grasp the fact that he was loved just for himself, regardless of the fact that he wasn't much of a person, just a broken-down former drunk, failed pugilist and a few other things he'd rather not recall. Doombie adored his friend Buster and welcomed him home. Charged with emotion, Buster became the child's willing slave, always anxious to please.

But Molly became more concerned. She discussed the child with a doctor and managed to persuade him to see Doombie, even though he was black, something she knew was necessary to mention beforehand, to avoid embarrassment. But Molly was now known as an excellent midwife, and the doctor dared not deny her.

His diagnosis only confirmed what she already knew. The boy was consumptive. Probably infected during his sojourn at the workhouse, where the disease was rife. He shook his head and prescribed medicines, which Molly already had through an arrangement with a friendly apothecary, as well as rest and good meals. He also suggested a change of climate, to fresh air. That annoyed Molly.

'What fresh air? We don't live in a city or a coal town. What better fresh air could he get than right here? We're only a few miles from the seaside.'

He shrugged. She was right. He had practised in London, seen plenty of consumptives there, where the usual advice was to take the patient to the Swiss Alps. But where did you go from here? Even the poorest had the best of climates in this country.

'Keep him well fed,' he told her. 'But call me if you see the signs. We may have to hospitalize him.'

But as he said it, he remembered that hospitals did not take black kids: 'Although I do feel, Molly, that you could nurse him just as well here. Better really. Kids fret in hospital.'

She understood. Buster did not. 'How could this happen to Doombie? You were a matron. You must know how to get him better. He'll be all right, won't he? He's only a little chap. He can't have that sickness.'

'Yes,' she said gently. 'You heard the doctor. We know what to do. Who better? We'll look after him. I thought we might hire a cart and take him to the seaside for a few hours. Doombie has never seen the sea.'

'Right! That's what we'll do. That will perk him up no end.' He was all for racing in to Doombie to tell him that they were all going to the seaside for a treat, but quietened down when Molly advised that the child mustn't be allowed to become too excited.

The riverboat, *Marigold*, had seen better days, but it was still the pride and joy of its master, Theo Logan, who preferred to be known as Captain. He had served some years as a lowly seaman in the British navy before distinguishing himself by breaking an officer's jaw and landing in a Tasmanian prison. For a lad who had escaped the slums of Glasgow to see the world, this was no great hardship, because the Lord had seen fit to provide him with an able body and uncommon strength, so he was equal to any punishments the warders cared to hand out. And they were many, for Theo was far from a model prisoner. He deeply resented his incarceration, believing that the officer had been a liar and a thief and deserving of the smash on the jaw when he'd tried to implicate this seaman in his wrongdoings; so he became well known to the prison authorities as a bad lot, truculent, belligerent and at times brutal. A loner, known to have a quick temper, he was given a wide berth by other prisoners, who did, however, enjoy the distraction of the Scot's rampages.

Two years in the Hobart prison was enough for him, though. When the opportunity of a prison riot presented itself, he escaped through the roof and disappeared into the waterfront fraternity based round dingy inns and bordellos, where he changed his name to Theo Logan, a name he wasn't likely to forget. It had belonged to the navy officer whose jaw he had broken.

Soon he was aboard a whaler, headed out to sea again, and for many long years Theo trolled the Pacific from Hobart to Chile, until he joined another ship, whaling in the gentler waters of Moreton Bay in Queensland, with their base in Brisbane.

And that was where the old salt met and married Marigold Frew, owner of the Ship Inn. It was said she was a harridan, a blowsy, foulmouthed old harpy, but no one would dare say it within earshot of her husband. They were soul mates, they understood each other, not a harsh word was heard to pass between them. Neither Marigold nor Theo had been married before because they'd lived hard lives and learned to trust no one, so it was a revelation to them, in their halfcenturies, to look through the smoke and gloom and come face to face with the one. After a time that couldn't be called courting, they made a decision, this pair of old-timers, and stepped out into the sunshine, trudged down to the nearest church and tied the knot.

There was no party, no wedding breakfast, because they considered what they did was their own business.

Theo worked in the pub, mainly as yardman, sometimes in the bar when it was busy, and often as her bouncer when needed, and the customers only noted the arrangement when the licensee's name over the front door was altered to M. and T. Logan. The regulars offered profuse congratulations, which were accepted with a free ale and an amiable nod, and otherwise life went on. The Ship Inn was always busy, no time for fripperies, but upstairs, when the last drunk was routed and the till was emptied and the doors locked and barred, Marigold and Theo looked at each other in wonderment. They were in love and they couldn't bear for anyone to know.

For her sake, Theo never mentioned that he missed the sea, the slap and the fall of the waves, the slosh of water beneath him, the stars, moonlight on the decks and the wild storms of the southern ocean. For his own sake he knew he could no longer handle ocean seafaring, what with his gammy leg that had been broken so often he couldn't recall the incidents, and his twisted wrist. That was why he'd settled for the less adventurous Moreton Bay whaling, but being a landlubber now did hurt a little. Still, he ruminated, you can't have everything in this life, and it was enough that he'd found Marigold. His wife.

They were blessed with ten years before Marigold sighed her last with a dignity that had never been afforded her earlier years. When she had the last heart attack, Theo closed the pub so that she could slip away in peace and quiet. Outside in the lane, loyal customers stood vigil with candles.

Theo never reopened the Ship Inn. He sold it quietly and went in search of a new life, finding it in a large ferry which he bought and renamed *Marigold*.

Then he became Captain Logan, plying back and forth along the Brisbane River, carrying passengers, light freight, mail, even livestock, in command of his own ship at last, and known all along the river as a grumpy old ferryman with a very quick temper, but reliable.

'Ah, yes,' they said. 'He's reliable all right.'

What they didn't know was his hurt. Theo missed his lady, her mad laugh, her pungent humour, her closeness. Not for nothing had he called her his better half. He had his boat but he was desperately lonely, and he knew that if he lived for a hundred years he'd never find another Marigold.

Theo employed two deckhands. He'd employed scores of deckhands, old and young, but they were all useless good-for-nothings, and they never stayed long; they were the bane of his life. On this day, returning to Brisbane, he'd picked up a cargo of potatoes and other farm produce, including tomatoes and eggs. Once they were loaded, keeping to his routine, he allowed the passengers to board, only to notice more bags of potatoes piled up on shore, bags that should have been loaded first to avoid injury to the lighter produce.

Angrily he shouted to his deckhands to fetch them, and the two lads began to push down the single ramp, upsetting passengers who were on their way up, and causing the Captain to shout even louder.

In all the confusion he didn't notice the small boy slip aboard and disappear below.

At last, though, he had his twenty or so passengers ushered forward so that he could collect the fares and issue tickets. The well-wishers were ordered ashore, after the last of the potatoes had been collected, and the *Marigold* was on her way, chugging down the winding river to the busy Brisbane wharves.

Bobbo was pleased with himself. He'd found a way to cross the big river. Hidden among the bulky bags in the hold, he took stock as his eyes became accustomed to the gloom. Spotting the tomatoes, he soon prised a fat juicy one from the top of a bag and dug his teeth into it. Two more eased the pangs of hunger, but since there was a chance he might find something else edible, he began investigating, only to be grabbed by Barney, one of the deckhands.

Delighted to find a stowaway, Barney dragged the squirming black kid up to the wheelhouse and dumped him at the Captain's feet.

'Who's this?' Theo shouted. 'Where did he come from?'

'Found him in the hold. And he's been stealing tomatoes. Look at him! A real mucky pup this one.'

Theo glared. 'Who are you? What do you think you're doing on my boat? Answer me quick or I'll throw you overboard.'

'Bobbo. Goin' home, mister.'

'Where's home?'

'Springfield.'

'Never heard of it. No Springfield on this run. What's a kid this size doing running around on his own? Where's your ma?'

'Springfield.'

'Where'd you come from?'

Bobbo jerked his head. 'Back dere.'

'I know that. What's back there?'

The child had no answer to that, so Theo gave up. No point in lecturing this kid about paying for tickets, or trying to make him pay for the tomatoes. It would be a waste of time.

'Put him back in the hold,' he snorted. 'I can't have him running loose. I'll shove him ashore when we dock.'

Barney ran him below deck and pushed him into the hold. 'You stay right there, and don't come out till I say so.'

That suited Bobbo. He curled up on the bags and dozed, happy to be crossing the river in such grand style.

When Barney finally came for him, he hopped to his feet and padded up to the deck. Then he stared at all the huge buildings.

'What this place?'

'Brisbane.'

Bobbo pulled back. He had escaped into the country from a big town and now they'd brought him to the same place, or maybe another town. He'd only wanted to cross the river, heading for bush on the other side.

'No! No!' he screamed, squirming away. 'This bad place. Not going dere no more. No!'

The Captain came down. 'What's wrong now?'

'He won't get off.'

'We'll see about that.' He picked Bobbo up, ignoring his screams, and lugged him ashore, dumping him on the wharf. 'Now be off with you, and consider yourself lucky I don't give you a hiding.' He gave a menacing stamp with his boot – 'Shoo!' – and sent the kid scampering away.

Right on two o'clock that afternoon, the *Marigold* swept out into the river to begin the return journey upstream. Rather than pay what he considered outlandish charges and levies for a berth at the Brisbane waterfront, Theo had negotiated a deal with the residents of Somerset, a small settlement far upriver. In return for basing the *Marigold* at Somerset, and providing them with regular transport to Brisbane, they agreed to build a wharf for him, and the arrangement was a boon for both parties. There were no charges for berthing at Somerset and the locals, especially the ladies, were delighted that at last the remote village no longer seemed cut off from the world. Between Somerset and Brisbane the ferry made six other calls, most of which were at landings that did not even boast villages, but farmers and their families soon took advantage of the new service. Even after several years on this run, Theo wasn't making much money, but then he didn't need much. He lived aboard the *Marigold*, having converted the rear saloon into a small galley and cabin, and at night he had his boat all to himself. A great joy to the Captain, who could often be seen, of an evening, sitting on the deck with his pipe and a shot of rum. As farmers are apt to do for a friend, they brought him fresh eggs, dressed poultry, or vegetables, refusing payment, but the Captain, with still enough Scot in him to find hand-outs difficult to appreciate, always managed to repay the kindnesses by delivering parcels or messages free of charge, or by leaving gifts for children at the landings. The grizzly old man had become a legend along the Brisbane River, his booming voice and irascible temperament more of a joke than a bother.

On this day he was carrying the usual complement of passengers up top and a cargo of timber in the hold, and for once, his deckhands agreed, everything had gone smoothly until Barney found the black kid in the hold again. This time he left him there and went up to report to the Captain.

'He's down there agin.'

'Who is?'

'The stowaway. The black kid.'

'What black kid?'

341

'The one we threw off this morning. He's down in the hold again, hiding in the stacks.'

'The same one?'

'Yeah!'

Theo exploded. 'Am I supposed to keep an eye on everything, you bloody fool? There's only one bloody ramp, can't you watch it? Or am I going to have to put up with stowaways every day? Get the bugger off my boat!'

'How?' Barney looked at the wide river rippling past.

'Pope's Landing. Next stop. Get him off and see that he stays off!'

To make sure he was rid of the nuisance, Theo watched as Barney pulled the skinny kid along the deck after the passengers had disembarked, but before they reached the planks that constituted a ramp, the child collapsed and fell into a dead faint on the deck.

Taken aback, and not a little annoyed, Theo strode down to look at the kid.

'Pick him up,' he said, 'and take him down to my cabin. I'll be down in a minute.'

His chores completed, Theo hurried down to the cabin and stared at the frail child on his bunk.

'Do you reckon he's sick?' Barney asked.

'No,' Theo said thoughtfully, cruel memories of his own childhood stabbing at him like a pain in his gut. 'No, just bloody starved.'

Archbishop Pedley was pleased to welcome Harry Broderick into the manse. He knew Harry's background. Who didn't? His fall from grace had been quite a scandal. But he had known Austin Broderick quite well, in a social rather than a religious capacity, unfortunately, so it would be interesting to receive one of the sons. The family was still important, as far as he knew, in the squattocracy. He smiled as Harry entered his elegant parlour, remembering that these fellows were known by friend and foe as 'the grass dukes' for their high living and huge properties. This Broderick certainly looked the part. He was tall and fair, with fine features, and his clothes, though tweedy country-style, were well tailored. And he had excellent manners, the Archbishop noted later, when morning tea was served.

Introductory conversation over, Harry came to the point of his visit. He was trying to locate three black children who had been removed from their tribal environment. The Archbishop was glad to know that Harry Broderick was taking an interest in the matter, which happened to be one of his own pet projects.

'It's a costly exercise for the church,' he explained, 'straining our budgets to the limit, what with the cathedral not paid off yet, and I fear it will cost a great deal more, but it has been very worthwhile, very worthwhile indeed. I can't tell you how much I appreciate it that you have come forward to see how the children are progressing.'

Harry put his teacup down quietly. 'Not exactly, sir. But I should like to hear how the system works, since you appear to know more about it than most people I've met. Everyone seems to be so vague about it.'

'By all means.'

While he talked, Harry listened without interrupting. This was the first time he'd met Pedley, and he summed him up as being an intelligent man, and a good man, not overly pious in his manner of speech. And yet . . .

'. . . So you see, this is really quite a stupendous challenge we have set ourselves, Harry.'

'And the aim is assimilation?'

'Of course. We can't leave the children to remain uncivilized, it is degrading to them and to us as their custodians. In colonizing this country we have a responsibility to the natives.'

Harry smiled grimly. 'In the north of this state there are many tribes who are fighting against colonization. Fighting for their very lives.'

'Yes, it's sad, but there's nothing you or I can do about that, is there, Harry? It's the way of the world.'

'I suppose so,' Harry admitted glumly. 'But tell me this. What about the parents of these black children? I believe they are distraught, and from my enquiries there must be thousands of them now who are losing their children.'

The Archbishop nodded. 'I am not unaware of this problem . . .'

'Hardly just a problem. It's pain, the worst kind.'

'We're trying to do what we feel is the best for their children.'

'Turning them into orphans?'

'If need be, because we consider that better than the alternative.'

'With no regard for the pain inflicted on the children and the parents.'

Pedley stiffened. 'I feel we are at odds here, and you surprise me. Many a station owner has asked the Government and the churches to remove the blacks from their properties.'

'I don't doubt it. Selfishness is not confined to colonial governments or churches; rather, they hide behind organizations like yours.'

The Archbishop was not happy with the trend of this discussion. 'It appears we do not see eye to eye on this subject.'

Harry nibbled absently on a butternut biscuit. 'Archbishop, bear with me. I am trying to understand your point of view.' He took a folded newspaper cutting from his pocket.

'Do you know of a Mr Tobias Waller?'

'Oh, yes. Excellent fellow. He writes very profound articles for the *Sydney Morning Herald* and for our own *Courier*. A thinker. I quite appreciate reading his articles.'

'Good. I have one of his articles here where he says that the stated aim of removing these children – I repeat, stated – is not assimilation, but the eradication of the Aborigines. And he's all for it. He considers them a scourge on the land. As he says here, in plain print, worse than dingoes. He says the only way to do this is to place the adults in reserves and take the children. Wipe out the language and their heathen practices.'

'Yes?'

Harry stared. 'Don't you find his attitude un-Christian?'

'An exaggeration, perhaps.'

'Then tell me what we're looking at here. Is it assimilation or is it eradication?'

The Archbishop shook his head. 'I fear you're allowing emotion to override common sense, Harry. You don't seem to grasp that we are doing what we feel is the best for these people.'

'You mean the people who owned this land in the first place? You didn't answer my question.'

'Well, then, I suppose one would follow the other. Eventually.'

Harry felt a nausea born of a hollow sense of hopelessness. If this man couldn't even conceive of a crime here, this man, so certain of his righteousness, what chance was there for the Aborigines?

He changed the subject. 'Do you know of a Church of the Holy Word? The name seems familiar to me, but I can't place it.'

On less prickly ground, the Archbishop was firm. 'There is no such church.'

'That's not my advice.'

'Ah, there was a fellow chasing about claiming he was the bishop of this so-called church, and he did have followers, mainly from New Zealand, I believe. But he was a charlatan. A thief of the first order.' He sighed. 'To my dying day I'll never understand how people can be so gullible, handing over their life savings to such rascals.'

Harry was shocked. Apart from learning more about the Anglican attitude to the children, he'd expected to be directed straight to the Reverend Billings and his church by an archbishop who would be sure to know about religious offshoots.

'Has he gone? This Reverend Billings?'

'No. That wasn't his name. Dashed if I can think of it now. He did have a house, that he called a church, on the outskirts of town, but it was sold. And he took the money. Some of his parishioners came bleating to me, but I'm afraid I couldn't rouse too much sympathy for them.'

'But what happened to the children?'

'What children?'

'This fellow, the Reverend Billings, took children, black children, from our station, claiming he would place them in their orphanage. My father gave him a donation to take care of those children. Where are they?'

'I've no idea. There is no church now, nor is there an orphanage in that name. I'm surprised that your father . . .'

'He was simply following your teachings,' Harry said angrily. 'He too thought it was for the best.'

As Harry was leaving, the Archbishop patted him on the shoulder. 'I think we have to agree to disagree, you and I.'

But Harry looked at him sadly. 'No, sir. We can't do that. I just hope that one day you'll come to realize that all God's people are not white.'

That night, staying at Fern Broderick's house, Harry wrote to Connie to tell her that this search could take longer than he had thought, because now he had no idea where the boys might be. He apologized, promising to write every day, even if his letters did arrive two or three at a time.

He began a round of orphanages, studying lists which contained not Aborigine but English names that had been assigned to the children. Finding them unhelpful, he walked through rooms full of sad, wistful faces, trying to remember what these kids, Bobbo, Doombie and Jagga, looked like, but for the life of him he couldn't recall. It was years since he'd seen them, and then only as babies.

In one place, though, someone remembered a kid called Bobbo.

He was what was known as a lay teacher, Harry discovered, a person without qualifications. But he soon found that none of the teachers at this orphanage had any qualifications, and they seemed to him more like warders.

'I might be able to remember,' the slimy character said, edging up to Mr Broderick. A half-crown helped.

'Yes. He was here. Bobbo. A real little brat. Never did nothin' he was told. Uphill job tryin' to learn him somethin'.'

Harry winced, hoping this fellow didn't teach English.

'So!' he said abruptly. 'Where is he now?'

'I dunno, he run off. Never saw him again.'

'Didn't you search for him?'

'Oh, yeah, we did that, but we got other kids to look after. Too many, if you wanta know. This ain't a prison.'

'But he's only about seven years old. Did you inform the police?'

'What for? Most of the runaways, they come slinkin' back when they get hungry enough. This one didn't, that's all.'

'That's appalling. A little child disappears and no one cares. It's a disgrace, and so is this place.' Harry peered down the long, dank passageway. 'It stinks. You haven't heard the last of this, believe me.'

The teacher squinted at him. 'Listen, mister. You do what you like, but this orphanage is a bloody sight better than where he came from. We only took him for a favour.'

Harry was suddenly alert. 'Where did he come from?'

345

'The workhouse,' he sneered.

'And you say he was on his own? No other small Aborigine boys with him?'

'No. We got other Abos here but they're older.'

'Who brought him here?'

'I told you. Some bloke from the workhouse. Jeez, I just thought, maybe he went back there.'

'Thank you,' Harry said angrily.

Within the hour he was confronting the manager of the workhouse, explaining his mission, but once again without any luck.

'I can't help you, Mr Broderick, I've only been here a couple of months myself, but I can tell you this, we don't take orphans in here. Sometimes children arrive with their mothers but we try to move them on as soon as possible. I make it a priority to place women with children somewhere else. Not the best environment for children, you understand.'

'But I have it on good authority that this child, Bobbo, was here, and maybe the others were too. Do you keep an account of the names of people who come in here?'

'Oh, yes, we do have a register. Most important. The Government grant is based on the numbers we take in.'

'Then would you mind checking the back registers? I should appreciate it.'

'Very well.'

They went into the office, where the manager took down large bound registers and placed them on his desk. Together they searched the lists, going back for months, concentrating on the ages of the residents, but the few children listed had all come in with their mothers.

The manager sighed. 'I'm sorry, Mr Broderick. I wish I could have been of more assistance to you, but as I said, orphans are not accepted here. It's against the rules. It's my guess, since you've already checked the orphanages, that they were farmed out privately by this Reverend Billings. I mean, he could hardly just leave them in the street. Scoundrels though they must be, these fellows . . .'

Harry was bewildered. 'I simply don't understand it. If they were charlatans, why would they take the children at all?'

'Did you give them a donation, perhaps?'

'My father did, I believe.'

The manager shrugged. 'Well . . .'

'No. That can't be right. If he just wanted the money he could have dumped the kids anywhere along the road, but he actually did bring them to Brisbane. One of them, Bobbo, was at an orphanage here.'

'Maybe the fellow at the orphanage was lying.'

'Oh, God, I hope not.'

The kindly manager escorted Harry to the gate, grateful for the donation of five pounds that his visitor had placed on his desk, but when he returned to his office, one of the charity ladies, Mrs Charmaine Collins, poked her head in the door.

'Wasn't that Harry Broderick?' she asked eagerly.

'Yes.'

'Oh, my!' She smiled mischievously, gossip-bound. 'He must be back in town then. Is his wife with him?'

'I wouldn't know.' He wasn't above a little gossip either. 'Who is Harry Broderick?'

'My dear! Quite a scandal.' Happily she outlined the tale as she knew it, and the manager was astonished to hear that this fellow had gone berserk in his own house with a gun.

'He seemed a very nice chap.'

'Ah, yes, the rumour has it that he was provoked. His wife, you know. Another gentleman was seen leaving the house, if you take my meaning. And then there was some fuss in Parliament. He resigned his seat as a result.'

'He was a Member of Parliament?'

'Oh, yes. And not so long ago either. What did he want here?'

The manager began replacing the journals in a tall cabinet. 'He was looking for some children. Three black children, quite young, I believe. But I told him that orphans were not accepted in a place like this. It was quite unfortunate, I had trouble convincing him. We even went through back registers . . .'

'But they were here.'

'What? How could they have been?'

'Someone dumped them at the gate. Matron was too kind to turn them away. Instead she was trying to place them.'

The manager pushed the last journal into place. 'I'll call her right away.'

'No, not this woman. The good matron, the one who retired before you came.' She grinned. 'Of course they wouldn't be in your register, it was against the rules. But she'd know where they were. And just a minute . . . one of our ladies took a child. A little black boy. Now, who was she? No, let me think. She was a silly woman, one of the dabblers as we call them. She came to help a couple of times, but was never seen again. Hopeless, never seen a scrubbing brush in her life.'

He was listening earnestly. 'I must find Mr Broderick then and tell him. Do you know where he lives?'

'No, but I can find out. Leave it with me.' Mrs Collins had no intention of allowing this intriguing story to slip away from her. Why was Harry Broderick making such a fuss about three black children? What was he up to now?

She left the manager's office, tied on her black apron, rolled up her sleeves and headed for the kitchen. Charmaine Collins would not neglect her duty to the poor. Harry Broderick would just have to wait awhile. But while she worked, she quizzed the other ladies working as her scullery maids in the ugly, steaming kitchen until they came up with a name. Mrs Smith. Mrs Adam Smith. Wife of some public servant.

Chapter Fourteen

At first Victor, and Louisa too, ignored Rupe. It was as if he didn't exist. Determined to play the hand his way, he pretended not to notice, taking his meals in the kitchen when it suited him, under the sullen eye of Hannah, who could not refuse to serve one of the bosses no matter the hour. Big house though it was, they did pass in corridors and outside, but no one spoke. The air, he smiled to himself, was ice. And that was the way he wanted it, because he was waiting for Charlotte to come down. A broken arm wouldn't keep her in bed, and the shock was fast wearing off in her delight that Teddy was still in the land of the living. In fact, most times when he'd popped in on her, she'd been happily reading story books to Teddy, since he no longer had a governess.

Rupe shuddered, and postponed that thought for another day.

Though the physical shock of her fall had worn off, Rupe knew that Charlotte was still angry. He'd listened to her complaints about the house and her garden, and nodded glumly, as if he agreed but would not like to comment. He knew his mother; the minute he voiced a criticism of Louisa, she was likely to turn on him. Charlotte was a contrary woman and he wasn't out of the woods yet. Fortunately, her mate Ada Crossley had gone home; you never knew which way Charlotte would jump with Ada stirring the pot. But there was no doubt that she was still cross with Victor for not letting her know exactly what had happened in the first place. For not keeping in touch with her.

Last night, in the quiet of her bedroom, Rupe had poured his heart out to her, telling her of his agony and his guilt when he had lost Teddy and feared he'd been drowned.

'I don't know how to face them,' he told her. 'What to say to them, and sure as hell they don't want to talk to me.'

'What about Cleo?' she asked. 'Surely she should bear some responsibility too?'

In apologetic mode, and this female presence, he changed his tune. 'We didn't even notice him slip away. You know how fast kids can move. It was only for a second, we were trying to identify different birds, and besides, he went towards the bush, away from the river, not towards it. He must have circled about. Just the same, I think poor Cleo has suffered enough. A horrible humiliation being ordered off the property.'

'What does she mean to you?'

He shrugged. 'She's a very nice girl. Comes from a good family. I had hoped . . .'

'I hope you kept your hands off her.'

'Mother, I told you,' he smiled, 'she comes from a good family. I wasn't to have her father arrive with the shotgun. Not that it matters now, I've lost her. I doubt she'll want to know any of us ever again.' Sadly he walked over to the window and stared out into the darkness. 'She was the first really intelligent girl I've ever met. She's very sweet, very nice, she's travelled the world, and I figured she'd be ready to settle down . . .'

'Good Lord. Are you in love with her? No one told me about this.'

'Who would? A little bit of jealousy there, I fear.'

'With Louisa?'

'What do you think? Cleo is wealthy, well educated, she lived in London for six months, and Teddy adored her. A bit much for Louisa to swallow, I suppose, when there was a possibility that as mistress of Springfield, she had run into competition.'

Charlotte handed Rupe her dinner tray. 'It seems to me that you're all getting ahead of yourselves here. I'm not dead yet, and this is *my* home.'

Which was exactly what Rupe had been driving at.

The following afternoon Charlotte told Hannah that she would be coming down to dinner and it was to be served in the dining room, despite Hannah's advice that the family preferred to eat in the breakfast room these days.

'And tell Rupe to be there,' she added. 'He will dine with his family. This "no speaks" business has gone on long enough.'

Deliberately, Rupe kept out of Victor's way. The shearers were due any day and Victor was busy clearing out the shearing sheds, so he rode out mustering sheep but came in early to hear the good news about the family dinner; and from one of the maids that Mrs Broderick had clashed with young Mrs Broderick over the rearrangements that had taken place in the front of the house in the absence of Mrs Charlotte.

'They've been going at it hammer and tongs, Mr Rupe,' the girl said anxiously. 'We've been moving furniture back like a couple of navvies.' She glanced up at him with a naughty wink. 'Best you stay out of the way. It's women's business.'

He gave her his sunniest smile, and patted her flirtatious bottom. 'I wouldn't miss it for quids.'

But he had. Charlotte was dressed for dinner in shiny black, with her hair pinned up over diamond drop earrings that he hadn't seen for years, and was arranging flowers in the parlour; only grevillias, probably the best she could find, he mused, since her English garden had withered. Charlotte adored flowers but it took a lot of work to nurture real blooms out here. You couldn't kill the red and gold grevillia with an axe.

She saw him. 'I expect you for dinner, Rupe.'

'I'll be there,' he chortled, and hurried upstairs. He showered and shaved, pomaded his thatch of blond hair, took out a dinner suit, not his best, with a dark velvet lapel and then went to a drawer and found a new shirt with a ruffled front that someone had given him. He was dressing for his mother, because he needed her on side, knowing that Victor, whose mind was on the station and its operations, had lost interest in the social side of station life. Not that he had ever had much interest in the first place; he was a man of habit, needing mothering in these matters. And Rupe doubted that, by the sound of things, Louisa was in any mood to further Charlotte's old-fashioned formalities. He added a slim black tie, tucked a gold watch across his waistcoat and lent a spit and polish to his black pumps, before checking the cheval mirror and descending to the parlour.

'Well, for heaven's sake,' Charlotte smiled, welcoming him into the parlour. 'You do look nice, and you're wearing that shirt I bought you last Christmas. I thought you didn't like it.'

'Of course I like it. I was just a bit shy of wearing all these ruffles. How's your arm?'

She looked down at the plastered arm in its black silk sling. 'It doesn't hurt, but it's itchy and the most awful nuisance. Would you like a sherry while we wait for the others to take their time?'

The dining room glowed. Amber glass lampshades lent warmth to the timber wall panels and softened the blaze of white damask on the long table. Evening light filtered through the lace on the tall windows framed by the luxurious green velvet drapes that had found their way back from the banishment of the linen press. Rupe smiled. They smelled a little of mothballs. So much for Louisa's short reign as innovator. The era of light and airy rooms had ended abruptly with Charlotte's return.

As Victor and Louisa hurried in, Rupe held the chair to place his mother at the head of the table, where once Austin had held sway, and settling herself, she acknowledged the thoughtful gesture with a gracious nod. But then she looked to the others.

Louisa was defiant in a neat blouse and belted skirt, and Victor, unaware of a problem, because he cared little about dress, let alone protocol, simply looked shiny and scrubbed in a clean shirt and cord trousers. If he noticed Rupe's formal attire he gave no hint, seeing that his wife was seated before he took his usual place at the end of the table, with Rupe on his left. Like any working man, he wasn't fussed where he ate; his interest was in the meal. Absently he picked up the starched napkin and looked to his wife.

'What's on?'

'Pea soup and baked ham.'

'Good.'

Charlotte, though, would not let this pass. 'Don't we dress for dinner any more?' she asked quietly.

'Oh, sorry,' he said, sounding less than apologetic, reaching for a warm bread roll and busily plastering it with butter.

'We agreed not to bother any more,' Louisa told Charlotte. 'As you know, we're trying to cut down on expenses, and it seems such a waste to be dressing for dinner every night in our good clothes when it's just us. And they take a lot more laundering than simple wear.'

'Suits me,' Victor added affably. 'I never liked stiff shirts anyway.'

'It seems a great pity,' Charlotte said, irritation in her voice now. 'We do have a tradition to uphold. We have always dressed for dinner. We don't live like farmers.'

'What's wrong with farmers?' Louisa asked, obviously still smarting from her demotion and the challenges of the afternoon.

'Nothing at all, dear, but we are not farmers. I like to keep a certain standard in my house. It's all too easy to fall into slovenly ways just because we're out in the bush, a long way from the hub. But you mark my words, once you let the standards slip, the staff will become slack too.'

Ha! There it is, Rupe mused as he ate a delicious onion-flavoured roll. 'My house.' That put Louisa in her place.

'Now, before we begin,' Charlotte continued, 'I notice that you people are not on speaking terms, and it has to stop. Thank the good Lord we still have our dear little boy, and that is all that matters. Rupe has something to say.'

He didn't stand. He simply turned to Victor and then to Louisa. 'I'm so very sorry about what happened. It was a nightmare for you, but equally for me. I won't try to offer you any excuses, that would be pointless. I just ask your forgiveness.'

Personally, he didn't care if they never spoke to him again, but he was acting under orders, Charlotte's orders, and he needed Victor back on side again.

'Can you do that?' he asked them earnestly.

'It's all right,' Victor said, nodding. 'It was a bad time for all of us.'

Louisa looked almost tearful at the reminder. 'Yes. It's over.'

'Thank God for that,' Charlotte said. 'Now it's my turn. We have the matter of ownership of Springfield to discuss. Does it belong to the family? Or just you two?'

Rupe groaned. This wasn't on his agenda. He let Victor reply.

'Mother, you know our position. We don't feel you were hard done by. I'm sorry we were a bit hasty about your allowance. It will stand. But the two blocks that you and Fern have freeholded must be returned to the Springfield estate. I am advised that we can set up a Springfield company which will encompass all the big runs, once freeholded, under our management. This will mean that we will keep the bulk of the property intact. I had thought of calling it the Springfield Pastoral Company, since only the homestead run can be known as Springfield Station now. Do you understand that?'

'Yes. I think it is excellent advice. But who will be the company directors?'

'Rupe and I.'

'And my rights are still being ignored. You want those blocks returned to you. We paid for them. We freeholded them. How do you propose we do that?'

'We'll buy them from you at the freeholding price. You won't be out of pocket. Under this law we would have had to do that anyway.'

She sat upright in the studded leather chair. 'Might I remind you that under the laws of business practice I'd be a fool to do that. One has to make a profit, Victor. And every day that you procrastinate, every day that you refuse to grant me my share of this property, the price is rising. By the time you get round to seeing my point of view, you may not be able to afford our land.'

Louisa intervened. 'Is it just you, Charlotte? Or will we have to face Harry's claim too?'

'No. Harry has indicated that he will not make a claim.'

Victor sighed, leaned forward, his elbow on the table, and scratched his neck. 'Then why are you doing this, Mother?'

'Harry is big enough to admit that he did provoke his father. My case is different. I have been treated unfairly. My brother partnered Austin when they pioneered this land, and despite promises, I got nothing out of that. And when Austin died he saw to it, magnanimously, that I would be housed and fed, like one of his damned merino sheep. Well, it's not good enough! I'm telling you both now, I haven't even started making life difficult for you. Keep in mind that if we do sell those blocks, the law states that the buyers must occupy within six months. You'll have strangers in the valley.'

Louisa was exasperated. 'Oh, for God's sake, Victor. I'm fed up with this. Give her a share.'

He turned on her, bewildered. 'You seem to forget that Austin made the rules here. I didn't. We owe him that respect.'

Rupe interrupted. 'I don't know about anyone else, but I'm starving. Do you think we could have dinner, Mother?'

She rang the little silver bell and the two housemaids, who doubled as waitresses, came bustling in.

While soup was being served, they all retreated into silence and Rupe took stock. He could see that Victor's stubbornly defensive attitude was no match for Charlotte's bitter determination. She wasn't dishing out idle threats; she'd batter her way through, trample them if need be, and Rupe would prefer not to be caught underfoot. She seemed to think that she had become a born-again Austin Broderick, tough, uncompromising. But she was wrong. Austin had toiled here, clearing land, fighting off not only blacks but other comers who had tried to ignore his blazed boundaries. He'd recognized that the great sweeps of pastureland beyond the valley could be wrecked by sheep without controlled stock numbers and efficient water supplies, and he'd worked intelligently to reroute creeks and dig wells. For many years he'd done his own droving, and shearing. Admittedly the money had rolled in with cheap land leases and high-priced wool, but he'd toiled and he'd lived hard. It could also be said that Charlotte had worked too, living in conditions that the family would now regard as real hardship: huts, cottages, no running water, just the basics of a roof and a camp kitchen, where she cooked for his stockmen. But that was beside the point.

She was wrong. Charlotte was no Austin Broderick. By sheer hard work and determination, he had whipped rough virgin land into his very own empire, and he would never have placed a square inch of it in jeopardy as she was doing. He would have known they'd all lose; he wouldn't have had a bar of this conversation about who owned what. Springfield mattered. That was the bottom line. He'd only left it to his two sons to keep the show on the road, to men who would not fail him. It had nothing to do with Charlotte. Harry, he'd been convinced, wasn't up to it; that left only Victor and Rupe, and Rupe knew that given more time, his father, who had become increasingly reliant on his eldest son, might even have left the whole shebang to Victor.

In fact, he mused, none of them had measured up to the big boss, they had always run a bad second to his dream for Springfield, which was now being threatened from within the ranks. And that could not be permitted. At least Rupe had the wit to appear weak, and by doing so had kept Charlotte on his side. After all, Louisa had taken the lead. It would be amusing to hang the blame on her when Victor protested.

'I have to say,' Rupe announced, 'that Louisa is right . . . although I wouldn't put it quite so bluntly. Since Mother really believes that she has been treated unfairly, I don't think that, as gentlemen, we can do other than stand aside. Family quarrels are so crass.' He gave his mother a winning smile. 'We should include Mother in the ownership of Springfield. One-third share.' He had deliberately repeated 'mother', not the insulting 'her' that Louisa had used.

'What!' Victor gasped. 'You were adamant that we should hold to Austin's wishes. He left Springfield to us.'

'Yes. But I realize now how deeply Mother cares about this.'

'Enough to threaten to fragment the property!' Victor snorted.

Rupe gave Charlotte an understanding glance. 'I don't think that would have happened. Mother was only working from a sense of hurt.'

Charlotte said nothing. Victor seemed intent on watching the maids clearing the soup plates and serving the next course. They placed tureens of vegetables on the table and took the platter of thickly sliced ham to each diner.

One of the girls addressed Charlotte before retreating. 'Mrs Broderick, the cook said to tell you there's plenty more ham. She's keeping it hot in the oven if anyone wants more.'

'Just a minute,' Louisa called to her. 'You forgot the mustard sauce.'

But Charlotte waved the maid on. 'It's quite all right. I told Hannah not to bother with the sauce. There's a white sauce on the cauliflower. We don't need two.'

Louisa pursed her lips and sat. Rigid.

Her husband didn't notice the exchange. 'All right. If you insist, Mother, and Rupe is now in agreement with you, I won't stand in your way. I'll have the papers drawn up.'

Cheered, she nodded. 'It's still in the family, Victor. But thank you. This ham looks delicious. Would you cut it for me, Rupe. This arm . . .'

Problems didn't affect Victor's appetite. He was halfway through his meal before he spoke again. 'I take it, then, that we can buy back your block and Fern's at the freehold cost price?'

'Yes.' Charlotte wasn't one to crow. She showed no emotion at all.

'And we will immediately put Fern's block on the market at a higher price. That's essential to raise funds. We are also tightening up our boundaries by selling off three other outlying blocks, which will relieve us of the necessity to employ outstation managers. You do understand why we must do this, Mother?'

'Yes. Very sensible. We're all agreed, then. It is a great relief to have this matter settled amicably. Would anyone like a second helping of ham?'

When both of the men nodded, she rang her little silver bell for service.

Charlotte wasted no time. The letter was written that night, signed by both Victor and Rupe and sent, first thing in the morning, to their lawyer, William Pottinger. Everyone was in a good mood again, except Louisa.

'Don't worry about Charlotte, she's just being a new broom,' Victor told her in the privacy of their room. 'Once she starts on her gardening again, and gets busy round the place, she won't bother you. Everything will be normal again.'

'I know. But it was so nice to be able to live as we wanted for a while. And don't remind me that it's her house. She's already made that plain. You realize that she has come off better than any of us, with the house and the share.'

Victor was tired of the carping. 'She is Austin's widow and this is her house.'

'And now, with no outstation, we can't get rid of Rupe either. I'm not still angry with him about Teddy, that's over, but he hasn't changed.

He's still as spiteful as ever. He went out of his road to show us up tonight. He could have told us he intended to dress for dinner.'

'Don't worry about Rupe,' his brother said thoughtfully. 'I don't think he's staying.'

'Really?' That was the best news Louisa had heard all day. 'What will he do?'

'He wants to travel. Go overseas.'

'When did you hear this?'

'We had a talk in the wool sheds this morning. They're all ready. Shearers should be here today. I reckon we'll have a bumper wool clip this year. The profits won't be so high because we'll have to put cash aside for freeholding, but the sale of those four blocks will give us a head start. I believe selectors are paying crazy prices to get in on the rush.'

'Yes, but what about Rupe?'

'Well, he's entitled to a share of the profits, a third share only, but that serves him right, for buckling under to Charlotte. Anyway, it will be enough to keep him in fair style out there in the wide world.' He laughed. 'I'm sorry about you and Charlotte, nothing can be done there, but at least I won't have Rupe second-guessing me at every turn.'

'Or sniping at me. I think it's a brilliant idea. He can swan round the world for the rest of his life for all I care.'

When Charlotte heard of this arrangement, Rupe was already packing. 'You'll do no such thing,' she snapped. 'This is the busiest time of the year and you're marching out and leaving Victor to do all the work. You get back into some work clothes and make yourself useful.'

'Mother, you don't seem to understand. Everything's under control out there. Victor and I have an agreement. I'll be leaving on Saturday.'

'You leave and you won't get a penny. I watched this happen with Ada Crossley's brother for years and years. The station paying him for no good reason. It won't happen here. You'll pull your weight.'

Rupe continued to sort through his closets. 'Ada's brother, old Judge Walker, wasn't an owner. He relied on Jock's generosity. This is a different situation. I will simply become a silent partner in this business.'

'Silent partner. I never heard of such a thing.'

'Well, you have now. I presume you will be taking your share of the profits too. Just as I will do. Neither of us is needed here, Mother, face facts. You're too old and I don't fit in.'

'Oh, you're a great talker, Rupe. You may be able to kid Victor into agreeing with you, but don't try it on me.'

Nevertheless, Charlotte was rather thrown off balance by his retort. Was she too old to be of use here any more? Was that what they thought of her? As she tramped down to the wool sheds in search of

Victor, she worried about her contribution. She helped with the cooking, she met the shearers and saw to it that they were all content with their temporary lodgings, she arranged the annual wind-up parties, she was always busy. Even in quieter times. There was always something to do. She tightened the scarf round her hair and hitched up her work skirt. Oh, no. She wouldn't allow them to pension her off.

She passed the pens where hundreds of sheep were being mustered for their turn in the sheds, breathing in the old familiar smell of the impatient, jostling animals, of their thick wool and their dirt and the ever-present clouds of dust. She passed men who acknowledged the lady of the house with a friendly nod, and panting sheepdogs that allowed her a quick gaze before they turned back to their charges, business as usual; and then she laughed. What a fool I am. Rupe could talk the handle off an iron pot, Austin always said. And he nearly had me in too. Damnit! I like living here. I like all this. The stink and the sweat of the wool sheds in action is only part of it. The station is alive all year round, it is always exciting, each season is different, and I'll be on my feet for a long time yet. Women do what they have to do on stations, big or small. They don't sign work sheets. And they don't have to give an assessment of their contributions to the workforce.

She decided not to bother Victor. It was more fun to hang over the rails and watch the sheep clambering up the ramps, while in the distance she could see more of the animals being moved forward like a grey carpet across the valley. Thousands of sheep, well cared for, well fed, were on their way to shed their precious woolly coats in preparation for summer. From habit she looked up gratefully at the blue skies. Bad weather spelled disaster for newly shorn sheep.

That night, though, she made her position plain. 'Rupe can go wherever he pleases. But under no circumstances will we bankroll him. Is that clear, Victor?'

'Yes. I know. He told me. He's threatening to cancel you out again. To renege on giving you your share.'

She smiled. 'I thought he'd try that on you. He's bluffing. Rupe knows where his bread's buttered. He won't take us both on.'

Charlotte was right. Rupe calmed down and Victor, now acting as peacemaker, persuaded him to stay on until after the shearing.

'When things are quieter,' he said. 'Just to give Charlotte time to get used to the idea.'

Louisa was unimpressed. 'She won't let him go. Now we really are stuck with him.'

At the same time, Theo Logan was stuck with this kid called Bobbo. It had taken weeks to get the frail lad back on his feet by feeding him a little more each day so that the small belly could cope. Even then, he hadn't been entirely successful, because the kid had broken out in boils all over his body and the doctor had to be called to minister to him. Theo knew about boils, but boils *en masse* gave him quite a turn. He thought it might be the dreaded chickenpox. He couldn't have that on board, his passengers would run a mile.

The doctor wasn't concerned, though. He lanced several of the boils – not an easy job, with the kid fighting, scared out of his wits – bandaged him to stop him scratching, and placed him back in his makeshift bunk in Theo's storeroom, with instructions to allow the poultices to do the work.

Although Theo put word out all along the river that he had a lost black kid on his hands, no one came forward, no one could identify him. And to make matters worse, the kid had become attached to him.

'Like a bloody dog,' Theo retorted when Barney mentioned this. 'Only because I feed him.'

But the two deckhands considered the situation very comical. They couldn't conceive how anyone could like their cranky boss, especially when he never had a kind word for the kid, short of grunts in his presence and instructions to the deckies to keep him out of the way.

What they didn't know was that at night, as the *Marigold* lay at anchor by the Somerset wharf, Theo sat with the child, keeping him company in an effort to alleviate his suffering. It didn't occur to him to tell Bobbo stories or to invent any childish games, because he had never had that experience himself; he simply lit his pipe and sat there surrounded by tight shelves of spare parts and tins of food and other odds and ends, thinking of nothing in particular, and the child did the same, until his eyelids drooped and he fell asleep.

When Bobbo began to recover from the onslaught of the boils, Theo deemed it time to find out who the kid was and where he had come from so that he could offload him. He didn't realize that his gruff approach endeared him to Bobbo, making the boy understand that this big man was not a threat. Willingly he answered the questions, insisting that he was going home.

'Over dere,' he told Theo. 'I go over dere.'

With difficulty Theo managed to discover that Bobbo and two of his friends had been brought to the town by a prayer man and his missus. He gathered that was a priest or a minister, which gave him no solace, since Theo had no time for religion except for the day of his marriage, which had been a necessity for legal reasons. For his part, to keep these conversations going, the Captain also had to answer queries thought up by the lively mind of this damn kid. Where was his missus? Where was his mumma? Did he own this big boat? Why didn't he have any sheep? Where was his mob? His people? And bit by bit, Theo gleaned a little more about the child's background.

Finally he worked out that the kid, and maybe several others, had been brought to town and put in an orphanage, but this one had bolted. Theo liked that. He didn't say so, of course, but respect grew for the sheer cheek of the kid to escape and try to find his way home. After all, the boy was no more than seven years old.

'You won't take me back to them bashers, will you, Captain?' Bobbo asked him earnestly, and Theo laughed. Bashers! He'd obviously learned that word from the other kids in the orphanage and it told its own tale. Interested, he asked for more information about 'that place', as Bobbo called the orphanage, and hearing from the wide-eyed fearful child, who was too young to lie, of the brutal treatment meted out there he was enraged.

'No, mate. I won't take you back.'

But then there was the problem of home, wherever that was. He had to explain to Bobbo that his home was not across the river. Not in these parts anyway, even if the boy did recall crossing the river over a big bridge. Amazing what kids noticed. He had to persuade him that it wouldn't do any good dropping him on the other bank. He'd only get lost again. His home could be hundreds of miles away. Then, with a sigh, he tried to make the kid understand what a mile was. That took time, because he had no concept of distance, but by this, Bobbo was aware of their daily voyages and the various landings, so Theo hoped the message was sinking in. He began to fear that his bolter would take off again and fare worse next time, so he lectured Bobbo sternly about staying on board until he could find his home for him, and Bobbo, eyes full of trust, agreed.

He had the run of the ship. He became known as the cabin boy, and his gleeful smile captivated the passengers, but always Theo feared for him. He was afraid the kid would fall overboard, so one Sunday morning, their day off, he instructed Barney to teach Bobbo to swim, while he watched from the deck, shouting orders as Barney led the kid down from the river banks into the softly flowing waters. Intrigued, men fishing from the wharf in the early morning watched the process, but then there was laughter all round. The boy could already swim like a fish. He left Barney floundering.

Gradually Theo began to piece Bobbo's life together. He had lived with his mob on a sheep station by a big river and had been sent away to be civilized. The latter he had gleaned from interested passengers, who were always keen to put in their pennyworth.

'A common occurrence,' they informed him. 'The black kids have to be removed from their tribes and assimilated into white society. It's for the best.'

A growl grew within Theo, who recognized the heartache this child had undergone, this child who still cried out for his mother in his sleep, and who cringed away from Theo in fear – even from Theo – when he forgot he was supposed to speak English and lapsed into his own language. He began to make more enquiries about this system

359

of civilization of black kids, by force, and the more he heard the less he liked it. He thought of his own mother, who had fought crushing poverty to keep her four kids together, and what a howl they would all have put up if someone had stolen one of the bairns away for their own good. To tell the truth, Theo was having trouble understanding any of this. From the way people talked, he had an inkling that civilization meant Christianization, and he had a deep suspicion of folk who had the effrontery to call themselves good Christians.

Time passed. Bobbo scampered about the boat on the heels of the deckies. They gave him jobs, like polishing the brass, wiping down the seats for the passengers and picking up rubbish, anything to keep him occupied so that he would not bother the Captain, and at night, as his health and the weather improved, he played on the top deck with rope quoits while Theo sat, resting and thinking.

The Captain still didn't know where this Springfield place was and he had become wary of asking. To him, the kid was like an escaped prisoner, and Theo knew all about that. If he did find Bobbo's home, who was to say the same thing wouldn't happen again? The kid could be returned to his orphanage, his prison, and there'd be no hope for him then. There'd be no one to stand up for him.

It wasn't that he was fond of the bloody kid, he kept telling himself. Insisting. It was just *someone* had to look after him. What if he did end up back in an orphanage? This type of kid would do the same thing again. He'd bolt. And he'd starve. Or he'd get into bad company. And it wasn't as if he was any trouble on the boat. He wasn't cheeky or anything. Truly, the Captain feared for his little friend if he set him adrift, so he had a good idea. He began calling the child Robbie after the greatest poet of all time, and when people asked, he informed them that his cabin boy's name was Robert Burns. Ignoramuses, all of them, they never saw the connection.

Fern was surprised to find Charmaine Collins on her doorstep so early in the morning. 'My! You're an early bird! Do come in, Charmaine.'

'Oh no, I won't hold you up. You're a busy woman. I was just wondering if you knew where I could find Harry Broderick.'

'Certainly do. He's staying here with me. Come in, I'll get him for you. I presume you do want to see him?'

'Yes, indeed. If I'm not intruding.'

'Not at all. It's nice to see you.' She led her visitor into the parlour. 'How is Angus? I hear he wasn't well.'

'He has recovered now. It was a mild heart attack. The doctor says he ought to retire but you know Angus. He seems to believe the entire law firm will collapse without him, even though both of our sons are there now.'

Fern smiled. 'He probably can't imagine his days without his legal

360

work. Whenever I think of retiring from the shop, I start to worry about having nothing to do . . .'

'Oh, you!' Charmaine snorted. 'You look as fit as a trout! You're a long way from retirement.'

'Thank you. I'm glad you think so. Just a minute . . .'

She came back with Harry, who was hastily fixing his tie. 'Mrs Collins. What a pleasure to see you again. You're looking well.'

Charmaine thought he did too. Clear-eyed, healthy. No sign of that so-called nervous breakdown. 'Thank you, Harry. I hope I didn't interrupt your breakfast.'

'No, the aunt here has me up and fed before she goes off to her office, deserting me.'

'Well, I won't keep either of you. I'll tell you why I'm here. I'm on the ladies' committee for the Welfare Association, and we are involved with the upkeep of the workhouse. That place keeps us busy, believe me. But that's another story. I saw you there yesterday, Harry. I believe you were enquiring as to the whereabouts of some black children.'

'That's right,' Harry said dismally. 'I'm looking for these kids and thought there might be a chance of finding them there. Unfortunately it was just another dead end.'

'But they were there!' she said excitedly. 'They were. I distinctly remember them.'

'The manager said they don't take orphans. We searched the books. There's no record of them. Surely he wouldn't deceive me?'

'Goodness, no. The poor fellow is doing his best against fearful odds. From what I recall, three children were dumped at the gate. One was called Bobbo, another one was Jack, I think, and . . . no, I can't remember the name of the third . . .'

'That's them!' Harry cried. 'Why didn't the manager tell me?'

'Because he didn't know about them. It was before his time. We had an excellent matron then, but she retired, unfortunately. However, she couldn't turn the children out, so she kept them there, off the record, you understand, until she could find homes for them. They had the run of the place.'

'Were they well treated?'

'They were not ill-treated, but it was hardly an environment for children, mingling with all sorts of riff-raff, as well as being unofficial inmates.'

'Who was this matron?'

'Her name was Molly Giles. Her brother worked there too. His name was Buster, not too bright, poor fellow, but good-hearted.'

'Is he still there?'

'No, he was put off in the general shake-up of staff.'

Harry sighed. 'I believe Bobbo was placed in an orphanage.'

'Yes. That'd be right. He went first.'

'He ran off from the orphanage. I thought he might have gone

361

back to the workhouse, but apparently not. I'll have to find Matron Giles. She might know where they are now.'

Mrs Collins, pleased with herself, smiled at him. 'I can do better than that. One of those children, Jack, a pretty little boy, was taken in by a Mrs Adam Smith. Do you know her?'

He shook his head. 'I don't think so.'

'I must admit I thought it was rather foolish of the woman at the time. I don't wish to be critical of her, because I know she thought she was doing a good deed, and indeed, one can't argue with that, but . . . what can I say here? She treated him extremely well, but he was like a doll to her. Sadly it was rather a joke among the ladies who visited her house. She dressed him up in fancy clothes. That sort of thing.'

'Is he still there? It sounds like Jagga.'

'Could be. I can give you her address. I haven't seen her for ages. She only came to the workhouse a couple of times. That sort of charity work isn't for everyone, you understand. Some women don't have the stomach for it.'

Fern produced pencil and paper and took down Mrs Smith's address. 'Do you happen to know that matron's address, Charmaine?'

'No. But she did tell me she was retiring to her cottage in Camp Hill. I'm guessing her address would be on file at the workhouse. She was a very efficient woman.'

Harry sat back. 'Mrs Collins, I can't tell you how grateful I am to you for all this help. It's just wonderful!'

'Then you might satisfy my curiosity. What's this all about? Who are these children?'

Harry didn't want to involve her in a discussion on the rights and wrongs of the disposition of black children, so he made his explanation short and to the point. 'We had an accident at Springfield. My little nephew fell in the river. He would have drowned had an Aborigine woman not spotted him and dived in to rescue him. Naturally we were all very grateful to her. It turned out that some time ago her little son and two others were taken from Springfield by missionaries to be educated, as part of the church and Government programmes, which I'm sure you know about.'

She nodded.

'So I promised this woman – Nioka, her name is – that I would look up those little boys and see how they were getting along. I felt it was the least I could do.'

She nodded again. 'Of course.'

'But when I arrived in Brisbane I discovered that these missionaries were fly-by-nights. Humbugs actually. They only used the story of helping the children to reap donations. The Church of the Holy Word no longer exists and the principals have fled. Having no further use for those poor little boys, they must have dumped them at the workhouse.'

'Shocking!'

'So you see,' Fern explained, 'what a spot Harry was in. He could hardly go back to the woman and tell her he couldn't find their children. Which one is Nioka's child, Harry?'

'Jagga. At least we've found him. That's a start.'

'Well, I'm glad I was able to help. I must be getting along now.'

'You mustn't rush off,' Fern said. 'Do stay for coffee, or a cup of tea.'

'No.' She stood. 'Thank you, Fern, another time. I've got a meeting to attend this morning, you have to get to that shop of yours, and I know Harry will be very busy today. But you will let me know how it turns out, won't you?'

'Of course we will,' Harry smiled.

'And do give my regards to Connie. How is she?'

'Very well, thank you. She's expecting,' he said proudly.

'That is good news. God bless you both.'

'I'm sorry, sir,' the maid said. 'Mrs Smith is not at home.'

'Oh. That's a shame. Would Mr Smith be in, by any chance?'

'He's at his office, sir. Would you care to leave your card?'

Harry's hand went to take out his wallet, but then he grinned, remembering he no longer carried cards.

'My name is Harry Broderick,' he said. 'When do you expect Mrs Smith back?'

'Not until this afternoon.'

'What if I came back at five?'

'I'm sure they'll both be in then.'

'Good. By the way, is Jack in?'

'Who's Jack?'

'The little Aborigine boy. Their ward, I believe.'

'Oh, no. He isn't here any more. He hasn't been here for a good while.'

Disappointment clouded Harry's face. 'He's not here? Where is he then?'

The maid, sensing a problem, backed away. 'I don't rightly know. You stay here, I'll ask Cook.'

There was a delay, but finally an angular, grey-haired woman came to the door. 'You looking for little Jack?'

'Yes. Actually I am. That's why I'm here.'

'And you are Mr Broderick?'

'Yes.'

'Why didn't you ask Mr Smith, at his place of work?'

'I don't know Mr Smith, or Mrs Smith, for that matter. I'm simply looking for Jack.'

'Why? Is he lost?'

'To me he is. And to his parents. He was taken away against their will, and they're very upset. I need to find him, madam. Can you tell me where he went from here? He was living here, wasn't he?'

She sighed, relenting. 'Yes, and a good little fellow he was too.' She stepped out on to the porch and took him aside. 'Listen, you won't tell anyone I talked, will you? Could be worth my job.'

'No. You have my word.'

'All right. Mrs Smith brung him home, tried to turn him into something out of a pitcher book, but he couldn't make no sense of this house.' She sniffed. 'Some of us have the same trouble, what with her airs and graces. He was homesick. Real miserable. Played up on her. Didn't mind the master, but what could he do? He's at work all day. In the end she got sick of him.'

'Sick of Jagga? I mean, Jack?'

'Yes, that's what I said. She lost interest, like she does with all her bright ideas. They never last long . . .'

'So what happened?'

'The master took him away. All dressed up nice he was too. Made me sick to see, it did, like an innocent puppy being taken to the pound.'

'For God's sake! Where did he take him? To an orphanage?'

'No. To the blacks' reserve, out past Ipswich somewhere. The missus was all talk about how well off he'd be there, with his own people, how she'd miss him and all that, but it was just excuses . . .'

'A reserve? At that age? None of his people are there. He comes from way out west.'

She frowned. 'How come he was in Brisbane? A little tot like that? Don't sound to me as if any of youse have been doing much of a job of looking after him.'

'I know. It was all a terrible mistake. That's why I have been trying to find him.' He took a half-crown from his pocket. 'This is from Jack. At least he found a friend in you. Thank you for your help. There's no need to tell the Smiths I called. I don't think we'd have much in common.'

'Looks like you've got another customer,' Buster said as he watched the big fellow dismount from his horse and hitch it to the front gate.

'Close those curtains,' Molly admonished him. 'It's rude to be peeping out like that. People will think you're spying on them. If he's got anything to say, he'll come to the door.'

Nevertheless, she did have a quick glimpse of the visitor and wouldn't have been surprised if this fellow was an expectant father, looking for the midwife. She waited until the brass door-knocker thumped, and opened up with a smile.

What can I do for you, young man?'

'Are you Matron Giles?'

'Yes.'

'May I come in?'

She ushered him into their tiny sitting room, glad that Buster had vacated, for there were only two armchairs. 'Now, what can I do for you?'

'My name is Harry Broderick. I come from Springfield station, up on the Downs. I've been searching for three little boys, three little Aborigine boys, and I'm told you might be able to help.'

Her heart sank. 'Oh, dear me. Do take a chair, Mr Broderick. I always hoped someone would come for them, but no one ever did.'

'I've heard from several people that you were good to them, and I can't thank you enough. We didn't know they were lost.'

'How can that be?'

Once again Harry related his story, and her reaction was outrage. 'Whoever thought of that idea of dragging kids away from their parents ought to be shot. Haven't we got enough beggars in our community without adding the blacks to them? I understand what you're saying, that these missionaries were humbugs – that's nothing new – but I have to ask you: why did you let them go?'

Rather than admit that the white folk at Springfield had given their approval, he answered lamely, 'I wasn't there.

'Look,' he added, 'I think I've found Jagga. He was with a Mr and Mrs Smith but they ended up sending him to a native reserve outside Ipswich.'

'Oh, dear God. Then there was Bobbo. We managed to get him into an orphanage . . .'

'He ran away. I'm still looking for him. I thought you might know where he is, and Doombie.'

She was very quiet. 'Doombie is here.'

'What?' His face lit up and he was almost out of his seat, but she motioned to him to be still. Her face was grave.

'Doombie was sickly at the workhouse. It's a hotbed of sickness, as you can imagine. My brother and I became very fond of him. We couldn't leave him there. When I retired, I brought Doombie home with me. He has been very happy here, he really has been, and it has been a great joy for us to have the child in the house.' She took a deep breath. 'Mr Broderick, I've had doctors to him, I've given him the best of care, but you might as well know, he has consumption.'

She took out a handkerchief to try to stem her tears, and Harry sat, stunned, distressed beyond words. He remembered those kids playing with Teddy, when he and Connie had gone home to Springfield for a break from city life, usually in the summer recess. They'd all been healthy and happy. At this minute, had he been able to get his hands on that rat of a Reverend Billings, he'd have beaten him to a pulp. He leaned forward, his elbow on his knee, and massaged his forehead, hoping the woman was exaggerating. Maybe she didn't want to give him up. Obviously she did love the child.

'Can I see him?' he asked, his voice a croak.

A voice from the passageway intruded. 'He mustn't be excited.' Harry guessed the brother must have been listening outside the door.

'It's all right, Buster,' the matron said gently. 'You bring in the washing.' Then, turning to Harry: 'My brother is terribly upset about Doombie. When the child first began to fail I had to ask him not to excite Doombie, because he loved to play with him. Now, it doesn't really matter any more, but I haven't the heart to tell him.'

'Oh, God. Is he that bad?'

'I'm afraid so.'

He followed her a few steps down a narrow hall into a very small bedroom. It looked like a hospital room, with a washstand covered in a white cloth holding a china jug and basin, and an array of medicines. A rack nearby held clean towels and a small rocking chair sat in the corner. The bed with its immaculate white sheets was only a single bed, but it looked huge when compared with its tiny occupant.

His dark skin was sallowed grey, his cheeks were hollow and thin arms rested on the covers, but his big eyes glittered with interest.

Harry swallowed a groan of despair. This was Doombie. There was even a family resemblance still; he could see Gabbidgee's facial structure and the wide, friendly smile. Poor Gabbidgee had always been a friendly fellow.

'You've got a visitor, darling,' Matron said. 'Do you remember Mr Broderick?'

'I hardly think he'd remember me,' Harry murmured, but Doombie thought he did.

'Him big boss,' he told her proudly.

'Springfield,' Harry reminded him, leaning over to kiss the child on the forehead, and taking his frail hand.

'Can I sit on the bed?' he asked the woman.

'Yes.'

He eased himself on to the side of the bed, not sure if he was causing any pain. 'I came to say hello. We all miss you, Doombie.'

To his surprise, Doombie broke into his own language, asking about his mother and father, as far as Harry could make out, so he made his best effort to reply in the dialect, which seemed to amuse the child. He was amazingly cheerful, but when he continued to rattle on in that language, Harry looked to the matron for guidance, wondering if this outburst might excite the patient. She nodded, encouragingly.

'Let him go,' she whispered. 'I think it is a relief for him not to have to be working so hard at English.'

Harry stayed. He had to resort to English to tell the boy about Gabbidgee and his mother, whose name he could not recall, and Nioka, chatting on as if they were all still at Springfield, just talking, pretending he could understand the child, who grasped his hand fiercely, as if afraid to let go of these beautiful memories.

Back in the sitting room, heartbroken, Harry asked, 'Is there any chance I can take him home to see his parents?' He was already thinking fast. He could telegraph Victor. Tell him to get the parents home. Nioka knew where they were.

'I'm sorry, Mr Broderick. He wouldn't last the distance.'

'I could take him by train. And then in a comfortable carriage. You could come too,' he said desperately. 'You could nurse him all the way. Please let me take him home.'

'I'm sorry. It's too late. Doombie hasn't much time left. You saw that fit of coughing he had.'

'What can we do? I can bring specialists. If it's money, Matron . . . ?'

She shook her head. 'I'd give anything to be able to reunite him with his parents, believe me, Mr Broderick. But you mustn't raise false hopes in people. The little love, he wouldn't make it.'

'I told him I'd come back tomorrow and bring him a present. Is that all right?'

'Yes. He likes ice-cream. That'd be a real treat for him.'

That night, Harry wrote another apologetic letter to Connie, but he had to leave it to Fern to explain the delay in an accompanying note. He was too upset to do it himself. Every day, without success, he scoured Brisbane for Bobbo, after his morning visit to Doombie armed with ice-cream and chocolate and fluffy toys. And in the back of his mind there was Jagga.

Harry and Matron and Buster were keeping vigil by Doombie's bed when the child, exhausted, closed his eyes for the last time, and Buster, the old ex-pugilist, wept as if his heart would break.

In Austin's time, mused Harry as the train charged across open country to Ipswich, travelling might have been slower but it was less complicated. When he had to come to Brisbane, his father would simply saddle up and head off. Several overnight stops made the journey a pleasure because other station owners welcomed the visitor. It was an opportunity for a yarn, comparing notes on the weather, wool and, of course, horses. Then the railway came. First to Ipswich and then stretching on to Toowoomba, and it couldn't be ignored, for speed was progress. Austin used to complain that you couldn't see anything from a train, and Harry was inclined to agree with him. He stared morosely out of the window. On horseback you saw the land, you noted the hints of changing weather, the greening after droughts or fires, the shy native animals, the sparkle of colour in what seemed drab bush. Always there was something different to come across. He looked at his fellow passengers, who seemed as bored as he was.

At Ipswich he'd have to leave the train and hire a horse to get himself out to this Aborigine reserve, bring the animal back later and then board a train again. To where? On to Toowoomba or back to Brisbane? It would depend on what he found at the reserve. Would Jagga still be there? The way these kids had been handed about, he very much doubted it, but he had to try. Harry dreaded being told that Jagga had been sent from there to a Brisbane orphanage. It wouldn't surprise him; the child was known as an orphan. What was the point of dumping him in an Aborigine camp among strangers? From what he'd heard, none of the blacks went there voluntarily, and they were all lumped in together no matter what tribe or clan. That in itself, to a man like Harry, who knew the blacks, spelled trouble. Their laws were very specific about skin associations.

When he stepped on to the platform Harry was so depressed he almost stayed to board the train again to head on up the range to Toowoomba. At least he had a horse stabled there to take him home. But once again, what home? To Tirrabee station and Connie? Or out to Springfield, where he would have to face Nioka and tell her he'd failed. Poor little Doombie had died, Bobbo could not be found, and her own son, Jagga, God help him, had been dragged from pillar to post and ended up displaced like countless others of his race. What if Bobbo and Jagga had caught consumption too? They wouldn't have any resistance either. Maybe that was why he couldn't find Bobbo.

That thought spurred him into action. There was still a chance of finding Jagga, and time could be against him. His conscience would not allow him to shirk this one last effort. Fruitless though it might be, it was another lead, and it had to be followed through.

Worrying about Connie, he prayed it wouldn't lead him back to Brisbane.

For a hired nag, this horse, a hefty bay, was splendid, and it took to the open road with such vigour that Harry guessed it rarely had the opportunity to be given its head. Probably only used by town-dwelling ladies and lads on fashionable local trails. He liked the horse and thought it was rather sad to have to return it to its stables.

'Sorry, old mate,' he said as they paced out across the plains. 'I'd like to keep you, but no matter what happens here, I have to get back on the bloody train. It doesn't detour like a man can do on a horse.'

Following the directions he had been given, back at the Ipswich stables, Harry came to the open gate of the reserve. There were no signs of any sort to designate the role of what appeared to him to be a treeless expanse of humpies and shanties, but by the gate was a neat timber building that had obviously been built by the state. It was an exact copy of hundreds of country police stations, with steps up to a narrow veranda and a counter directly inside the front door.

Several oddly clad Aborigines who were hanging about the entrance looked at him curiously as he passed by, and he nodded to them. 'Where's the boss?'

They pointed up the steps and he strode on by with a nod. He did not notice the black child in a grubby white shirt who had come scampering round the corner, only to stop dead and stare at him, scratching his head.

Jagga checked out every new arrival in his constant watch for his friends, and although he had no children with him, this big white man, he knew, was someone. Someone familiar. He stood for a moment, rubbing a bare foot against the other leg in an awkward stance, as he searched a confusion of memories. This man, he knew, was a big white boss. From somewhere. Somewhere? And that somewhere was a good place.

He followed him up the steps, sneaking a look round the door as the visitor started to talk to the camp boss, who was standing behind his counter. He couldn't figure out exactly what they were talking about, but then he heard his name. The white boss had spoken his name, not Jack, but Jagga. Jagga! He inched across the wooden floor and tugged on the newcomer's jacket, so lightly, so carefully, that it was hardly a movement.

The camp boss gave a big, booming laugh. 'You're looking for Jagga, mate? The little bugger never misses a trick! Who's that on your coat-tails?'

Harry turned about and stared at the kid. He was so accustomed to failure that he was suspicious. He didn't recognize this grimy child. How could he? Victor and Rupe knew Jagga better than he did, he'd been living in Brisbane for years. What a fool he'd been to think he could just walk in and claim any of these children.

'Are you Jagga?' he asked.

'Too right, boss. Me Jagga.'

He could be anyone, Harry worried. Aborigines, and not only the kids, were famous for telling white people what they wanted to hear, with scant regard to fact.

There was a wooden bench along the wall, so Harry walked over and sat down to talk to the child. It would lend insult to injury if he brought the wrong one home. For all he knew, Jagga could be a name as common as Jim.

'Where do you come from?' he asked.

'Out dere.'

'What's out there?'

Puzzled, the child shook his head.

'What's your mother's name?'

That too posed a problem. 'Maggie?' the child offered enthusiastically.

'She's the old girl that's been looking after him here,' the manager told Harry.

'Springfield,' Harry tried. 'You know that place?' He was being careful not to prompt.

'Yeah. Good place that,' said the boy.

'What sort of place?'

That didn't help either. Jagga couldn't offer any further information on the subject.

369

'Do you remember Mrs Smith?'

'The pretty lady? She comen back for me?'

Harry still had a nagging concern. Was this really Nioka's boy? What if he'd answered to Jagga just to please the white boss? He should have stayed and spoken to Mr and Mrs Smith to find out what they knew about the lad. If he had talked to them about his family. There was no proof, really, that this child was the right one. Only hearsay.

He decided to test the boy.

'Is your name Billy?'

He blinked. 'Not Billy, mister.'

'Is it Bobbo?'

The child's eyes lit up with excitement. 'You got Bobbo, mister? You bringin' Bobbo here? You tell him Jagga mind him real good.'

'Who is Bobbo?'

'He me friend. You got Doombie too?'

Harry sighed, took the child in his arms and hugged him. 'You remember Springfield, don't you? Your mummy, Nioka? She sent me to find you. She's waiting for you. I'm going to take you home.'

'Nioka. You bring my mumma here too?'

'No. I'm taking you home.' Harry was so relieved, he felt emotionally drained. He looked over to the manager of this place, expecting a similar reaction, but the fellow's face was set hard.

'I thought you was just a visitor. Don't be filling his head with this tale. He can't leave here. They're all wards of the state. Once they're in here, they stay.'

'You don't understand. This was all a mistake. He shouldn't be here. This child has a home at Springfield station.'

'Never heard of it.'

'I wouldn't expect you to. It's a long way from here, out on the western Downs, but the child belongs there and I have to take him home.'

'Oh no you don't. Not without the permission of a magistrate.' That's the law.'

Harry argued, cajoled, wondered if he should offer a bribe, then had a better idea.

'You don't seem to realize who I am, sir. I am Harry Broderick, a Member of Parliament, in the Premier's party. I doubt the Premier will be pleased to hear that you place the merits of some country magistrate above the rights of a legislator. Sign this child out immediately!'

The lie worked. The paperwork took a bare few minutes. The child had no belongings to collect. Harry picked him up and marched out of the gate with him, placing him on the horse and mounting up behind him. Neither of them looked back.

As the bay took them out on to the long, sandy road, Jagga was bewildered. And probably not for the first time, Harry thought.

'Where we go now?'

'You ever had a ride on a train?'

'No . . . ooo.' The dark eyes lit up with awe. 'A real train?'

'Yes. Then we find your mummy.'

After the excitement of the train came the more tedious leg of the journey. Harry collected his horse and rode out with Jagga mounted up in front of him again, strapped to his belt in case he dozed and fell. So as not to tire the child, he rode carefully, spacing the journey out over several days by staying with friends along the route.

The child was a chatterer but his talk was disjointed, confused and laced with a bravado that saddened Harry, who realized it was an instinct to survive in a bewildering world. To pass the time and keep Jagga occupied, he resorted to the childish games of counting kookaburras, or magpies, or black horses. After rest stops, he'd switch to pointing out plants, trees or flowers, giving the English names and asking Jagga to provide the Aborigine equivalent. At least the games provided some mirth and competition, fending off the boy's restlessness to some degree.

By the time they were, finally, past Cobbside and on the road to Springfield, the boy was quiet, but Harry knew he was wide awake, doing what children do best, observing intently without comment. Jagga was quick-witted. Did he feel he knew this road? Harry wondered. Was it reminding him of the strangeness of his departure? Did he really believe he was being taken home to his mother, or was he steeling himself for another disappointment?

For Harry, there was anguish in the seeming droop of the dry bush, in the hollow quark of noisy friar birds and the brooding eyes of watchful crows, as if his secret was known only too well, and the loss of two bush children weighed heavily.

It was dark when they rode past the tall pines, making for the lights of the homestead. Jagga was sitting sideways, asleep at last, leaning against Harry's chest. He didn't have the heart to wake the boy, even to tell him he was home.

They were all amazed when Harry marched into the house carrying Jagga, but he grinned at them and went on through to the kitchen, knowing he'd find Nioka out there somewhere.

She stood at the door, dumbfounded, when Hannah called her, and for a minute she could hardly believe her eyes, but there he was, her boy, her Jagga, drowsily stirring in Harry Broderick's arms, and behind him, crowding into the kitchen, were all the others. Missus Louisa was crying. Then Nioka moved quietly, cautiously across the stone floor, around the large scrubbed kitchen table, tears streaming as Harry handed her her son.

Later, Harry sat outside with her to answer the inevitable question: 'Where are the others?'

371

Broken-hearted, Nioka blamed herself. Sobbing, she told Harry she should have been minding them herself that day, not leaving the children to others who were too shy to put up a fight. She was shocked to hear that Doombie had died so far from his family and his Dreaming, fearful that his little spirit would never find its way back. She was afraid that Bobbo, too, had died, and Harry tried to convince her, without much success, that her nephew would come home one day, just like Jagga.

'Another Mrs Broderick, my auntie,' he explained, 'has promised that she will keep looking for Bobbo. She lives in Brisbane. She'll find him.'

Eventually, he sat down for dinner with his own family to explain the search to them. Knowing that recriminations were pointless, because they really were upset by the death of Doombie and the loss of Bobbo, and by the horrendous tale of the missionaries.

'I never did like that bastard,' Victor said.

Then Harry looked at them, Victor and Louisa and Charlotte, all hugely interested in his travels . . .

'Where's Rupe?'

Charlotte shifted uncomfortably in her chair, and sighed. 'That's another story.'

Chapter Fifteen

Charlotte was feeling rather smug. She'd had two letters from her new lawyer, Mr Winters. Both were business-related, but the second ended on a more personal note, hoping that it would not be too long before she came to Brisbane again. The town, he added, was coming along in leaps and there was much to see.

Her cheeks tingling, she thought it was quite forward of him, but at the same time she defended him. Why shouldn't he be a little forward if he felt like it? People were entirely too stuffy about these things. Besides, he was a personable chap and, she'd ascertained, a widower. Mr Winters, more than anyone else, understood how remote a widow felt, even in family circles. When she'd first met him, she'd been startled that she found the gentleman quite attractive, but of course she hadn't mentioned that to Fern. Finding a man attractive and being interested in him were two different things. She didn't want Fern teasing her. Anyway, Charlotte knew she was no oil painting; why would such a charming man be interested in *her*, apart from business?

Still, she smiled as she wrote her reply, expanding into a cheerful description of busy days on the station, with so many shearers hard at work in the famous wool shed. It was nice to have someone to write to, even if the correspondence was only based on polite pleasantries. Nevertheless, she kept his letters in her room, away from prying eyes.

Softened by this exchange, Charlotte looked kindly on Louisa at lunch, which they usually took together. The men in the family rarely came in, unless they were working close by. And at shearing time they ate with the workmen at midday.

'I was thinking,' she said, 'that we ought to get away from Springfield more often. It doesn't seem right for you to have to be buried out here. Or me, for that matter.'

Louisa gaped. 'Like when? Victor thinks he's chained to the station. He thinks everything will collapse if he leaves, even for a day.'

'I know. He works hard. But Rupe's here. You ought to make time to take a few weeks off. Go to Brisbane. Or the seaside.'

'Can we afford it?'

'Dear me. A cottage by the sea, down at the south coast, can be rented for a few pounds. And Fern would put you up in Brisbane. It's up to you. Austin took time off whenever it suited him. Why shouldn't Victor? And while you're here, I don't need to be about. I think it would be nice to be able to spend time in Brisbane. That town is coming along in leaps and bounds, you know. There's so much to see. Really, you ought to plan to go to the seaside in the summer and Brisbane in the winter.'

Her daughter-in-law gulped. She passed a bowl over to Charlotte. 'Would you like some banana custard?'

'Yes, please. And I'll have some cream too.

'I would have liked to take more holidays when Austin was alive, when money was no object. We could have gone anywhere in the world but he only liked to go to Brisbane to catch up with his friends. Don't let that happen to you, Louisa. We'll get over this bad patch in a few years and the Springfield Pastoral Company will be more valuable than Springfield ever was, with the price of land sky-rocketing.'

Faced with this burst of benevolence, Louisa was afraid to say too little, or too much, for fear of breaking the spell, but she had to react. 'I hope we can convince Victor,' she mumbled gratefully.

On the other hand, Charlotte's youngest son was furious with her for upsetting his plans. Victor was weak. He'd always been weak, jumping to Austin's tune, and now to their mother's. How dare she tell him what he could and could not do! Who did she think she was? It was unbelievable that she should be able to step in and bully Victor into reneging on his promise to allow his brother to leave, with an annual remuneration. They didn't need him here, he was only playing second fiddle to Victor, and it was obvious that this would be his role for the rest of his life! And what if he married? They'd probably be magnanimous and give him a suite in this wasps' nest.

Well, if they thought he would settle for that, they had another think coming. Rupe considered reneging too. So much for Charlotte's gratitude! He'd stood up for her, allowing her into the firm, and what did he get in return? A big fat nothing. Maybe he ought to advise the lawyers that he'd changed his mind. Blow this new scheme laid out by Victor to form the Springfield Pastoral Company right out of the water. But he knew that, financially, that would be a serious mistake. If he blocked Charlotte at this point, the same thing would happen all over again. He'd known all along that she was not bluffing, regardless of what he'd told them.

Round and round the arguments raged in his head while he worked in the stinking wool shed, gathering up fleece and tossing it into the moving crates in the wake of the shearers, no more important in this system than Spinner, a blackfellow, who was working up ahead of him. Rupe couldn't shear sheep himself. He'd never learned, nor did he wish to. Victor could, at a pinch, but he preferred to leave the job to the professionals. It didn't seem to bother him that he, too, was no more than a labourer in the wool shed, an odd-job man, working where he was needed, all for the good of the family firm.

'Well, bugger them,' he muttered. They weren't going to turn him into a stockman. A half-shorn sheep slid away from a shearer's hands and Rupe kicked it, viciously, back into place.

'Hey! Fair go, mate!' the shearer protested, but Rupe ignored him, marching outside to have a smoke.

Victor's idea was brilliant. All the divisions of Springfield they'd marked off were of a size to be regarded as sheep runs, or small stations in their own right. Victor had decided that they should have new names, and Louisa and Charlotte were given the honour of naming them. They chose to call them after trees, Black Wattle station, Needlewood station, Mudgee station, Stringybark, and so on. Rupe wouldn't have cared if they'd called them by number, but listed as stations owned by the Springfield Pastoral Company they would be impressive.

The Government was now taking another measure to check dummying – the buying-up of more of their own land by squatters over and above the maximum – by transferring administrative powers from the Brisbane Lands Office to a local Land Commissioner, who would recognize any rascality, and Victor was very happy about that. The new Land Commissioner was an old mate of Austin's who had already indicated to his son that he would look the other way when it came to the Broderick lands.

Then there was the matter of Government-required improvements on these new stations, which had to be shown to inspectors within a certain time to prove that they were not being snapped up by speculators. Improvements quite often meant residences, even agriculture, but Victor had discovered that he could get round that requirement by some strategic fencing and new dams.

Rupe listened to Victor's explanation of the new processes of freeholding, which entailed licensed surveyors, notices in writing to the court sittings, and applications for Certificates of Fulfilment of Conditions of Purchase to be posted in the local Lands Office, and inserted three times in local papers, but it was all too complicated for him. He deemed it wiser to let Victor get on with founding a new empire of stations owned by the Springfield Pastoral Company.

If he threw a spanner in the works now, by denying Charlotte access to the company, he knew he would be cutting his own throat. Wrecking the birth of a magnificent family company.

He ground the cigarette butt in the dirt. Although he'd never say so, he had to hand it to Victor; he'd gone through those Government regulations with a fine-tooth comb, looking for loopholes, better than stupid Harry could ever have done.

At least Harry was out of the picture, one less to share with. Rupe grinned. Old Harry had done the smart thing marrying Connie Walker, but then he'd blown it. If he'd played his cards right, he'd be managing the entire Walker holdings now, instead of that pathetic Tirrabee.

Rupe returned to his own concerns and his rage at the way he was being treated. If he did not wish to live out here in the backblocks, they could not make him. But he would need money and he worried that they would refuse to pay him his share of the profits, the annual apportionment that was his right.

He stomped angrily away from the sheds to stare at the long drive that led from the homestead out to the main road. To freedom.

Then I'll sue them, he smirked. They won't like that. Another family scandal! And I'll win, because there's no law that says that as a legitimate part-owner I have to work here, any more than Charlotte does. I can turn that argument back in on them.

But whether they pay up on time or are forced to do so by the courts, he worried, there's still the problem of my upkeep in the meantime. I'll have to think on that. I suppose I could borrow from friends, but loans have to be repaid.

What to do when he left here, though? Hanging about Brisbane, living on loans, was a dead-end prospect, hardly the ticket to the sort of life he envisaged for himself, so Rupe had to give this serious consideration before he made a move.

Then it came to him. Cleo! With luck she'd still be in Brisbane, staying with her aunt. There was nothing to stop them picking up where they'd left off. She had been keen to marry him, she was in love. That wouldn't have changed. And how romantic it would seem for him to come after her, in person. He would go to her door like a real suitor, not the way they'd been here, meeting on the quiet; take her out, whisper sweet nothings, propose to her again. It would work. He could suggest they visit her father on his plantation in the north, where he could formally request Cleo's hand in marriage. Staying with her family for a few months would eliminate the need for board and lodgings, a huge saving. Not to mention a holiday in itself. It would be fascinating to visit the far north, see those tropical coastal towns. Rupe had always been keen to experience the tropics, the land of waving palms and balmy blue seas. The more he thought about it, the more excited he became. It would be heaven after this summer dust bowl. He might even like to live there. Her father could probably be encouraged to buy them a house, preferably near one of those sunny beaches, to keep his daughter within reach. It must be sad for him to have Cleo living so far away from home.

Cleo had said that Cairns was the nearest town to their plantation, and from what Rupe had read about the easy-going life in those frontier towns, it sounded just the place for a gentleman of leisure. Later they could afford to travel – or he could, if she was home with babies – but what a superb location, where a man could forget winter. And sheep. And his lousy family. Just sit back in the luxury of the tropics, and enjoy life.

He was so entranced with this plan, he didn't even consider returning to the sheds. The only thing holding him back now was cold, hard cash. Rather than having to borrow from friends, which was demeaning, to say the least, maybe there was another solution. Maybe there was . . .

'Where's Rupe?' Charlotte asked as they sat down to dinner. 'He's never on time for meals. You ought to have a quiet word with him, Victor. I don't think I'm in the good books at the minute. It's not fair on Hannah to be held up like this.'

'Me have a quiet word with him? I'll wring his neck. He just wandered away this afternoon, hours before knock-off time. He knows I need every hand in the sheds. He's just a bloody loafer.'

They began their meal, but when Rupe still didn't appear, Charlotte decided he must have come in during the afternoon to take a nap, so she sent a maid up to rouse him.

When the girl returned to tell them that Mr Rupe was not in his room, Victor nodded. 'I know where he's got to. There's a dance on over at Jock's place. A lot of our lads and the shearers went after work.'

Charlotte sighed. 'He could have said so. But a dance? Why didn't you and Louisa go?'

'Because we're not very popular with Ada Crossley,' Louisa said.

'Oh, goodness. You don't want to take any notice of Ada. She can get on her high horse at times, but she means well.'

'I hadn't noticed,' Louisa murmured, but she managed a smile, which surprised Victor and caused him to ponder that the two women seemed quite affable this evening. There was an absence of their usual sniping. Not for the world, though, would he comment; best to leave well alone. He launched into an enthusiastic report of the day's operations, pleased that the shearing was going smoothly and the weather was holding up.

'I miss Jack Ballard, though. I have to be everywhere, keeping them all moving. It was a mistake lending him to Harry at this time, but what else could I do?'

Louisa smiled. 'You did the right thing. We were both so grateful to Harry we'd have given him half the stockmen if he'd asked. Jack will be back soon. Harry said he wouldn't keep him long. He wouldn't have asked if he didn't need him. Your brother isn't as experienced in running a station as you are, darling.'

'I suppose so.' Mollified, Victor looked over at Rupe's empty place. 'Tell Hannah if there are any chops left, I'll have them, since Rupe's gone walkabout.'

In the morning at first light, Victor was in the kitchen with Hannah, nursing a mug of tea while she cooked his sausages and eggs, when a spokesman for the shearers came to the door.

'We've got a casualty, boss. One of our shearers, Les Bragg.'

377

'What happened to him?'

'Got boozed at the dance last night. Fell down and broke his wrist. He can't work.'

'All right. Send him up and I'll pay him off. Everyone else fit for work?'

The shearer laughed. 'They'll suffer, but they'll work.'

'Good.'

Victor sat at the scrubbed table, enjoying the breakfast that Hannah put in front of him. This was his favourite time of the day, and his favourite mealtime, because he didn't have to talk. Hannah understood that, and left him in peace as she began her day's work, allowing him to envisage with military precision the number of sheep his stockmen could bring up, in stages, without overstocking the maze of pens, or keeping the shearers waiting.

The sun was casting a pink dawn, which was a good sign, warmth for the shorn animals. He drank his second cup of tea, stood, thanked Hannah and headed for his office to put up Les Bragg's pay, deciding he might as well take the pay envelope to the sheds himself rather than wait for Bragg to come up to the house. Then he remembered Rupe, who hadn't surfaced yet.

'I don't care if you've got a king-sized hangover,' he muttered, taking the stairs three at a time, 'you'll front up like the rest of us, mate.'

But when he looked into the room, he saw the bed hadn't been slept in.

Why am I surprised? he asked himself. The bastard got boozed too, and stayed over. Rupe's a boss man! On principle he'll take his time getting home.

Annoyed and frustrated, Victor went back down to his office, knowing that he couldn't make Rupe work. He wondered if he shouldn't have a talk with Charlotte. It was more annoying to have to put up with Rupe loafing about the place than to let him go.

He took out his wages book. Worked out the number of days that Bragg had been working, and opened the safe to draw his pay from the wads of notes set aside for this purpose. All the shearers had to be paid in cash.

Then he stared into the dark interior of the heavy safe. It only had two ledges, containing papers and a cash box, a steel cash box. But the box was gone.

Disbelieving, he rummaged about, even though it was obvious that a box that size couldn't be hidden under a few papers.

Victor sat back on his haunches, stunned. 'We've been robbed!' he whispered. He looked about the room, bewildered. That box had contained hundreds of pounds, the pay for the shearers as well as an extra fifty or so for emergencies.

When his glance settled on his desk, he gave a sigh of relief. There was the cash box, large as life.

Embarrassed, he climbed to his feet. 'I must have left it out myself. What a bloody fool. You've got a safe and you forget to use it.' Although he couldn't recall leaving it out, relief flooded over him, along with a vow not to do such a stupid thing again. Not, he supposed, that anyone here would steal the money, but still . . . unwise.

The second shock had him reeling. The cash box was empty. He slumped into the chair by his desk. Who would do this? Not his own men. One of the shearers? Some of them were strangers, others barely known to the family. They were itinerants. But would one of them brazenly walk into the house and do this? Unlike Austin's rooms, Victor's office opened on to a courtyard that led through to the back yard beyond the kitchen. Could a man steal through the courtyard at night without the dogs creating a racket? Not likely. Victor found himself gazing at the windows, not fancy French windows here, because his office did not open on to a veranda, just plain windows.

What thief would bother closing the window after him? The only other access to this room was through the house.

Slowly, bile rising, Victor left his office and went upstairs. Before he raised the alarm, before he began accusing someone, he ought to check. No one need ever know about his suspicions if – as he hoped – they were unfounded. Rupe was still not in his room. His brother checked the big chest of drawers and the wardrobe. He knew every stitch of clothing that Rupe owned, and all the good clothes were gone. An ominous silence hung over the room as Victor saw what remained: work boots, work shirts and battered trousers, bush hats . . . Gone too, from the dressing table, was Rupe's silver brush and comb set. As if to further upset himself, as if he needed any more proof, Victor walked over to the washstand. No shaving gear, not even a toothbrush or dental paste. A clean sweep.

His brother had stolen away. And a large amount of cash had been stolen. Too much of a coincidence to be ignored.

'I don't believe it!' Charlotte gasped. 'How could you even suggest such a thing? It'll be one of the shearers. You get down there and demand that money be returned before the police are called in! And if you won't do it, I will.'

She swung her legs out of the bed, not caring that her nightdress was hiked up to her knees. 'Give me a hand! No, not you, Victor. You go and do as you're told. Louisa, just help me to my feet. This damned nightdress feels like a bloody straitjacket dragged on over this great lump of plaster. I'm not wearing one any more, not until they take this cast off.'

Despite the seriousness of the theft, Louisa grinned. 'I'll warn all comers.'

For propriety, Victor made a quick exit, but he had no intention of accusing any of the shearers. He didn't want to believe that Rupe could be guilty either, but everything pointed to him. Or did it? There were a few questions he could ask without giving the impression that anything was amiss. He ran down the back stairs and headed for the sheds.

'Was the safe locked?' Charlotte asked her daughter-in-law as she shed the billowy nightdress.

'It's never locked. You know that.'

'So that's our first lesson,' Charlotte grumbled. 'Make proper use of the damn thing. Pour some water in the basin for me, will you? I'll have a wash and get dressed right away.'

But Louisa sat her back on the bed. 'Don't be so independent. Sit there and I'll sponge you first. You'll feel better.' She sighed. 'There's nothing much we can do.'

'You don't really think it was Rupe?' Charlotte asked, a querulous note in her voice.

Louisa poured water from the china pitcher into the matching white basin. 'There doesn't seem to be any other explanation. Victor is terribly upset. He came up to me with a face as white as chalk. I thought he was sick. And he was, near enough. He went over and over what had happened, for a good hour, before he decided he would have to tell you.'

'Just the same, he shouldn't be jumping to conclusions.'

'You can't call his reaction jumping to conclusions, Charlotte.' Louisa dipped the sponge in the cool water and then squeezed it. 'Now sit still.'

While she bathed the woman and went through the awkward process of helping her to dress, Louisa tried to be noncommittal. She listened to Charlotte's anger, knowing that it was spiced with fear, and she felt sorry for her. From the minute she'd heard Victor's shocked story, Louisa had been certain that Rupe was the culprit, but she let him work through it himself rather than rely on her judgement, which could be construed as biased. Then, when he finally decided he'd have to tell Charlotte, he insisted she come with him for moral support. And just as well. Even now, Charlotte was trying to lay the blame on everyone except Rupe. Even on Victor.

'Are you sure the money is missing? It's quite possible that Victor has simply mislaid it. He can be quite absent-minded, you know.'

'We both searched the office, Charlotte. Only to set Victor's mind at rest. The cash box was open on the desk. That was clear enough.'

'But to be blaming Rupe . . . He only went to the dance last night. He'll be home soon.'

'With all his clothes? If you're ready, we can go down now.'

Charlotte fingered her hair nervously. 'I'm not going anywhere. I want to wait here for Victor. If we have things to talk about, best we do it here in my room, not downstairs with maids wandering about. I don't want them to think anything is wrong.'

380

'Hannah might, if we don't go down to breakfast.'

'Damn the breakfast!' Charlotte said illogically.

Louisa sighed. 'Well, I have to get Teddy dressed. Can I send you up some breakfast?'

'I'm not hungry. I told you, I'll wait here!'

After she had fed Teddy and made lame excuses to Hannah, who was bewildered that neither of the women seemed interested in breakfast, Louisa called to Nioka.

'Would you take Teddy for a walk? I'm busy this morning.'

The child was delighted. He loved Nioka and followed her about like a lamb.

'Can we go down and see the sheep?' he asked. Nioka nodded, pleasure lighting her face too. Louisa was just about to ask the black woman to be careful with him among all that boisterous activity when she checked herself. Nioka was the last person who needed to be told to take special care of her son.

When they had left, she took a cup of tea and sat on a bench on the back veranda, waiting for Victor, wondering what would be worse, a thief among the men, or a thief in the family.

It was frustrating, then, to see him return with one of the Springfield men and, with a smile for his wife, take the fellow on through to his office. What was going on? Maybe the problem had been sorted out after all. Victor hadn't seemed even slightly concerned.

Louisa decided she'd better take a tray up to Charlotte, who must be a nervous wreck by this.

On her way up, she was met by Victor, who opened his mother's door for her.

'What's happened, Victor? Has the money been found?'

He shrugged, ushered her inside and closed the door firmly behind them. Then he addressed both women.

'The priority is the cash. I have just sent to the bank for more. I must have it on hand to pay the shearers. I've got one leaving tomorrow. He broke his wrist so I told him he could rest up today. Any excuse. The bank won't ask questions, nor did the messenger, but I did mention that I must have under-calculated the amount I needed.' He looked at them grimly. 'Some miscalculation.'

Charlotte was on the defensive. 'Why did you have to do that? Didn't you bail them all up and advise them of the theft? Demand that the money be returned?'

'There was no need. Rupe has packed up and left. He did not go to the dance last night. One of the stockmen saw him riding out yesterday afternoon. He did not take a stockhorse, so he wasn't doing any work, he took Piper Lad.

'What conclusions would you draw, Mother?' he added bitterly.

'Yesterday afternoon?' she echoed. 'For all you know, Rupe might

381

have had an accident. A fall. He could be out there hurt.'

'If he's hurt, not on the property but on the main road, where he was heading, the stockman who just went to replenish my cash box will find him, won't he? We might even get our money back.'

'You're being sarcastic now!'

'No. I'm only thinking that the bugger has a head start on me of about eighteen hours, or I'd go after him. It's too late. He's gone and so has the pay.'

Charlotte shook her head. 'I can't believe this. There has to be some explanation. Rupe wouldn't do a thing like this.'

'Perhaps you'd like me to call the police?' he asked her quietly, but when she would not answer, he nodded. 'I thought so.'

'What's another story?' Harry asked, but Charlotte delayed her reply for the sake of privacy.

'We've finished dinner. Let's go into the parlour. We'll have coffee later.' She placed her napkin on the table, stood firmly and led them from the dining room.

Harry blinked, confused, as they trooped into the parlour and his mother instructed Victor to close the doors. Louisa was unusually quiet, Victor had seemed in a bad mood from the minute he'd walked in the door, and all through dinner, all through his account of his search, Charlotte had been impassive, almost unconcerned. It was by no means the reception he'd expected. He wondered if he had offended them by interfering, but if so, too bad.

Charlotte sat in her chair. 'Tell him, Victor.'

'Tell me what?'

'You asked about Rupe,' Victor said heavily, 'so I guess you might as well know.' He outlined the events concerning the theft, and the disappearance of their young brother, and then he sat back with a shrug.

Harry gave a low whistle of surprise. 'When did this happen?'

'Two days ago.'

Charlotte leaned forward to confront Harry. 'Do you think it was Rupe? I mean, it could have been anyone. The men are still all here, but one of them could have stolen the money and buried it until he was ready to leave. Do you see what I mean? That way he wouldn't be drawing attention to himself.'

Harry looked at her thoughtfully. 'It seems to me that the person who stole that cash couldn't care less about drawing attention to himself.'

'What do you mean?'

'Exactly.' Victor seemed relieved. 'That's what I've been trying to tell you, Mother. Rupe couldn't have made it more obvious if he'd run up a flag.'

Charlotte turned on Harry. 'You think he did it? Your own brother?'

'Yes.'

'Oh, dear God!' A flush crimsoned her face and she tried to cover it by searching her sleeve for a handkerchief. 'What can we do now?'

'What have you done?' Harry asked.

'Nothing, of course. Victor sent to the bank to replace the money, and I suppose that's that.'

'But what brought it on? Did you have a row or something?'

'Not really,' Charlotte said, but Louisa intervened.

'Yes, they did. They finally came to an agreement that Charlotte should own a third share of the property, which will be known as the Springfield Pastoral Company, and will encompass all the runs that they freehold.'

'Good. I'm glad to hear it.'

'But Rupe wanted to leave . . .'

'Uh-oh!' Harry grinned.

'Yes. He didn't like living here.'

'Or working,' Victor snapped.

'So Victor agreed that he could leave,' Louisa continued, 'and still receive an annual cheque as a one-third owner of the property.'

'Very generous, but not unheard of,' Harry commented. 'You were actually paying him to stay away, Victor.'

'Not exactly,' he muttered.

Charlotte spoke. 'Of course you were. And I wouldn't have it. Definitely not. A young man like Rupe, what sort of a giddy life would he live without any responsibilities? Without having to lift a finger to support himself? I still won't allow it.'

'By the sound of things there won't be much to share anyway,' Harry said, 'what with the costs of freeholding.'

'We're taking care of that. We're selling the outer runs to consolidate our boundaries. We'll have less acreage but a more compact set of properties that we can manage more easily from here.'

Harry was interested. 'That's an excellent solution. I was wondering how you would cope . . .'

Charlotte interrupted them. 'You can talk about that later. What can we do about Rupe?'

'I don't know.'

Victor frowned. 'You could suggest something.'

'What do you expect me to say? He's your problem. I'm not connected with the Springfield Pastoral Company in any way. Remember, Victor? Whether you like it or not, whether he works here or not, Rupe won't be backward in claiming his share of the annual divvy-up.'

'I'll bloody dock him what he has already taken. Stolen!'

'He'd be aware of that. He's not stupid.'

'Harry,' his mother looked at him earnestly, 'I was hoping that you'd go and find Rupe. Talk to him. Tell him that he must come back, and he must return that money . . .'

'No fear. I have to go home. I've been away longer than I expected. I'll be leaving in the morning. My shearers are due.'

'I can't go after him,' Victor said. 'You've got my foreman.'

'Come off it, Victor. You wouldn't go anyway.'

'So we just do nothing?' Charlotte looked to Victor.

'Not unless you want me to charge him and have the police haul him back.'

Louisa had been listening carefully. 'Does anyone mind if I have a say?'

'By all means.' Charlotte sat back, defeated.

'We can't drag Rupe back here, and to be truthful, I don't want him back. How big is Springfield compared to Tirrabee, Harry?'

Surprised by her seemingly irrelevant question, he answered simply: 'Oh, Lord! Springfield is ten times the size of Tirrabee.'

'Really. And what is your salary?'

'Ninety pounds a year with the house and upkeep thrown in. I'm on a pretty good wicket, considering it's a dream of a station, sheltered by the hills and well watered.'

'Thank you. In which case, as manager of Springfield, I think Victor should be paid at least five hundred pounds a year.'

'That's outrageous!' Charlotte cried. Victor, too, seemed to be shocked.

Harry laughed. 'No it's not. It's logical. You'll never find a better manager than Victor.'

'No one in the world gets paid that much money,' Charlotte objected. 'Besides, we can't afford it.'

'Then the firm should owe it to Victor until we can afford it,' Louisa said firmly. 'Victor is the manager, he's entitled to a decent salary. The present arrangement is no longer acceptable, Charlotte. Either Victor is paid, or we leave.'

'But five hundred pounds!'

'That is a lot,' Victor agreed, but Louisa knew the point was won.

'Four-fifty then,' she put to Charlotte.

'Three-fifty.'

Louisa smiled. 'Done. As long as Victor is paid and is still entitled to his remuneration as shareholder, I won't begrudge Rupe his share.'

'When he comes back, he'll be entitled to a wage too,' Charlotte said, 'but we will of course deduct the money he has already borrowed.'

Victor looked at her incredulously. 'Borrowed? The hell he borrowed! Listen, Mother, you'd better get this straight. As long as I am manager of Springfield, Rupe is out. I won't have him back. Not after this last episode. Not under any circumstances. And as for his share, there won't be much for him for a very long time.'

'You can't mean that,' she said miserably. 'This is Rupe's home.'

'He can visit, but he doesn't live here any more. Not as long as I'm running the place.'

'But if he isn't here, and his share of the profits won't amount to much, especially after your salary has to be paid, what will he live on?'

'He's got a head start with the shearers' pay.'

'But after that goes?'

They all knew that Rupe was capable of spending the money he had stolen in a matter of weeks if he went on a spree in Brisbane, but Victor had made his decision and gave no indication of relenting. He took a cigar from a humidor and offered one to Harry.

His mother watched them clip the cigars and light them. 'I'm waiting,' she said. 'If Rupe can't come home, how will he support himself?'

Harry luxuriated in the expensive cigar, a rare treat for him these days. 'He could get a job,' he grinned. 'They say it's great for character-building.'

Before he left, Harry had another talk with Nioka.

'Will the rest of your mob come back now? I can assure you that no more of your children will ever be taken from here again. Victor has promised. He'll even build a school for them.'

'I don't know, Harry. I'll send them messages. Tell of poor Gabbidgee's boy gone. Tell of my Jagga home and your good kindness. Tell of Bobbo still lost. Then they decide. But I stay here with my Jagga if the missus let me. My sister gone, someone has to wait for Bobbo. You think that all right? They let me stay?'

He gave her a hug. 'Of course. You've got your room out there now. Everyone will be happy for you to stay. But it would be good if the others come back to their old camp. Better here, Nioka.'

'Spinner say more strangers comen to Springfield, push everyone out.'

'No, not with Victor in charge. Springfield's safe with him.'

As he walked away, she called out to him. 'When you get your baby, you bring him to see us?'

'I certainly will,' he smiled. He wondered if Nioka had said 'him' by chance, or if she, too, had foreknowledge of the event. Then he shrugged. Enough of that nonsense. It was time to get on with his own life.

With a wad of cash in his satchel, Rupe thought better of staying with friends. Instead he installed himself in the fashionable Gloucester Hotel, a mecca for well-heeled country folk, and although he was still in his riding clothes, he made straight for the Bushmen's Bar, driven by a thirst that had been building over the last forty miles of that long, dusty ride. Never in his life had he been so pleased to see again the wide drift of the Brisbane River, and he rode over the bridge with an excitement that he hadn't felt in years.

He wasn't troubled by the reaction back home. He knew very well they wouldn't call the police. They'd be furious, but what did he care? He had simply taken an advance on his entitlements. Victor was an excellent manager, he didn't need an offsider.

He grinned, thinking of Louisa. He bet she wouldn't really care that he'd left, no matter how much she grizzled with them about the circumstances of his departure. And as for Charlotte . . . she'd brought this on herself. Invited by her sons to join the firm as an expression of good will, she had no right to start laying down the law. He hoped she realized now what a mistake she'd made. He and Victor had had an agreement. She shouldn't have interfered.

As he leaned on the smart marble counter, one boot on the shiny brass footrest, he thought of his father, and gave an involuntary shudder. If Austin had been alive, he'd have come after him with a shotgun!

From down the bar a voice called, 'Well! If it isn't Rupe Broderick! Where have you been hiding yourself, mate?'

He looked down to see a collection of familiar faces, picked up his glass and moved to join them. This was the place to shake off the dust of Springfield for good.

Some time during the rest of that boozy afternoon, followed by a hell-raising night, he managed to send a polite note to Cleo Murray, telling her he was staying at the Gloucester for a few days, and asking if he might call. This time, the formalities had to be observed.

The next morning he slept late, with only a hazy recollection of more bars, a music hall, flash women hanging about him and his mates, and some bawd screaming at him to be paid. Whether he paid her or not he couldn't recall, but it didn't matter, he'd only had a pound or so on him. The rest of his hoard was hidden here in his hotel room. In a sudden funk, Rupe leapt out of bed and checked the bottom drawer of the wardrobe, relieved to find the money intact. Then he felt good. Alive. No longer held down by the family.

As he shaved, the mirror told him more good news. Reminded him that he was handsome, better-looking than his brothers, even Harry. And those good looks had had the ladies flocking about last night. That much he remembered. Must have been early in the night. They drooled over his long eyelashes and said he had naughty eyes. Maybe he did, when it suited him, he grinned, wiping the blade on a cloth.

He wondered when he'd hear from Cleo, not doubting for a minute that she would respond. Thank God he'd remembered where the aunt lived; she'd told him often enough, skiting, in fact, about her aunt's lovely home at Yeronga, on the banks of the river. He'd known that she was trying to impress him, but why bother when the real family wealth was up north with the father on that big sugar plantation? He'd read recently that the price of sugar was going through the roof, with jam factories springing up in the major cities. Queensland was the only place in the country where sugar could be grown successfully, because they had the climate and a surfeit of cheap black labour, imported from the Solomon Islands. It all sounded so marvellously decadent, like tales of the planters in the tropics of the Americas, lolling about in white suits with long drinks and scads of servants.

But that was in the future. Right now, Rupe was starving. He needed a good meal. He trooped down to the dining room in time for lunch. As he ate a mixed grill and pudding he returned the shy, sweet smiles of some really pretty girls who would have made this sunny day even brighter had he not begun to worry about Cleo. What if she had already gone home? What if she refused to see him? She had been chucked out of Springfield rather unceremoniously. But he hadn't done that. It wasn't his fault.

As he strolled from the dining room, Rupe was irritated, thinking that he was stuck here now, forced to hang about to wait on a reply from Cleo, when there were plenty of other things to do in this interesting town.

A porter intercepted him. 'Mr Broderick . . .'

There it was. A letter in a pink-tinted envelope, addressed to him in Cleo's neat handwriting, noted: 'By hand'.

She was pleased to hear from him and invited him to call that afternoon. Rupe nodded, smiling. Of course she would. Why had he worried?

He decided, having observed gentlemen in the hotel, that he needed a complete new outfit, so he dashed across the road to the Elite Gentlemen's Outfitters, where the Brodericks were well known, and indulged himself, airily charging all of his purchases to Springfield.

When he emerged from the hotel in a dark frock coat – the new length, much shorter these days – slim striped trousers and a top hat, he was brimming with confidence. He took a horse cab out to the address in Yeronga, paid the driver and stood before tall iron gates, studying the beautiful gardens within.

Cleo was right; the grounds were sufficient to tell him that this was a residence of note. Undeterred, he pushed through the side gate and walked up to the house. It was certainly not on the grand scale of the Springfield homestead, which made him feel better, but it was a lovely house, single-storeyed, more like a retreat, with its sandstone elegance resting gracefully behind a row of archways in monastic style.

He was not prepared for the stern woman who answered the door. She had to be among the ugliest females Rupe had ever seen, with a face, he thought, like a potato and her hair plastered down into a central parting that added nothing to her appeal. Only his glance at the stodgy dark taffeta dress with chunky sleeves and a pearl brooch at the stiffened neckline told him that this was not the housekeeper.

He learned that she was expecting him, that this was Miss Murray,

Cleo's aunt, and, while he was still standing on her doorstep, that Cleo was not well. That she was not really up to visitors, but he might as well come in, since it appeared he was invited.

Simmering at her rudeness, Rupe kept a smile on his face and followed her through the spacious house, noting the expensive carpets and display cabinets that held shelves of delicate china. Then she showed him into a long room at the rear of the house and he looked about in wonder. It was a sun room, he supposed, glassed on one side with windows that were misted by sheer white floor-length curtains. All the furniture was white cane, upholstered in white, so the blaze of greenery was a shock. He was met by a profusion of pot plants, standing palms, hanging baskets and, at the lowest level, rows of energetic ferns. There were even orchids, languid purples and pinks and whites hanging lethargically as if bored by this exotic landscape. The air was fetid, unpleasant.

He turned to the aunt, proffering compliments. 'You must have a gifted gardener, Miss Murray. The plants are magnificent.'

'I am a botanist,' she replied curtly. 'Cleo is waiting for you.'

Only then did he see her, away to his left, sitting determinedly on a small sofa, clutching a cloth purse, looking as if she was waiting for a long-overdue bus. He smiled as he walked over, realizing that in her white muslin, half hidden by the greenery, she was effectively camouflaged. No wonder he'd nearly missed her.

On closer inspection he decided that this room didn't do much for her. It was full of energy, making her look sallow and lifeless, and her dark hair, hanging limply round her face, lacked the sheen of the glossy *Monstera deliciosa* leaves that competed nearby.

'How are you, Cleo?' he said cheerfully.

'Very well, thank you, Rupe.'

A voice behind him contradicted. 'She is not well at all. Sit here, Mr Broderick.'

The aunt indicated a sofa facing Cleo, part of a trio of couches that formed a neat little conversation nest. Or would have, he thought, had not Miss Murray decided to occupy the third, placing herself as chaperon between them, making conversation difficult.

'I'm sorry to hear that,' he began, wondering what sort of a sickness caused women to put on weight, because she looked decidedly flabby. Worse, he groaned, decidedly unattractive.

'. . . Still, the weather is improving, so much warmer now. I venture to say that will put the roses back in your cheeks.'

She nodded. 'Yes, indeed. I'm sure. And yourself, Rupe? How are you?'

'Fine. Yes, keeping very well. It's a pleasure to be able to get to town again, to see all the sights.' He chatted on for a while and then, in desperation, since Cleo wasn't helping, turned to the aunt. 'Do you enjoy Brisbane, Miss Murray?'

'As much as anywhere, I suppose. I find the winters most pleasurable. And of course I keep busy.'

'So I see. It is obvious your talent does not simply reside in green fingers. Where did you acquire your knowledge of botany?'

'Kew Gardens,' she replied, taking it for granted that Rupe knew where they were located, which he did not. 'I worked there as an unpaid assistant for three years, learning as much as I could, then I returned to Australia . . .'

At least he had broken the ice. The woman talked at length about her career, her abiding interest in native flora, her work these days with the curator of the Brisbane Botanic Gardens, while Rupe feigned interest, wishing she would go away and give him a chance to talk to Cleo, instead of boring him with long, involved discourses on native acacias.

'There are hundreds of species of acacia, mimosaceous genus, and we keep finding more,' she told him.

'That's amazing,' he enthused, thinking that they were all still bloody wattles to him.

It was becoming obvious that his first visit to Miss Murray's home was to be short and sweet, since no move was made to offer him tea, so he looked about him with a sigh. 'I suppose I should be moving along now. Business appointments in Queen Street, you know.'

That seemed to wake Cleo a little. 'But you will call again?'

'If I'm invited. Of course.'

She shuffled nervously. 'I wanted to ask you. How are Louisa and Victor?'

'They're fine. Busy working out how to dud the Government out of freeholding payments.'

Miss Murray was suddenly tense. 'What? I don't understand.'

Rupe launched into a complicated version of the Alienation of Lands Acts as both a ploy to delay his departure and small revenge on his hostess, hoping she would find this as boring as her botanical lectures had been to him. Gradually, though, he sensed disapproval. Thinking he'd been too facetious in his talk of dudding the Government, and the Brodericks' attempts to dummy land, he backtracked.

'I can't say that I approve of those tactics; after all, give unto Caesar . . .'

Cleo looked up with a deprecating smile. 'Render . . .'

'I beg your pardon? Yes, of course. Render unto Caesar.' He returned her little smile with a dazzling one of his own, to show he had not taken offence at the rebuke. 'No doubt, Miss Murray, your niece is an excellent teacher.'

But the woman's pudgy face had gained shape, a jaw jutted and the pale eyes were set hard. 'I presume the Louisa you mentioned is your sister-in-law, Mrs Broderick?'

'Yes.'

'She treated Cleo very badly. We haven't forgotten that.'

Rupe nodded. This explained the lack of hospitality. 'I know she did, that's why I'm here. I've come to apologize. But you must understand, Miss Murray, as I'm sure Cleo does, that it wasn't my doing. I was distraught at the time. Everyone was . . .'

'You could have stood up for Cleo. I am led to believe that you were a friend of hers, and yet you let them treat her like that . . .' She was furious, nose twitching, neck as stiff as a poker.

Cleo tried to intervene. 'I never said I was angry with Rupe . . .'

'No. You didn't say you were angry with any of the Brodericks.' She turned on Rupe. 'That girl arrived here distraught, hysterical. I know it was a tragedy; but no one offered her any kindness, and I repeat, not even you, Mr Broderick.'

'How could I? I had no idea what was happening. I'm still quite hazy. My brother was so upset I had to leave the station temporarily. I know now that Cleo was treated badly. But so was I. As a matter of fact, that's why I have left the station for good now. When I returned, their attitude to me was so unbearable I had no choice. Weeks of being shunned in my own home was just too much.'

'You've left?' Cleo was astonished. 'Oh, Rupe. I'm so sorry. What will you do now?'

'It's not a great problem. I'm still a major shareholder in the Springfield Pastoral Company. I won't starve. Actually, I'd thought of going north. Having a look round, you know.'

The aunt was relenting. 'They drove you out too?'

'I'm afraid so. Even though Teddy was found fit and well, they were uncompromising, they blamed me for what could have happened. What *could* have happened! It was so unfair of them to carry on like that . . .'

But Miss Murray had gasped, a great gulp of air, as if in shock, and Rupe stopped, looking from one to the other as a sudden silence struck the room. Maidenhair ferns, hanging from a basket above him, seemed to shiver as if their warm haven had been turned into an icebox. Roses had returned to Cleo's face: scarlet spots like daubs of rouge stood out against her pale skin.

The aunt's question came with a savage jerk of her head. 'Cleo! What was that child's name?'

'Teddy,' she whispered.

'Did I hear aright? Did I hear him say that Teddy is fit and well? Did I?'

Cleo gulped. Speechless.

'Mr Broderick, did that child survive after all?'

'Yes. I thought you knew. He did fall in the river . . . I thought you knew . . .' He was blathering now, babbling. 'He did. Though we weren't to blame. He slipped away on us, that's all. The way kids do.

390

But an Aborigine woman saw him and rescued him. She took her time bringing him in, from the other side of the river . . .'

Damnit, he told himself. What's the difference? He smiled at Cleo, kindly this time. 'So all's well that ends well. I'm glad that I am able to be the bearer of good news.'

There was that silence again. That ice.

'Do you realize what you people have put Cleo through?' The aunt was livid. 'You selfish, uncaring wretches! Did no one think to inform Cleo that her pupil, the child who was in her care, had not drowned? That he was, after all, fit and well, as you say? Do you mean to tell me it was all a mistake?'

He tried to placate her. 'Miss Murray. Please. Hear me out. There was such excitement, such relief when he was found that no one thought . . . I mean, I took it for granted that Louisa would have written to Cleo. Explained what had happened.'

'Did you really? You have just told us that your sister-in-law does not have a forgiving nature, even in the light of a tragedy avoided. Why would you take it for granted that a person like her would write to Cleo? Why didn't you write? It has been weeks, and all the time this poor girl has been suffering, blaming herself for the death of a child!' Her voice was raised to a screech.

'You don't understand . . .'

'Oh yes I do. I find you a very devious piece of work, sir. Now you might excuse me. Cleo, see to your guest!' She stamped out of the room.

Thank God she was gone. He moved over to Cleo, taking her hand, almost on one knee before her. 'Dear Cleo. My love. Had I known you were going through such suffering I'd have written, I swear I would. I thought you knew.'

'How would I know? No one told me. There was nothing in the papers and why would there be? A tragedy that turns out to be not a tragedy . . .' she broke off in tears, but struggled on, ' . . . that happened hundreds of miles away.

'It's hardly news!' she added wildly. 'Even if you are the famous Brodericks. I have been so sick over this, I haven't been able to face anyone. So ashamed! And you let me suffer.'

'Cleo, I didn't mean to. Honest. I missed you . . . We have to talk. We have so much to talk about . . .'

She stood, pushing him away. 'No we don't. Get out!'

'You can't mean that. You're just overwrought.'

So was he. Rupe couldn't believe that this frump of a girl was actually throwing him out.

'Can't you forget all this and remember what we meant to each other, Cleo?'

But she backed away from him, tears streaming down her face. 'Go away, Rupe. Please.'

The aunt was standing at the door. 'I have your hat, Mr Broderick. I'll show you out.'

No doubt it was a fine day. Rupe lifted his hat and acknowledged two elderly ladies who, smilingly, pointed this out to him as he passed by. The sky was a sweep of blue, not a cloud in sight. Tiny birds flicked and twittered through the trees, unaware, he noted meanly, that a hawk hung above them, so high it appeared almost motionless. A dog dozed at a gate, not even bothering to twitch his damp nose at this person walking along his snooty street.

Rupe kicked the gate angrily, and the dog came awake with a yelp, but by the time he'd adjusted to a bark, Rupe was turning the corner. He couldn't believe that those women, those nobodies, had had the gall to show him the door. And why? Because Cleo had been too damn stupid to find out what had actually happened at Springfield. She could have written to Louisa. A letter of condolence would have been in order, if she'd been so sure that Teddy had drowned. Then Louisa would have replied. Set her straight.

In his anger and resentment, the actual sequence of events at that time had become foggy, and he was in no mood to dwell on them. So what if Cleo hadn't been told? She ought to have been thrilled when he gave her the good news.

'Oh no,' he muttered. She was too busy playing the martyr, feeling sorry for herself. Surely she didn't think, if Teddy *had* drowned, Rupe would ever want to see her again. She wasn't sick, she was just stupid. And as plain as mud. He wondered how he had ever considered marriage with such a graceless lump. Even if the family was moneyed. She'd never fit into society anywhere.

Rupe strode on, bravado lending jauntiness to his step. He refused to think what he would do next. There were other fish in the sea. In the meantime a man could have plenty of fun in this town, and he'd been starved of fun for far too long.

The Bushmen's Bar was crowded with men returning from the annual yearling sales that had been held at the racecourse that morning. Rupe wished he'd gone there instead of wasting his time with Cleo and the ugly aunt. It would have been a damn sight more interesting. But forget about them, he told himself as he joined in the excited talk of who had paid what for bloodlines, who had paid too much, who was the proud owner of the colt from Kerry Star, imported from Ireland.

Champagne flowed. No one cared who was paying. Pound notes were slammed on the counter and bettered by more genial hosts, to be rescued by busy barmen and dumped, soggy with champagne, into overflowing tills. But in all the talk and the back-slapping and the singing and the drunken boasting, Rupe heard another tune. He heard whispers, and wary asides, and he saw groups huddled in corners, only two or three men at a time, caught in serious discussion.

While he drank with his own mates, chortling over old yarns, he watched these men, knowing that something was up. But what? He moved closer to Lindsay Knox, a fellow he'd known at school, who seemed to be the focal point of the mystery.

'Were you buying or selling today?'

Lindsay grinned. 'Neither. I heard your old man died. Sorry about that. Did you come in for the sales?'

'No. I just decided to give myself some time off from the station. Take a look around. Maybe travel a bit.'

'Oh, yes? Where are you off to?' As he spoke, Rupe could see that Lindsay wasn't much interested in this conversation. The question was limp, distracted, and his eyes were not waiting for a response, but were already looking elsewhere. Rupe, though, persisted, determined not to let him go just yet.

'I haven't decided,' he said firmly, edging to block Lindsay from moving away. 'I was thinking of going overseas, but they say you should see your own country first, so that you know what you're talking about. I might go up to Cairns. Have a look at the tropics. Hot weather and hot women go hand in hand, they say.'

It must have been the mention of women that brought Lindsay's attention slewing back to him.

'Why Cairns?' he asked suddenly.

'Why not?' Rupe's sly smile was intended to convey the impression that he knew more about the sexy ladies of the north, but Lindsay wasn't buying it.

'Come on, old mate. Don't kid me. You're in the know.' Swaying slightly, he leaned on the bar. 'I think I'm a bit drunk. Might as well go the rest of the way. Pass me another bubbly, Rupe.'

It was as good as done. Rupe commandeered two overflowing glasses. 'Good luck!'

'Never a truer word,' Lindsay laughed. 'When are you going?'

Rupe guessed he must mean Cairns, and played along, curiosity dogging him now.

'Any day. What about you?'

Lindsay transferred his weight from the counter to Rupe's shoulder, and confided in him. 'I'll tell you what about me, mate. I'm off. I wouldn't miss this for quids. But I need a partner. None of these blokes suit me, if you know what I mean. A lot of them are all talk. And I don't know if they'd have the stamina, but you and me, we ought to join forces. What do you say?'

Puzzled, Rupe drank his wine, searching for an appropriate response.

Finally he decided to appear cagey. 'I'm not sure we're talking about the same thing.'

Lindsay's voice dropped to a whisper. 'Oh yes we are. We're talking gold, and you know it.'

Gold! Rupe was stunned. No wonder the word was only whispered about. Where was this gold? In Cairns? There had been huge gold strikes all over the country, but in the far north? Not that he knew of. That was what came of living out in the backblocks. You missed out on what was really happening.

'A partnership?' he said. 'I'll think about it.'

Yes, for a half a minute, he told himself.

The next morning a cold-sober Lindsay Knox brought his map and plans to Rupe's hotel room so that they could talk freely. Rupe soon saw that the map, which only listed coastal towns, not goldfields, wasn't much use, but that didn't deter him.

'Where is this place, exactly?'

'It's called the Palmer River. It's up there somewhere. We can get directions in Cairns. But speed is the order of the day, Rupe. It's only a whisper so far, but once the word's out we'll be lucky to get on a ship.'

They talked for a while, getting nowhere. Rupe learned that there were goldfields at a place called Charters Towers, south-west of Townsville, and suggested they ought to go there first, but Lindsay disagreed.

'That place is overrun with diggers. The gold would be gone by the time we got there. I thought you wanted to try the Cairns trip, because that's where I'm going, with or without you.'

In the end, Rupe asked for a couple of hours to make some enquiries.

'Where? Don't you go spilling the beans all over town.'

'I won't do that. I know an old bloke who works in the Lands Department, he was a good mate of my father's. I'll see what he can tell me.'

Leo Marshall had indeed been a friend of the late Austin Broderick, which was why he took the lad out into the back lane to talk with him. 'Your dad was good to me. He found me the job here in the first place, when I was down on my luck. Been here all these years. Close to retirement now. Oh yes, I know about the Palmer strike, it'll be headlines any day. We got wind from the Mines Department. It isn't anywhere near Cairns, but you'd have to take ship there first. Then get another ship on to a settlement called Cooktown, way up at the mouth of the Endeavour River, where Captain Cook repaired his ship after it was damaged. You'd have learned about that at school, I daresay.'

'And that's where the gold is?'

'No. You'd then have to trek inland, south-west for about a hundred miles as the crow flies.'

'But there's gold at this river?'

'Yes.'

'Plenty of it?'

Leo sucked on his pipe. 'A healthy strike.'

'A hundred miles isn't far. We could do that in a couple of days. Ship up there and then ride in. It'll be a breeze.'

'That's where you're wrong. It's dangerous. Terrible country, fever-ridden, no supplies, and worse, the blacks there are hostile, and there are plenty of them. I'm giving you good advice right here. Don't go. Don't let anyone talk you into it. That place is too dangerous.'

'It can't be that bad. Obviously gold miners are already there.'

'At great risk. The men who got out safely have made that very clear. You don't need to go up there, Rupe; the trek to the Palmer over a jungle range through territory held by the fiercest black tribes in the country would be a living hell. It's only for desperate men, not for the likes of you. The Palmer will not give up its gold easily. You mark my words.'

Rupe did mark his words. The ones about the location of the goldfield and the ones about there being plenty of gold. He passed on this information to Lindsay, who was impressed.

'Good work. I found out there's a ship leaving for Cairns tomorrow. What do you say? Is it a goer?'

'Yes!' Rupe was bursting with excitement, but he tried to keep calm. 'We'll buy all the equipment we need in Cairns, but we'll need guns and ammo for protection from outlaws.'

'Of course! Where there's gold there's outlaws,' Lindsay agreed enthusiastically.

'We'll buy them here in Brisbane, though. They'll be cheaper.' And not so much in demand, he added to himself. 'But not a word to anyone, Lindsay. We'll just slip quietly out of town tomorrow. Is that all right with you?'

'Couldn't be better, partner. While they're all still talking, we'll be on our way.'

Only then, when it came down to assessing costs, did Rupe discover that Lindsay could only put up fifteen pounds. No wonder he needed a partner!

Nevertheless, Rupe had heard enough of Leo's warnings to know that a partner was essential. If they were to be mixing with desperates, he'd need someone to watch his back, so better the devil you know than picking up with some stranger. He worried a little that Lindsay was treating this as a lark. True, he was well built, and fit enough to handle tough diggings, but he was no bushie. He had lived all his life in Brisbane; his father was a doctor, a specialist of some sort. How he'd go on the trek that Leo had described was not clear. But that was Lindsay's problem.

'Can't you get your father to back you?' Rupe asked.

'No. I've run out of credit there.'

Rupe couldn't give up now. 'All right. I've got enough. We'll pool the cash for the time being, and you can pay me back out of our earnings.'

'In gold, mate. To the penny!' Lindsay laughed. 'Let's go down and celebrate our last night in civilization.'

'Yes. But you keep your mouth shut.'

Rupe had a fair idea of what they'd need in supplies and equipment to head inland from this Cooktown place – enough to last them for months, plus packhorses – so he wasn't inclined to spend too much or to allow Lindsay to be volunteering to shout drinks. And the next morning, faced with the hotel bill, he worked out another way to economize.

He'd already bought the tickets, and now sent Lindsay down to claim two decent bunks on the coastal steamer, while he packed his bag. Then he dropped it out of the window into a thicket of oleander bushes.

Dressed in his new clothes, carrying only his top hat, he approached the clerk at the desk to inform him that he was expecting guests for lunch.

'When they arrive, please place them in the reading room. I shall be back shortly.'

'Certainly, Mr Broderick.'

With that Mr Broderick strode out of the front door, placed his top hat jauntily on his head and walked away. Never to return. He ducked round the side of the hotel, collected his bag and made his way down to the wharves to find the ship that would take him to a life of untold wealth.

But a guest did come. The nervous young lady was escorted into the quietly carpeted reading room, with its frosted windows and its firmly upholstered chairs and its green and gilt lamps and paintings of rustic scenes on the walls.

Cleo hadn't slept a wink all night. She felt they'd been too hard on Rupe, what with the shock and all. She was mortified when it dawned on her that her reaction had been atrocious. Instead of being over the moon at the miracle of Teddy's survival, she'd attacked Rupe for not letting her know. Or her aunt had, she couldn't recall. She still wasn't well. Or she hadn't been yesterday, anyway. But on waking this morning, that great weight of guilt and shame had gone. Teddy was alive! She went down on her knees by the bed and thanked God in His mercy for this deliverance. But what about Rupe? She owed him an apology. What if they *had* just forgotten to tell her? Or taken it for granted that she'd hear the good news? Wouldn't they have been in such euphoria that no one but Teddy mattered? Who was she to think that the Brodericks would remember her at a time like that?

Her aunt's reaction at her humiliating dismissal from Springfield was understandable, but not a little illogical, Cleo realized now. Though the finger of blame pointed squarely at the governess, all Miss Murray saw was her niece arriving back on her doorstep, totally shattered. And so she had taken her side. It was natural.

And then Rupe had walked into her withering dislike of that family, which had coloured Cleo's confused reaction.

Now she was sorry. So terribly sorry. Rupe had come for her as soon as all the hoo-ha had died down. Probably as soon as he could get away from the station. And he had looked so handsome! So sweet and so lovable, with that gorgeous smile. She clutched her town handbag, the one with the amber trim that she'd bought in London, and looked down at her hands. She was wearing the two large diamond rings her mother had left her. She hadn't taken them with her to Springfield, feeling that jewellery of this sort would have been out of place for a governess, and out of place on a station. But now she could wear them, they were correct in town, as was the large diamond brooch in the shape of a feather that glittered on her lapel.

Cleo sat for a long time in that chair facing the wall, rehearsing what she would say to Rupe. She would apologize, of course, and tell him how happy she really was to hear about Teddy, and ask him to forgive her, again. But most of all, she had to reassure him, to let him know how much she appreciated his visit. He did love her, she'd seen it in his eyes, that sweetness when he'd first looked at her at her aunt's place, and she had noted his disappointment when Miss Murray had lodged herself protectively between them. If only they'd been able to have that time together, alone, none of these misunderstandings would have taken place. Cleo wasn't one for blame, she did understand how much her aunt cared for her; but so did Rupe, and he wasn't given a chance.

That was why she'd made an excuse to leave the house on her own. She had to find Rupe. To explain. Apologize. And, damnit, to let him know that she did love him. Somehow.

She consulted her little gold fob watch. They'd said he'd be in for lunch but it was nearing two o'clock. She walked out to the porter's station, avoiding the desk clerk, who was busy anyway, and asked a nice lad if he would check the dining room for Mr Rupe Broderick.

Finding that Rupe had still not appeared, she asked the very nice young man if he could send a note up to Mr Broderick's room, advising him that a visitor was awaiting him in the reading room.

'By all means, miss,' he said. 'And when he comes in, I'll be sure to spot him and send him your way.'

'Thank you. You're so kind.' This time Cleo took a chair facing the door. A gentleman offered her a newspaper, which she declined. There was a lot to think about. It would be a good idea to invite Rupe to come north with her, because she was planning to go home and visit the family. How marvellous if they could go together. Engaged. She'd always dreamed of taking her fiancé home to meet the family. They'd like him, they really would.

The hours dragged, but she didn't mind waiting. After all, Rupe was not expecting her. Why would he, for heaven's sake? And he had so many friends in Brisbane. The Brodericks were as well known here as they were in the country.

But even for Cleo, the wait became too much. Especially in a fashionable hotel like this. She became acutely aware of formally dressed ladies drifting by the door as pages came by to light lamps, brightening the room; and of a surge of activity in the foyer, and she knew she'd have to relinquish her vigil or look a real fool. Gamely, she approached the reception desk once more to ask that same clerk to take a message for Mr Broderick.

'Would you tell him . . .' she began.

But the fellow glared at her, snorting through a thick brown moustache: 'Mr Broderick is no longer resident in this hotel, miss.'

'Oh! Oh! I'm so sorry. I beg your pardon!' Cleo stumbled outside, embarrassed. Disappointed that she'd missed Rupe. Terribly disappointed. He'd probably gone home. Damnit! Oh well. Such a shame to have missed him, but she'd write to him. Looking on the bright side, she thought that it would be easier to explain everything in writing. She wouldn't be so intimidated that way. Not so nervous.

She hailed a horse cab and climbed in, resigned. In a letter she'd be brave enough to tell him that she still loved him, something she wouldn't dare say to his face. All was not lost. Rupe had come for her, after all.

As the ship cleared the river and headed out into Moreton Bay on its voyage northwards, Rupe had forgotten Cleo, and Springfield. He was not interested in the dusky shoreline, only in the predominance of men, gold prospectors, on this ship. With his partner, and a bottle of rum, he sat at the back of the saloon, dreaming of what he would do when he struck it rich. Dreaming. Even Lindsay was quiet. They were at peace, he and his partner. The last peace Rupe would ever know. So it was fitting that he should be allowed this gentle interlude, sea calm, moon riding high on a balmy night.

The two voyages, to Cairns and on to Cooktown through the waters guarded by the Great Barrier Reef, were to Rupe sheer joy. He was freed of family restraints. Free at last. He wished he could sail on forever through these aqua-blue seas, with not a worry in the world. He wondered why he hadn't walked away from the dust of Springfield years ago, because this was the life.

He wasn't a Broderick any more, he didn't have to answer to anyone. He was just another bloke among a host of merry men, on the adventure of a lifetime.

He didn't feel the spear, it was only like a thud on his back, until Lindsay tried to pull it out and his scream echoed into the darkness of that awful night. He tried to talk, to tell stupid Lindsay to wait until morning, to wait for daybreak, because as sure as hell Lindsay would get lost. But poor bloody brave Lindsay was dragging his body deeper into the scrub, away from the trail, thinking he was doing the right thing. No sense of direction. No bloody sense of direction. The blacks had gone. There was no need to panic any more. Rupe thought of Kelly. His father's partner. He'd died by the spear too, but worse. So this wasn't so bad. He tried to tell Lindsay about Kelly but his voice seemed to be lost in the shuffle and rush of an oily stream that gushed from the slippery heights above them.

He heard Lindsay gasp and slide away through the slimy undergrowth, too weak to crawl back. He'd been sick for days, battling a fierce fever and debilitating diarrhoea, but he'd struggled on, apologizing. Always apologizing, insisting that once they got through to open country, out of this mosquito-ridden jungle, he'd be all right.

Darkness was swift in this land. And total. Not even a sliver of moonlight could pierce the ancient canopies of tree and vine that wrestled for space, but Rupe didn't mind. He was only lingering for Lindsay's sake. He'd turned out to be a bloody good mate. With all the life force left in him, Rupe willed him to go back, to save himself. All he had to do was let go. It wasn't a matter of strength, the mud and the long slope would do its work. If he kept on sliding down through the night, by morning he'd have a view of the sea, and that was half the battle. Then he'd be able to pick up a trail, come upon other diggers who wouldn't deny help to a sick man.

Lindsay must have heard him. 'Rupe,' he called, his voice faint and raspy. 'We didn't make it. We didn't even get there.'

The hurt and the disappointment were understandable, but unimportant now. Why didn't Lindsay know that? The priority now was to get out, go down to the coast.

Lindsay was muttering, trying to reassure him. 'Don't worry, mate. We'll be all right.' His breaths, short and wheezy, gasped out words that Rupe couldn't hear. 'I won't leave you.'

But Rupe had gone on ahead of him.

Coda

Seven Years Later

The two ladies met in the pleasant tearooms that overlooked the Brisbane River, and greeted each other with hugs.

Ada hadn't seen Charlotte, now Mrs Craig Winters, for more than a year, so there was much to talk about. They were still chattering, both talking at once, when the waitress approached to lead them into the sunny alcove reserved for favoured customers.

'This is delightful,' Ada said, looking about her. 'I must tell Connie to remember this place when she comes to town.'

'How is she?' Charlotte asked as they were being seated.

'Oh, very well. And Harry too. Since Pa's death he's been a tower of strength. He's as good a manager of our station as Victor is of yours. And you should see them together. It's like Pa and Austin all over again; when they're not comparing notes they're arguing, competing . . .'

'But they get on well?' Charlotte asked anxiously.

'Of course they do. It's all bluff. Underneath they are the best of friends. Connie and Louisa get along well too; those two girls are the mainstay of social life in the district. But I have to say, Harry is my favourite. He's such a dear.'

'So I believe. I heard you introduce him as your son-in-law.' Charlotte smiled.

'Oh, well. Poet's licence. Allow me that. I never had children of my own, and it's wonderful to have grandchildren. Their boys call me Grandma. Such a delight. Now that she has two sons, I'm hoping Connie will give me a granddaughter.'

She stopped. 'Oh, my dear! I hope you don't mind. I know they're your grandchildren, but they call you Nanny. I'm not really usurping your status. Or their Walker grandmother. She never comes out to the station anyway.'

'No, it's all right,' Charlotte said sadly.

But Ada Crossley, in her forthright way, could not let this pass. 'If I've upset you, Charlotte, you say so. I didn't mean any harm. I mean, the children are still Brodericks. Please don't take my little whim unkindly.'

Charlotte gazed out of the windows at a small ferry plying the river. 'No, it's not that.'

'Then what is it? Something's wrong. You'd better out with it before Craig comes along. You're not unhappy in the marriage? I heard you two are like a couple of turtle doves . . .'

'We are.' Charlotte hid her face from her friend as she found a handkerchief in her purse to head off the tears brimming in her eyes. 'It's nothing like that. It's . . . Oh, Ada, it's Rupe's birthday today.'

'Oh, dear God.'

They sat in silence until Charlotte could compose herself.

'No word?'

Charlotte shook her head. 'We've made enquiries all over the world, because he used to say he wanted to travel. But nothing. All we know is that he was in Brisbane for several days after he left Springfield. He called on that girl, the governess. He was with friends at a bar in Brisbane, but then he disappeared. We haven't heard a word since then.'

'Oh, well. Knowing Rupe, he's probably in Europe. Living it up. He'll come home one of these days and surprise you. You know your boy. He'll be at the door as if nothing has happened.'

'I don't think so,' Charlotte sighed. 'The Pastoral Company is doing well now. I've set up a trust in Rupe's name, and every penny that is owed to him from the annual share of the profits has been paid into that trust religiously.'

Ada tried to cheer her. 'Well then. He'll get a lovely surprise. I'm guessing, going on our figures, which will be much the same as Springfield, that your prodigal son will come home to find he's a wealthy man.'

Charlotte turned to her. 'I can only say this to you, Ada. I know Rupe. He'd know the money is there. He wouldn't just leave it there for years. Rupe's the sort of person who could never have enough money.'

She looked down at her hands, clasped together as if in prayer. 'No. Rupe's dead. I know he is. His brothers know too, but we keep up this pretence.'

'Oh, my dear. I'm so sorry.'

Charlotte's voice was anguished. 'How long should we go on pretending, Ada? We've never had a service, not even a memorial service. He's never been laid to rest.'

Ada, close to tears herself, could not help. 'Charlotte, dear, I really don't know. I think you would have to discuss this with Craig.'

Charlotte's husband was in his rooms, waiting for Teddy Broderick. Every second Saturday, young Teddy was given leave from his boarding school to come into town for lunch with his grandparents, and although Craig was only a step-grandfather, he looked forward to the treat as much as the other two did. Teddy was a fine lad, tall for his age, with the strong Broderick features and a touch of copper in his hair which delighted Charlotte. All three of her sons had inherited their father's blond hair, but this time round, as Charlotte often said, her red hair had got a look-in.

Victor teased her about that. He said that when Teddy came back to the station and life in the sun, his hair would fade to fair as it had been in his much younger days, but Charlotte wouldn't have it, claiming the red would become even more prominent. It was an ongoing family joke, especially since Harry's sons had retained the fair-haired Broderick strain. Craig Winters smiled. His marriage to Charlotte had brought him more blessings than any man had a right to expect. Childless, he now had a family as well as a good wife, and he loved them all dearly.

His clerk knocked and entered his office to announce, with a sigh, that a client was waiting in the anteroom.

'Who is it? I don't have any more appointments.'

'It's a Captain Logan,' the clerk said, sniffing, raising his eyebrows derisively. 'Or so he says.'

'Did you tell him this is a half-day? I'll be leaving shortly.'

Whether he did or not was not to be discovered, because a burly man in rough seaman's clothes pushed past the clerk and limped into the office. 'I won't keep you long, sir. I just want you to write me will, only a few lines. Are you capable of doing that, Mr Winters, or should I push on down the street and find another legal light?'

Craig stared. The old fellow's ruddy face was almost hidden by a coarse grey beard and clipped side whiskers; and a black cap, which he hadn't bothered to remove, was set firmly on his head, the peak near to beetling eyebrows and hard, mean eyes.

Craig looked at his watch. 'I don't have much time really.'

'I can pay, if that's what's bothering you. I only want you to write a will.'

'It's not the money . . .'

'Good. We're all busy, Mr Winter, this won't take long.' Logan planted himself on a chair facing Craig's desk and called to someone outside. 'Get in here, Robbie lad. You have to hear this.'

Craig gave up, knowing it would be easier to deal with this pesky fellow than to try to turn him away. Then he blinked as a black youth poked his head in.

'Come on, come on!' Logan said impatiently. 'Sit yourself down there. This gentleman hasn't got all day.'

The youth wore the same type of clothes as Logan: a black jerkin, dungarees and canvas shoes. He was, Craig noted, neat and well scrubbed. Reluctantly, the lawyer sank into his chair and picked up a pen.

'Very well. What can I do for you?'

The Captain, if indeed he was a captain, since he had no brass or insignias to bear out his claim, wasted no time. 'Good. Write this down. My name is Captain Theo Logan.'

'Theobald?'

'What? No, just Theo. And this here is Robert Burns. He's my lad, I brung him up. Works on my boat. You might know her. My riverboat. The *Marigold*?'

'Ah, yes, I do.'

'On her. Then you know who I am, right?'

Craig nodded, writing. He could place this Captain Logan now, he was well known on the river. Known as a character, and that was undeniable, he thought, now that he'd come across the Captain in person.

'It's like this. I'm getting on in years. My eyesight. Not too good these days. Nor is the ticker. So I asks meself what's going to happen to the *Marigold*, and him, if I kick the bucket. And I have to answer meself. Now Robbie there, he knows the boat and the job, been working on the *Marigold* since he was knee-high to a grasshopper. So I want you to write this will for me, leaving the boat and all my worldly goods to him. You got that straight?'

'Yes. Now I'll need your addresses.'

'You got them. The *Marigold*. We both live on board. He's an orphan. He's got no one but me. When I go, the Marigold will be his livelihood. He don't know nothing else.' The Captain leaned forward. 'You look like an honest man. I want you to take care of this and make it leak-proof, if you get what I mean. I don't want no jokers taking away his rights, just because he's a blackfellow. Too many bastards out there ready to pull tricks on blackfellows, and it's not going to happen to the *Marigold*, or to him. See what I mean?'

'Yes. Quite.'

'Then that's all there is to it. You write it down for me and we'll get out of your hair. Let you go home.'

'Just a minute. I'll draw up this document for you, Captain, that's no trouble, but it will take a little time. I can have it ready for you next week.'

'I wanted it now. I've got the cash with me.'

The lad, Robbie, stood up and tapped Logan on the shoulder. 'Leave it, Captain.' He turned a wide, self-assured grin on Craig. 'This gentleman knows what's best. He has to do it right. Put it all down proper.' His voice was suddenly gentle as he looked back to Logan. 'You're not going to die next week, or next year. You got it started, that's what you've been pining to do. We'll leave the work to Mr Winters now.'

Grudgingly, the old man heaved himself out of the chair. 'You better be right. I don't want this mucked up.'

'I'll attend to it, Captain Logan. I'll draw up your will and it will be ready for you to sign next week.'

404

'All legal then?'

'My word, yes.'

'Good. We'll shake on it.' He reached over and the heavy paw crunched Craig's outstretched hand.

'You too, Robbie,' Logan barked. 'You shake hands. You got yourself a lawyer now, and you see you do as you're told when the time comes.' He winked at Craig. 'Or I'll send a debbil-debbil after you.'

But then he caught Craig sneaking a glance at his watch again, and was irritated. 'No need for hints, mister. We're going!'

The lawyer rushed an apology. 'No! No! I'm sorry. There's no hurry. I was just checking the time because I'm waiting for my grandson. He should be here by now.' He liked referring to a grandson, a little excursion in pride, and then he realized that this man, Theo Logan, shared that pleasure. He too had acquired a grandson, in the shape of this genial black youth. God was in his heaven.

'He's about the same age as you, Robbie,' he added, and was rewarded with a slow nod of appreciation from the Captain.

Teddy took his time strolling along Queen Street towards Grandpa Winters' office. He was always in two minds about these Saturday outings. They were a kind old pair, these grandies, not as stuffy and pompous as Judge and Nana Walker who claimed him on the occasional Sunday. Not too often, thank God, he mused. It was horrible having to sit through afternoon tea with them, having to listen to the Judge lecturing him on the behaviour and misbehaviour of minors these days. And he was mean, never gave him so much as thrippence, while Grandpa Winters always slipped him ten shillings. He grinned. So did Nanny.

Nevertheless, it was rather boring to have to endure the same old questions over lunch with them, while the boys back at school were setting up for the usual sports afternoons. On the other hand, they always took him to keen places where the food was glorious and he could eat his head off. And he could go back to school afterwards and make the other kids drool by describing in minute detail every skerrick he had devoured, especially the desserts: rainbow ices, three-tiered chocolate cakes with inches of mushy icing and gallons of whipped cream.

That reminded him, he'd better get a move on. He left the store where he'd been admiring the latest in flash bicycles, and stepped out more strongly. Judge Walker had taken it for granted that when he left school he would go to university and study law, and he knew that Grandpa Winters would like that too. They'd even prevailed on his father to encourage him, but Victor had said it was up to the boy.

'Sure is,' Teddy remarked to himself. He knew better than to instigate an argument with the cranky old Judge. Boarding school had taught him to keep his mouth shut if he didn't want to get into

405

fights, so he did just that, listening politely, saying nothing. At Judge Walker's house that was acceptable. Children were expected to be seen, not heard. But he had his own plans. As soon as he had done his time in boarding school he was going home to Springfield. Teddy knew, he'd always known, he belonged on the land, and he was ready to start right from scratch, working as a stockman and earning his way to the top.

His father would be happy, real happy, no doubt about that, but he'd been so bullied by old Grandpa Austin he wouldn't try to influence his own son in any way. He wouldn't even talk to him about his future, which Teddy had found frustrating until Uncle Harry had explained this to him. Adding that Victor was a man of few words. He wasn't given to momentous discussions, and he hated arguments. He just wanted the best for his son.

'But *your* way,' Harry had added. 'It's not that he doesn't care.'

Teddy liked Uncle Harry. He was a laugh. He never asked permission of the Head to see him, as the rules stated. He just turned up in the schoolyard on the odd occasion when he was in town, bearing large tins of toffees or biscuits which he said would add to his nephew's popularity.

'They sure do,' Teddy grinned, as he crossed the busy street.

Harry agreed that if Teddy's heart was at Springfield, then that was where he should go. For a couple of years.

'What then?' Teddy had asked, surprised.

'Then you go back to school. There's an agricultural college opening in Victoria. It's called Dookie. These days you need to know more about raising sheep than just mucking in as a stockman. Give yourself a couple of years in that job, then get down to Dookie and really learn how to run a station.'

'Why can't I go straight from school?'

'Because you'll be sitting in a bloody paddock. They've only started building it. Anyway, a few years working on the station will give you practical knowledge. And don't tell me that just because you grew up at Springfield you know all about the job. You don't.'

So that was the plan.

'Should I write and tell my father?' he'd asked Harry.

'Yes. Put him out of his misery. He'll be proud as hell. But you'd better shape up with your schoolwork. I hear your reports are only middling. You'll look a real ass if you can't get in to Dookie. There'll be a rush for starters, so they'll only take the cream, the dunces can forget it.'

All of a sudden, to the surprise of his teachers, Teddy Broderick had stopped cruising along, and turned into a swot. There were adventures ahead, not the least of which was travelling to the far-southern state of Victoria to learn how to take his place beside his father.

As Bobbo ushered the Captain through the anteroom he was sad. Terribly sad. The ready smile had disappeared. He'd only played this part on the Captain's angry insistence. He hadn't wanted to come here at all. This talk of a will, a death pact, frightened him. To him it was like playing with fire. Like teasing the spirits. Like walking over your own grave and defying the elements. Asking for trouble.

They'd argued over this for months until the Captain said he'd go on his own. But Bobbo couldn't allow that. The Captain was sprightly enough on the boat that he knew so well, as sure-footed as a goat. But in a town, with traffic a constant danger, he might as well be blindfolded. His eyes weren't just not too good these days, they were failing fast. He could get trampled by horses if someone didn't go with him. There were so many conveyances hurtling through the streets.

Bobbo had talked to friends among the regular passengers about this ailment, and they'd recommended doctors, but would the Captain go? Not on your life. He said his eyes were in God's hands, not in knife-wielders', and Bobbo couldn't argue with that. In fact he agreed, but went on worrying.

Although he'd been known as Robbie all these years, and hadn't minded it at all, accepting the change as the Captain's right to call him what he liked, he still clung stubbornly to his own identity. He never aired it, he just held the name to himself like a treasure that he could not relinquish. Bobbo was the last frail connection with a family that he knew existed, but was lost to him. He rarely dwelled on that part of his life, because to do that was to dredge up a sad dream, which still occurred, of his mother drowning, not in a river but in safe waters. That was the confusing part. Accustomed to the river and its moods, he doubted that dream. But one thing he did know was that she'd called out his name in that recurring dream, and in that name was love, beautiful, hugging love. Sounded stupid, he supposed, as the years stretched, as he worked his way on this boat from cabin boy to first mate in a crew of three. Their deckhand was a Chinee, Willy Chong. He'd lasted for years now, because he was a good hand, smart and reliable, and deaf. The Captain's abuse and insults didn't mean a thing to him. He just kept on smiling in that mad way.

So they'd become a family. A nice family, Bobbo thought. Together and yet not. All three living on the boat. The Captain with his undeniable status. Willy, who was about twenty years old, silent about himself and who he was. Bobbo, not a little ashamed that he was emerging into manhood but still yearning for that hugging love that these two men could not give him, worked hard at pushing away that soppy old tale about going home, because he knew that, had his home existed, the Captain would have found it for him. Like a talisman, though, he kept Bobbo. He was his twin, his confidant. His friend.

But the Captain was so bloody independent. He absolutely refused to be seen in this swanky lawyer's office with his walking stick, so Bobbo was careful with him on this shiny linoleum. He looked down the long corridor that led from the street to this particular office, and saw a tall kid walking towards them.

Mr Winters' grandson, he surmised, peering. About his own age. Taller than him. But skinnier. Bobbo was proud of his hard, muscular frame now, the first time he'd ever given it any consideration. He could wrestle this kid to the ground in a flash. He took note of the kid's posh clothes, boater hat, striped blazer, natty trousers and shiny pointed shoes, and turned his nose up in derision as the boy came closer.

Years of deferring to passengers caused the Captain, and Bobbo too, to stand aside and allow the youth to make for his grandfather's door, to enter those hallowed offices, and he did so with a polite nod of thanks to them. Bobbo liked that. Often people pushed past the Captain as if he was of no matter. Some of them were terrible rude.

The Captain had already set off, heading for that sharp rectangle of light, one hand on the wall to steady himself, but Bobbo delayed, his eyes following this boy, the grandson who pushed the door open so confidently. Curiosity had him peering into another world, the world of a posh schoolboy whose grandfather was a significant person. A lawyer. He wondered what it must be like in the high-class white world. Pretty good, he supposed.

That snooty clerk in the outer office had reminded Bobbo of clerks *he*'d had to deal with, mean individuals who worked in dingy waterfront offices, and who made him wait, treated him like dirt because he was an Abo. Not that Bobbo gave a shit. He gave as good as he got. But Mr Winters' clerk had given the Captain that same icy, insulting stare, as if he had no right to be in there, dirtying the air, or the floor, or whatever he was paid to protect.

Fortunately, what with his bad eyesight, the Captain hadn't noticed, or they'd have been out of there in a flash. Or that sneering little gent might have got his neck wrung.

Thinking of this, Bobbo lingered. He just wanted to hear the reception that this kid, his own age, would get. The kid in the posh clothes, with the power to smash that sneer if he felt so inclined. He prayed that the clerk would be rude to the boy, though he knew it wouldn't happen.

He heard a chair being pushed back with a scrape as the clerk leapt to his feet and exclaimed a greeting, all smarmy and oily. His voice was high-pitched, servile, and Bobbo crowed, delighted, as he heard: 'Oh, good morning! I'm terribly sorry. Good afternoon, it's well past twelve. Good afternoon, Master Broderick. Come right in, your grandfather's waiting. Come right in . . .'

The voice faded but Bobbo stood, rigid. Something stirred. Something important. He stood transfixed, wanting to go back in there, to follow a vague sound, or a thought. He didn't know. It was that kid. His name maybe. Was that it? He couldn't go on, and he couldn't go back. His feet seemed immobilized. He needed to go after that boy, the rich boy. To grab him, hold on to him, beg him to stay, talk to him! Wildly, his mind careened into a spiral that focused on the kid himself. He knew him! Bobbo was sure he knew him! That smile of his, that he'd appreciated, had been real. Gentle. Friendly. He knew him from somewhere.

'Are you going to stand there all day?' the Captain barked from down the long passage, breaking the spell.

And Bobbo began to let go. Where had he got the idea that he knew a posh kid like that? The name itself had only been a signal to alert him, it had drifted into time, lost in his concentration on something real, that boy, his own age. He even moved a few steps back to the door, hearing the voice as the kid was being greeted by his grandfather, hearing laughter and games, smelling a kitchen warm with women and the heat of fresh bread, inhaling dust, ever-present dust, seeing the joyful respite of a river and the rope they used to swing out . . .

'What's the matter with you?' the Captain shouted, his cramped frame silhouetted against the entrance, and the moment slid away.

Bobbo came to his senses, wakened from that impossible nostalgia. He shook it loose, wondering what had brought it on. Probably because that boy had been polite to an old man and a young blackfellow. That didn't make him a friend. He hadn't even noticed Bobbo. And why would he? Nevertheless, it had been a peculiar experience. He'd never mention it to the Captain, who'd think he'd gone off his head.

'Are you going to stay there all day?' the Captain yelled angrily.

Bobbo shrugged. 'No. I'm coming.'

As he walked away, Teddy Broderick opened the door to see what the fuss was all about, with that old man shouting down there at the entrance to the block of offices. But all he saw was the black lad hurrying down the corridor. For a second there he felt the same sweet nostalgia. When he'd been very young he'd had black playmates and they'd always had a special spot in his heart.

He too shrugged, and turned back to wait for Grandpa Winters, who'd said they mustn't keep Nanny waiting but was still fiddling about in his office.

When Teddy looked again, the old man and the young blackfellow had both disappeared.